Abiding Darkness
Volume Two of *The Tellers' Tale*

by Lorraine DeWolf

Abiding Darkness
Volume Two of the Tellers' Tale
Lorraine DeWolf

A Cornerstone Book
Published by Cornerstone Book Publishers
Copyright © 2013 by Lorraine DeWolf

Cornerstone Book Publishers
New Orleans, LA

First Cornerstone Edition - 2013
www.cornerstonepublishers.com

ISBN: 1-61342-095-1
ISBN-13: 978-1-61342-095-9

MADE IN THE USA

Dedication.

To Jeff and James Horner,
whose magic can make even dark hearts light

Abiding Darkness
Volume Two of The Tellers' Tale

ABIDING DARKNESS

Prologue

"Elya!"

A voice, sharp with insistence, slapped at her telling, tolling mind. The world shuddered violently, and she shuddered with it, aimless and ungainly as a ship swamped in treacherous seas. Floating treasure sloshed, swirled — images, sensations, thoughts and feelings, the belongings of many others.

She was a dark-eyed man frowning out over a city gate. She was a dark-haired woman riding away from that gate on a sturdy roan. She was the razor-sharp and cold-eyed warder riding at the woman's side. Then the light pulled her upward, and she became the hawk skimming thermals high above it all.

"Elya!"

A vicious current of energy hooked her, dredged her up. The hawk, the warder, the girl sank into the depths, while the bulk that was Elya rose to a tumult like wind-scoured waves. Voices uninterpretable as the sea's rose and fell, then receded. Elya became Elya again, a single body cast up, half drowned, upon a stony shore.

She opened her eyes.

The world was a gray haze, a globe of mists. Then the grayness formed up into ranks. For a moment those ranks looked like the trunks of tightly packed, pale-barked trees. But then they flattened out to become wooden planks in a rough-hewn wall.

Elya blinked at the wall. It reminded her of rotting, uneven teeth. She tried to lift her head, but her body flopped, loose and unwieldy as a skin half full of water. Her water-logged limbs pushed at the darkness beneath her, and it slithered into a pile of damp, papery leaves.

Her own memories stirred within her. *Gatekeeper?*

She rolled off her leafy bed seeking the Gatekeeper's eyes, those guiding stars of multihued light. She saw stone floor instead — thickly carpeted in dead leaves the color of faded black velvet — and warped gray walls propped beneath a partially collapsed roof.

Gatekeeper!

This was wrong, all wrong. Where was the Gatekeeper? And what had happened to her once cozy cottage?

Elya shook her head hard, a dog trying to clear a water-logged coat. She wanted desperately to vomit for there was a burbling heaviness like an ocean of salt water swelling her insides. The pressure of it tasted like nectar and gall.

She needed the Gatekeeper.

Clenching her teeth against the urge to spew her guts onto the floor, she launched herself to her feet, headed for the open doorway, and stepped out into an atmosphere as final as a slammed door.

She froze, heart contracting.

Hoary old age had come to the timeless Twilight wood. All was diseased whiteness and dusky deathly light. The very air smelled of rot, and the slender twilight trees dropped a steady rain of gray-black leaves.

What has happened to this place?

"You!" a voice answered.

She locked her lips against a desperate urge to spew bile and ambrosia, and turned to confront a marvel surmounted by a wonder.

A creature stood on the Twilight path, a creature that would have jarred a lesser mind and jangled a poorer imagination. It bore a vague, nightmarish resemblance to a horse. But its hooves were cloven, and its hide shone dappled silver like the surface of the moon. Beneath that silver stretched bones and sinews devised by the architects of madness, and a cruelly spiraling horn jutted from its forehead. Its eyes were windows on oblivion.

"What are you doing?" demanded the voice.

Elya dragged her eyes up to the roughly triangular shape of darkness crouched astride the moon horse.

"Doing—" she began, only to gag on her bottled-up Telling. The darkness of the rider, a blackness purer than black, appalled like the monstrousness of the horse.

That blackness loomed larger and larger in her vision, then produced a quite ordinary, man-shaped hand.

The hand was reaching for her.

"Don't!" Elya commanded.

The hand withdrew, opening a wider gap in the blacker-than-black and exposing a shirted forearm and a booted leg. The forearm was encased in white linen, the boots were leather.

Elya, born to strangeness as to recklessness, made the necessary mental adjustments that would enable her to see beyond the cloak of pure Midnight to the shape of the hooded rider crouched beneath. "Who are you?" she demanded.

The rider stiffened. "The keeper of these lands," he answered.

Elya lifted her chin. "You lie! I know the Gatekeeper, and you are not her."

"Nothing is definite in these realms," returned the rider, pressing a booted leg to moonscape hide. "Where is the Gatekeeper? What have you done with her?"

"Done with her?" barked Elya.

"You reek of power, power you stole from this place."

"I—" Elya began to protest as her mind opened on the hinge of his words and the Telling foamed upward, coating her tongue with sweetness. *Tellers! What have I done!*

She began to run, stumbling, then jogging, then loping through the rain of leaves. "Where are you going?" the moon-horse's rider sang-out behind her.

"Back!" Elya shouted between breaths. A moon soared level with her shoulder, and she panted at it. "If I don't I could collapse this dimension entirely."

"Collapse it?"

"The power you said I stole—it must have gone into my Telling—but the Telling isn't done. It will draw more power—unless I get out."

The moon soared in front of her. Elya pitched to a halt, colliding with chill silver flesh and unnatural sinew.

"You are a Teller?"

Elya considered the cold beneath her fingers. It was hard to speak and not vomit at the same time. "Yes, but I lack my full power. That is why I came to the Gatekeeper. I did not realize that she would take power from this place."

"*She* drained the power?" the rider exclaimed.

Elya pressed her lips into a hard line as her insides spasmed. The Twilight wood spasmed as well, and Elya's mouth filled with a sweet searing while branches thick as a man's arm began cracking and tumbling down through the falling leaves.

"Come up!" the rider commanded, holding out a hand.

Elya did not have to be asked twice. The whole wood was rippling like an image mirrored in running water.

The monster horse bounded forward, soaring with moon-like sereneness through crumbling white wood and then slipping around an invisible corner to carry them down into a blackness like freezing waters. Elya looked back to see an image of white woods dwindling like a lighted doorway seen from a fast-moving boat.

"Get me to the gate," she gritted through the energy rising in her gorge.

"The Gate is closed! That is why I came looking for the Gatekeeper!"

Elya was up to her groin in freezing black waters now, but the shape of the monster horse was changing. Its dappled moon-flesh was stretching out, curving upward like a cup made to bear them.

Elya's lips bubbled nectar and bile. The urge to vomit was overwhelming now. *I can't hold on*, she thought.

Then let go, another thought answered as the Telling, surging from the back of her throat, broke the seal of her lips and exploded outward in words that tasted of frosted wine and ashes.

Elya sank again into a vast, dark ocean of words and thoughts, sensations and feelings.

Book ONE: The Road to Empyre

Chapter 1: The Healer of Greenwood

In the crisp cool of early spring, Colin Blackhammer finished setting out his healer's garden. He planted the latest bush, a small holly-like shrub with a peculiar spiky leaf, watered it well, and then stepped back to contemplate the results. The rough rectangle he had spent the last month hacking out of a neglected corner of the Blackhammers' yard was greening up nicely. It included many unusual specimens from Millicynt Encanta's garden, although Millicynt herself would never see them.

Millicynt Encanta was dead, her remarkable garden gone to seed and the wild.

Colin sighed, collected his gardening tools, and headed for the nearest shed. When he emerged from it, the setting sun was sowing the village rooftops with orange fire.

"Healer!" someone called out, and he turned his head to see Mistress Raines hailing him from the road.

Reanne Raines fingered her shawl. "You should be resting, not gardening," she scolded. "We kept you awake two nights running."

"I napped earlier. How is Trist feeling?"

"Much better. Thanks to your medicines."

Colin smiled. "I will come and look in on her later."

Reanne Raines smiled back. "Much later." She held out the basket she carried. "Fresh cured ham and bread. Make sure you get the lord's share. You could stand more meat on your bones."

Colin took the basket. Mistress Raines nodded. "Healer," she said formally. Then she hurried up the road, leaving Colin wondering at the changes time can bring.

4

Only a few months ago, he'd been a mere apprentice and a dying one at that. Attacked and wounded gravely by a pair of men in motley, he should have bled to death on the forest floor. Only Garvin Blackhammer's intervention saved him. Garvin found his son, carried him home, and sent for Old Marge Frickers from Fairway to do the rest. Old Marge, the oldest healer in the district and the wisest next to Millicynt Encanta, arrived just in time to keep Colin from succumbing to blood loss and infection. She salved his wounds and stitched them, but she could not refashion ruined flesh. Colin's right leg and arm would never be the same.

He woke to disability and the death of his long-time mentor. Then he learned that the person he felt closest to, Emily Sayer, had departed for parts unknown.

The sum of these losses was more than his traumatized mind could digest. He spent weeks brewing anger, several more sunk in depression, until an epidemic of winter pneumonia forced him to reassess his own gifts for healing. With half the district sickened and Millicynt dead, the village had no official healer of its own to call upon. It was up to Colin to avert disaster.

He managed the crisis better than anyone expected. The sick villagers recovered, Old Marge declared him a "major talent," and the guild of healers adopted him as one of their own. Colin's long apprenticeship in the healing arts ended, and his professional life began, bringing with it a new impetus for closing old wounds. He bandaged his grief with work: studying late, serving others, and seeking the advice of more experienced healers when he could.

He might walk with a limp, but he had never held his head higher. And yet, when the light was just right . . .

He looked up the road, half dreading, half hoping to glimpse a jittery shadow lurking among the roadside trees.

The trees were empty, their shadows ordinary, like the shadows escorting the two riders coming up the road.

Those riders seemed an oddly mismatched pair. One rode a tall, long-limbed roan; the other, a short, rough-coated pony. The roan looked amiable, the pony fierce, not at all like the fat, placid beasts kept hereabouts.

The riders pulled up at the smithy's gate. Then the rider of the roan raised her face, and Colin dropped his basket.

"Emily?" he breathed, breaking into a hobble. "Emily!"

She was through the gate and leaping for him, so exuberantly that she nearly knocked him off his feet. He felt her hair slide across his cheek, heard her laugh, or sob, into his ear. "Colin! Colin! Tellers, but it is good to see you!"

"You're here," he muttered, "You're actually here!" He wrapped his good arm around her waist, then pushed her away to get a better look at her. "Whatever are you wearing?"

"Warder clothes," she laughed, and bowled him over with another fierce hug.

Colin yelped, and she stepped back, hands to her mouth. "Did that hurt? I'm sorry. You look so well, I quite forgot—Are you well?"

He smiled, feeling well—deeply, soulfully well. "I'm a tad stiffer than I used to be."

"You could be dead!" she declared, then blanched and dropped her eyes.

Colin laughed. "Same old blunt Emily, I see." She *was* the same old Emily. Or were her cheeks a bit leaner, her eyes a bit brighter?

Over her head, he caught sight of his father emerging from the smithy. Garvin was wiping his hands on a scrap of leather. He seemed to take in the scene with his usual laconic expression, until his eyes slid past Emily to the second rider and his heavy brows shot up into his hair.

Colin's eyes leaped to the second rider as well, tried to pin him down, failed, and tried again. There seemed to be a blur upon his vision, a distortion like the rain that sluices a windowpane. "What in Tellers'—" he began.

"What what?" Emily asked, smiling up into his face. Then she followed his eyes and firmed her voice. "Oh. Let me introduce you." She tugged, but Colin's feet refused to budge. "Come on, Col," she urged. "He won't bite you—at least, I think he won't."

The other rider poured from his pony. How to find a face in all that fluidity? "Colin, I would like you to meet Faryn of House Warder. Faryn, this is my dearest and oldest friend, Colin Blackhammer."

Did the other man smile? Colin couldn't tell. He did perceive a pair of eyes the color and temperature of icicles. "Pleased to meet you," Colin heard himself murmur, while Emily yelped, "You're doing it again!"

"Doing what?" he shot back in confusion, but Emily was glaring at the man called Faryn.

Colin looked back at the stranger, and his skin tried to crawl toward his scalp. The elusive quality enveloping the other rider had parted like a curtain or a veil, exposing a countenance lean and alert and dominated by those icicle eyes.

"That's better," approved Emily, while part of Colin's mind shook and gibbered.

"You're back," Garvin Blackhammer rumbled warningly from deeper in the yard.

Emily's hand bit into Colin's. "Yes, thank you, Master Blackhammer," she answered. "It's good to be home."

As darkness came on, Colin set out tankards of cider and platters of bread and ham for his guests in an uncharacteristically empty Blackhammer kitchen. Emily dug into the food; Faryn ignored it. Colin toyed with a tankard and concentrated on not looking at the other man. He had the distinct impression that the warder was measuring the surroundings to within a hair's breadth, and he didn't like the sensation at all.

He focused on Emily instead, sharing the news and dickering about old times, but soon she began to trouble him as much as Faryn did. Though she laughed and joked like before, there was a peculiar tension in the set of her shoulders, a shrillness to the flights of her voice that said she was less pleased than she acted. Her attention often drifted, her eyes sliding away from his to fasten on thin air as if tracking a sound only she could hear. She always came back to him, but those momentary absences were disturbing.

When he told her about his healer's garden, she demanded to see it, and he escorted her outside, leaving Faryn alone at the table. She stood for a long time amid the freshly turned rows before turning back to him. "I'm glad you saved so much," she said, her voice sinking into the downy night. "Millicynt would be pleased. You paid such a high price for knowing her."

He limped closer to wrap a reassuring arm around her shoulders. "Oh, it's not so bad. You'd be surprised the number of chores a bad leg and a weak arm can get you out of. I'm enjoying myself immensely."

They stood for a while in companionable silence, and it came to him that she had said almost nothing about the things that had happened to her. With a nod toward the house, he began, "So, is he a friend of yours?"

"Faryn? Yes. I mean I suppose so. But he's also a condition of my being here."

"A condition?"

"Grandfather wouldn't let me make the journey without him."

Colin stiffened. "Grandfather?"

"My grandfather. I told you about him in my letters."

"You did not."

The look she directed at him blended amusement with irritation. "I did so. I distinctly remember it."

"You wrote about the city Cyr, a Lady Syrene, Blayne, a Lord Keeper."

"Exactly. Grandfather is the Keeper."

"The Keeper is your grandfather?"

"If being the father of my mother makes him so."

"You never told me you had a grandfather."

"I didn't know."

Colin blinked. "Oh."

"To put it mildly."

"Why didn't *he* escort you home?"

Her face grew wary, elusive with evening shadows. "I didn't want him to," she snapped. "Besides he's a busy man." Abruptly, she stared off into the night.

"You dislike him."

She laughed softly and shook her head. "No. Although I thought I did. I thought a lot of things actually, none of which proved to be entirely true. But that's all behind me now. I'm here at last, in a place I do know. I just hope here remembers me."

"Of course it does." He caught her hand in his long one and pulled her close enough to bend down and give her a kiss, but she pulled away before their lips could touch.

"What's wrong?" he asked, trying to keep the hurt out of his voice.

"Nothing."

He tightened his grip on her hand, felt the cool iron of her ring, and held it up toward the moonlight. "You kept it."

She pulled her hand away. "Colin, I've only come back to the Greenwood for a little while. I'm not staying."

He stood very still, trying not to think, not to shout "You're going back to Cyr."

"Tellers, no! It was all I could do to get out of there. Between Grandfather and the Steward and—Well, let's just say that it took every ounce of strength and guile in me to get this far. But I have farther to go, Colin. Much farther." The words seemed to tumble out of her.

Colin had never thought of shaking any woman, but he shook Emily now. "Going where?" he demanded.

They were both shaking by the time he was done. "South, Colin," she whispered. "South, all the way to the Empyre."

"The Empyre?" heaved Colin.

"Yes. It's Beth—you remember Beth." As if anyone who had caught sight of Emily's Southern friend could forget her. "She needs me, and I think she's going to need you too. That's why I came home, Col. I want—no, I *need* you to come with me."

The early hours of the next morning found Colin sitting alone on the edge of the Blackhammer front porch with three words banging about in his mind: *Come with me.* Such simple words. Was that all it took to erase months of effort and achievement? So she wanted him to go with her. Did she understand what it would mean? She was asking him to leave his family, his friends, his new position, all he had cared about and accomplished since she disappeared out of his life. And she wasn't even being completely honest with him about it. She said that she needed to help her Southern friend, but Colin sensed that this was only a partial truth. He knew Emily, her loyalties, her obstinacies, her caprices. He knew when she was running toward one thing to escape from something else.

And what was she offering him in return? Not herself certainly, not with her aversion to his kisses, her forced ebullience, her mental absences.

So he sat, elbows on knees, painting the darkness with his doubts until the darkness began to assert its own meaning. Somewhere off down the dirt road an overeager rooster crowed. Was that a shadowy figure hunched waiting just inside those oak trees? The door to the house opened, and his father stepped onto the porch in a monolithic creak of timbers. The blot of deeper darkness vanished.

"Been out here all night?" Garvin rumbled.

Colin stretched his painfully stiff leg. "Couldn't sleep."

"Care to help me open shop?"

It was the first time in many weeks that Garvin had made that request—Dax was Garvin's assistant these days. Colin shook his head. "I wouldn't be much help. I think I'll take a walk instead." He stood up gingerly and eased away from the porch, conscious the entire time of his father's stolid scrutiny.

His feet—steady left and halting right—took him where they would, past dozing homesteads and into the Greenwood along a trail as familiar as the lines on his palms. When he came to the meadow that marked the boundary of Millicynt Encanta's land, he paused for a moment to stare through morning mists at the place where the cottage had once stood.

Slowly, he climbed its hill. A seared patch of roughly rectangular ground and a pair of crumbled chimneys were all that marked the house's location. Nothing grew there. But in the overrun garden, weeds and cultivars vied for supremacy. He limped toward the forest line and spotted an eerie phantom shimmering just beyond a stalky white rose. Then the wavering dissipated, and the lean face of Faryn emerged, sharp beneath a dun-colored hood.

"Good morning," Colin said, with courage pitched somewhere between the warder's absolute silence and the early morning's hush.

"Good morning," Faryn returned in hovering voice.

Colin looked about, shivering. "I don't know why Emily insisted on staying out here. You could have spent the night with us."

Faryn's lean face twitched. "Lady Emilyn did not wish to disturb."

"Lady Emilyn!" Colin laughed, then registered Faryn's expression and sobered. "No Blackhammer is going to be disturbed by her."

"But they might be disturbed by me."

Colin coughed.

Faryn's icy eyes were unrelenting. "You do find me disturbing, do you not?"

Lost to tact, Colin settled for frankness instead. "Very."

Faryn laughed, a surprisingly human and amiable sound. "Come then. Allow me to soothe your discomfort with some tea."

"You drink tea?"

Faryn laughed again.

Emily was sitting by a campfire laid between two enormous old trees. She looked pent up and exhausted, although she smiled to see Colin.

"Rough night?" he commiserated as he eased himself down beside her.

"Rough joining," remarked Faryn, pulling a kettle off the fire and proceeding to brew tea in tin cups.

Emily glared hot pokers. "Just a bad dream."

"Were you being hunted by a shadowy figure?" Colin asked, thinking of his own nightmares.

Emily looked surprised. "Yes. I was being stalked by Roland."

"Who's Roland?"

"A famous warrior. We Midlanders call him Dorlan. Isn't that right, Faryn?" She flicked the words like ashes.

Colin turned a surprised face to the warder. "Dorlan! Do *your* people tell stories about him too?"

"About Roland we tell many."

Colin leaned forward. "Do you tell the one about him cheating Death? That's my favorite."

"Which one is that?" asked Emily.

Colin turned his smile on her. "You know. You tell it better than I do." Emily looked away.

Colin swung back to Faryn. "It's the one where Death, who has been hot to catch Dorlan for ages, finally tracks him down in this very forest. But Dorlan, instead of being afraid of Death, jumps down from his horse as soon as he spies him and kisses him on his cold, hard cheek. 'Dear Death!' he says, 'We meet at last! Welcome!' Naturally, Death is surprised. And Dorlan says to him, "Relieve me, Death, for my life is become a shadow and a plague. I was born a fighting man, as well you know, but no being in this world is capable of withstanding me. I am far too tricksy and tough for other men. But you, dear Death, you can give me the battle my weary being craves. Every creature knows that your embrace is unbreakable, your blows irresistible.'

"So, Dorlan begs Death to give him one last good brawl, and Death agrees. Then Dorlan proposes that they hold the fight in the underworld so that all of Death's subjects can see. They go down, and the fight begins. It goes on for an age and a day, so long that Death actually finds himself growing weary from it, but Dorlan—why he's just as fresh as spring green. So, Death draws back and looses his deadliest blow. Nothing happens. Over and over again Death tries to knock the life right out of Dorlan, until he's about done in himself with the effort. Then Death cries out to Dorlan. 'You trickster! What sort of cheat have you devised now?' 'No cheat of mine,' laughs Dorlan. 'You cheated yourself. Any fool knows that you cannot kill those welcomed already into the land of the dead.'"

Colin grinned, and Emily chuckled, but Faryn's light eyes glinted coldly. "That's a dangerous telling," he said.

"Oh?"

"You left Roland in the underworld."

"That's how the story ends," Colin shrugged.

"No. Roland escaped the underworld, to his enemies' everlasting regret."

"How?"

"He bought his freedom, by promising the death of another, one almost as powerful and elusive as himself."

"You mean he killed someone else?" Colin frowned. "That isn't very nice."

"Roland isn't nice," agreed Faryn.

Emily lifted her chin. "Whose life did he take?"

Faryn's light eyes locked onto hers. "The life of the Steward's only child and heir."

Emily wandered to the bottom of the meadow, feeling very small and forlorn against a towering backdrop of sky and trees.

"Missing her?" Colin murmured, coming level.

"Always. But just now I was thinking of all the books she owned, books I might have read."

"If you'd had time."

"If I had made the time. She encouraged me to, but I was always running off into the woods instead, pursuing figments of my imagination."

"As I remember it, some of your figments weren't all that imaginary." Colin rubbed his side.

Emily closed her eyes. "Beware the stories you tell."

"What's that?"

"Something my mother used to say to me when I was little." Her lids lifted. Her eyes were dark. "I didn't understand what she meant back then. But I'm beginning to. I wish she and Millicynt had done more to prepare me."

"I never knew your mother, but I knew Millicynt. She would have done anything for you. She loved you."

"Can love fight off death and darkness? Can it teach me how to help my friends instead of hurt them?"

Colin hunched his shoulders and slid his hands into his pockets. "I'm just an ignorant country fellow, but to my way of thinking, that's not the point."

"Then what is?"

"To keep trying. Love can help anyone do that."

"Who dares call you an ignorant country fellow?" Emily proclaimed. "I'll clobber the next person who says it."

"I'm glad you have such a good opinion of me because I've recently decided to share my brilliance with the wider world."

"Oh?"

"A bunch of barbaric Southerners to be exact."

"You're coming with me!"

"I can't very well let you go off alone. You need someone level-headed to keep you out of trouble."

She was practically climbing on him now. Colin lost his straight face and his balance, but even though his leg hurt badly, he didn't complain.

Emily pulled back and took his face in her hands. "You are the best friend a girl could ask for," she whispered.

"Yeah. When should I pack?"

Emily glanced up the hill. "Not just yet. First, we have to figure out how to escape Faryn."

Colin's smile flicked off. "Faryn isn't coming?"

Her fingers flew to his mouth. "No! And he mustn't know what we're planning."

Colin jerked his head away. "Are you mad?" he said.

"Keep your voice down. His hearing is very sharp."

But Colin's indignation would not be contained. "Here's hoping he hears!" He pointed a finger at her face. "The only reason I agreed to this harebrained scheme was because I thought he would our guide. What do you know about the Empyre? What do I know? He on the other hand — Well, I don't think it much matters whether he knows the Empyre or not. With his help we might stand a chance, a very slim chance, of actually reaching the Empyre. Without him . . . Tellers! Sending us off to the rescue of a mysterious Southern lady is like sending lambs to a shearing. Dorlan's grief, Emily! What were you thinking?"

"Does every man I care about have to treat me like an idiot!" Emily fumed back. But the ire in her face soon fizzled, leaving behind a desperation that wrung Colin's heart. Almost, he regretted his tirade, until he saw the old glint of stubbornness surfacing in her eyes. Grabbing her by the shoulders, he said her name like a warning.

But she pulled away, speaking hotly, "And this is the man who tells me to let love be my guide. Well, Beth is going to die if we don't go to her. I've seen it. I feel it. And as a friend who loves her, I can't let that happen, not without doing everything I can to prevent it."

"But that's not your only motivation, is it?"

Emily froze. Then she burst into tears.

Inwardly, Colin groaned. Why did it always take him this long to realize that he had lost the war before it had even begun? He set his face and stared off into the distance.

When Emily calmed down, she waxed apologetic, too apologetic to Colin's mind. "I'm sorry," she said, with an impressive show of contriteness that Colin only partly believed. "I should have known better than to ask. It's not as if you haven't suffered enough for knowing me."

"Oh, spare me the histrionics," snapped Colin. He sighed. "I can't believe I'm saying this, but if we actually want to have any idea what we're doing, we'd better go talk to my father. Tellers be good, I can only imagine what he'll say."

When they finally cornered Garvin Blackhammer, he didn't say anything—at first. He listened with his characteristic taciturnity and a steady lifting of brow.

"Are you mad, girl?" he rumbled when they had both done.

Although Emily was sick to death of that question, her response was frank. "Probably."

Her admission seemed to soften the smith. "It will take you more than a month to reach the City of the Sun," he rumbled, "assuming you reach it at all, and when you get there you will still have no way to reach your friend. You do realize what she is?" Emily nodded. "Then you must know that Empyreal princesses do not loiter in public streets."

"Empyreal princesses!" blurted Colin.

Emily was attending to Garvin. "I believe the powers will offer us a way."

"You have a lot of faith in the powers considering the mule kicks you've earned lately."

Colin stared. He had the disturbing feeling that more was being said than he realized.

Emily thought for a moment, seemed to resolve some internal conflict. "There is this," she said, holding out her right hand. A silver leaf mark shone faintly from the center of her palm. Colin inhaled. He'd mostly forgotten about the strange mark. Garvin Blackhammer held Emily's eyes. "She gave it to you, did she?"

Emily's reply was not without pain. "The night the darkling creatures attacked."

Garvin nodded. "Neither the mark nor the powers served her all that well in the end," he commented.

"No, but her death wasn't entirely in vain either. The talisman that this mark commemorates has finally returned to the lands of men."

"I heard," the smith remarked flatly. "I figured you were behind it."

"You did?"

"I manage to keep up with the news, and in certain circles, the appearance of the Shield was very *big* news."

"And will you help us get to Sun City?" Emily held her breath as she waited for his answer.

It was several long, painful moments in coming. "Getting you to the city is not the problem. Getting you away from that warder is."

Emily jumped at the opening. "I may have a way to lose him, once I know our road."

Garvin Blackhammer's expression dripped doubt. "What do you know about warders, girl?"

"I have spent many weeks among them, and I've thrown Faryn off my trail before. When he loses it this time, he'll have to return to his Lord."

"You should have spent even more time among them if you think so. What warders ward, they never give up. He would no more return to his Lord having failed of his mission than a man under a death sentence would present himself to his judge. Even if you do escape him, he will hunt you, with all the unimaginable resources at his command."

"I've dealt with warder magic before."

"Have you met their hawks and hounds?"

"Hounds?" said Emily.

Blackhammer's derisive grunt said that her ignorance was as wide and deep as the sky.

In desperation, Emily added, "Look, I don't care if he finds me eventually. I just need time to get Colin to Beth before the baby is born. Then Faryn can do whatever he wants with me."

"Baby!" blurted Colin, who was still wrestling with the notion of rescuing Empyreal princesses.

Blackhammer lifted a hand for silence. "Give me a few days," he said.

Chapter 2: The Tomb of the Cyros

Some days after the Shield bearer left Cyr, the Lady Syrene wed Lord Corwyn Abrille. As Lord Abrille was a scion of House Steward, citizens from across the Northland came to pay their respects. Among them was a representative of Castle Numyn named Blayne.

He stood apart from the crowd, in essence as in substance, an unapproachable green-eyed paragon only incidentally shaped like a man, but he missed nothing that went on around him, including the currents and crosscurrents of emotion eddying the throng. It did not matter that he could not feel such emotions for himself. He had long ago learned to perceive their physiological effects in others. To Blayne, every human feeling gave off its own distinctive vibration, heat, and smell, according to its own unique chemistry.

So, he was also instantly aware when a presence nearly as void of feeling as his own entered the room via a shadowy second-floor gallery.

He tracked its movements until it caught wind of his awareness and slipped away in a ripple of rose-silk cloak.

He did not bother trying to follow. He headed for the Lord's library instead, turning heads and talk as he went.

The large book-filled room he entered breathed quiet and order. Its sole occupant, a man plainly dressed, sat before the large western-facing windows with an open and unread book upon his outstretched leg.

Blayne did not bother announcing himself. He moved to one of the windows, ineluctable as the light, and noted the sunset staining the manicured grounds.

The other man spoke. "Nice party?" he asked with typical irony.

"As predicted."

"I gather Syrene managed to overcome her enthusiasm for your attendance."

"But not her indigestion. I think Grandfather chose me as his representative just to give her stomach pains."

Alsandyr laughed softly. "I'm sure he did. Meredyth has never liked Syrene."

"He encouraged Lord North to adopt her as heir, and he expresses great confidence in her abilities."

Alsandyr chuckled. "I didn't say his dislike was rational. Sometimes two good people just end up developing an aversion to one another."

"As enemies sometimes develop an affinity," returned Blayne with his usual indifferent directness.

"Just so," said Alsandyr. The sun was now halfway below the horizon. Blayne turned away from it to see Al gazing straight into the heart of that dull-orange ember.

"Your lady was in attendance."

To all outward appearances the comment had no effect on the dark-haired man, but Blayne knew better. He shifted his stance and noted with something approaching admiration how Al controlled his heartbeat, his breathing, his countenance.

This remarkable self-control was in part a family trait, in part a product of intensive training. Clinical detachment was a hallmark of the Stewards, whose particular gifts required them to take the long view. But, like all mortal men, Al was susceptible to strong emotion. Unlike most, he was capable of inflicting widespread harm with it.

Blayne continued. "Alysse fled as soon as I spotted her."

Al kept his own eyes on the western horizon. "She is still uneasy with people."

"It is more than that. Something has changed."

16

"She is weak, tired."

"Not in the evenings." Blayne spoke the words blandly, disinterestedly. "People say that she walks abroad at night and tires only when the sun rises."

Al set aside his book and rose.

Blayne moved to block the way. Behind his eyes a green sun was rising. "How long, Alsandyr, will you permit her to deteriorate?"

The dark-eyed man stared coolly back. "Alysse is not your concern," he said and turned to walk away.

Blayne caught his shoulder. "She is everyone's concern," he remarked factually. "If she has been re-infected, she is a danger to us all, and particularly to you."

Al glared at the restraining hand. "Some dangers are worth risking."

"Even if it only increases her body's pain? Grandfather called your refusal to interfere cruel."

The dark eyes lifted. Now Al's black gaze seemed to drink in all the remaining light, and the air about him shimmered with silent thunder. Blayne executed the subtle shift in balance that would permit him to ward a blow.

"It was you who awakened her," Al said, his voice deceptively easy and low.

"It was Emilyn," returned Blayne.

Neither man moved. "She did it for you," Blayne added clinically. Al took one sharp precisely measured step away from Blayne's hand. Then he exploded into action, so violently and suddenly that even Blayne could not but be driven backward into bookcases. "Blast her. And blast you," Al snarled, his eyes holes on oblivion.

Quite disinterestedly, Blayne noted that he was being choked. Calmly, he began prying Al's fingers back.

With a grunt Al released him.

Blayne drew his sword. Al stared at the blade for a moment, then he moved. Two slender bars of steel kissed and then flashed into blows. Books and furniture flew. Blayne parried each assault clinically. Al was good, but Blayne was inhuman.

The duel was short but satisfying. When Blayne determined that Al had done enough damage, he quit holding back and rushed his colleague's guard. Al's sword went spinning away from him. Al himself flew backward into a bookcase while Blayne swung neatly out of the charge into an indifferent stance.

For a long time, the two combatants just stared at one another, Blayne blandly, Al inscrutably. Al's right hand was bloody. Blayne's face was empty, though his eyes blazed like twin green infernos.

"Wild as a warder," he commented.

Al frowned and slid down the bookcase to the floor, dropping his forehead into one hand. "Blood and fire! What is wrong with me?"

Blayne sheathed his blade and, with the tip of his boot, tossed Al his sword.

The dark-eyed man batted it aside. "Daemons, but I'm tired."

"The air is clearer."

Al's gaze sharpened. "What do you mean?"

Blayne shrugged. "You've been brewing anger for weeks now. It was beginning to slop over and affect other people's thinking. I was growing tired of it nipping at mine."

Al, with one arm resting atop his bent knee, studied him. "My anger bothered you that much!"

"Not as much as your preoccupation. We need you sharp and clear-headed, Alsandyr. Meredyth insisted on as much when he ordered me here."

"What does Meredyth have to do with this?"

"He warned me that your problems might require outside intervention."

"Are you saying that you deliberately goaded me into a fight?"

"Meredyth suggested talk. Fighting tends to work better. There was a time when fighting was your chosen method of release."

"Times have changed."

"Your temper hasn't. You have hard decisions to make. You cannot hide from them behind your ire."

"Is that what you think I've been doing?" said Al incredulously. For a moment the air thickened with new menace. If Blayne had been more human, he might have winced. Instead, he stabbed to the heart of the issue. "Every moment Alysse continues here, she increases our vulnerability to attack or dissolution."

Al was pulling himself to his feet. "And what would you have me do . . . kill her?"

"Yes."

The bottom seemed to drop out of Al's black eyes. "I cannot do that," he whispered. "As I love my own soul, I cannot."

"Then she will kill you."

Al ran his hands through his hair. With all the disinterestedness of his colder heritage, Blayne observed the gesture and saw through it to the tangled heart of the truth. "Ah." He crossed his arms. "If you honor her, Alsandyr. Release her. Do what you must before it is too late."

Al spun away, kicked a book lying on the floor, and watched it smack into a bookcase in a flutter of pages. "Would you look at what she has done to me?" He cast a black eye over the mess around them. "I always said she was a disaster! She appears from out of nowhere, ignores the rules, rewrites others, does what no one else would dare and then disappears the way she came, leaving me to deal with the damage."

Blayne raised a quizzical brow. "You are speaking of Emilyn. You did not have to let her go."

Al started laughing. "Let her go!" He flopped down into a chair. "She strong-armed me. Can you believe it? Me!"

"You played with fire."

Al's body went taut, but his tone, when he spoke, was philosophical, "Yes. And I deserve every blister I get. But what about the others? What about Alysse? Should she and her father have to pay twice for my mistakes?"

"You ask pointless questions. There is only action and reaction, what is and what must be done."

Al's smile was rueful. "Exactly. And all action sets off an infinite chain of reactions. Some we can see, others we could never apprehend. If you saw things as I do, you might not consider the matter so simple."

If the fight with Blayne cleared Al's head, the time spent setting the library to rights composed it. Feeling more focused than he had in days, he made his way out of Cyr city via the newly opened western gate and stepped onto the sheer rampart of earth that skirted its eastern escarpment. Although the evening was lightless, but for a sprinkling of stars, he picked his way across the steep slope easily, following the path workmen had trod.

The entrance to the caverns cut a jagged crack across the softer darkness. He could have lit the lantern he carried with him; he did not, choosing instead to make his way by memory and steward sight through spaces redolent of water and stone.

The first great cavern, still lit by workmen's lanterns, made him feel like he had stepped into the belly of a decomposing leviathan. Great ribs of stone curved out of the floor to a roof dripping with reddish stalactites like shreds of flesh. Other blobs of stone melted like organs across the floor.

In the middle of it all stood a middle-aged man busy packing away picks and brushes. "Lord Alsandyr!" the man said as he looked up. "Back so soon?"

"Master Rycard," Al nodded. "Are you done for the night?"

"I might as well be. The rest of the workers disappeared as soon as the sun set. A superstitious lot, they are." Rycard's voice was as dry and dusty as the artifacts he unearthed.

Al smiled his sympathies. "You must be patient with them. Not so long ago wights were swarming all over this hill."

"All the more reason for them to set aside childish fears. If a twilight denizen does decide to come for them, no city wall will stop it."

Al followed Rycard to a worktable that held a large sheet of paper upon which a partial map of the cavern floor had been sketched. Almost absentmindedly he said. "Northlanders grow up hearing all sorts of stories about the people of Twilight, but relatively few have personally experienced enough magic to really believe in them."

"Foolishness!" huffed Rycard, snapping his leather tool kit closed and slapping at the dust on his knees. "Why else would your order exist, or mine? What do they think the Lord Steward spends his time watching out for?"

Al frowned to himself. "What every other political leader does, I imagine. His own interests." He studied the items on the table. "Find anything of interest?"

"Much to make a historian's mouth water, little that addresses the Keeper's or the Steward's particular concerns."

"Nothing to explain the wights' behavior?"

"What can? Certainly not animal bones or a few jars of water-damaged scrolls."

"Were the bones unusual?"

Rycard snorted. The thin line of his mouth curdled. "If you are asking if they belonged to monsters, I have to disappoint you. Stag bones, bear bones, the usual trophies of an avid huntsman." He snorted again. "But there is one thing you should see. This way." He motioned Al away from the table toward a shadowy bend in the cavern wall. Picking up a lantern and adjusting its shutters, he made it shine a more focused beam of light. "A few days ago some of my better diggers began working on this."

Al's eyes roamed over the elaborate relief carving. "A hunting scene."

"What period would you say?"

"Well, Bandyr held lordship 300 or so years ago. But judging from the style of the carvings and the dress of the figures, I'd say these were older than that"

"A safe answer," sniffed Rycard. He flicked the lamp's light to another part of the wall. "And now what do you see?"

The nebulous circle of light hovered over a larger, more elaborate carving of a single horseman riding at full gallop and pointing a long spear at the end of which hung a crescent moon. "What do you think?" pressed Rycard.

"Another huntsman," said Al, glancing at Rycard. "Why? What do you see?"

Rycard's narrow face radiated excitement, so Al leaned in to examine the riding figure more minutely. "Why is he spear-hunting at night?" he wondered aloud. He ran his hand over the relief. "And why is the style of this carving so different from the others? The weapons are wrong too."

"Exactly."

"A different period."

"Altogether. Whoever did the more recent carvings tried to match them to the older one — they did a poor job though. I would estimate that this carving predates the one next to it by five or six-hundred years."

"That old! Cyr didn't exist then. This area was wild."

"Very wild," agreed Rycard as something awfully close to glee tried to blunt his sharp features. "But you are missing the best part, seer. You of all people ought to be able to see it."

"See what?"

"The meaning. Consider the period, the figure, the fortress, the great wards you yourself called to life."

Al looked at him blankly. "I don't follow."

Rycard's eyes moved back to the carving. "A thousand years ago, this land was in a turmoil like nothing it has seen since — until now perhaps. The place we today call Cyr was part of a vast no-man's land contested by humans and shadows. The Steward's reach had not yet extended so far. But that does not mean that men were not dwelling here. Men of particular purpose might have found good use for the caves beneath this hill."

Al picked up the scholar's trail of thought. "Warders. You think that this was a way station used by warders."

"More than a way station. It may well have been one of their ancient refuges."

"That would explain the wards at the base of the old fortress," Al mused. "But if it were an ancient warder fortification, why didn't the Lord Warder mention it?"

"I cannot speak for the Lord Warder. But I can say that the evidence is pointing to warder occupation."

Al shook his head. "What would wights want with a refuge of warders? Such a place should have been repellant to them." Al crossed his arms. "Is there other evidence besides this single carving?"

Rycard spoke tartly. "A man with the sight shouldn't miss the evidence that's under his nose."

"What? This?"

"Think about the dating of this carving and look at the rider again, Lord Alsandyr."

Al looked, this time calling upon the sight.

Behind him, Rycard spoke in a voice suddenly soft. "A thousand years ago the Houses experienced one of the great calamities of their history. What began as an age of unprecedented prosperity, discovery, and cooperation collapsed into an age of conflict and catastrophe. The Tellers alone were spared, for, as the story goes, they had already withdrawn from the world of men. It was during this age that two of the great talismans vanished."

Al was listening to Rycard, but at the same time he was riding the sight to a different level of awareness, a place where the stone carving before him took on life and movement, became a silver-haired man, riding at breakneck speed toward a darkening horizon, and in his hand—

Al snapped back into the present, rocking on his heels. The rider, fixed and stony, stared ahead, locked in colorless flight, and from his spear jutted a threatening shape like a crescent moon.

Behind him Rycard sighed, "And now he sees."

Excited in his own right, Al hissed. "This crescent shape, it isn't the moon; it's the warders' device."

"Yes. A crescent like a "c" and down here if you look carefully you will find other letters."

"Cyros," murmured Al, wondering how he could have missed them.

"Precisely so. Literally, C Yros in one of the languages of the time, or translated Crescent Lord."

"Roland," breathed Al.

"The secret consort of Illyria. The wielder of the second lost talisman. Known to many historians as Cyros Roland simply because they do not know that C Yros was an honorific specific to the Lord Warder."

"Wasn't Roland the last to bear that title?"

"Indeed. When he disappeared after the drowning of Illyria, he left without passing on his Lordship. Legend says it was many years before the crescent mark finally reappeared among the warders. And even when it did, some doubted its legitimacy. The warders have never again referred to their leader as the Crescent Lord. Of course, I'm assuming that we members of House Keeper have their history correct, the warders not being known for sharing. It is a pity the Lord Warder has left Cyr. I would dearly love to get his opinion on this."

"So Roland himself might have lived here."

"The better to fall upon his enemies."

"And to visit the land of his lover."

Rycard nodded. "The Gap is not many leagues from Cyr. Alberyc always claimed that the Gap marked the northern border of Illyria's lost land."

Al spun away from the wall, then pressed his fingers into his closed lids.

"Reservations?" demanded Rycard.

"Oh, no. If anything it's too perfect. Only a short time ago Illyria's talisman, the one Roland himself was alleged to have cast into the sea, made its way here."

Rycard shuffled his feet. "You asked about other evidence," he said. "If you are still interested, I can show you something else."

He led Al out of the large cavern and into the smaller one neighboring it. Al had seen this cavern only once, and he had scrupulously avoided thinking about it since. Then as now his mind began hemorrhaging images as soon as he entered it—Alysse entombed, Blayne pierced by light, Emily wading into a sea of grasses, and lastly and most powerfully of all, a dark beast that ripped Al's own neck open with a claw of blackened steel.

Recovering, he saw Rycard standing before the great stone box that dominated the space. "Now," Rycard was saying, "You must understand that I have not yet had time to study these carvings as closely, but I think even you can see their relation to the Roland carving."

Al moved forward and squatted down to put himself on eye-level with the procession of carved figures moving around the box. "You think this box was carved around the same time as the image of Cyros Roland?"

"Yes. And if I'm right, I know who carved them both."

"Who?"

"A sculptor named Kevyn of Esande. Here is his mark." Rycard pointed to the cornice decorating the top edge of the box.

"What do you know about him?" Al asked.

"Quite a bit. The archives of Numyn contain several of his more famous sculptures, remarkable things. His dates correspond roughly to that of the Steward Ayr."

Al quirked a brow. "The period would be right then. Grandfather has long suspected that Ayr was the Steward who betrayed Roland." He let his hand drift over the bumps and ridges of stone.

"If anyone can know for certain, it would be Lord Allyn. Unfortunately, stewards guard their history almost as jealously as warders."

"Was Kevyn a warder?"

Rycard coughed. "Actually, no. That is what makes this so interesting."

Al's look was sharp.

"Kevyn was born in Esande, which in some stories is the name given to Illyria's land. And Kevyn himself was the father of Ruyth, who eventually became the first Keeper in Castle Numyn. So Kevyn must have been a Keeper by heritage, and he was also a favorite of Ayr. In his old age Ayr commissioned a number of works from Kevyn, including his own tomb." A long finger brushed the identifying mark Kevyn had chiseled in the stone.

Al peered where Rycard pointed and realized that Kevyn's signature was not the only writing on the tomb. Rycard translated, "Ayr by Kevyn. For the C Yros. May he forgive and find rest."

Al threw the scholar a shocked look, and Rycard responded with a cynical smile. "Smacks of confession, doesn't it? Apparently Ayr repented of his misdeed and tried to make what amends he could. He commissioned this for Roland. He many have even arranged to have it placed here."

"To act as what? A monument to the man he helped destroy?"

"Or, judging from the size and dimensions of the box, to serve as his tomb."

"But that doesn't make sense. Roland vanished into the wilds. No one knows how or where he died."

Rycard was nodding, his eyes glazed with thought. "Perhaps Ayr did."

Something cold and heavy as a stone settled in Al's chest. "Do you think that the Cyros actually rested here?"

"I've seen nothing to indicate it, but it is always possible that his body was here for a time, then removed at a later date."

"Could the shadow brethren be looking for Roland?"

"You will have to determine that, seer."

Rycard left a short time later, but Al lingered, unable to turn his back on the puzzle before him. He circled the tomb for while, then settled himself into a natural indentation in the stone and fell into a darkly contemplative mood. From this angle he could see two of the tomb's three undamaged sides and the figures moving relentlessly in frozen procession across them. They seemed to be trying to lead him toward something, but his usually potent powers of vision refused to respond. It was as if some power in the great tomb itself were preventing him from exercising his gift.

Eventually he fell asleep and awoke sometime later with a stiff neck and a massive headache. The lantern Rycard had left shown fitfully upon the base of the tomb. He started to rise, then froze as his ears picked up a strange muttering.

Guttural and deep, the sound of it scratched at the silence and seemed to come from the vicinity of the tomb.

Carefully, quietly, Al put a hand to his sword and shifted his legs under him. A moment later, he saw a delicate white hand work its way around the edge of the stone box. His own hand bit into the hilt of his sword so hard that the capillaries in his skin broke.

Moving like a four-footed animal, Alysse crawled around the corner of the carved tomb. Dressed in a nightgown of lawn and lace, she looked delicate, fragile, but her face was twisted into a rictus of hate or pain, and her flesh shone with a faint radiance like the soft illumination seeping through a window shade.

Despite his horror, Al had to fight an impulse to go to her, to try to call her back to her gentle human self.

Then Alysse began to keen. "Where?" she cried, "Where? Four for the four houses; to flesh, heart, mind and soul; to past, present, future and always." Like a long-limbed bug, she scuttled with startling speed around and around the tomb. "Yes," she hissed. "But incomplete, ruined, iced in fresher stone. Except for you, you little witch, you little thief!"

Aagh!" she wailed, crouching low. "Here, all here and yet the answer is not!" With frantic hands Alysse began to claw at her face and scalp, strands of hair slipping through her fingers to the floor. At last her feverish movements eased, and she curled up like a sleeping child and grew still.

Limbs aching with the effort, Al slowly slid forward, and scraped a boot heel against the stone. Faint as the sound was, it was more than enough. Alysse's large eyes shot open and locked on him.

"Alysse," he breathed.

In an instant, she was on him, pressing him back into stone. At first, Al tried to push her back. But that was a mistake. With a casual twist of her wrist she broke his hold and slammed him violently back into the rock. The force coming out of her frail-looking body was stunning. Thoroughly winded, he could do nothing but gape like a fish while she wrapped her narrow hands about his wrists and held him. "Alsandyr, my love," she breathed, and for a second she was the sweet faced, sad-eyed beauty he had loved.

"Alysse, please" he begged. "Let me take you back to your rooms. You are not well."

"Would you, Alsandyr? Take me? You never visit my rooms anymore." Her breath was strangely cold on his face. Her lips iced his own, "I miss you."

He rolled his head away, and she bit his cheek. More alarmingly, he could feel her biting at the edges of his mind. He hardened his shields and fended her off, but she breathed a bitterly cold fire. Like true fire, it seemed to suck all the air into itself, until he was gasping. "Taste, my love," Alysse whispered persuasively. "Then we can be together."

The fire in her was intoxicating indeed, but even as it coursed into his blood stream, he could feel it changing. This was not his first exposure to such fire, and his already sensitized body instinctively countered its effects. At the same time he could sense another mind leaping awake inside his own and pouring power into him. As from a great distance, he could hear her voice calling, "No! Let him go!" Golden fire erupted from his right hand, silver from his chest. Alysse leaped back shrieking and fell away.

Burned out he sagged toward the cavern floor, while her pale form scuttled back into the dark. When he could move again, he used the little energy he had left to send a mental summons the one other person he knew would hear him.

Syrene found him leaning against the great tomb.

"Alsandyr, what has happened?" she cried. Her normally smooth countenance was pinched with fear.

"Go to Abrille and your uncle. Warn them that Alysse is re-infected. But tell them not to try seeking her out until I come. Even if I can find her, it will take a team of talented practitioners to subdue her. And for heaven's sake keep your own guards with you. She could strike at you next."

Even in the near dark, she broadcast distress. "Alysse! I thought—"

"We all did. But either her restoration wasn't complete or something changed. She's more dangerous now than ever."

"Oh, my poor cousin. Is there nothing else we can do?"

"Nothing you can do."

26

It took him some time to persuade her to leave him, but when she had gone, he returned to scrutinizing the tomb. Alysse had expected something from it. What? Holding out Rycard's lantern, he circled it, gazing with sight-opened eyes. On the east side, strangely clad figures battled heroically with a massive shape wrapped in fire. On the long side facing north, carvings told the story of Roland and Illyria meeting and loving. The damaged western side was obscured by hardened dribbles of once liquid stone, but the Shield bearer was there, looking something like an ancient knight with the great talisman hung upon her left arm. With a sigh, he knelt and touched her. And then his thought was winging across the leagues to where the real Shield bearer sat cross-legged in front of her campfire. She looked frightened and upset, but at least she wasn't alone; the cold-eyed warder named Faryn crouched nearby.

Almost, he called her name, but he decided he had distressed her enough for one evening. From her expression, he could guess how much she had felt of his confrontation with Alysse.

He let the image dissolve into the stony solidity of the carven tomb. Using its edge, he levered himself upward and felt a small part of the carved cornice give way to bounce with a crystalline ring across the cavern floor. Retrieving it, he found that it was small cylinder carved in something like marble or alabaster with the symbol of the Orb etched upon it.

"Blood and fire," he hissed. His fingers tested the Orb mark, then raised the cylinder to his lips. When he blew into it, it gave no sound.

The great tomb heard, however. The bottom of it filled up with the ghostly image of a robed man, which melted almost immediately into letters spun of silver fire. Ancient they were, in style and language, yet Al's mind digested them like they had been fashioned in the current tongue.

Can the broken be whole,
the sundered united?
Let sinister knows what dexter does
and the parted be requited.

In tomb living was the Crescent interred,
age wrapped in age to lie
till the sighted go blind
and sons their true selves find,

til blood with blood is repaid
and empires bow dismayed.
Then shall the thorn of death worm free,
night fall, and Cyros rise,
a new moon over a waterless sea.

Chapter 3: The Lady Alyra

Al spent the next several days working to locate Alysse, but her rooms and her belongings yielded no clues, and all the link of joining told him was that the Lord's daughter was no longer in the city. Apparently, Alysse had devised some means of limiting his awareness of her.

Tired and deeply depressed, he again retreated to the lord's library, there to obsess over the verse uncovered in Roland's tomb. It burned in his mind's eye like a brand, and yet it resisted the power of his sight. When he tried to use his powerful inner awareness to peer beyond its silvery surface meaning, it blinded him with brightness.

He turned to researching it in other ways. He wrote it out exactly as he saw it in his mind, then translated, analyzed and coded its contents in various ways, supplementing his own considerable knowledge with information from the library's resources. The language it was written in and the reference to House Crescent seemed to date it to the age of Roland, but he could make nothing of the references to blood or sons. Had Roland had a son? Surely not. Historians would have mentioned it. Of course, they tended to neglect the subject of Roland in general, and recorded nothing about him after the drowning of Illyria.

His investigations ended up generating more questions than answers. Only one thing was absolutely clear. The verse was a clue to the location of the second great talisman, the warders' missing Crescent, sometimes known as the Talon or Thorn. As such, it belonged to the members of House Warder.

Yet Al made no attempt to communicate its discovery to them. He spoke of the verse to no one, not even Blayne, and guarded his investigations into it as closely as he guarded his own soul.

He was aware of the irrationality of his behavior. He upbraided himself for it. He knew that no charm meant for warders could bring good to a steward like himself, and yet he did not speak. He could not. It was as if the shining silver lines had set a seal upon his lips.

One morning as he wrestled with these things, he received a summons from Syrene. "Have you word of Alysse?" he demanded as he swept into the large salon Syrene used for private audiences.

Syrene was standing in the middle of the room looking uncharacteristically insecure in her own domain. "You have a visitor, Alsandyr," she said, flicking a wary glance over her shoulder.

Al followed that glance across a wide expanse of scrolled carpet to a woman standing at the far end of the room. "Mother!" he spat.

His mother turned around. In her youth, Alyra Goodwin had been called the "jewel of the North." Even in middle age, she remained darkly, strikingly beautiful—her figure lithe yet seductive, her skin creamy and offset by ebony hair and large inky eyes. Yet Lady Goodwin's physical attractiveness paled in comparison to the force of her personality. At once cool and intense, distant and alluring, she exuded power and a distinctly feminine charm. When Lady Alyra entered a room, she filled it, like the aroma of a subtly intoxicating perfume.

Al could feel his mother's charm sliding around him now, coaxing him to relax, be reasonable, yield. In deference to Syrene, he tolerated it. His eyes, however, glinted obsidian.

Syrene's normally mellifluous voice sounded tinny in his ears. "Your mother arrived earlier this morning, Alsandyr. I tried to send you word."

Alyra approached her son, smiling relentlessly. "I wonder that Alsandyr did not sense it for himself," she commented as she laid a hand upon his cheek.

Al endured the touch. His voice, however, went hard and flat as a plank. "I've been busy."

"So I have heard," his mother replied. Her inky eyes drank him in, widening as some even darker thought disturbed their black depths. "But it is more than that."

She turned to the fourth person in the room. "It is more than preoccupation, Blayne. There is a shadow on my son's thoughts."

Blayne spoke from the window. "I see no shadow," he said indifferently, "Only two minds."

Alyra turned back to her son, studied him as if he were a knotted thread she was about to untangle. "Two minds. Two natures."

"And being pulled by both of them," Blayne clarified.

Al crossed his arms. "Shall I lie down while you two dissect me?" he snapped.

Syrene dropped her eyes to the floor. Alyra's widened. "Testy as well!" she commented.

Blayne shrugged. "He is still less trying than most mortals." His gleaming green eyes slid to Syrene, who stiffened in offense.

"How touching to hear you say so," Al remarked.

Alyra's voice deepened, turned heavy, rounded and yet impersonal. "He will prove more trying yet," she said. "But you must not desert him, Blayne. The way to your heart and your heart's desire lies through him."

Then as quickly as her tone of portent had come, it departed, swept away by Alyra herself, who now spoke with brusque directness. "Join me for dinner, Blayne. We have much to talk about. For now I must speak with my son." Stepping to Al's side, she slipped a languid hand around his arm. "Come, Alsandyr," she said and walked him from the room.

Al dropped all pretense of tolerance as soon as they were alone. "Why are you here, Mother?" he demanded when they had wandered far out onto Lord North's well-kept lawns.

Alyra squared shapely shoulders, seeming to admire their flowering surroundings. "I wanted to see you, of course. Is that not reason enough to come? Wilhem sends his love."

"How is Father? And Jules and Jorge?"

"They are all well. Dale has a new baby daughter." Alyra's fingers plucked a round red rose from a mounded bush.

"He wrote me. Three girls!" Al smiled.

"He and Riza kept hoping for a son even though I warned them they would never have one."

Al's smile flicked off. "They are entitled to hope. Father, I'm sure, is ecstatic."

The long fingers of Alyra's left hand twirled the rose. "The spoiling has already begun. I'll never understand his pleasure in all the playing and pouting."

"You wouldn't. You've never had much patience for children. It's a wonder that you ever inconvenienced yourself enough to have me."

The expression Alyra turned on him was polite. "What do you mean?"

"Nothing. I was only observing that you are your father's daughter—clear-eyed, logical, and anything but maternal."

"I was maternal enough to raise you."

"But not to love me. A family failing, I believe."

His mother let go of his arm and slapped his face. The blow was light, but so abrupt that he couldn't process it before he felt its sting.

Alyra spoke levelly. "Never say that to me again. I have loved you as deeply as a mother can."

The shock worn off, Al sneered, and spoke with a surge of anger so intense it overwhelmed reason. "A pity then that you couldn't show it," he snapped, bitterness like grit in his teeth

Then he heard himself, and shut his mouth, blinking. By heaven, his self-control really was deserting him!

Alyra, who almost never lost hers, studied him quite objectively. "Two minds indeed. Blayne, as usual, misses nothing." Her thoughts coiled like smoke about her son's mind. "How long have you been like this?" she asked, raising an eyebrow.

"Like what?" evaded Al, still fighting to rein in his anger.

"You know what I mean. Your emotions are running amok, overrunning your controls."

Al took a step away from her. "It is nothing. I'm just tired."

But the touch of his mother's mind intensified. She caught his arm, and he felt her concern washing over him like cold water. "You have seen something," he murmured in surprise, "something concerning me. It frightens you?"

Alyra sighed and looked out over the lawn. "I have always seen things that frighten me for you, Alsandyr."

"One good reason for keeping your distance as a mother," Al remarked ironically.

Alyra pointed to a marble bench "Sit," she ordered. The day was overcast, but the ground before them shimmered under a strange wavering of light. Al looked up and saw the Shield Light, the Keeper's recently recovered talisman, glimmering atop its black granite pedestal.

Alyra gazed at it also, then sat down next to him and, with one slender hand, turned his face away from the talisman and toward her. "You are confusing misunderstanding with lack of affection, my son. If I was distant with you, it was out of an excess of caution, never from lack of love, though I grant you that we of the Steward's house are not known for our demonstrativeness. We are both bred and trained to keep our feelings in check, to be ruled by reason and objective thought rather than feeling. But that does not mean that we do not have feelings. I have always loved you, Alsandyr, as I love my life. But you — you were — "

Her son's voice was wry. "What?"

"You must understand, my son. You are the child of my body, but in many ways, you are not the child of my mind. From the beginning, you were different."

Al started upward, turned his back on her disdainfully. "As I have been told time and time again. I never see Grandfather but he is quick to point out that I am flawed, too impulsive and unpredictable, as like to act on intuition as reason."

"You are certainly restless and quick to action, fierce in your dislikes and your loyalties alike."

"Most unsteward-like," he sneered.

"But you are a steward. And I did all I could to help you realize that aspect of yourself even when my lessons frustrated and confused you."

Al turned back to her, shaking his head in disgust. "You should have known it would not work. Shearing the sheep won't change its blackness. Why, by all that's infernal, didn't you have another child, one more suited to the office. Better yet, why didn't you step up and accept the heirship yourself. Grandfather would have been relieved to bestow it on you."

"Because I couldn't."

"Couldn't what? Be Steward and mother? Other women have."

"I wouldn't."

He frowned at her. "Why not? Were you so eaten up with pride that you couldn't admit your mistake in marrying a man without power? You could have set Wilhem aside, taken a more suitable spouse. We all might have been better served if you had."

"Alsandyr, stop." Alyra said it softly, but her thoughts slid over his burning ones like chill waters. "You were the child I wanted. That is all you need to know. If I refused to give my house another heir, it is because I believed then and believe still that you will be a Steward like no other."

He laughed to hear her delusion and pressed the fingers of his right hand into his eyes as if to push back a more searing thought. "A Steward like no other? A Steward who can't think clearly or see objectively. And look at me now. By the powers, I feel like I could lash out at the entire world."

Her hands caught his arms, held him. "The emotionalism is not you, Alsandyr," she said, "but it is something you have brought on yourself."

He pulled his fingers from his eyes, looked into hers, and saw that she had raised them to the strange artifact hanging above their heads like an ax poised to fall.

With a groan, he dropped back to the bench. "Tellers, I'm an idiot."

His mother's voice held both affection and reproach. "Did you really think that you could join with her and not pay the price?"

32

His voice testified to his own disgust. "I suppose I was expecting something different."

"From the Keeper's House? Did I waste all those hours I spent teaching you their history? How in ancient days it was called the House of the Heart, sometimes the House Compassionate, because it is the unpredictable but inescapable power of the heart it wields. You may reign over the seat of your reason, but where your feelings reside, she will guide and rule. And because of your earlier actions, the effect is compounded."

"I bound myself twice."

"So you did. Through two women you have laid yourself open to an alien house. Naturally, you find your emotions getting the best of you."

"So now I have to fight them as well."

"Your instinct has always been to fight. Perhaps you should try something less confrontational. Have you tried communing with her instead?"

"She won't open up, or listen. She resents me, her own power, and our connection, as no doubt she should. If only she hadn't kept pushing me away."

"If you are confused, imagine how she must feel. She needs your experience Alsandyr, your cooler head and knowledge. You both must learn to manage your impacts on each other. As for Alysse—"

For a moment, the Shield's light seemed to darken. "Alysse," Al breathed.

"You are in great peril. She will never quit pursuing you until you find the strength to sever your link. And that may be beyond you now." Alyra's lovely face had gone white, her voice opaque.

"Is that what you have come to tell me?"

"No, that much you knew already."

Al swept a hand through his hair. "Then you've come to reproach me for not killing her as soon as the opportunity presented itself."

Alyra took his right hand in both of hers. "I told you. I came to see you." Unexpectedly, she wrapped her arms around him and held him close.

Al had no memory of his mother ever hugging him like this. The gesture set fear like frostbite in his bones. "Mother?" he said hoarsely. And when his mother did not answer, he spoke sharply. "What have you seen, Mother? Tell me."

Alyra sighed. "Nothing, my son. For many weeks now I have tried to envision you, but I have gotten nothing—nothing but writhing dark."

Al went to see Lyr. The old man welcomed him with typical sprightliness and ushered him into a chair.

"I hear your mother is in town," Lyr winked as he busied himself serving tea.

"You hear everything."

"I make every effort to. A pity I wasn't there to witness your heartwarming reunion."

Al's smile showed its edge. "If you join us for dinner, you'll find warmed heart all over the menu."

Lyr laughed, waving a hand. "Ah, no! I worship your mother, my boy, but I would sooner confront the heads of all the houses — as I did none too recently you will remember — than dine with her."

Al chuckled, "Why, master, what have you ever done to incur her displeasure?"

"Well, let's see. My first mistake was probably declaring myself her master in the schoolroom."

"She was that difficult a student?"

"Indomitable is the correct word. Brilliant, yes, and about as cooperative then as she is now."

"And she criticizes me for being a fighter."

"Yes, well, your mother wages war in an entirely different fashion, but she is no stranger to conflict. Now, she can't be the only reason you have come to see me."

"No. I wanted to show you something that came into my possession not long ago."

Lyr sipped his tea and nodded.

From his coat pocket, Al pulled out a small book. Its leather cover was scuffed but supple and stamped on top of it was the shape of the Keeper's mark. Carefully he handed it to the old man.

Lyr took it with equal care. Its pages, when opened, spilled forth a riot of color.

"Are you familiar with it?" Al asked.

"Alberyc," the old man muttered, and the look he shot Al from beneath his wild white hair was almost sly. "Where did you get it?"

"Emily gave it to me before she left for the Greenwood. She claimed it belonged to Alysse, but I never saw such a thing in Alysse's possession." He was looking at the old man almost sternly. "Did you give it to her?"

"No," Lyr said bluntly, transformed suddenly into a very sober and very wise old man. "I am familiar with this copy, but I haven't seen it in, oh, nearly three decades."

Al sat forward. "There are others?"

"At least one other that I know of. That other copy was in the Keeper's Library at Numyn."

"Was?"

"It went missing, about the time that Blayne was born. The council was quite dismayed by the loss of it."

"And do you know where this copy comes from?"

"The last time I saw it, it was in your grandfather's possession."

Al sat back in amazement. "A book with the Keeper's mark?"

"Yes. There was a mark impressed upon the copy in the Keeper's library as well, but it had been obliterated long ago. If I remember correctly, the librarians descriptions made no mention of it."

Al's intent gaze hovered over the old man. "Have you read either version?"

Lyr smiled to himself, leafing through the pages slowly. "Have you?" he teased before answering his own question. "No. And why? Because it can't be done."

Al sighed. "The little I tried to translate came out as gibberish. Sentences, even words, like a bastardization of true language and defying all logic."

"The histories do say that Alberyc was mad."

Al agreed, "His book would certainly convince."

"However," Lyr continued, "A few of the more daring scholars have suggested that Alberyc was merely madly cunning."

"You think that the books are a code?"

"If so, a bafflingly complex one. But it is an interesting idea."

Al sat back, pondering. Then he reached into his pocket again and pulled forth several sheets of carefully folded paper. Offering them to the little white-haired man, he said, "So how, master, would you explain these?"

Lyr accepted the pages and opened them to the lamplight.

The change their contents wrought on him was immediate and extreme. His pale face grew two shades paler, and the lines in it deepened to rocky chasms.

"Master?" said Al, sliding to the edge of his seat.

Lyr did not seem to hear him. His bird-bright eyes were darting back and forth across the lines of writing.

He read the pages through, once, twice, three times, and when he sat back all his native energy had evaporated. Al could not remember ever seeing the old man look so weary.

"What is it?" he demanded.

But Lyr only shook his head, his gaze turned inward toward thought or memory.

"You recognize the writing," Al insisted. "Whose is it? Emily thought Alysse wrote it, but I know better."

The old man did not seem to hear him, so Al sank into a crouch beside him. "Lyr, what about the verse at the end? Could it have been buried in the book?"

The old man's hand shot up. "Not now, Alsandyr. Not now." He motioned for the younger man to move and rose heavily to his feet.

Al's face grew stern, commanding. "Lyr, I need to know."

But the old man rounded on him with such ferocity that even Al was taken aback. An instant later Lyr's manner and expression softened. One of his hands, as light and bony as a bird's claw, caught Al's arm in a surprisingly firm grip. "Please, my boy, not now. You have given me much to think on, much to think on. I need time to sort out the facts before I attempt to answer any questions."

Al left the master's house more troubled in mind than when he had entered it. The tangle of questions snarled about him had only grown, leaving him restless and pent up, with a raging headache to spare. He could have kicked the first creature unlucky enough to cross his path, but he was so busy sifting details that he did not notice the shabby-looking person who skulked not far behind.

When he turned onto a particularly narrow street, two more men materialized beside the first, but by this time Al's pace had quickened as he approached an intersection with a wider way. Then a hunched figure scuttled out of the shadows ahead of him and blocked his path.

"Lord," it croaked.

Al halted, his right hand drawing back the edge of his coat to grip the hilt of his blade. "Yes," he said politely. He heard footsteps rushing behind him and spun, but his attackers were on him before his blade came free. He snapped the whip of his thought into them instead.

The mental attack rebounded with skull-shattering force, and his assailants carried him to the ground.

A scuffle ensued, short and violent. Two of the initial attackers fell wounded, but others rushed out of the darkness. Al kicked and struck at them all, but they weighed him down. Desperate, he tried once more lashing out with his mind. Again, his thought sprang back upon him. Then one well-executed stroke to his temple knocked him nearly senseless. He sprawled on the cobbles. When the stars behind his eyes faded, it was not a thug's face that he saw, but the once lovely and familiar face of Alysse North.

"Greetings, my love," she hissed. Her breath rattled over him, smelling of frost and charred flesh. With an almost filmy hand she raised a narrow needle of bone. "Greetings and goodnight," she cooed, and jammed the needle home.

Alyra Goodwin's dinner party had been over for hours, but the table remained uncleared, and the servants like the guests had been dismissed.

. "Let me go and search for him," Blayne said for the fifth time as she stood with her back to him, arms crossed at the window.

"Absolutely not," Alyra returned. "Not until the Lord's soldiers complete their investigation."

"If your suspicions are correct, he will be dead or gone from the city by the time they discover anything." Though his words were grim, Blayne spoke them indifferently.

Alyra met his indifference with remorselessness. "Then I will have only myself to blame. We cannot risk losing you too. We do not know what traps Alysse and her Twilight masters have laid. In a few hours it will be dawn. You can try tracking them then."

"Your strategy is sound only if they leave me something to track. Dead is dead, lady."

Alyra studied his perfect and perfectly disinterested countenance and wondered, not for the first time, if there were another reason why she was keeping him near her. All her legendary steward self-control seemed to be failing her tonight, and she yearned for Blayne's cold-eyed distance and objectivity.

A rap on the door brought her head around. Lord North stepped into the room and held up a dusty garment that drew from Alyra a faint cry.

Blayne's response was more pragmatic. "How much blood?"

"Not much. We believe he has been taken. A guard at the eastern gate noted an unusual group of wagons rolling out of the city several hours ago."

The impossibly beautiful half-breed nodded. "I will start there."

"Wait," the lady ordered. She looked hard at Lord North. "Where was the coat found?"

"In the south quarter. Apparently, he had just left the home of the master named Lyr. Lady, I cannot begin to express my shock and dismay at this development. I will send word to your Lord father immediately."

"I will speak with my father myself, Lord North. But I thank you for your efforts. Please continue them, and I will join you when I am done here."

If Lord North balked at being summarily dismissed in his own home, he forbore to show it. Perhaps he knew the lady's formidable nature, having played at courting her in his younger days. With a gracious bow of sympathy, he draped the coat on a chair. "Take as much time as you need," he said. "I will wait outside and escort you to the council room when you are ready."

Alyra lifted a brow, but did not object. She waited for him to leave, then approached Blayne, who was riffling the pockets of the coat.

"You must get to him as soon as you can," she ordered. "He is not dead. I know it. He will now focus on surviving and escaping. Do not give up on him even when all seems most hopeless."

"I do not answer to hope, and I never give up on anything, lady," said Blayne with a blandness that shut down argument.

She smiled her rue. "I know. I speak more to myself than you. I just hope you understand how much we all stand to lose in him."

"I understand that there is a job to be done. That is all I need to understand, unless you have information that will help me to locate him." He raised his head to fix her with the glow from his lambent eyes.

Alyra shivered. "I think of him and try to use the sight and all I see is blackness, blankness."

Blayne dismissed the statement and unfolded the sheet of paper he'd just pulled from the coat's pocket.

The lady, however, was not done. "But I see many things concerning you." A small smile of cunning played about her lips. "What did Alsandyr tell you of your cousin's plans?"

"Emilyn?" Blayne shrugged as his eyes skimmed the pages. "She has returned to the Greenwood."

"With no intention of staying there."

Blayne lifted his head. "Her guardians will ensure otherwise."

"I doubt it. Like all her house, she is dogged where loyalty is concerned, and her loyalty is driving her south, to the aid of a friend, an incomparable beauty called Empyre's daughter, who is also growing in power."

In the dimly lit room Blayne's eyes began to burn a brighter green. "Bethnara. She is in danger?"

"As is the child growing within her."

Even the indomitable Alyra quailed to see the transformation those words wrought. All semblance of humanity evaporated from Blayne's countenance, leaving behind the revelation of a creature perfect in power and utterly alien in its intent. The sight left the Steward's daughter feeling almost helpless, as if she dared to hold a tiger by a thread.

"Bethnara is pregnant?" Blayne said the words slowly, flatly, indifferently. "Does Alsandyr know?"

Alyra dipped her head, never taking her eyes off him. "Yes, through the girl."

"He kept it from me."

"Only because he feared for your safety and the safety of our land."

Blayne's eyes flamed, though he spoke as disinterestedly as ever. "You are a fool to tell me this now. I could leave for the Southland tonight, abandon your son to his fate and secure my own." His words were soft, but his barely restrained otherness was suffocating.

"If you do, your son as well as mine will die. There is a power gnawing on the roots of the Empyre that even you cannot master. I have seen it building; I have seen it breaking free. If you go to your princess now, you will only hasten her destruction and your own. And your son, if he lives, will be consumed to the restoration of an ancient enemy. You need Alsandyr."

"Why?"

Alyra's certainty faltered. "I—I cannot say. I only know that he must go south with you. Only with his aid can any of you come safely through the ordeal ahead."

"If you lie—"

Alyra's eyes flashed. "Stewards do not lie."

"No." Blayne's eyes burned into hers. "Not when they have partial truths to call upon." But he withdrew his aura of unspoken threat and held out to her the piece of paper he had pulled from Alsandyr's coat pocket.

Frowning, Alyra took it, read it. Then she called upon the sight and read it again. "Where did he get this?" she gasped.

"I do not know. But judging by his notations and his behavior recently, I would say he has been working on it for several days."

Alyra brought hand and paper to her mouth.

"I will send word when I can," said Blayne, moving to the door.

"No! Wait!"

Blayne stopped, looked at the lady, who seemed to be staring wide-eyed at the disarray of her own thoughts.

"The situation is more complicated than I thought," she said. "Let Lord North's men try to pick up Alsandyr's trail. You must go to the Lord Warder." She held out the piece of paper to him. "Find Sandyr Ash and give him this. Tell him that his son has gone missing and that more than the Lords of Twilight may be behind it. Make sure he knows that it was Alsandyr who was in possession of this verse."

Alyra saw a hand-picked group of men ride off into a graying dawn. Twilight denizens would be no threat to them for now, but who knew what human opposition they might encounter. She wondered where Blayne was on his road and pressed cold hands to her tight belly. It was time to leave the wide terrace and settle into the trance that would initiate contact with her lord father. His response would be acid-contempt and anger, but she would endure it. She had known little else from him since the fateful day when she broke her house's oldest rule. Whether she could handle the wrenching losses to come was less certain.

Pulling her shawl around her, she turned her back to hope and the dawn, and discovered a small, grave bundle of authority standing in her way.

"Master Lyr!" she said in surprise.

"Alyra," said the master in the very tone he must have used to cow her in the classroom.

"You have heard about Alsandyr?"

"Of course!" snapped the little old man, peering up at her from beneath his wild white hair.

"Then how may I serve you, master?"

His sharp little eyes dug into her own. "Your Lord Father lied to us, Alyra. Have you been lying as well?"

"What?" Her voice cracked upon the stones.

Without breaking his mental hold on her, Lyr pressed into her hand a set of pages. He waited silently while Alyra looked them over. Her eyes had only to graze the writing to recognize it. "Dyre," she whispered.

"Indeed," answered Lyr shortly. "What really happened to your brother, Alyra?"

Chapter 4: Boxes

Six days after Emily's return, Greenwood village witnessed the marriage of Lettie Harrington to Cal Whitfield. The ceremony was held at noon in the village council chamber. Then the villagers broke ranks to set up for the real festivities, which would begin at sunset.

In a back bedroom of the Blackhammer homestead, Emily dressed, choosing one of the everyday garments made for her in Cyr. It was a color of red that her grandfather called the heraldic color of House Keeper. According to him, it suited her.

Giving her crimson skirt a final swipe, she opened the bedroom door and discovered a stranger lurking outside. Hands on hips, she studied him. "If you don't move, you might just pass for a common-as-dirt Midlander."

Faryn looked almost stiff in his borrowed Midlander clothing. "I still do not understand why I must attend this . . . what do you call it?

"Wedding celebration. Don't warders hold weddings?"

"Why would we?"

Emily blinked, raised a hand as if to pull words from the air. "To . . . to honor a couple's promise to be committed."

Faryn quirked a brow. "All warders *are* committed — to their work."

Emily opened her mouth, closed it and tried again. "Yes, but married couples agree to be committed to each other. You know, to be exclusive."

"Ah."

"Warders do eventually become exclusive?" She flushed.

"Rarely."

"Rarely?" It seemed that Garvin Blackhammer had been right — she knew almost nothing about Faryn's people. "You mean that a man and a woman may sleep together for years, even have children, without making each other any promise for the future."

"A man and a woman may promise what they like. We consider the act of formally contracting such relationships rather barbaric."

Emily gaped, and Faryn's stiffness dropped away. Suddenly he was all warder and closing in on her with a speculative look. Emily dropped her eyes. She could tell that her response both interested and amused him.

"This offends you," he said.

"Well," she huffed, then floundered. "Well. What if a woman wants a man all to herself?"

Faryn smiled wider. "She tells him so."

"And what if he doesn't want . . . that."

"He tells her so, and they negotiate a compromise."

"Warders must be the most understanding people on earth," she spat disgustedly.

"We do not fight nature." The way he was peering into her eyes made her feel as simple and transparent as spring water.

Emily glared. "You consider it natural for men and women to sleep with whomever they want whenever they want?"

"Yes, and pleasant too."

"Until the woman gets with child," she snapped.

One corner of Faryn's mouth actually twitched as he looked at her. He seemed to be working to suppress a laugh. "Why would that change matters?"

"Well, who raises it?"

"The community, of course."

"And what about its parents?"

"They are a part of the community."

"Even if—" She gave up. "Here let me fix your collar."

He leaned into her a little, and she smoothed the material over his vest, biting her lip as an unexpected thought occurred to her. "Faryn, you do realize that Midlanders have, um, much stricter views on intimate relations."

His icy eyes swiveled to catch hers. She was sure he was laughing at her now. "How so?"

"The young women you meet tonight may be quite flirtatious."

"And?"

She drew herself up sternly. "You must not treat their flirting as an invitation. Unless you want to hold a wedding of your own."

He laughed out loud. "You have no reason to worry. Word of the prudishness of Midlanders has reached even House Warder."

She was searching for a retort when a creak of the hall's floorboards announced Colin's arrival. He was shaved and brushed and dressed in his best clothes and almost twitching with anxiety. She could have pinched him. Faryn's inherent watchfulness needed no encouragement.

Colin nodded to the warder uneasily. Faryn nodded fluidly back and followed the Midlander's gaze to Emily, still standing in the bedroom doorway.

"You look nice!" Colin blurted, his face reddening.

Emily beamed. "Do you like it?"

Colin jerked his chin awkwardly as his eyes slid from her face to the open neck of her bodice then jumped away. "It's very—" he coughed, "flattering."

Emily tossed her head. She didn't have to look at Faryn to sense the amusement emanating from him. "Excellent seamstresses," she pronounced primly, "One of the advantages of living in a big city. Shall we go?"

The green before the inn overflowed with smiling, laughing people. The inn itself eddied thick with them. As Emily waited in line to give the bride the traditional kiss of blessing, she found herself trying to swallow a lump in her throat.

When the bride and groom made their way outside, the real celebration began. Out came the fiddles and pipes, the smoked meats and pies, the casks of good ale. Emily led Faryn and Colin into the throng, surprised to find herself the recipient of much attention and goodwill. Girls she had rarely associated with exclaimed over the rich color of her gown; young men made free to take her hand and welcome her home; and older villagers spoke reverently of her aunt.

At another time, Emily would have enjoyed the warmth of their attentions. Tonight, she could only pretend to. Inwardly, she was dashing through a thousand disastrous scenarios, every one of which made smiling hard. And Colin wasn't helping. He seemed ready to yelp at every move from the warder padding close on both their heels. And Colin wasn't the only person that Faryn disturbed.

It was painfully apparent that the villagers did not know what to make of this familiarly dressed stranger who stalked like a wolf among lap dogs. Emily had repeatedly warned Faryn to squelch whatever mysterious element of his power screamed "unnatural" to ordinary folk, but one can't expect a predator to act like prey. With or without his magic, Faryn was dangerous, and on a gut level all the villagers knew it.

Just as Emily began to despair of ever escaping him, a larger presence loomed at her shoulder. Garvin Blackhammer made a short comment to someone else nearby then growled, "You and my son should dance."

The smith stepped away as soon as the words were out of his mouth, and Emily grabbed Colin by the coat. "Come on, Col, I feel like dancing."

Colin looked at her blankly. "Dancing! You never . . ."

She jerked him to silence and propelled him toward the dancing ground.

Faryn let them go, running a sharp eye over the faces of the excited, jovial people around him. They reminded him of children—big, soft, ignorant children. An adult would not ignore the fiends scratching at the door.

He circled the dancing space slowly, sidestepping a group of giggling young women who threw him admiring looks. He barely glanced their way. He knew he had only to hold their eyes to see them shrink like mice before a snake. He wondered that Emilyn didn't realize the serious threat he posed to ordinary people if he let down the guard on his magic for even a moment. He didn't let down his guard of course. He hadn't challenged his way up to seventh by being careless.

His eyes settled on a swirl of brilliantly red gown and the girl in it. She was speaking intently to Colin, and Faryn smiled to himself as he imagined what she was saying. She was planning something; every quivering line of her body, every uttered word, every flicker of lash shouted it. And the young man also sang with tension. This Colin was in deeper than he could know, for what the bearer of a great talisman willed no inexperienced village youth could hope to resist. Yet this Colin possessed more toughness and talent than he knew. Real potential there.

"Master Faryn," said a deep voice, "Would you permit me to stand you a drink."

Faryn turned to face the big man he had heard approaching. He calculated the tensile strength in the tall body, the balance and control, then smiled into the steady brown gaze. Mental strength was there as well. "Just Faryn," he said to Garvin Blackhammer. "I am not thirsty at the moment. Later perhaps." He slipped into the dancing crowd.

Stepping carefully to the music, Emily and Colin lumbered through one dance and into another. "If your leg is hurting, we can stop now," Emily said. "I just wanted to get you away from Faryn."

Colin looked offended. "What's that supposed to mean?"

"Don't get angry. I didn't like the way he was watching you. If we are going to pull this off, you can't look like you are about to jump out of your skin."

"I'm fine."

"You're as twitchy as a scalded cat, and I've a hunch that Faryn can smell nervousness from five leagues off."

Colin looked over his shoulder. "Where is he?"

"Somewhere over there. Quit looking. It's as suspicious as twitching. Did you give your father the drugs?"

She saw his throat move. "Yes."

"Enough?"

Colin scowled at her in irritation. "Yes! When it comes to sedatives I do know what I'm doing."

"Then quit worrying."

"I'm trying, but you won't shut up about it, and —" Colin winced.

"And what?"

"I can't help wondering what warders do to people who try to drug them." His words ended in a dying groan.

Emily rolled her eyes; the music rolled to a stop. Then Colin yelped and bumped into the couple behind them. Turning, Emily yelped as well for Faryn had somehow materialized right beside her.

"May I?" the warder asked, bowing gracefully and holding out a hand for Emily.

Colin blinked, then threw Emily a delighted look. "Certainly!" he said, and handed her over.

"What are you doing?" Emily demanded as the pipes and fiddles spun up.

But Colin was already limping away. "Try not to act twitchy," he called merrily as Faryn set a hand on her waist and spun her into the dance.

She expected awfulness, awkwardness for she was no dancer and warders didn't spend their time practicing their country reels. But Faryn's grip was firm without being tense and warm without being alarming. Emily found her own physical tension dissolving, her instincts improving. Faryn moved and Emily moved with him, as naturally as water follows a channel. The tempo increased, and they moved faster, until Emily marveled at the soaring sensation building inside as her feet kept perfect time. What was it Beth had once said? That dancing with a suitable partner was like flight?

For the first time in her life, Emily realized that a dance could end too soon. As Faryn spun her to a halt, she couldn't stop herself from panting, "That was wonderful! Your dancing is . . . a marvel."

The light-eyed warder looked amused. "Why wouldn't it be? I'm a master of my body, and any child could commit these steps to memory."

Emily laughed breathlessly. "I don't know many that could execute them like you do?"

"Shall we go again?'

"Yes. Yes, please!"

Emily danced two more sets with him, but by then, several other young women were hovering nearby, eyes greedy for a turn. At Emily's insistence, Faryn agreed to partner a few. And Emily, seizing the opportunity, went in search of Colin and his father. She found her friend surrounded by a group of young women, all talking animatedly and admiringly with the village healer. Their open expressions made Emily wince with guilt. Greenwood village had more than a life of healing to offer Colin Blackhammer, though by the looks of it Colin had not yet begun to notice. She wondered how he would react if she made sure that he did.

Faryn bowed to his giddy, young partner and easing the mental control he exerted on her gawky mind and body, walked away. He found Emily and Colin easily enough. They were standing near the trestle tables sipping beer and chatting with a collection of other young people.

Not far away stood Garvin Blackhammer, big, dark and solitary as a mountain bear. The smith held the warder's gaze as Faryn approached. "I didn't know warders danced," he rumbled.

Faryn smiled to the bottom of his gray eyes. "We prefer to do it with knives."

The smith snorted.

"I would like that drink now," said Faryn.

Garvin glanced at the makeshift bar. "I could offer you ale, but as I understand it, warders don't like most spirits. Still, I may have something to your taste."

Faryn nodded and, noting Emily's position, allowed himself to be led back toward the inn. 'You seem very familiar with my order."

"I encountered a few warders when I lived in the capital."

"Who was your regimental commander?"

"You see the soldier in me then?"

Faryn nodded, "Sound training leaves its mark. I did not expect to find a guard of the Steward's city here."

"No more, I am sure, than I expected see a warder dancing on the village green." He motioned to the young man behind the makeshift bar to get out of the way, stepped behind it himself, and dug out two rather dusty glasses. Bringing them back, he added, "My commander was Holdstock, but those days are long over. I'm a smith and family man now." Blackhammer held out one glass out to the warder. Then he reached into an inner pocket and pulled out a dusty, tightly stoppered bottle. "Fire whiskey," he rumbled holding it up. "A weakness of warders, I believe. Once a weakness of mine." He opened the bottle, offered it to Faryn to sniff, and poured a small amount of liquid into both glasses.

He drank first, a small taste only, wincing at the intensity of the burn that followed the strangely light liquid down his throat.

Faryn swilled his like spring water, then looked thoughtfully at the glass.

Garvin Blackhammer was not a man to hold his breath for fear, but even he found inhaling difficult in that moment. The part of his mind that wasn't focused entirely on the warder recalled the words he had had with his son earlier that morning.

"You made it clear."

"You said you wanted to coat the glass."

"You're sure it is tasteless?"

"As near as I can be, Papa. Millicynt trained me to heal people not poison them."

"Tell your conscience to relax. We are aiming to slow him down, not kill him."

"Yes, well, if the drink is as potent as you say, he shouldn't be able to taste anything."

"Let us hope so. Warders have extremely acute senses. How much?"

"A drop, no more. Tellers, Papa! Not two! You could kill him!"

"Warders also have extremely fast recovery times. What would kill a normal man will likely give him little more than a headache."

Now, as Garvin watched the warder drink, he concentrated on keeping his heart rate steady, his breathing even. There was no turning back now. Either the warder would drop or Garvin would, probably before he saw the weapon that felled him. Icy gray eyes locked onto the smith's, and Blackhammer raised the bottle again in a silent salute.

Faryn smiled and held out his glass.

When Emily saw the smith and Faryn drinking side by side, she began nudging Colin in the direction of the woodwright's shop. People parted, came together. She pushed Colin through a momentary gap and into the dimness between buildings. Together, they scurried around the baker's shop and across a wagon yard to the woodwright's place. Its doors, thrown open to the evening, beckoned. And just as Garvin Blackhammer had promised, two open crates awaited them. Emily contemplated the rough wooden boxes for a long moment before swallowing hard and climbing into hers.

47

"Not too tight," she warned Colin from her crouched-down position. But she couldn't stop her breaths from coming fast and shallow as he dragged the lid over her head.

"She is gone," said the warder, having swallowed his fourth mouthful of fire whiskey. He turned fixed, cold eyes on the smith.

Garvin Blackhammer assumed that his time had come. With more resignation than hope, he inched his hand toward the knife at his back, and vowed he would at least draw it before Faryn struck. The warder's gaze caught the movement. He blinked, then blinked again. His eyes seemed to frost over as he took a single step forward. Then he fell.

Minutes seemed to lengthen into ages as Emily waited in stifling dark that smelled overwhelmingly of pine. Her left palm was already sticky with sap. Somewhere beyond her wooden world there was a scuffling like feet moving across a dirt and sawdust floor. Muffled voices spoke of the road and the weather. They approached, receded, approached again. Then she and her rough confines were being lifted. She pressed her hands and feet into the corners trying to balance her weight against the shifting wood. She got splinters and a bruised shoulder for the effort. Then, with a tooth-cracking jolt, her crate was plunked down and shoved forward.

The small sounds around her changed, spoke of harness and open spaces. A motion of a different kind began, a gentler jarring. With a shaky sigh, she gulped down all her uncertainties and tried to settle in for the ride.

Garvin Blackhammer stumbled into his house.

His wife, Kaitlyn—who should have been at the party but, being precognitively female, wasn't—saw the lean form draped across her husband's shoulders and cried out, "Garvin!"

"Don't ask," grunted her husband. "Just show me where I can put him down."

His wife's lips thinned, but she did as he requested without another word. Guiding him to Colin's room, she arranged the sheets and pillows then helped her husband drape Faryn's lean limbs atop them.

Together they stood looking down at the warder lying prone in their house.

48

"He looks dead," hissed Kaitlyn around her husband's broad shoulder.

"Nah," grunted Garvin. "But you and the children should sleep at the inn tonight. He won't be happy when he wakes up."

Kaitlyn Blackhammer seemed to bite down on her words. "And what about you?"

"I'm used to daring death."

Kaitlyn frowned at him, but her eyes soon returned to the warder, the relaxed limbs, the clean features, and closed eyes with their long sweep of lash. When she spoke again, her voice had a hitch in it. "He's not all that much older than Colin, is he?"

"Not in years, but he has seen things ordinary men can hardly imagine."

"Will you be able to handle him?"

"No. But as I promised, I'm going to try."

His wife pressed herself against his broad back. "And Colin?"

"Be proud, Kaitie. Our boy's a man now and ready to make his own way in the world."

He grimaced as he heard his strong, proud wife gulp back a sob.

The ruts and holes of the road beat Emily into semi-consciousness where she loitered in a terrible dream. She was locked in a box. She wanted desperately to get out, but she couldn't even move her limbs, and the more she struggled, the more pressure she felt upon them. With tremendous effort, she willed her terribly heavy lids to open and beheld crawling, creeping lines of darkness. She tried to cry out, but the dark seemed to have clamped a heavy hand over her mouth. She tried to push out with her weighty arms, but they refused to move. The world had contracted to a narrow space barely wide enough and long enough to accommodate her body, and all about her were those inky lines of writhing, constricting blackness. They were squeezing the breath and pulse and life right out of her. "I'm dying," she thought panicking. "They're going to bury me. They are going to bury me alive!"

Pain bloomed in the crown of her head. With a start, she came fully awake. "Ow!" she hissed and raised a hand to her bruised scalp. The wagon must have jounced so hard that it slammed her head into the top of the box.

The crate lurched. She hissed more defensively, and gazed at the planks of pine surrounding her. This box wasn't so bad. It was roomy in comparison to the one in her dream, and sunlight oozed between its boards. Then there came a sharp sound and a thunk above her. She tilted her head and saw a narrow bar of metal poking into her prison. The bar pried upward and the world opened up to light. Above the light, a jaunty voice said, "Let's see what prize we've claimed, Artie!"

Emily found herself blinking into a sun-shadowed face. The face let loose a laugh. "Why it's nothing more than a ripe, red apple, Artie, all juicy and sweet.

"Who are you?" she croaked in a voice she meant to be firm.

The head laughed again and wagged its thick red beard. "Correction, Artie, it's a talking apple we've got ourselves! We'll be rich men yet!"

A thick arm reached down, pulled her none too ceremoniously to her feet. Emily gasped to feel the blood gush back into unused limbs. She would have fallen if two thick arms hadn't lifted her up and set her on the bed of the heavy wagon.

Reeling, she fell against its rails and stared balefully at her savior. The speaker was a short, but incredibly stocky man of middle years wearing a lopsided grin. "Take care there, Apple," he laughed. "We wouldn't want such a nice ripe piece of fruit falling and getting bruised."

"Who are you?" she demanded again.

The man wagged a chunky finger in her face. "Just a moment there, my sweet, let me see what other windfalls we have aboard."

As Emily watched, he went to work on one of several other crates.

"Ho, ho," he barked as he lifted the lid. "Carrots, this time, Artie. We'll feast like kings."

He reached in a thick arm and pulled a groaning Colin Blackhammer to his feet. "So, Carrots, do you talk too?"

"Gagh!" moaned Colin.

"Carrots here is taking exception to our handling, Artie."

"Who are you?" Emily demanded a third time, her voice piping shrill. Then another man, rangy as the red-bearded man was blocky, leapt up into the wagon. This man's face was nut brown and twisted in a scowl, and he ignored her completely as he wrapped his lean arms around her bulky crate, somehow managed to lift it off the wagon's bed, and then launched it over the wagon's side. Dumbfounded, Emily watched it sail down into shadowed space.

Their wagon, she realized, was parked on the very edge of a steep and deep gully.

Another blocky shadow rose over her, and a second crate flew outward into space, splintering itself upon the scrub and rocks below.

"What did you do that for?" she blurted. Artie's scowl deepened, and he jumped out of the wagon.

50

"Oh, don't mind him, Apple," declared the stocky man. "Artie's not much of a talker. Disappointed hopes and all that."

"If he's Artie," interrupted Colin, who was chaffing his bad leg, "who are you?"

"Why I'm Reggie, of course. Don't you remember me, Carrots?"

Colin stared. "Remember you?"

"Why sure. I used to dandle you on my knee when you was just a little tyke."

"You're joking," said Colin.

"I sure ain't. I well remember the way you gnawed my fingers. You had the orangest hair I ever saw. Told your mother, she'd better take extra care or she'd mistake you for one of your vegetable cousins and chuck you in the stew."

"Time," snarled Artie from the front of the wagon and whipped its four mules into a walk.

If Artie wasn't a talker, Reggie exceeded garrulous. He talked as steadily and incessantly as the wagon's wheels turned. Emily was briefly inclined to think him a simpleton, but then she noted the quickness with which he took in the world around him and the deft way he handled the long blade sheathed at his side — she had been around Al and Blayne long enough to recognize the habits of experienced swordsmen. And then there was Artie. He might not speak, but his manner like his blade said plenty.

"How exactly do you know my father?" Colin asked Reggie before they had been long on their road.

"Oh, your pa and I are old colleagues of a sort. You might say we were in the army together. Those were the days, I can tell you. Hasn't he ever told you about them?"

From the driver's bench came a bark of a contemptuous laughter.

Emily was all astonishment. "Your father was a soldier?" she said to Colin.

Colin cocked his head. "I suppose so. He never talks of it."

Reggie nodded. "Well, Gar always was a miser with his words."

"But—" Emily began, only to feel Colin brush her to silence.

"So where are you taking us?" the younger Blackhammer continued conversationally, and Emily marveled to hear his composure.

"Best not to discuss that just now. Wouldn't want the word leaking out."

Colin looked at the empty woods around them. "Is someone listening?"

Reggie chuckled in good-natured appreciation. "In Greenwood forest everything has ears."

They camped that night a half-mile from their road near a fast-moving stream. Reggie took elaborate precautions with the camp. He set things out most carefully and sprinkled the earth with some odd dust before he would let them alight from the wagon.

"Stay close," he warned. "We don't want to leave too much scent."

When Emily and Colin were fed and huddled before a niggardly fire, Emily dared to ask, "Do you travel to the Empyre often?"

Her words seemed to drop like pebbles into the purl of the evening for Reggie had grown strangely quiet as darkness fell, and the ill-natured Artie had absented himself entirely.

Reggie looked at Emily out of fire-riddled eyes. "I've been down to the Empyre a few times," he admitted. "Been some years though. If what I hear is right, it's still a snake pit."

Emily frowned. "So you are not happy to be going back?"

"Going' back!" Reggie whistled soft and low. "Ah, no. I'll not visit that daemon hole ever again, and thank the powers for it. Too much hereabouts that needs my attention."

Emily stared. "But I thought . . ."

Colin put a restraining hand on her arm. "Aren't *you* the guides my father hired?"

Reggie was chuckling to himself. "For this part of the journey sure. For what lies further on, I'm afraid not."

Colin leaned forward. "Then who?"

Reggie took a long swill from his water bag. Wiping his mouth on his sleeve, he said, "Best wait and see."

Cocooned in night and wilderness sounds, Emily tried to sleep. But every time she began to doze, the ground, uneven and unyielding, nudged her awake. Already she missed Faryn. He could coax hospitality from even the bleakest landscape.

To take her mind off her physical discomfort, she tried mapping the journey ahead, but her thoughts kept turning to the past instead, to Cyr and the road she had traveled there and back. She experienced a mental fugue of images—Blayne, Beth, Al and a face made of rainbow fire.

She shivered and huddled into her blanket while high above her the trees swayed and sighed, their sound moving her toward a shadow of rest.

Once again, she lay entombed in a narrow coffin. Her heart fluttered, a wild thing caught in twin nets of blackness and panic. She opened her eyes to impossible darkness scrawled on impenetrable black. Dark symbols like evil snakes curled sinuously around her. Her instinct was to cry out and beat against the walls of her prison, but no sooner had she opened her mouth than those twisting lines of darkness began to pour into it, effectively stoppering the sound.

Be still. Just a dream.

Yes, she told herself. Only a dream. But the darkness was so constricting, so suffocating. Involuntarily she gasped for air, and her muscles tightened.

Relax! Don't fight it.

But even as she willed her limbs to loosen, shaky sobs were building in her chest. Deep in her throat, she moaned.

Your panic is feeding their power. Relax.

Was that true? Did the blackness around her, like the power of the wights, draw energy from her own fear? Emily quit resisting and with a shudder let the sinews of blackness envelop her. They snaked all over her, but gradually, the pressure they exerted eased.

Good girl.

I have to be calm, she told herself. She tried to imagine the darkness as a comforting thing, a soft, all enveloping blanket, but she could feel the sinuous threads in it moving against her, winding round her like poisonous serpents bent on swallowing her whole.

No!

Not a blanket then. Something smoother, almost liquid, like a sea of black. She imagined she hung suspended in it like a string of kelp. What had kelp to fear?

That's better.

Better? It was better. The bands of darkness still swam about her, but they no longer threatened to choke her life out.

She floated in dark and felt her heart's beat begin to ease, until her breaths began to move in and out like gentle waves. The lines of deeper black began to resolve themselves into patterns strange yet familiar. Their blackness too resonated in her memory. She had seen darkness like this before, a darkness so deep it seemed to have its own radiance.

Where?

I can't quite remember.

Relax. Don't force it.

She deliberately eased herself deeper into the black. There! That symbol. Wasn't it familiar? Across her inner eye shot a vision of a falling star, a multihued radiance plummeting across a jewel-strewn sky of pulsing black.

Very good. It is vital we remain calm. Otherwise, we can't begin.

Begin what? She let her light-starved eyes trace another shape in the living lines.

Thinking our way out of this box. Do you hear that sound?

Emily's eyes snapped open. She turned her head. The fire was ashes, Colin was a mound of shadow lying near her, and the sky strung between the tree limbs was fitful with stars.

The wind intensified, bending the tops of the trees. It more than sighed now. It moaned, lifting up on its softer sibilance, a sound like distant howls.

Reggie had said that the wind had ears. Tonight it had a voice like the baying of a pack of dogs.

A flash went off in her brain. She rolled quickly to her knees, heart hammering in her chest. Could it be? Where was Reggie? Which direction was the road?

She took a moment to orient herself, cudgeling her brain into remembering where she lay in relation to their way, and then she heard the stream's gurgling voice.

Casting her blanket from her shoulders, she felt for the two slender bars of silver sheathed at her waist.

She slipped into the trees and scrambled up the embankment to the meager road, hardly aware of the uncharacteristic precision with which she did it. Only when she stood in the middle of the dusty ribbon that was their way did she stop, her head swinging back and forth in search of she knew not what. All seemed quiet enough. But once again her ears pricked to a faint, fell cry.

Two shadows separated themselves from the tangle of black beneath the trees.

"Hey there, girl!" called the thicker one. "What're you up to?"

Impatiently, Emily gestured for silence.

"Reg?" warned the leaner figure.

"Quiet!" hissed Emily as her ears picked up another faint, high call.

Reggie and Artie acquired weight and dimension.

"Do you hear that?" she demanded of both men. Reggie's vague face radiated all the doubtful goodwill of a rational man trying to commiserate with the insane. Artie's face scowled even as his mouth chewed furiously on the stick jammed into its right corner. "Hear what?" he snapped.

"That whine."

"What?"

"In the wind."

Reggie actually frowned. "Girl, the wind often whines."

Emily looked up at the trees and said, "Even when it has stopped blowing?"

Both men grew ominously still, their heads cocked.

"Do you hear anything?" Reggie hissed Artie.

"Only quiet."

"Extra quiet?"

Emily stamped her foot. "Whether you hear it or not, I do! And I know what it means. They have our trail. We have to get moving."

Reggie shrugged at Artie. "A Shield bearer would probably know," he conceded.

"I'll get the wagon," scowled Artie.

But Reggie caught his arm. "No. We should leave the wagon and ride. That way we can separate if we have to—not that they won't catch us anyway."

Emily took command. "Get the mules ready. Once we are on the road, I will do the rest."

She ran for Colin and shook him awake. Together they snatched up bedrolls and helped Artie load the most important packs onto the mules.

"Lots of hunters use dogs," Colin commented to her once they were jogging down the road.

Emily was leaning over her gawky mule's neck like it was a courser. "At night? In the middle of the wildest part of the Midlands?"

"What do you know about this part of the Midlands?" demanded her friend.

"More than you obviously."

"Oh! You've become a geographer, have you?"

"I've looked at a few maps. I assumed someone should. Clearly, I assumed right."

"Don't get snippy with me. You're the one who dragged me into this."

"You two make it damned hard to listen," snarled Artie as he jogged his mule past.

Chastened, Emily clicked her mouth shut.

Slowly, the eastern sky began to lighten, and Emily began to look for other smaller trails diverging from their main one. She scrutinized every one that she saw no matter how unpromising it seemed. She was waiting for one to speak to her and trusting in the power to steer her a course.

Reggie reined his mule back to hers. "If you are right about those hounds, you'd better do something soon."

"Not yet," she answered through gritted teeth.

But a short time later, they crested a hill like a nobby island in the sea of vegetation, and Emily yanked her mule to a halt, struck by the sight of several chipped obelisks of stone like petrified fingers jutting skyward.

She slid down her mule's flank.

"Whoa there, girl!" Reggie called sharply, kneeing his floppy-eared mount her way. "Best not stop here."

Emily ignored him. She was studying the tracks that sloped away from each of the three obelisks, the third of which lay half-toppled into a tangle of thorny black vines.

"Emily?" Colin queried as he rode his mule closer.

Emily approached the trunk of a shattered tree half smothered in impenetrable arms of blackthorn. "There has to be another way," she murmured, peering into the weave of vegetation.

"What are you talking about?" Colin asked.

But Emily's eyes were reading the web-work of vines as if they were words in a book and recalling another crossroads, one bathed in jeweled radiance beneath a burning black sky. "I know this place. I've been here before."

Reggie chomped his red beard. "I doubt that, Apples. Even brigands avoid this crossroads. It has a bad reputation."

"Is that so?" Emily smiled to herself, took a step back, and pointed to the track that ran past the most upright obelisk. "Where's that road go?"

Reggie shrugged his thick shoulder. "West to Hardgrove. That's the way we need to go to reach the merchants road that will take you south."

And the one we were on?" She pointed to the track that they had just come down.

"Stuart's Road it is called hereabouts, but it runs all the way to the Northern border, where it becomes Old Steward's Road."

"And this one obviously runs east toward the mountains."

Ill-tempered Artie cursed. "What's your point, girl?" he sniped.

Emily threw him a look hard and haughty. "Where is the rest of the road running south?"

Artie looked at Reggie and rolled his eyes. Reggie sighed. "Men make roads as they need them, Apples."

"You yourself called this place a cross roads. And someone *made* a fourth way, the one that lies just behind this curtain of blackthorn."

With a harsh burst of bitter laughter, Artie jerked his mule around. Reggie cast him a sympathetic look.

Emily sniffed. "I'll show you." She stalked to the net of vines, pulled out one of her tiny daggers and made a series of quick downward motions. The vines parted like spun sugar, uncovering a moss-furred fourth obelisk and a track like a tunnel running through the thorn. By the looks of it, the obelisk had lost its top ages before.

"Blood and fire," hissed Reggie.

And a high quaver split the early morning air. Everyone looked up.

"Throw the supplies on my mule!" Emily ordered as she jumped to follow her own command. "Colin and I must go on alone."

"We must what?" objected Colin.

"Reggie and Artie have helped us all they can. We will take this way, and they will keep riding west to confuse the trail."

"What about the guides my father arranged?" Colin protested. Emily quit grabbing items long enough to sweep all of them with eyes fiercely, colorfully bright. The vivid colors in those eyes reached into the men, compelled them, and before any of them realized what they were doing, the mule was loaded, and Emily was leading it into the tunnel of thorn.

"It's been good to know you, Carrots and Apple!" called Reggie waving from the head of the western road and blinking rather dreamily as his legs nudged his mule. Artie, dazed almost scowl-less, said nothing, just pressed his own and Colin's animal after.

Colin shook his head like a man trying to throw off a blindfold. He had awakened from the spell to find himself standing under an arch of thorn bushes. The spiky blackthorn was all around him like a cage and pricking at vague memories of a different track also walled in thorn. "What are we doing?" he murmured at Emily. The words came out thick and syrupy. "We can't go on alone!"

Emily ignored him, clucking at her mule to send it trotting deeper into thorny shadow. Then she squatted down in the loam.

Something in her intent expression made Colin drop down beside her.

"Say goodbye to where we've been, Col," Colin heard her say in a voice windy with portent.

"Goodbye?" he breathed.

She smiled at him, but there was a terrible tension in her face undercutting the smile. "Once I'm done, there will be no going back," she explained. Then she took a small silver dagger from her waist and set it tip-down in the earth.

That tip drew a line across their track. Then Colin felt all his doubt and bewilderment curdle to horror as the world beyond that line — obelisk, brush, light and dust — fell away into misty nothingness.

Chapter 5: Lost Road

Al's captors let him out of his coffin-like box in the evenings, only for a short time, and only to take care of the physical necessities.

He groaned as two men jerked him up by his aching arms and tossed him unceremoniously on the ground. All he wanted to do was lie there, taking in the clean smell of grass and drinking in the moon's wan light, but he willed himself to move, to pull in his knees and roll up onto them. It was awkward with one's hands nerveless and tightly bound behind one's back.

A heavy boot buried itself in his side. "I said get up and relieve yourself," a gruff voice growled.

He rolled over, gasping for breath, caught it and started laughing. "Happy to, just come a bit closer." His voice, thin and ragged from disuse sounded strange to his own ears. It also earned him another kick for his pains.

"We don't have time for this," a cleaner, colder voice said. "Get him on his feet." Again hands grabbed him by his awkwardly pinned arms and yanked him upward. They marched him into the trees.

He allowed himself the fleeting hope that tonight they would be impatient enough to free his hands, but they preferred to handle his clothing themselves. Then they dragged him back toward the camp.

"Eat, dog," said one as they plunked him down on his knees before a bowl of scraps.

Al considered the food, his tightly wrapped wrists, and cast a dangerous eye over the men crouched around him. Most were gobbling down their own food. He spoke brightly. "Allow me to thank you gentlemen for your tender attentions. I rarely get such preferred treatment from my friends." He nodded at the thickset fellow who had kicked him. "You—I'm sorry but I didn't hear your name—have been particularly thoughtful." The man regarded his tin plate balefully and kept shoveling food into his mouth.

"Do you imagine yourself an amusing fellow, Lord Goodwin. Or do you just enjoy the sound of your voice." This from a lighter-voiced bald man, the fellow in charge. No mean ruffian here, but a hardened and efficient professional.

"A man must have something to hold on to," shrugged Al.

The man shook his shaved head and skewered a chunk of meat with his knife. "A man in your position should concentrate on holding on to his life."

Al smiled more broadly. "Oh, come now—captain, is it? If your masters wanted me dead, you would have cut my throat days ago."

The bald head lifted, exposing eyes sere as the sunken planes of the face. Leaning forward the man said, "I doubt they would mind me taking your tongue."

"With whom then would you converse? Your colleagues' conversation hardly sparkles."

Another man growled, "Leave the dog his tongue, Captain. How else is he to lap up his dinner?" There was a round of appreciative laughter.

Al didn't care. Repartee wasn't the point. He was trying to size up the captain, noting his gear and form, the suggestive shape of the half-hidden tattoo on his neck. Growing desperation and the bald man's blatant stare made him contemplate something more daring.

Charily, he reached out with the power.

The effort spun him into a black inferno, and he collapsed into an agonized heap.

The bald man's laugh was savage, and Al mentally kicked himself. The bald man's challenge hadn't been a mistake. He had locked eyes with Al in order to goad him into a painful lesson.

Resting his throbbing head on the earth, Al listened to the other man approach. "Save your energies, lord. You will have better uses for them soon enough."

This time, Al made no attempt to respond. There was no point.

"Give him a few minutes to appreciate his predicament," the leader said to his men. "Then make sure he eats even if you have to stuff the food into him. We want him strong enough to enjoy what's coming." With a careless laugh of his own, the captain walked off into the night.

A short time later, the mercenaries dumped their prisoner back into the box. Al had to lock his jaw against the cry that welled up inside him. All too soon the choking symbols descended. Again, he went deaf, dumb and blind; again his limbs succumbed to a freezing rigidity. Locked into a body still and cold as one in the clutches of death, his still vibrant spirit sought out another means of escape. Forsaking the flesh, it fled into a different kind of bondage and found itself traveling a new and very different road.

The road Emily had chosen was indeed a strange one. What had started out as a brush-choked path soon widened into a broad, even inviting, avenue of moss-encrusted, limb-littered stone. The massive quarried blocks of it implied that it had been constructed to withstand many, many centuries of heavy traffic, yet mile after mile it ran before them silent and empty but for a scattering of leaves and broken branches. Sometimes it snaked its way onto the backs of sun-crested hills, sometimes it dipped deep into forested valleys where mists hung like a pall, but always it seemed a thing apart from the land, a vast, ancient, silvery serpent bent on winding its way back into the nether realms.

Haunted, Emily decided, was the only way describe it, and in her mind she often likened it to the twilight roads she had traveled. But where those roads swarmed thick with the sense of watchful alien presences, this one cried out for a presence of any kind. In the ivy-coated woods that grew dense upon it, no birds chattered, no insect voices sang, even at night. The road ran so empty, so silent that it seemed to be listening, perhaps for the voices of its long-forgotten builders.

As their journey went on, the unrelenting silence of it dragged at Emily more than the stiffness of her tired muscles and the weight of the pack on her back. Nor did it help that after days of traveling together, Colin still avoided talking to or even looking at her.

Emily felt certain she understood his problem. She could almost see the practical Colin warring with the Colin who had faced darkling magic and met a nonman and stepped off the edge of his known world. She respected his need to resolve the conflict, but his aloofness made her feel almost as lonely and bereft as she had when Millicynt died. During her most trying days in Cyr, she had clung to her memories of the Greenwood and especially to her friendship with Colin as the only things that were truly and completely hers.

She should have realized that no bond is unbreakable. She had roamed farther than most and walked roads mortals rarely traveled, and she had come back changed in a way that even she had yet to define. Now Colin had seen something of that change, and even his sturdy love and loyalty had been shaken. Once again, Emily found herself bracing for the death of something she could not bear to lose.

"Let's stop here," said Colin, breaking into her thoughts, and Emily sighed and nodded.

The mule, remarkably placid for his kind, immediately stopped too and began chomping at the ferns growing beside the road.

"Don't let him step off of it," Emily warned.

Colin glared at her, while the mule continued lipping fern. "I heard you the first time."

Emily shriveled. "It's just that I don't know what might happen," she apologized.

"Seems like you don't know an awful lot," Colin growled, and began digging through his pack.

Hurt, Emily walked off to the other side of the road and sat on the trunk of a fallen tree.

Colin didn't seem to notice. He chewed furiously at a leathery strip of dried meat, and contemplated the road darkly. "I hate this place!" he expostulated, and chewed even harder.

"It is a bit unnerving," agreed Emily.

"Unnerving! It's horrible." His warm brown eyes stabbed the air. "League after league of unmarked stone. I can't begin to tell where we are or how far we have come."

"We could be in Faryn's clutches by now."

Colin glared at her again. "Tellers make it so! What I wouldn't give for a warder's company."

Emily jumped up. "Stop it!" she shouted. "Why don't you curse the one you really hate—me."

Something like shame darkened Colin's face. He looked away. "I don't hate you," he mumbled unconvincingly.

"Tellers, you don't! I presumed on our friendship and dragged you away from your home. I persuaded you to give up the office you always wanted, the very work Millicynt trained you for. But most of all, I cut you off, from your world and your family. You are so angry with me right now you could spit iron." She finished breathing hard.

"Being angry isn't the same as hating."

"Well, give yourself a little more time. I'm sure you'll work up to it."

Now Colin was on his feet, fists clenched at his sides. Through gritted teeth he said. "How dare you tell me what I feel! Hate you? What I hate is my own stupidity. Even when you went away from the Greenwood, I never quit thinking of you. I thought of you almost every day. I thought to myself, she'll come back and then we'll get married."

Emily fell back to the trunk with a plop. There it was at last. What was she to say?

Colin looked away down the road, looked back at her, opened his mouth and shut it. At last he sighed and said what needed to be said. "But we're not ever going to get married, are we?" His words were almost plaintive. Emily bit her lip.

Suddenly, he was squatting at her knees. "Why are you even still wearing the ring?"

It was Emily's turn to look away. "It's not your ring!"

"I gave it to you."

"But you didn't make it!"

For a second Colin's gaze turned inward.

Emily let loose a humorless laugh, "You should have paid more attention to the Dorlan stories. The gifts of magicians are always two-sided."

Colin stood up. Emily expected him to walk away, but he only stood over her staring ruminatively. "You love him," he said at last.

Emily dismissed the idea with a wave of her hand. "It's not a question of love," she said.

"Then why do you dream of him?"

"Don't be nonsensical," she snapped, standing. She tried to edge around him.

Colin caught her arm. "You talk in your sleep, Emily. Especially since we've been on this damn road."

Emily flushed scarlet, then went white as chalk. "Don't," she said shaking her head and holding up a hand between them.

"Why not?"

"Because." But Colin with his air of sorrow and studied patience deserved a better answer. In a small, unhappy voice, she said. "Whatever he is to me it hardly matters. He has a life and duty before him that I cannot share. We come from two different worlds, and in two different worlds we will remain."

When Colin didn't reply, Emily dared to look back up into his face. The compassion she saw there broke her heart all over again. With a dry sob, she hugged her dear friend and said, "I'm so, so sorry."

He patted her back awkwardly and said, "Yeah, well you aren't the only one." They stood together for a long moment; then he pulled back and peered into her face. "And stop with this two worlds nonsense. He may make magic rings, but you cut slashes in the world with magic daggers. Sounds a heck of a lot like the same world to me."

If their strange road had a memory, that memory must have been stirred by the laughter that suddenly fluttered up from its hushed stones. The unbearable tension between them finally broken, Emily and Colin put aside the waiting silence and made a merry supper of their dry provisions. They talked as they always had, picking up the threads of an old friendship with banter and gossip and silly stories. They would never again be carefree innocents, but they could renew the bond of friendship that would keep a part of that innocence alive as long as both of them lived.

"We'd better get going," said Colin after a while. "At the rate we're walking, it will take us months instead of weeks to make it to the southern border."

"You are right, of course," nodded Emily, brushing crumbs from her skirt. "But something tells me we'll make it in plenty of time."

"More of your magic?" returned Colin with a suddenly sour look.

"No. It's nothing to do with me, and it's not *my* magic. It's the road. Sometimes, especially at night, I get the feeling we are still moving, even though we seem to be standing still."

Colin nodded, "I know what you mean. It feels like the road itself is moving."

Emily gave him a mysterious smile. "Perhaps it's not such a bad road after all. Just lonely." She looked at the road and her smile turned sad. "I feel rather sorry for it."

The road responded.

"Sorry?" It said. "What an interesting choice of words. I've seen a few travelers on this road, but none that ever expressed sympathy for it." The voice was light and quick, but full of complex undertones, and once Emily had gotten a hold of her leaping heart, she discovered it belonged to a hatted figure standing at the head of their way.

As she and Colin scrambled to their feet, the figure came walking slowly toward them, easing down the road's gentle incline.

Of average height he was and slender, and in his left hand was a long black staff intricately carved. From his shoulders hung a loose-sleeved robe of brilliant blue, but a shade darker than the broad-brimmed, flat-topped hat he wore on his head. The head beneath that hat was mostly shadowed, but Emily could see a generous mouth and firm chin framed by hair that looked almost white, but which, on closer inspection, proved to be threaded with pale gold.

Like the protective male he had been raised to be, Colin stepped forward to greet the stranger, his hand wrapped firmly around the hilt of his dagger. "Evening, master," he said, flicking a warning hand at Emily behind him.

"Evening," said the stranger, stopping a few feet away and smiling toothily.

I know that smile, thought Emily, and then frowned, for she was certain she did not know the man.

"May we be of some assistance to you?" Colin asked, falling back on the customary formulae for want of any other plan.

"May be," said the man, "And it may be that I can also be of assistance to you."

Colin looked uncertainly at Emily.

"Do you know where this road leads?" she asked.

"Not that we're lost," Colin added.

"Oh, no. You don't look lost," said the stranger with exaggerated gravity, and he flashed white teeth again.

"Well, if you are wanting provisions, we don't have many," continued Colin, a warning flavor in his voice.

"I'm not hungry."

"Then how can we help you?"

The brim of the hat dipped as the man shifted the butt of his staff across the stones. "Let us just say that I'm rather tired of traveling alone. The heaviness of this road takes the spirit right out of man. I was wondering if you might permit me to walk along with you for a while."

"Well," drawled Colin, trying to think of a polite way to refuse, but Emily interfered again.

"Where are you going?" she asked. She could feel the stranger looking at her from beneath his hat's brim.

"South."

Colin's lips thinned with suspicion. "But you just came from the south."

"Oh, I was merely resting ahead. When I heard your voices I thought I would take a look. You seemed like such a nice young couple that I couldn't resist introducing myself."

Colin narrowed his eyes.

"Do you travel this road often?" asked Emily.

"Quite often."

"So you are familiar with the passes through the southern mountains?"

"Very.

"How far are we from them?"

"Some weeks. A bit more than your provisions will allow, judging by your packs. But I know the plants and animals here about. I could help you extend your provender with forage."

"There are animals around?" said Colin in disbelief.

The man smiled more broadly. "They don't often wander onto the road, but yes. Come now, talk it over between yourselves, and I will wait for your answer." And with that he swung aside and seated himself on the same fallen tree Emily had used earlier.

"We should accept his proposal," said Emily with certainty.

"Are you out of your mind?" hissed Colin, shocked. "We don't know anything about him. He could be a thief or some more dangerous sort of outlaw."

"I don't think so." Emily watched the stranger scratching at the stones with his staff.

"What if he clocks us over the head with his stick as soon as we fall asleep and steals all our goods," whispered Colin furiously.

"Of course! Why didn't I think of that?" retorted Emily, slapping her forehead in mock reproach. "A mule, a bundle of dried meat, a set of dirty clothes and his fortune will be made."

"This isn't funny. We have some money, and he could be a stone-cold killer."

"Then why did he go to the trouble of introducing himself? Wouldn't it have been simpler for him to wait until dark and rob us while we slept?"

Colin turned away with an explosive sigh, but Emily could tell by the slope of his shoulders that he had already begun to relent. He cast a worried look at the seated man. "The problem is, what's to stop him from following us anyway."

"Exactly," affirmed Emily. "Better to make a friend than an enemy."

Colin didn't look convinced, but he called to the hatted man while Emily observed with curious eyes. The stranger leapt lightly up from his trunk.

"My friend and I have talked it over, master," Colin said when the stranger once again stood before them. "We too find this road rather lonely. If you would like to walk along with us, you are welcome."

The stranger nodded.

"But," said Colin with sudden sternness as he drew himself up to his full lanky height. "I warn you that this lady's safety is my responsibility, and I will tolerate no threat to her." Emily gaped at him, not sure whether to feel grateful or ridiculous.

But the generous mouth beneath the hat became so solemn it looked almost sad. "You have my word that I will honor you both as my dearest companions," said the stranger in reverent tones.

Colin blinked, then held out his hand. The stranger looked at it a moment, then bent into a stunningly fluid bow instead. Colin's hand dropped.

As the stranger straightened, he smiled more broadly. "Glad to have that settled," he said in almost merry tones, and with the end of his staff he bumped back the brim of his hat.

Both Emily and Colin stared. The lean face now revealed looked little older than Colin's, but the eyes, set deep into it beneath pale, angled brows, were large, predatory and dominated by irises yellow as gold. Owl's eyes, thought Emily, wolf's eyes, and finally remembered to breathe.

Chapter 6: Shade

The stranger called himself Shade, and Emily soon came to regret championing his cause. He exhibited oddities of behavior that worried her and positively infuriated Colin. He claimed to have traveled widely, but he joined them without pack or provisions of any sort, avoided most of the labors of travel, and in no way behaved like a man interested in companionship. Early in the day, he generally strolled along with them, tapping his staff on the stones as if content to let the quiet and their legs eat up the miles. Occasionally, he whistled a sad, foreign-sounding tune that seemed to hang in the still air over the road like the fog. If Colin or Emily asked him a question, he might answer it briefly or shrug it off entirely. Once or twice, he pointed out a tree or shrub bearing nuts or berries.

As soon as the sun had arced high enough to shred the fog and touch the road, they usually turned to find him vanished into trees without a word about where he was going or when he would return. This behavior enflamed Colin, and the smith's son worked himself into a frenzy thinking that Shade would return with a whole band of bright-eyed renegades. When that didn't happen, Colin prayed that Shade — that worthless vagabond as he called him — would stay gone for good.

He didn't. He always reappeared toward evening, slipping out of the ivy-draped trees around the time Emily and Colin had finished setting up camp. As they went about tending their mule and preparing their evening meal, Shade selected a likely looking resting place and stretched out with all the indolence of a well-fed tomcat.

"What do you do out there?" Colin flared up one miserably damp evening as he struggled to light a fire in a bundle of soggy, decaying sticks. His question was a slightly different version of the one he had repeatedly hurled at Emily, and she winced to hear his ungracious tone.

Shade didn't answer immediately. So Colin looked up from his tender to glare at the other man, who sat with his back propped against an encroaching tree, his hat lowered over his face, and his well-worn boots stretched toward the still unlit fire. "Well?" Colin demanded.

"I scout," Shade replied. His words skipped across the road light and quick despite being spoken into the crown of his hat.

Colin scraped his flints more furiously and more sparks flew. "What is there to scout? There are no people, not even a sign of them. You claim there are animals here abouts, but I've yet to see so much as a sparrow."

Shade tilted his hat brim. One white-blonde eyebrow and one golden eye gleamed. "Perhaps you should look more carefully," he said.

"Really? Prove it."

"Colin," murmured Emily warningly.

Colin turned his glare on her. "If our new companion wishes to teach me the error of my ways, far be it from me to keep him from it."

"Oh, put your flint away, and stop trying to start fires, Colin," Emily returned in exasperation. She tossed an apologetic look at Shade. "He's actually quite good-natured when he has a roof over his head and a feather bed to sleep in." She pulled a face at her friend. "Roughing it makes him irritable."

"Roughing it is not making me nearly as irritable as he is," muttered Colin, jerking his chin at the lounging man and stubbornly going back to scraping flint.

Shade studied him for a moment with an inscrutable eye, then flashed his long white teeth. Quick as a blink, he swung his black staff and smacked it against the tree. The tree shivered and a sharp report reverberated down the empty road. A few leaves drifted down. Then Shade zipped his staff forward as if to pluck one of them out of the air and, plop, caught a furred and clawed bundle instead.

As the dazed squirrel scrabbled for purchase, Shade turned the staff and drew the small creature in close. His wide golden eyes seemed to absorb every detail of the little rodent with the remorseless curiosity of a child studying an insect. The squirrel, no bigger than Emily's hand, undulated his bushy tail and tiptoed back and forth along the stick while chattering wildly.

Emily let loose her amazement in a laugh—it was funny to see the tiny squirrel hectoring the man who had so efficiently netted it. Colin whooshed. "That was lucky," he gasped.

Wide gold eyes fastened on him. "Was it?"

A shadow of a doubt crossed Colin's face. He opened his mouth to respond but had difficulty shaping the words. "How did you—?" His voice trailed away.

"I looked, I listened," Shade said. He brought the squirrel nearly to his nose although his eyes held on to Colin. Strangely, the feisty little rodent made no move to leap away, even when the golden-eyed man prodded it with a long finger. "This little one's curiosity got the better of him. He is young and full of himself, so he went a bit too far out on his limb. He should learn to be more cautious."

Emily could see the muscles in Colin's jaw jumping. She noted how he leaned forward as if bent on confrontation. "Or what?" he breathed, balling his hands into fists.

Shade gave Colin such a toothy grin that Emily half expected to see him pop the hapless squirrel, fur and all, right into his mouth. Instead he flicked the end of his staff and sent the squirrel spinning through the air and careening onto the middle of the road.

"Oh," gasped Emily, her heart going out to the mistreated creature. "Poor thing," But the squirrel jumped up as if it had never struck stone at all. Hopping on all fours, it chattered and whisked its tail reproachfully at the three of them.

Emily smiled her relief, and tossed the little creature a piece of cheese. Then a silent but deadly shadow swooped down out of the trees and with talons outstretched struck the preoccupied rodent.

Both Emily and Colin blinked, and the great horned owl dug its talons deeper into its twitching victim and blinked slowly back. Then, in a flare of soundless wings, it lifted off and floated back into the trees.

"In this world, my friend," said Shade, "it pays to stay alert."

Emily's hands dropped to her side; Colin's had curled into fists so tight the knuckles showed white. "That was cruel," he said in a voice tight with fury. He glowered at the man seated across from him.

"That, my boy, is life."

Colin straightened. "I'm not a boy."

"Then quit inviting me to treat you like one."

Colin paled, and Emily put out a warning hand, hoping to cut him off before he did anything rash. The nature of the bristling tension between the two men defied her understanding, but she knew Colin well enough to recognize that Shade's remark would fire his festering resentment. Colin, however, surprised her by suddenly wilting under the blond man's unrelenting stare. Kicking his uncooperative stack of wood in defeat, he said, "I give up. Clearly, I have no more chance of winning a fight with you than either of us has of setting fire to wet wood." Sick with self-loathing, he turned away, and Emily, concerned, again reached out to him.

Shade smiled broadly and, with movements light and quick as his laugh, rose and snapped his fingers at the wood. There was a hiss and then a rush of air. The wet wood burst into flame.

"You know what this means," Colin said to her the next day when Shade had once again absented himself.

Emily looked at him in surprise for he had spoken hardly a word since the night before. "Do I know what what means?"

"This Shade business," said Colin, lowering his voice and ducking his head. He ran a wary eye along the curtain of trees.

"What about it?" sighed Emily.

"We're as good as caught."

"What are you talking about?"

"Shade's a warder, Emily. Faryn must have sent him to guard us until he himself can get here."

"A warder?" she blurted, loud in disbelief.

"Quiet! Do you want him to hear us?"

"What makes you think he's a warder?"

"Are you teasing? Have you seen the way he moves? He is as strong and fast as Faryn and even more cold-blooded. And what kind of senses does it take to pick a squirrel out of an entire forest and catch it with your bare hands. He has to be a warder."

Emily bit her lip and tried to dismiss the idea. "He caught the squirrel with his staff," she equivocated.

Colin looked at her like she must be joking. "And did you see the way the creature obeyed him?" he continued. "That owl too."

Emily shook her head. "I can't believe it."

"Why not?"

"I've been around warders a bit more than you have, Colin, and if Shade's a warder, he's like none I've ever seen."

Abruptly, she went silent, meditating.

"Oh? And just what makes him so different?"

She brushed an unfinished but troublesome thought aside. "Well, you've seen Faryn. You've even witnessed some of his magic. Warders are, I don't know, vaguer, harder to pin down."

"Harder to pin down! Now I know you're joking. What I know about Faryn stacks up to volumes compared with what I've been able to determine about Shade."

Emily wagged her head, trying to focus her thoughts. Colin's idea perturbed her, and yet she couldn't quite figure out why. "I see what you are saying, but physically speaking, Shade's entirely different. He is absolutely present, a law unto himself. Warders tend toward the fey and elusive, like people whose minds are tuned to a different world, while Shade delights in tweaking this one." She shivered, "Think of the way he relished talking with you last night."

"Toying with me, you mean," grumbled Colin, but Emily was relieved to hear that he sounded far less bitter than the evening before.

"Perhaps. He does act a bit like a cat who has been at the cream but who still can't resist tormenting the mouse that crosses his path. He just can't help himself. He has been programmed to be a hunter."

"Like a warder," finished Colin.

"Actually, now that I think about it, I find that he reminds me more of Blayne." As her own words came home to her, she halted swaying. The half-formed thought that had been plaguing her had just flicked into focus.

Colin, however, continued walking. Throwing his hands skyward, he gave up, "Fine! Ignore what's right in front of you. But don't be surprised if you wake up one evening to find Faryn, with Shade's help, trussing you up like a freshly plucked chicken."

When Shade appeared in camp that evening, he dropped two dead rabbits before their fire.

"What's this?" goggled Colin.

Shade bared his teeth, "You said you were tired of jerky."

"Oh. Yes."

Shade lifted a white-blond brow. "Can you skin them?"

"Of course," retorted Colin, puffing with indignance.

Colin did skin them, quickly and cleanly, while Shade looked on in approval. Soon, the two men were engrossed in a debate over the best way to snare rabbits.

As Emily stirred the pot, she marveled to see them conversing with all the ease of old acquaintances. Where had yesterday's barely restrained aggression gone? Men, she decided, operated according to a ridiculous set of rules—all that hackle-raising and posturing to end up communing around the same fire.

She settled down to sleep feeling strangely comforted, even as she steeled herself for the unpleasantness to come.

For many days now she had dreamed of lying frozen in snaky, suffocating darkness. And now the dreams were getting worse. Almost as soon as she fell asleep, the darkness wrapped itself about her like a winding sheet. It no longer terrified as it once had, but only because she now understood that she wasn't alone.

"How long are we going to have to endure this?" she complained. And got no answer.

"Do you hear me?" she asked. But the only other awareness she sensed lurked deep inside in those snaking lines of black writing.

She felt the first small flutterings of the old horror.

"Why don't you tell me what's going on?" she asked, but the question only rebounded into her own mind. "Give me some kind of answer at least, so I'll know you are all right."

Could it be that she really was alone this time? "I'm here," she called again, then whimpered to herself, "Where are you?" Black fire licked at her thought.

She could feel her heart beating like the wings of a trapped bird. It's just a dream, she told herself, but as no answering reassurance came, every additional instant in living darkness ate further into her fragile courage.

As her own impulse to struggle grew, her inner desperation struck a heartbreakingly plaintive chord. "Please don't leave me."

Something shivered in that darkness, slowly stirred. The black lines of fire flared blacker and clamped down tighter.

"Tired," came the sluggish, reedy thought.

She grabbed at it, held on. "Let me help you."

"No use."

"You only need energy. Take some more from me. I've plenty to spare."

She could feel the other receding. "Just hold on to me," she said.

"Time to let go" came the weary reply.

She reached out with her heart, her soul. But it seemed she tried to grasp running water, and she wept as she realized the impossibility of it all. The tighter her grip, the faster the other slipped away. Was he to escape her so easily? She quit thinking like a fist and imagined herself a basin instead. She opened up completely, stretching out to enfold him as the land enfolds a river. The embrace was a mind-bending one. For the first time, she felt the full weight of another soul pressing into her. Strange thoughts flashed through her like bright fish. Deep currents ate away at her foundations. Waves eroded her shores. It was a defiance of the self more complete than mortal consciousness could bear.

But the power came to her rescue. The burden grew light. She was transformed from a riverbed into a lens capable of drawing all light to her. She drew his essence in, felt it and focused it.

Light exploded outward, and the black lines shriveled like vines thrown into a furnace.

She flared awake, throwing her arms wide as if to release the sunburst within her. The sickle moon offered her a cool caress and a lopsided grin, a grin that almost matched the smile of the one sitting beyond the embers of their fire.

Night had dropped a curtain over Shade's face, but beyond its shadow were the glowing embers of his eyes, burning like distant suns. "That was impressive," he said.

Chilled, Emily clutched her blanket to her. "What are you?"

"You don't know?"

At that moment, the only thing that Emily knew with any confidence was that she was afraid to know. "Colin says you're a warder."

The twin suns picked out Colin's sleeping form before sweeping back to her. "What do you think?"

"I think," she paused to swallow. There was a dryness in her throat like dust. "I think you are some sort of half breed."

Heavy lids shaded the eyes to golden slits. "Because?"

Emily stoked her flagging courage. "Because you avoid the direct light of the sun. Because right now your eyes shine with inner fire. Because when you want to, you move more like a wight than a man. Because you seem without remorse."

"And only a child of Twilight can be without remorse," he agreed almost sadly, but there was a mocking edge to his voice.

"Yes. No. I mean . . . I don't know what I mean." She dropped her chin onto her knees, recalled other remarkable faces she had known—Millicynt's, kind but resolute; Meredyth's, stern yet understanding; the Steward's, proud but at the same time dreamy-eyed. Quite unexpectedly she recognized the common-as-clay traces of loss underpinning them all. With a wrench of heart, she thought of

Al, laughing through both pain and regret. She set his face next to the most extraordinary face of all, one filled with eternal, multihued fire. Her thoughts broke from her, skittish as wild horses, uncertain of the direction they should take. "Well, the wights certainly have no reason for remorse, do they? Life can't really injure them, whereas it sentences mortals to all sorts of torments. Sickness, old age, death, sorrow — these teach people remorse."

"And love." The voice dipped lower as if to duck beneath a breath of night wind.

"What did you say?"

Shade's burning eyes slid away from her searching ones, but when he spoke, the complex undertones of his voice drew her in. "Love also teaches remorse."

She thought of all she had learned of her family history, of her own experiences and sighed. "Yes." Another idea drove self-pity away, and she knitted her brow. "But how would a half breed know that?"

The glowing eyes were steady, fearless, a predator's eyes. The predator answered her with a toothy smile.

Emily shoved aside her alarm. She sat forward, open and eager as an acolyte seeking answers to burning questions. "My cousin Blayne would give anything to know love, but he feels nothing at all. How is it that you do?"

The smile softened, grew more mysterious. "Life, as you said, teaches people."

"So Blayne can learn to love?"

"Perhaps. If he lives long enough, and if he is willing to pay the price."

"How did you?"

Shade stirred the fire's embers with his staff. "That is a very long story."

"Then tell me a shorter one. Tell me what it is that you want with us."

A chunk of wood succumbed to flame, sending a wash of red light across Shade's suddenly ageless face.

Galden Madson, former Captain of the Capital Guard, took the stair treads two at a time before leaping the remainder of the distance to the cellar floor.

"What happened?" he barked at a man crouched and shrieking on the floor. Madson prodded the man with his foot only to withdraw it as the crouching man lifted a blackened visage and wailed louder.

Galden swept a hand over his bald head. Two more of his men came running up from the undercellar. "Corg, Needle!" Galden shouted. The men altered course immediately, skidding up to him as their hands clenched and unclenched. "What in the name of all that's infernal is going on?" Galden demanded.

"The box, sir," panted Corg.

"The box, Captain," echoed Needle.

Galden's cold eyes bulged. He tightened his grip on his own blade. "Yes?"

"It burst apart," said Needle.

"Exploded, sir," gesticulated Corg with outflung arms.

Galden reconsidered the burned man as Corg hissed, "Dast and Ivon were on watch, as you ordered. Dast was struck in the face. Ivon was killed."

Galden set off through the low hall, sword extended. The plaster walls and stone floor ran smooth and unblemished except for a wash of light from oil lamps, but the large room at the end of the hall was hazy with smoke and littered with splintered wood. Galden scanned the large, low-ceilinged room carefully before stepping into it. An acrid smell assaulted his nostrils, charred wood crunched under his feet.

"Where is the prisoner?"

"We are not sure, Captain. He may have been killed in the explosion."

Galden's look said they were both fools. "No," he stated grimly. "He's looking for an exit or hiding." He cocked his head as he heard footsteps approaching from behind. Moving carefully to the place where the box had lain, he bent and picked up a fragment of wood and watched it crumble to black ash that glittered gold.

"Could *she* have done this?" hissed Corg, folding his thickset body into a squat and running a hand across the sooty floor.

"No, she could not. For now, the magic our master deployed keeps her at bay."

"How can you know for certain?"

"Do you doubt our Lord?"

Corg dropped his own eyes, studied the outline of the box scorched into the floor. "Then it was the prisoner."

"It was he." Galden dusted his hand on his trouser leg, and watched a handful of other armed men jog into the room.

"Do you want us fetch him?" asked Corg.

Galden stared off into the deeps of the cellar. "No. Keep your distance until I speak with the Lord." He tossed a set of keys to one of

74

the new arrivals. "Move the men back outside, then lock the gates. Let the prisoner stew in his own juices." Sheathing his blade, he headed for the stairs. At the foot of them he stopped, turned, and gave the hard men behind him an even harder look. "Oh, and should Lord Goodwin decide to present himself, make sure you avoid meeting his eyes."

Al adjusted his awkward grip on the dagger to better saw at his bonds and nicked his wrist for a fifth time. He cursed, a low snarl that rolled into the shadows, where it met a distant metallic clang. He lifted his head, listening. If his captors intended to make an appearance, they were very slow in doing so.

It could mean only one thing: they knew he was still trapped, out of the box, but imprisoned all the same.

Of course, they might be struggling to regroup. By now, the entire troop would be reevaluating just how dangerous he could be. They couldn't be looking forward to cornering him, considering what had happened. Abruptly, he remembered how it felt to be on fire, to see the deadly black lines flashed to nothingness like shadows erased by the sun. Much of what happened immediately after the box flew apart eluded him. He recalled shouts, a pair of surprised eyes. He remembered reaching out for the consciousness behind those eyes with a fiery hand.

He shuddered. What had she done to him? To both of them? Though physically beaten, he pulsed with inner energy. He felt as light and buoyant as thistle down, and if he let himself, he could still smell and feel and taste her coating him like the resinous smoke from the box. Once again he had tried to exert control, and she had overmastered him. How? Perhaps he had unwittingly given her the means by escaping into her and joining her on that strange road. The link had certainly extended his own flagging energies. In the last few days, it had actually kept him from going mad. But, at last, when he knew his own life was fading, he had resigned himself to releasing her, lest she be dragged down with him. As his strengths could become hers, so could his weaknesses, and her burdens and dangers were great enough already—take the mysterious presence with her on that strange road. Bitter as the admission of defeat had been, he had known it was time to minimize the bond and let go. But, as usual where Emily was concerned, he had miscalculated. He had not counted on her obstinacy. She had fought back, and succeeded in actually strengthening and intensifying the bond.

A strand of rope at his back parted. He worked his wrists free carefully, loosening the cords until he could slip them over his hands. A coil of rope hit the floor.

So, now what? It was either escape or die on his own terms. Anything less could spell disaster for the Keeper's house as well as his own. He studied the knife in his hand. He certainly didn't want to die, and he wasn't a man to give up easily. He was used to fighting hard and pulling off unlikely victories. But matters had proven more complicated than he had imagined. Who were these mercenaries who held him? What was their connection to Alysse? And where had they come by power as subtle and deadly in design as the spells sunk into that box? Those spells were malicious yes, but not the sort of magic employed by shadow brethren. Who then had arranged his abduction? And for what purpose? He felt certain he would learn soon enough. But it frightened him to think that there was an adept in the world audacious enough to direct such arts against the Steward's own heir. It implied a betrayal the likes of which no house had seen in centuries. More alarmingly, such a practitioner would undoubtedly know how to use his captive to harm countless others, including the woman he was joined to.

"Damn it, Emily," he muttered. "When will you learn to listen to me?" Then he laughed. He could see her standing in front on him, hands on hips, eyes flashing as she spoke with asperity. "I got you out of the box, didn't I?"

"Out of the briar and into the bag," he murmured, recalling a Midlander saying, and began exploring his prison.

The place known as the Crow's Nest sat in the northernmost foothills of the eastern mountains near a no man's land of wilderness. Despite its unprepossessing name, it had once been a large and gracious estate, one of the most gracious and influential in the entire Northland.

A quarter of a century of abandonment had blunted its glory. The sprawling hulk of the house now languished in a landscape gone wild. Its roof sagged, and its wide windows stared emptily at gardens thready with overgrown shrubbery and fountains choked with decaying leaves.

And yet there were fresh signs of life about it—smoke drifting from a chimney, freshly churned gravel, clumps of horses picketed in the yard, men skulking beneath the eaves.

Inside, the stirrings were more vigorous. Dusty hallways and wide rooms clamored of booted feet, clashing arms, and rough voices. Once empty parlors billeted an odd assortment of individuals who concentrated on polishing their gear and casting dice.

In one of the house's more quiet rooms, Galden Madson stood with the tips of his fingers resting on a slab of oil-slicked stone. "The box was utterly destroyed, my lord," he gasped out, sweat beading his shaved head. "The pieces of wood that remain have been charred to coals."

A passerby looking in would assume that the Captain speaks to someone else in the room. In fact, he speaks to a person many leagues away, a person whose inaudible responses fill the room with weighty silence.

"We have made no attempt to secure him as yet, lord. He cannot escape the cellar, and I thought it best to speak with you first, in case he had prepared some other nasty surprise."

More weighty silence. The door guards shift edgily as the Captain's breathing grows more strained.

"We have not seen her for the past three nights. She took Tallwood, then disappeared."

Oppressive silence. Galden knits his brow like a man fighting a savage headache.

"Yes. Lady Malamot says she has heard rumors of a connection. She has confirmed that all three heads of the houses met in conference at Cyr."

Crushing silence.

"Her ladyship remains cooperative. Do you wish us to attempt to find this girl?"

Silence so heavy and lasting so long that the guards cast wide-eyed looks at each other. Their captain's head now hangs upon his chest, and he breaths in shallow gasps.

"As you command, my lord. We will prepare the necessary safeguards."

Galden is staring fixedly at his shaking hands. He inhales deeply, then lifts his fingers from the stone — and collapses into a ball of quivering flesh.

His guards run to him. "The draught!" the captain rasps. "Give me the draught!"

One of the guards pats at the captain's tunic, pulls out a vial and pours its cloudy contents into the captain's drooling mouth. Again and again, Galden swallows, gulping the liquid down. Then he lies back on the dusty floor and waits for his agony to abate.

Some time later, Galden Madson, paler, stiffer, and slower than usual, exited the room of the speaking stone. He was intercepted by a small female in an exquisitely cut gown of deepest jet.

"You spoke with him," cried the woman, bobbing her ash-blonde head. Her sharp-featured face might have been attractive but for the displeasure digging furrows about her small mouth.

"I did, my lady," replied Galden, bowing with a refinement completely at odds with his shaved head and mercenary attire.

"Well? Did you tell him about the searches, the spies?"

"I told him what he wished to know."

With a snort of disgust, the woman turned away only to spin back around. "Did you tell him that the Steward knows? Did he say when he will move?"

"No, Lady, and I would no more presume to ask him than you would presume to accost the Steward."

"That spider!" spat the diminutive woman.

"A most subtle and deadly spider, lady. My lord will act only when he is secure in the outcome."

"But not for me?" the woman said, lifting her head haughtily.

"He will not forget how you have served."

With a dissatisfied flare of skirt, she hurried away, and Galden continued down the hall, gesturing to the reliable Corg.

"The trap is set," he said. "We need bait."

"One of her ladyship's men should do. Young Hark perhaps."

"A rather pretty youth," said Galden thoughtfully. "Find him. Take him to the front garden after dark and bind him to one of the stakes there. We want our daemon lady to know that she's been invited to dinner."

Al's explorations yielded little beyond the obvious fact that he'd been stowed in a complex of cellars. The low-vaulted chambers, lit by occasional lanterns, contained many heavy-beamed shelves of the kind designed to hold casks of wine and barrels of foodstuffs. But all were empty except for dust and an almost magnetic dullness that his magic could not penetrate.

He ran through a list of the great houses he knew and tried to recall which if any were abandoned. A few came to mind, but none seemed to be the right distance from Cyr, assuming that his estimations on the speed and duration of their journey could be relied upon.

After scouring the deepest part of the cellars, he silently worked his way back toward the entrance. He found the room that had held the box littered with debris and deserted. The hallway leading out of it was covered with a dense iron gate secured by several enormous locks.

Briefly, he thought about testing the locks with his knife and just as quickly discarded the idea. They looked intricate, and the knife was no pick. He also considered sinking some sort of protective magic into the iron that might delay his captors, but he knew that the warding power that worked so effectively against wights would have less impact on ordinary humans, especially in this place. The powers of the houses had developed in the service of humanity, not in opposition to it. The situations in which he could work magic against ordinary mortals were more limited, and these men had access to potent magics of their own. To master any of them, he would need to be in close proximity, and the men would need to be relatively few in number. The well-informed Captain would know as much.

He wound his way back into the deepest room, the smallest of all of them, collecting or dousing lanterns as he went. Here too, massive, floor-to-ceiling shelves divided the space. He muddled through a number of strategies as he stared about, and eventually found himself standing before the shelves lining the back wall. There was definitely an aura of old but potent power here, a whisper coming from beyond the back wall.

He studied the rough wood backing of the shelves, then reached in and rapped. The sound was higher than it should be. Cautiously, he sent a mental probe into the spaces beyond the wood and all but recoiled at the sucking sensation that brushed his mind. It was as if the space behind the wall drank power.

Instead of retreating, he began looking for a way in. He pulled at the shelves, but they seemed solid. Kneeling, he moved along them until he came to a join. He ran his right hand slowly up the seam in the wood. When it reached chest height, a soft light flared into a startlingly familiar shape — the Steward's orb. Something behind the wood clicked, and the wall of shelves swung slightly ajar.

He studied the narrow opening for a long moment before picking up his lamp and opening the hidden door wide enough to slip inside.

At the bottom of a short spiral stair, he found a perfectly round room, whose contents made him loose a low whistle of appreciation. The flickering light of his lamp revealed a great curving wall faced with hundreds of stone cubby holes stuffed with books, scrolls, and a few odd-looking artifacts, all neatly and precisely shelved. The polished black floor held two delicately incised chairs and a simple design of mosaic tiles—a larger version of the Stewards' orb. And, in the exact center of this gleaming floor stood a massive but simple white pedestal, atop which rested the thing emitting the sense of pulling.

Slowly Al walked toward it. The room sprang to light. Symbols carved deep into the domed ceiling emitted a soft golden radiance that the item atop the pedestal seemed to repudiate.

He approached it with the wariness one reserves for a rabid animal.

It looked like nothing more than an anvil-sized chunk of stone, flat at the top like an anvil but denser and much, much darker and shot through with delicate veins of color like black opal. It looked completely inert, but it pulled at the mind in a deeply disturbing way. And the nearer he came to it, the greater the pull became. Though it gave off no sense of awareness, it oozed an abiding, insatiable thirst for the power, a thirst that fascinated and sickened.

Chilled by premonition, he backed away.

An long time later when Galden Madson led a small troop of his best men down into the same room, they found the prisoner lounging in a chair, seemingly absorbed in a crumbling sheaf of parchment.

"What an interesting place you have selected for my prison, Captain," Al said without looking up. "And what a treasure trove of antiquities you have put at my fingertips."

He raised his head to meet the captain's distrustful glare and smiled to see the the bald man avert his eyes.

Weapon at the ready, Galden moved a bit deeper into the room, motioning for the six men accompanying him to array themselves along the wall running around them. "None of these things will help you," he said blandly.

"Are you sure?" the other man teased.

"Quite sure." The captain's tone slapped the air. *This lordling certainly has the family arrogance,* he thought. *Even beaten and filthy, he manages to condescend.* The observation did not endear the prisoner to him any more than the dagger dangling from the prisoner's right hand or the bared flame of the lamp set on the arm of his chair.

"What have you done with the other lamps?" Galden asked nodding at the remaining light. Were those splashes of lamp oil on the nearest wall?

"Oh, I found I really didn't need them. What have you done with the rest of your men? Their numbers seem sadly reduced."

"Their numbers are more than sufficient for this parley."

A black eyebrow shot up. "Parley? Captain, have you come to negotiate your surrender?"

Galden's cold eyes grew colder. "Do not delude yourself, Lord Goodwin. There is no way out for you. Many more men stand ready in the rooms above, all protected by potent charms. It's time for you to choose how you will serve us."

"How generous of you to give me a choice."

Galden was curt. "I doubt you realize how generous we are willing to be."

Was that a flicker of interest breaking through the other man's watchfulness? Galden tasted satisfaction, but spoke as if he hadn't. "It may surprise you to learn, Lord Goodwin, that we have no interest in taking your life."

The Steward's heir smirked. "Not that my death would be a disappointment to you."

"Not to me. To you it would be a grave disappointment indeed, and we *will* kill you if we must, but we would prefer for you to cooperate. In exchange, we promise to leave you with your life."

"A most tempting offer, assuming that I value my life that much."

"You should value it if you value the well-being of those you are bound to."

Although the young lord continued to lounge in the chair, he shifted his grip on the dagger he held.

Galden kept his eyes on that dagger. "I am given to understand that you participate in a peculiar sharing of power that allows you to, among other things, accomplish feats like the one that killed my men and destroyed the box."

All semblance of good humor drained from the prisoner's manner.

Galden continued, "I am also given to understand that the rewards of this sharing come at a price."

A slight shift in the position of the other man's wrist brought Galden's sword up. "Don't do it, my lord," he snapped, eyeing the dagger. "You can't hit me, and you will only anger my men."

"What makes you think I would waste a good blade on you?"

Galden reconsidered. "Suicide? Have you no real regard for the life of the Shield bearer?"

The other man blinked. His words frosted the air. "You dare to threaten a second House?"

Galden held up an admonitory hand and spoke as his lord had instructed him. "We mean her no harm. It is you who endanger her. You must realize that what you experience she will experience also. As the test of the box proves, your bond is unusually strong. If you kill yourself now, you may drag her down with you. And even if you don't, you will do irrevocable harm to her mind and spirit. On the other hand, if you cooperate with us, she will be set free from your increasingly perilous union."

All the men in the room tensed as the young lord leapt to his feet. He stood before them absolutely still, eyes wide in his drawn face, invisible fingers of black thought threatening to menace them all. "Why should I believe you?"

Galden felt the charms tattooed on his body begin to tingle. "You should trust in your gifts of power. What does the sight tell you?"

He glanced into the prisoner's face just long enough to see dark eyes grow both sharp and distant. Almost he could feel their inky blackness peeling back the layers of his skin, lancing into his thoughts. The protective spells inked on his body flared burningly cold, and the stabbing black gaze recoiled from its own ricocheting power.

Long moments passed, then the Steward's heir spoke in an even but deadly voice, "What do you want from me?"

"Nothing more than your inheritance," Galden responded flatly.

"Inheritance?" The young lord took a step forward.

Galden raised his blade warningly.

"And if I do not agree?"

Galden smiled. "We will take it anyway. Neither a dagger nor a minor conflagration will prevent us from ripping it from you, and in a way that stabs to the heart of the Keeper's house as well as your own."

Lord Goodwin held them in a standoff for a bit longer, but in the end, as Galden's master had predicted, he gave in. "What would you have me do?"

The answer was exactly what Alsandyr's premonition had warned him it would be. After he slid them his dagger, they caught him by his arms and marched him toward the strange stone. He tried to reach out for their minds, but found his thoughts sliding off a slick surface of magic. Again he crossed the outer ring of the floor's design, and again the ceiling blossomed light. Galden, still holding his sword, moved to stand on the other side of the pillar holding the stone. Then he nodded at the man on Al's right, who grasped the younger man's wrist in hard fingers and raised Al's right hand palm out.

Galden nodded at the mark shining there. "Place your hand on the bloodstone, my lord, and we will leave you in peace."

Al swallowed, his breathing suddenly shallow.

"Now, Lord Goodwin or the forcing will begin," Galden growled.

Al fixed him with a killing look, but slowly lowered his palm to the stone. As soon as he touched it, he gasped and grew markedly pale, while the opalescent veins in the stone began to beat with light and life. Shallow breaths quickly turned to low groans.

To Al it seemed as if the bones of his hand were bending and cracking under the stone's overwhelming pull. When his captors let go of him, he dropped to his knees awash in mingled helplessness and agony. He knew he had no more hope of pulling his hand away from the stone than he had of yanking his mortality from his flesh and bones. The stone held him fast, and slowly but surely drank his power.

The day after Emily dreamed of burning a malicious box to cinders, she and Colin topped a rise in the road and got their first glimpse of the red rock massifs that marked the southern border. Like the shoulder blades of buried giants, the peaks rose above the declining mountains, sheer and barren.

"That has to be Red Gorge," said Colin tugging at the mule's lead.

"So soon!" murmured Emily. "It's only been a few days." She felt curiously lightheaded as if the bright morning air had seeped into her bones and leavened them.

"And Red Gorge is still days away," came Shade's light voice.

Emily eyed him over her shoulder. The blue-robed man stood lower on the road amid a clump of tree shadows. He never had told her what he wanted from them, and now Emily frowned to see how unguardedly Colin spoke to him. Shade listened, leaning on his staff as a gentleman might lean on a mantelpiece. At the same time his golden eyes, strangely bright beneath the shady brim of his hat, stalked Emily.

Their expression said that he knew what she was thinking, so she hardened the protective bubble screening her thoughts. Shade only smiled. Then he slipped past Colin into the trees, leaving Emily bristling. She knew a dare when she saw one.

"What are you doing?" called Colin sharply. And Emily realized that she had pursued Shade to the tree line and now stood with one foot barely resting on the road and the other completely off it as she peered into the underbrush.

She jumped back in surprise. "Nothing," she lied.

"How many times have you said we shouldn't leave the road?" Colin warned, looking at her worriedly.

"I know," she shot back. "It's just . . ." she peered harder. "I can't help wondering what he's doing out there."

Colin choked. "And this from the woman who scoffed at my worries!"

Emily had the grace to look sheepish as she walked back to her friend.

"What's the matter?" Colin pressed as they crested the next hill.

"Hmmm?" muttered Emily, distracted by her own thoughts.

Colin caught her left wrist and pulled her to a halt. "Stop that!"

"Stop what?" she returned in confusion.

"Stop rubbing the mark on your palm."

Emily looked down and slowly uncurled the fingers of her left hand. Her palm was red, but the mark gleamed as silver as ever.

"What is worrying you?" said Colin patiently.

"I'm not worried," she lied.

Colin held up her marked hand. "This says otherwise. You know, the week before we left the village, I thought you were going to dig a hole in your palm you rubbed it so much."

Emily glowered at him, but he countered her irritation with such steadiness that she gave up and gave in. "You'll slap me when I tell you," she warned.

"Will not."

"Will too."

"Will not!"

She smiled—as he had intended her to—and gave him a gentle shove. "Only because you are the best of friends."

"Only because my father forbade me to slap girls—even annoying ones," Colin winked and dodged her half-hearted blow.

"Are you saying that you *have* thought about slapping me?" she laughed.

"Emily, I doubt there is a male who knows you who hasn't thought about slapping you at some time." And he threw up an arm as she swung at him again. Catching the offending hand, he pulled her back into a walk. "So, what is it?"

She sighed. "I don't know. Just promise me you won't let Shade get too close."

Colin flung back his head in a plea to the heavens. "You're right," he groaned, without any trace of good humor. "I *am* going to slap you."

"And you have every reason. But I'm more worried about you getting too comfortable with Shade. I just want you to be more careful."

"Isn't this a case of too little, too late? We couldn't escape him if we tried."

"No," Emily agreed fretfully.

"So what is it you think I can do? I have to say he's kept his word. He's even begun to help lately."

Emily shook her head, trying to put into words a feeling that defied rational analysis. "I'm not saying that we need to take any particular action against him. It's not our physical safety I'm worried about. I just want you to be careful how far you trust him." She paused, crooked her brows. "He doesn't have to mean us harm to bring us harm."

Colin stopped walking. Emily put a hand to his mouth as her gaze turned more deeply inward. "I told you that I don't think Shade's a warder. But that doesn't mean that I don't think he's dangerous. In some ways I think he's more dangerous than a warder ever could be."

Colin frowned and slipped a question through her fingers. "What's more dangerous than a warder?"

"A creature of Twilight."

Colin stared, then laughed, but there was an edge to his laugh that suggested panic. "Are you saying that you think Shade's a type of wight?" His words ended on a croak.

Emily withdrew her hand, putting one finger to her own lips. Keeping her voice low, she said, "Not exactly, but I think he is very close to that world. And the longer I know him the more convinced I am." She tapped a finger against her lips, feeling for the words that would explain without terrifying. "He's like the talisman I carried," she said thoughtfully. "A thing outside that somehow finds its way inside, a thing so strange it defies belief, but too terribly real to be denied. To reach out to such a thing is to be shaped to its purposes, its designs."

Colin's expression said that he feared she was sliding into paranoia. He put his hands on her shoulders. "Emily, what exactly are you trying to tell me?"

She looked up at him without seeing him. "What the Steward once tried to tell me. Don't fall too much under his shadow, Colin, or stand too directly in his light. Don't let him in here." She put her fingers to his chest and looked deeply into his face. "To do so is to open yourself up to unimaginable consequences."

They walked on, Emily worrying about driving Colin away, Colin worrying about losing Emily.

As ordinary twilight descended and they began to set out their camp near one of the odd streams that sometimes cut across their road, he lifted his head and said, "You've never talked about the talisman before."

"Yes, I have."

"No, you haven't. All I know is that you found it. You've never told me what it was or how you used it."

She lowered her head to the sticks she had been gathering. "Because there is nothing to tell."

Colin snorted, "You have some nerve saying that after your earlier attempt to scare me with it."

"Colin, please. I wouldn't know where to start, and I couldn't explain if I did."

"I have to see it for myself, eh?"

Emily turned away, "Tellers grant you never do," she whispered. Then she winced. Wasn't he here with her now, in this strange place, among even stranger company? And wasn't he here because she had asked it of him? And didn't she know deep down inside that the Shield was far from done with her? And didn't one thing inevitably lead to another, as the Steward would say?

Shade reappeared when the last of hint daylight was draining from the sky. They enjoyed a stew made of the hares he had caught and a starchy tuber that he said would taste like potato. The food tasted good, but Emily couldn't eat. As the star field wheeled, her lightheadedness translated itself into a dreadful anticipation like the nervous tension infecting a cavalry before the charge. Her eyes began darting about, giving her brief, disconnected glimpses of her surroundings: Colin's hand before the fire, Shade's balanced negligently upon his knee, the overlapping limbs of the trees, the hints of pattern in the stars, and the darkness looming in between.

She gave up on the food, stood, tried to stretch, and felt the far-off thunderclap of something going horribly wrong. Like the whispered report of a distant catastrophe it broke upon her mind.

An ordinary mortal might have fled the ill omen of that report. But Emily wasn't an ordinary mortal. And she wasn't one to cower before intimations of disaster. Without regard for her personal safety, she summoned the power and set her spirit shooting across the leagues. She was a Keeper after all, and the first to carry the talisman of that house since Illyria's day. She decided, all unknowing, exactly as Illyria had.

Colin heard Emily cry out and, whirling, saw her collapse to the ground. Dropping the pan of food he was holding, he scrambled to her side. At first, he thought she had simply fainted, but when she didn't rouse immediately, he began checking her head and neck for injuries. Perhaps the fall had hurt her. The boneless way she lay draped across his arms frightened him, but something in the heat of her skin, the flutter of her heart frightened him even more.

"Get the small pack of herbs in my bag," he commanded Shade. The pack hit the ground.

The pan of hot water he requested was a little longer in coming, but by that time, Colin was peeling back Emily's eyelids and sucking in his breath over what he saw. Her irises seemed to flicker with multicolored light.

He tried everything he could think of to wake her, pungent salts, cold water, certain stimulants, shouts. Nothing had any effect.

He got her laid out on blankets with Shade's help — though he never caught the strange traveler touching anything.

"I don't understand," he said shaking his head, his face pale and tight with worry. "If I had to guess, I'd say she's having some sort of fit, but Emily isn't prone to fits, and she's looked and acted fine all day. I know of no illness that can come on so suddenly."

In his light-limbed way, Shade had squatted down by the unconscious girl's head. "Nothing?" he asked and the sound of his voice made Colin's skin prickle. In the unnatural quiet of the road, his light voice reverberated strangely, almost as if it carried its own dark echoes.

Colin looked up, but all he could see of Shade's face beneath the wide-brimmed hat was a solemn mouth and firm chin. Abruptly, he took Emily's face in his hands, and with his thumbs, he folded back her eyelids. The flickers were still there. "It's more of this infernal magic," he muttered out loud.

"And what do you do for magic?" asked Shade.

Colin looked into eyes that glowed a fiery gold. "How should I know?" he snapped.

Shade rested his elbows on his knees, letting his staff fall against one shoulder. "Some healer you are!"

"I don't see you trying to help her!"

"Because I can't."

"Well, if it's magic we're dealing with neither can I!" Colin flared around a painful tightness in his throat. Aggravated, he thrust out an arm, pointing to the other side of the road. "Just leave me alone and let me do what I've been trained to do."

"Very well," said Shade, though he made no move to rise. He watched Colin adjust the rolled up blanket that served as Emily's pillow, then said, "But, if that is all you are going to do, she will die."

Colin glared furiously at the other man. "How . . ." he began, and then dismissed his own question with a shake of his head.

"How do I know?" pressed Shade.

"Go away, Shade," said Colin, his eyes on Emily's pale face. "I don't have time to play games with you."

"I don't play games," answered Shade in a layered voice that tugged like an undertow. "Unless you consider life itself a game."

Outraged, Colin leapt to his feet. "My friend is sick. What exactly do you hope to accomplish by provoking me?"

Shade bowed his head, but he took hold of his black staff and rose. When the brim of his hat finally lifted, the eyes beneath were burning like miniature suns. Throwing his hand up against that awful light, Colin fell backward to the accompaniment of a roaring in his ears. Clear and crisp above that roaring came Shade's sigh and his words. "What a trainer hopes to accomplish with a balky horse, I imagine. I do hate to see good material wasted."

Magic! More magic! Colin struggled to wrap his mind around it, but the voice in his ears, the same voice permeating his mind, beat at him. "Where exactly do you think your power to heal comes from?" it mocked. "From the knowledge of a few herbs, the wisdom of a few old wives? Do you really believe that your teacher drew her success from such mundane sources? Enter the Empyre under that delusion and you carry your death with you."

Without growing appreciably in volume, the voice intensified until Colin threw both his arms over his head in a vain effort to block it out, and yet no amount of pressure exerted on his ears dulled its volume by one whit. He was on his knees and whimpering by the time it released him.

"Please," he cried. "Please. If you know magic, use it to help her."

"I told you," said Shade in a suddenly ordinary voice, bending down to the stricken younger man. "I can't."

Around the protective shield of his arms, Colin whimpered, "And you think I can?"

When the golden-eyed traveler didn't answer, Colin glanced up. Shade stood leaning on his staff, hat cocked back and eyes burning with a cold calculation that smarted of contempt. "Come," he said and squatted again by the stricken woman.

Thinking of Emily, Colin bowed his head.

"Lay your hands on her," Shade commanded, jerking his chin.

"Where?" bleated Colin and flinched as the bright eyes stabbed into him.

He took a deep breath, studied Emily's limp form and for some reason felt compelled to press his hands down on the valley between her breasts. He could feel the heart beneath her ribs laboring. It galloped as if she were racing uphill.

"Now what," breathed Colin to his unexpected mentor.

"Tell me what is wrong with her?"

"I don't—"

"Use your gut, boy, your instincts."

Colin concentrated until a sweat broke out on his brow, until he had basically given up hope, and then experience and exhaustion took over. For a moment, he forgot about friendship and became just a healer. For a moment, Emily was no longer Emily, but just another patient. He stepped outside his own feelings and let her body speak to him—the hot flesh and rushing heart, the shallow breaths and flickering fire in the blood. Beneath it all, he encountered hollowness.

"She's not here!" he exhaled.

"Yes," nodded Shade. "She's gone to him."

"Him," agreed Colin.

"But this is a journey she must not take. This fight she cannot win. Call her back."

Colin shook his head in confusion. "Call her?"

The golden eyes burned into him. "You know her," they said, "Now call her."

Call her, thought Colin. He set his shoulders and pressed down on her chest and called, with his hands, with the muscles of his back, with the focused effort of his mind. Beneath his hands he felt Emily's heart leap and begin to slow, and he knew she heard, although she did not return. Soon her heart sped forth again.

"She hears me," he breathed in amazement, "but she will not come."

"Make her."

"How?"

"She is still tethered to her body, draw her back into it."

"I—" he choked, but he was already sinking in, flowing past his hands to touch with fingers the intangible cords of her being. The smooth cloth of the flesh and organs, the tough fibers of muscle, the web-work of bone. He touched them all, but instinct told him he had to go deeper still. Matter gave way to energy, a dance of radiance, and in the dancing sparks he discovered rainbow radiance and a chord of woven light. This chord he touched and felt the consciousness at its other end twinge. Wrapping invisible hands around it, he pulled, trying to bring her near. As he pulled, he felt the chord pulsing with energy.

At the same time he understood that the energy flowing through it was steadily diminishing.

She resisted the pull with all her might, until he felt his own deep sight failing. One last time he yanked upon the luminous tie, then surfaced gasping. His shirt was soaked, sweat dripped from his nose, his hands shook.

"She will not come," he panted. "She's ghastly strong, and stubborn."

"Aye," hissed Shade, "they were ever so?"

"They?" he heaved.

"The Keepers. Ever loath to relinquish what they take to heart. 'Tis a pity." Did the golden eyes dim? Did a shadow deeper than the fallen night cross the traveler's face and try to pull it back into darkness.

Colin tried to blink the strange illusion away. "Now what?"

Shade rose. From an impossible height he spoke down to Colin, and his golden eyes flamed "It is over," he said in a voice like the wind.

"No," yelled Colin and thrust a hand out to grasp the robe of the receding form. "There has to be something else." An inescapable cold like the frost that kills the flesh coated his fingers, but he ignored it. "Do something!" he pleaded.

"I told you. I can't." The light voice was retreating, like Shade himself.

With numb fingers, Colin clutched at the icy darkness. "Please. There must be something else we can try. I'll do whatever you say."

And suddenly Shade was back. "Words I always like to hear," he returned in a voice like the leaping of light off a mosaic of mirrors. He flashed his teeth, and his eyes flamed brighter, casting their golden radiance over all his face.

Colin held his breath, somehow certain that he teetered on the very edge of an abyss. "So you *do* have the power to help her," he quavered. His once numb fingers had begun to sting.

"I never said I didn't?"

"Then why did you—?"

"I have to know you are willing to pay the price."

"The price?"

The white teeth gleamed, and the golden eyes ravaged like a lion on the kill. "My dear boy," Shade said, "There's always a price."

Emily heard Colin when he called her, felt him struggling to bring her back—Who knew he had such strength in him?—but she could not worry about that now. She was too busy trying to staunch a mortal wound. The glassy globe of contracted consciousness slowly emptying of light and life withstood her invasion no matter how she clawed at it. If only he would let her in. She looked down into the recesses of that directionless inner space and saw a black hole sucking up all his vital energies. It was killing him. It was killing a part of her.

The tug on her consciousness grew stronger, but she dug in her metaphysical heels and fought to chip her way into the globe. She knew she was growing weaker, but she couldn't find the self-interest to care. Something more precious than life itself was being stripped from her, and she had to throw everything into the fight.

Cracks now appeared in the surface of the other's mind, terrible harbingers of the implosion that must come. She dug into one of the wider cracks to pry it open.

And felt her left hand speared by a bar of light. Fast to the earth it nailed her, yanking her across the leagues back to where her body waited.

Her eyes and her mouth flew open. A wail rose to admonish the star-dusted sky. "No!"

She flung herself side to side, struggling to tear herself free of the cruel instrument that had staked her to the road. "No, no, no," she cried. Her fingers clenched carved wood and sizzled, but she didn't care. "Let me go! You must let me go!"

Shade's staff, drilling the mark on her palm, held her fast. "Welcome back," he grinned down at her.

In one of the overgrown gardens of the Crow's Nest, a young man, drunk on wine, slurred defiance and wrestled with a set of chains that bound him fast to a large wooden post.

"Wha' kinda joke's this?" he shouted, imagining the smirking faces of his compatriots. "I'll cut ya for this!"

He planted his back against the stake and jingled the chains binding his arms into a more convenient position. That was when he heard a voice coming from a stand of shrubs like a wall of shadow.

"Is that my love?" the voice said softly, sweetly, persuasively.

"Who's there?" demanded the young guardsman. He was sobering up quickly.

"I feel you, my love," sang the voice.

The guardsman stumbled as his eyes detected movement in the shadows. "Cut this out, you mongrels," he snarled and strained to see his comrades' faces in the deeper darkness.

"Shhh," answered the voice, from somewhere on his left side.

The young guard spun about fighting his chains as his anger gave way to a slow, building horror. "Who are you?" he cried.

"Over here," said the voice.

It now came from directly behind him. The guardsman spun again, as far as his chains would allow. He could see nothing but a tangle of shadows and the suddenly menacing hulk of the house.

His chains rattled faintly as the violent shaking in his chest translated itself to his limbs. "Heaven's lights," he hiccoughed and began again to curse.

A light flickering in the corner of his eye brought his head round. Eyes wide and mouth falling open, he watched a shining woman slip out of the trees. At first, he was mesmerized by her beauty. She shone and moved with a silky, gleaming grace that made his heart leap.

She was tall and white, with her hair seemed to be threaded with fire, and she wore clothing so stained and torn that it revealed a seductive swell of breast and shapely length of leg.

Involuntarily the guardsman licked his lips even as a part of his mind cried out in terror.

Some yards from him, the woman halted her weaving advance. "You're not my love," she said sadly, her lips pursing into a tempting pout. "Where is my love? They took him from me, and I need him." She bowed her head, causing her hair to fall over her shining face. "I'm so lonely, so hungry."

"Lady?" croaked the guardsman, his heart galloping.

Her head lifted ever so slightly, and her eyes shone out from under her brow like evil stars. She was on him before he knew it, moving less like a woman than a strangely articulated insect. Now he could see how her flesh was as parched and shriveled as scorched leather, how here and there the fire inside her had eaten all the way through the skin to lick at the air with tiny multicolored tongues.

He started to shriek when she sank her teeth and talons into his face. "So hungry," she growled and shoved him writhing into the stake.

Inside the manor, men rushed to finish packing gear, while others called for supplies and mounts.

Galden Madson swept past them all, heading to his own temporary quarters.

"What now?" asked Corg, jogging beside him.

"What do you mean?"

"Should some of the men remain to keep watch on the prisoner?"

92

Galden barked a laugh. "Not unless they want to be eaten by her."

"What if he escapes?"

Galden halted, rounded on the shorter man. "Our lord promised to leave him his life, so leave him his life we will. He won't go anywhere. He's fixed to the stone, and as it feeds on him, its other protective magics fail. When they do, she will come for him." Galden began walking again. "He'll wish we had killed him before she's done."

The troops of men departing the house were so caught up in the chaos of breaking camp that they never noticed the stranger among them. This man, dressed nondescriptly and wearing a hat low over his forehead — which might have seemed an incongruous garment on any less hectic night — stalked among the others, swiveling his head slowly from side to side.

At one point another man called out to him and tossed him a bag. "Take that to the south picket," the man ordered. The stranger nodded and moved on, tossing the bag aside as soon as he rounded a corner into an empty hall. He picked up the trail of two younger men conversing intently as they walked.

"The lieutenant just seized him, I tell you. Right in the middle of the game. No explanation at all."

"He must have done something."

"What? And why tie him up in the yard? He's out there right now."

The man following them stalked closer and asked in a strangely disinterested voice, "Have they moved the prisoner yet?"

The two young guardsmen spun about, faces thrown open in alarm. "Damn, fellow, are you trying to scare us?" one cried.

"I asked if they have moved the prisoner," repeated the hatted man.

"What prisoner?" they returned.

"The one Captain Madson took from Cyr."

The guardsmen eyed him doubtfully. "We don't know about any prisoner," the stockier of the two said. "We're the Lady Malamot's men. If you want to know what your Captain's up to, go ask him."

"Assuming you're that stupid," snorted his companion.

The two turned to walk away, but the hatted man slipped round them. "Hey!" one exclaimed, the sound dying in his throat as the hatted man raised his head and fixed him with glowing green eyes.

"And where would I find Captain Madson?" the green-eyed man said softly.

The two guardsmen hastened to give him their best guess.

Captain Madson was in the mansion's library supervising the moving of his master's speaking stone. It was one of his lord's more valuable possessions, and he wanted to make sure it was handled properly.

Elsewhere in the room, the lieutenant named Corg was carefully packing away Madson's papers and belongings. Neither he nor any of the other men were aware of the hatted figure listening to them from the hall.

Madson followed the stone bearers out the door. Corg was left alone with an armload of document cases and several rolled maps. He did not see the man who snatched him into the darkness of a neighboring room.

What Corg did eventually realize was that he was choking. Into his fading sight swam an oval dominated by glowing green eyes. "Where is the prisoner?" the green-eyed daemon said in a flat voice that plucked the nerves along Corg's spine.

"You filthy—" Corg croaked.

The iron hand at his throat squeezed harder, and Corg's curse came out as a raspy breath. "The prisoner," the daemon repeated. Panicked Corg struck out with his arms and legs until the green-eyed man rammed a knee into his chest.

"The prisoner," the daemon said one final time, allowing Corg a gulp of air.

"I'll never tell," Corg choked out.

"You will," said the green-eyed man matter-of-factly, then raised a hand, set his thumb to Corg's nose, and began slowly to press it in.

It didn't take Blayne long to extract from his captive the information he wanted. He knew pressure points in the frail human body that mere men would never imagine, a few of which, stimulated properly, broke the mind wide open.

While the Captain's and Lady Malamot's troops dispersed into the night, Blayne ghosted through largely deserted corridors looking for the entrance to the cellars. When he found it, he paused, head raised like a wolf scenting the air.

What would have been a well of dark to ordinary men was as good as daylight to Blayne. He slipped unerringly through the blackness, responding to the faintest currents of air, until a faint fitful glow beckoned him to the spiral stair. Down the steps, he flowed, smooth and silent as the light itself, narrowing his eyes as his ears detected a low hum well beyond the range of human hearing.

Without any trace of emotion, he stepped into the hidden room and took in the strangest of scenes: Alysse, glowing like a fairy moon, save where her clothing and flesh were stained dark with gore, and in her arms, a darker, limp form.

With dagger and blade drawn, Blayne moved toward the burning woman. Alysse's head jerked up, her star-white eyes touched him briefly, and then she went back to stroking the man she held.

Blayne rushed her, streaking like a bolt. Alysse was ready. Without releasing the man she held, she shoved Blayne across the room.

Blayne used the momentum to spin into another perfectly balanced stance. With glowing eyes, he studied her, knowing that he now had her full attention.

"What have you done to him?" she demanded in a ghostly voice that flickered through its pitches like fire.

Blayne's response was to dance forward while calculating just how swiftly she could move. His blade scored a line across her arm, releasing more tiny tongues of iridescent fire.

With a savage hiss, Alysse snatched at him. "You will not take him from me," she blazed and then began to moan, a low keening sound that rose into a high mournful howl and stirred even the hairs on Blayne's neck. "His energy is almost gone," she cried.

Blayne's eyes flicked to the unconscious man. He noted how all of Alsandyr seemed to dangle from Alysse's arms except for his right hand, which was splayed upon a rock shot through with throbbing ribbons of color.

The light in Blayne's eyes waxed brighter. He attacked the possessed woman again, probing. Again, she lashed out, claws flying faster than any mortal could see. Blayne's face split in a mirthless grin, and he moved in for the kill.

Death did not come quickly. He had to beat her in increments with quick slashes and small stabs, for, though she bled fire, she did not die, and soon she learned to hinder his attacks by using Al as a shield. Blayne heard his colleague groan.

Then Alysse released the darker man, letting him fall like a bundle of rags, and jumped behind the pedestal holding the strange rock. Blayne jabbed across it, feeling as he did so the rock's intense magnetic pull. Alysse caught his sword blade in one frail hand, and with the other she snatched at his dagger, closing her fingers on his fist. Slowly and inexorably she bent his wrist backward. Blayne's grip on the dagger loosened. The blade dropped free, hit the stone, bounced and clattered to the floor. Alysse now pulled on Blayne's blade, drawing him closer to the stone. Blayne tried to twist his blade free, but it only bit deeper into Alysse's enflamed flesh.

"Why do you fight me, brother?" Alysse asked, and the inhuman fire in her eyes leapt to meet his own. All traces of the sun-loving mortal she had been disappeared as her flesh drew down over bone, shrinking it into a wraith-like mask.

Blayne called to Al through gritted teeth, "Get up, Alsandyr. Take my knife and finish her off." Al groaned again.

Alysse's starry gaze brightened.

"Hurry, Alsandyr," commanded Blayne, straining to hold the deadlock. He could feel the stone's pull increasing. "Do it now!"

Beyond the strange, living fire that was Alysse, Al moved, groping for Blayne's knife. It seemed to take him forever to find his feet. But when he did, he raised the knife over Alysse's glowing shoulder, where it hung for an instant, before descending with savage power into the daemon lover's neck.

Again and again the knife bit. Blayne saw Alysse's delicate neck shredded, saw her head loll, saw her body collapse onto the stone. Then he and Al were flying through the air as the whole room erupted into rainbow fire.

Emily sat on the trunk of a fallen tree staring absently into the distance. Colin had tried to get her to lie down, to drink something. She did not even seem aware of him.

In the end, he decided that all he could do was drape a blanket over her shoulders and wait for her to return. It hurt him to see her so devastated. For a brief moment he thought about the bargain he had made with Shade on her behalf and hated her for the making of it. Still, he couldn't, wouldn't abandon her now. They had known and cared about each other too long.

The night moved on in wheeling banks of stars, and finally, when dawn began to spread its thin fingers up from the horizon, Emily spoke in a broken rush. "I told you not to let Shade get too close," she hissed. "I don't even know if he lived or died." She clenched the blanket she wore with her marked hand.

"He's alive, Emily," Colin reassured her. "I'm sure of it. He's too capable to be otherwise."

"I pray so," she said, breaking into quiet sobs. "But he's still lost to me."

Chapter 7: Curses

Al opened his eyes to benign blue sky and smiled, relieved to have finally awakened from the terrible dream. Then he felt the emptiness gnawing at his insides and the dead weight of his disempowered limbs, and wished he were dead.

Overhead the wind whispered, tree limbs quibbled, a circling hawk screamed. Much closer, there was the snap and crackle of a fire and the clink of metal.

"There is tea if you want it," said a disinterested voice.

Al turned his head. Blayne sat across the fire, studying Al like a pig meant for slaughter.

Al did not care. He went back to accusing the offending sky.

"You should drink something. You look very bad."

Al laughed joylessly, and tried to focus on less material matters. "How did you find me?"

"Alysse. They used some sort of magic to hide their trail, but they could not hide hers. She must have used the link to follow you."

His heart lurched. "What happened to her?"

Blayne's perfect indifference acquired a touch of curiosity. "Don't you remember?"

Al moved painfully to sit up. The dull, thick stolidity of his body, the hole where his power had been disgusted him, but he balled his hands into fists and strained to keep his voice even. "Not all of it."

"The stone took her."

"The stone?"

"The one that held you. What was it?"

Al's head began to ache. He discovered that he was using all his remaining strength to fight an anger so deep it threatened to swallow him whole. "He called it bloodstone."

"Who?"

"The good captain."

"I have never seen its like. Have you?"

"No." Al clambered to his feet. He needed desperately to get away, but he was swaying, and the world was spotty with shadows. He sank to his knees, holding his head. "Maybe I should have some of that tea."

Blayne was blandly obliging. Al took the tin cup in shaking hands and sipped. "What's become of the renegades?"

"Their trail leads south."

"Are we following them? We'd better be. I have a score to settle with the fine Captain."

"You are in no condition to follow anyone. I have been hauling you through the countryside like baggage for two days."

"Two days." Al groaned.

"I was concerned that you might never regain consciousness."

"Concerned? You?"

Blayne shrugged. "In a manner of speaking."

"Never mind. How many days are we from Cyr?"

"Many."

"Surely we are closer than we were."

"We are not going to Cyr."

"We are heading to the capital then?"

"No."

Al lifted his head, shook it. He found focusing difficult. "We aren't going to Cyr, we aren't going to the capital, we aren't chasing our enemies. Exactly where are we headed?"

"To the Settlement."

"The Settlement? What settlement?"

"You'll see."

Al shut his teeth on his growing irritation. He decided to ignore Blayne's built-in obtuseness and get to the critical point. "Well, I am awake now. I say we head for the capital instead. It is vital that I speak with my grandfather."

"Corwyn Abrille has undertaken that mission."

"Abrille?"

"He found us yesterday morning. He will take word to the Steward."

Al shook his head again. "I wish you had spoken with me first."

Blayne raised a questioning eyebrow. "You were unconscious."

Al ground his teeth, but managed to hang on to his temper. Sometimes dealing with Blayne was like dealing with a child. "Abrille doesn't know all that I do. We will make for the city."

"No, Alsandyr, we will not."

Al stared, and Blayne looked unwinkingly back. So Al spoke slowly and distinctly, holding on with what energy he had left to his patience. "Listen, Blayne, and try to understand. This attack wasn't just on me," he swallowed. "It was a direct assault on the Steward's house, one that could have enormous repercussions for all the houses. It is essential that I communicate with Allyn."

"You could try to speak with him mind to mind."

Al stood up, reeled with dizziness, cursed, and threw his cup across the clearing. "I can't."

"You are very ill, Alsandyr. We will go to the Settlement."

"You go to this settlement!" he shouted, his vision going black. "I am going to the capital."

He started to walk to it and stumbled into a tree instead. As he sagged there panting, he heard Blayne say, "No, Alsandyr, you have other obligations now. You will go with me to the Settlement, be healed, and then you will lead me south to Bethnara and my child."

The world seemed to be sidestepping him. He clung to the tree in a vain effort to hold on. "Your child? Who told you—" He never finished the question, for the world spun toward darkness, dragging him with it.

Just before he hit the ground, Al realized with chagrin that he was actually going to faint.

For the next two days, he suffered the excruciating humiliation of being hauled through wilderness like a sack of flour. Too weak to walk or ride steadily and growing weaker, he had to be shoved into the saddle and then tied to it. When Blayne decided to camp, he was hauled down and put to bed like a child. He was even fed like a child because his hands shook like pennants in a high wind.

"Your fever is growing worse," Blayne blandly commented one night.

Al cursed him, using language that would make an old soldier blush.

Blayne held out a cup of tea.

Al cursed him again, in a voice more wind than word.

Blayne lifted the suffering man's hand to take his pulse and studied his palm. "The mark is looking worse as well." His uncompromising green-eyes probed Al's pale face. "Why aren't you fighting harder?"

No longer able to muster the energy to speak, Al cursed him in his heart.

Blayne stood, peered down at him. "Stop being childish, Alsandyr, and start making a serious effort to survive. Otherwise you will never get your revenge."

It was something to think about. In the morning he managed, shaking violently, to drag himself into the saddle, and he actually snarled like a wild animal when Blayne moved to fasten him to it.

"I have to, Alsandyr," said Blayne coolly. "You can't afford to fall."

It was just as well, for Al slipped in and out of a fevered sleep and passed much of the morning slung over his horse's neck. Even when his eyes were open, he wandered in hot, throbbing darkness. Sunk in a soul-sickness more profound than any mere ailment of the body, he was oblivious to the sheer-sided trail they rode, to the clear air that greeted them as they broke through the timberline, to the strange escort of vaguely discernable figures that led them through a narrow pass.

Someone was speaking to him of things and people he thought he knew. Being tired, he tried to push the voice away. It receded, and a warm liquid filled his mouth. He choked on it, then swallowed, then choked again.

Darkness came and went. He was aware of people around him. They were strange and towering, but beyond them loomed even taller trees. These should have stood aloof against the brilliant blue dome of the sky, yet they seemed somehow to bend intimately over him until he could pick out the texture of their bark, the edges of their leaves. They seemed to whisper to him in wind-strung voices.

A pressure began building in the air around him, causing his breathing to become more labored, his ears to ring. He closed his eyes and felt the pressure crawling like a beast onto his chest. There it squatted, undulating its long tail, gripping his body in taloned limbs, brushing his face with feathered wing tips, until it leapt into his mouth like a fish. It tasted of earth and honey and mountain water. It swam into the very heart of him and filled him with a heat and energy as soothing as sunshine on a cool day.

"I am dying," he thought and opened his eyes a final time. The last pictures to penetrate his darkening brain were the faces of a black-haired woman and a white-haired man.

The white man and the darkly beautiful woman walked side by side but an arm's length apart, far enough to keep even the edges of their garments from touching. Their faces and voices, like the high valley around them, exuded serenity, yet there hung between them a tension deep as the force that pushes up mountains.

"It was gracious of you to let me come," the dark-haired woman said.

"You are his mother. He needed you."

"Perhaps. But it was your blood and your house that saved him."

The white-haired man studied the tips of his soft boots. "He may yet die."

The black-haired woman did not speak for a long moment, but her air of elegant hauteur deepened. "He possesses more strength than he realizes. He will survive. The powers will not let him off so easily."

100

"I suspect you are right."

She turned her face toward him. "Your interests in this matter aside, I deeply regret further embroiling you in the politics of my house."

"A betrayal as dark as this one concerns us all."

"Yes," she sighed and looked off into the trees, unaware that his ruby eyes watched her.

"You should go to your father," he said.

"I will leave tomorrow. But my old teacher has gone ahead, in a high dudgeon too. My father has much to answer for, and Lyr will not make the answering easy, even for the Steward. I still cannot believe that Dyre could live."

"And yet this development with the second talisman troubles me more."

"Wasn't it to be expected, what with the Keeper's shield coming to light, and in Cyr, too? I know my father feared just this sort of concatenation."

"The talisman of House Warder, Alyra, is not the Shield Light, just as the gifts of Warder House are not those of House Keeper. Although we warders were formed to keep the peace and in many ways hallow peace more than other men, we are at heart a bloody and dangerous race."

"I have not found the members of house Steward all that gentle or safe."

"But you are made to watch and guide and shape events. We are built to kill. It is a dark gift, so it is fitting that our great talisman is also dark. In our lore it is sometimes called the Talon of Death."

"All the talismans are perilous. We have long known that."

"But ours is particularly inimical, even to the other Houses, and perhaps mankind as a whole. That a clue boding its return should come to one born of the Steward's line augurs ill for the Steward who found it."

She stopped, her dark eyes searching his face. "Even if he has blood ties to your house as well?"

He refused to meet her eye. "The first and only warder to bear our talisman was Roland."

"Yes, the great hero of your house, Illyria's beloved."

"That is how your history remembers him. Warders know a rather different version of him." Sandyr Ash was looking off into the distance at a point where the valley dived down to meet the great plain that lapped the mountains' feet. "If half the tales we have of him are to be believed, the Cyros Roland was undoubtedly the greatest warder who ever lived. And we revere him for it, but we also speak his name with caution. If there was greatness in him, there was also a great and terrible darkness as well. Roland served this house, and he almost singlehandedly destroyed it. Yes, he taught us to act and think like our enemy, but he played havoc with the rules, bringing us ever nearer to the twilight realm so that we became a people set apart. And he and he alone bore our talisman. Until then the great relic remained in our most sacred place, the place it was laid when it first came out of the east. No one dared to touch it. No one could, and live."

The lady's dark eyes grew deep and strange. "And this is the man the Steward Ayr betrayed."

"Yes. To his and our everlasting regret," he gazed into her eyes for a long time as if he saw in them the ghosts of the past, but at last he stepped away and said, "Come with me."

He led her to the clearing where Alsandyr's life had been saved the day before. At its center was a great flat rock cracked across its center, the same rock on which the servants of Warder House had laid her son.

"This is where the talisman lay until Roland raised it. The story goes that when he lifted it up, the stone cracked through and a spring of water gushed forth. Roland told the people that the spring was a promise to them from the earth itself. The waters, he said, would run pure and sweet as hope so long as the warders served the living faithfully."

The lady's heart contracted to see the hint of smile on his face as he said, "Shortly afterward, Roland went to the war that saw him strike like lightning at the lords of twilight and claim the love of Illyria. You know the essentials of what happened between them. You know that Ayr betrayed them. You do not know that after Roland lost Illyria, he returned here for the express purpose of setting a curse on the Steward's house. He himself carved those marks at the bottom of the stone."

She looked to where he pointed. Just above where the boulder met the grass, letters of an ancient language had been incised. Sandyr translated, "Till blood is repaid by blood, death by death, weep not nor quench any thirst. Death in life to the seer until he tastes true death from me."

Her face when she lifted it mingled questioning with concern. The white head nodded. "His curse against your house. Legend has it that the spring dried up on the day he carved those words, and the stone has been dry ever since."

Her hands gripped her elbows, "Hope dried up." Then she thought of something else and said almost accusingly, "And you dared to lay our son here?"

"It was the only way. I hoped that the ordeal Alsandyr suffered would prevent Roland's oath from recognizing him as the Stewards' heir. It seems to have worked, for now. But you see why I fear for him."

But her mind had flown back along the years. She sank to the springy turf, her dark gown billowing around her like a black cloud. "What have we done?" she cried.

In his pale face were the stirrings of sympathy and something more elusive. "What in all fairness to our people we had to do," he said softly.

She could only stare up at him in horror. "But to think that we may have handed Roland the means of exacting his revenge, and through our poor son."

She hung her head, and for the first time in many, many years wept.

Al knew he dreamed, but he held on to the moment anyway. It was a bright spring day, and he was standing outside Blackhammer's smithy, shaping a piece of iron with his bare hands. Without fire or forge, he worked it, and the iron yielded to his touch as if it were clay. Soon he held a crescent of metal so perfectly black that it looked like a sliver of pure night fallen to earth. As he raised it to the light in admiration, he heard a familiar emphatic voice. He turned his head to watch the dark-haired girl and the smith's son pass by and felt the iron, blade-sharp, part the skin of his hand. The blood welled up. He gazed perplexed at the capricious thing he had made, and out of the corner of his eye caught another flicker of movement. There in the deeper shadows of the smithy, a man-shaped shadow stood and watched. Al held a hand over his sun-shot eyes and stared harder.

The world shook. A hand was prodding him awake. He dragged open his eyes and met Blayne's uncompromisingly luminous stare. "You have slept enough for today," the half-breed said. "You should get up and exercise. The sooner you get your energy back, the sooner we can leave."

Al grimaced. "This is awful. Either I'm still alive or you have died as well and followed me into the afterlife. Either way, I lose."

"Quit talking and get up. The Lord Warder wants to see you later."

Al sighed, but rolled off his cot. As always, the remarkable speed of his recovery surprised him. He marveled at how well he felt physically, especially considering the delirium of days before. His fever was entirely gone, and whatever magic the healers of House Warder had used, it seemed to have infused his muscles with the old tensile strength. He had grown thinner of course, but the color had returned to his skin. If he continued to eat as he had been, he would soon fill out again.

None of this, however, began to touch the overwhelming absence inside him. Where once he had pulsed with power, he now felt cold and dead. Yet Blayne, the healers, and the Lord Warder himself all acted as if he should continue like nothing had happened. Al wasn't at all sure he could.

He pulled on his new, oddly loose clothing, and stepped outside the tent that had become his temporary residence. As usual, he felt that strange disorientation that came with taking in a world that seemed somehow both unreal and more real than any other place he'd ever known. To either side of the shallow valley, trees stretched elated arms to the morning air, and above them the towering mountains exulted, balancing on their flanks the delicate weight of ice and snow. From the foot of his tent, the valley bottom rushed away in amber and emerald waves, a grass carpet dotted with the most delicate flowers. To look at it, the whole place existed as a work of nature unblemished by human touch.

But appearances, like everything else about the valley, were deceiving. He knew he had only to walk into the trees to enter an alpine forest filled with ghostly warders.

As if this thought were a summons, one of the valley's elusive residents came stalking out of the trees. She was tawny-haired and hostile-eyed, though her hostility seemed as inaccessible as the rest of her.

"Blayne wants you to know that he is waiting for you in the high clearing," she said.

Al nodded. "Thank you — Callyn, is it?"

She had begun to turn away, but when he said her name, she gave him a last long, measuring look. "I have seen the Keepers before. But you are the first seer I have met," she said.

That struck a blow to his vitals. "No," he said harshly, "I am not," and moved quickly past her.

Blayne was prowling the clearing when he arrived, looking as sleek and full of easy power as a lion. He insisted on putting Al through several drills, as if the Steward's heir were a warder in training. He seemed convinced it would speed Al's recovery. Then he insisted on their sparring. To Al, the bout felt like an exercise in mediocrity. Without a steward's supernatural clarity of vision and precognitive quickness of reaction, he couldn't begin to handle Blayne. He was forced to scramble up and down the glade like a sheep being tormented by a young wolf.

For the twentieth time, Blayne executed the feint that had sent Al stumbling to his knees nineteen times before, and a pain that was more than the scream of overextended muscles shot through Al. Seething with helpless fury, he hurled his blade at the chest of his green-eyed foe.

Blayne dodged it with a slight turn. "Now you will have to retrieve it," he said not letting his guard down for a moment.

"No! I'm done," spat Al, and climbing to his feet, began to stalk away. A steely point pricked his neck.

Outraged, he rounded on the green-eyed man and slapped the blade away.

"That's better," said Blayne. "Now, at least, you are trying."

Al squared his shoulders and prepared to walk away again.

Again, Blayne's blade nipped him, this time on the cheek.

Executing a half turn, Al said succinctly, "Stop it."

"You will have to make me," said Blayne with perfect disinterest.

The glade erupted in sibilant laughter. Al looked around in surprise and saw that a crowd of cold-eyed warders had gathered among the trees to observe their bout. Another wave of humiliation washed over him, followed closely by a tidal surge of fury. He drew himself up and said as calmly as he could, "Enough." Then he resolutely turned his back on his tormentor.

With a mocking slash, Blayne's sword parted the sleeve of his tunic and scored a thin line across his upper arm.

Al froze. And so did the clearing. It was as if the entire valley had suddenly caught its breath. Then the whole world contracted into an icy ball of hatred—hatred for the inhuman creature that plagued him, hatred for the alien house that scorned him, hatred at himself for being only human.

He stood there on the verge of exploding and actually heard Blayne relax his grip on the hilt of his sword. Before he had even finished thinking about the attack, he found himself atop his old comrade. Savage as any lion maddened by baiters, he fought Blayne for control of the blade that now represented nothing less than all the pain he had ever endured and longed to re-inflict.

Thus began a brutal and engrossing fight. To hisses of appreciation, they rolled across the grass, trading blows. Again and again Al was bashed and buffeted, but Blayne's crushing blows only fueled his savage determination to win the fight.

Eventually, inevitably, Blayne, the man of more than mortal blood, got the upper hand. He used his superior strength to pin Al to the earth and pressed the other man's wrist tight to his back. "Truce," he said.

"Never," spat Al, but his fury had already begun to slacken. The last of the madness draining out of him, he started to laugh weakly. Only then did Blayne release him and rise.

Al sat up, still laughing, or weeping, he wasn't sure which. The onlooking warders had gone silent, but their keen eyes seemed to gleam satisfaction. He stared unapologetically back at them and felt that he was really seeing them for the first time. Then Blayne's hand cut across the scene. Al frowned at the long perfect fingers for a long moment, then finally allowed himself to be hauled to his feet.

As their observers melted away, Blayne set his hand to Al's shoulder. "Warder medicine agrees with you," he said with an unusual air of satisfaction. "I have never seen you move so fast." For the first time in many days Al's face broke into a real smile.

Neither man noticed the two figures standing farther back in the trees.

"He is like a dying man—drowning in the knowledge of all that he must lose," said the first healer to her lord.

The Lord's pale features remained severe, but his ruby eyes smiled. "Or like a drowning man clawing his way back to life."

Blayne led Al to the Lord Warder's dwelling as the shadows of the mountains were descending on the valley. Al expected another tent like the many scattered throughout the vale. Instead, Blayne guided him up the sheer side of the mountain to an eyrie-like cavern fronted by a large, columned pavilion that hung over the mountain's tumbled flank. It was a place that breathed ease and enchantment. The air this high—light and cool and splendidly pellucid—unburdened the body and enticed the eye toward the plain beyond. As Blayne greeted the other warders gathered there, Al stood near the pavilion's edge and contemplated the trick of light and shadow that had sunk the warders' valley in silver twilight while firing the far plain red-gold. Somewhere nearby he could hear water falling.

"That gap in the mountains at the valley's end is called the Dawn Gate," said a soft voice behind him. "It is said that the first warder returned to the lands of men through it."

Al turned slightly and caught the steady red gaze of the Lord himself. "After the great war," he added.

"The Great Catastrophe, as we call it."

The topic kindled a welcome, purely intellectual curiosity in him, one that he had begun to doubt he would ever feel again. "What does your house say about the enemy that was defeated in that war?"

"No more and probably less, I think, than the Steward's house. Most of it sounds like the stuff of nightmares."

The white man lapsed into a polite but expectant silence. Al thought he knew what the Lord Warder waited for, but he had to swallow gall to say it. "A second time, my lord, you have saved my life. I am deeper in debt to you than ever."

"But not grateful." It was a statement, not a question.

Unable to hold those bloody eyes, Al dropped his own. "Forgive me. I fear I am still adjusting." There was bitterness as well as heat in his voice.

The Lord Warder smiled and waved a dismissive hand, "Oh, you need not apologize to me. All warders know life for the dubious gift it is. Come and eat."

He led Al across the great blocks of the pavilion's floor to a long and low table loaded with bowls and platters. Already other warders were seated crosslegged around it and partaking of various aromatic dishes. Al noted with interest the informality of warder society that allowed the lord's men to indulge in his board before the Lord himself was even seated.

A stranger to nearly every person there, Al moved to sit near Blayne, but found himself redirected to a place near the Lord's side instead.

It was a good meal and a relaxing one. Al came to the Lord Warder's table armed with the experiences of a diplomat's son, one well practiced in making the best of tedious state dinners. But he found he had no need to exercise his skills. The warders treated him as casually as they did each other. They acted like comrades bent on relaxing after a long journey. They spoke little and softly and seemed more interested in enjoying the food and fiery drink than society. It was an atmosphere he could appreciate. There was nothing to interfere with the pure and simple pleasure of good food and a glorious evening: no banal or boringly conventional conversation, no awkward self-consciousness, no duty to please. The warders took their world and each other at face value and asked nothing more. And if any of them felt put off or offended by the presence of a burned-out seer, none showed it. Perhaps they knew they no longer had anything to fear from him.

He forgot his statecraft and concentrated on his food. It was robust and delicious, and sapped by his skirmish with Blayne, he couldn't seem to get enough of it.

The end of that meal found him rapt in the calm of a sublime evening. The lamps hung along the pavilion had been lit and a portion of the cloth roof rolled back to reveal an evening sky heady with stars. Then Blayne's dry voice cut through his abstraction.

"Alsandyr and I must depart for the Empyre soon."

Al blinked and, looking about, realized that all the guests but him and Blayne had left the Lord's table. The Lord himself was there, flanked by a silent black-haired warrior with fierce blue eyes.

Blayne was looking at Al. "As I have repeatedly told Alsandyr, time is running out. We must reach the City of the Sun before my son is born."

To Al, the statement irritated like a badly stitched wound. He was growing tired of Blayne's assuming things on his behalf, but he reminded himself to argue the point later. Tonight, he was a guest of the Lord Warder.

Then he heard the Lord acquiescing to Blayne's proposal. "What did you say?" he demanded.

The Lord Warder turned to him unblinking red eyes above a maddening hint of smile. "Blayne is right. You must head south very soon."

Al straightened his shoulders and matched him stare for stare. "You aren't actually endorsing this plan of his?"

"Important events, world-altering events, are even now taking place in the crown city of the Empyre, events you and Blayne have had a hand in making. It is fitting that you go there to meet them."

"And how would you know? If I remember correctly, it is the members of House Steward, not House Warder, who augur the future." Al regretted the retort even as it left his lips, but he did not back down.

The Lord Warder appeared unmoved. "Because only stewards have the sight?" he asked, but his soft voice held a warning flavor. "All the Houses were made to serve the world. And the sight is only one of their ways of shaping world events."

"I fear you underestimate what the sight can do."

"As I fear you overestimate it and underestimate me." The red eyes latched on to him and refused to let go. "The sight may not be in our arsenal, but we have other powers which suffice, including the ability to recognize disturbances in the natural world. The reverberations of important events speak to us in the wind and the waters and even mute stone." Abruptly his red eyes moved to Blayne. "And we understand the nature of our brothers in Twilight as no Steward can."

Shaken, Al took a deep breath. "And you would let that nature drive Blayne to his own destruction."

From the white lord stole a palpable exhalation of power, one that awakened a primordial fear. It forced Al to re-acknowledge the new, insupportable truth about himself.

He bowed his head, knowing he no longer had the right to speak on matters of power. He looked at Blayne. "I should have told you about your son," he said. "I didn't because I feared it would lead you into a trap." His voice faltered. He seemed to taste the dregs of a nightmare. "Trust me when I say that a journey to the Empyre will strip you of the thing you want most."

Blayne shifted slightly forward. "What thing?"

Al looked away.

Blayne continued. "Was it the safety of Bethnara that prompted you to withhold the truth from me? Was it the child, Alsandyr? Or were you simply acting the Steward and using my ignorance to your own ends?"

The accusation stung. Al climbed to his feet. "Do what you must, and the world be damned for it," he said, "but as you are my friend, I will not help you to your own destruction."

Blayne checked him with words like a wolf's bite. "As you call yourself my friend, you will — if that is what I ask of you. I have helped you to your desires. Now you must help me, whether it leads to my destruction or your own." His perfect and perfectly unfeeling face offered no quarter.

Al's black eyes narrowed. Both men seemed to have forgotten the two warders present. In a voice strung tight with suppressed emotion, Al said, "What is it you think I can do?"

"Your mother said you would help me secure Bethnara and my child."

"My mother! So, it was she who told you about the child! Devious, meddling woman. Well, her cleverness has caught her out this time. She spoke too soon!" He bent over the table and shoved his right hand under Blayne's nose. "You've seen this. Do you not understand what it means?"

In the center of Al's palm, where once the Steward's mark had gleamed, lay an ugly black spot like an irregular stain on the skin. Blayne regarded the spot indifferently, but Al's expression said he was sickened to his core by it. "The bloodstone did more than nearly kill me and consume my mark," Al hissed. "It consumed my gifts. All of them. Even if I wanted to help you I could not. I have no power remaining to help you with."

"Do courage, skill, and intelligence count for nothing then?" The question was the Lord Warder's. Sometime during the exchange he had risen, and now he stood with his back to them looking out over the star-lit valley, white as a ghost or a wight against the starry sky. "Imagine what an unfriendly world this would be if ordinary people thought so little of their gifts."

He turned and flashed them a real smile. "And what would become of all mankind, the members of the houses as well, if such gifts ceased to exist?" The look he directed at Al chastised. "No, Alsandyr, you go too far. There are many forms of power in this world. Some may seem small and simple and common, and some may be mistaken for greatness, but none of them should be denied."

He studied the younger man. "Any man as blessed as you certainly shouldn't complain. Even stripped of steward magic, you remain a formidable friend, and foe. You have been educated by the finest minds of your house. You have had training in arms that most other men would envy. And let us not discount your connections and experience. You have friends in all of the houses and most of the ruling families of this land. You have traveled widely and seen wonders few other magicians can imagine. And yet you stand in my court and dare to assert that you have no power." His almost smile grew secretive, and he moved back to the head of his table. "Surely, you can come up with a better reason for refusing your friend aid."

Al exhaled. "Fine," he said. "I concede the point. Unfortunately, what Blayne asks of me would require the use of the exact type of power I seemed to have misplaced."

"And yet Blayne must go south by hidden roads, and you must go with him."

"Why?"

"Because many different powers and the agents of those powers are converging on Sun City, and some of those powers are inextricably bound up with you. There is also this."

He held out to Al a much-folded piece of paper.

Al opened it and started. "Where did you . . .?"

"Blayne brought it to me. Your mother tells me that it was written by you."

"My mother! She is here?" He glanced around as if half expecting to see Alyra emerging from the shadows.

"She was, for a brief time, when you first came to us."

The old resentment rankled in his breast, and he looked off into the night. "She didn't even speak to me," he said.

"It hurt her to see you so ill, more than you can imagine."

"It's never easy to stomach a cripple," he admitted bitterly.

The Lord's response was immediate and sharp. "No more than to stomach an ungrateful son."

Taken aback, Al shut his mouth. The Lord sank crosslegged to the stones and gestured curtly to the fourth man with them, the fierce-eyed warder who had remained silent and unresponsive throughout their discussions. This man, sinuous as all warders, now disappeared into the cavernous recesses of the Lord's house.

"Come. Sit," the Lord Warder commanded, and Al had to obey, though he could sense displeasure emanating from the Lord like winter's breath. Apparently warders held mothers in great reverence.

"Tell me exactly how this verse came to you."

Rather humbly, Al did, watching with something like relief as the familiar feline serenity seeped slowly back into the white lord's face.

"What did your researches into it uncover?" the Lord asked when Al had finished.

"Nothing. Cyr's library contains few resources touching on the warder's talisman, and almost nothing about Roland. According to the histories I examined, he disappeared with the Shield after Illyria died. Of course, I did not have access to Numyn's or my grandfather's libraries. I might have discovered more there."

The lord's mouth curled in a humorless smile. "Unlikely."

"Why?"

"Because Roland was very good at covering his tracks. He may have been the most subtle, and devious" — this with a hard look at the younger man— "leader of any house who ever lived."

"Do the warders know what happened to him?"

"Some of it. And some of it bears on your journey south."

"How?"

"Do you really wish to know? Think carefully before you answer. When this verse came to you it might have been the ghost of Roland himself reaching out to you. And Roland's touch can be terrible indeed, especially to one of your heritage."

Al looked down at the table. He thought of the ugly blot staining the palm of his right hand. "All Roland can take from me is my life, which I'm not all that worried about losing."

"Be careful how you tempt fate, Alsandyr," warned the lord. "None of us know the preciousness of life until we feel it slipping from us."

Al nodded meditatively. "Just tell me."

"After Illyria's death Roland returned to the Settlement. He brought with him the talisman of our house, of which he was the first and last bearer, and certain treasures he recovered from the drowned wreckage of the Keeper's land. But he remained only long enough to lay certain powerful spells designed to punish the Steward for Illyria's unwarranted death. Then he disappeared into the great Wyrmwood, the remnants of which men today call the Greenwood, and from there he traveled south by secret and dangerous ways. Sometimes moving in our world, sometimes crossing the border into Twilight."

"Why?"

"The stories say it was in penance for the crime of cleaving to Illyria. Others claim that he sought a way to purge himself of his loss. A few suggest that he had long ago made a bargain with the Moon Queen who ruled the south, a creature of formidable power. All of these things are in part true, but there was yet another reason why Roland turned his attention to the Empyre."

"There was a child," said Al, his eyes grown distant.

"Yes. And our legends say that Roland went south seeking the son Illyria had borne him."

"But why would Illyria have sent their son to the Empyre?"

"She didn't. When the child was born, Roland brought him here, fearing the wrath of the other houses. But as time passed and the child seemed in no danger, Roland permitted him to return to his mother. The boy was with her on the day the great wave came. Illyria had enough time to place him in an artifact of the old world. Some say it was the Shield Light itself. But whatever it was, by some miracle or magic, when the wave struck, the artifact bore the boy up and carried him out to sea, where he was discovered by slavers bound for the Empyre. Sailors all along the coast still tell stories about a mysterious craft bearing an enchanted child in it. But it must have been Roland's magic that told him the boy was alive. He went south with the warders' talisman to retrieve him."

"And?"

"Neither he nor the talisman returned."

"And the child?"

The Lord Warder raised a hand, and the black-haired warder came forward bearing a very large and ornate scroll made of hide and wood and gold.

Carefully, the Lord Warder unrolled all but the last portion of the scroll upon the long table. It was a complex genealogical chart.

"Here are the lines of the Lord Warders since before Roland's day."

Al scanned those lines eagerly, genuinely fascinated. "I didn't think warders kept such records." Moving up the table, he pointed. "Here is Roland."

"Yes," said the Lord Warder. "And that character stands for Illyria. Even now we are careful to avoid a direct reference to the merging of the houses."

"But his line is broken," noted Al.

"Until here."

Al looked to where the Lord pointed. "Yes!"

"About five hundred years after Roland's disappearance a man of the south made his way to this very valley despite the many protective magics laid around it. He said that he had often dreamed of this place, and that in the dream a figure like Death had come to him and enjoined him to seek our valley out."

"Not Roland's son, surely."

"No, but a direct descendant of him."

"And your people were able to confirm this?"

"Oh, yes. The man was marked."

"With the symbol of your house?"

"Yes. And in another way as well. You see, something in Roland's heritage was strange beyond that of the other warders, and that strangeness left its mark on his son. So when the Southern descendant of Roland and Illyria made his way here, the people took one look at him and immediately recognized him as a descendant of Roland."

"Because?"

"Because that man was bleached white as snow."

Al let out a slow breath. "Like you."

"Exactly like me. Roland's descendant went on to become the next Lord Warder, and since that time all lord warders have been descended from Roland's line."

"And Illyria's too. Have they all looked like you?"

"No. When I was born, my people took it as a great and terrible omen for I am the first in many generations to be so marked."

Al stared into the middle distance, his internal eye full of images of the past, the odd glimpses of history he had been granted by the sight, history and imagination. "This lost descendant who returned to the fold, he didn't bring Roland's talisman with him, did he?"

"No."

"But now I seem to have discovered directions for retrieving it."

"Which is why you must go south with Blayne."

"But I am of the Steward's line. Roland would never permit his talisman to come to me."

"Which is why I will go south with you," returned the Lord Warder.

Chapter 8: On the Fringes

The road broke its promise to Emily and Colin. Instead of continuing to lift toward the bare red bones of the pass, it plunged down into a steep and rugged series of dim valleys. The curtain of enclosing trees finally parted to allow them a glimpse of the misty, inaccessible dales beyond, but then jagged boulders closed in upon their oddly elevated road, steering them away from any attempt to cross over into those haunted lands, and usually a thick tunnel of fog cut them off entirely from their surroundings.

The mood of the three travelers had also taken a downturn. Colin went about the business of travel as methodically as ever, but his shoulders were bent, and he moved like a careworn old man. Emily had retreated into a haze of heartbreak, and even Shade had grown shadier. Shadows seemed to hover about him. His cloak and hat looked more black than blue, and the pervasive mists leeched the gold from his hair and eyes. Even his voice sounded darker. Sometimes it penetrated Emily's gloom enough to send shivers of foreboding down her spine.

She tried to remember her old sense of purpose. She tried to care — about Colin, about Beth, about herself — but she just couldn't. She seemed to have expended all desire in the fight to hang on to something she had run away from in the first place. She seemed to hear her mother telling her, "Be careful the stories you tell." Well, she had told herself a pretty fiction this time, and now she was paying a hefty price.

She looked up as an unexpected gust of wind roiled the fog surrounding them. Shade turned into the wind, which blew harder. "Storm coming," he said, hanging on to his hat.

"A storm," said Colin in astonishment. "Really?" The wind whipped the words from his mouth. The mule laid back his long ears and neighed.

"We should keep moving," said Shade. He strode on ahead of them. Colin moved closer to Emily. "Come on," he urged, as if he doubted she had been listening.

"Hurry!" Shade was far ahead, beckoning, his figure half dissolved into flying swathes of fog.

Colin hunched into the wind and tugged Emily and the mule after. As they walked, the wind grew stronger and somehow colder, but the fog refused to break up and no rain came. The road, steeped in a twilight that defeated the eyes almost as readily as true darkness, seemed full of shapes. Emily began to get the prickly sense that they were being watched by invisible eyes. She didn't care. The emptiness inside her had cut her off from the rest of the world like a thick pane of glass.

"Shade?" Colin called. He pulled her harder. "Shade!" he yelled louder.

"Where's he gone?" Emily murmured looking around.

"Damn this fog! He's ahead of us somewhere. Walk faster."

They walked until the darkness was so complete that Colin was no more than his warm hand and an intermittent rush of garbled grumblings.

"We will have to stop, Col," she said wearily. "Light a fire. Shade will see it and come to us."

Colin tried, but could find nothing to burn. "Would you believe it," Emily heard him grumble, "Not so much as a twig!"

"There must be some trees up ahead."

"If only we had a torch."

"Go ahead and look. I'll wait."

"And leave you here alone? What if I lose you too? Would you even remember to look for me?"

"Of course," said Emily, but her listlessness didn't convince.

Colin's voice cut through the dark. "Snap out of it, Emily! You're the one who got us this far. I'm counting on you to take us the rest of the way."

Although she knew he was right, she couldn't make herself try. The effort wearied so.

The wind had died, and the air thickened. They sat down where they stopped and waited, the mule chomping at the collar of Colin's shirt. Occasionally Colin called Shade's name, but the heavy silence that swallowed each call only disheartened more. Not one star came out to greet them.

Emily was about to lie down to sleep, when a flash like a firefly's blink caught her eye. She leaned forward over her crossed legs and gazed off into the blackness. There it was again. "I think I see fire ahead," she said.

"What?" Colin barked. "Where?"

"Right there." Emily reached out, found his shoulder, then his face and aimed it in the right direction. "See," she said.

"But—"

"There! Did you see that? Shade must have managed to build a fire."

"He would if anyone could," admitted Colin, but his voice betrayed his doubt.

"Shall we follow it?"

"It's still awfully dark. What if one of us falls? A twisted ankle would put quite a damper on the rest of the journey."

"You wanted to find Shade and you wanted me to snap out of it. Here's a good way to accomplish both."

"Oh, all right. But go slowly."

They did go slowly, at first. But as the gleam grew brighter and steadier, shining in and out of hummocks of rock, their pace quickened.

It was a fire, a large one, and Emily thought she detected a figure moving before it. "It's him!" she exclaimed and actually felt the stirrings of something like her old enthusiasm. She quickened her pace and stepped confidently out into thin air.

She didn't remember much of the fall, except for a brief sensation of bruising, but she came round to aching darkness moments or hours later. Places all over her body ached, including her jaw, but none of her limbs screamed serious injury. She gingerly rose to her feet and saw above her, shining amid shards of perfect black, a dusting of stars. She had fallen into some sort of gully, which meant that the road must be above her. She called out to Colin and Shade repeatedly, and got nothing but a hoarse voice for her pains. She tried to climb out of her stony trap, but the cruel boulders hanging overhead pushed her back. She moved along the gully instead, still calling as she searched for an easier route upward.

The gully abruptly turned shallow. She clambered up the side of it and discovered light. Surely it was Shade's fire, small with distance. She hurried down a gentle slope covered with grass, but before she reached the bottom, a second fire blossomed some distance from the first. She stopped in mid stride, thoroughly confused. A moment later a third, even more distant fire sprang up between the other two.

She sank down in the grass, biting down hard on one knuckle. Could Colin and Shade have lit three fires to try and draw her out? Or were these the fires of other travelers, outlaws of the type said to stalk the Southern border.

Desperation carried her forward.

The fires grew steadily larger, and yet her eye failed to discern a single living soul moving in all that wide land. Only the merry whine and cackle of the great flames spoke. Huge they were and set far apart, and they danced with undulations of deeper color like figures moving within them. The more Emily looked into them, the more she wished she hadn't. There was a familiarity to the way the figures in

116

the fires danced that unnerved her. She passed between the two closest fires into a great triangular meadow and stepped onto ground littered with man-made objects— shallow bowls and carved sticks of wood, books, spinning wheels, cauldrons, glass balls. The light of the fires played over these objects in a way that made them seem almost animate.

She hurried on, arriving at a point equidistant from all three fires, and stepped onto a another triangle made of paving stones. A familiar symbol sprang to light.

It shone out of the side of a squat stone pillar, on top of which rested a wooden bowl bearing a single red-orange fruit. The fruit looked something like a pomegranate, but it glowed brightly as if it burned with its own inner fire, and its smell was luscious. Her mouth watered. Reaching out, she took the weight of it into her palm and saw the mark on her palm flare silver like a warning. Yet the luscious scent of the fruit was tickling her nostrils and teasing her lips. She brought its soft, round flesh to her mouth.

"If you eat of it, you can never go back," said a familiar female voice laden with the timbres of many, many other voices.

Emily looked over her shoulder. A robed figure stood behind her. "I know you," she said.

"Do you?" The robed figure pushed back its cowl. Emily saw the face of the woman, half in light half in shadow. It was neither young nor old, plain nor pretty, but it unburdened the soul like hearth fires.

"You gave me the Shield," Emily said

The woman might have smiled, or not. "You won it."

"Or it won me."

The woman bent her head. "There is that aspect to it."

Emily looked again at the fiery fruit she held. "And now I have another choice to make." She ran her thumb over the juicy flesh of the fruit, then placed it back into the bowl, but the fruit rolled back so that her thumbnail pierced its thin skin ever so slightly. Absentmindedly, she licked the drop of moisture away.

A taste exploded in her mouth, a sensation like nothing she had ever known, except perhaps for the wight's fiery kiss, but this was even more intense, like unquenchable desire and its fulfillment all in one. As the bright tang coated her tongue, she felt her whole body growing light and warm and realized she *had* known its like before, in some other time, some other place.

"You will have to live with that," said the woman almost ruefully. "But I suppose you deserved it."

"Deserved it?" said Emily in alarm.

The woman smiled. "A mixed blessing, but a blessing all the same. You have a long way to go, and that little taste may help you to get there."

"Oh." Struck by a sudden fear, Emily asked, "So I can still leave?"

"Mostly."

"Mostly? How does one mostly leave?"

"The same way one mostly stays," said the woman. "Or mostly loves," she added.

Emily winced. "What do you want from me now?"

"The question is what do you want of us?"

"I don't understand. Your fires drew me here."

"But you chose to come."

"I was trying to find someone, someone else."

"But you came anyway."

Emily looked at the fire behind the woman, squinting her eyes to shut out the sight of the forms moving within it. "The grass was littered with objects. Where have their owners gone?"

"They are not far away."

"But not here?"

"Not in any sense that you would understand."

Emily looked harder at the left-hand fire, narrowing her eyes against the forms moving within it. "This place is different from the high place where I found the Shield."

"In some ways, it is nearer to men's world."

"Is that why I didn't have to work so hard to get here?"

"That is one reason. Another is that you are now closer to our world."

Emily looked down at her hands. "Because of the Shield."

"All things come at a price."

"What price will I have to pay for responding to your fires?"

"That depends on what you do because of it."

"So I am supposed to do something here."

"You are doing something, here and elsewhere."

"But you cannot tell me what?"

"It is not for me to tell."

Emily nodded. She had expected as much. "Did you light the fires to draw me here?"

"Yes and no. Once every few centuries, when circumstances are right, the fires bloom, a summons to the three houses, a gesture to the half living and their three children, a prediction of the children to come."

Emily tried to make sense of that. "Three fires for the three houses. But once there were four Houses."

"Once and always."

"The Tellers' house we call the fourth one. Why don't you light a fire for it?"

"That is a good question."

"So answer it."

"First you must show us that you know the tongue."

"The tongue?" Emily asked. Closing her eyes, she remembered the way the game was played. The powers would help only those who helped themselves, and the only answers this woman would accept were the ones Emily brought with her. With the lingering sweetness of the strange fruit pervading her mouth, she thought of tongues, the tongue she tasted with and spoke with and once upon a time kissed Alsandyr with; the tongue that was the language the first tongue spoke, and the tongue that embodied flame, that which burned yellow-orange and that which waxed iridescent with color. So many different tongues, but all reaching, dancing, entwining, telling. Smiling to herself, she traced a symbol onto the top of the stone pillar holding the bowl. It was the same shape as the symbol that had burned on the pillar's side, and as she finished tracing it, both signs flared bright, and the fiery fruit in the bowl burst of its own ripeness, exposing a blood-red heart speckled with dark seeds.

"That is the Teller's Tongue, the sign of the fourth house," sighed the woman, and opened her hand to the flame etched night. "And here you find the fourth house."

"Here?"

"And everywhere. But always at the center." She raised her arm in a sweep of dark sleeve and pointed at each of the fires. "Three houses lie on the margins, body, mind, and heart, and here at the center lies the fourth house."

"So the fourth house isn't really lost."

"Lost to some." The woman's mouth quirked.

"How so?"

The woman touched Emily's chest. "Have you ever tried to put a finger on your soul?"

The question fed a more troubling thought. "Not mine, no, but I may have inadvertently touched someone else's."

"Yes." The affirmation raised the goose flesh on Emily's arms. "And so you come again to us. You have shown us that you have the tongue, now tell us what you want."

One answer was obvious, and yet it seemed the wrong choice. "Will you answer one more question for me first?"

"If I can."

"What is the power of the Teller's house?"

"You know."

"Telling."

"Yes."

Behind the woman two of the great fires danced, and Emily watched the figures moving in them, figures that now seemed to beckon to her. "But what does it mean? The powers of the other houses represent specific links to body, mind, and heart. So, the heart connects and feels, the mind interprets and knows, the body senses and acts. What is the power of the fourth house, the power you call Telling?"

"The power to relate them all."

"Relate them? You mean connect them."

"And separate them."

"How can it do both?"

"All things do. Is a bridge a bridge without the span that it crosses? Or light, light without the darkness it expels? Do words speak without the spaces between and behind them? Any relation is built upon the gap it crosses. And in the dance of gap and relation is the telling — conception, possibility, attempt."

Emily shook her head. "I'm not sure I understand. Why then it is forbidden for the houses to intermix?"

"All things come at a price. Men know this. It is the everywhere-written law of their world, but fearing the law, they declare certain acts forbidden. All things are possible, if one has the means and the will to bear the cost." The woman turned her head as if responding to a distant call. "Our time comes to an end, tell us what you want."

Emily's heart fluttered up into her throat. "If I asked you to give me back something I lost, could you do it?"

The woman looked back at her with large, knowing eyes. "Are you willing to pay the price?"

Emily swallowed her heart. "I think I would be willing to pay any price, but —" she sighed — "I also think the price would not be mine to bear alone." She heaved a bigger sigh as her mouth remembered the strange, stirring taste of the fruit. It tasted like love, she realized. She looked at the darkness between the fires. "And I have no wish to force my debt on another person. I guess I will just have to learn to live with this feeling too."

The woman had disappeared back into the folds of her hooded robe, and her robe seemed to be disappearing into the groping darkness. "Quickly, now, tell us?" Her voice seemed to come from far away.

The fires were blurring into streamers of red and gold as real night slashed into them. "Tell you—" murmured Emily. "Tell you—" she whispered, growing dizzy as the fire and darkness slipped away.

She woke to a fog so thick that all she could make out was a suggestion of rising ground and the circle of tall grasses surrounding her. She sat up slowly, lifted her hand to wipe the damp hair from her eyes and stared. Her right arm was black and blue. Her right hand, half buried in grasses, was balled into a tight fist.

She lifted it into her lap and uncurled her fingers slowly. Four tiny jet-black seeds rested upon her life line.

Images of fire and darkness, a woman's face, a red-gold fruit washed through her. She closed her fist tightly on the seeds and looked about. The day had stolen upon her like a thief. Tellers only knew where the road lay.

Then the silver air shimmered with a high howl.

Eerie as the keening of a lost soul it floated through the fog, leaving her wide-eyed and listening. Then it came again. But from which direction? The muffling fog made it nearly impossible to tell. This second howl was followed by high-pitched yelp, a ghostly belling that soon divided into two.

She broke like a deer from cover, bolting heedlessly into the fog in hopes of putting the terrifying sounds behind her. She topped a rise, tripped, and sprawled upon stony earth, gathered her feet under her, and rushed forward again. The yelps were growing louder, the ground steeper and stonier. Soon it was rising before her like a wall. Tiny seeds bit into her damp palm as she climbed. She tried brushing them off on her skirt, but they seemed stuck to her flesh. She pushed on, scrabbling from boulder to boulder up the steep incline. Here or there, the earth turned traitor, becoming an incline of loose shale that ate relentlessly into the little progress she made, but she kept on pushing upward. Finally, her questing hands discovered a stony shelf. Grunting, she heaved herself up onto it, lay panting on the edge. A keening yelp sent her scurrying higher. She raced across shelf after shelf, taking them like gigantic steps, until she ran out of shelves completely.

She stood atop a broken peak of red stone in a maze of other red ridges all rising out of a sea of mist. The fog here at the top of the world was thinner, and she could see the red rock falling away from her in knife-like edges.

Hearing a low growl right behind her, she spun about. She dared not go back, but she could not go forward either; the next closest ridge top was many feet away across a deep cleft in the rock.

The unseen creature behind her keened louder.

It was close now, very close. She spun and got her first sight of one of her pursuers as it came slinking to the top of a nearby ridge. In color it matched the silvery gray of the fog except for a staining of black on large pointed ears and oddly clawed feet, but it only incidentally resembled a dog. It was as tall as a small pony and whippet thin, so lean it looked starved, and its enormous eyes gleamed scarlet.

As she watched, it balled itself up and sprang easily, silently across a huge gap to a nearer ridge top, where it lolled its tongue at her out of a long snout ragged with dark fangs.

A moment later a second silvery shape appeared behind it.

"Say goodbye, Emily," she whispered to herself.

"Be still," a light voice answered.

Emily nearly lost her shaky purchase on the stone. "Shade?" she cried. "Help me!"

"Be still," Shade said again.

"You be still," she spat.

"They won't hurt you."

Emily laughed. "What fool would take the chance?" She craned her head looking for the blue-robed man and found him standing on the next nearest ridge, leaning on his black staff, and gazing at the creatures menacing her with something like fondness in his face.

"You have done very well, my lads," Shade said to the awful dogs. "But you should go back to your master now."

Cringing, Emily looked again at the dog creatures. The nearest one was shaking its head as if to throw off a collar.

"Go now!" Shade commanded, in a voice that leapt like lightning and dissolved like thunder.

Both dogs shied. They glared at Shade out of blood-red eyes and whined with all the voices of the dead, but they also slunk away, sliding back into the curtain of fog.

Emily transferred her amazement to Shade, but he only zapped her with his voice. "Jump," he ordered, and her legs obediently launched her into the air.

Chapter 9: The Face of Midnight

On the day Al Goodwin began his own journey toward empyre, he stood before the great flat-topped stone at the center of the warders' clearing. A pack of supplies was at his feet, but his eyes were on the marks etched upon the base of the rock, marks the Lord Warder had translated for him.

So Roland had it in for him as well. No matter. Al no longer wished to avoid death. He welcomed a chance to spar with it. Better to die fighting than by slow degrees. "Come and get me," he said quietly to the stone, a hint of a smile playing about his lips.

Then he looked up as a strong breeze set the grove's great trees to muttering amongst themselves. Day was ceding the land back to night, and he was alone, but for Blayne, who was as indifferent as the great rock and even less communicative.

A flicker of white announced the coming of the Lord Warder. He appeared in the gap in the opposite end of the clearing, and Al felt the entire grove resonate to his arrival. The power of this place must be truly astonishing if a burn-out and a seer by birth could feel it.

At the Lord's heels strode the laconic, black-haired warder Al had first seen at the Lord's table. This man, Al now knew, was the Second Warder, and his face revealed no more of what went on behind it than a closed door. Yet he exuded loyalty to his Lord. In fact, the cast of his features suggested close kinship, not that the relation would have had any bearing on his status. Warders attained rank through combat, not by birth. As Second, this man was a power in his own right and positioned to succeed to the lordship of the house, whether he was related to the present Lord or not, unless another should arise to defeat that claim. What must he think of his Lord's decision to undertake an impossible quest in a foreign land with only a half-breed and a burned-out seer for company?

"Are we ready?" the Lord asked in his quiet, even voice.

Al glanced at Blayne, but the green-eyed man looked worlds away. "We await your direction," he answered formally.

The Lord Warder smiled for real. "But you, Alsandyr, will show us the way."

Al lifted a brow.

The lord's smile widened to a wolf's grin. "Place your hands on the stone marked by Roland."

Al looked at the great stone, then looked at his palms. The black spot on the right one gaped like a wailing mouth. He shoved it hard against the stone. Rather to his disappointment, he felt only roughness smoothed by time and a faint residual heat from the sun. He closed his eyes in frustration.

And the whole world turned.

His eyes flew open. The great shattered rock was the same, but the grove had changed in some inexplicable way. The trees were more vivid now, brighter, darker, greener, deeper, and each seemed to shimmer with life. Al blinked, trying to confirm the report of his merely mortal eyes, and beheld a robed and cowled figure slide out of one of the tree trunks. Then another robed and cowled figure emerged from a different trunk, followed by another and another. Al yanked his hands off the stone, but the figures and the new depth to the surroundings remained. He looked about. At the base of every tree lining the clearing but one, a robed figure waited.

"Who are you?" he breathed.

The Lord Warder answered. "Men and women of our house. Those who have held lordship since the first days."

"Are they ghosts?"

"Not precisely."

Why is there no figure by that tree?" Al gestured with his chin to a slender specimen.

"That is Ash, my tree."

"And when you are dead?"

"My consciousness will join with it."

The prickles along Al's skin intensified. "So when your body dies, your essence remains tethered to this world."

"Yes."

Al shut his eyes as if to deny the unthinkable. "Heaven's merciful lights! Will you ever be free?"

"It is the fate of those who lead this house to serve for as long as our house does, and we may not be entirely free of it so long as the need for our house remains."

Al wanted to turn to the lord, to ask him why he would reveal such a disturbing secret to an outsider, but he dared not take his eyes from the waiting figures. "Which one is Roland?" he asked.

The name struck the air like a silent crash. A giant ripple of energy swept in, then out, and the mouths of the waiting figures began to move, shaping a word that built into a whirlwind roar. Al ducked his head, but the sound was like the earth's rumble, a thing so great and deep it was heard in the marrow of the bones.

Al called out to the white lord, "Which tree is his?"

The Lord Warder answered quietly, as if he either were deaf to the ghostly chant or knew it for the insubstantial thing it was. "It is not here. As I told you, Roland never returned. The sapling planted to receive him wilted and then vanished altogether."

124

Al could have shouted his pain and frustration. What exactly was going on? He glared helplessly at the figures chanting around him. "Stop!" he roared.

And they did stop, though the aura of expectancy they exuded intensified until it raised the hair on Al's neck. They now looked past Al, to the large gap in the clearing's trees. Al turned to look there as well and saw shadows coalescing.

A massive mountain cat the color of a starless night padded out of the trees. At first, it swung its large head from side to side as if scenting for prey or danger. Then its great yellow eyes lit on Al. Al laughed in disbelief, and the great cat charged, bounding then soaring over the flat stone to descend directly upon him.

Slammed to earth beneath hundreds of pounds of snarling cat, Al cried out, twisted, and felt the cat's hot breath rake his cheek. Grasping his knife, he struck upward with it, heard a deep yowl, and felt the cat's weight vanish. He uncurled slowly to see the other three men in the clearing watching him almost meditatively.

"What is this?" Al demanded.

The Lord Warder's red eyes actually smiled. "A well-executed blow. You will pay for it I fear, but our path is marked." As Al watched, he stooped to the grass and raised blood-smeared fingers.

His black-haired Second hissed in surprise. "He *is* out there."

"He never really left us, Cayne," returned the white man. He pointed his unnaturally pale face toward the gap's shadows. "Tis a pity we no longer have Illyria's daggers. You will have to seal the gate behind us as best you can. When the inevitable battle begins, those consigned to Twilight may seize the chance to push through."

The dark warder dropped his surprise like a broken knife, hardened his face back to a bleak mask. "And you?"

The white man answered with his customary hint of a smile. "I know my way, and I am ready for it." He glanced at Blayne, lingered a moment over Al. "If in a month's time the Cyros is not come, you know what you must do. See that the Keeper understands it as well."

The black head bowed, and the Lord Warder gestured to the two younger men. "Come," he said.

Al had walked in Twilight many times. Not long ago he had forged a way through its creeping malignancy for the warders, who were being prevented from defending Cyr by the wights laying siege to it. At that time, with the sight and the power on his side, he had been able to slide into and out of its otherness like water.

But none of his earlier experiences quite prepared him for the world he encountered now. It was as if he had stumbled into pure enchantment, a place where precious stones could be made malleable and forced to take root and life. He seemed to stand in a woody parkland beneath massive trees made of smoky quartz, onyx and emerald, and at his feet sprang flowers, grasses, and mosses spun of flawless ruby, peridot, and sapphire.

And all was lit in the most delicate radiance, an inner fire fed by the brutal nonlight streaming down from a jewel-studded midnight sky.

"The Powers be good," he breathed as bone-deep cold bit into his flesh and queasiness took hold of his mind. This place tore at the will and concentration the way the outlaws' stone had torn at his power. Were it not for the white light pouring from hand of the white-haired man standing next to him, Al would not have known where to anchor his fraying thoughts.

"The realm of Midnight," announced the white Lord, gesturing with his shining hand. "You have not seen it before."

"No, though it is like the places glimpsed in dreams. Why do they covet our world so, if they have all this?"

"Why did the truth about the Grove appall you? A prison is a prison, no matter how tricked out it may be. Imagine then what any prison means to one who must endure it until all worlds' end."

"It is terrible!" Al could feel his mind scrabbling for purchase on a steep and shifting slope.

"But beautiful. Brilliant and barren as diamond and twice as hard."

Al hunched into his tunic and shuddered more violently. "I did not know that warders ventured so deep."

"No other member of my house does, and many of the Lords who preceded me were unable enter so far." The white face swung away, toward a vista that included a darkling valley. "In my lifetime, only one other mortal has penetrated this deep into Midnight."

"Not the Steward, surely. My grandfather loathes all things Twilight." Al fought to hold the image of the white Lord and his shining crescent mark firm against the overwhelming unreal of their surroundings.

The Lord Warder's voice came to him across the gulf of that wonder. "So he would have you believe. But I speak of another, a ward of my house who went on to win back the first great talisman."

"Emily," Al breathed, and for a moment, the mind-rending otherness of Midnight receded somewhat. "She's better at keeping things from me than I thought."

"We must hurry. Look to your friend."

Al turned, struggling to fend off brutal beauties galore, and saw Blayne kneeling amidst moonstone and pearl. The half-breed's face and his form had not changed, and yet he looked like a completely different man.

"Blayne?" Al asked, shaking his head to clear it.

Blayne's wide gaze stumbled into his, the eyes like blown-out candles. He looked like a man stricken to his core.

"Blayne!" Al breathed more sharply.

Blayne's face broke open on hope and terror. His normally flat voice shook. "I feel, Alsandyr. I feel . . .".

"It is his mortal part he feels," the Lord Warder commented, ghosting to Al's side. "The pressure this place exerts allows him to feel it."

Struggling to keep his own mind from sliding further down the glassy slope of Midnight, Al said, "You knew this would happen to him?"

"I knew limitations were placed upon Blayne in both worlds."

Al frowned. "So his twilight kin withheld his mortal part from him."

"Not they. They have no such power." Into Al's sliding thoughts swam the face of the white lord, mouth grim, ruby eyes ruthless. "His mortal capacity for feeling was withheld by the Keepers."

"Meredyth!" Al could not contain his shock.

"With the aid of the Council of Numyn."

"Why?"

"Because they knew enough of the history of the other half breeds to fear what he might become. But we must speak of this later."

Together they hauled Blayne to his feet. The green-eyed man tried to resist them, feebly at first and then more frantically, but the Lord Warder gazed deep into Blayne's darkened eyes and gentled him to compliance. Around Blayne's tawny head, Al tried to catch a glimpse of the Lord's countenance. He found that focusing on the white lord helped combat the glassy disorientation of Midnight. "Meredyth told me that Blayne was the only hybrid ever conceived of his house."

The Lord Warder's eyes looked ahead, along their gemstone track. The lights of Midnight streaked his pale hair with rainbow fire. "And so he is. Whatever men's legends say, there have only ever been three half breeds, each one begotten by the Lord of Twilight on a mortal woman from one of the three houses. Through the girl Emilyn, he might have fathered a fourth and final one, the most powerful and dangerous of all. But you intervened. Come."

The Lord stepped off the path into a gap between jewel trees. "There has been no half-breed of the Steward House," Al protested. "No steward would allow it."

The Lord Warder's voice swam in rainbow fire. "And yet Steward House was the first to conceive one. Your Steward grandsire could tell you as much were he less jealous of his knowledge and protective of his honor. Many things are possible, Alsandyr, and for the Houses many things were preordained, including the birth of these bastard children. Such was the price of power."

Al stumbled on a gleaming onyx root. "But the houses' powers hail from the talismans. I have seen it in my dreams. And Emily saw it as well."

"Only in part. The talismans opened the door, but it took the joinings to pull us through."

"Joinings." The word dredged up a delicious memory of gold and silver fire. A door opened in Al's mind. Disconnected images, the accumulation of a lifetime of information and sight-fueled vision began to come together, like the building blocks of a complex edifice whose dimensions were only slowly emerging.

"Joinings, yes," the white lord repeated. "Something you possess a talent for." He lifted his pale head as if harkening to trouble ahead. They had reached a clearing where slender trees glowed softly like pillar candles around a heavier tree, woody, dead and dark.

Al swallowed. "I've seen this tree."

"And she sees you," the Lord Warder replied, moving closer to the dead tree. It was a hulking, aged thing whose trunk divided into three heavy boughs, one of which seemed twisted and ripped off, so that the stump of it looked like an elongated head tilted backward.

"This was not in Midnight," Al said.

"She is where she needs to be. First she was, eldest and wildest. Leave Blayne and come and greet her."

"Her?"

"Do as I say."

Blayne's arm slipped from Al's freezing fingers.

"Touch her," said the Lord Warder.

"Why?"

"Just do it."

Al set his left hand upon the tree. And the Lord Warder struck. An instant later Al realized that a knife had been sunk hilt deep in his hand. As he watched the blood begin to well around the guard of it, his vision seemed to bleed as well and a savage beast roared inside him.

With no thought for the pain, he yanked the knife from his flesh and struck out at the Lord Warder. The Lord dodged the blow mercilessly, neatly, almost meditatively, and slammed Al hard against the tree.

Past the pale arm jammed hard against his throat, past the fury ringing in his ears, Al heard Sandyr Ash whisper, "Be still, Alsandyr. She had to taste your blood, to know your call."

The beast that was Al thrashed and snarled. Laughter soft and cold. "You find your instincts overwhelming now that your gifts as Steward are gone. But master your nature you must, lest it master you. Submit, Alsandyr, and I will let you go."

Al tried instead to curse the Lord roundly. The pressure on his throat increased until breath and fury abated. Midnight shrank into a kinder darkness.

"What have you done to me?" he croaked when he could see again. He was on his hands and knees amid a scattering of topaz and carnelian, the awful weight of Midnight's strangeness squeezing him.

"Awakened what was dormant," spoke the Lord Warder. "Get up. They are coming."

A pale hand caught him beneath the arm and yanked him sharply to his feet. "Mount," the Lord Warder said and shoved him toward one of two sloe-eyed forms whose shapes, like the sharply twisting horns jutting from their foreheads, roiled the mind.

The Lord Warder mounted in one smooth leap. "Get up," he said, "and bring Blayne with you."

Somehow Al obeyed, his wounded hand splashing blood on Blayne and his mount's gleaming silver coat. They rode, for eons or an instant, while Al labored to breathe and his mind thinned to a flimsy cobweb spun upon a lacerating world of alien energy. Only the throbbing of his left hand kept his consciousness from fraying into it.

To either side of him loomed the gem-like trees, but something darker tracked his movements. Sometimes it resembled a large animal of indeterminate shape, a great wolf perhaps or mountain cat; other times it looked to be a striding man; but always, it shadowed him— body, mind, soul. Then his mount reared, and all the wondrous, terrible vision of Midnight collapsed into a shape of living flame.

I saw a man made of fire, all colors of fire. The words Emily had once whispered on a cold winter's night now blew like winter wind through his shreaded mind.

He lost himself in a face formed of rippling multihued light. Slitted pupils called him into inferno, and he went, would have passed into those flames completely and perished in them, but for the lines of silver fire that sprang up like bars across his mind. Then a shadowy tangle of muscle, tooth and claw leapt in front of his horned mount to snarl and slash with glassy claws.

Flaming eyes scorched the great cat, but could not consume it. Inferno eyes danced like laughter. "Take him then," a mind-voice chimed, "as I take what is mine."

The great crouching cat lashed its tail, and the flaming eyes bored into the slumped form in front of Al. "Wake, Blayne, and greet your father."

"No," Al croaked as Blayne raised his tawny head.

"Would you keep a father from his son, blind man?" the inferno eyes chimed. "Come Blayne. Join me and be made more."

Somewhere far away the Lord Warder was shouting. Al saw a pale hand wielding a white wand spit a whip made of silver light and lash the alien air with it, saw a flaming violet sword sever that light and slash across the white man.

"No!" someone screamed, someone whose hand burned like a stake was being pushed up through it.

"Run!" another voice cried.

Help me, Al's frayed and dissipating mind whimpered. Then the wound in his hand erupted in a darkness that became a hoary black tree. The burning man vanished behind that tree, while Al's monstrous mount leapt away, streaking luminous beauties into rainbow.

They flew through the forest of living jewels toward a bridge of crystal, and then they were upon the bridge, where cloven hooves rang like glass cymbals. The monster horse reared and spun, dashing both Al and Blayne to the glassy stones.

Al struck hard and rolled. Blayne slid to the bridge's edge, began climbing awkwardly to his feet.

And a burning form came sailing down Midnight's black radiance on wings of rainbow fire, seized Blayne in burning arms, beat its fiery wings once, and yanked the half-breed upward into brutal anti-light.

Al lay gasping upon icy glass unable to catch his breath no matter how he reached for it. A black shape came prowling onto the bridge, stalked over to him, and planted midnight paws on his caving chest. Mind and body screamed when five-inch fangs sank deeply into Al's shoulder and began dragging him like so much dead meat into dead dark.

He woke clutching at his savaged shoulder. Feeling no answering pain, he sat up and pulled the fabric of his tunic away from his chest.

The flesh underneath was sound, the skin unblemished and unbroken. Had it all been a dream?

His hand gave back to him the image of a narrow whitish scar, the mark left by a deep wound long since healed.

Not a dream.

He looked around. All was grassy quiet bathed in mist. What had become of his companions?

Blayne, he remembered, was gone, snatched into darkness by his infernal kin, but the Lord Warder might be anywhere in this world or the next. As for himself, he had no idea where he was. Slowly, he stood up in eddying gray. The mist obscured everything—damn his merely ordinary sight. He set off anyway, picking his way from rock to scrub, scrub to rock, until darkness began to swallow everything. Then he knelt and spent some time trying to build a fire among damp grasses while he waited for the fog to roll back.

Finally, the sky uncovered its familiar dusting of stars. He stood up, determined to steer a straighter course, and saw a fire bloom in the distance. The Lord Warder? He set off toward it, easing down shadowy slopes, but just before he reached it, another fire bloomed and then another. He stopped, noted their symbolic triune arrangement, and thoughtfully resumed his course.

As he came to the first of the large, strangely quiet bonfires, a prohibitive bar was laid across his waist.

"Not for you, my man," said a light voice riddled with dark undertones.

Al pivoted, took in the size and shape of the cloaked and hatted figure standing at his side. "And why not?"

"Because if I cannot cross over neither can you."

"Are we connected in some way?"

A chuckle emerged from the voluminous garments. "Not in any way that you would see. But then you don't see much these days, do you?"

Al went very still. The figure tilted its hatted head. "There are connections and connections," it said, "some more exploitable than others. But you can chalk this particular prohibition up to petty maliciousness on my part. I simply dislike the idea of you doing what I cannot."

"Regrettably, stranger, what you like matters not at all to me," responded Al just as lightly, and brushed the other's stick aside.

It slammed into his gut and then leapt up to pound his face. Al dropped to his knees, hand pressed to burning nose and the warm slickness trickling from it. The hatted man squatted down, propping his thick staff on his shoulder. "I wouldn't try that again if I were you," his layered voice said solemnly. But Al could hear the laughter running beneath the solemnity. He pressed his nose harder and cursed.

"You curse a lot these days," said the other mildly and offered him a hand up. When Al ignored it, the smaller, lighter stranger snagged him by the tunic and hauled him to his feet anyway.

Al, unused to being plucked back into line like a wayward child, re-evaluated his opponent. Without the sight, he could make out little of the other's characteristics, until the bonfire's light slashed the shadows beneath the stranger's hat and kindled a hot, yellow glow in the stranger's wide eyes. Then Al felt his heart stutter, and the mouth beneath the hat smiled. "Now he begins to see. Step aside, my man, and let us talk."

Eying the staff, Al reluctantly obeyed. The stranger set off into the night, and Al followed, watching with fear-salted admiration as the stranger waded to a rocky bluff and began bounding up it like a mountain goat. Al climbed more slowly, pulling himself up the sheer stone until his eyes anchored him in light. The stranger was sitting, legs dangling, upon a wide shelf of rock. A merry fire burned near him.

Al dusted himself off and sank down cross-legged beside the fire. The stranger stroked the butt of his staff. One long finger swiped at it and then dipped into the man's mouth. "Not much of the seer left in you anymore, but the blood is still good. And blood is what matters most to Bloodstone. But by now you know that."

"Power seems more to its taste," snapped Al, feeling the beast curled inside him beginning to stir. He studied the stranger's generous mouth, firm chin. The rest of the face lay hidden beneath the hat's wide brim.

"It might seem so, but it is the blood that matters. For the taste of blood willingly given, bloodstone will return much, including the power to consolidate, conquer and heal."

"So why did it drain my power when I touched it?"

The generous mouth seemed to smile, though the wavering light of the fire made it hard to be certain. "Because the one who used it to trap you wanted it to. By itself the stone would have held you prisoner until it gradually drew your blood into it or until you tapped enough power to break free, but your enemy is more creative and knowledgeable than that."

"So this enemy wished to destroy my power or perhaps a piece of my house."

The mouth smiled for certain this time. "Oh, no. His schemes were far more lucrative. He would never waste power that could be appropriated."

"Appropriated?" whispered Al as his persistent anger contracted into a hot kernel of fury.

"Your seer power is not gone, Alsandyr Goodwin, sometime Steward's heir. Oh no, it is alive and well, only in the possession of another."

Al forgot his fear of the stranger in his coal-black fury at the unseen enemy. "Who?"

"One close to you."

"I knew I should have gone to Allyn," Al growled — then allowed himself a short, bitter laugh. "Although he is probably relieved to be done with me."

The stranger's mouth turned down. "I thought you were supposed to be bright? What exactly does the Steward stand to gain by losing you?"

"A more suitable heir."

"Don't be a fool. He may not approve of all your impulses, but he is hardly blind to your value. He is the Steward after all. For him, your benefits far outweigh your inconveniences. Through you he has been able to influence all the houses."

"He has openly resented my reaching out to them," Al argued.

"You of all people should know that what the Steward seems and what he is can be very different things."

Al narrowed his eyes against the disturbing seeming in front of him. "You assume a lot about the Steward and his house."

"I have made it an object of study for some time. And, at long last, my study has rewarded me — with you."

Al allowed himself a slow, knowing smile. "And what exactly do you expect to get from me?" he asked quietly, sure he knew the answer, but curious to see how the other would respond.

"Your life," admitted the stranger, the complex undertones in his voice playing over Al's skin like tentacles.

"Don't you mean my death?"

"Sometimes the two are one and the same thing."

"I suppose that is true. Well, I'm here. Why don't you do it now?"

The other laughed brightly. "What kind of dabbler do you take me for? If it were simply a matter of killing a Steward, my work would have been completed centuries ago."

"What then do you require?"

"A number of things. But ultimately, a willing sacrifice."

"It's a pity you didn't come to me right after the stone took my powers. You could have had my head then, and been welcome to it."

The other clucked impatiently. "And still he refuses to understand. Since when have stewards been so thick?"

Al suffered the insult graciously. "I'm a defunct steward, remember?"

"Perhaps that is part of it. More likely, your warring instincts are muddling your wits. Take it from one who knows, it is never easy to bear the competing demands of very different heritages, and you have been in the habit of using one heritage to suppress the other for half a lifetime."

To Al the other's cryptic comments were tiresome; almost as tiresome as this morbid game of treating death like a theoretical exercise. "What sort of sacrifice do you require then? Since a simple willingness to die isn't good enough for you."

"Suicide is not sacrifice, even if one tricks another into doing the dirty deed. The spell requires the true spirit of sacrifice, life given for life. And sacrifice requires nothing more and nothing less than the absolute love of life on the part of the giver."

Now it was Al's turn to laugh. "You want me to love my life, so you can take it from me?"

"So you can give it up for another. Only then will the exchange have force and meaning, true power."

"And then you can rain destruction on the Steward's house at last," said Al flatly.

"If that is what it takes."

"Even if I could learn to love my life again, I would never betray my house."

"Not even if that house betrayed you?"

Al blinked, thought for a moment, and said, "Not even if it were my own mother who ripped the power from me." But his words lacked force.

"Close, but not quite. And what if your house were about to turn on the others?"

"My grandfather may be ruthless, but he would never permit such a betrayal."

The man half hidden under the hat poked his stick into the fire. The flames leaped up. "Your grandfather will not live forever. What then?" His question was just louder than the whine of his fire.

Al looked into that fire and saw figures moving in it. He stared harder and the figures solidified. For an instant he almost believed the sight had returned to him. He could have cried for joy. Then he saw the stick weaving through the flames, saw it stir the figures into familiar faces and forms all broken and bleeding, except for the last, who was laid out on glittering stone like one dead. "Emily!" he hissed and almost burned the tips of his fingers. The figure melted back into pure fire.

"Oh, yes. Even she will fall before what is to come – unless you halt the power awakening in the south."

"And fulfilling your curse will enable me to do that?"

"That and more."

"You really do think me a fool. When do the dead accomplish anything?"

The generous mouth looked almost sad. "When they leave their mark on the living."

Al drew his hand across his mouth. "Another pretty paradox. Why should I trust you enough to believe anything you say?"

The sadness curved into a smile. "What else can you trust? Deep down inside, you know that you are moving to your end, and when you meet your enemy, you will begin to understand why."

"So tell me of more of this enemy."

"I've told you all you need to know for now."

"And what of the Lord Warder? What of Blayne?"

"They will find you eventually. But beware. Blayne will be changed, and twice as dangerous for it. Even now he is being tempered in Midnight's fires. Once he finds what he seeks, his instinct will be to cross back into the darkling realm. You or the Shield bearer must prevent this at all costs. Use everything and everyone at your disposal."

Al swept a hand through his hair. "I feared he would be lost." His mind slipped into another vein of thought. "This terrible power that is awakening in the South, is it his son?"

"That child may yet become the terror you have seen, but what awakens now is ancient and hungers to claim Blayne's unborn for herself. First, she was, and time has only strengthened her power and madness." The wide hat had fallen entirely over the face.

"Is she the enemy you spoke of?"

"She is the enemy of all, and she answers, when she must, only to her even crueler father."

"What does she want with Blayne's child?"

"Exactly what we all want: an heir to unite the peoples, a living being to make what is broken whole. But where the Houses were built to forge that unity in life and light. She and her Twilight ancestor would forge it in oppression."

"Can she be stopped?"

"Only by the power that imprisoned her in the first place."

"Let me guess, the second talisman, the very touch of death," said Al hollowly.

"And someone willing to embrace that death." The brim of the hat suddenly lifted, and for the first time Al looked full into the face of a legend. His breath caught. The other's eyes were the panther's hot golden orbs, but his generous mouth curved gently as he swung his black staff out over the fire. The flames licked it thirstily, but the black wood neither smoked nor burned. "This," came the complex voice, "is the Staff called Life. When you see it again, you will know that your time has come."

Chapter 10: Crossing Over

For Emily the trip down the spires of red stone was arduous and harrowing. But Shade didn't give her time to think about anything but keeping up. He leapt sure-footedly from boulder to boulder, his loose coat billowing behind him, and Emily had no choice but to follow, gulping back terror and trying not to look down into the gloomy crevices perforating their path. Eventually they emerged from the fog above a narrow canyon of rounded red rock where the sunlight seemed to hover close amid stark wedges of shadow.

Shade pulled his large hat low over his ears, hunched into his swirling robe and stuck his black staff out as he had so many times before to guide Emily across the last crumbling gap between them and the road.

Puffing, she landed squarely on the road's massive stones and heard Colin Blackhammer bark, "Where have you been!"

Emily located his tall form a few feet away. "Col! It's good to see you too."

"Good to see—" His words got tangled up in his growl. "Do you have any idea how frantic we've been?" He flicked a dubious glance Shade's direction—the hatted man had retreated into the hard shadows beneath a wall of red stone.

Emily put her hands to her hips. "I wasn't exactly happy about being lost myself. Didn't you notice when I fell? I called for you, but you didn't answer. I had to start searching for you. Fortunately, I wasn't seriously injured, or I'd still be lying there waiting for you." She shuddered. "One night alone was bad enough."

Colin's eyes widened. He seemed to work to suppress some emotion. When his lips moved, they released tightly controlled words. "One night? Emily, you've been missing for four days."

The red stones all around them seemed to lunge forward and fall back. The curving road leered. "Four days?" Emily repeated, not really understanding what she said. She gave her head a little shake. "Four days," she said more loudly, and the shrillness of her tone scraped at her own ears. "That's not possible."

From the shadows where Shade stood came a dry but heavy-laden chuckle.

Both Emily and Colin looked him. Then Emily remembered the four seeds in her right hand. All four were still there, strung like beads along her lifeline, tiny nodules of who knew what. She picked at one of them with her thumb, but it lay like a splinter just beneath her skin. She put her hand in her pocket.

She didn't try to tell Colin what she had seen and done, and Colin didn't ask. He was too busy fuming about Shade, who had stalked off down the road, hugging the shadows to its left side. "He found me right after you disappeared," Colin complained. "I wanted to look for you, but he wouldn't hear of it. He kept prodding me with that stick of his and saying we would find you ahead. I shouldn't have listened."

"But you did find me," Emily dared. "And we are ahead of where we were."

Colin blinked at her; his glower deepened. "Still, I should have made him look."

"Can you imagine anyone making Shade do anything?"

Colin hunched his shoulders, looking at her more closely. "At least you're back," he said. And Emily knew he was speaking of more than her physical return. Side by side, they took the bend in the road and entered a smaller canyon whose farthest wall was punctured by a rounded hole like a window.

"Come and see," called Shade from the shadows. At his feet, the dressed stones of the road broke up and petered out.

Together Emily and Colin walked forward and looked down on a desert rolling like a golden sea.

Shade pointed his staff at a ribbon of lighter gold running east to west. "Your road," he said.

"Where's Sun City?" Colin asked peering at the blank horizon.

"That way. If you go quickly, you should reach its margins in one day or two."

"I've heard that it is immense."

"The City is large indeed, and proud of its immensity. It is dangerous too, as full of vices as beauties. You will have to be careful."

"How do we get down?" asked Emily looking all around. Knowing they were so close made her itch to move on. Colin, however, stood stiff and silent.

"Over there," answered Shade. He pointed to a gap between two slabs of red stone. Emily hurried to it and discovered a steeply eroded trail curving between walls of red boulders.

"It looks tricky," she commented.

"It is," agreed Shade. "But at the bottom is a shallow cave with a deep pool. Be sure to rest and fill your water bags there before you take to the main road."

Emily turned him. "Aren't you coming with us?"

"No." His generous mouth drew down. "My road ends here."

He beckoned to Colin, pulling the younger man into shadow. They spoke but a moment. Then Shade held out his staff, and Colin took it into his own two hands.

Every nerve in Emily's body started to sing, while her mouth went as dry as dust. Colin turned away, took the mule's lead in his hand, and guided it to the steep and sliding trail, where he disappeared in a hiss of cinder.

Emily turned her alarm on Shade, and the mysterious wanderer accepted her challenge, stepping out of the shadows into a full-blown sunlight that electrified the blue of robe and hat. Dazzled, Emily raised her hand against that light, and still it stabbed her eyes, searing them until she dropped them earthward.

She saw Shade's boots gleaming; she saw the hem of his blue, blue robe; she saw the sand, bright as a carpet of gold running under and around him.

He casts no shadow! her mind shouted at her as some invisible force propelled her backward onto loose scree that swept her down and away.

Emily's ankles and calves were cramping by the time the steep and twisting trail finished carrying them down from the heights.

"Here's the cave," Colin called from ahead. It was the first time he'd spoken to her since he'd laid his hands on Shade's staff.

She approached him cautiously, uncertain what he would do when their eyes finally met. "I'll help with the water bags," she offered, turning to the mule.

"Don't bother." He sounded calm enough. "It will be dark before long. It might be best if we camped here tonight. It seems isolated enough, and who knows what we will meet on the road."

She looked around. "I wouldn't mind resting a while," she admitted.

By the time they finished setting out camp, the sun was setting, and Emily was looking longingly at the cave.

"What is it?" asked Colin, watching her from across the fire he'd built from tough, thorny scrub.

"I'm just thinking how nice it would be to have a bath and wash my hair. It's been weeks since either of us has been clean." She wrinkled her nose at her own musky aroma.

Colin leaned back against his pack, and settled Shade's black staff across his sharp knees. "Go ahead. I won't look."

"It wouldn't be right to dirty the water," said Emily unhappily.

"You won't. The pool's obviously fed by some sort of spring. Just be careful not to get sucked down.

Emily's eyes brightened. She hopped up and dug down in her pack for the thin bar of soap she had packed.

When she returned, Colin looked to be asleep, but the fire was bigger than ever and the food packs were laid out.

"You should try bathing yourself," she encouraged.

His eyes opened. "If you think you can stay out of trouble, I will." He took Shade's staff with him.

When he was done, and drying his hair at the fire, Emily asked, "Do you miss him yet?"

"No." Colin's tone was curt.

She studied the fire-eaten planes of his face. "What did he say to you up there?"

Colin lay back on his blanket with a huge yawn.

"He said something to you," Emily pressed.

Colin rolled, deflecting her question with the thickness of his shoulder.

"Won't you tell me?"

He bolted upright. "You won't talk about the talisman."

Emily floundered. "That's different!"

"Is it? Are you sure?"

She clamped her mouth shut, knowing he had a point. "Is it that you no longer trust me?" she asked.

"No!"

"Then what?"

"Because I can't, Emily," he shouted, his voice booming off the nearby rocks. "Do you understand? I can't? Shade forbade it."

"Shade's not with us anymore?

Colin looked at her in amazement and laughed. "Do you really think he has to be here to make good on his promises?" he said.

Emily shrank down into her own blanket, and Colin rolled back onto his side, clutching Shade's staff close to his body. Around the painful lump in her throat, Emily whispered, "I'm sorry, Col."

Something between a laugh and a sob floated up from Colin's huddled form. "You and me both, Emily," he replied.

They set off the next morning at the first dusting of dawn, Colin in the lead and Emily drawing the mule behind her. By the time the sun was all the way up they had reached the flats, and soon after, they met the road, a ribbon of lighter, finer dust cutting sharply across the empty landscape.

The journey thereafter tested their patience and endurance in new ways. The featureless road ran level and straight as a beam of light beneath a bleached dome of heavy heat.

By midmorning, they were sweating heavily and happy to squat in the stingy shade afforded by the mule and a clump of low, thorny shrub. They drank only enough to take the edge off their thirst and pulled extra shirts from their packs to drape them over their hot heads. "So much for yesterday's bath," Emily sighed, wiping perspiration from her eyes.

Colin leaned back on his elbows. "Please. The last thing I need to think about now is cold water. How can people live here? There's nothing but dust and heat and thorn bushes. What do they do for water?"

"Actually, there is a lot of water. But it's down deep, under the sand, so the people here have to dig for it. We'll probably come across one of the Empyreal wells before we reach the city."

"The Empyreors dug wells?"

"How else were they going to promote commerce? The wells support the caravans, and by Empyreal decree, their water is available to all who travel the Empyre's roads."

"Makes sense. How else would you get people to cross this wasteland? The city must have a thousand wells.

"I'm sure it has many, but Sun City gets much of its water from aqueducts that run out of the southern hills."

"Aqueducts?"

"Elevated structures topped with immense cylinders of clay pipe that carry water from the Sankal Mountains. The Empyreor's city may lie on the fringes of a desert, but historians describe his palace as holding rivers of water. The streaming waters of the Empyreal palace are regarded as one of the great beauties of the southland and a testament to the Empyre's wealth and might."

"I can't believe there are mountains out there?" Colin peered doubtfully into the brilliant haze.

"They lie behind the city."

Colin looked west to where the light of the sun seemed to shimmer about a collection of brighter shapes. "Where did you learn so much about the Empyreal City?"

Emily fanned her face with an ineffectual hand. "I did a lot of reading while I was in Cyr."

His brown eyes scrutinized her. "You had time to read *and* recover the Keeper's talisman?"

She met his eyes briefly before looking away. "Until Lyr started teaching me, there wasn't much else for me to do. I was just a homeless foreigner."

The expression in Colin's eyes was unreadable, but suddenly more than the heat oppressed her.

"What did he teach you?"

When Emily did not say, Colin made a sound of disgust. "Never mind. Don't tell me. I'm sure I don't want to know." He jammed the butt end of Shade's staff into the sandy soil, his fingers unconsciously tracing some of the staff's strange markings, the muscles beneath the smooth skin hard as rock.

"What is it?" Emily dared to ask.

"Nothing." His eyes squinted into the horizon, but his gaze had turned inward. "I'm just reminding myself how little I know you anymore."

"That's not true! You know me better than anyone."

"How can you say that? Every time the events of the last year come up, I learn something new about you—Cyr, warders, the Keeper, the Steward, this talisman you hate to talk about."

She finished the thought for him. "And now you are caught up in the strangeness too."

"Am I? I don't know. I can't be sure. And that's the most terrifying thing of all. I thought we were together on that damn road, but twice you abandoned me. I keep wondering what you will do next—sprout wings and fly away."

"I wasn't trying to abandon you," cried Emily in a low voice. "Those things just happened."

"Did they? Did the road just drop out from under you? Did that magician drag you out of your body? Or did you get so caught up in the magic that you essentially forgot all about me?"

Emily recoiled as if he had struck her. She wanted to rail at the injustice of his accusation, but in some unswept corner of her own mind a voice was clucking that Colin was right. "I did get carried away," she admitted. "From now on, I'll make more of an effort to talk to you before I let go and leap."

Colin's mouth narrowed into a dissatisfied line. "You could promise not to leap at all."

Emily ducked her head. "I've carried one of the great talismans, Col. In Lyr's words, that makes me a pawn of the powers."

"That's supposed to comfort me?"

"No. When it comes to magic, there's little comfort to give. But it is the truth as I've come to know it, and it may help you bear your own burden." She jerked her chin at the black staff he was cradling. "Sometimes trying to fight the magic is the worst thing you can do. You have to surrender to the current and ride it through the difficult times."

"So hang on and hope for the best."

"You could always try enjoying the ride."

"Hah! Shade would appreciate that sentiment."

"Would he?"

"To him, life and death are a lark."

"That staff is no lark," she said darkly.

Colin studied it with a somber expression of his own. "No."

Although Emily itched to know what he was thinking, she did not ask.

Noon saw them slogging through heavier heat. Though they had been on the road for hours, they had encountered only one other traveler, an older man riding a small donkey and leading another loaded down with packs. He came up behind them as they reached an inviting clump of palm trees. When they pulled aside under them, so did he.

He was a small man, neat looking despite the dust of the road, and he wore a loose, hooded robe over a long buttoned tunic. He hobbled his donkeys and adjusted some of his packs; then, to their surprise, he approached them, folding back his hood to reveal a short steel-gray beard and dark eyes, alert but benign.

"Greetings, fellow traveler," he said bowing to Colin.

Colin rather awkwardly bowed back. "And to you, master."

The little man smiled. "I do not mean to intrude upon your rest, but I wondered if I might share this shady grove with you."

Colin raised his brows. "Of course. The grove doesn't belong to us."

The little man bowed again. "Ah, yes. But to you go the rights of the first arrival, and I would not wish to intrude. I am Abreem Imharta."

"Are you familiar with Sun City, Master Imharta?" blurted Emily, anxious for information.

Abreem Imharta looked at her in surprise, and Colin jumped to cover the moment's awkwardness. "Forgive my sister's abruptness, Master Imharta. She does not mean to offend. We are visitors to the Empyre. Midlanders. My name is Colin Blackhammer, and hers," he cleared his throat, "is Emily."

Sister? Emily's eyes accused from beneath lifted brows, but Master Imharta's surprise had turned to understanding. "Ah, I see," he said graciously. He now bowed to Emily. "Greetings, good lady," he said. "You honor me with your address. The pleasure of ladies' talk is one that I am not much accustomed to."

Emily smiled. "Why?"

Abreem's benign eyes smiled back. "In the Empyre, it is considered rude for a man to address a freeborn woman. But your customs are not ours, and the gracious man puts the ways of his guests before his own. Allow me to welcome you to the Empyre and offer you its hospitality. I would be honored if you would break bread with me."

Colin shifted. "But we have no bread, Master."

Abreem smiled through his beard. "Ah, but the bread would be mine, goodman, as is the invitation. Please, come, and join me in my afternoon meal."

Abreem did indeed have bread — stiff, flat, honey-coated, circles of it — and bags of dates and raisins, and even some tart slices of sugared oranges and lemons, all of which he offered to them with a rich crumbly cheese that melted like butter on the tongue. It wasn't long before both Emily and Colin were luxuriating in the unexpected largesse.

They ate leisurely, urged by Master Imharta to rest while the sun declined. Emily and Colin asked many questions, and Imharta answered them all. They learned that he resided in the city, and he proved it by giving them detailed descriptions of the great city's many and varied quarters, castes and customs. He made it sound as exotic and rich as the cheese he urged them to eat.

"May I ask what work you do, Master Abreem?" Colin asked while the Master was packing away the remains of their repast.

"For certain," said Abreem. "I am a teacher and translator."

"What do you translate?" Colin asked.

"Languages, naturally, ancient and modern."

"I thought the people of the Empyre used the same tongue as Midlanders."

"Many do," Abreem agreed, "But the light of the Empyre is long, shining even into the far south where there are tribal cultures that never knew the influence of the Great Confederacy. And there are remnants of the ancient tongues as well, languages that linger in the North and Midlands as well as the Empyre, such as those written on your staff."

Colin looked down at the thick rod he held. "My staff?"

"It bears the lettering of many tongues. Didn't you know?"

"No," gulped Colin, running his fingers over the marks.

"What does it say?" asked Emily.

Imharta shrugged. "I do not know. I would have to examine it more closely to see."

Colin thrust the staff forward. "Look then, master," he said. "But don't touch."

Imharta blinked in surprise, but dutifully bent over the extended rod.

"Turn it please," he asked as his eyes moved up the staff's length.

"What do you see?" urged Colin.

"Ancient Sardic, Ancyrian, Halish and Inginar, Caresh even Malpronian, as well as the Confederate tongue that gave rise to our common one. And there are some markings I cannot classify." He raised his eyes to Colin in wonder. "Where did you get this?" he asked.

Colin pulled the staff back. "It doesn't matter," he said. "What do the languages say?"

Abreem frowned for a moment, then smiled again. "One word, I believe, repeated over and over."

"Just one?" said Emily, disappointed.

"Yes," answered Imharta transferring his sage look to her.

"And what word is it?" asked Colin.

"Life."

"Life," Colin repeated, opening his eyes wide.

Later when Colin was preparing their mule for the road, Emily approached the little scholar independently. He was standing by one of his donkeys, adjusting the straps on its packs.

"Thank you for the meal, Master Imharta?" she said by way of opening the conversation.

Abreem Imharta's expression of mild surprise melted into an avuncular smile as he turned to her. "You are most welcome," he bowed.

Emily bit her lip, suddenly unsure how to proceed. Then she pushed ahead. "I was wondering if you could tell me about the Empyreal palace."

Imharta frowned and his smile grew abstracted. "What do you wish to know?"

Emily tried to keep her voice light. "Have you been inside it?"

Imharta shook his head, chuckling. "No, good lady. Though I have been honored to serve the Empyreal house in small ways. I have never been granted an Empyreal audience. One must be much more than a poor scholar to receive such a summons."

"One has to be summoned?"

He looked amused. "Unless one is of the blood Empyreal."

"Oh," Emily's shoulders slumped.

"For certain, you may see the palace from the outside. Even its great wall is impressive, and there are many places in the city that afford fine views of it."

"I was rather hoping to see inside."

He shook his head. "Regrettably, I may not assist you there."

Emily smiled through her disappointment. "No. I suppose I was silly to think so. Please forgive me for interrupting." She started to move away, only to turn back as Abreem cried out. Packs were slipping from the donkey's back and spilling their contents onto the sandy soil.

"Oh," Emily exclaimed as Abreem fought to catch them. Another pack hit the dirt, and a batch of papers flew out. Emily jumped at a page floating toward her and, catching it, went stock still as she beheld the image sketched upon it.

"Where did you get this?" she exclaimed.

Abreem was on his knees scrapping together the rest of the papers. "They are sketches. From the ruins of Ab Syminal."

Emily stared. "Ab Syminal?"

"Ancient ruins out beyond the Min Jar desert."

"I thought you studied languages."

"Ruins are full of languages. The remnants of them," Imharta stuffed the papers in his pack, then reached for a small hammer. "Those in Ab Syminal date from the time of the Great Confederacy."

"And what is this word?" She hurried to him, pointing to a curious set of sinuous markings repeated many times across the page.

Abreem peered at them. "Strange." He stood up, took the sheet from her hand to inspect it more closely. "I don't remember sketching this. It could be writing, but more likely it is a device, a design or sigil of some family of the Great Confederacy. It rather resembles a flower, does it not?" He bent to his materials.

"And what is the Great Confederacy?" pressed Emily squatting down beside him. "Is it another name for the First Empyre?"

Imharta's head lifted sharply; his brown eyes radiated concern. "There is only one Empyre, lady," he said softly "and death comes to those who say otherwise."

But Emily shook her head stubbornly. "No. There was another Empyre, long ago. Northlanders know of it. Their histories say it lasted almost a thousand years."

Imharta raised a warning hand and spoke like a stern schoolmaster. "We Southerners do not speak of it. Those were brutal and barbaric times when Sards occupied the land and people indulged the most deplorable vices, worshipping the vagaries of the changing moon rather than the steady light of the sun." His voice sank lower. "Heed me, good lady, and do not speak of other empyres again, not while you dwell in this land. The agents of the One True Empyre would take great exception to it." His earnest brown eyes interrogated hers. "Do you understand?"

Emily was not at all sure that she did, but she could see that Abreem Imharta believed in what he was saying. "I understand," she repeated. "I will not speak of it again."

Imharta's face relaxed into a smile. "That is very good." Reaching for a bundle of rags, he changed the subject. "Now, about the Great Confederacy. That is truly ancient history. Almost no one remembers it anymore, and yet it may have dominated one of the greatest ages of man. It was a vast alliance of city states, you see, that held the peace from the Black Mountains of the far North all the way to the Southern sea of Serpentia."

"I've heard of a similar alliance," said Emily. "It ended in a cataclysm?" She blinked as her mind drew an unexpected connection between that alliance and Imharta's sketch.

"You know that story?" Abreem asked, and shook his head in pity. "Legend, lady, not history. But the Confederacy itself was quite real. The evidence is everywhere for those who know how to look."

"Evidence like that?" Emily nodded at the drawing in Imharta's hand. He lifted it, smiled rather bewilderedly, and pointed to another mark on the paper.

"For certain. Do you see this symbol? It tells me that the Confederacy united peoples north and south for it contains word forms peculiar to both regions. And these markings here — they are a record of plague deaths over two thousand years old. They tell me that disease took a terrible toll on the Confederacy near its end."

He told her other things as she helped him repack his tools and supplies, but her own mind was occupied with a different charting of history. And when she left him to his packs and donkeys, she took a moment to trace the mark she had seen in his sketch in the sand. It was easy for her to remember it for she already knew most of its parts by heart — the Orb, the Crescent, the Shield and the Teller's Tongue — the four marks of the four houses. But here they were incorporated in a single design and all connected by one sinuous line. In all her studies in Cyr she had never seen them so united. In fact, the histories she had read stated that the Teller's mark had been lost for more than a millennium. What did it mean that all four marks had appeared together here and now in one design copied by a Southerner scholar studying ancient ruins? And why had the design come to her?

For a moment she dipped back into that carefully cordoned off area of memory where she kept all that was unbearable or unbearably precious to her. She again became a witness to Cataclysm, a young man dying in a poisoned and burned land. Again she was pursued by beings alive with internal flame. Again her hand moved across something whorled like a tortoise shell but larger and incredibly light.

She opened her hand and looked at the mark on her left palm. The mark was the Shield, and the Shield, the mark. That much had become clear in the moment the Keeper's talisman revealed itself to her. Was the same true of the other talismans as well? Were their marks made in their image? And did they all come out of the same horrifically dark place? Why hadn't she ever considered the possibility before?

Seeing the marks joined together in the symbol at her feet made her once again recall what the piercingly insightful old Steward had said: *One thing leads to another.* Just as the sinuous line in this the symbol moved from one mark to another.

What would happen if all the talismans returned?

The three travelers returned to the road as a small company, hoping their newfound companionship would eat up the uneventful leagues.

By late afternoon, their empty road had merged with a wider one beaded with travelers. There were boys driving small herds of shaggy goats, men driving wains or wagons, riders on long-legged camels. Abreem pointed to a smudge on the flat, western horizon. "Sun City," he announced.

Then a cart rushed past them as cries sprang up in the rear. A camel rider came next, galloping past in a plume of dust. Soon all the travelers around them were running and shouting.

Master Imharta seemed to listen to their cries for a moment, then yanked his little, short-legged donkey aside, and hurried it off the road. Uncertain what to do, Colin and Emily followed. "What is it, master?" Colin cried. "Where are you going?"

"Run!" Imharta cried, legs pumping furiously at his donkey's sides. A dozen or so dark-skinned horsemen cut through the empty landscape, spewing clouds of dust, and swung wide to encircle all of them.

A man wearing a rough cloak over armor made of leather and metal disks eased his blowing, stamping horse closer. His face beneath its black hood was a maze of crimson tattoos, some of which struck Emily as familiar, but before she could determine why, a cold female voice rang out.

Emily followed that voice to a female rider wearing robes as crimson as the men's tattoos. This female, sitting astride a lathered, long-limbed horse, spoke no language Emily had ever heard, but her tone left no doubt as to her feelings. Someone was in a heap of trouble.

As the woman finished speaking, two of the robed men leapt down from their horses and yanked Abreem off his little donkey. The woman spoke again, and Abreem answered from his knees in a pleading, shaking voice. The woman cast her red hood off, displaying a forehead tattooed in vivid blue. She barked an order, and the man to the left of Abreem wrenched the little man's arm behind his back.

Abreem screamed.

"Stop!" cried Emily.

Colin cursed and reached to hush her, but Emily would not be denied. An energy to rival the Southern sun was building inside her. "Why are you doing this?" she shouted at the red-robed woman. The woman shot her a look of utter contempt and spat another sentence. The air about Emily thickened into a strangle hold.

Emily ripped it to shreds with her mind.

For a moment the tattooed woman's face opened wide, then she whipped out a strongly curved saber and spurred her horse at Emily. Abreem screamed again, and Emily drew one of her little knives to meet the blade flashing down. The smaller blade sheered the saber off at the hilt then swept back to take the hand holding the hilt as well. Hilt and hand dropped to earth in a puff of dust and a splash of blood. The tattooed woman's eyes flew wide, and her lips skinned back from ivory teeth. "Aaiee!" she wailed as the entire landscape seemed to gasp. Then the robed men yelled and kicked their whinnying horses while Colin yanked Emily from the mule's back. Emily hit the dirt hard and balled up amid stomping hooves.

She tasted dirt, lifted her head, and saw a saber knick Colin's shirt. Colin answered with a blow from Shade's black staff, and the robed man went flying out of the saddle like the sky itself had yanked him from it. Then a tattooed man leaning from the back of another tall horse grabbed Emily by the hair, pulled her screaming to her feet. She sank her tiny blade deep into his leg. The man let go only to be ripped from his saddle by a flying, snarling shape. Emily took one look at the silvery monster dog savaging her attacker and began scuttling backward. Another hand hauled her around by her collar.

"Get behind me," said Faryn in a level but unbroachable voice.

"Colin!" cried Emily, holding out a hand.

"Colin's holding his own."

Looking past Faryn's shoulder, Emily saw that it was true. Colin's hair shone deep red in the late light of the sun as he held off three saber-wielding riders, none of whom seemed particularly interested in moving closer. When one finally did, Colin knocked him clear to the margins of the road, where he landed without moving again.

In the meantime another, larger group of men was converging on her and Faryn, who kept shifting to put himself between Emily and the men stalking them. But where Emily and Colin fought with the desperation of people who expect to lose, Faryn moved with the perfect composure of a man who knows he cannot. Not since she had watched Blayne in the practice yard at Cyr had Emily seen a man shift so seamlessly from feint to blow. Men and horses struck at them, and Faryn struck back without looking the slightest bit rushed or off balance no matter how he was pressed. The horsemen retreated briefly, fanned out and closed in again. As one pounded forward Faryn spun himself and Emily aside, slashing at the horse's leg. Down the horse went, throwing its rider over its head, at which point Faryn leapt to sink his knife into the tossed rider's throat. Two more horsemen rushed them from either side in a pincer-like movement, but a blur of growling motion ripped one from the saddle while Faryn's thrown knife took the other in the throat. As the rider fell backward, his spooked horse careened off into the dry plain dragging him from a single stirrup.

There were only five men left now, and the leader of this remainder, a large man, called out to Faryn in snaking words.

Faryn echoed the rider's speech.

The man glared, barked at the others, and two of them hurried to collect the fallen form of the crimson-clad woman. Then the entire group galloped off the way they had come.

Sick with relief, Emily sank to her knees. Faryn, however, had other ideas. He motioned to Colin and then let out a piercing whistle. A clear whinny came back, and out of the seemingly empty landscape galloped three wild-eyed ponies, tossing bristling manes.

They ran right up to Faryn who whispered to them and rubbed their shoulders and then led one over to Emily. "Mount," he ordered.

"I'm not going back," she warned him, doing her best to look resolute.

Faryn froze her with his stare. "The Sards may return. If they do not, Empyreal soldiers will come. We must leave this place. Mount." He stalked to Colin, who listened attentively, then swung his lanky form up onto the nearest pony.

Emily was looking at the mangled form lying nearest her. "These people are Sards!" she squeaked.

"Yes, Sards," answered Faryn.

"What did they want?"

"It does not matter. They will want you now."

"Because I defended myself?"

Faryn raked her with his icy eyes. "Because you killed one of their priestesses."

"I didn't mean to kill anybody," argued Emily.

"What you meant is irrelevant. Sards respond to what is done."

Abruptly, Emily saw the sense in getting away. She moved to mount her pony, but glimpsed the hunched and moaning form of Master Abreem. "Master," she called, moving toward him. "Master, what did these Sards want?"

Faryn yanked her back.

"He's hurt," she protested

"He is not your concern."

"He helped us."

"And brought a pack of Sards down on you."

"So we abandon him without even asking why?"

At that point, Faryn actually stalked off to collect the injured Southerner.

He kept them galloping through blank wilderness well into the night. Now and then Emily saw gleams in the distance that must have been lights from the city, but it was a long time before she caught sight of any buildings. When she did, they appeared beyond an unexpected patch of green, a thirsty lemon grove. Here, at last, Faryn called a halt to their flight.

As Emily slid wearily from her pony, Faryn busied himself in some arcane manner about the grove's perimeter, and Colin hobbled over to help Abreem.

"How bad?" Emily asked him when she had found her legs.

"Bad enough that he has fainted," said Colin. "He has a dislocated shoulder and a mild head injury, but he will heal."

"I'm glad."

"Here, you can help me put his arm back in the socket. It's best we do it now while he is still unconscious."

While Emily held on to a strip of cloth around the southerner's chest, Colin manipulated the arm. The arm bone went back in with a pop, and Imharta cried out, but never awoke.

By that time, Faryn had built a small, sunken fire, one that cast hardly any light. Colin set a pan of water boiling over it, dug a packet of herbs out of his pack and poured a liberal amount into the water. Some of this strange soup he spooned into Abreem Imharta's mouth. Then he returned to the fire and poured two whole cups of it.

"Here," he said, handing one to Emily. "It will help our bruises." Over the rim of his own cup he looked at the ever-alert warder. "There's plenty for you too, Faryn," he offered.

The warder smiled. "I am well thank you."

Colin nodded. "We should be thanking you. Things would have gone very badly for us out there if you hadn't showed up."

"You fought well," said Faryn frankly. Emily saw his eyes move to the staff Colin held. "That is a remarkable weapon you have."

"It's not mine," said Colin gruffly.

"You wield it like it is."

Colin shrugged.

"How long have you been following us?" Emily demanded.

Faryn's cool eyes slid her way. "Since you left the village of course."

Colin looked worried. "You didn't hurt my family, did you? It was my idea to drug you."

"They are fine. After I awoke, I let your father hold me until he felt you had put enough distance between us and then I left. Your parents never even saw me go."

"So why did you wait so long to confront us?" asked Emily.

"I lost your trail." His light eyes latched on to Emily's. "Just as you intended, Shield bearer. It wasn't until you reached the Red Hills that I discovered it again. If it hadn't been for the hounds, I might never have found it."

"Those awful dogs are yours?"

"They belong to House Warder, but I was given charge of them for this mission."

"The Lord Warder wants me back that badly, eh?"

"He wants you kept safe."

"Well, I'm almost to the city now. I'll be fine."

"I doubt that."

"Well, I have no intention of going back. I came here to help Beth, and I won't leave until I've found her."

"Naturally."

"So what now? Do you just knock me over the head and haul me off against my will? Or are you planning on siccing your hounds on me?" She looked uneasily into the shadows behind the warder. The hounds were nowhere in sight.

"I will keep watch on you as I was instructed to do."

"You aren't planning to take me back?"

"No."

"I don't believe you!"

"Why not? You don't really think that the Lords of the three Houses believed your little story about wanting to settle down in the Greenwood. You are the bearer of the Shield Light. You could not settle down if you wanted to. That is why the Lord Warder gave me the task of protecting you on the next stage of your long and dangerous journey."

Emily stopped, stared and then stuttered. "Are—are you saying that the Lord Warder knew I was making for the Empyre?"

"Certainly. He told me to guide you here. I would have, if you had asked me to."

Beside her, Colin emitted a sound like a whimper. Emily's face grew hot. "You mean I—" She cut herself off and flung one arm out to include Colin. "*We* made all those plans for nothing?" Colin's whimper had now intensified to a gurgle.

Faryn shrugged. "Your plans worked well enough, and you managed to survive your worst blunders. Plus, you shortened the journey by several weeks. Fortunately, I too know roads through Twilight, and I was able to keep up. Of course, if you had asked me to guide you, I could have shortened the journey even further."

Colin was laughing so hard now that Emily began to hope he would choke.

Later that evening, Emily fell into a doze where the tangible things of the real word melded disturbingly with the pearl and horn of dreams. She sensed the men lying near her, the ground supporting her body, the odorous whisper of the thirsty, forgotten lemon trees. But part of her soared above her surroundings to a height where vast areas of land shrank into a delicate and rippling landscape.

To the west, lay the expansive maze of Sun City, now little more than a pool of fog, except for the massive, squat fortress crouched at its center. This fortress was perfectly black, so black that it made the night seem gray by comparison, but Emily's eye penetrated it easily. She saw small, foggy shapes moving within, perceived the foggy dressings of gold and silver like veneer upon the blackness. Once, she saw something that sparkled like a bright gem. But her eye was drawn ever deeper down into the heart of that darkness where she glimpsed a cold inferno like a distant twinkling star. The star moved. It spiraled inward, spiraled out, reached some limit, and began circling inward again. It left behind it a trail of light as slick and faint as snail tracks.

To the east, lay a great desert like a swollen sea. Here thousands of human fires burned and voices, small with distance, cried out. Emily heard their rolling chant, but quickly turned her attention north where a road like a river of quicksilver running between and through the hills wove in and out of crevices of shadow that were gateways to different dimensions. Beyond this road she saw the rippling hills of the northern Midlands and the plains of Cyr. She even saw beyond Cyr to other cities and a great lake of water crowned by the stateliest city of all. This city basked in a soft yellow light as warm and inviting as the golden glow of a lamp.

"Emilyn," said a rather weary voice.

"Grandfather?" she responded automatically.

"Are you already to the Empyreal city then?" The question wrapped around her, heavy and dreary as wet wool.

"Yes."

"And alone."

"No. Not alone. Faryn found me, and Colin is with me too."

But the voice continued as if it had not heard her. "A pity. His binding was all for naught then. Well, it cannot be helped now."

"I'm not alone, grandfather," insisted Emily, anxious to lift that terrible heaviness.

"Emilyn?"

"Yes, grandfather. I am here. I am well."

"You must be very careful."

"I know."

"You cannot imagine what is ahead. And the one who might have helped and guided you is lost to us now."

"Faryn can protect us."

"Faryn cannot protect you from the eldest and purest. Nor from Blayne, nor ..."

"From Blayne?"

"It will be up to you to help him, Emilyn."

"Help him? I don't understand."

"So much has happened. So much unexpected, dire."

"Dire? Why? What has happened to Blayne?"

"He is coming into his own I fear, and none will stand in his way. His father will see to that. But your blood relationship gives you power. Remember Millicynt's binding. Use it when the time comes. But beware."

"Yes, beware of Blayne."

"Beware your own power. It will grow faster now, and you cannot know what it might demand of you. We counted on Alsandyr to help you direct and constrain it, but the Shield —"

Something even heavier than the weight of the Keeper's voice was weighing her down, this time from the inside. The sensation dimmed the glow and shape of the city by the lake, which seemed to be dissolving into smoke.

Her grandfather's voice became a whisper for all that it seemed to strain to shout across a great distance. "Hear me, Emilyn. The Shield . . . the Shield."

"What of the Shield?" she tried to call back, but her throat felt thick with sleep.

"It comes to li —"

BOOK TWO: Night Rising

Chapter 11: Princess in Waiting

Sun City—vast, ancient, splendid and corrupt. In a large house on very quiet street in the least remarked quarter of this sprawling city, a veiled woman hastens, without appearing to hurry, down a wide, tiled corridor. She passes many soldiers, all of whom look sharp though they are in fact grown dull with inactivity.

The woman arrives at a set of doors flanked by more guards and, waving a hand adorned with many delicate rings, passes within. The rooms she enters are dim and cavernous, cool compared to the heat outside. They are also mostly empty.

Throwing back her veil, the woman weaves her way past a few low divans and tables to a set of elaborately carved wooden screens that depict an oasis in whorls of light. Sliding one of these doors aside, she steps out into blindingly brilliant sunlight.

The small, high-walled courtyard burns white with light, and at the center of that whiteness stands a princess, with her face lifted to the noonday sun.

"Highness!" protests the woman, raising a hand against the light and the heat.

The princess turns to her. She wears a sleeveless silken gown several shades lighter than the lapis lazuli of her eyes and the sunlight tugs golden highlights from the bronze of her hair.

The woman takes a few quick steps forward, then halts abruptly as if deciding to hang back. "You should not expose yourself to this heat."

"I was cold. I'm always cold these days, Miri."

"Cold?" Miri echoes feebly, choosing to ignore the chill in her chest that mocks the warmth of the air. "You may have a touch of the heat sickness. Come inside."

The princess smiles at her. "But it isn't heat sickness," she says. She looks at her bare arms, holds them out toward Miri. "I never feel hot, and I never brown, let alone burn. Even the noon sunlight cannot warm me."

Miri looks at the princess' pale flesh, creamy as the limestone walls around them and just as immune to the sun's rays. She swallows hard. "You have been blessed with a strong body."

"I have been blessed with a child who draws all heat from me."

Miri hisses, glances behind as if to confirm that they are truly alone. "You must not—" she whispers.

"Must not what? Speak of the child I carry? But Jazim will learn of it soon enough, long before I am ready to give birth. All your watching and scheming and planting of false evidence cannot prevent that."

Miri presses her lips together.

The princess looks into the sky. "I dreamed we were back in the Greenwood last night."

"My princess—"

"All was changed. The wood had swallowed up the manor, the village, everything. In places it wasn't even a wood any more but a great maze of corridors like giant tunnels. I ran through them, calling. Do you know for whom I called?"

Miri holds herself very still.

"My child's father. Blayne. The heartless monster I fled. I called for him over and over again. I wanted him, desperately. Gods of light and sand I want him even now."

"Please, my princess, do not speak of—that."

"Of Blayne? Why? Because he was my lover and took what my father would have sold to a lesser man, or because he wasn't really a man at all."

Miri sucks in her breath, then speaks fast and hard. "Because you are in danger, and your child with you."

The princess brings her eyes down from the sky. "Dear, Miri," she says sadly. "You have sacrificed so much looking after me."

Miri's mellow voice breaks on something like a sob. "What mother wouldn't do at least as much to protect her child?"

"A surrogate child."

"The only child I will ever know?" Miri holds out a shaking hand.

The princess takes it in her cool one and suffers herself to be led inside. She lounges as Miri makes tea in a delicate brass pot and pours it out in small dishes.

"I saw Ogren," Miri says softly.

"Yes?"

"They have him confined at the other end of the house."

"Did he speak to you?" asks the princess.

"No. Not that it matters. Only you can comprehend his speech. But they did not let me that close to him. Nonetheless, he saw me. Of that I am certain. He changed color ever so slightly."

"Are they treating him well?'

"What is well for a nonman? He seems as impervious as a stone, but he also no longer intimidates the guards as he once did. They have become so used to him they behave quite negligently."

The princess lays her cheek in one hand to gaze into the beyond. Miri avoids looking into the princess' eyes. She does not like the way they glow a deep virulent blue in the manufactured twilight of the room. Folding her hands together, she says softly, "I have been thinking."

"You are always thinking."

"I have been thinking about Ogren."

Her princess floats back from beyond. "How so?"

"He could take you out of this place."

The princess lifts her head. "Take me where?"

"Anywhere you want to go, somewhere safe, even to the home of his people perhaps. Jazim may treat him like a prisoner, but he has strength and knowledge no mortal can test, and ways of moving no mortal can know. He can use them to disappear. He can use them to disappear with you."

"And then what?"

"Then you will be free."

The princess' mouth curves into a slow, sad smile. "You know better."

Miri's head dips. "You would at least be free of Jazim," she says. "And the prison he has made for you here."

"You mean the prison my father has made for me, to shield himself from my curse."

Miri stiffens. "How many times must I tell you that there is no curse?"

The princess sighs. "The Greenwood wasn't the only thing I dreamed of last night."

Miri clasps her ringed hands. "You shouldn't listen to dreams."

"How right you are! If I had not, I wouldn't be pregnant and alone."

"Not alone!" Miri objects softly. She reaches out. "Never alone."

The princess looks at the ringed hands grasping her left one. "It was the old nightmare again," she says. "The one where I am a little girl sleeping in my bed and I hear a terrible voice in the walls."

"It is just a dream!"

"'Come to me,'" it says. 'Come, little one.' But I don't like the voice. It's cold and hard as crystal. I cower down under my blanket and close my eyes, but the voice gets closer and closer. And then I feel an icy breath upon my ear, and I jump up to run but a hand sweeps out from under my bed and grabs my leg, a cold hand, a white hand."

"All people have nightmares."

"Not nightmares like mine," the princess says and, pulling back the folds of her gown, extends a pale leg marred by a set of red marks like blisters left by fiery fingertips. Her eyes glow an even brighter blue.

The lovely mouth beneath those glowing blue eyes smiles gently. "You hope that I did it, even if it means I am mad. Poor Miri. Do you think I am mad?"

Miri does not respond.

The Princess sighs again. "Whatever I am, it is getting worse as my child grows."

Miri closes her eyes. "This is what comes of taking a daemon lover."

"Aye," says the princess. "And of carrying his daemon offspring, but Blayne didn't put anything inside me that I wasn't primed to bear. I did not know what I was running toward when I ran to him, and I understood only a little more when I fled him. But over these last months I have come accept one thing. I *am* cursed."

"No!"

"Yes. That is why a creature like Blayne could give me a child. That is why there can be no more running for me now. Wherever I go the curse must follow."

Miri sinks back into her chair. "Then what?"

"I must see my father."

"Jazim will not let you. How many times have you asked, and how many times has he refused?"

"He claims to act as my father commands."

"Why would a dying Empyreor refuse to see his only child?"

"A child he banished to the Midlands."

"A child he sought to protect."

"He thought only of his own safety!" The princess hisses the words. Rising, she stands over her waiting woman.

And Miri tries not to cringe into her chair, suddenly afraid of the incomprehensibly beautiful creature looming over her. The Princess' face is an ivory mask with flaming sapphire eyes. "He knew from the beginning that I was cursed, and he now fears to confront what I have become."

"He could have had you put to death at any time," argued Miri. "If he was so afraid of you, why did he send you away instead?"

The blue light of the Princess' eyes is merciless. "Why indeed?" she snaps. Turning away, she sweeps to a nearby table and lifts a book from it. "I took this from Jazim's library the last time I had an audience with him. It is a history of the Bet Anari Empyreors. Listen to what it says about my father."

158

At the time of his father's death, Bethnarian was called "the Unlikely." The youngest child of Betanar II by a minor wife, he was, by nature, studious and retiring. He lived content on his country estate while his far more powerful half brothers, Beltand and Bertran, contended for the throne. It was only when his brothers' strife opened the Empyre to foreign incursion that Bethnarian stepped out of the shadows. While the forces of Beltand and Bertran slaughtered one another on the plain of Ab Nagnar, word came to Bethnarian of an army of Sardic raiders preparing to invade Sun City. Cobbling together a third army, he rode out to meet them, and his troops scored a tremendous victory, despite being vastly outnumbered. The Sards fled back into their great desert, and Bethnarian's forces pursued them, emerging many days later with a band of Sardic hostages, including several high priestesses, and other tokens of treaty. A few days later, a Sardic raiding party fell upon the forces of Beltand as they were retreating from Ab Nagnar. Beltand was killed outright, leaving Bertran first in succession. Not long afterward Bertran was struck down as he rode in royal procession from Kal Naib to Ab Siminar. A Sardic assassin's dart took him in the throat. Studious and retiring, Bethnarian the Unlikely became first in the line of succession, and on the first day of the festival of the Ninth Moon, he ascended the Sun Seat as Empyreor.

"Do you see?" the Princess urges, closing her book.

"See what?

"My father wins a major battle with the Sards, and shortly thereafter, both of his elder brothers are killed by Sardic agents. Bethnarian must have made some sort of treaty with the Sards, a people known for magic and daemon worship. He bargained with the sworn enemies of the Empyre, thinking that he had outmaneuvered them, until his queen gave birth—to me."

"You believe that the Sards laid a curse on your life."

The princess' blue eyes burn. "You have never wanted to believe in the curse, but assume for a moment that it is real. Can you think of a people better suited to effect it?"

Night comes swiftly in desert places, but Beth felt the darker hours approaching long before the light disappeared. She felt it in the coolness spreading across her skin, in the lightness of her bones.

She called her waiting woman to her in the little courtyard. Miri watched the darkness at the back of the house as she addressed her princess, "You are certain you want to do this?"

Beth nodded. "It's the best plan under the circumstances. I must have leverage to force any acknowledgement from my father. The

Prince of Carnis can give me that leverage." Her pale hands were lightly clasped together. "You are certain Jazim set A'Carnis free?"

"He must have. The guards snicker at the Prince's outrages all the time. He is quite the political operator and lover of blooded women."

Beth nodded. "Summon Ogren then."

Miri dipped her head. Moving to the center of the high-walled courtyard, she slipped from her gown a small cylinder of what looked like alabaster. Slowly, she raised the cylinder to her lips and blew. It emitted no sound that a person could hear, but for a moment the bars of metal stretching over the high-walled courtyard seemed to hum in sympathy while the acrobatic swifts wheeling high in the evening blue swerved sharply and scattered.

Ogren heard the call. He materialized in Beth's bedchamber at midnight as if he had melted through the walls and bars. Seeing him step out of an empty corner made Miri turn white. But Beth, who had appeared asleep, simply opened her eyes and laid a white hand on the vaguely monkeyish face bending over her. Ogren trilled, and Beth said, "I am glad you are well, and I thank you for waiting so long. Now, I need you to find A'Carnis and deliver this. Make sure you give it to him and him alone." She pressed a small slip of paper into the nonman's hand.

Two days later, just before midnight, Beth was pacing her little courtyard unable to sleep when an unexpected eruption of sound shattered the house's quiet and set a cold fire sweeping through her thoughts. The fire flared into a second consciousness—stronger, sharper, crueler than her native one—that flooded her nostrils with scents of sand and iron and fading heat until the night seemed sharpened on a whetstone. Her tongue tasted blood.

Miri! she thought, for the waiting woman had left the apartment a short time earlier to spy on the rest of the household. The cold consciousness sent her gliding calmly into the front room to sit down to await developments.

Soon the noises in the house were translated to sounds of raised voices and blows. Then the heavy doors to her apartment were thrown open, and a group of silent, massive savages entered. Warriors by bearing and attire, they wore black robes over bare chests and loose pants. Each carried a variety of weapons and had sun-darkened skin adorned with elaborate tattoos.

From beneath her veil, Beth watched them fan out from the door, pointing their curved blades at her until a soft command splintered the air. Then the warriors shifted, permitting movement at the back of their ranks to become a parting at the front, and a much smaller robed and hooded figure stepped through.

Beth rose, frowning. "You are not the Prince of Carnis?" she said as her nose picked up the acrid scents of blood and adrenaline while the coldness inside her danced.

"No!" said an unmistakably feminine voice from the depths of the heavy robe. "I am judgment." And a slender, bejeweled hand shot forward.

Beth could only watch the hurled blade come, a splinter of death flashing light as it tumbled. Her normal mind was frozen in shock, but the cold, clear consciousness smiled. It told Beth when to raise her right hand into the air and how to snag the dagger by the hilt so that its blade stopped a finger's breadth from her chest.

The knife wielder sank to her knees, uncovered her head, and bowed toward the floor. "Greetings, Daughter of Night," she said.

The marked men dropped to their knees as well.

Beth lifted her eyes from the knife, considered the woman kneeling before her, noting the way her fair hair and light eyes netted the candlelight. "Get up," she commanded, turning the knife she held.

The woman rose, and Beth descended on her, knife poised to strike. Neither the woman nor her guards flinched.

"You tried to kill me," said Beth softly, speaking through the will of the cold consciousness inside her. She pointed the knife at the woman's robed chest.

The woman smiled and answered in a voice thick with foreign accent. "The knife would not have harmed you, great lady, only a pretender."

"Who are you?"

"Those in the City know me as the consort of the First Prince of Carnis. But I am also L'eret, a granddaughter of the high priestess of the Jur'gon tribe. You sent a message to my son. I come instead." The Lady Carnis' light eyes gleamed.

"I offered an alliance to your son, not you." Beth listened in amazement to the icy clarity of her own voice. "I should cut your throat," she said, and realized that she could cut a throat, without horror or remorse. The cold consciousness offered her that much ruthlessness and more.

"As the Daughter of Night wills, so it must be," recited L'eret Carnis.

The coldness inside Beth smiled. She looked again at the blade in her hand and saw staring from its hilt the face of a woman with diamond eyes. There were serpents in the woman's hair, and serpentine letters all over the blade.

"If you will let me, Great Lady," said L'eret Carnis, "I shall escort you from this wretched place to more suitable quarters."

"Where?"

Lady Carnis bowed her head. "The Empyreal palace," she answered, "even as you requested."

The cold consciousness smiled wider; it instructed Beth to nod her head.

She was hurried through the house, past broken porcelain and bleeding bodies that made her weaker human heart cringe with horror and guilt. All was eerily quiet. "Where is my waiting woman?" some remnant of the warmer, softer Beth asked. "Where is the Lady Inimiri Dahar?"

L'eret Carnis pretended not to hear. But the cold consciousness whispered otherwise. It observed that the Lady Carnis knew things she wished to hide. The Princess stopped walking. "I will not leave without Lady Inimiri," she hissed.

L'eret Carnis bent her head. "Great Lady—"

Beth stared at her, frigid with alien energy.

L'eret Carnis spoke to the floor. "This way."

They led her to a room sticky with drying blood, and there, covered in more of it, lay the crumpled body of Lady Inimiri Dahar. Beth cried out in horror as grief like a deluge overwhelmed the cold consciousness. "Who did this?" she cried, falling on her knees, and holding Miri's bloody form in hot, weeping eyes.

"It must have been the Prince of Serpents' men, Great Lady," Lady Carnis replied. "We found her thus. Now please come. You can do nothing for your servant, and the Prince of Serpents' spies are everywhere."

They dragged her to her feet and pulled her through more rooms to an outer yard where many armed men milled about. Beth was lost to all of it, lost to everything but sorrow like a river in flood.

"This is Injak," said L'eret Carnis as a massive hulk of tattooed muscle took hold of the weeping princess. "You will ride with him." She threw a heavy cloak over the princess' form.

Injak carried Beth on his tall horse down countless dirty alleys to a small house deep inside the city. In a windowless but luxurious room filled with silken cushions, he left her to her grief. She wanted to sink beneath the waves of her sorrow, to, at the very least, lose herself to unconsciousness, but horror, regret and a resurgent cold consciousness would not permit it. When a serving girl appeared, bearing water and a plate of fruit, Beth shoved her away. The girl stumbled and fell, blinking eyes the milky color of blindness.

At dawn, more massive tattooed men came for her, escorting her into yet another high-walled courtyard. To one side of this courtyard, squatted a large, elaborately carved black palanquin hung with white curtains. Waiting beside it was the Lady Carnis, dressed all in black except for the jeweled bracelets and rings adorning her arms and fingers. A morning wind off the desert stirred the Lady's dark veil.

"We will go to the palace now," said the L'eret Carnis as Beth looked at her vacantly. "There should be no questions when we enter the gates." She motioned to Injak, who knelt by the palanquin and adjusted the bottom carving so that it folded down. Inside was a narrow, padded space just large enough to hold a person lying prone.

"You will ride in here."

Beth bestirred herself. "I do not like tight spaces."

"If you truly wish to enter the palace, this is the safest way. Come, Daughter of Night. Honor your waiting woman's sacrifice and take action. Your father and your destiny await."

A flickering cold consciousness propelled her toward the palanquin.

The ride to the palace was not uncomfortable. The bearers were powerful and well trained, and there were many holes in the palanquin's elaborate carvings that would have afforded her intriguing glimpses of the City had she been inclined to look.

She lay numb to it all—the walls of stone and plaster, the broad plazas full of noise and color, the open-air stalls reeking of dung and pepper and rotting meat, the buildings crowned in green terraces and ridged domes.

Then they passed into a wide boulevard, and the palanquin stopped between immense walls of black stone. Iron gates clanged. Orders were sung out. The palanquin rocked and moved on, greeted at intervals by more clangs and more cries of command. Beth's compartment was dusted by a shimmering of light as they crossed a large body of water on a narrow stone causeway. Edging the causeway were tall water reeds, lotus flowers, and palm trees. In the distance were immense boxes of black stone.

The black boxes advanced until they hemmed the palanquin in. The palanquin settled to the ground. Footsteps retreated into quiet, and the wooden carving over Beth's compartment opened up, revealing the enigmatic tattooed face of Injak. The Sard kept his eyes on the ground as he helped her to climb from the small compartment.

She stood in a narrow corridor of black stone.

"This way!" hissed the Lady Carnis, "Hurry, before the palace servants appear."

Beth followed the ripple of the Lady's black silk into an abrupt moderation of temperature. She now stood in a large round room with a sloping floor. The room's colorfully tiled walls were curved inward toward the ceiling where they converged into a single point. The whispers of her slippered feet came back to her as she moved across the floor. "This is the Chamber of Echoes," announced the Lady Carnis. And the walls returned, "chamber, echoes, chamber, echoes, echoes."

They passed into a second chamber and then a third. Then they entered a space that was not a room at all but an immense cylindrical hollow like an enormous well. Its sides were lined with enormous blocks of black granite, which soared straight up to a sun-punctured dome and plunged downward into unseen depths. At different places along the well's wall, openings had been cut so that delicate streams of water poured themselves down the well's sides.

"This way Highness," urged the lady Carnis, gesturing her toward an opening in the landing on which they stood. But Beth turned to look at the sunlit hole in the dome instead. "My father waits in the Courts of the Sun," she said.

"The Empyreor's sun is setting," L'eret Carnis answered impatiently. "Now is the time for the Courts of the Moon." Beneath her black veil, Lady Carnis's eyes gleamed blue. "This way, Great Lady," she urged, setting foot on the top step of a spiraling stair.

Still Beth lingered, tasting something in the atmosphere of the well that spoke to the abyss of her grief. She tried to remember the High Court of the Noonday Sun with its golden splendors haloing a father who had rejected her. *Father, I've finally come home*, she thought.

And her nose filled with a terrible stench, a reek of imminent death. In an instant she knew she could follow that scent like a hound on the blood trail through the maze of halls above all the way to the fearful, suffering soul that leaked it. The new life growing inside her jumped in eagerness or protest, and her mind drew back, while her hand came to rest reassuringly against the swell of her belly. The Court of the Noonday Sun must wait, though its ruler would not wait for long.

She followed Lady Carnis down the stair into a series of darkened rooms and through them to a large pillared space hung with gauzy fabrics of rainbow hues.

"I know this place," said Beth.

"The Lesser Court of Veils," nodded L'eret Carnis.

Beth held out a hand to their fabric-strung corridor. The Court of Veils was the ceremonial court reserved for the high ladies of the Empyre, one of the few places in the palace where they could shed the veils they donned at puberty and wore for the remainder of their lives.

She had played here as a young child, running through the filmy curtains and piling up the silken cushions in order to jump into them while, in the shadows, eyes looked askance and voices whispered.

"Great Lady?" Lady Carnis asked. They had come to another of those ubiquitous wooden screens.

Beth shook off her ghosts. "The court is so empty."

"The other ladies wait upon the Empyreor in the Court of the Noonday Sun. As he sickens, they spend more and more time near him, playing at the politics of succession from their husbands' sides."

"But not you?"

The Lady barked a derisive laugh. "I take little interest in such affairs. My husband, like his Empyreal aspirations, is dead." The Lady unlocked the screen with a large key and then slid it back to reveal a narrow stone passage

The passage was poorly illuminated. The Lady Carnis walked forward past narrow wooden doors looking up at a ceiling embossed with female faces. Under one of these, she knelt and, pulling a small knife from beneath her veil, pried up a large floor tile.

Beth looked into the hollow space revealed. "We are going down there?"

"We must take care to avoid Jazim's spies while we prepare you to meet your father." The Lady Carnis flung back her veil, swung her skirted legs into the square of darkness, and dropped from sight. "Come down," her voice urged.

Feeling strangely disassociated from her bulky body, Beth lowered herself to the floor and peered down into it. She could just make out the pale oval of L'eret Carnis' face at the level of her ankles. The lady's hand guided her foot to the rung of a ladder.

The tunnel at the bottom was squat and featureless and brimming with dark.

The older woman climbed back up the ladder to reaffix the floor tile, and the darkness became complete. Then a bud of orange light bloomed and divided. The Lady Carnis blew out her tender. "This way," she said holding high a corroded oil lamp.

"Where are we going?" Beth asked.

"To the throne room."

"But the throne room is stories above us."

"I speak of the Empyress's throne room."

"Empyress? There hasn't been an Empyress since the ancient days. Wasn't Zardan the last Empyreor to grant his consort that title?"

Her speculations in that direction ended as the passage sloped steeply downward, split into two, then split again. Both times the Lady Carnis took the left-hand opening. Then she and her lamp disappeared around an edge of darkness.

Beth stood alone in a passage that was cool and damp and full of whispering. Cautiously, she rounded the corner and confronted wetness leaping off a curtain of water shimmering with silvery light.

The whispering was louder now.

"Through here," called the Lady Carnis, and her hand guided Beth past the falling water into a dimly-lit chamber containing a double circle of immense columns. The space was impressive, but what drew a sigh of surprise from Beth's lips were the dozens of narrow sheets of clear water falling through the chamber. They hung among the pillars like glass curtains, and struck the chamber floor with almost no splash, for the stones beneath her feet were riddled with slots and holes that permitted the water to pass right through it. The sound the falling water made filled the huge, round space with a loud whisper that was both hypnotic and eerie.

Looking up, Beth discovered that the pillars, all of varying height, supported a complex network of immense beams, the sources of the thin curtains of water. And much farther overhead, more than half hidden by the beams, she could just make out a yellow disk like a sickly cousin of the sun, the source of what little light filtered down into the chamber. She realized then that they must be at the bottom of the immense well.

The Lady Carnis had removed her veil entirely and moved so that the nearest fall of water mirrored back a runny image of her holding her lamp.

"The Greater Court of Veils, Great Lady," she bowed.

"The greater one?" asked Beth. She brushed her own veil back from her damp face and surprised L'eret Carnis into gaping. Beth did not notice. She was taking in the eerie atmosphere of the chamber, with its ceaseless crowd of hissing voices, and feeling the cold consciousness inside her rising like a vapor.

Lady Carnis shook herself free of a net of beauty and said, "Before the Empyreors laid claim to this land, women ruled it. And in this chamber the most powerful among them met—to judge and worship and plan, but most of all to learn how to see through the veils between the worlds. The Empyress herself taught them, and they passed the skill on to their daughters."

"Does my father know of this place?" said Beth.

"Yes. But only those who belong to the ancient sisterhood come here now."

"Sisterhood," murmured Beth, wandering between curtains of falling water, and slipping deeper into the cold consciousness with every step. "Tell me about this sisterhood."

"The Great Lady should see the place prepared for her first," Lady Carnis redirected.

"Place?" scoffed Beth, "Down here?" Her eyes had begun to gleam like sunlit sapphires even in the semi-darkness of that deep place.

"We must begin somewhere," L'eret Carnis answered, bowing.
She led Beth beyond the watery curtains to the further side of the chamber where a low hallway bled yellow light. Beth followed it into a luxuriously furnished cavern of a room in which sprawled the Prince A'Carnis. He rose smoothly as the two women entered, then folded himself into an obsequious bow. He looked very rich and very handsome, as elegant and arrogant as a prince of Sun City should be.

"Highness!" His tone was unctuous, his manner virile.

Beth felt how his eyes pressed against her face and pulled her veil over it. The prince's mouth smiled.

"You were told not to come," hissed the Lady Carnis, guiding Beth toward a seat on a rich divan. She seemed angry to see her son.

"I was anxious to confirm the suitability of my arrangements, my mother. Tell me, highness," he begged of Beth, gesturing widely, "have I done enough to soften the rough edges."

"Leave us," ordered his hard-eyed dam.

"But who will wait on you while you talk and plan? There is food and drink."

His mother frowned at him, then nodded curtly. "Very well. Bring us chocolate."

With a sensuous smile, the handsome Prince of the Empyre bowed his way out of the room.

Beth followed his departing figure with bemusement. In the Empyre, women bowed to the authority and power of men. How was it that so slight a woman as the Lady Carnis should disdain so rich and powerful a son?

"Is this where you expect me to stay?" she demanded regally, while an image of Miri slain flashed into her head, searing her to the core.

"You are in the palace, Great Lady. Your enemies are all about you now. It is best you remain hidden until your son is born."

Beth stiffened as a freshet of emotion broke through the suffocating insulation of her grief. "My son?"

Beth stiffened as a freshet of emotion broke through the suffocating insulation of her grief. "My son?"

The Lady Carnis's expression turned sly. "You are far along with child, are you not?"

"Whether I am or not, I did not invite you to speak of it," snapped Beth.

The lady lowered her eyes, but her mouth curved. "As the Great Lady commands."

Beth exhaled.

"You need not be afraid," L'eret Carnis continued. "I will guard your secret and your son. He is destined to rule an Empyre greater than any this world has seen. He will stand with one foot in two worlds and unite them."

Beth said nothing. Her tongue had turned to clay.

Prince A'Carnis swept back into the room bearing a tray. Deftly, he set shallow dishes of thick black chocolate before the princess and his mother.

"Drink," he urged, smiling seductively at the younger woman.

Beth took the warm bowl into surprisingly cold hands. "Did you escape Jazim, highness?" she asked sliding the bowl under her veil, "Or did he let you go."

The prince bowed deeply. "I stood most courageously on my political clout, and he released me once we crossed the border."

"To release then," said Beth, lifting the bowl of bitter chocolate to him.

A'Carnis' eyes glittered. "And all its delights," he returned, lifting his own. They drank together.

"You spoke of realms being united, Lady Carnis," she continued, lowering her cup. "Have you designs on the North as well as the South?"

The Lady Carnis laughed, a brassy sound that hurt Beth's ears. But the princess covered her discomfort by taking another long drink from her cup of chocolate. From out of the corner of her eye she watched A'Carnis slip behind her.

The Lady Carnis set her own bowl on the low table. "The Steward and his ilk are children. They only play at a power that is yours by right. And your son will have even greater magic!"

Beth's chocolate-coated throat heaved. "I told you not to speak of that," she husked.

The sly look spread across the lady's Carnis's face. "Your son or his magic? Ah, it embarrasses you for my son to hear. Do not worry. He knows his place."

Beth doubted it. She shifted her position on the couch to include the prince in her line of view and felt a wave of dizziness roll over her. Then her sight began to blur, melting the room into blobs of color. Suddenly, she was finding it difficult to keep her head up. The cold consciousness hissed a warning, but Beth was already falling backward into the cushions of the divan.

The room was swimming, and the Lady Carnis floated in it. A moment later A'Carnis floated into view as well. "She is pregnant!" he expostulated. "Not by some idiot cowherder, I hope!"

His mother snorted. "Quiet, fool! She is the daughter of eternal night. No ordinary man could survive her embrace, let alone impregnate her!"

"Some magician might—"

"No. I think not," returned his mother, gazing hungrily at Beth. "It was a daemon lover, wasn't it, Great Lady? One with power and seed strong enough to take root in you."

Beth tried to speak. "I . . . want."

The Lady's expression softened. "No, no, daughter of night. No more wanting for now. Your desires have done enough already, and without goading from us," she laughed in genuine amusement. "How it will gall your sire when he discovers it! Then shall he know that his sun has gone out."

An invisible hand was pressing Beth's lids closed though she moaned and fought to lift them anyway.

"Let go, daughter of night," Lady Carnis' throbbing voice hissed through Beth's drugged brain. "Rest and drink in night's presence. It will take all your power to bear the heir the Empyre needs, the son I was made to raise."

"As opposed to the one you already have," sneered Prince A'Carnis. "Shall I guard her?"

"Urttah will watch her."

"The witch! You trust her?"

"I trust her knowledge of the power. She will know best what to do."

Beth felt a finger graze her cold cheek, but she had no strength to turn her head and bite it.

"A pity," said the Prince with a note of genuine regret. "I would dearly love to stay and learn what one experiences in the arms of a daemon."

Lady Carnis's voice slapped at his. "The power would consume you like fire consumes straw. Now come!" The divan vibrated and silks and silken footsteps whispered away.

Alone at last, Beth yielded to the downward pull of the drug and let unconsciousness like an ocean of grief close over her.

What called her out of bottomless blackness was an infants' wail. Beth sat up in alarm and found herself in her old room at Greenwood manor. Her hand went to her belly, found it taut and flat as it had once been. Panic set in. Where was her baby? That awful woman must have taken him. She leapt from the bed and rushed into the hallway outside her room, but it wasn't the warm wood panels of the manor's halls that greeted her. This was a hallway of wet, weeping stone. She could hear her child crying, and she ran toward the sound. Other voices crept in under the crying. The damp tunnel changed into a room hung with sheets of fabric. Now she was running through silken curtains and twisting in order to elude the pale arms that reached out to grab her. The baby's wail was growing fainter. She dived under a swath of green silk and found herself running barefoot down a wooded track. The great limbs of Greenwood Forest hung over her like the fingers of outstretched hands, but she rushed on beneath them toward the sound of the crying child. Ahead of her on the track a net of light-spangled shadow resolved itself into the retreating form of a tall, tawny-haired man.

Beth let loose a sob of relief. "Blayne?" she screamed. "Blayne, help me. They've taken our baby."

But even as she stumbled toward him, he crested the rise of a low hill and disappeared over it.

"Wait!" Beth sobbed.

She climbed the hill and found herself dashing down a neat track of gravel amid a lushly cultivated garden full of ornamental shrubs in tall marble urns. She could no longer hear her baby crying, but she ran on anyway, praying that she had not lost the trail.

At last she stepped onto a large marble terrace, cool in the first of the evening. Overhead the sky was a brilliant cobalt blue flecked with early stars. At the opposite end of the terrace stood a young woman in a green dress. She appeared to be speaking heatedly to someone screened by branches. Then she shifted her stance slightly, and Beth saw her profile.

"Emily?" she gasped. "Emily!"

But Emily did not appear to hear her. She was looking defiant and gesturing sharply.

170

Beth would have run to her, but as sometimes happens in dreams, her legs seemed mired in molasses. She cried louder, "Emily, it's Beth? I'm here. Won't you look at me?"

And Emily turned.

Beth held her breath in hope, but a dark-haired man stepped out of the shadows and stared across the terrace straight into her eyes. Beth realized that she knew him. She also knew that he, unlike Emily, could see her. He fixed his eyes on her so exactly and with such intensity that their weight was like a wind in her face. The man said something to Emily that made her look sad. Then Emily shook off her sadness and stepped away from the man, and the landscape changed again.

"Emily," Beth whispered, and watched Emily scan the grove of dusty trees in which she now stood. "Beth!" Emily demanded. "I'm here. Where are you?"

"Here," cried Beth, her heart surging with hope. "They have locked me in the Empyreal Palace and they have taken my baby."

Though Emily's eyes continued to search the grove in vain, her voice now came to Beth as clear and firm as if they stood face to face. "I'm coming, Beth. Do you hear me? I'm coming."

Beth awoke to lamp-lit cushions and carpet. Her hands went immediately to her abdomen, which was reassuringly round. Slowly, she sat up, careful to give her woozy head time. Then she lashed out, kicking the table and sending the bowl of drugged chocolate flying to the floor. She was a prisoner again, only without Miri.

She dropped her head into her hands and wept until the well of tears was exhausted. Then she began to think. At least she was inside the palace now, closer to her father than she had been since childhood, and Emily was coming. Why this last thought, so irrelevant, so ridiculous, the report of a mere dream, should have comforted her she could not explain. She only knew that it did comfort her, like the touch of a friendly hand.

Crunching broken porcelain beneath her slippered feet, she set about exploring her prison. She had gotten herself this far; she could get herself farther. It was a sentiment that the cold consciousness approved of by flickering along her bones like fire. She could hear it humming in her mind, promising to shrivel the aspirations of lesser beings. But Beth took no comfort from its song. The cold consciousness was too cold, too calculating, too alien. And it exerted a terrible pressure on her familiar self. Powerful it might be, but it was untamed and dangerous as well.

171

There was a rusty iron gate at the end of the hallway leading to her room, but it sagged against one wall. "They have forgotten to lock us in," Beth breathed to the child inside her. Hope stirred as she peered into the darkness. True night had come to the bottom of the well, the great chamber of falling waters.

Alone in the darkness, Beth experienced that chamber as a living, breathing thing speaking in the voice of many waters. Which way to the exit tunnel? The chamber's restlessness made it difficult to determine, so she began walking the well's perimeter with one hand held to the wall, knowing she must eventually come upon the passage leading to the upper Court of Veils.

The wall ran sticky but otherwise unobstructed for many feet, curving ever so gently around her. When her hand met falling water, she pushed through it to the stone behind, ignoring the way her sleeves filled with water that coated her bodice.

Her arms and chest tightened with chill, and the cold consciousness began to loom larger in her mind. Her sight grew keener. By the time she found the cleft where she and the Lady Carnis had entered, she could see the falling waters like silver-chased banners among the thick columns. There was a thick iron gate stretched across the corridor's watery opening that was fastened with chains. She pulled and pushed at it, but though it shifted, it did not yield.

Gulping down disappointment, she moved on, while the massive chamber whispered its secrets and the silver-chased waters rippled with ever shifting images. At a point squarely between two massive columns, her freezing hands discovered a third opening. This one was wider than the others, and the air wafting from it felt warmer and drier than the air of the chamber. It smelled different as well, not unpleasant, but thick with a complexity that teased her memory. She leaned slightly into it, but her eyes could not penetrate the passage's darkness. A small gust of warmth hit her face, smelling of onions and pepper. It was followed by a guttural snicker.

Beth flung herself backward with a gasp, fell through a stream of water, and landed hard on one hip. Pain knifed up her side, but it couldn't keep her from scrabbling at the carved stone floor as a shadow slid from the dark opening into silver-chased twilight.

Beth found her feet and took off through the dark, hands out before her. She tried to dodge pillar and water alike, but she only careened from one to the other, her soaked gown coiling about her legs and further encumbering her flight. Yellow light directed her toward her lamp-lit room and the sagging iron gate that might afford her a moment's protection. Something caught her skirts and brought her down. Her head cracked into the floor and light exploded behind her eyes.

She awoke a third time choking, sprawled upon rough carpet and silk cushions. A cup had been shoved against her lips, and she spluttered back the liquid pouring from it. She was coated in wet silk and freezing. A black-hooded figure crouched near her.

A raspy cross between a hiss and a cackle emanated from the hood. A wide-knuckled hand set the cup aside. The cowl slid back, exposing a female face like an image made of melted wax. Its key features seemed largely to have dripped away. Where the nose should have been two uneven nostrils gaped surmounted by a narrow triangle of scarred skin. The mouth was a mere slit above the lumpy chin. The flaps of skin that passed for eyelids were so taut they would have difficulty closing. The eyes behind them, however, were sharp and clear, dark with shining whites.

Shock gave way to horror and horror to revulsion. Beth flailed and struck out.

A thick-knuckled hand caught her wrist.

"Lift her," rasped the largely immobile slit of a mouth.

"My pleasure," answered a male voice. Beth rolled her head and saw A'Carnis moving toward her. He slid his warm arms beneath her wet skirts and, grunting, lifted her from the floor. The cowled figure disappeared from Beth's sight.

Too weak to object, Beth let herself be draped like so much wet silk upon a divan.

The scarred face returned. "Blankets," it hissed.

"Pah, you old witch," returned A'Carnis, but he disappeared as scarred hands began peeling back wet silk.

"L—leave m—me alone," stuttered Beth through shaking lips. The slitted eyes regarded her imperturbably. "I am Urttah," the slit mouth said. Wet silk was yanked to Beth's waist. Deft and quick Urttah stripped the princess of her clothing, then began packing cushions about her.

"Gods and Daemons," choked A'Carnis from somewhere else in the room.

Urttah's head turned, Beth's lifted. A'Carnis stood a few feet away, looking hammer struck.

Too cold to even flush at her nakedness, Beth stared back.

"Give," Urttah hissed, descending upon the overawed man. "Leave," she ordered, and shoved him out of sight. In a trice she was back and draping a thick woolen blanket across the princess' form. "Rest, young one," Urttah croaked.

Rapt in Urttah's dark stare, Beth did.

Chapter 12: Sun City

Emily and Colin spent two days hiding in the lemon grove, while Faryn came and went, eventually disappearing into the city with Abreem Imharta and his donkeys. On the morning of the third day Emily awoke dusty-eyed and cranky, to find Faryn crouched before the ashes of their evening fire.

"You're back." She grated in a voice gone sour

"For now. I am returning to the city this morning. I will try to be back before dark."

Emily rubbed her scratchy eyes. "Doing *more* reconnaissance?"

Faryn's light eyes gleamed in a measuring way.

"I want to go with you," Colin announced from the opposite side of the camp.

Emily snorted, but Faryn cocked his head. "Very well," he said.

Emily rubbed harder. "You mean we can finally leave this place?"

"Not you. You will stay here."

Emily gaped in disbelief. "Alone!" she protested.

"Is that a good idea?" asked Colin in a rather alarmed voice.

"No," Faryn replied, "But then she won't be alone." And, smiling his most feral smile, he whistled sharply. Two large silver and black shapes came loping through the lemon trees, wolves out of a child's worst nightmare. Their strangely dark fangs gleamed and their red eyes burned, but they came and sat before Faryn like well-mannered lap dogs. Emily sucked in her breath.

"You can't intend to leave me here with those—" she began.

"The hounds will take care of any unexpected visitors to this grove, and the grove will do the rest."

"I will not sit here while those things lick their chops at me," Emily protested, her voice climbing into its upper registers.

"They will only trouble you if you attempt to leave my circle," said Faryn, smiling at her in a most infuriatingly smug way. Abruptly he glided closer and held out his hand. "Your daggers please."

Emily's hands jumped to her belt. "These are Illyria's daggers. They were given to me by your lord. You have no right to take them."

"So I should give you the chance to pull the same trick thrice? My lord would be most displeased."

Emily gripped the delicate silver hilts more tightly. Faryn smiled. Then he moved. Before Emily could pull either dagger clear of its sheathe, he had somehow twisted both knives away from her. Emily stood blinking, Faryn grinning. "Move beyond this clearing," he said to Colin over his shoulder. Then he pointed a dagger at Emily. "You, stand close to the fire pit, or this will be uncomfortable."

"That again!" she complained. "It didn't work the first time."

"It will now," Faryn smiled, and drew from his robe the narrow switch she'd seen him handle once before. With a warder's native grace, he moved from tree to tree touching the trunk of each one, while Emily followed him with furious eyes. The limbs of the lemon trees swayed in what Emily thought was a wind off the desert. Then she realized that all the limbs of all the trees were moving inward toward the fire pit regardless of where they stood, and a creeping sensation moved up her spine. Faryn was talking to the trees, and the trees, even these unfamiliar Southern trees, were responding.

As Faryn finished joining his irregular circle, he cried a strange word aloud and Emily felt the air snap. There was a brief, overwhelming scent of lemon blossom, and a rustling of leaves like whispering.

Faryn turned back to Emily smiling. "Now no one may enter or leave this circle until I return. And no one outside it will be able to see into it. Expect us near evening."

In a ripple of dun tunic and poncho he passed through the barrier he had created, setting the air about Emily to rippling like the surface of a pond.

"Colin," protested Emily.

But her friend only grinned at her from outside the circle and slipped off into the trees.

The city Colin and Faryn entered was a series of beige stuccoed boxes stacked irregularly atop one another. On the roofs of some of these boxes, Colin saw green things growing and swathes of what looked to be colorful cloth, and here or there a thickly shuttered window or wooden door perforated the beige.

As they threaded their way down one narrow cobbled alley into the next, Colin considered the ribbon of the sky above them and wondered how people could live in such cramped quarters.

"Wait here," Faryn said as they came to a wider way, and vanished around a corner.

He returned with a bundle of cloth, which proved to be two deeply hooded robes of dark, heavy cotton. Faryn handed one robe to Colin and donned the other himself.

"Is this how warders move so secretly through the world?" questioned Colin as he pulled the hood over his head.

"One way. But I would not have bothered with disguise if you were not with me."

"Oh?"

"Warders have even better ways of making themselves inconspicuous."

"Such as magic."

"Such as taking routes that other people overlook."

"You mean twilight roads. Does the city have them?"

"Twilight can penetrate anywhere. The roads of that world are not fixed like those in ours, but move to the power's whims."

Colin recalled the strange atmosphere of the road he and Emily had traveled while Faryn continued, "But I would not cross over in this city. Like calls to like, and there is a deep affinity for Twilight in this place that might stir the darker powers within it."

To this Colin could only shrug. "So what way would you have taken?"

Faryn's deep hood turned toward him. His finger pointed up.

Colin looked at the sky in bafflement. "Do warders fly too?"

Faryn's grin was mocking. "No, Midlander. But roofs provide any good climber with a quick and largely unhindered route through most cities." His hood swung away.

Colin squinted upward. "We could have tried that way, you know. I'm a pretty good climber myself, even with my bad leg." He spoke confidently, encouraged by the warder's uncharacteristic loquacity.

"Not good or quick enough. Not yet. You could learn to be. If you had grown up in our society you would have learned how to push the limits of your mind and body much sooner."

"I thought one had to be born a warder."

"In as much as one is born with a warder's power, that is true."

"Well, I'm no warrior, though my father may once have been."

Faryn's light eyes flickered at him from inside the hood. "It is a pity he didn't instruct you. You might have discovered more benefits of your warder heritage."

Colin stumbled.

"Warder heritage?" he blurted. He wanted to laugh. "You think I have warder blood!"

Faryn's shrouded eyes met Colin's squarely. There was amusement in them. "I know you do."

Colin stared. "Impossible. My people are Midlanders."

"You father was not born in the Midlands. Perhaps your mother was, but she carries our heritage inside her."

"That's ridiculous," Colin gawked. Then his face sobered as some connecting thought moved across it. "Anyway how could you know?"

Faryn flashed his toothy smile. "It is rather obvious really, though not in any way you can yet imagine. It is where your talent for healing comes from, as well as your own physical strength and resilience."

Colin shook his head. "Warders heal?" he said.

"Our healers are the finest of all the houses, save perhaps for those of the Tellers'. Millicynt Encanta herself spent time studying with our First Healer. No doubt, she recognized your warder heritage from the beginning."

Colin clutched at the warder's shoulder. He was feeling queasy beneath his dark hood. "She trained me because she was good and kind."

Faryn, suffering himself to be so held, stared back. "And because you had magic, plenty of it. I have seen you call upon it not only to heal but also to defend the Shield bearer."

Colin clenched and unclenched his jaw. "How and why would a member of the warder clan end up in a tiny Midlander village?"

"No doubt for the same reason a Keeper's heir did. Not all those born into the houses choose to play a part in them. Some, like Lady Millicynt, go their own way. Occasionally, they take ordinary lovers. The land you call the Midlands was once part of a larger territory defended by House Warder. In those days, most people flocked to the Steward's banner or the Empyreal scepter, but we held the buffer lands between, including the western slopes of our mountains and the great Wyrmwood that stretched from them to the sea."

"Wyrmwood is the old name for the Greenwood," Colin remembered.

"And that wood is still home to some who bear the blood of our kind. It remembers what they have forgotten. Your father may be a vigorous man, but your mother and her family were something more. What name did your mother's family go by? Alder? Holly? Not Fir or Oak obviously."

"Rowan," said Colin hollowly.

"Ah, yes, fire-crowned Rowan." Faryn brushed Colin's hand from his shoulder and stepped ahead of Colin into a wider way. Way led to wider way, and the light grew steadily hotter and brighter. Then they were rounding a corner into a brilliant disarray of noise, color, and pungent smells, all steeping in a blinding refraction of light and heat.

Colin squinted, and stumbled as a troop of half-naked boys the color of roasted nuts, ran past on bare feet. Behind them came a palanquin borne by four heavily muscled men in sleeveless tunics and striped headscarves. More palanquins moved in the distance along with horses and camels and people of every color and stripe. They had stepped into a vast plaza.

Faryn moved quickly across it, passing two enormous reservoirs of water where children played and horses and a few donkeys bent to drink.

They encountered two more of these great open plazas as they wound their way deeper into the enormous city. Then they turned into a more squalid section where lopsided buildings of mud brick fought with each other for very shred of space. The people here looked duskier, acted shiftier. They hugged the buildings' walls as if to avoid being noticed.

They ended up on the dirty doorstep of a building that looked as if a stiff breeze would crumble it.

Faryn did not bother to knock. His hand jabbed something slender into the door's lock and popped the door open.

They entered a narrow, dim and rickety hallway, then walked down a flight of uneven steps into a wider but dimmer hallway. Faryn moved without a sound, but though Colin tried to be quiet, every scrape of his soles seemed to rend the musty air.

Metallic hisses cut through the dimness, shadows leaped, and hands shoved Colin into a wall. There were grunts and scufflings and the clatter of a blade skidding across stone. Dim figures seemed to be knotting and unknotting about a flitting form.

"The children of Rygel are not what they once were," Colin heard Faryn say brightly.

Harsh breaths and harsher voices clashed together. The man holding Colin snarled, "We have your companion, assassin. Surrender or we will cut him down!"

Faryn's voice smiled. "Do not do it, friend. I would not harm a brother of the blood."

"Brother of the blood?" said a wearier voice from the depths of the hall. "Who are you, stranger? Speak truth now, or I will spring a trap to kill you one and all."

"I am a servant of House Warder, sent to you by the Lord himself."

There came a collective inhale in which even the dust motes in the air seemed to hang motionless.

The threadbare old voice spoke again. "If that is true, why did you not simply announce yourself?"

"For the same reason you set traps — prudence. But I did use the front door, as a gesture of goodwill. If I wanted you at my mercy, I could have infiltrated this house in a hundred different ways."

Colin heard what he took to be a snort. "And who *is* the Lord of the Taloned these days?"

"Sandyr Ash, who came to you as a young man and swore to honor Rygel's children as his own brethren."

An easier silence.

"Come then, warder," said the worn voice.

Colin was marched quickly the length of the hall into a dim room, whose interior seemed all the more obscure for the bars of light streaming from what appeared to be slatted windows.

On the far side of this room, partially obscured by that light, waited a robed and cowled figure among an array of other men.

"Step forward, warder, if that is what you truly are, and let the brethren bear witness."

Faryn materialized at Colin's side and slipped into the center of what seemed to be an intricately inlaid floor. Immediately a portion of its complex pattern began to glow in a blue-white shape like a crescent moon.

"Ah," said the worn voice of the robed man. "And the other?"

Hands shoved Colin forward. "I'm no —" the Midlander tried to protest as he stumbled toward Faryn and the glowing symbol began to shine more brightly.

"Ah," said the aged voice. "I would not have thought it."

"My companion has come rather late to his gifts," explained Faryn.

The robed figure pushed through the bars of light, and Colin saw an old man's face, white bearded and skull-like beneath a fine wrinkling of skin. It was a face that struck him as having been ravaged by time and care. The eyes in it were so sunken that Colin could make out nothing of their shape or expression. But the knobby hand rested on the hilt of a long curving blade with sureness and strength.

"You are Janeryc," said Faryn, bending his head.

"I am."

"My lord will be pleased to hear that you still serve and guide."

"As I am pleased to hear that he has fulfilled his people's hopes. He was so wild when I knew him that I despaired of his ever achieving lordship — much as his masters did no doubt. When your brethren finally came for him, I thought they would have to kill him to take him back."

"The road to power is never easy, particularly for the lords of our house. And he is the greatest we have known in many, many years. He still speaks with great respect of you."

The wrinkles in the face deepened, and the skull nodded. A second hand emerged from behind the old man's back and gestured to the waiting warriors surrounding them. In a procession of footfalls nearly as soft as Faryn's, they retreated.

"Come," said the old man when they were alone. "Share a meal with me and tell me what the Lord Sandyr wants of his old ally."

In a sunny, elegant room quite at odds with the building's crumbling exterior, the old man and the young warder talked, sitting crosslegged before a low table.

Colin stood apart, gazing past the two men into his own memories. He was envisioning his energetic mother, her calm face and quick tongue and hands. He saw her making dinner, working in the garden, scooping up one child as she herded another.

Out of those memories arose a hazier one of a grandfather he had barely known, a man who made his living as a hunter and trapper in the deep woods. Kaitlyn's father Labyn Rowan had been a stern and secretive man, but he had trained his daughter to wield a knife better than most men, a skill she'd used to unexpected effect when she'd bested the hand and heart of a young Garvin Blackhammer in a knife-throwing contest.

That recollection brought Shade leaping to mind. What had the golden-eyed traveler said? "I do hate to see good material wasted. Where do you think your power to heal comes from?"

So Shade had known from the beginning, just as he had probably planned to give Colin his staff from the beginning, and that knowledge somehow made the strange burden and the even stranger truth easier to bear.

"A girl, you say," Janeryc was murmuring.

"A very special girl," Faryn replied. "But you can judge for yourself. Vouch for her safety, and I will bring her here to meet you."

"Of what interest is a Midlander girl to me?"

"Of what interest is the Shield Light?"

The lines in the old man's face knitted together. "The shield. *The* Shield."

Faryn nodded once. "The Keeper's talisman has returned to the lands of men."

The white beard wagged, words snaked through it. "Can the other be far behind?"

"My Lord thinks not. The age foretold by your people and mine may finally be drawing near."

The old man straightened. "Bring her to me. Yes, bring her at once."

Chapter 13: Predictions

The Lady Inimiri Dahar paced the aisle between two walls of grain sacks as if she were hoping to trip over the solution to her predicament. Every now and then she tossed a speculative glance at the massive creature squatting at the end of that aisle. He, for his part, seemed no more animated than the sacks.

When Bethnara was taken, Miri had been arguing with the captain of the household guard. It had taken her a moment or two to realize that the doors to their room had burst open and by then a group inked Sards was descending upon them. The Sards made short work of the Captain and then turned on her. Something sharp stung her in the neck, and the whole room started to spin. She awoke hours later covered in dried blood and cradled in the arms of the nonman giant. Ogren was loping through a dawning city.

On a crumbling rooftop in a derelict quarter, he finally set her down. Miri tried to hold a hurried and very broken conversation with him. "Why did you leave her?" she kept crying at him. Then she collapsed to the rooftop in shock.

That night they took shelter in a crumbling house on the edge of one of the City's worst slum quarters. They spent several miserable days camped there while Miri devised a plan.

With Ogren's help she made several forays into other areas of the city, acquired a few helpful tidbits of information, and eventually harnessed enough courage to approach Dahim Rujak, a first cousin and old friend. The risk paid off. Her cousin was as delighted as he was stunned to see her. He took her in and hid her in one of his many warehouses, not realizing that he would be hiding a nonman as well.

Although crude, Dahim's warehouse was a palace compared to the prison cells reserved for the Empyre's criminals or the dumps where the murdered went to rest. It was also a good location from which to ferret out information on the family Carnis. Miri felt certain that it was A'Carnis who had staged the assault on the house. It was he whom Bethnara had reached out to, and the family Carnis was known to have blood ties to the Sards. In fact, A'Carnis' mother was rumored to be more than half Sard. She was also said to practice magic.

It wasn't long before Miri turned to magic as well.

It had been almost two weeks since Bethnara's abduction, and Miri had yet to find a single clue as to the existence or location of her princess. It was either turn to magic or give up altogether.

Now, as Dahim Rujak appeared around a hill of spices, Miri stopped her pacing.

Dahim was a small man, ashy blonde like Miri and elegantly attired in the silk tunic of a prosperous merchant.

"Well?" Miri demanded.

"He will be at the Dal Awiri chocolate house."

"Tonight?"

"Tonight."

They set off into the warm Southern night.

"Let me call a palanquin?" Dahim begged as they hurried along the crowded streets.

"I prefer to walk," insisted Miri. "It is less conspicuous, and I have spent far too much time sitting." She peered through her heavy veil at lamp-lit stalls smelling of roasted goat and lamb, at customers milling and chattering. "The streets seem crowded tonight," she commented.

"The festival of the ninth moon is only a few weeks away. People like to begin their preparations early. Do you remember the fireworks we used to set off during the festival? We once set several bolts of my father's best silk on fire."

Miri snorted. "Yes, we were quite the daring little rascals then."

"And you the most daring of all."

"Oh for such youth and carelessness of heart."

"Yes," commiserated Dahim. "But the gods are supposed to frown on those who live in the past."

"And they are at their cruelest when they make our dreams come true. Or so we were taught. But I do not believe in the gods, Dahi. You know that."

Dahim flashed her a smile, then looked over his shoulder. An unexpected quiet had overtaken the street.

"What is it?" asked Miri softy, as he pulled her toward a narrow alleyway.

Other people were also hastening from the street as a larger cluster of alarming persons came shuffling down it, moving at a steady, rhythmic pace and waving their arms in serpentine patterns. Their robes and faces were streaked with a substance that shone in the dark, and the leader of their procession wore an immense living serpent about his neck. "Open to receive the Goddess's light!" he cried as he swayed, and his followers shouted, "All praise to the Queen of Broken Light!"

Miri and Dahim retreated deeper into their alley. "Servants of the Broken Light!" Miri hissed. "I thought Bethnarian banished them."

"Once upon a time he did," answered Dahim. "But his rule fails, his soldiers patrol less often, and the sects multiply. Rumor has it that the Empyreor has embraced many strange faiths in his quest for healing."

"Nonsense," Miri retorted, "Bethnarian is no superstitious fool, whatever his subjects may be. How barbaric this place seems to me now!"

"Were the Midlanders so much more cultivated? From what I hear, they are provincial in the extreme."

Miri had to smile. "Provincial, yes, and quiet-living. But they school their children and avoid the more wanton cruelties."

Dahim clucked, "I fear the Empyre is too old and vast to ever be so kind. Perhaps the best we can hope for is that its decadence will inure it to the peculiar perversities of the Sect of the Broken Light."

"Meaning?"

Dahim's solicitous hand guided her onto a wider way. "You know their prophecies about the destruction of the Empyre? Well, lately they have begun to speak of the author of that destruction, an immortal god-prince borne by a woman of Empyreal blood. The Empyress of Night they call her. The queen-dam of their longed for destroyer."

"They dare to use the term Empyress?"

"Shocking, isn't it? The word used to cost a man his tongue, if not his life, but these days the Servants proclaim it to the skies, and no one dares complain."

"When — when is this queen due to arrive?"

"The Servants say she is already among us, preparing to birth her son into the world on the Festival of the Ninth Moon."

They had reached the foot of the wide steps leading up to the chocolate house. Miri paused. "I've never really believed in magic, Dahi," she said, "Do you?"

Dahim shrugged, "People I trust believe in it."

"And you trust this man?"

"I do not know, cousin? I know him as a very astute, very discrete businessman, but there are other stories —" Dahim gazed up the steps.

"Some people say he can predict the future, extract truth from lies, make fortunes or break them. But he is an outsider."

Miri laid a hand on her cousin's arm. "And what did it cost you to persuade this 'outsider' to see us?"

"That does not matter now." Dahim coughed. He slipped her arm around his. "You asked me for help, and once, a long time ago, you helped me."

Miri nodded, and together they mounted the wide steps.

At the top was the arbor-shaded terrace belonging to one of the city's finest chocolate houses. Here, beneath silken lanterns hung so as to cast pools of colored light, the highborn denizens and merchant princes of the city lounged, ate candied fruit, and talked politics while sipping the bitter drink that only they could afford.

Dahim and Miri found the object of their search seated at a low table tucked into a quiet corner with an excellent view of one wall of the Empyreal compound. He sat alone drinking wine, instead of the ubiquitous chocolate.

"Good evening to you, Master Scryos," bowed Dahim.

The other man raised his head, rose smoothly to his feet. "Ah, Lord Merchant Rujak," he returned, bowing back in a wave of gray-silk sleeve.

"Allow me to present the widow Dahar, a relation of mine by marriage," said Dahim, smiling up at the taller man.

Scyros bowed again, and Miri found herself riveted by the tall stranger's cool but unequivocal countenance.

The master named Scryos had hair and eyes as dark as any desert nomad, and he wore his loose Southern attire like a native, but his feet were shod in spurred boots instead of slippers, and the cast of his sun-tanned features was foreign.

With a gesture at once gracious and austere, Master Scryos bade them sit. "I did not know, Dahim, that you were a connoisseur of chocolate," he said as he gestured to a server.

"It is, I confess, rather rich for my tastes," Dahim admitted. "But every now and then I indulge."

"Allow me to indulge you tonight."

Dahim bent his head in acceptance.

"And what would please your lady companion?" asked Scryos, following protocol by addressing the male escort of the woman to whom he had only just been introduced.

"Chocolate?" Dahim asked Miri, and Miri gave him the faintest of nods.

The server backed away.

"Your company is an unexpected pleasure, Lord Rujak," continued Scryos. "I was just regretting having to spend such a fine evening alone."

Is this man even capable of regret? thought Miri and dropped her gaze as Scryos' eyes flicked her way.

The two men conversed languidly about the weather, the price of goods, and the problems of provisioning caravans while Miri sat still and silent. She found it a relief to do so for it gave her time to think. This Scryos was far more than she had expected, and she was trying to decide how much she wanted to confide in him.

When the chocolate came, Miri slid her cup carefully under her veil, and all three members of the unlikely party fell into a companionable silence, the two Southerners sipping chocolate while Scryos swirled his wine. Miri could feel Dahim searching for a polite way of introducing the real purpose of their visit.

At last Dahim set down his half-empty cup and spoke. "It is generous of you, Master Scryos, to share your news on the trade. Your own successes are legendary."

"Oh?" said the gentleman.

Dahim cleared his throat faintly. "You must know that many of my fellow merchants credit you with extraordinary abilities.

Scryos looked mildly amused. "Is that so?"

Dahim hung on to his uncomfortable subject. "They say you can divine the truth about many things."

The tall man smiled. "So now they are calling me a diviner."

Dahim looked away, but Miri leapt at the opening, raising her eyes to the Scyros and saying, "It is my . . . daughter. She has gone missing, and I was told that you might be able to help me find her."

"Your daughter," said the tall foreigner with a smile dangerously close to a sneer playing about the corners of his mouth.

Miri looked down at her folded hands. "She disappeared several days ago, while visiting one of the poorer quarters of the city. Her escort thought that she might have been taken by slavers." She passed a hand over her eyes, surprised to find herself weeping over her own lie.

"Look at me," Scryos commanded.

And Miri raised her eyes to a stare like a black awl. She began to tremble.

The tall man moved as if to rise.

"Wait!" Miri reached for and caught his wrist. It was a brazen gesture, but she was desperate past caring. "I wish to know where to

look for her. But if I cannot know that, I need to know that she lives."
Real tears were trickling down her face.

The Scryos looked at her hand, then stabbed her with his eyes.
"Give me the item you brought with you," he commanded.

Miri yanked her hand back as if it had been burned.

Scryos waited, and Miri swallowed her astonishment, fumbled at
her sash, and drew forth a delicate piece of carved ivory.

Scryos lifted the little comb out of her fingers and held it to up to
the lantern light. Plucking from its teeth a single long strand of hair, he
looked at the strand for a long time and then his mouth curved in a
smile of perfect serenity. "Nobly born. Nobly besieged," he said.
"Look for her in the places of the noble dead."

From beneath the eaves of the chocolate house, another man, his
face shrouded by a light hood, observed the threesome's odd exchange.

It had taken Jazim, Prince of Serpents, some time to locate Inimiri
Dahar's hiding place—a delicate piece of work made even trickier by
the agents of the family Carnis, who had their own reasons for wanting
to tie up this particular loose end.

Until tonight he had been content to let his spies monitor her
movements. She was neither threat nor help to him at this point. But
when his men announced that her cousin was inquiring into the
whereabouts of the foreigner called Scryos, Jazim moved to take matters
into his own hands.

Now, as he watched the tall Northlander exiting the chocolate
house, he wondered if his overconfidence had caught him out. The
scene he had just witnessed added a new layer of complexity to an
already troubling situation. On the surface, the man called Scryos lived
like a wealthy exile, dabbling in trade and lurking about the margins
of Southern society. In actuality, he managed a complex network of
mercenaries and spies, one that might surpass Jazim's in size and
influence. For years Jazim had longed to penetrate that network, only
to have the Empyreor himself forbid him to interfere on the grounds
that Scryos' schemes had nothing to do with the Empyre.

But now Jazim wondered if there might have been more behind
the Empyreor's command. Bethnarian was as canny and ruthless a
ruler as the South had ever seen. It was unlike him to turn his back on
any threat, even a small one, and Scryos' had connections to the Sards
that went very deep.

Rising from his seat, the Prince of Serpents prepared to follow the
small couple now scurrying from the chocolate house. At the same

time, he considered carefully what he already knew, that the man who called himself Scryos was the only male to circulate in Sardic society without wearing the bands of bondage.

Chapter 14: Awakening

Down in the deeps of Sun Palace, Beth brewed rebellion despite being steeped in luxury and indulged in her every whim.

She wasn't fooled by all the petting and pampering. She knew that she was a prisoner, just as she knew that her jailers' indulgences had less to do with her than the child she carried. The Lady Carnis wanted Beth's baby. She looked upon it as some sort of god, and she would do all she could to ensure its safety, even if it meant taking abuse from its useless mother.

Understanding this, Beth pressed her advantage.

She demanded things — clothing, baubles, furniture. And, as the exorbitance of her demands grew, the real battles began. Beth turned up her nose at their proposed compromises, whined and complained, refused to eat, stamped her feet, and generally made a royal pain of herself. She proved marvelously gifted at it. She was after all both an expectant mother and a princess.

She pouted and complained until her chamber overflowed with lovely objects, and her captors nearly fell over themselves trying to appease her. In particular, they liked plying her with food, dishes fit for an Empyreor's table. They fed her so much, so often that Beth expected to grow fat. Only her belly swelled; the rest of her remained thin, much to the concern of the Lady Carnis.

At first the Lady was the only person besides the omnipresent Urttah to visit Beth's underground chamber, but when Beth complained of loneliness, a few other thickly veiled women arrived. They never showed her their faces, but they sewed for her and read to her and tried to coax her into conversation, until Beth began shouting at them to go away. She shouted so loud that L'eret Carnis came running. The women never returned, but A'Carnis reappeared. His company, unlike the women's, proved amusing, so she permitted him to return. Return he did, nearly every day, bringing with him such little luxuries as ladies like — fresh flowers and perfumes, swaths of richly colored fabric. Beth never truly trusted him, but as the days passed, she warmed to his cajoling ways. He was an informative as well as diverting companion, and Beth could revel in the fact that L'eret Carnis bitterly disapproved of his visits.

Today, he was entertaining her with a strategy game called Kafaq and the gossip of Sun Court. "You could have heard a feather hit the floor," A'Carnis said, as he moved a game tile.

"You expect me to believe that a prince's wife would wear pantaloons to court?" Beth's expression dripped doubt as her eyes moved up and down the table.

"But she did! Bright red ones and belted with gems."

"I don't believe it! Miri always said that no respectable woman shows so much as an ankle bone."

"Oh, her pants hid her ankles. They were quite voluminous—her pants, I mean. In fact, they might have passed for a skirt if she had stayed still." A'Carnis laughed. "Instead she flaunted the split in her legs, disgusted the Empyreor, and humiliated her husband. I fear that his reputation will never recover."

"And the lady herself?"

"She was beaten of course, in full view of the prince's entire household. Her legs will never again be worth flaunting."

Beth gasped, "How horrible!"

"I couldn't have put it better myself. A woman in pantaloons is hideous!"

"I was talking about the lady's beating. She may have broken with custom, but did she deserve such treatment? Whom did she slight or harm?"

"Besides her husband, you mean?" A'Carnis was laughing wholeheartedly now. "There are few crimes more serious than breaking with custom, Highness! Murder and treason perhaps. I fear your time away from the Empyre has corrupted you terribly."

Beth arched a delicate brow. "Because I think women should have the right to choose some things for themselves?"

A'Carnis pretended to choke. "In the patriarchal Empyre? You jest with me, Great One."

"Women are thinking beings, Lord Carnis."

"Did I ever say otherwise? You have met my mother, have you not? She plots circles around most men then drowns them like unwanted puppies. But even she bows to propriety because she understands that there is only one thing men fear more than the power of other men, and that is the power of women. With good reason. Women give birth to us, nurse us, rear us, and seduce us no matter how high we rise." He was looking at her intensely now, his gaze deep and his voice earnest. Almost, he looked like a man in love. Then the look evaporated, leaving behind his customary mien of princely boredom. In a more normal tone of voice, he added, "Besides no woman really wants other women to wield power. Jealousy is woman's vice, and insurance for our twisted and perverse code of conduct."

"Which code of conduct is that?"

"The code, princess, that calls concubinage and wife-beating exercises in nobility, and the wearing of pantaloons a lashable offense. The same code that regards an overtly independent woman as slightly more dangerous than a full-on traitor."

"I cannot believe the women are so minded."

"You might think differently if you had seen their faces when their foolish sister entered in pantaloons. I tell you every female eye flashed a death sentence, and every male's a rape."

"If that is true. It is no wonder your mother speaks of men with such . . . dislike."

"Dislike! Hah, call it what it is — disdain."

"So she really does despise them?"

"Every one of them, including me. My mother is three-fourths Sard, and Sards are matriarchal. Women rule the tribe, and one's position in the society is determined by one's mother."

"A society ruled by women," Beth mused and moved a tile. "And what of the men?"

A'Carnis answered the move. "The men are slaves. The most powerful warrior has less status than the lowest woman."

Beth chewed on that. "Even a woman's husband?"

A'Carnis' laugh held nothing of humor in it. "Sardic women don't marry! Not by choice. They keep stables. Children never even know who their fathers are."

"But the men are physically stronger. Why don't they revolt?"

"And risk having their throats cut on some bloody altar? Sardic women have terrible powers, highness. And they worship cruel gods."

"There is one male your mother seems to honor." Beth lifted her eyes to his, held them. "My son."

"Because you, my queen, are a demigoddess, and your child will be the true god who delivers the Empyre back to its first people."

"The Sards," said Beth.

"So you *are* reading the book I gave you." A'Carnis raised an admiring brow. "Very sneaky."

Beth couldn't quite suppress her own smile. She shoved one of her tiles forward. "So, is that why your mother married an Empyreal prince, so that she could pave the way for her people's second coming?"

"My mother was a political hostage."

"She was forced to marry your father."

"Yes. Not that she suffered the degradation for long. She poisoned him when I was small."

Beth's pretense of polite interest folded. She looked up to see the Prince's face bleeding horror. "You know this?" she whispered.

"I saw her do it."

"Why are you telling me?"

"So you'll be ready when the time comes."

"Ready for what?"

A'Carnis' voice dipped low. "To deal justly with her. You have the power, and you have seen how handy she is with drugs. Imagine what she is planning to do with them once you have given up the thing she really covets." A'Carnis was leaning toward her now, all suggestion of urbanity gone.

"You would side with me over your own mother?" Beth breathed.

"My mother has already sided against me."

Beth had heard enough. A'Carnis's words were stirring the cold consciousness inside of her, which had already been restless of late. It seemed to hunger, and its hunger was now directed at the blue-eyed man. To quiet it, she gathered her skirts, rose, and took a few steps away from the table.

Immediately, she heard — no, felt — him close in. He was standing right behind her, close enough to wrap his arms about her.

"You presume, my prince," she said warningly.

"I do," he murmured to her ear, still without touching her. "And for that offense, I offer up my life. Let her do with it what she wills for I have seen her in all her glory." Beth turned around. Their faces were no more than a breath apart, and she could feel the cold consciousness licking its lips over the lusciousness of him. *Down*, she thought with the force of that coldness, and A'Carnis dropped to his knees.

"And do you see me now?" Beth breathed.

"Now and always. When I close my eyes at night and when I open them to the sun. I cannot *not* see you, my queen." His fierce blue eyes dilated to darkness. "Once I was lost in the dark, but at last, I have seen the light. And she is glorious. So long as I live I will serve her and her fire."

He caught her hands and set his lips to them. Beth felt the strength and heat in those hands. Even more palpable was the admiration coursing through from him. It was like cool water to a person lost in a desert. Reaching out with some sense beyond sense, she took a deep draught of it, tasted nectar, and felt the cold awareness roar to life.

Chapter 15: Life Among the Dead

Shrieks rang through the huge well's deep spaces, starting as low groans and building to high screams that caromed off the wet stone.

In the smaller room beyond the chamber of pouring waters, three veiled women struggled to restrain a savagely writhing form. "Let me go!" shrieked their silk-swathed prisoner. A delicate claw shot out of the tangle of limbs and drove diagonally into the face of one of the women. She fell back with a shriek, her veil ripped, her cheek raked to blood.

"Quiet!" cried Lady Carnis from the doorway. Ripping off her own veil, she yelled at the scarred woman standing at the princess' head. "How long has she been like this?"

"Some time," replied Urttah impassively.

The lady dashed forward running restless eyes over the struggling woman. "Why didn't you give her something?"

"I did," Urttah answered flatly, "She should be sleeping now." Urttah's eyes rested on the sweat-sheened head below her. With one hand, she lightly grazed the damp hair, now plastered in sweat-darkened tendrils across the contorted features of the face. For a moment the princess quieted. The cobalt blue eyes opened. "Please make it stop!" she begged. Then the lids screwed shut, and the furious writhing began again.

"By the Infernal, what happened?" Lady Carnis demanded.

"Ask him!" said Urttah pointing in the direction of one sloping wall.

A'Carnis stood against that wall, motionless, pallid, his eyes locked on the writhing woman.

Flicking her robes behind her, the lady of Carnis stalked to him. "You fool!" she spat. "What have you done?"

His eyes tracked the princess' face. He seemed not to hear.

The Lady raised a clenched fist and drove it hard into his handsome face.

Her son's head jerked sideways, but his attention turned on her with ponderous slowness.

"Again I ask you, what have you done?"

"She did it," said A'Carnis slowly, "to me." Already his eyes were shifting back to the desperate struggle.

"Please!" wailed the princess in piteous tones.

Lady Carnis grabbed his chin in one steel-tipped claw. The many rings on her hand sparked. "If the child is harmed — You will tell me exactly what happened!" Muttering low she began to summon the power to compel him.

Her son's hands shot forward, shoved her violently. The Lady Carnis sprawled, her head snapped back, and with a crack that split the air, struck stone. She spasmed once and grew still.

A'Carnis ignored it. He waded into the tangle of stunned women, shoving the two nearest aside, and hoisted the princess into his arms. Without a word he carried her from the room.

The veiled women cawed in dismay and fluttered toward L'eret Carnis like confused crows. Urttah ignored them also and stalked after the son instead.

A'Carnis was in the center of the waterfall room. Laying the moaning princess upon the grating, he heaved at a large section of grating, pulling it upward and revealing a narrow ribbon of tiled stair leading into deeper depths.

"Where are you taking her?" Urttah rasped.

"Out of this hell hole."

The burned woman clucked. "If you take her from this charmed place, we may not be able to hold her."

A'Carnis' grimace became a snarl. "Hold her! Witch, you should worship her!"

Urttah's cackled a warning. "The ancient charms cool her fire, protect her as well as the child."

"Right now they are killing her."

The princess moaned as he hefted her again in his wiry arms. Cradling her head against his collarbone, he began the tricky descent, leaving Urttah to follow after using one hand to slide the incredibly heavy grating back into place.

"If you do this Lord Carnis, beware," she warned as she followed him down a midnight corridor.

The Prince was murmuring to Beth. "You want open air and sunlight, don't you, my queen? I know. I have heard you protesting the cold."

The princess gave a small sob.

Urttah came abreast of the Prince, now holding high a lantern that illuminated wedges of their strange surroundings. They had left the narrow corridor beneath the ancient court of veils and entered a bizarre warren of disintegrating rooms, the remains of a different and long forsaken Empyre. Splendor there was in those rooms, and great treasure. But little of it was visible now. Gold and lapis lazuli, silver-trimmed malachite and pearl, ivory and jade—all reposed under a thick veil of dust and a hush as deep as the grave.

As they passed beneath a set of intricate arches carved like festoons of lace, Urttah redirected the Prince's footsteps. "This way. We must not pass too close to *her* den."

A'Carnis halted, his eyes probing the shadows. "Even here," he muttered. "Gods!"

"Yessss," cackled Urttah. "She senses the young one's power and aches for her revenge." She pointed. "This corridor will take us to the necropolis. There is power among the tombs of a different sort that may ease her suffering."

A'Carnis followed the corridor to an elaborate stair paved in black marble and topped in doors of stone barred in iron. Huge and heavy, those doors were, made to withstand assaults from forces beyond man's imagination, but so cleverly hung that when unbarred they swung open to the press of a single hand.

They stepped into fresh air and sunshine. The sky overhead was pale blue, and before them stood a gateway to a city of stone monuments, the resting places of the great lords and ladies of the Empyre.

A'Carnis looked down and smiled to see the princess' blue-tinged lids open lazily, unveiling a deeper blue.

"Come," beckoned Urttah, pulling the hood of her robe low. She hunched into the voluminous fabric and hurried up an alley running between lavish tombs toward a hilltop crowned with the most extravagant tombs of all. These were the mausoleums of the dead Empyreors, and they encircled the only living thing to permanently inhabit that sacred ground, a tree so massive and old it dwarfed the great tombs about it.

When Beth touched A'Carnis's mind to redirect the thoughts and feelings inside him, she altered something in herself as well. It was as if a key snicked inside a rusty lock, and a door flew open, permitting energy like wildfire to surge through her and scour the softer, weaker places clean. New channels were seared across her mind and will. In an instant, she was being broadened, made larger, more expansive. She was also being hollowed out.

That aspect of the experience was terrible enough, but as the energy bored deeper, it unleashed a chaos of emotion, feelings so various, deep and rich that Beth felt she would go mad under the onslaught of them.

At first she thought these feelings came from deep down inside her, but as she struggled to accommodate them, she realized that they were different, alien. In fact they poured from the people around her—the women in the room, the prince called A'Carnis, and the thousands of distant but still vital beings who scurried like ants through the palace rooms above. Just as she had tasted the sickness and fear of the dying Empyreor on the day she entered the Well, so she now tasted the feelings of the Empyreor's subjects and servants. Terror and delight, anger and satisfaction, lust and love—they gushed upon her like a nectar of the gods too rich for mortal palate until she felt she must split at the seams.

All she could do was scream and scream and pray for release, weeping fleetingly for the second, more fragile life she carried within her.

An ordinary woman would have died. But where Beth's human self failed, a stranger, inhuman heritage blossomed. The cold consciousness took over, sipping, then gulping at the emotions passing into her, consuming the choicest ones and growing stronger and fatter until it began to fill in the newly hollowed cavities within her.

The physical pain of transformation eased, and the spiritual suffering increased tenfold.

She screamed from terror now as well as pain. The Beth she had been, had believed herself to be, was burning away, and being replaced by a cold, clear ruthlessness. She tried to fend that ruthless consciousness off, just as she fought the hands that tried to hold her down, but she could not escape the fire infecting her blood.

Then, mercifully, warmth struck her face, and a gentle pulling like roots tugged her earthward. The cold consciousness receded, and she was Beth again.

She fluttered her lids open and beheld a softly shifting pattern of cool blue and deep green. She felt as light and resonant as the many-chambered shells the sea throws up on the Empyre's western shores. At the same time, she felt possessed of a newfound strength, like ore purified by heat and hammer into a delicate but strong blade.

"She seems better now," a masculine voice said.

Gingerly she turned her head. A'Carnis was bending over her, and behind him hunched the scarred figure of Urttah. "My baby?" Beth said, lacking the energy to fill out the question.

A'Carnis glanced behind him.

Urttah exulted. "He thrives. The power is much to his taste."

Beth closed her eyes in disgust and spoke to A'Carnis. "Where?"

"We are in the Empyreal necropolis."

Beth sighed, opened her eyes to the limbs of the great tree arching over her. "A burial ground."

194

"You needed fresh air, Great Lady," he murmured.

"The fresh air of the dead," whispered Beth. She tried to laugh, coughed instead.

"The dead know rest, and they tell no secrets," rasped Urttah. "You asked for sunlight. Here you will have it. Here you can walk in the daylight and still remain hidden."

"No," said Beth, the new-forged steel in her body breaking into her voice. "No more hiding. I will see my father now. Either you take me to him, or I will go myself."

A'Carnis threw a questioning look at the witch, but Urttah spoke with a note of triumph in her voice. "Rest and recover first, and then we will go."

When Beth felt stronger, A'Carnis carried her to Moon Tower. This long abandoned tower, built in a style radically different from the rest of the buildings in the palace compound, stood on the northern edge of the great necropolis like a sign post for the dead. For long years only rats and bats inhabited it. Recently, its upper floors had been swept clean and furnished by Urttah herself. It was to one of these upper floors that the witch directed A'Carnis, and it was in one of the upper rooms that the princess, curled upon a divan, dreamed the old dream.

She was little child again and lying in the long, low bed where her nurses always laid her. She was supposed to be asleep; but she lay awake worrying about the strange shadows the lighted lamp cast into the room's corners and hangings. Sometimes she heard voices in the shadows, and those voices frightened her.

In an effort to make herself invisible to them, she lay very still and quiet beneath the blankets while the lamp's teardrop of flame dwindled and the shadows grew larger.

"Little one," came a voice a shade louder than the child's own breathing. "Precious one, come to me."

Little Bethnara tried not to move. She screwed her eyes up tight and hung on to her blanket. But the voice was persistent and growing louder. "Little one, I need you," it whispered as it sidled closer. "It's Mother. Come to me."

Bethnara quaked. Her mother should not be here. Her mother was dead. She had died when Bethnara was born and now rested with the other dead queens in the great necropolis behind the palace.

But the voice entreated her again and again by the name of mother while little Bethnara shook harder. She did not want to go with the owner of the voice. She knew that those who were carried to the necropolis never returned. She had been to the houses of the dead when her great father's second queen died. She remembered how cold and dark those houses were. She remembered how the hollowed-out faces of the older dead had lifted empty eye sockets to the gold and silver ceiling of the Empyreal vault.

The voice loomed close, closer than it had ever been. It seemed to speak to her from the shadows just beneath her bed. "Little one, darling one, let Mother care for you."

"No, no, no, go away," whispered the terrified child, gathering her knees under her. Something beneath the bed was moving, slithering across the floor, creeping up the side of her mattress. Bethnara bolted, turning and leaping the other way, dashing to the door across the room.

When she reached the empty corridor, she stopped, turned slowly back to look. The room and its wide bed were empty in the lamp's soft glow. Only the shadows jiggled.

Then long white arms grabbed her from behind, yanked her in tight, and Bethnara screamed and screamed as hands on those arms plunged long white fingers straight into her child's heart.

The dream chased Beth from sleep, so that she woke frightened and terribly disoriented. But she wasn't alone—Urttah skulked close by, ready to feed her, dress her, carry her across the floor.

It took her three days to grow strong enough to walk any distance, and as soon as she did, she went in search of her mother, disdaining Urttah's hisses of scorn. She found that enigmatic lady among the gilded tombs of the tree-crowned hillside, in the massive mausoleum of the Betanari Empyreors. Bethnarian's first queen was memorialized by her name and family insignia—a heraldic design of a shield resting against a sprawling tree surmounted by a sickle moon. Beth interrogated the emblem as she tried to piece splinters of history into a portrait of the woman who'd given birth to her. The image she arrived at was faceless, voiceless, and full of contradictions—beauty and fear, love and despair. She thought of the long years spent in exile, of the unearthly beauty and power of the father of her child, of the power building inside her, and she could not help but curse the woman who had abandoned her into these troubles.

Her curses faltered as fresh footsteps profaned her solitude. Up the tomb-fronted avenue came four half-naked men clad in long white loincloths. They carried on their shoulders the ends of long poles strung with silver buckets full of sacred water. But they moved slowly, arms outstretched like blind men, for they were blind, and deaf and dumb as well. They had been made so in a ceremony of mutilation as old as the Empyre itself, for they were the caretakers of the great tree, and every few days they marched forth to water its roots, which were said to bind the spirits to the earth.

Beth pressed herself into an embrasure as they passed, repulsed by the idea of such mute, blind subservience to the dead. Laying a protective hand over the child in her belly, she hurried away. It would not be long now, Urttah had said, before the baby was born. A month or so, no more. It was time she quit interrogating the dead and confronted the living instead.

She set off for the palace and came upon Urttah and A'Carnis instead. They stood by the gateway leading to the great necropolis doors as if guarding it. Beth stiffened, clenching her fists. She had been prepared to face the witch for the scarred woman was never very far away now, anxious to ensure the health of mother and growing child. But A'Carnis came as both an unexpected and unwelcome sight.

"Why are you here, Prince?" she demanded, her voice sharpened by alarm at the stirring of the cold consciousness inside her. "Urttah told me that your mother is ill."

A'Carnis brilliant blue eyes flashed into Urttah's. "My mother is dying, Highness," he bowed. "Her skull has been broken."

"All the more reason for you to remain by her side," snapped Beth.

"She will not miss me. I hoped that you, my queen, might. I come bearing gifts."

"I have no time for gifts," retorted Beth. "I go to find my father." She moved to walk between them.

A'Carnis cut her off, spoke humbly. "The gifts I bring, Highness, are meant to enarmor you for that meeting."

Beth's smile mocked him. "You are trying to divert me, Highness, but it will not work. I said I would see my father, and I will."

"How? By losing yourself in a warren of tunnels you do not know how to navigate, or by throwing yourself on the mercy of the Empyreal guard?" A'Carnis's voice soothed, but his light-blue eyes blazed concern. "How will that guarantee you the audience you seek? Is it not more like to earn you a cell in an Empyreal dungeon?"

"Let us help you," rasped Urttah.

Beth flung her arms wide in exasperation. "When?"

"Tonight." hissed Urttah.

"Tonight," confirmed A'Carnis. "When the Empyreor retires."

"You would conduct me to him?"

"I would. I told you as much," rasped Urttah. "No Empyreor can hide from me."

Beth narrowed her eyes, "Why should I believe you?"

"Come to the tower and see," suggested A'Carnis.

A nut-brown girl stood in Beth's tower apartment. Small, but well-proportioned, and wearing a bronze collar like a manacle about her neck, she prostrated herself on the stone floor as soon as the prince and princess appeared.

A'Carnis moved to look down on her. "I believe you have wished for a more gentle and pleasant companion than this old hag," he said with a negligent wave at Urttah. He prodded the girl with his toe. "Rise," he ordered. "Let the great queen examine you."

"Who is she?" said Beth confusedly.

"A slave of mine. She was taken in a raid on the desert of Nom, but she has served me faithfully for some years now." Beth watched the way A'Carnis caught the girl's jaw in his hand. It was a possessive gesture that made Beth curious about the connection between them. Immediately, the cold consciousness leapt to oblige her, sucking in a spicy brew of emotion that left her in no doubt as to the nature of master and servant's relationship. She was not surprised. It was no secret that the Princes of the Empyre made free with their slaves and servants.

"What makes you think I want one of your bed slaves for a maid?" snapped Beth.

A'Carnis turned in surprise, releasing the girl. "If I have overstepped—" he began.

Beth flicked a hand for silence. "Send her away."

"Naj here is thoughtful and dutiful and entirely loyal."

"To you."

"And since I am entirely yours, my queen, she must be." His voice cajoled while the feelings emanating from him poured over Beth thick and sweet as honey.

"Let her stay, my queen," rasped Urttah, and Beth looked at her in surprise. "We must prepare you to meet your father. The girl will be useful."

"Just so," said A'Carnis, brightening. "And that brings me to the second part of my gift." He snapped his fingers at the girl, and she backed quickly out of the room then returned a moment later, holding a wisp of cloud studded with miniature moons and stars.

"What is this?" snapped Beth.

"A gown fit for the Empyre's queen," said A'Carnis, bowing low.

198

The girl Naj lifted the gown higher so that the sprinkling of diamonds and seed pearls sewn to the fine lawn shimmered.

Naj bathed and dressed her new mistress, and shortly after sunset, Urttah and Prince Carnis escorted Beth into the underground palace. The Princess peered into the buried rooms in wonder. "What is the place?" she asked.

Urttah's voice rattled across the floor. "A part of the Empyre that was, the one the usurpers' wish to forget."

"Why does no one use it now?"

"For the same reason they do not use Moon Tower," volunteered A'Carnis. "It is a haunted place." The prince was acting edgy, almost nervous

Urttah snorted. "And so it is. Quiet."

Beth had assumed that they would pass back through the watery Court of Veils to access the inhabited areas of the palace, but they did not. Instead Urttah led them to a tall but narrow door fitted with an enormous lock. Carved upon this door were figures of naked men and women writhing as if in torment, centered in it was the more familiar image of a beautiful woman crowned with serpents.

Quickly and silently Urttah lifted the bars. Then she fitted a key into the lock and turned on the princess and A'Carnis. "We must go quickly and quietly here and in the dark," she hissed. She grabbed Beth's suddenly cold hands and pressed a fold of her robe into them.

"Keep hold," she rasped.

Beth nodded, and A'Carnis doused the light.

They heard a key turn, the door open. A breath of air like the wind that runs before a grass fire smote Beth's face, hot and dry and tinged with smoke. Then it was gone, and she was being pulled through the door and pressed aside. The door closed, the lock turned, and they shuffled forward as quickly as their searching feet would allow. They could not have gone more than thirty paces before Beth heard another lock turning. Another door opened on a very narrow hall lit by a single small wall lantern.

At the end of this very narrow passage was a stair that went up and up to another narrow corridor with a couple of openings onto other passageways, but Beth saw no other lanterns, and there were no windows to admit outdoor light.

At last they faced a third door, which Urttah also unlocked with a key. It opened into a pillared rotunda of a room whose curving walls were covered entirely with shelves of books and scrolls.

"You, wait," Urttah said to A'Carnis.

The prince gave her a mocking bow, then caught Beth's hand in his two strong ones. "You are the hope of this Empire, my queen," he said. "Make the Empyreor see it as you have made me."

Urttah broke his hold with a wrench of her own melted fingers and tugged the princess forward. Beth was slow to respond. She was absorbed in the surroundings — the pillared library with its marble floors and gilt and leopard-skin divans, the wide passageway opening onto a golden anteroom of rich carpets and gemstone mosaics. So much of what she saw fanned the embers of distant memory, but none of it was as powerful as the taste and smell of death and fear that came pouring into her. It was the same death and fear that had assaulted her on the first day she entered the palace, and it made the cold consciousness lick a thousand tongues.

Passing between a pair of golden doors, Urttah towed her to a much smaller room dominated by a long, low table layered with parchment and a great low bed covered with cloth of gold. At the table sat a man in silk of purest white and wrist guards of finely beaten gold. It was from this man that the waves of pain and fear beat.

Urttah swept forward. She did not announce herself, and she did not bow.

The man's head came up. Beth saw the light from the crystal-paned lamps on his desk chisel out the planes of his face, the curve of his finely aquiline nose. She pressed a hand to her mouth.

In a voice thinned by illness, the man said, "What do you want, witch? Is your mistress hungry again? Four strong youths have I offered her this month, and now she craves a fifth?"

The faded voice faltered.

Urttah cackled, "No, Bethnarian, self-styled Empyreor. I am come on another matter."

The seated Empyreor and the hideously scarred woman glared at each other. Then the Empyreor turned his head and stared full on the breathtaking sight hovering at his chamber door.

The bitterly tired expression on his face never changed as he took in the form of his daughter — tall, white, and slender as a water sprite dripping diamond and pearl — but Beth felt the shock waves rocking his inner world. They crashed like ocean waves into the hollow spaces within her and set the cold consciousness singing in triumph.

Bethnarian, Empyreor of the South, Scion of the Sun, turned back to the witch woman. "I told you I did not want to see her."

"She wanted to see you," returned Urttah. "Is she not beauty itself to behold?"

200

With arms enfeebled, the Empyreor pressed himself to his feet. Breathing hard, he limped across the black marble floor until he stood before his daughter. Bent by time and care he had to look up to study her face. "Oh yes," he said his voice dripping disgust. "Beautiful as the stars that flame to earth, beautiful as a killing frost, beautiful as the kiss of death to a suffering man."

Beth heard the acid in his words but could not react to it for the roaring hunger his powerful feelings evoked in her. Then the Empyreor smiled and briefly became the man a lonely little princess remembered. Beth shoved the daemon hunger down and away, and the roaring subsided.

"Have you come to kill me, daughter?" her father said.

It took Beth a moment to digest those words. "No," she whispered, horror stricken. "How could you think so?"

"Pity. It is what you were born to do, and there is little enough I savor in life any more." He looked down at the swell of her belly. "I see you are a woman now, and have already met the man, the one whose seed could survive you. Almost I wish I could live to see the fiend call down destruction on this nest of vipers."

He turned away, shuffled up to the fire. "Why are you here, if not to pull the Sun Scepter from my hands and plunge it into my heart?"

She might have said I come for your blessing, Father, or I come to prove myself a dutiful daughter, Father, but she knew now that her darkest memories of him had not lied. He had never loved her, never wanted her.

"I've come for answers and, when you are dead, to offer what leadership I can to our people," she said.

The Empyreor laughed, "And what a glorious leader you will be with your daemon beauty and your daemon consort at your side." Bethnarian threw a sharp look into the shadows beyond the doors. "Where is he?"

Beth lowered her head, the diamond pins in it sparkling like tears. "He is not here."

"He lies in wait then?"

The tears were real now, welling up in her eyes, falling like a scattering of gems. "No, Father, I fled him many, many months ago."

Suddenly, she was across the room on her knees before her terrible sire and holding pleading hands up to him. "Oh, Father, I know I have done wrong. You were right to doubt my fitness, my purity. I was weak. I gave myself up to something both more and less than a man. But as I am your daughter, I am willing to do all I can to make amends for it. I gave him up to prove my loyalty to you and the Empyre, in hopes that you might one day find me a worthy daughter. I will give up even this child if you demand it."

She heard the sharp hiss of Urttah's indrawn breath. The witch-woman was cursing, but Beth did not care. Her father was looking down at her with an unreadable expression.

"How did you meet him?"

Beth sat back on her heels and dropped her face to hide her shame. "Does it matter?"

"Oh, yes. Tell me. Was it a natural thing, or were you bewitched?"

"Bethnarian, Empyreor, you go too far," spat Urttah."

"Quiet, witch! My daughter says she came here for answers. I believe I'm entitled to a few myself."

"I met him in a wood."

"And?"

"And what else must I say. I lay with him."

"Did he woo you?"

"Yes."

"How?"

"With a look, a dance . . . a kiss," her voice sunk low as if she wished to bury her words along with the memory."

"One dance, one kiss! You are an easy morsel, daughter."

The words stung. Beth shook away the pain. "No!"

"But you wanted him."

"Yes!

"So you had him."

She was angry now. "Yes! But were it not for exile, I might never have met him. If you had only cared for me as a father should—been less the Empyreor and more the man. But you cared for your power and your reputation instead. You listened to the soothsayers, and you sent me as far away as you could, to a strange place without family, without friends. Why wouldn't I turn to the first man who wanted me? I thought he loved me."

"Love!" the Empyreor almost yelped the word. Laughter rattled in his throat, but the shades of bitterness haunting his face deepened. "You love! You!"

Beth was sobbing now. "And why shouldn't' I? The lowest slave can have love. Why not me? I wanted his love. And I wanted a parent's love. They say you loved once. You loved my mother. Miri always said her death broke your heart. I can understand how you might hate me for taking her from you, but if you honor your memory of her, shouldn't you look upon me with some favor?"

But the Empyreor's face had hardened to a mask of horror. "Loved your mother?" he said in amazement. He jerked his eyes away from the weeping woman at his knees and locked them on the hideously scarred one standing apart.

"You have not told her," he said.

"Not yet. She is not ready," responded Urttah.

"Get her out of my sight until you do," said the Empyreor and limped into the shadows beyond his chamber door.

All the next day Beth's brain beat to the terrible rhythm of her father's parting words while the cold consciousness inside her flickered like laughter. "Told me what?" she shouted at the witch-woman skulking in her chamber. "What were you supposed to tell me!" and when the scarred woman did not respond, she hurled a volume of the Empyreal chronicles at her. Urttah ducked and held her silence, and Beth hurled the full force of her flaming anger at her like a brick. "You know what he meant, witch! Tell me now, or get out!" Urttah departed, as if real bricks were being thrown at her.

Beth tore through another volume of history. Nothing. Nothing! What terrible secret were they withholding from her? She dropped her increasingly bulky body across the divan and fumed herself to quiet. Then tears began to trickle from her eyes. What evil could her mother have done to earn such hate? Beth looked at the name she had scrawled across the top margin of one of the books. Lady Janera Cyronian. Her mother. According to the chronicles, Janera came of an ancient and respected family. She had brought Bethnarian wealth, intelligence, resourcefulness, and an unimpeachable reputation. All the chroniclers said that Bethnarian had loved her well.

They were married two years before he became Empyreor, and she became pregnant with their first child only a few months after he claimed the throne. That child the Empyreor would name Bethnara.

All the chroniclers agreed that Janera had died in childbed, as Beth had been told many times. Why then did Bethnarian speak of her with such loathing? Could the relationship have been less loving than it seemed?

Recalling an interesting passage from one of the histories, Beth went searching for it and after long minutes stumbled across the desired page and paragraph. *"That the Empyreor should name Jazad commander of his armies surprised many who did not know Jazad's close connection to the daughter of the sea lord Cyronian."*

Beth bit a nail. Could Janera have been the reason for Jazad's promotion? Did the Empyreor suspect that there was more between Janera and Jazad than friendship? Might Jazad have planted a cuckoo's egg in the Empyreal nest? If so, why would the Empyreor have retained Jazad as commander of the Empyreal armies and later promoted his son to the same position? The theory seemed ridiculous.

Frustrated, she tossed the book aside and walked heavy-hearted to the great window that dominated her apartment. She could see the Empyreal city spreading out from the palace complex like a carpet, rich textures dwindling into smudges as it touched the horizon.

Moving in the twisting alleyways of that city were countless men and women, small and invisible as ants, yet free in ways she had never been. If she had not been born the unwanted child of an Empyreor, she too might have walked beneath the sun instead of skulking in shadows. The thought made her eyes sting and soon she was crying again.

When the knock on her door came, she had no voice to answer it. She waited for Urttah or Naj to enter, but A'Carnis appeared instead. "My queen," he said with a florid bow, then he saw her face and hurried to clasp her hands. "Why does the great Queen cry?" he begged in tones of genuine dismay.

Beth wanted to send him away, but she felt too weak to stand.

A'Carnis held her up, guided her to a divan.

"You need food, rest. Let me fetch you something."

"No, I'm just tired and dizzy," she said clutching one of his arms, "Just let me lean on you a moment."

He settled onto the divan, cradling her head at his collarbone. Beth could hear his heart beating, could smell and hear and feel the pulse of his devotion. That devotion was like food to the starved child inside her. It made her want to press her body close to his adoration and draw its heat into herself. She ran a hand up his chest, felt his devotion flame to full-blown desire. With her whole body, she sensed how desperately he wanted her.

Her own barely banked fires rose up, and the cold consciousness took command. She lifted her head and drew his face down to hers, relishing how he clutched her as their mouths met. His kisses were hot and sweet, but it was his love and need she wanted. She opened her mouth and drank it in, and the more she drank the greater his love and need became and the more she thirsted.

She did not know exactly when his desire turned into fear; she only knew that his fear tasted even more sumptuous than his adoration. She pulled him closer, deeper, supped on him like he was the very stuff of life itself and when he gave up his last heartbeat to her, she ate that too.

It was Naj who found them, Naj who screamed and screamed to see her lovely prince burning from the inside out while a bright-eyed daemon crouched atop him. Naj screamed, and the unbelievably beautiful daemon watched her, until Urttah, coming suddenly upon the scene, caught the desert girl by her hair and slit her throat.

The sun had turned the color of rust when Beth struggled up out of a fearsome nightmare to see Urttah bending over a strangely translucent corpse. The features of the corpse were unmistakable. They belonged to Prince A'Carnis.

In a rush, Beth remembered what she had done. Had Urttah not been there she would have run mad.

"No, no! No!" she shrieked, as the scarred woman worked to restrain her. "Tell me it isn't so. Make it go away. Make it not be so."

"Quiet, young one," rasped Urttah, squeezing the princess' wrists.

Beth pushed violently at her. "Let me go! Get out! You did this to me. I don't know how. But you did it. You are a monster," she cried, and a terrifying thought bit into her. "Gods and Daemons! What are you doing to my child? Are you trying to make him a monster too?"

"Quiet, great lady," croaked Urttah in a tone reminiscent of strain. "Only be quiet and be still, and I will take care of the rest."

"Take care, witch? You've cursed me forever. Is that why you imprisoned me here, to call up evil spirits to possess me?" But then Beth remembered A'Carnis' face, her hunger for his agony, and she sagged into her caretaker's hold sobbing uncontrollably.

Urttah eased her onto a divan, and knelt beside the stricken beauty, brushing tangled hair from flawless features. Her hideously scarred face seemed to be trying to contort itself into a mask of commiseration. "Why do you weep? Only accept what you are, revel in it, and you shall weep no more."

The incredibly blue eyes, liquid with welling tears, blinked. "And what am I?" the princess asked hollowly.

Urttah stroked the tormented head. "The culmination of centuries of effort and power. The one true heir to Empyre, terrible to mortals because you are beloved of the Gods. Remember that and forget the rest."

"I cannot forget," moaned the younger woman. "I will never forget—unless—" Her brilliant blue eyes yawned wide, and drawing on the power inside her, she leapt up, dashing the witch to the floor. In the blink of an eye she stood upon the very edge of the great tower window.

"No!" rasped Urttah, holding out a scarred claw.

Beth only smiled and shoved one slippered foot out into open air.

"Don't you dare!" cracked a voice as gently forceful as Urttah's was cruel.

Beth's head shot up.

Lady Inimiri Dahar stood in the chamber's doorway, clad in a beggar's robe and turban. "Don't you dare abandon me," she said, voice breaking on a sob, "Not after I have fought so hard to find you again."

"Miri," whispered Beth, and slid down the window's enormous casement to the tower floor.

Chapter 16: Bargains

Amber robe billowing, Jazim, Prince of Serpents, strode through the massive public chambers leading to the Empyreor's private apartments. In the gaps between enormous gilded columns, robed men and veiled women whispered together as he passed. Jazim ignored them all.

At the golden portico, he confronted sentries wearing shiny gold breastplates over long split-seam tunics of whitest linen. Their wicked looking golden pikes clashed an acknowledgement, then drew back to let him pass. In the room beyond he encountered several of his master's many adjuncts and secretaries, as well as Bethnarian's Major Domo, a man named Caphal.

"He awaits you, Highness," said this austere individual in a papery voice. Caphal gestured, and a silent body servant, face parallel to the floor, immediately ushered Jazim into a more private room. This room was large and gracious and lacking entirely in a fourth wall. Where that wall should have been an enormous terrace spread, filled with potted orange and lemon trees that had been seeded with vividly colored parrots.

The Empyreor of the South half reclined on a golden divan, while over his head massive silken fans beat, their ropes wielded by servants stationed along the edges of the room. At his feet stretched a tiger's skin. At his head knelt a veiled woman with a leather case beside her.

It had been several weeks since the Prince of Serpents had visited his master's lair. On sight, he judged Bethnarian to be as alert as ever. Yet the hollows in the Emperor's cheeks and around his eyes, the looseness of his golden cuffs, testified to the relentless progression of his disease.

The Empyreor greeted him blandly. "Welcome back, Jazim. How fares my Empyre and my army?"

Jazim bowed, casting a curious eye at the kneeling woman whose thick rope of long white-blonde hair exceeded the length of her dark veil.

When he looked back at his Empyreor, Bethnarian was watching him intently, light-blue eyes cold as a snake's.

"Does the Great One wish me to report?" Jazim asked with another glance at the woman.

The Emperor waved a negligent hand, "Of course." His cold gaze moved to the woman and warmed a degree or two.

In language so circumspect as to constitute a code that only the Empyreor could decipher, Jazim passed on information sifted from his countless agents and commanders. He touched on the deployment of men, on the activities of members of the most powerful families, on the religious fanaticism sweeping through the poorer quarters of the city.

"The Sect of the Broken Light," said the Empyreor meditatively, and he began to cough — a rough, searing sound. He pressed a swath of crumpled linen to his face.

The veiled woman moved forward on her knees to collect the blood-spattered cloth. "Great One?" she said in a soft, husky voice. She held out a small, unstoppered bottle of liquid.

Bethnarian's fit of coughing had sunk him deeper into the cushions of his divan, but he took the bottle and drank its contents. Then he held out a suddenly feeble arm to the woman.

"Allow me," said Jazim, sweeping forward to his master's aid.

"No," the Empyreor commanded in a voice that cracked. "Vyara will do it."

Jazim retreated, watching the woman with greater interest. She moved gracefully about the divan, raising the Empyreor and propping cushions about him. The light penetrating her veil gave Jazim cloudy glimpses of her figure. But it was the thick white-blonde braid of her hair that most drew his eye.

As she knelt before the Empyreor again and spoke in a low voice about treatments for pain and insomnia, Jazim watched the Empyreor's face.

At last the Empyreor motioned the young woman to her feet. "Go now, my dear," he said, "But come again early tomorrow. None of these charlatans who call themselves physicians relieve my sufferings as well as you do.

The young woman bowed deeply and departed, unaware that Jazim's gaze rested on the seductive sway of her hips.

Alone with his Lord Commander, the Empyreor held out a more imperious hand. "Come," he rasped. "Let us walk."

"Are you feeling well enough, Great One?" the Prince asked.

"Yes, yes," spat Bethnarian impatiently. "Vyara has eased my pain, and now we must speak in private. Help me up." He leaned heavily on his general's arm as they moved slowly into the grove of potted citrus trees.

"I did not know that the Lady Vyara was attending you," the Lord Commander said after a while.

"I summoned her myself. She has great talent in the healing arts."

"And you are fond of her."

Bethnarian threw him a sharp sideways look. "I am," he said.

"She has grown into a very attractive young woman."

"And a kind one. She favors her mother."

"Even more your late wife, Janera, I think."

Bethnarian's look was sly. "What are you suggesting, Jazim? Vyara is my niece."

"By marriage only, Great One."

"You cannot think I have more carnal designs upon her."

"I would not object if you did, Great One. She looks fit to bear strong sons."

Bethnarian abruptly withdrew his arm. He swayed as he stood before the Prince, but he stood, and his eyes were glacial. "I am a dead man who has already buried three queens and several more favored concubines. Vyara is a child, an adopted daughter. I will hear no more of ugly insinuations."

Jazim bowed low. "Forgive me, Great One, I did not understand." Carefully, he proffered his arm.

Bethnarian took it. "It is forgotten. I know that you cannot understand. Men like you and I must come very close to death indeed to remember the pleasure of innocence."

They walked some more, until the Empyreor asked Jazim to help him onto a bench of richly carved sandalwood. By then the Prince of Serpents had worked up the courage to broach his most prickly topic. "You have a blood daughter, Great One."

Bethnarian raised cold eyes. A slight cough shook him. "Have you found her?"

208

Jazim folded his hands behind his back. "I believe that I have. The evidence indicates that she is hiding somewhere in this palace."

The Empyreor's eyes followed the squawking flight of a yellow and blue parrot. "I know," he said.

Jazim's face betrayed none of his surprise, but behind his back, his hands clenched. "What would you have me do?" he asked.

Bethnarian watched the parrot, but spoke to the point. "You? Wasn't it you who allowed her to escape in the first place?"

Jazim sank to his knees. "Has the Great One decided on my sentence?"

"Oh, get up, you fool," hissed the Empyreor. "I forgive you. I don't even really blame you. It was I after all who ordered you to keep the nonman close."

Now surprise did break over Jazim's face. "And my incompetence which let your enemies in. Such incompetence cannot be tolerated." His amber eyes burned fiercely.

"No? Well, I will think of some suitable punishment for you. In the meantime, you will continue to serve me. You are far too prudent to do otherwise. But do not mistake me. I am as wise to my daughter's character as I am to yours. Those who attempt to wield that particular weapon against me will find that it turns in their hands, as the family Carnis has already begun to learn."

"You do not fear her?"

"Not for myself." The Empyreor began to cough into his sleeve, and a long time passed before he was able to speak again.

Jazim stared at the bright blood staining the spotlessly white garment. The Empyreor picked up the thread of his thought. "I fear for my land. What will happen to all that I, and my father, and my father's father built? What will become of the Empyre and our ways?"

"If you ask it, I will take her life myself."

"Hah! And hand them the victory?" rattled Bethnarian, laughing deep in his tattered chest. "No, no, my friend. I will keep my oaths and my power while my life lasts and see what I can make of her desire to please me."

"You have spoken with her?" said Jazim incredulously.

"I have. It is strange. The taint is unmistakable, and yet—" The Empyreor's voice trailed away, and Jazim wished he could see the thoughts churning behind the aquiline profile. "In some ways she too is an innocent."

"She is a child of the ancient darkness, Great One. I beg you, as I have before, to put her down. At least imprison her, if you dare not kill her."

"I did that once before, and what did it accomplish? I went so far to remove her from this land entirely, thinking that I might yet find a way to sire a more natural child. But I only played myself and my land right into their hands. I am cursed, and if there is any good to be salvaged from that curse, she is the key to it. You must leave her to me."

"And what of the Sards?"

Bethnarian sighed. Something like sadness eased his face into the hawkish visage of a much younger man. "I am not blind, Jazim. I too see them gathering like crows before a feast of death. They may get their feast, but you need not fear that my daughter will help them to it. The Sards are fools. They believe that the orchestration of her begetting and the heaping of offerings on the altars of daemons has earned them the blessings of their cruel gods. But gods do not bless men; they devour them. To the gods, men are just beasts built for herding and slaughter."

Bethnarian stopped speaking, for Caphal was approaching.

"Great One," bowed the Major Domo. "The representative of the one called Scryos has arrived."

Jazim held himself very still while the Empyreor granted the audience, but when Caphal moved away, Jazim made haste to voice his concern. "That one may also be mixed up in your daughter's return. I can assure you that he is thoroughly mixed up in the schemes of the Sards."

But Bethnarian only laughed weakly. "Oh, Prince Jazim, how your conscientiousness amuses me. Don't you realize that I already know?"

As the cool winds of evening swept across the city, Miri hummed and brushed her princess' hair, delighting in the thick, cool weight of the amber locks. She was at peace for the first time in weeks, so she refused to look back on the horror that she had intruded upon in reaching for that peace.

"What do you remember of my mother, Miri?" asked the princess in a weary little voice.

Miri thought carefully before answering, wielding the tortoise-shell brush mechanically. "Very little, highness. She died before I came into your father's service."

"But you visited the court when she was queen."

"A few times, yes." Brush, brush.

"What was she like?"

"Queenly, and people who knew her spoke of her as a woman of great generosity and grace."

"Is it true that my father married her because he loved her?"

Miri frowned at the bronze tresses. "Who can know besides the Empyreor himself? But there seemed to be great affection between them. I have told you as much, many times."

"Was she beautiful?"

"More striking than beautiful I would say." Brush, brush, brush.

"Then I do not favor her?" There was no hint of vanity in the question, only a profound tiredness.

Miri opened her mouth, but failed to find words.

"Did you hear me, Miri?"

"You are tall like she was."

"Was there anything strange about her?"

The brush seemed to meet resistance.

"You can tell me." The princess said softly.

"And I would, if there were anything to tell," replied Miri in a mixture of sternness and reassurance.

Beth's head turned slightly. "Then why are you afraid to answer my questions?"

The brush slipped from Miri's fingers and clattered to the floor. The waiting woman bent slowly to retrieve it. "I am not afraid."

"Don't think you can fool me, Miri. The power in me can taste your anxiety as it tasted my father's hate and A'Carnis's lust."

"Highness," hissed Miri.

"Just tell me. What was wrong with my mother?"

Miri closed her eyes. She walked around the princess and knelt down before her, resting her own warm hands on Beth's cool ones. "Nothing. Nothing was wrong with the Lady Janera. She came of an ancient and noble family; she was loved by the people, and she exuded honor and integrity."

"Then why am I evil?"

"You are not evil," Miri admonished.

"You saw what I did to A'Carnis."

Miri set the brush aside. In a voice low but firm, she said, "Do not speak of it. The Lord Carnis overreached, and fate punished him for it. There has always been power in the Empyreal House, and the wise never forget to fear it."

"So I am an instrument of fate?"

"The great are always so. Your father could tell you as much. His decisions have been life and death to many, many people. It is a cruel burden, but one that the sons and daughters of Empyreors have to bear." She rose, picked up a lock of hair and coiled it atop the princess' head.

"Do you think this power inside me comes from my mother?" asked Beth in a suddenly far-off voice.

Miri swallowed, trying to overcome the sudden dryness in her mouth. "Who am I to say?"

"Urttah has implied . . . "

"Do not trust anything that that creature tells you," hissed Miri, bending sharply to the princess' ear.

The interrogation ended there, but the shadows had drawn close about them once again, and Miri worried about the look in her princess' eyes. Suddenly, the wind's moan through the large window of the tower made her think of the whine of lost souls.

As Beth picked at her afternoon meal, Urttah slipped into the apartment, and Miri stiffened with distrust. The waiting woman made no effort to hide her intense dislike of the witch, and Urttah for her part ignored Miri, content to let the waiting woman take over the management of an increasingly unmanageable princess as long as it soothed mother and baby.

"Your father wants you," Urttah announced.

Beth rose from her chair, rocking the small table in front of her. "My father," she echoed in a suitably hollow voice.

"Now?" Miri demanded.

"Even so. He charged me with escorting his daughter to him."

Miri threw a worried look at her charge. "Let me go instead. He appointed me your guardian. Perhaps I can explain—"

Beth regarded her with a queenly air. "Explain what? How I devoured the life of A'Carnis? No, Miri, that is my responsibility. I am in my father's house. I must do as he bids me. Help me dress."

Entering the Empyreor's bedchamber, Beth saw the same royal bed, the same low table, the same fire and aquiline profile eclipsing it.

She smoothed the midnight silk of her gown against her thighs and prepared for judgment. "You sent for me, Great One?"

"I did," said Bethnarian. His light eyes raked her form. "Good. Your veil is thick. It quite obscures your face. You will join me at court tonight."

Beth's eyes widened in disbelief. She took in his lavish robe and collar and then looked down at her own subdued attire. "I thought you summoned me to—" Words dried up. "I am not dressed for Sun Court," she finished in a weak little voice.

"It does not matter." He tried to rise, grasping at the table and exhaling in a grunt.

"Let me help you." She hurried to his side, skating on his pain.

Bethnarian flinched from her touch, but did not shake her hands off. Slowly, he leaned his weight upon her, leaking fear, calculation, and a physical pain that made Beth suck in her breath.

Bethnarian was watching her closely. "The Prince of Carnis wasn't enough to sate you, eh?"

Now Beth flinched, and clamped her lips over an urge to vomit. Bethnarian seized her hand, clenched it painfully. "Oh, yes, I heard." His light eyes seared hers. "You feel it, don't you? The pain I'm in." His voice was hard.

Beth looked away. "Yes."

"You quite enjoy it."

"No!"

"Do not lie to me. You cannot. I know you better than you know yourself."

Beth said nothing.

"You drink my pain like wine. You swill it. And that is not all that you drink, is it?" he demanded.

Her body and voice stiffened. "I do not know."

The Empyreor snorted his disgust. His eyes raked her over coals of contempt. "Don't equivocate, daughter mine. We both need to know the extent of what you can do. Reach into me; tell me what you sense."

His disdain forced her past hurt, past guilt, past fear. She took a long drink of him. "I sense that you are angry, but cold as well, calculating. You hate me, although you seek to convince me otherwise. Most of all you are deeply, terribly afraid. You fear death."

"Hah!" barked the Empyreor and coughed until a ruby froth bubbled up in one corner of his mouth. His claw of a hand dug into his daughter's arm. "You should do quite well tonight. Give me that napkin," he pointed. "And let us go.

"What do you expect me to do?"

"Exactly what you just did: read people. Only this time you will read my subjects instead of me."

They walked through his apartment into a palace of enormous gilded corridors fired by sconced torches and shining bronze chandeliers.

"Did Urttah tell you about my abilities?" Beth dared to ask.

"Why would she need to? I've told you that I know you, daughter. That includes your more pestilential gifts."

Beth exhaled, matching her smooth steps to his halting ones. "And my mother?" she pressed. "Did she have gifts as well?"

She felt a wave of horror roll through him, forced herself to dive into it as he whispered, "Oh yes, she had gifts. Those gifts and more."

Then he began to explain in more detail what he wanted from her. Guards snapped to attention, servants eddied about them, and a pair of gigantic blood-red doors yawned open. Beth heard the heavy, shimmering roll of a beaten gong and followed the Empyreor into the Court of the Noonday Sun on crashing waves of sound. The torch-lit throne room, constructed to set off a series of perfectly round arches built to look like concentric rings and adorned in semiprecious tiles in all the colors of the sun, painted a brazen halo about her father's frail ivory figure. At his feet shimmered a moving floor of molten gold.

The Empyreor stepped onto the golden walkway spanning this moving floor, which was nothing more than a wide but shallow pool of running water bisecting the court. Paved with gold, this pool served to both adorn his majesty and insulate it from the courtiers and princes crowding its edges as he passed.

A pair of guards escorted Beth after her father. She was grateful for their obscuring bulk for she was struggling to keep her head above the undifferentiated ocean of collective feeling rolling out of the assembled nobles like an invisible tidal wave. She focused on the walkway, and gradually, the wave subsided. She saw a great fish the color of pearl floating in the golden stream.

The Empyreor was now hobbling up to his high seat, a rounded bench backed by a huge golden disk. Beth was shown to a curved bench on the lowest step of his dais. She sank to it gratefully for emotions were boiling all around her—hunger, satiation, defiance, adoration, anger, lust, petty jealousy, vanity, and an ennui nigh unto death. They weighed her body down as they stirred the cold consciousness to a blaze.

The Empyreor tapped his scepter on the arm of his Sun Seat, and the glittering crowd of nobles surged forward. Nobles were announced. Nobles were dismissed. And through it all Beth had to sit still and concentrate on sifting one individual's emotions from the vast collective. It took great effort. The cold consciousness seemed to want to slurp up every emotion it touched, preventing her from focusing on the complex emotional narrative underlying the whole person.

Gradually, her control improved, and she learned to sip at various states of feeling like a bee sips the nectar of various flowers.

She grew aware of the sound of her father's scepter tapping. What had he said? That three taps meant that she should pay particular attention to the words and feelings of the individual standing before him?

She heard the tap, tap, tap more often than she would have liked, but she concentrated hard and managed to harvest a few impressions.

By the time the gong of ending sounded, she was sick with headache and fatigue, and the baby was moving ferociously. It was all she could do to rise to her feet and follow the Empyreor out. The throne-room doors closed, and she grabbed her belly and gagged.

"Bring the lady a basin," Bethnarian ordered as he moved on. Beth did not throw up, but she leaned on the servants who came to her, too tired to contemplate the fresh emotions swirling around her.

They led her back to Bethnarian's apartments, where the Empyreor waited on a golden divan to grill her. The grilling lasted the remainder of the night. Beth knew he saw her physical discomfort and mental fatigue, but he kept her up all night anyway.

From then on, Beth spent most of her time in her father's apartments and attended court regularly, always entering behind the Empyreor, and always sitting on the Empyreal dais apart from the other members of the court, who were never permitted to address her.

Bethnarian never said what he thought of the information she gave him afterward, but she must have pleased him in some way. Soon he began ordering her to sit in on the smaller audiences he held in his extensive apartments. At one of these, she finally came face to face with Jazim, Prince of Serpentia. They met as indifferent acquaintances, each more invested in pleasing their terrible master than in accusing the other.

One afternoon when her father was resting and Beth was reading in the library off the Empyreal bedchamber, she heard the Empyreor cry out and saw his body servants run for fresh linen and basins of water and herbs. Moments later, the doors to the private apartment opened, and two men in dark robes and turbans were ushered into the Empyreal bedchamber. The Empyreor's cries and coughs only intensified, so Beth made her way to the chamber door and saw the robed men trying to bleed a flailing, coughing Empyreor.

"Stop!" she cried.

The men froze in surprise.

She moved to her father's head, anger like a fire in her belly. "He does not want this," she said, shoving the nearest man away. "Move."

Both men shrank away from the bed.

Beth sat down next to her father, passed a hand over his moist brow. Deep coughs wracked his thin body, and he clutched at his chest as if to claw his failing lungs.

On impulse, Beth lifted her veil and looked deep into his eyes. "Peace, Great One. Be quiet, be still." She imagined her will enveloping him like flaming wings.

The Empyreor's eyes widened in fear, but his clutching hands loosened and fell away. His coughing eased, and a soft moan escaped his slack and bloody lips.

"What is it?" she whispered to him.

The slack mouth groped for words. "Don't," he slurred. "Don't take me. Not again."

Beth dropped her veil. "Sleep" she commanded, tightening the flaming wings of her cold will about him. The fading eyes closed.

She turned on the other men in the room. "How often does this happen?" she demanded.

They looked at each other. "Often, lady," said one of the turbaned men.

"What do you do for it?"

"We give him medicines. We bleed him when the fits become most severe."

"Bleed him!" said Beth disgustedly. She looked down at the dark spatters on the sheets. "I think he has lost too much blood already. Are you the best healers this city has to offer?"

One of Bethnarian's body servants spoke up. "They are not healers, great lady. They are physicians."

"What does that mean?"

"No one trained them to heal," the servant explained. "They belong to a guild that studies the stars and the shifting of the sands to diagnose diseases of the body, which they treat with expensive concoctions of gold and silver."

Beth stood up, and the two physicians shrank toward the door. "Where are the Empyreor's real healers?"

The body servant answered. "The Lady Vyara comes and tends him when she can. She has great skill at healing." He looked a question at another servant. "I believe she came not long ago."

"Well, send for *her*," Beth ordered, and when no one moved, she barked the order again.

216

Two of the body servants disappeared at a run. Beth regarded the two turbaned physicians in disgust. "Expel these fools," she commanded. And the physicians began squalking as two other body servants herded them through the door.

Alone with her dying father, Beth sat down to wait for the Lady Vyara.

The lady arrived a short time later, and seeing that the Empyreor was attended by only body servants and a single noble woman, she immediately threw off her veil, rolled up her sleeves, and went to work.

Through her own veil, Beth watched the noblewoman care for the unconscious man. The Lady Vyara was every inch a noble woman and yet there was nothing of the jaded court sycophant about her. Though young, she exuded a gentle, open intelligence that warmed like sunshine. She was very attractive, and yet her face was more interesting than beautiful, with doe-like brown eyes, set over a delicately hooked nose and full mouth. Her face had an exotic, sensual cast that went well with her figure's generous curves. Her hair, however, was her glory. Beth had always considered her own sun-streaked tresses blonde, but Lady Vyara's hair made Beth's look brown as bark. Thick and very long, it was the color of sun-kissed linen.

When Vyara finished her examination, she addressed Beth. "Tell me about his symptoms," she said in a rather husky voice.

"He had a coughing fit, which was exacerbated by the quackery of a couple of soothsayers calling themselves physicians."

Vyara shook her head and sighed. "I have told him to send those fools away. But he is desperate enough to try anything." She laid her hands on the sleeping Empyreor and closed her eyes. "It is strange: the crisis has abated, but the heaviness of his sleep seems wrong." She opened her eyes, and looked at Beth. "It is as if someone has drugged him."

Beth's heart bumped, and her eyes fell to her father. "Is the sleep hurting him?" she asked.

Vyara slid her hands to the back of the Empyreor's head. "Quite the opposite. It should give him a much-needed rest. He pushes himself too hard, and pain is the result. It robs him of sleep. I have told him to take a sleeping draught when he can't rest, but he always refuses, he says he is afraid of his dreams. Keep the physicians away from him, and he should do better." She offered the sleeping Empyreor a rather sad smile.

Beth rose. "I will, and I will stay with him tonight. Is there anything else that I should do?"

The Lady Vyara shook her white-blonde head. "Make sure he takes some medicine for pain when he awakens. I wish I could do something to stop the progress of his illness. I have tried, but it would take a healer far more talented than myself to check it. Let him rest, and I will come to see him again tomorrow."

Vyara lifted her small trunk of medicines, and Beth rose. "You could remain here," the princess proposed. "Caphal can assign you quarters, and then you can look in on the Empyreor during the night."

"I would, lady, but I have other patients to attend to. I will go now and trust you to watch over him." Vyara smiled at her, half turned away, then turned back. "What, lady, shall I call you?"

Beth thought for a moment and said, "You may call me Beth."

"Lady Beth," said Vyara, tasting the name. "Are you a relative then?" she smiled.

"Yes," Beth said, feeling a twinge of guilt for being so circumspect with someone so open.

"I am glad. He could use a good nursemaid. I would stay with him more, if I were not needed elsewhere. He has been a good to me and kind to my mother. He should not be alone in his illness."

Beth sat with her father through the night, but in the morning she left him with his body servants to return to her tower rooms for a quick bath and change. Strangely, she didn't feel the slightest bit tired. If anything, she was more hopeful than she had been in a long time. By the time she returned to the Empyreor's apartments, the Lady Vyara was closeted with him, and Beth was directed to the Sunset Chamber that opened onto the great citrus-garden terrace. In the morning light, the trees shone emerald and alabaster.

Caphal met her there, his spare face expressionless and his hands tucked into the sleeves of his dull, dark robe. "Highness," he said, for he was one of the few Empyreal servants to know her proper station. Not even the Empyreor could keep secrets from Caphal.

"How was the Empyreor when he awoke?" Beth asked.

"Much better, Highness."

"He awakened on his own?"

"Just before Lady Vyara arrived. Shall I have the servants bring you refreshment? Chocolate perhaps?"

"I was hoping to see the Empyreor."

"I am certain he will send for you soon."

"Very well," sighed Beth. "Chocolate it is."

Caphal bowed and backed away. Beth turned to inhale the fragrant air, then called, "Caphal?" The Major Domo halted in mid-retreat. "Please ask the Lady Vyara to attend me when she finishes with the Empyreor."

Caphal's face, inscrutable at the best of times, stiffened ever so slightly, and Beth automatically reached out to stroke his feelings. There was dutifulness, respect, and discomfort. "I will make your desire known," Caphal equivocated, and made what was, for him, a hasty exit.

Beth understood. The Empyreor did not want her having any more contact with the Lady Vyara. Lady Vyara, however, had her own ideas. As Beth sat breakfasting on chocolate and a selection of cool ripe fruits at the far end of the terrace garden, the young healer came hurrying toward her. Beth automatically reached for her veil, but she did not don it fast enough.

Vyara was upon her and speaking in a breathless voice, when she managed a direct look at Beth's face and stopped dead, doe-eyes flung wide and smile faltering.

Beth stiffened as well, but she did not turn away. She was the Empyreor's only living child, and by the gods, she would skulk no longer.

Vyara seemed to be having difficulty finding her voice. "Oh, daemons and darkness, Lady Vyara," spat Beth impatiently. "What *have* you come to say?"

Vyara's large eyes blinked. "I—I," she stuttered. Then, to Beth's surprise, she dropped to the bench beside the princess. "Lords of Light, Lady, but you are beautiful."

Beth wanted to cringe. "Am I?" she asked bitterly.

"You must know it."

Beth waved the comment away, but Vyara could not contain her awe. "I understand now why the Empyreor is so protective of you."

"What makes you think he is?"

Vyara smiled, and a small dimple peeked out of her left cheek. "I may not attend court, but I hear the gossip. Everyone is speculating about the mysterious woman who sits at the Empyreor's feet. They think the Empyreor is soon to have an heir."

Beth stood up. "The Empyreor already has an heir," she snapped.

Vyara blinked. "I'm sorry?"

"The Empyreor has a daughter. Does no one remember this?"

"Does she still live? I had heard that she was deformed and died as a young child."

"Really!" blazed Beth.

"But even if she had lived, she would not rule. The Empyre needs a royal son, may the Gods grant that you bear one."

Beth almost choked. "What?" she demanded, staring at Vyara out of wide, shocked eyes.

Vyara's expression turned confused, then embarrassed. "Have I spoken in error? Are you not carrying the Empyreor's child?"

"The Empyreor's child!" Beth spluttered, unable to master outrage. "Is that what they are saying?"

Vyara blushed. "What else would they say? Only the most favored of concubines ever sits at the feet of the Empyreor."

"Concubine!" exploded Beth. "Does the Empyreor know that his courtiers are saying this?"

Vyara ducked her head. "I would not presume—" she began.

"Well, I will!" heaved Beth. "I am no concubine! And I am not carrying the Empyreor's child. I *am* the—"

"Vyara!" barked a thin, yet steely voice from the trees.

It was the Empyreor. He was dressed in loose robes and leaning upon Caphal's arm as he hobbled toward them. "I thought I told you to go directly home!" he shouted at the young healer.

Both Vyara and Beth jumped—Vyara to her feet and Beth to a slightly different position near the bench.

"Father!" she accused, feeling the irritation spewing from her father fall like salt on her own open wounds.

"Father?" Vyara gasped, shooting another wide-eyed look at Beth. "Are you—?"

Bethnarian cursed and hobbled faster. "You blasted innocent, Vyara!" he choked between ragged breaths. "Why didn't you do as you were told? Do you think me so invalid that you have nothing to fear from my displeasure?" his voice trailed away into a wheeze.

"Would you let the whole court believe I am your concubine?" raged Beth in return.

"You are his daughter—his daughter," mumbled Vyara, going largely unheard.

"You *were* someone's concubine," flared Bethnarian at Beth. "Why should I bother to hide it?"

"Because I am your *daughter*, and this baby is your grandchild, and we are all that will remain of you, you monstrous fool!" Beth bellowed, following up her words with a lash from her cold consciousness.

The color drained from Bethnarian's face, and he sagged against Caphal's arm.

"Stop it, both of you!" Vyara cried.

Bethnarian slipped to the terrace, while Beth, realizing in horror what she had just done, yanked the power back into herself.

Vyara hurried to the fallen man and spoke to him with the ultimate authority of a healer. "Breathe, Great One. Breathe. Just relax and breathe."

Beth slunk closer. "Is he all right?" she asked.

There was reproof in Vyara's glance. "He is not, but we may hope this latest crisis will pass. Caphal, help me take him to his chambers." The Major Domo and the pale-haired girl carried the sagging Empyreor away. But Bethnarian summoned Beth to his rooms a short time later. Beth did her best to act contrite, and the Empyreor, quite surprisingly, spoke to her without rancor. "Yesterday, my illness forced me to cancel a critical audience. I must hold it today, and I wish you to attend. You will need to be particularly alert."

"Of course, Great One," responded Beth.

"Good," said Bethnarian and closed his eyes.

Beth rose to leave.

"Do not go," said her Empyreor father. "Sit with me."

Beth sat.

Sometime later, she followed him to a lofty side hall, a much less ostentatious space than the great throne room where the princes of the city paraded their homage.

The first man to be announced was small fop reeking of self-importance. Beth tasted the shallow self-absorption pouring out of him and promptly withdrew her power. Here was a pampered baby of the minor nobility if ever there was one.

With a florid bow and an elaborate wave of hand that set his many rings to glittering, the fop held forth in a stentorian clang, "Great Bethnarian, Empyreor of the South, Scion of the Sun, Conqueror of the Moon, Master of all the lands between Bedad and the sea, I come on behalf of Marbek, Prince of Cadash and Kos, Count of Deshad, Son of Bertran, who sends you his greetings and blessings for the future."

"Greetings to the Prince also," said Bethnarian in an excruciatingly bored little voice. The Empyreor passed his hand before his mouth as if to stifle a yawn.

Although Beth had good reason to resent her father, watching him play at politics made her admire him as well. He knew just what to do to rock the little egotist back on his heels.

The fop cleared his throat. "Marbek wishes you to know that he has defeated the tribes of the deep south in your name and that he desires to lay his plunder before the Sun Seat."

Bethnarian feigned another yawn. "What exactly does this plunder entail?"

"Rubies and diamonds from the far mountains, gold from Infarek, pearls from the Shallow Sea, slaves beyond number, and countless hot-blooded daughters of the desert chieftains."

"Yes, yes, Count Yadak," yawned Bethnarian. "But how is my dear nephew?"

"Nephew?" thought Beth and shifted in her seat, and she dipped back into the pool of self-importance that had so irritated her moments before. There was more than self-importance sloshing inside the fop after all. He had a secret.

Bethnarian listened to Yadak sing the praises of fearless Marbek, and Bethnarian's daughter listened to Yadak's secret. At one point, as her father lapsed into another fit of feigned disinterest, she dared to speak for herself.

"Is Prince Marbek enjoying the comforts of Sun City now that he has returned?" she asked the Count. In the high-ceilinged chamber her voice sounded small and strange to her ears, but the fop nearly jumped out of his robe. His rings glittered frantically as they dove to conceal themselves in the folds of his loose garment.

From the corner of her eye, Beth watched her father sit forward to better absorb Yadak's reaction. Bitter blue eyes briefly met her own. Then Bethnarian raised the back of his hand to his mouth again, this time to stifle a smile. "My dear, Yadak," he said with something like a desperate attempt at enthusiasm. "You should have told me at once that the Prince is in Sun City. I so look forward to embracing my nephew."

"I . . . I . . . I, ahem" stuttered the fop.

Bethnarian saved him the trouble. "Marbek must come to court. Yes, yes, at once. We must hear his tales of adventure and triumph. The ladies especially, I know, will delight in it, as they always delight in him." The Empyreor permitted himself a naughty laugh. "Tell him to expect Jazim to send his finest captains as escort. It would not do to have the hero of the Empyre arrive at the palace without an honor guard." He nodded at the Empyreal guardsman stationed nearest his high seat. "See our most excellent Count Yadak back to his patron, Imir, and wait there for my dear nephew's reply."

The stammering, flapping, glittering messenger was flushed from the hall.

222

The Empyreor cursed and then he began coughing.

Body servants hurried up the steps of the small dais with fresh linens and bottles of soothing liquid. The Empyreor waved them aside.

Beth drifted up to him, knelt down. The Empyreor shrank from her, coughing violently and screwing shut his eyes.

"Look at me, father."

"No!"

"Then you must stop and rest now."

"No," he croaked, waving his hand.

"Then let me help you."

His blue eyes glared at her for a moment. Then he nodded once.

She laid her hand on his, felt his adamance and a tight coil of frustration and suffering and fear. She touched them lightly, smoothed them out like silk. The Empyreor's tight chest loosened and his ragged coughing eased. Sighing, he leaned back against his high seat.

"Better?" Beth asked.

"Yes."

Beth drifted back to her seat. Minutes later Bethnarian waved the doors to the high hall open again.

Beth paid scant attention to the new supplicant at first. She was thinking of her father's pain.

"Master Scryos," said the Empyreor in a voice scoured thin over threads of steel.

The tall man at the foot of the dais folded himself into an austere bow.

Bethnarian glowered. There was no pretense of the doddering and world-weary ruler about him now. "You come later than expected. I am not used to having my summons ignored."

"Forgive me, Great One. I was ill not long ago and the recovery proved more difficult than I expected."

"*You* were ill?"

"Unfortunately, yes."

Bethnarian tapped his fingers impatiently on the arm of his throne. The triplicate sound nudged at Beth. She set aside her father's feelings and tried to focus on the man in front of her. "Strange," Bethnarian was saying, " I have never known you to be ill before."

"It is a rare occurrence I admit," the visitor replied as Beth reached out for his emotions. She struck a glassy wall instead. Surprised, she pressed at it, thinking the barrier was some unexpected failing of her concentration. The wall remained — slick and dark and utterly impenetrable.

With her peculiar powers held in abeyance, Beth took a good long look at the man whose mind had defeated her. For an instant she was certain that she had seen him before. A second look, however, convinced her otherwise. If she had seen him, she was certain she would never have forgotten it. He might submerge the force of his personality beneath nondescript dress and a quiet manner, but his strength and power were such that they easily bled through.

He was speaking to her father of caravan profits, his expression cool and collected despite Bethnarian's obvious displeasure, and he countered the Empyreor's hard stare with an equalizing distance. He was very tall, with hair nearly as black as his eyes, but his face, like a few faint peculiarities of pronunciation, proclaimed him a foreigner by birth, and he exuded a foreigner's disinterest in Empyreal authority. Although, he stood on the floor looking up at the seated Empyreor, he held himself with a confidence that put the two men nearly on a level.

Beth wondered if her father realized the degree of the other man's arrogance, and decided that he did by tapping into the intense dislike now circulating freely through Bethnarian's body. The Empyreor was thumping the arm of his chair emphatically now. "Very good, Master Scryos. Have your factor report these incomes to my secretary, and we will look into the other opportunities in the region as our business permits."

Scryos inclined his head. "As the Great One wishes."

"Are there any other financial matters you wish to discuss with me?"

"Only one. I thought I should inform you of my decision to divest myself of certain transportation interests in the eastern districts."

Bethnarian knuckled his chin meditatively, blue eyes aglitter. "Hmmm. Would those be the very lucrative interests?"

"They would." White teeth flashed. "Which is why I thought the Empyreal Purse might desire a first-look at acquiring them, at a very fair price, of course. I do not forget the favor the Empyreor has shown me."

"What prompts this divestment, if you don't mind my asking?"

"Personal matters."

"Nothing concerning the Sards or their westward incursions, I hope." Bethnarian's voice was soft, but his daughter felt the force of will behind his words.

"The Sards are hardly a personal interest of mine, although they have sometimes been amenable trading partners."

"The recent rumors of unrest in the North, then?"

Scryos' mouth pursed slightly as if he checked an impulse to laugh. His black eyes gleamed. "I admit to a certain fascination with the news coming out of that land."

"Jazim tells me that you have also relocated some of your operations to the Midlands."

"I am honored that the Prince of Serpents takes so much interest in my activities."

"Honor me, not him," snapped Bethnarian, and he stifled a cough. He leaned forward to glare at the dark man and said in a voice a little above a whisper. "I sense that you are planning on leaving us, Master Scryos."

The other man gave the Empyreor a small bow. "I fear I must."

"Not before you fulfill certain obligations to me. Otherwise I fear news of your activities may reach certain lords of the North." Bethnarian spoke ominously, but then his face went gray and he slumped in his seat. Alarmed, Beth moved to catch him, but found Scryos standing in her way. "Never fear, Empyreor Bethnarian," the dark man said. "I keep my promises. Allow me to call my servant."

Between rattling breaths, the Empyreor waved his permission.

The guards opened the hall doors and a slave boy scurried forward. Kneeling he offered up to his master an ironbound casket. Scryos took it, smiling. "The last time we met, Great One," he said, "you asked me to procure a rather rare item for you. Here it is." Dipping his head, he offered the casket to one of the guardsmen.

Beth almost reeled at the surge of hope and doubt coursing from her father. She reached for her seat, and Scryos' hand found her instead. The baby inside her turned violently, and Beth gasped and pressed a hand to her side. Then Scryos' mind and hand were moving away.

Bethnarian, meanwhile, had taken the little casket on his knees; his thin hands moved over it restlessly.

"I would not open it now, Lord Empyreor," Scryos warned

Bethnarian glanced at his daughter, then locked eyes with Scryos. "What of the other?"

The Scryos' dark eyes smiled. "In bygone days, they used to say that luck comes in threes."

Bethnarian frowned. "And what is that supposed to mean to me?"

"It means, Bethnarian, Empyreor, that your luck is coming. But it will require something from you to activate it."

In the Empyreor's face, anger warred with hope. "What?" he asked.

Scryos' eyes seemed to bore into the sick ruler. Beth brought her hands to her heart, for she was suddenly terribly afraid for her father, as if the dark man were holding out to Bethnarian ruin disguised as hope. She wanted to speak, but her abdomen hurt so as to make breathing difficult. Before she could intervene, Bethnarian's colorless lips moved again. "What would you have of me now?"

Scryos' dark gaze seemed almost pitying. "A small thing, a familiar thing where Empyreors are concerned — one death."

Beth found her breath. "No!" she hissed.

Bethnarian's face was a death mask. "Whose?"

"A traveler's, one of three coming down the old northeast road."

"Thousands frequent that way?"

"This one is rather special."

"How will I find this traveler?"

Scryos gave a low chuckle. "You will not need to. He will find you. I need only your assurance that you will take him in and give him what he wants."

Bethnarian had closed his eyes. "One more death, and then the long nightmare will be over," he said bitterly. Beth could have wept for him, but her sorrow like her voice was locked behind an icy wall of fear. She sensed a terrible finality in the moment that she longed to turn aside. The cold consciousness could feel it too, but it hungered to hear the black bargain struck.

The Empyreor nodded his head. "So be it," he declared.

For the first time, Scryos' mouth smiled, and the fear holding Beth silent released her. "Father, what have you done?" she whispered, and felt a tearing in her belly that knocked her to the floor.

They carried her back to the Empyreor's apartments where Urttah quickly appeared to hover over her — the witch woman found ways to shadow her that even the Empyreor could not fathom. Vyara was also there, with a healer's kind face and even kinder hands.

"Don't," Beth whispered as Vyara moved to lay those hands upon her. She feared what the healer might discover.

Vyara only smiled reassuringly and pressed her hands to Beth's belly anyway, closing her eyes as if to concentrate all her attention in her sense of touch. That touch was gentle and firm. "What a healthy and strong baby." She breathed, her eyes opening wide. "I reach in and the baby reaches back. It is eager to be born."

"But there is blood," rasped Urttah. After Vyara's warm and soothing tones, her voice abraded.

Blood! Beth struggled to press herself into a sitting position.

One of Vyara's hands pushed her back. "Only a little. It is not unusual, especially in the late stages of a pregnancy." She removed her hands. "How do you feel?"

"Fine," said Beth rather curtly.

"Do you feel any pain?"

"My back hurts."

Vyara nodded, "Contractions. Just little ones, practice for the hard labor to come, I think. You should be fine. But lie down for the rest of the day."

Servants came and put Beth to bed in a high room just off the Empyreor's chamber, a room with gold-coffered ceilings. This is where I should have been sleeping all along, Beth thought as Vyara came to perch on the edge of the bed. "You are carrying a big, healthy child," she said. "And your baby is an active one. I wonder you can sleep at night."

Beth's sighed. "I'm finding it more and more difficult." She did not mention the fact that other things tended to disturb her sleep even more. "Thank you for coming to check on me."

"I never left. I am afraid I defied the Empyreor again. I could not leave him looking so weak. But I am glad that I could help you as well." Vyara dropped her large eyes to Beth's belly. "What a joyous thing it must be to feel a new life growing within you."

Beth bit her lip. She cared about her baby with all a mother's instinctive protectiveness, but nothing about the experience of carrying it had been easy, much less joyous. Was joy, she wondered, what more ordinary mothers felt?

"Do you want children, Vyara?" she asked, although the warm feelings flowing from the healer were all the answer she really needed.

Vyara laughed. "Many. I am the only child of what is now a very small family, and I can think of nothing better than filling a house with happy, noisy children."

Beth thought of her father, the stories of his grief at her mother's death. At one time, Bethnarian himself might have hoped for the same. But he too had ended up with a surprisingly small family.

Vyara patted her hand. "Rest. I will go see the Empyreor now." She started to rise, but Beth caught her wrist.

"You are certain my baby is well?"

Vyara tilted her head. "Absolutely," she said. "The child is doing far better than his weary mother right now."

Beth gripped her wrist more tightly. "So everything is . . . right with him?"

A tiny line formed between Vyara's pale brows. "Him? Are you so sure it is a boy?"

Beth shrugged. "Mother's intuition. I just wondered if you felt anything strange."

"Strange?" The line deepened. "How so?"

Beth let go of her wrist and turned her face away. "Never mind. I have odd fancies sometimes."

"Many women in your condition do. Do not let it worry you." Vyara's warm voice hugged her. And then she was gone, leaving Beth to lie in her strange, quiet room and long for a sleep that would not come.

Beth did not see her father again until the next evening as Urttah and Miri were readying her to join him in court. Miri was not happy about her doing so, but Beth insisted that she felt fine. The Empyreor had insisted that she wear the pearl and diamond dress that A'Carnis had given her.

"Let me see her," his worn voice commanded as the two women finished up.

Beth went to him, with her waiting woman walking behind her in a trail of veil like ivory mist.

"Lady Inimiri," Bethnarian said, acknowledging the waiting woman. His skin looked chalky, but he seemed more vigorous.

"Lord Empyreor." Miri bowed.

Bethnarian turned from her to the paragon that was his child, and smiled a cat's cold smirk of satisfaction. "Come daughter," he said.

As they moved through the blazing corridors surrounded by the finest of the household guard, she dared to ask, "Did you get all you hoped for from your audience with the man Scryos?"

The Empyreor's mouth twitched. "That one gives nothing, but I got enough. Tell me, what did you think of him?"

She hunted for the words. "He reminded me of you, Great One. A man who is used to getting his way."

The Empyreor snorted. "He has had his disappointments."

"It does not show."

"No," returned her father gruffly. "He is made of sterner stuff than that. What did your other abilities tell you?"

Beth tripped a little on the trailing material of her skirt. "Very little."

"You could not read him?"

"Not at first."

Her father's gaze was sharp. "But you saw something."

"He seemed to open his mind to me for a moment."

"And?"

"He keeps his feelings tightly controlled. There was nothing in him that I could reach." She thought of Blayne, but he at least had felt physical passion and seemed to want to feel more. She was not sure that this Scryos was capable of either. "I am glad I did not have to be close to him for long."

"And yet I once toyed with the idea of wedding you to him," said her father bluntly.

She stared at Bethnarian in shock that devolved into distaste.

Her father waved away her dismay. "Do not worry. He would not have had you. He has another wife in mind."

And with that insult he led her into the golden heart of Sun Court.

Beth's concentration was poor on this night. She couldn't seem to put her most recent conversation with her father out of her mind. What game was Bethnarian playing at in telling her about his plans for her and Scryos? When exactly had he considered foisting her off on the foreign merchant? Had that been before or after he had given up on having other children?

The great gongs crashed. The lords and ladies of the court turned to take their places for the main event, and two rows of the Empyreal guard came marching across the gleaming expanse of the floor. They took up positions before a crowd of blooded citizens, opening a wide avenue on one side of the enormous hall.

The light reflecting off their brassy armor made it difficult for her to see the man walking between them. She did not behold him clearly until he reached the Empyreal dais.

"Marbek, dear nephew," cried Bethnarian, descending from the Sun Seat to beam benevolence on the auburn-haired giant of a man who stood before him.

Marbek bowed deeply, then raised his burly arms and cried out in a deep voice. "For our beloved Empyreor. All praise and honor to the Great One!"

Pipes skirled and drums pounded while wave after wave of red-clothed servants and porters brought forth chests of treasure, the plunder of many fiefdoms. Behind these came more soldiers bearing ceremonial short swords and many chained slaves, most of them young, comely women.

Standing serene in Empyreal white and gold, Bethnarian smiled at it all. Then Marbek dropped to one knee. "All for you, Great One."

"Ah, Marbek, will you ever disappoint?" Bethnarian beamed. He said it so sweetly that only Beth felt the irony underlying the question. The Empyreor briefly rested a frail hand on one of Marbek's broad shoulders. Then he raised both his hands to the assembly. "The Empyre's most daring prince has returned. Welcome him!" A cheer went up; a roil of mixed emotions swept across the court. Beth caught a flutter of dark cloth out of the corner of her eye and saw that Jazim, black and gold as one of the great desert vipers, had come to stand on the other side of the dais.

Bethnarian raised Marbek to his feet, kissed his cheeks, first right, then left, and bestowed him upon the adoring throng. Then he turned for his throne, and his facade of avuncular pride melted into glittering menace.

Beth kept her eye on Marbek for the remainder of the evening. Here, she realized, was a serious contender for the Sun Seat, a truly impressive figure of a man. But for Ogren, he was the tallest person she had ever seen, taller even than the dark man called Scryos, and as well built as he was tall. He looked every inch the warrior and moved with the terse, muscular economy of a man practiced at action. He was also, Beth admitted, very attractive. Not pretty as A'Carnis had been, or even truly handsome, but radiating an aura of fierce masculinity. With his deep-set blue eyes made bluer by his olive complexion and auburn hair, he reaped a broad swath of devastation among the women and even some of the men of the court. They flocked about him, and he accepted their fawning as his due.

Once or twice his hot eyes skimmed her, but so quickly that she would have doubted his interest, had she not possessed other abilities. Prodigiously popular he might be, but prodigiously vain he was also, and his ambition exceeded even his conceit. Already he saw himself as lord and master of the hall—investiture being no more than a formality—and he intended to crush with ruthless ferocity anything or anyone obstructing his route to Empyreal glory.

The realization made Beth look more thoughtfully at Jazim and wonder what he thought of Marbek's presumption. The Prince of Serpents had remained standing upon the lowest level of the dais, guarding his Empyreor. Beth could feel the waves of protective vigilance rolling off of him. It made her smile, and when Jazim finally turned his hawk eyes toward her, she dared to show him that smile, earning herself an amber-eyed blink of surprise.

The Empyreor departed the throne room on Marbek's arm. Beth and Jazim left later, as a couple. They did not speak to each other during the long walk back to the Empyreor's apartments, and Jazim promptly handed her over to her father's pleasure. She found

Bethnarian resting in the great sitting room that fronted the terrace grove.

Without turning to look at her, he said, "Come into the light, my dear, and take off your veil."

She obeyed, puzzled by his unprecedented use of an endearment. Then he said, "And you too, dear Marbek. Join us."

As Beth stiffened, the auburn-haired warrior stepped out of the shadows of the terrace and ran hot eyes over her face and form as he moved aggressively to stand beside her. Beth was tall for a woman, but this man's height made her feel almost doll-like. It was a sensation she did not like. She reached back to retrieve her veil.

"Leave it, daughter dear," her father ordered. "We are all family here."

Beth threw him an affronted glare, angry at his pretense of fatherly devotion. Bethnarian smiled as if he hadn't noticed and motioned her to sit.

Marbek sat as well, on the divan directly across from hers, from which he could peruse her face and form at his leisure. He spoke not a word to her, and answered her father's questions quite curtly, but Bethnarian kept the talk going until almost dawn, during which time Beth felt Marbek's vaunted ambition coil outward to encompass her.

When her father finally dismissed her to her rest, she was damp with impotent outrage. What was her father playing at? One moment he treated her like a valuable ally, the next he dangled her before Marbek like so much raw meat. How it made her miss Blayne. Unfeeling he might have been, but he had never so demeaned her. He might not have loved her in the mortal sense, but he had always acknowledged her as another thinking creature and a power in her own right. And on that bitter irony, she went heavily to her rest.

Chapter 17: Daemon's Delight

Days later, in the balm of the early evening, Beth wandered beneath the potted orange trees of her great father's private terrace— quiet now that the raucous parrots had flown to their roosts. The city was a labyrinth drifting ever deeper into night, and the palace was its heart, a heart as dark as the fear building inside her.

The cold consciousness was growing, in power and hunger. At night it came on particularly strong, licking through her veins like wildfire, overpowering her real self, enflaming her dreams.

Last night all of her dreams had been of fire—a cold, relentless, multihued fire that infected and then consumed everything it touched. She saw the Greenwood burning and Sun City too. She saw A'Carnis writhing in it and Miri running from it. She even glimpsed Emily with eyes aflame. "Run, Beth!" her friend cried, before disappearing behind a wall of rainbow fire. When she did run, deep into the shadows and hollow stony spaces of the Empyreal palace, she heard sobbing and a man's desperate voice crying out, "No, Janera! No!"

From out of the dark at the end of the corridor came another voice like a breath of midwinter.

"My dear one, my sweet one. Come!"

Beth shivered just remembering that voice and turned from the terrace wall as she realized that someone was watching her. The cold consciousness had whispered it to her in a thousand flickering tongues.

The towering bulk of Marbek emerged from the tree shadows. The calmness of her voice surprised her. "Prince Marbek."

Marbek moved closer, took on color and definition. "Princess."

"Shouldn't you be waiting on the Empyreor?" Although she did not like this man, Beth kept her courtesy. It would not do to insult a prince of the blood. She drew her veil about her.

"I came out to see the stars," said Marbek, "and I find the brightest of them walking beneath the orange trees." He meant the statement for a blandishment, but he spoke it like a man who believes himself to be in command of both stars and trees.

Beth was incensed. "A rather tired compliment, don't you think, Highness? Men since the Empyreor Idar have been comparing women to stars."

She turned to walk away, and her trailing veil caught on Marbek's foot. The Prince had set his gold sandaled foot upon the trailing edge of it.

"And receiving the gratitude of the women so complimented. Kneel and show me your face," he commanded.

Beth crossed her arms, and Marbek yanked the veil from her head.

"How dare—" she hissed, putting her hands to the disarray of her hair.

Marbek's eyes glittered as, lunging, he seized her jaw in his large hand and set his hard mouth upon hers.

Beth reacted by raking her nails down his cheek. Marbek hissed and slapped her, hard. While her head was still ringing, he caught her up in his arms and kissed her until her mouth opened.

For Marbek is was like sinking his tongue into the sweetest of fruits and the bloodiest of meats. He tasted her juice and soon he was craving it in a way that made all his muscles ache. His heart began to race; his breathing came in thick, fast pants. His lungs screamed for air, but he simply could not stop kissing her, though parts of his mind were winking out like stars at morning.

Then he heard a shriek that scored his ears the way the princess' nails had scored his face, and an invisible shockwave knocked him, sweat plastered and trembling, to the terrace.

"Nephew!" cried Bethnarian in a frail, mocking voice. "Where is your courtesy? You should ask me before helping yourself to my delicacies. You are not Empyreor yet."

There was a terrible chill in Marbek's fluttering chest that made response impossible, but his dazzled eyes still hunted for the beautiful curves of the princess' face. She lay sprawled upon the stones, only feet away from him.

"You are lucky I intervened," Bethnarian continued moving out of the shadows of the trees. The Empyreor was all in silhouette, except for his right hand, which pulsed with multihued light. "A moment more and she would have killed you. As it is, I fear you will have been quite weakened and someone else will have to die. One of your lackeys I think. That fool Yadak perhaps. Yes, that simpering peacock was made to be eaten. Caphal! Have the guards fetch Count Yadak to me, and call the witch."

Bethnarian's gray form moved closer. "Be happy, dear Marbek. Now, instead of working against me, you can work for me, while basking in my tender loving ministrations. You will find that I am a good uncle, unfailingly cautious and protective and where my relatives are concerned."

Marbek tried to lift his head, managed a moan instead.

"Now, now. Don't whine," said Bethnarian. "I warned you that overweening pride packs a terrible cost. Focus on learning that lesson and I may let you live."

Later, in a round, torch-lit room known only to the Empyreor and a handful of his servitors, the witch woman Urttah stood guard over a silk-swathed figure held by chains to a symbol-coated floor. The figure plucked at the shackles on her wrists and shook her long hair back from a breathtakingly beautiful face. "Where is he? Where is my love?" Her voice was cream and crystal, and her eyes were blue flames.

"He comes," rasped the scarred woman.

The bronze and ivory woman rolled her head, and her burning eyes narrowed at the sigils carved into the room's walls. "I want my love."

"And you shall have it, that and more," rasped Urttah.

Beauty rose, sleek and deadly as a serpent, and even the witch woman retreated before it as the twin blue flames of the Princess' eyes seared scarred flesh. "Are you afraid of me, Urttah? Don't be afraid. I can taste your bitterness, your pain. I can take them away." She reached out to the witch woman, while every sign in the room, even those etched into the ceiling, leapt to sun-gold light. Both women recoiled, the fairer horror shrieking and flinging up her arms.

The sun-symbols went out, and Urttah, hunched over her own extreme pain, hissed.

Sounds of voices and marching feet drifted into the room via one of the two narrow, arched doorways that opened into it.

"My love," whispered the radiant woman and her eyes brightened.

The officiously self-important count named Yadak squeaked as he was shoved through the nearest door. Then the door slammed shut, and Urttah's scarred mouth stretched. "Count," she rasped.

The Count recoiled to see the scarred creature standing before him. "What is this?" he demanded. "Who are you?" Then his eyes moved to the bronze and ivory idol standing at the center of the room, and his face broke open on wonder.

"She is beautiful is she not, Count?" said Urttah. "She is your empyress. Kneel before her."

Weak-willed Count Yadak did as he was told, stumbling forward and falling upon his knees before the woman with the glowing lapis lazuli eyes. "Most beautiful," he rasped.

"So paltry, so weak," beauty lilted. "This is not my love."

Urttah's scar of a mouth twisted. "Call him dinner then."

Long white fingers brushed the kneeling man's forehead. Beauty bent its head, bringing shining eyes closer to Yadak's bulging ones. "Dinner? Little man, are you my dinner? Are you delicious?" She kissed him lightly and Yadak groveled in her embrace. "Yes," she sang, "Dearest, delicious dinner."

Yadak moaned.

The draining begun, Urttah squatted down to watch.

Bethnarian was sitting slumped in his bedchamber when the witch returned from the feeding. "Is it done?" he said tiredly.

"It is."

"Will she continue to be of use to me?"

"The room's spells drew some of the energy from her as she fed. Once the sun is up, the daemon will submerge, the mortal re-emerge. I will see to it that she spends time out of doors in full sun. It should help to keep her colder fires banked."

"And what of the danger?"

"Keep your pawns and princes in their places and all will be well. And do not think that you can wriggle out of your doom with the paltry relic you conceal in your robe. If the princess does not deliver her son while she belongs to neither realm and yet partakes of both, your piddling empyre will pay the price. Those are the terms of the bargain, and eternal night will hold you to it. So be a good empyreor, Bethnarian, and don't invite punishment from another quarter."

The Empyreor's lips skinned back from his teeth. "Leave me, witch," he spat.

Urttah turned away. But she spoke again when she reached the margins of the room. "If you don't keep your little trinket away from my sister's flesh, self-styled Empyreor, I may take your punishment into my own hands." In a rustle of heavy robes she departed.

Chapter 18: Small Thefts

Zabet, the conjurer—some called him thief—sat in the back room of his father's seedy sundries shop and rolled a coin across his knuckles. The coin was a pure gold Empyreal completely unsuited to its cheap and filthy surroundings. And Zabet, who was as round as he was ruddy, and he was very ruddy, was the cheapest and filthiest thing of all. He hadn't washed in days, and he wore a caftan that looked as if it had been pissed on by a dozen desert cats and spat on by a caravan of camels.

Zabet lifted his round head and rolled his round eyes as he heard his father stumping through the family living quarters. In point of fact, neither Zabet nor his father spent much time there. Both were opportunists and itinerants by nature, as likely to hole up in someone else's den of vice as occupy their own rat-infested one.

Zabet the elder conjurer stuck his long, thin face around the doorframe, and his son made haste to flip his golden coin into a concealed pocket in his filthy caftan.

The elder Zabet, as skinny as his son was fat, scowled ferociously. "You have visitors," he spat and almost fell into the room as three tall men shoved past him. Two of those men wore the black-leather, metal-studded armor of Empyreal soldiers. The third wore a loose hooded robe over a golden silk tunic that struck amber from his eyes.

Zabet leapt from his chair and, with movement amazingly nimble for such an obese man, began bowing deeply and often. "Most honored Highness," he cried. "Welcome! Welcome to my humble abode."

Jazim, Prince of Serpents, gripped the hilt of his saber and glared.

Zabet fell forward and began bowing repeatedly and often. "Please, oh Prince—allow my worthless father—to present you with a chair—while I prostrate myself—before your glory." Whale oil would not have flowed more smoothly than Zabet's voice.

"Be still, Zabet, you cur!" barked the Prince of Serpents with quiet authority. "You are irritating enough without all the tail wagging." He nodded a dismissal, and his men filed out while Zabet the Elder bolted for the proffered chair. The emaciated old man returned a moment later with a rickety goat-hide chair that he plunked down beside the prince.

Both Zabets now bobbed over their knees. "What might the magnificent Lord Commander want with us?" Zabet the Younger groveled.

"Your head, if you don't shut up. Send your father away."

With a cry of joy the old man threw his eyes heavenward and clasped his hands. "Thank you, oh prince of princes. Thank you! Thank you!" With a last malicious leer at his son, he fled the house entirely.

Zabet the Younger scowled at the place where his father had been. "And hell and damnation to you too, you evil imp," he murmured.

"Sit," commanded Jazim.

Zabet gathered his caftan, jumped up and sat.

"Tell me, Zabet, how is business?"

"Wretched, Highness. Our clientele is sooo poor. And the imp, my father, wants sooo much for the garbage we sell. I keep telling him to lower his prices."

Jazim's lips thinned. "But just yesterday you were seen enjoying the best of wine and women with Horek the Repellant. Trade on the black market must be quite lucrative."

Zabet grimaced. "And the Empyreor's cut is coming, Highness. I promise you that."

"Tell me about your most recent acquisitions."

"Ah, yes. There is a shipment of gold from the southern mountains and some excellent emeralds from Harod. It would be my honor to gift you with one, Highness." He measured Jazim's indifference and added. "Or three."

"Anything else?"

Zabet coughed delicately, grew even ruddier. "Ahem, yes, well there are those items borrowed from the less than vigilant—secret ledgers and other incriminating evidence, a first-born son or two. Nothing terribly valuable."

"Borrowing means returning, Zabet," said the prince.

"And the items will be returned, Highness, as soon as they are paid for."

"And what of the more unusual items coming out of the east? How is your trade in those?"

Zabet's fat, dexterous fingers flexed. "The wealthy are always in the market for good Sardic tapestries and pottery, Highness. But I have never taken much interest in their crafts."

Jazim grabbed Zabet by his filthy caftan and pulled him in close. "I'm not talking about rugs and pottery, dog, and you know it."

Zabet quit dissembling. "If you are referring to items of a more arcane nature, I have nothing. Such goods must be specially ordered, at great cost I might add. However, such is my admiration for you, Lord Commander, that I would be more than willing to—"

"How about obtaining another item like the one you recently procured for the man called Scryos?"

Zabet's round eyes popped. "Highness! Please don't speak of him! Only a dirty scoundrel would stoop to doing business with a foreigner."

Jazim smiled gently. "And you are dirtier than a beggar's ass, Zabet. Don't bother lying to me. I already know that he used you."

"For what?"

The tall prince dropped a marked piece of paper into Zabet's lap. Zabet glanced at it, and his cheeks grew even rounder.

"I have Inris in custody, Zabet," the Lord Commander hissed. He has already talked. In fact he has proven quite eager to do so."

Zabet dropped pretense. "Good luck making sense of it," Zabet mumbled.

Jazim moved as if to box the thief's ears for insolence, then held off. "So you know about Inris' madness. Have you also heard that he blames you for it, you *and* Scryos? He curses both of you most creatively."

Zabet's round eyes rolled, glassy as marbles. "I know nothing," he squeaked.

One of Jazim's long brown fingers stabbed at the drawing. "But you *have* seen this stone before."

Zabet shook his head, and his belly jiggled like a waterskin. "No, no, no!" he insisted. "You can kill me, but the answer is and will always be no."

Jazim crossed his arms. "I won't kill you, Zabet. I want you to live, in the lowest dungeon of the foulest prison, while bits and pieces of you are slowly, precisely broken upon the machines of torment."

Zabet closed his eyes. A bead of sweat trickled down his temple. "Better your torments than his."

Jazim cocked his head. "Than whose? Scryos'? Has he threatened you?"

"He doesn't have to? Just look at Inris."

"You blame Scryos for Inris' madness?"

"Stop saying his name! Do you not know that the man can pick thoughts out of the air?"

Jazim scowled, then wrapped long fingers about the hilt of the saber at his side. "The heat has finally cooked your brains Zabet if you fear a Northlander spy more than the right arm of the Empyreor. You will tell me about this medallion now, or I will start carving the design on that gem into your chest!"

Zabet laughed bitterly. "I have nothing to tell. I know nothing, I saw nothing. I was just the middleman. Inris was the procurer. He brought the item to me in a casket that I never opened, and I passed it on to that foreigner. Only he knows what the stone is for. Question him if you doubt me. I'm a dead man anyway."

"You are a fool, Zabet." Jazim spat his disgust. "He has scared you with phantoms. Have you forgotten how bad I can make things for you?"

Zabet gave another despairing little laugh. "We are both fools, Highness. I thought I could bargain with evil, and you think you can conquer it?"

"Did you call me a fool?"

Zabet sagged as Jazim whipped his saber free of its sheath. "At least I'll have a better death than poor Castak," he muttered.

Jazim's brows rose. "Castak the smuggler? What happened to him?"

"Exactly what has begun to happen to Inris, or anyone else who meddles in that black magician's affairs. Castak learned from Inris that a certain party was paying handsomely for a mineral found in the far east. He tried to intercept a shipment. He ran shrieking mad afterward and eventually bled to death through every hole in his body."

Jazim furrowed his brow. "You think Scryos was responsible?"

Zabet raised his eyes from the saber long enough to answer with weary exasperation. "Who do you think the shipment belonged to? The man's daemon spawn, I tell you. I doubt he takes any more interest in the Empyre than you or I take in a colony of ants. He is working toward some other goal."

The silver line of Jazim's blade swept back, and Zabet shut his eyes.

He heard a muffled curse, the thudding of booted feet, and then the sound of a door opening. Street sounds blossomed, and Zabet opened his eyes to find himself alone.

He collapsed into a sweaty heap of fat. Then he jumped up, collected what valuables he could, and ran. He knew Jazim's spies would try to follow him. He had to laugh at them for trying. They would never keep up. It was Scryos' magic he feared, Scyros's magic he longed to escape. Only with luck and the blessings of the gods might he reach open desert and live to run another day.

A talented thief and illusionist, Zabet easily slipped the spies' pursuit. He had grown up among thieves and smugglers and knew routes through the great city that even Jazim's agents could not imagine. He cut through back alleys, safe houses, sewers, even private residences, and by the time he had reached the margins of the Golden Quarter, where the city's most powerful merchants did business, he had lost them all — all of them but one.

This last hooded pursuer proved alarmingly resourceful. Time and time again Zabet thought he had confused him, only to spot him coming around the next corner. Grudgingly, Zabet saluted the man's skill. Then an absolutely terrifying thought turned his admiration into horror and set him running again, harder and faster than ever.

Abandoning cleverness, Zabet made a beeline for the beggars' quarter, the most pestilential and violent part of town, a place even a prince of serpents would fear to slither. Perhaps his pursuer would think twice about following him there?

His strategy seemed to work.

He dropped out of sight behind a pile of stinking refuse, then slipped up a shadow-haunted back alley littered with the corpses of cats killed by giant rats.

And found his hooded pursuer waiting for him.

Heart hammering like war drums, Zabet watched as the robed figure cast back its dark hood. Zabet glimpsed black hair, black eyes and choked on a scream.

Then the dark man spoke. "Zabet?"

Zabet's joints turned to water. His kneecaps collided with stone, and he dropped his forehead into a pile of stinking refuse.

Footsteps approached. Out of the corner of his eye Zabet glimpsed a well-heeled boot. "Are you ill?"

Zabet rubbed his cheek against the dirty stones like they were made of down. "Am I ill?" he crooned. "Is a man who wakes from the nightmare of his own death ill? No. Call him the most blessed of men. The gods love Zabet still."

His pursuer's response was wry. "Knowing something of you and your gods, Zabet, I doubt that."

Zabet sat up and took hold of the other's woolen robe with pudgy hands and shook it. "Oh, trust me, my friend. You are the answer to a most fervent prayer, a good omen for remarkably bad times."

"I wouldn't be too sure of that either."

Zabet brushed the warning aside. "Such cynicism. In this wretched world, the smallest good fortune is cause to celebrate. And today my enemy has been transformed into my friend. That is a miracle only the gods could create. That you should look so much like him and not be him — well, as I said, it is more than a god-loving man would hope for."

"And what, Zabet, besides loose purses and even looser women, were you hoping for?"

Zabet grinned up at the other and winked. "A touch of good magic. Ah, but I forget my manners." He let go of the taller man's robe and climbed to his feet. "Welcome back, Al of the Northlands, welcome to my nasty, depraved, jewel of a city. Now, let's get out of this sewer hole and find one we can drink in."

He led the Northlander to a beer-maker's stall in a marginally better quarter. Zabet swallowed his first watery beer in one gulp then sat peering over his second mug at his companion. The man that Zabet knew as Al appeared to be soaking in the brilliant havoc of the streets. He had his own mug of beer in front of him, but he hardly touched it, and although he appeared to lounge comfortably in his chair, he kept his hood up and one hand on the hilt of the blade at his side.

Zabet set his own mug down on the scarred boards of the table. "Looking for that terrifying friend of yours?"

Dark eyes slid his way, and the air about Zabet seemed to grow thick with hostility. "Have you seen him?" asked Al.

"Me? Gods, no! Would I be breathing if I had? The glorious devil can't stand me. Soon slit my throat as look at me. Then again, I doubt he feels the least bit of compunction about slitting any throat." Zabet winked an eye. "I can't help but wonder how you manage to keep the beast on a leash."

"He's not a dog, Zabet," returned the other.

Zabet held up an apologetic hand. "No, no. Of course not. I never meant to imply –" Zabet's thick, agile fingers picked at a splinter along the table's edge.

"You still haven't told me why you were running," prompted Al.

Zabet's eye's jumped to the other shadowy figures in the establishment. Most were robed and turbaned men who mumbled into their cups. "Not here," Zabet hissed. "Not now. When we are alone."

Al's dark brows rose. "Is it the Prince of Serpents you are afraid of?"

"You saw him? Pah, of course you did. Those sharp eyes of yours never did miss a thing."

Those sharp eyes cut Zabet off in mid digression, and the fat man took a long swill of beer, then wiped his lips on the back of his hand. "Jazim's not the problem," he confessed. "Well, not the most serious problem, but more of this later, when you can ward out those who might be listening with more than their ears."

Al was looking out into the street again. "What makes you think I'm not warding us now?"

"Here?" Zabet's round eyes popped. He leaned over the table. "Can your wards block *all* spells?"

The handsome face swung his way; the lips curved faintly. "What do you think?"

Zabet licked his lips, torn between suspicion and hope.

Al's smile widened into a persuasive grin. "Why don't you tell me about this magician you fear?"

Zabet spilled his guts. "He is one of your kind, I think. But I have never seen a magician work the way he does. I thought you Northlanders were sworn to use your magic to protect men."

"And why is this bad magician after you?"

"I arranged something for him. I didn't want to do it. But he wasn't going to give me a choice."

"Then he should be in your debt."

"He should, but, ah," Zabet shook a sausage finger, "I might have taken a few liberties with his instructions. And now I am afraid this Scryos will find out."

"Scryos." The warm air turned sharply oppressive, hard to breathe.

Zabet wiped his forehead with a filthy sleeve. "Scryos, yes. Or so he calls himself."

"And what exactly did you do for this Scryos?"

"I helped him to procure a rare gem," panted Zabet.

Al smirked. "Still haven't licked that bad habit of yours, eh, Zabet?"

Zabet tried to expostulate between pants. "If I had refused him, he would have killed me! The rumor was that he had already eliminated a handful of other procurement specialists. So when he came to me, I made damned sure to be accommodating. I hoped to buy myself some time. But Scryos coerced me into the deal. I took precautions, of course. I farmed the job out to an old colleague and acted as the middleman only, handing the item off to Scryos as soon as it came to me. I even sealed it in a protective Sardic casket—you never know what residue these objects of power might leave. The point is I gave Scryos as little reason as I could to resent my continued existence." Zabet clenched his teeth. "But then Inris, the thief I hired, fell ill, and he put the Prince of Serpents on to the matter. And so, today Jazim appears at my door and starts spitting the name of Scryos' to the twelve winds."

Al had crossed his arms. "What kind of gem did you steal, Zabet?"

The fat thief shook his head sadly. "Procure, my friend, procure," he whispered. "One with some old lettering on it, ancient Sardic I believe. Why Scryos wanted it, I don't know. I don't want to know."

Al loosed a dry chuckle. "Because you think not knowing will protect you."

"Won't it?"

"No. Power calls to power. Balances of power have to be paid in kind. If you managed to transfer a thing of power to a magician, you bound yourself to him through it. When and how he strikes at you will be determined by the nature of the thing you took."

Zabet screwed his round eyes up as if struggling to absorb this esoterica. He licked his lips again. In a sick whisper, he said, "Scryos has been making people go mad and gush blood."

Al's eyes narrowed. "Not pretty."

"No."

"You said the jewel had writing on it, Sardic writing. Did you 'procure' it from the Sards?"

"I couldn't. Scryos' requirements were very specific. Also, I'd already persuaded Inris to take the job, and he would never steal from the Sards. No man who values his life or his freedom gets within fifty leagues of the clan territories—if the men don't flay and kill you, the sorceresses brand and geld you. Scryos had told me where I could locate the item, but that alone presented problems. I felt I needed to know more, so I sent Inris to an expert of sorts, a scholar named Abreem Imharta. Imharta is a very traveled and learned man. He has been east many times, and he knows many strange languages. If there were any particular dangers associated with the jewel or its markings, Imharta might be able to tell us."

"And did he?"

Zabet ran his tongue across his upper lip. He seemed to be trying to read his future in his mug of beer. "He confirmed the likely location of the stone, and he warned Inris to avoid physical contact with the jewel. He said it might be poisoned."

The dark-eyed man was sitting up now while Zabet slumped, dripping and gasping like a fish yanked out of water. "And where did Inris find this item?"

"Beneath Sun Palace."

Al's eyebrows shot up. "The Empyreal Palace?"

"Yes. But not the one everyone sees. The other one, the ancient one underneath." Zabet's eyes were bulging now. He inhaled in short gasps, and his chest heaved. "Help me," he croaked, clawing at his chest.

The darker man didn't look the least bit worried. "Breathe, Zabet," he said flatly,

"Scryos?" gasped Zabet, panic in his face.

"Anxiety. Just breathe. Slowly."

"Dying?" wheezed Zabet, pounding on his chest. The Northlander kicked him under the table, and he gasped in air. It felt like a slab of granite had been lifted off his chest.

Al the Northlander smiled humorlessly. "So Inris went into the labyrinth," he continued, "and brought back an ancient artifact that had been hidden there."

"In the old palace. Yes."

"And how did he enjoy the experience?"

"He seemed fine, physically."

Al's laugh was contemptuous. "But now he is mad?"

"That was Scryos."

"Maybe not."

Zabet blinked. "I know it was him. It had to be."

"If Inris went into the labyrinth beneath the palace, he was exposed to more magic than Scryos or any other man could muster."

"Magic? In the palace? No, no. The Empyreors would never have permitted it."

"The Empyreors helped put it there. Trust me there is magic in every stone of that building. The whole place is rotten with it. In fact, if this Scryos is what you think he is, your best bet of escaping him is to find yourself a hiding place in or around the palace. The power laid there is layered and very complex, and much of it is, let us say, inhospitable to my kind."

Zabet puffed with hope. "Can it destroy him?"

"Hardly, but it can confuse or block his own power. Make it more difficult for him to spy you out."

Zabet was licking his lips furiously now, his face as knotted as the tangles of his thought. He lifted his mug in salute. "I knew you were a turn of good fortune, old friend. Thank you."

The other man looked amused. "You are welcome. And now I have a request to make of you."

Zabet winked teasingly. "If it is magic stones you are after, I'm afraid I have recently gone out of the business."

"Actually, it does concern a stone, but all I want is information."

"What kind of stone?" Zabet sipped his beer.

"Bloodstone."

Zabet choked, spluttered, and rolled accusing eyes. "Are you playing with me?"

Al lifted a brow. "Why?"

"I told you about the jewel I procured for Scryos, didn't I? Three guesses as to type of stone it was?"

The Northlander's expression never changed. "Bloodstone," he said softly.

Zabet nodded. "Imharta told Inris the name. He is quite interested in the stuff. He thinks it has special properties. Something about harnessing energy of one kind or another."

"Imharta knows about bloodstone."

"Yes. And he is not the only one. Imharta studies bloodstone, but my sources tell me that Scryos collects it. He's been shipping raw chunks of it into the Empyre out of the east for years."

"Then why hire you to locate another stone?"

"I imagine it has to do with the quality of this stone and the markings on it. Scyros was most particular about both."

Night was creeping up from the gutters and the cracks in the squalid sun-baked streets when Al parted ways with Zabet. He felt rather guilty about doing so for the illusionist, for all his unsavory habits, wasn't all that bad. In fact, his unsavoriness made him both amusing and useful. Al had no problem bending rules or even disregarding them, but he hated deceiving others to their harm.

Zabet had trusted in Al's ability to protect him, because he believed in the power he had seen Al use years before. But Al's power was gone, and his more ordinary gifts would amount to a hiccough in the eyes of any serious practitioner. If Zabet was in danger from this Scryos, Al had only increased that danger by persuading him to talk.

Scryos, he thought, savoring and cursing the name as he wove his way through the packed streets. The name alone meant more than a Southerner like Zabet could know.

It was an obvious variation on the Northland word *scryer*, which any member of the Steward's house would recognize as an ancient name for seer. Al himself had been trained in the art of scrying, and his grandfather was the foremost scryer in all the lands. Water, mirrors, panes of glass, fire, the constellations, all might be used by those born of the Steward's house to summon visions of surprising clarity.

Al slipped around a group of turbaned women, thinking of a dark night licked by firelight, a panther's eye, and a layered voice saying, "What if your house were about to turn on the others?"

What if? He could do nothing about it. He was a seer no longer, and only those who possessed a steward's power could be expected to defend the first house. But, if a rogue seer *had* succeeded in evading his grandfather's all seeing eye, more than the Steward's house might be in danger. A renegade who secreted himself in this ancient city might hatch all sorts of malicious schemes because the City of the Sun had long defeated the Stewards' oversight. It, like the Fortress at Numyn and the Warder's Settlement, was seeded with a wild magic that resisted all attempts to penetrate it. And now that power appeared to be waxing.

Al realized that his mind was made up. He might not be a seer anymore, but he was a fighter and the old loyalties weren't dead in him yet. He retained the history and lore and philosophy of his house. Let the mysterious master of the staff called Life scheme as he would, he could not prevent Al from pursuing other goals until fate rose up to meet him. Besides, Al's issues with bloodstone were personal.

Bloodstone had taken Al's power. Bloodstone had left him permanently marked with a blot of evil. Bloodstone had been his enemy's weapon of choice, and bloodstone seemed to be this Scryos' hobby. Until either Blayne or the Lord Warder found him, Al was free to do as he liked, and he what he liked was learning more about this Scryos and the stones he coveted.

CHAPTER 19: In Service

In the great house of the Lord Janeryc Cyronian, a serving girl named Emily Sayer balanced a heavy tray on her forearms and mounted a shallow, turning stair. In the afternoon light, the great rectangular stairwell, lit by a series of barred slits of windows, brooded in premature dusk, and Emily, stepping into that dusk, shivered. As the sound of her footsteps drifted like leaves through the quiet, she felt, again, the bleakness saturating the entire house. It had been many days since the Lord Cyronian had installed her and Colin in his home as servants, and she still wrestled with its atmosphere of pervasive and permanent gloom.

On the looks of it, the house of the Cyronians should have shone with light and life. Although built in a severe Southern style, its square, high-ceilinged rooms were large, airy and gracious, opening onto wide pillared walkways and fountained courtyards. Its furnishings were made of rich woods and strewn with bright cushions. Its stone walls and floors were adorned with vividly colored tiles and warmed by thick tapestries and carpets.

And all this vivid splendor was meticulously maintained by a staff of neat and efficient servants, who kept the inlaid floors polished, the divans and tables oiled, the courtyards and terraces swept clean, and the potted foliage pruned and watered to lushness.

Even so, the house had a dim, gray atmosphere like the emptiness of a tomb. There were only a dozen or so regular residents occupying the sprawling enormity of it, and the majority of those were servants, most of whom had a knack for ghosting about the place. Only three of the residents were family members, and one of those, Janeryc, was hardly ever home. His mansion might look luxurious, but it felt more like a house of the dead.

Approaching the great, carved door on the top landing, Emily carefully maneuvered her tray to one arm. Porcelain dishes clinked, and a hastily muffled curse slipped her lips. Only when she got the contents of the tray under control did she lift her hand to knock.

As usual no one answered. So Emily quietly pushed the door in and announced herself. It would not do to surprise the resident of these rooms. She had done so once before and paid a heavy price for it. Now she looked about, gripped her tray tightly, and cautiously stepped around a basket overflowing with rolls of silk yarn.

At a low table resting near a great barred window, she set her tray down. "My Lady, Janys?" she called, keeping her tone pleasant and soothing. "Lady," she called again after a moment. Finally, she heard a whisper of sound. It came from the room connected to the one in which she stood. "I have brought you your supper," Emily called, peering into the dimness. Another rustle and a whisper that might have been hastily muttered words.

"Won't you come eat?" Emily cajoled.

Silence.

Emily sighed heavily and let her eyes drift to the scene beyond the window. Out there the sun shone bright, and a whole world hummed with full-blooded people leading full-blooded lives while she languished here, in this heavy palace that chafed at the heavy places in her own soul.

She turned back to the depressing disorder about her. She knew her duty — she had been lectured about it often enough in the last few days. "Lady," she insisted. "I was told to make certain that you eat. Will you please come to the table, or shall I bring the food to you?"

"Go away," came the anxious reply.

"Not until you have eaten, my lady."

"I am not hungry." But the speaker was closer. Emily could see her pallid figure hovering in the doorway between the rooms. Holding herself very still, Emily spoke as pleasantly as she knew how. "Come and eat. Benja tells me that she has made your favorite."

"I told you. I am not hungry."

"Now, now, lady, do you want to upset your daughter again? You know how she worries when you don't eat."

The nervous figure scuttled closer. "You should be caring for my little daughter instead of pestering me."

Emily sighed again. She tried a different tack. Pointing at the tray, she said, "Look I have brought you some young leaves from the orange trees. See what a pretty shade of green they are. And here are a few wild flowers I found growing in the kitchen garden."

"Wildflowers?"

"Yes. You asked for new things to draw. Come and sit, and I will bring your sketching pens so that you may draw them."

The hovering figure scampered into the window's light, and its shaggy head ignited into a halo. According to Benja, the Lady Janys' ivory hair had once fallen smooth as silk clear to her ankles. These days no one could stop her from chopping it short. It stood out in tufts around her thin face, and still she complained that it interfered with her "work."

Janys, thin and clad in wrinkled and fraying silks, moved to kneel at the table. She clucked and cooed over the limp little flowers lying in one corner of the tray. Then she began snapping the fingers of her left hand, while poking the picked flowers with the index finger of her right.

Emily moved quickly into the other room. She knew what Janys wanted, pens and sketching paper. It took her a long time to find them. This second room was even more cluttered than the first, piled high with rolled carpets, jumbled furniture, several spinning wheels, and discarded items of clothing and personal effects that the Lady Janys refused to let the servants clear away. The sketch paper was not where the lady normally piled it, so Emily had to work her way through various piles of items until she reached a narrow door that was always kept closed. Emily had never been allowed through that door. As far as she knew, no one but Janys, her daughter and Janeryc ever passed through it. But just now it lay ever so slightly ajar, and for a moment, Emily was sorely tempted to peek around it.

A flurry of thin limbs and silk prevented her. Janys had gusted past her to slam the door shut.

Panting, her spiky tresses sticking up about her head, the lady Janys leaned against the door and cried. "Spy!"

Emily silently ran through every curse word she knew. She could tell that the wild-eyed Janys was on the verge of one of her famous fits. "No, no, Lady. I wasn't spying! I wouldn't do that to you."

"Liar!" cried the pale woman, her ravaged face contorting. 'You want to steal my secret! But you will not succeed. The guardian will not speak to you!" She flailed at the younger woman.

Emily backed away, holding up her hands in surrender. "Please, lady, I wasn't snooping, I swear it. I was only trying—"

"Snooping!" A confused look crossed the other woman's face. In her markedly southern accent she said, "What do you mean, snooping?"

Emily opened her mouth to answer and had a better idea. "If you will come back to the table, I will tell you."

Curiosity got the better of the madwoman, and by the time Emily had settled her at the table, Janys had forgotten the door incident. She was drawing and opening her mouth for the food that Emily spooned past her lips like a happy child. But there was nothing childlike about the brilliant images that Janys' thin fingers generated. Emily couldn't help but marvel at them. Janys' expression might be that of a simpleton, but her drawings were those of a genius.

"Your flower is beautiful, my lady," she said warmly.

Janys frowned and stuck the tip of her tongue between her lips. "It is fair. But Janera will like it."

"Janera, your sister?" Emily prompted, breaking the rules, again.

"Yes, my sister! Stupid girl."

"Did—does Janera draw?"

"No, she is much too busy at court. Uncle says she will make our fortunes yet."

"She must be very gifted in her own right then."

The brown eyes of the madwoman lifted from the paper and latched onto hers. "She never comes to visit me anymore," Janys whispered.

Emily started to act as if she had not heard. "The light is failing, lady. Let me clear these things away."

Emily reached for Janys' plate and a claw-like hand caught her ear, pulled her close to the madwoman's ravaged face. A jolt went through Emily, and Janis's wide brown eyes seemed to clear while her slack face acquired maturity and dignity. "They killed her, you know?" Janys said.

Emily looked into Janys' face, saw pushing through it the ghost of another woman, the woman Janys might have been. "Who?" she said. "Who killed Janera?"

"Bethnarian and those Sardic witches." Janys' fingernails dug sharply into Emily's arm.

At that same moment the door to the room opened and a lightly-clad figure slipped through it, raising the blue smoke of its veil from its face.

Janys' sooty fingers grabbed Emily's arm. "It's her," she cried. "Janera! She will not rest with the other dead."

As Emily looked toward the door in dismay, the visitor moved deeper into the room. "It's not Janera, Mother," she said. "It's me, Vyara."

"Vyara?" squinted Janys.

The Lady Vyara moved to her mother, touched her lightly, then bent her own pale head and bestowed a kiss on the crown of Janys' ragged one. Accusing eyes jumped to Emily. "Have you been encouraging her to draw?" Lady Vyara said.

Emily clenched her jaw, hating the way those eyes made her feel.

Vyara drew herself up and spoke in a level voice that could not quite conceal the dislike running beneath it. "Did you give her this paper?"

Emily contemplated several answers.

One of Vyara's ivory brows went up. "Did you?"

"It is her paper; I merely brought it to the table."

"So you *did* encourage her to draw."

Emily was having a hard time controlling her own anger. "You wanted her to eat," she said in a rising voice.

"I did not want her tricked into it with a distraction that will only disturb her more."

"She was happy."

"You do not understand. She may look happy, but drawing brings back memories, and memories cause her confusion and distress. Tonight she will not sleep, or if she does, she will have nightmares." Vyara sighed. "Why is it that you cannot do as you are told?"

Emily aimed her eyes at the floor. They felt hot enough to burn a hole through the carpeted tiles.

"Well?"

"I was only trying to help," she muttered.

"From now on you are to do no more and no less than you are told."

"She brought me flowers, Janera," Janys interrupted. "But I am done with them now. Will you take them to my little Vyara?"

Emily heard Vyara's indrawn breath, and dared a peek at her. The blonde girl's eyes were wide and wet.

Embarrassed, almost remorseful, Emily looked away. "I am sorry, lady. I was not intending to upset her. I think it actually helps her to be busy. She shouldn't always be lurking in these upstairs rooms. You should encourage her to go outside more."

Vyara dashed her unborn tears away and blazed forth. "Be quiet! You are not here to suggest but to obey. If you cannot do as you are told, then I will order my uncle to dismiss you."

Emily blazed back. "Don't do me any favors! Keep your poor sick mother shut up if you like. I'm done here!" Turning on her heel, she strode to the door. Just before she slammed it, she heard Janys cry out, "Bring me flowers, girl!"

She pounded down the stairs, enjoying the way her stomping made war on the house's quiet. A lone servant emerged from his self-imposed limbo long enough to stare at her as she stalked through the halls. Crossing a minor courtyard to the smaller building that held the servants' quarters, she ran up a much narrower stair to a rooftop terrace and found Colin Blackhammer repotting an orange tree. Colin looked up in time to register her expression and went back to potting the orange tree. "What did you do this time?"

Emily glared at him. "What makes you think *I* did anything?"

Colin shrugged. "Oh, I don't know? Experience maybe." He smiled to himself.

"Amusing. I'll have you know that I actually got Janys to eat. And for that her daughter threatens to have me dismissed."

That caught Colin's attention. There was a warning flavor in his voice as he said, "Be careful, Emily."

Emily raised her hands to the heavens. "Haven't I tried? I know I'm terrible at being a house servant, but you and Faryn and Janeryc didn't give me any other choice."

"Really? And that's why you can't go half a day without stomping or complaining or fuming at our new mistress?"

Emily glared at him, a picture of indignation. "I can't help it if she hates me."

Another voice answered. "A convenient excuse since it gives you the right to hate her back."

Emily looked up at the roof of the building that walled one side of the terrace and saw Faryn's supple boots dangling from it. She set her hands on her hips. "Where have you been?"

"Around and about."

She traced the shape of his head against a backdrop of blue.

"Have you found a way into the palace?"

In a flutter of garments Faryn pushed off, dropping a good fifteen feet to land without a sound on the blocks below. "Perhaps."

"Well, get more definite. As of tonight I will need another job and another place to sleep."

The warder's cold eyes held neutral, but Colin groaned. "I thought you said that Vyara only threatened to dismiss you."

"She did. I quit. I'm sick of the arrogance of noble women."

"As opposed to the arrogance of Midlander women," commented Faryn equitably.

Colin snorted a laugh, and Emily shot him a hard look, lifted her chin, and took the moral high ground. "I'm not the one pushing people around."

Colin's amusement turned into incredulity. "No. You are just the one pushing back."

The warder, who stood with his shoulders propped against the wall, grinned like a wolf.

Emily swung away. "You know what I mean."

"What you mean is that if anyone is going to do the pushing it should be you," said Colin.

She set her hands on her hips, reproaching him with her eyes. "Fine. Blame it all on me."

"I don't blame you. You obviously can't help it. You were born pushy, and people have indulged you."

"What?"

"It's probably all the special treatment you got because you were Millicynt's niece. While the other village girls spent their time learning how to respect their elders and run a household, you spent yours running through the woods and turning up your nose at anyone who criticized you for it."

Emily was offended. "You make me sound like a spoiled child. I worked too."

"Not the way the rest of us did. Not in the fields or sheds. Not like a person who wanted to be a part of that life."

"For somebody who worked so hard, you certainly found a lot of time to spend with me."

"I wouldn't have if Millicynt hadn't taken me on as an apprentice. I'd have spent most of my waking hours in my father's shop or learning some other trade."

Faryn's soft voice interrupted. "The endless toil of the common man."

Colin looked piqued. "It keeps nations fed and clothed and sheltered."

The warder's light eyes gleamed. "Did I say otherwise?"

"Well," Colin huffed and turned back to Emily. "The point is I'm not surprised that you and Vyara act like nervous cats around each other. But I am amazed that you aren't concentrating on getting what you really want. You said we came here to see your friend, Beth. To do that you need Janeryc's help. Why not put up with his niece for a little while? It's a small price to pay if you consider the reward."

"Well said," commented Faryn.

Emily turned away frowning. All petulance seemed to drop from her as she looked toward the dark shadow in the southwest that was the Empyreal enclave. So close and still a world away. "I just don't understand why you, Faryn, can't slip me in. Warders can be amazingly discreet when they need to be."

The gray-eyed man crossed his arms. "I told you: it is not that simple."

"Why not?" she demanded, venting her frustration.

"There are other powers in the world besides warders."

"You fear the thing lurking at the roots of that place."

The warder's eyes seemed measure her resolve. "Power calls to power. But even if I could get you into the palace, I could not ensure that you would reach the princess. Our best chance of success lies in using more conventional and legitimate means."

"Janeryc."

"Yes."

"I don't trust him."

Colin volunteered, "He's been helpful so far, and the Lord Warder sent us to him."

"Why?" Emily aimed the question at Faryn, who shrugged.

"I do not know the Lord's mind."

Emily regarded him intently. "But you know that Lord Sandyr owes a debt to this man."

Faryn's expression had grown enigmatic.

Emily stomped her foot. "Why won't you tell me more?"

"It is not my place."

"Even if it may bear on the outcome of my mission and yours?"

"You are as safe here as anywhere, and safer than you will be once you make contact with Bethnarian's daughter."

"I'll be the judge of that."

"What do you have against Janeryc?" pursued Colin.

Emily ran the back of her wrist across her forehead, her face tight with worry. "I don't know. But something's not right. I can feel it. And it's not just Janeryc. It's the whole family, something's off about all of them."

She looked at the two men regarding her blankly and threw up her hands. "Can't you feel it? The deathly atmosphere that hangs over this place. It's like a curse, a suffocating curse that presses all the life and breath from you. No wonder Janys is mad. I'd go mad too if I had to live under this pall."

Colin frowned and looked an inquiry at Faryn, who shrugged his shoulders. "It is a quiet house," the warder returned. "But I sense no curse here."

Emily collapsed in silence just in time to see a veiled head topping the final step of the stair. She croaked a warning at Faryn, but the warder was already disappearing over the side of the terrace. Colin rubbed his hands anxiously, hurried to Emily and hissed. "Let me handle this."

Emily hissed back. "Have at it! She likes you."

Vyara emerged on the terrace, and Colin immediately folded himself into a bow as deep as his stiff leg would allow. Then he yanked Emily's sleeve until she bowed also.

The Lady Vyara's soft veil floated about her. Through it, Emily could see how the younger lady's eyes lingered on Colin before jumping away. "Girl," Vyara said to Emily and paused. "Emilyn," she amended.

"My lady?" Emily purred with exaggerated humility, flicking Colin a smug sideways glance.

"I have come to ask your pardon."

Emily's head came up. "My lady?" she said, and heard Colin cough back a laugh.

Vyara clasped and unclasped her hands. "I have wronged you. You meant well, and you could not have known how seriously drawing affects my mother's condition."

Silence reigned until Emily realized that Vyara was waiting for her response. "How is your mother?" was all that she could think to say, and winced.

"She is sleeping. It is a good sign."

"It relieves me to hear it, lady," said Emily and felt Colin nudge her with his elbow. Swallowing her pride, she added, "And I apologize for acting on impulse. I should have asked permission of you or Benja before encouraging her to draw."

Vyara permitted herself a dignified nod. "You will stay of course. Lord Janeryc wants it so, and I will not have it said that I dismissed a servant unfairly."

The last comment rankled, but Emily let it slide. In a voice approximating gratitude, she said, "My lady is kind."

Vyara brushed gratitude aside. "I would like you to accompany me on an errand tomorrow."

"As my lady wishes."

Vyara nodded again. Her eyes flicked back to Colin. Abruptly, she turned to walk away, her rounded shoulders slumping as if she felt all the sorrow hanging over her house descending upon her. Then the trailing gauze of her gown tangled her feet and she stumbled and pitched forward over the steep stair. Both Emily and Colin jumped, but Colin reached her first.

"Thank you," gasped Vyara, clutching his tunic. Colin nodded and very deliberately removed his hands from her person. Vyara, however, hung on to him.

Emily cleared her throat, "Lady Vyara, are you well?"

Vyara remembered herself. Her hands flew up from Colin's chest like startled birds.

Colin spoke carefully. "If you are injured, Lady, I can go for Benja or Dejan."

Vyara turned and fled down the stair.

Colin loosed a breath. "That was close. A step or two more and she would have fallen."

Emily shot him a look of amazement. "Oh, she's fallen alright," she said.

Chapter 20: Nighttime Encounters

Abreem Imharta, scholar of the Empyre, cowered in his narrow bed in his austere bedchamber and listened to the breathing of the house. He had been home for many days now — having been deposited on his doorstep early one morning by the cold-eyed man named Faryn, whose every movement threatened to overturn Abreem's straightforward notion of reality. Abreem had not seen the man since. And he was profoundly relieved about it—at first.

Then he began to fall apart. Not physically. Physically, he mended. His arm hurt less; his bruises faded; he grew strong and steady enough to return to his studies. But his mind—his mind cracked.

He grew increasingly distracted, almost paranoid. During the day, he jumped at every movement and noise. At night, he fought to sleep. Only when he had exhausted himself by tossing and turning after it, did he finally nod off and then he descended into dreams that shocked him back to wakefulness.

He assumed he had been traumatized by his violent encounter with the Sards. After all, he had witnessed the killing of a Sardic priestess and narrowly escaped being killed himself. But the fear that gnawed his insides seemed of a more insidious character. It dwelled upon things unreal, turning mere shadows into monsters and filling his dreams with a voice that crackled and hummed like fire.

Abreem tried to ease his apprehensions by telling himself that he lived in an excellent quarter of the city, that he had two live-in servants keeping guard upstairs, and that his dreams lacked substance. But he still could not shake his fear.

On this particular night, he grew so exasperated with himself that he threw back his bedclothes and tip toed through the hall to the servants' back stair. Better to risk confronting monsters than to be driven mad by shadows. His footsteps filled the air with whispers only slightly less loud than the rasp of his breathing and the boom of his heart.

Room by room, he searched his house—and found nothing. The sitting rooms were dark and neat, the doors to the outer courtyard were locked tight, the wide-arching front hall reposed in shadow. Then he started down the narrower corridor leading to his workroom and library and saw a ribbon of golden light seeping under the library door.

He stopped breathing, which made his heart thump louder than ever. Thoughts of dark men, hard hands, and darker purposes fired his nerves. He told himself to stay calm; he told himself to think; he told himself to run for the servants. His scholarly self reminded him it was just a light—just a light. One of the servants must have left a lamp burning.

He set his hand to the door's handle, and silently levered it open. Then he thrust the door inward so that it banged into wood.

The sharp sound reverberated into silence.

His wide eyes lighted on a single dancing teardrop of flame. As he watched, the laughing flame steadied itself behind its glass shield. He exhaled. All else was as exactly as it should have been—his library chairs and long reading table; the bookcases, dense with their orderly holdings of books and manuscripts.

Grumbling, he shuffled to the table and lifted the lamp's globe to blow out the light. The little flame flickered again, directing Abreem's eye to the gold-leafed title of the book on the table. His grip failed him. The globe fell, struck stone, and shattered into a thousand gleaming splinters.

A hard hand seized his injured arm and shoved it to the middle of his back, while another hand dug into his throat, choking him in mid-wail.

"Master Imharta, I presume," said a cool, distinctly foreign voice.

Cocooned in pain, Abreem gurgled. The grip on his injured arm eased, and he sagged in his attacker's grip.

Hands and words propped him up. "Relax, Master. I am not interested in hurting you. I am just looking for information."

In some part of his brain inured to fear, Abreem placed the voice's accent. He reached for words, missed them, and settled for bobbing his head.

"Promise me you won't try to shout, and I will let you go." The voice like the words reassured, but something savage stalked beneath.

Abreem blinked away tears of pain. He nodded more firmly despite the hand gripping his throat.

"Promise? Believe me, if you try anything, I will decapitate you before you finish opening your mouth."

Abreem nodded again.

The hands let go. Abreem bit down a moan as his overextended joints shifted back into place. Something sharp and cold as splintered glass nicked the flesh of his neck.

"Turn around slowly," the intruder said.

Abreem did. He found himself confronting a tall, dark-haired Northlander whose fierce gaze held no congress with the hint of smile upon his face. The tip of the unremarkable saber the man held rested just to the left of Abreem's sternum, precisely above his heart.

With his free hand the Northlander gestured. "Please, master, take a seat. I hadn't planned on speaking with you yet. But since you have seen fit to join me—"

Abreem looked around as if he expected to find the furniture rearranged.

256

"Why don't you try that one?" remarked the dark man dryly and pointed.

Abreem limped to the designated chair, cradling his aching arm, and eased himself down into it. All the pain in the world seemed to have lodged itself in his shoulder, but strangely enough, his fear was gone. For some inexplicable reason, he felt more safe now than he had in weeks. He also felt curious. He noted how the tall man came to stand within easy striking distance, though he leaned comfortably against the edge of the heavy library table.

Abreem's eyes moved about the room looking for other nasty surprises. "What do you want?" he husked, his voice catching on a prickling in the air that made him want to cough.

A dark eyebrow lifted, a dark eye gleamed. "I told you. Information. I hear that you are a very knowledgeable man."

"Is that why you are helping yourself to my books?" asked Abreem, and flinched at his own temerity.

The invader smiled more broadly and gave a little laugh.

Abreem's response was polite. "If you wanted to speak with me, you could have requested a regular meeting during day-time hours."

Another low laugh, which for no discernable reason raised the hairs on the back of Abreem's neck. "Could I now? That is a comfort to hear. Unfortunately, my leisure time is not what it used to be. Besides, I prefer to do certain work at night."

Abreem swallowed. "What knowledge would you have of me?"

The intruder's smile withered. "Knowledge pertaining to bloodstone."

Abreem stared. "Bloodstone?"

"Yes."

"You will find none of it in my house."

"But you know of it."

Abreem crooked his brows, glanced at the tell-tale book on the table. "As you can see."

"Yes, the book has proved most interesting, but a well-read man like yourself, master, must have gleaned knowledge from many books, as well as other sources."

Abreem looked at the blade aimed at his chest, followed it up to the steady hand that pointed it, stopped short of the intruder's eyes. "There is little enough to tell. Unless you are interested in old legends."

"Let's start with what you consider to be the facts and move on from there."

The intruder reasserted his pleasant little smile. The scholar dampened his lips and felt his way into his subject. "Bloodstone is one of several forms of rock containing active forms of energy. It is known to radiate this energy. Some believe that Bloodstone has the unique property of being able to absorb and store energy."

"Is the stone found here?"

"The older histories suggest that it was brought to the Empyre."

"From where?

"Different chroniclers say different things. I doubt that anyone knows exactly where to mine it anymore, even the Sards. It is very rare. The first Empyreal records of it date to about the time of Ambyre the Heretic."

"So shortly after the first Empyre's fall."

Abreem's curiosity deepened. "You are familiar with the unofficial histories."

The invader did not comment. "So it is not native to the Empyre?"

"No. The Sards, who particularly value it, claim it came out of the East. They employ it in certain rites." The prickling in the air intensified. Abreem coughed and his voice faltered. Suddenly, there seemed to be a weight on his chest. He had to suck at the air while the shadows in the room took on a life of their own. The shadow of the mere man before him seemed to have grown fangs and claws so that Abreem began to wonder if he actually sat in the stolid and comfortable confines of his little library or if he had slid into yet another nightmare.

"What else do the Sards say about it?" the cool voice prompted.

Something in the voice reminded Abreem of the fiery voice in his nightmares. He watched the intruder's looming shadow and answered like a man in a dream. "They keep their lore secret. But if you look deep into the old stories, you can find the outlines of the tale that seems to have shaped their culture. A great magician discovers the first stones of the blood. He brings them to our land. He tears their empyre apart, and uses the stones to cast the Sards into the desert. So, the Sards hate and fear bloodstone, yet prize it above all things. They keep it in nested boxes carved with special symbols."

"Why?"

"Probably because they know it is toxic to the body. It cannot be handled for any length of time without making the holder very ill."

"Even ordinary men?" asked the intruder softly.

Abreem's head gave a little shake. "Ordinary?"

"Never mind. What are the symptoms of this illness?"

"A general wasting accompanied by madness and eventual death."

"Have the Sards found a way to prevent this illness?"

"I doubt it. But they are an ancient, bloody, and superstitious people, the last remnant of the Empyre that was. They believe the blood magic of the stone can compel the daemons they worship. The lives of mere people, even their own, mean nothing to them by comparison."

"How do they call on the power of the stone?"

Even lost in a dream, Abreem did not want to answer. He shook his head warningly. "Why would I know? I am a citizen of the Empyre."

"But in your quest for knowledge you have run across clues to their practices, haven't you?" The man reclaimed Abreem's attention. His eyes were earnest.

Abreem blinked. "What I know and what I suspect are two very different things."

"Sometimes suspicion is all we have to guide us."

Abreem knit his brow, then nodded. "The Sards have a saying, 'Blood calls to blood, stone to stone.' They are known for making offerings."

"Let me guess. Blood offerings."

Abreem nodded. "The blood of animals, of men and women, even children. Life blood. They seem to believe that the stone is alive and aware, that it thirsts for blood the way men thirst for water and life. So they pour living blood on the stone to awaken the old blood inside it."

"Blood inside the stone?"

"Because of the veins of color in it, you see."

"Whose blood?"

Abreem shrugged.

The man leaned forward, and his great beastly shadow once again flexed its claws. "Whose do you think, Master Abreem?"

Abreem shivered. "It is just legend," he explained.

"Whose blood?"

It seemed as if the man's great shadow pinned him, while the man himself drew the answer out of Abreem with impossibly dark eyes.

"The blood of the Unstoried," said Abreem.

"Unstoried?"

"The Untold, if you prefer. Either translation is like to be inexact. In certain Sardic legends he is referred to as the Womb of the Gods, but you Northlanders I think call him the Ancient One or Ancient Enemy."

The man blinked. The blade over Abreem's heart dipped just a little. The shadow was just a shadow, the man just a man. Abreem dared to glance into a face hollowed out by a care too great for its years. *He is a young man*, realized Abreem, and felt a sudden impulse to reach out and console the invader.

"The ancient enemy's," the stranger said. Then his dark head whipped round. For a moment he stood listening to a sound only he could hear.

Thoughts of consolation evaporated from Abreem's mind for he could hear sounds too, sounds of stealth from the hallway outside. But when he shifted forward in his seat, the intruder's sword jumped up to kiss his jugular vein.

"Please," hissed Abreem, raising a steady hand.

The younger man leaned in and said in a low voice. "I'm afraid you have other night visitors to greet, master. If you are as wise as people say—"

"Please—" whispered Abreem again. "Don't leave me."

The man blinked in surprise, and the handle of the door moved. In three strides the intruder was across the room and disappearing into the deeper darkness between bookcases.

Abreem was left alone to confront the men who opened the door.

In their heavy robes, they appeared as little more than shifting shapes of darkness, but gradually, the light of the lamp separated them into stark, sinewy men with faces parched to leathery toughness and painted in intricate designs. Sardic warriors.

Abreem met them with resignation bordering on relief. These stalkers he understood, and some part of him, he realized, had expected them all along.

As the first of the brown-robed men flowed toward him, Abreem tried to draw himself up. The Sard's skin was very black, but his hair had turned white, and when Abreem read the marks of power on his lined face, some of his resignation chilled to fear. This man was a warrior of exalted order. The other two were also important, but much younger, though just as lean and hard with desert deprivation. Their marks as much as Abreem's familiarity with Sardic ways told the little scholar just how valuable a target he had become.

The elder Sard murmured something indecipherable in his native tongue. Then he spoke more loudly to Abreem, using a thickly accented common tongue. "Where heart breaker?"

Abreem briefly considered responding in Sardic, opted instead for the language of the Empyre. "I do not know what you are talking about."

He expected a blow. But the elderly Sard only looked at him, unequivocal as his naked blade. "You find Bin Edath, the city that was."

Abreem swallowed. "If you mean Ab Syminal, I was there. But I swear to you I brought only drawings back with me. Take them if you want them. They are over there."

The Sard glared down at him. From beneath his robe he drew a chain of iron links from which dangled a large drop of faceted crystal. "Look," the Sard commanded, holding the crystal only inches away from Abreem's nose.

Seeing less to fear in obeying than in not, Abreem looked. The crystal's internal intricacies pulled at his eye, and he followed its swing into a confounding maze of fractured light, at the heart of which nestled a tiny and terrible splinter of pure dark. The splinter widened into a wedge and then a chasm. On the other side of that darkness a flaming figure stood. The figure spoke and Abreem's mind cracked open.

A crash and simultaneous jolt of pain yanked him out of the abyss. He was lying on the floor, a shout dying in his burning mouth while a black form reeled across his line of sight, smashed into the wall, and crumpled into a heap at its base with a saber protruding from its chest. Abreem tried to raise himself onto his good shoulder but, feeling tiny bits of glass slicing into his hand, dropped back and saw the chair he had been sitting in lying on its side. The library table was a pile of planks, but somehow the lamp upon it still burned bright atop broken wood.

A darting and heaving tangle of limbs spun into view. Sards! And something else that fought with brutal efficiency and a wild animal's ferocity. The Sards fell back.

Abreem pressed himself to his knees and half crawled, half scooted to the limp figure lying against the wall. Setting one foot against the dead Sard's chest, he heaved until he drew the bloody length of the Northlander's saber free.

Then the gentle scholar rose and stumbled toward the fray, confounded by his own intentions. It took him as much as his enemies by surprise when he swung the sword at the nearest Sard's neck.

The sword bit. Blood spurted, and the younger Sard stumbled and dropped while Abreem's first home invader snatched the advantage. He threw himself at the elder Sard, who, strong and crafty and wise though he must be, lacked the younger man's feral strength and intensity. The Northlander feinted back, drawing the white-haired Sard in, then spun sideways. The two men, white-haired and dark, swung together for a moment. Then the white-haired Sard grunted, grinned into his enemy's eyes, and slid slowly out of his hold.

The Northlander's face burned. He turned hot animal eyes on the waiting scholar, and the feral energy emanating from him pushed Abreem back across the room. Then the wildness ebbed, leaving behind a faintly bemused and blood-spattered man.

The white-haired Sard was not quite dead. He coughed and raised a feeble hand, then said something in his hissing language. The Northlander, forgetting Abreem, bent over him. The Sard mumbled again and, bubbling blood, died.

From their respective corners, the two survivors contemplated the carnage.

It was the Northlander who spoke first. "My Sardic was never very good. Do you know what he said?"

Abreem swallowed and cleared his throat. "Something about the Captain of Night and the Son of Morning."

"The Son of Morning," the Northerner repeated. He turned a thoughtful look on Abreem. "What kind of man earns the dispatch of not one but three Sardic assassins?"

Abreem pushed himself off the bookcase. "What kind of man dispatches such assassins?"

The Northlander grinned. "I took care of two. You finished the third one." Squatting, he began rifling the folds of the dead Sard's robe. "Search the other two," he ordered.

Abreem did as he was told, swallowing his distaste. When he looked again at the Northlander, the man was dangling the Sard's crystal.

"What is it?" Abreem asked.

His night visitor didn't answer. He only stowed the crystal inside his robe. "We need to get rid of these bodies," he said.

Abreem stared at him. "We! As far as I am concerned, this is a matter for the Empyreal guard."

The Northlander rested his elbows on his knees and fixed Abreem with a mocking look. "And how will you answer their questions? Is there any answer that will satisfy the Empyreal interrogators?"

"That is not my problem. My duty is to speak the truth as far as I know it."

The Northlander laughed. "The truth is as likely to kill a man as save him, especially when the Empyre's agents are involved. But setting that aside, do you honestly think you can admit to being targeted by Sards without casting suspicion on yourself? The Empyreor is dying; mistrust is everywhere. Believe me, if you depend on the Empyreal guard to put an end to your troubles, you will only earn yourself a lengthy stay in the Empyreal dungeons."

Abreem blinked rapidly. "The Empyreor knows my reputation. He and I share similar interests in the Book of Nyte. I have spoken with his secretary numerous times."

"And I'm sure the Empyreor's secretary will be more than happy to clear his busy schedule to help you explain why three Sardic assassins died in your home."

"You only press me out of fear for yourself," accused Abreem.

The man dropped his head and shook it. When he raised it again, he said pointedly, "I won't be here when the guards come."

Abreem's shoulders drooped.

The other smiled. "Come now, Master Abreem. You can trust me. You already have, and I would say that your trust has paid off, wouldn't you?" He gestured at the dead Sards.

That point Abreem couldn't very well argue. "What would you have me do?" he groaned.

"That's the spirit!" The dark Northlander encouraged and flashed him a most disarming smile.

Bethnarian, Empyreor, brushed aside the ministrations of his body servants and entered his great garden room alone. Another night of public ceremony, another night of gilding the canker at the heart of his realm. He cast off the Empyreal robes, tossed his scepter upon a leopard-skin divan, and mentally calculated the depreciation of his Empyreal authority. All the great families of the Empyre had attended tonight's court. But several had sent heirs once or twice removed, and of the first sons who had appeared, fully half divided their attentions between Marbek and Bethnarian. Marbek himself had left early, still surrounded by an Empyreal "honor" guard. Add to that the troubles with the Flame Eaters in the poorer quarters and the encroachments of the Sards, and all indications were that the Empyre was preparing to tear itself apart.

He moved toward the fireplace that dominated one wall. A roaring fire had been built in it that did little to assuage Bethnarian's chill. He always felt cold these days, cold to the bone.

At least his pain had abated. He reached beneath the golden torque at his neck and stroked the strange stone lying against his skin. He was grateful for the temporary relief it afforded, but he had no illusions. His disease progressed. The stone could not stop it, only enable him to bear it better by masking pain with a strange euphoria.

But, soon, very soon, the stone too would turn on him, and the pain would return hundredfold. Then he would know that the time had come to put the gem to its final use. He would bear it down into the winding corridors beneath the palace complex, and with or without the key to the labyrinth, he would call and she would come. He had no real hopes for success, but the ghosts of his past demanded that he try. Then and only then could he dare the final journey into permanent dark.

He stared into the yellow fire with his hands behind his back. Its light reminded him of ripples of firelight on white-gold hair. Would he see her on the other side, as the priests of the gods claimed? Would she acknowledge him if he did? Pray the gods grant him this one act of atonement to lay at her feet.

Movement elsewhere in the room drew his attention. Idly, he raised his head, expecting to see Caphal shuffle forward. But the form that gathered itself into the light was yet another ghost—one couched in flesh.

The Empyreor did not flinch, though the aura of danger about the visitor was palpable. His mouth thinned to a grim line. "You have returned."

The visitor dipped his head. "As I promised."

"That was many years ago."

"Many more would have to pass, before I would forget my oath."

Bethnarian turned, shuffled to the nearest divan, and eased himself down onto it. He motioned for the other to sit as well. "Please," he said, indicating the gilt chair across from him.

The corners of the visitor's mouth deepened in the merest hint of a smile. He moved to stand near the fire instead so that the firelight turned his white hair to gold and his red eyes to drops of blood.

"I trust you spared my household guard getting in here," commented the Empyreor dryly.

"I had no need to disturb them."

"Did you scale the walls then? Or simply fly over them?" His words dripped sarcasm.

"I found the hidden passages beneath your halls far more convenient."

"Hmm. You look well. It would appear that your masters finally found a way to tame that bloody disposition of yours."

"You, on the other hand, look like a walking corpse."

Bethnarian grunted a laugh. "Not so tame after all."

"My kind never are. But I am the master now. And you are still the Empyreor. Is it all you hoped?"

Deep lines formed about the Empyreor's thin mouth. "Do not mock me," he said in deadly earnest.

Lorraine DeWolf

"Mock you? I wouldn't dream of it. All power comes at a price. Believe me, I know."

"Yet your words smack of 'I told you so.'"

"*Janera* told you so."

Bethnarian's right hand closed into a fist. "Do not speak that name to me!"

The Lord Warder slipped into the chair. He smiled widely this time, but his smile was a predator's toothy grin. "I tried to save your wife."

Bethnarian's answering smile was nearly as carnivorous. "Whereas I killed her."

"You did, and now the time has come to pay the debt in full."

The fingers of Bethnarian's right hand began to beat a rapid rhythm on the arm of the divan. "And you are come to ensure it. How it must please you to play the cruel hand of fate to one you despise so much!"

"What pleases me is irrelevant. I swore an oath to your dying wife."

"You would have taken her away from me." The words were a comment rather than an accusation. Bethnarian's gaze had turned inward.

"I would have offered her a life away from the power of her enemies. One where she could have reached her vast potential."

"But she chose me instead," Bethnarian said.

"Yes, she loved you."

"Too much."

"Enough to try to put herself between you and your damnation."

Bethnarian's cool eye returned to the Lord Warder. He pressed himself to his feet and tottered to the fire, holding his arms across his chest as it to stave off an icy blast. "And did she learn to hate me at the end? She must have if she made you swear to avenge her."

"Her thoughts were not for herself."

The Empyreor turned back to his visitor. For the first time, his face registered surprise.

The red eyes of the pale lord flamed. "If she hoped to avenge anyone at all it was her child, your son."

Bethnarian bowed his head. "Then tell me, how do we do this? Will you slay me now, or let me suffer longer."

The white man's smile deepened. "Oh, no Bethnarian. You cannot get off that easily. Janera shall have her revenge, but on her true foe, and you will be her instrument." The white lord rose. "For many years my people have watched the evil rebuilding in the heart of this land, even as Janera and the rest of her family did. But we alone have

265

kept alive the secret to its destruction and the locks that up to now have contained it. You must help me put an end to it."

A fierce light filled the Empyreor's eye. "Then it can be done. The monster can be destroyed." Decades seemed to drop from his face, and his voice regained its old note of ringing command. "Tell me!"

The Lord Warder's expression remained sober, but his blood-red eyes smiled. "First, you must do something for me. Then, and only then, will I give you the keys to the labyrinth and your redemption."

Emily woke abruptly from a dream of fire to the reality of it.

Night robe flying behind her, she rushed out of the servants' quarters and into the great courtyard to see several of the tall windows and doorways of the lowest floor of the house fringed with flame.

The scene inside was chaos. Servants ran hither and thither carrying small rugs and basins of water. Fire was climbing a wooden screen and belching smoke along the ceiling. In one corner of the room, the aged retainer Dejan was beating a burning chair.

"Colin?" shouted Emily.

Dejan pointed toward the room beyond. Emily grabbed a pitcher full of water from a passing servant and threw the water on the chair. Then she ran back out to the courtyard to dip the pitcher in the fountain.

It seemed like she ran and dipped and doused for hours. In fact, the fires were extinguished rather quickly. The bulk of the house being constructed of stone, there was little besides furniture and tapestries for it to burn. But restoring some semblance of order took much longer. It was some time before she had a chance to locate Colin.

She found him in another wing of the house with the lady Vyara. The young Lady Cyronian was veil-less—except for the glory of her ivory hair—and her face like Colin's was streaked with sweat and soot. On the floor beside her lay the unconscious form of her mother, Janys.

"What happened?" said Emily, stepping aside as white-haired Benja came in with a basin of water.

Vyara fastened tired eyes on the Midlander. "I told you she would dream. Why did you ever bring her those flowers?"

Emily stepped back. "You mean—"

Colin said softly. "Janys set the fires."

Emily was horrified. "Why?"

Vyara turned her bright head away, and Colin spoke instead, "She was crying that Janera told her to do it—to burn down the house and destroy the family along with it."

266

"Tellers!" breathed Emily. Overcome with remorse, she crouched down next to the unconscious woman.

"Don't you touch her!" Vyara cried. "Haven't you done enough already?" She glared at the Midlander.

"Lady, please," interposed Colin. "I know you are upset, but I need you to focus on your mother."

The look Vyara gave him merged fear with hope. Knowing there was nothing she could do, Emily departed to shoulder the burden of Vyara's anger alone. "I'm so sorry, Vyara," she muttered to herself. "So sorry."

Colin found her resting against the side of a large fountain and staring up at the stars. Without a word, he sat down next to her.

Emily spoke without looking at him. "How is she?"

"They have taken her back to her rooms. She should sleep now." He looked down at his hands. "I touched her. It was strange. I've never tried to heal madness before."

"Were you able to help her?"

"I don't know. Her mind is so fractured, and slippery as glass. It seems cracked from the inside out. Vyara allowed me to give her some herbs that will help her rest." A note of wonder entered his voice. "Vyara's a healer too. Did you know that? I could actually feel the energy coming out of her"

Emily wearily rolled her head toward him. "Really? Do you think she sensed the healing energies coming from you?"

"Probably. But who knows what Janeryc has told her."

Emily studied his profile with eyes grown deep. "I don't think Janeryc tells her much of anything."

"Why don't you go to bed? There will be plenty of work to do tomorrow."

"I couldn't sleep."

He gave her an exhausted smile. "I know what you mean. Every time I close my eyes I see fire and that poor, wretched madwoman."

Emily looked back at the stars. "Vyara was right; I'm responsible for all this."

"I wouldn't dwell too much on what Vyara said. This isn't the first time that Janys has endangered her family."

"I'm still a bad influence, Col. I shouldn't be here. I feel it in my heart."

Colin sat straighter. "Don't be foolish," he chided.

"I'm not. Power calls to power. You heard Faryn say it. I have heard Faryn's betters say the same thing. There is something dead in this house that is trying to find its way back to life. But I fear that the only thing that I am waking is darkness. Look what came of my spending time with Janys. I had only to touch her, Colin, to feel something change—only I was too bent on nursing my own resentments to pay attention to it. And now this."

"Emily, Janys is mad. She was mad long before we came here, and she will be mad long after we leave."

"This is different, and Vyara knows it. If you can't believe me, try believing her. Why else would such a sensible young woman treat me like the clap of doom? I'll tell you why, because the healer in her knows that I am dangerous. Tonight's fright only loosened her tongue, allowed her to say what she has been thinking all along: I'm trouble."

"You didn't make Janys mad. Vyara was distraught. She wasn't thinking rationally."

"Magic isn't rational, Colin. Or it operates according to laws beyond mortal conception. But that doesn't mean it's not real. I need to leave this place soon, or worse will happen."

Colin clasped her shoulder with a sooty hand. "Emily, this wasn't your fault. I know that. Deep down inside Vyara knows it too. You were both upset and tired. Tellers! I'm upset and tired. For the time being, forget Vyara and your fears. Get some sleep. I bet you will see things very differently in the morning."

Emily said nothing, but she sighed. Morning wasn't that far away.

Emily did sleep; Colin saw to it by slipping a few drops of one of Millicynt's extracts into her tea.

He considered dosing himself as well. But remembering the unpredictable Janys, he tucked his pack of herbs under his arm and mounted the side stair that led to Janys' chamber door.

A muffled voice urged him to enter. It was Vyara, a silver-limned silhouette standing against the great barred window. "Have you come to see my mother?" she asked. He noticed that she wore no veil and did not bother to turn her naked face away from him, so he tried to point his gaze elsewhere.

"I want to make sure that she is reacting properly to the medicine."

"Of course." Vyara escorted him into the room where Janys lay. To the right of the bed sat Benja, who frowned to see the Midlander man trespassing in her lady's suite.

Vyara lifted her chin. "The goodman has come to check on Mother. Go to bed, Benja. I will keep watch for a while."

Benja rose slowly, departed in a grumble.

"I'm offending her by coming here, aren't I?" Colin asked, as he sat on the bed and took the sleeping lady's wrist in his fingers.

"Benja is not accustomed to having young men wait on my mother. But she will do as I say."

Colin nodded, and Vyara continued in a low, earnest voice. "I felt what you did earlier. You calmed the voices in her mind, closed some of the old wounds. Many times have my uncle and I tried to do the same. Always her madness has defeated us, and my uncle is the strongest healer I know."

Colin ducked his head and concentrated on the patient. Carefully he slid the part of his consciousness that allowed him to perceive a body's workings into the sleeping woman. Janys' body, worn to fragility by time and care, still functioned well. It was only when he went into her mind that he felt the terrible swelling that was symptomatic of her overthrown psyche.

Caught up in the "feel" of his patient, he instantly perceived the warm touch of Vyara's hand. Soon she was touching him in another way, filling him with a gentle presence that bolstered his own insight. With her help he probed the cracks of Janys' mind — great, jagged rendings that occasionally belched geysers of emotion. But these were only the symptoms of the disease; the source lay deeper, beneath the broken mental crust of consciousness. Millicynt had taught him many years ago that the minds of all beings were layered. The deeper you went the more fundamental the energy of the mind became. Janys' mind seemed fueled too intensely. To tame her madness, heal her wounds, one would have to tame what raged beneath.

Yes, a softer mind whispered in agreement. Holding his breath, Colin slipped inside a spectacularly large crevice in Janys' broken brain to descend toward the heat and pressure that had created it.

Everywhere about him sparks flew between nodules of light. Some glowed softly like lamps. A few were bright as the sun, and then there were those that burned deep red or swallowed the light altogether. He studied one of these more closely, noting the incredible dark energy it held, and then he reached out and touched it.

His mind bucked and screamed, casting his invisible companion aside. Power exploded into his unprotected mind like lightning, illuminating strange pictures — a man holding a tall shield and calling out in a forlorn voice; that same shield filled with dancing light; a woman in a high place looking out over a sea that ate up the whole

269

horizon; a small white-haired child, naked and crying hysterically upon a sandy shore; that same child older and entering a fortress of shadows and fairy light; and last of all, a winged darkness like black lightning cleaving the sky.

He felt his own skull crack. Then he was free, and the terrible pain and images were dissolving like dying embers. He saw ceiling above him, and felt a weight across his chest. He pushed at it. "Get off," he croaked.

The weight lifted. Vyara's face, orange and black except where lines of brighter light streaked her cheeks, hovered over his. "I thought I had killed you," she cried.

Colin couldn't really make sense of that. "Did you want to kill me?" he asked.

She laid her face in the crook of his neck and sobbed, "I am sorry. I am sorry. You were in such pain, and I couldn't help."

Gradually, he recalled the facts. His hand touched Vyara's sobbing head. "Lady, I think you should get off of me," he suggested.

Vyara pulled back. "I have offended you," she said. She looked mortified.

Shifting out from under her, Colin answered, "No, but your family would not approve."

Vyara's mind was elsewhere. "I do not please you," she whispered.

Colin started to laugh. "Please me? Tellers! Who am I to be pleased? You are a lady, beautiful and noble and kind."

Vyara knelt so still that her half-lit face resembled a beautiful mask. Then her lips curved in a shy smile. "You think I am beautiful," she whispered.

Colin blushed. This wasn't entirely new territory for him. He had enjoyed his share of summer flirtations. Then again, he had never imagined flirting with an exotic Southern beauty. He swallowed, searching for a suitable reply, one that would keep him out of trouble with the Empyre and the lady.

Vyara thrust caution aside. Touching his cheek, she said, "You too are beautiful Colin of the Midlands. I thought so the first time I saw you."

Leaning in, she kissed him.

Colin felt a tightening in his gut, accompanied by a rush in his veins that set his heart racing. "Lady?" he whispered. He was telling himself he should run and hoping more than anything he could stay.

Vyara made the decision for him. She continued pressing her warm lips to his until the rush turned to intoxication and delirium.

Chapter 21: Reunions

Emily groaned as someone began shaking her. Rolling over, she opened her eyes. "For the love of heaven, Colin, I just got to sleep." But it wasn't Colin leaning over her cot. It was the Lady Vyara.

Emily sat up. Dark still gripped the windows, the half-open door. "Lady?" she asked, in a voice melding surprise and concern.

"It is time to go," said Vyara, raising a lamp.

"Go where?"

"On the errand I spoke of yestereve?"

"Oh." Emily ran her hands through her disheveled hair, remembered the chaos of the night before. "Is it that important then?"

"More important than ever, I think," said Vyara, pulling a very dark veil over her face. "Hurry. I will wait for you near the servants' portico."

Dawn was just beginning to snuff the stars as the two young women slipped from the house by a servant's door and headed off into the gloom of the streets, Vyara muffled in heavy robes, Emily wearing a headscarf. The lady carried a small covered basket on her left arm.

This early in the morning, the city streets ran to cool and quiet, but there were a number of shadowy figures lurking in doorways and around street corners. They filled Emily with trepidation and seemed to concern Vyara as well for the Lady Cyronian tended to hug the walls of the buildings they passed as if anxious to avoid being molested. In an ominously silent quarter dominated by elaborately carved and pillared buildings so old that they were slowly collapsing into their own dust, Vyara finally stopped, looked all about, then darted through a dim colonnade into an alley ending in a very narrow locked gate.

"Where are we?" Emily asked as Vyara fumbled with the lock.

"Quiet!" Vyara hissed, then added in a low voice. "This is the old compound. The Empyreal guards patrol it now, and others as well." She opened the squeaking gate and motioned Emily inside.

They had entered a large and upward-sloping yard paved with interlocking slabs of stone broken up by row upon row of low-growing citrus trees. As Vyara fastened the gate, Emily stepped under the trees' canopy. Some of the branches in that canopy were dead, some were dying, and some were yet green with leaves, but all the branches sprouted from trunks thickly gnarled by time.

"Watch your step," Vyara warned as she led Emily uphill over a network of shallow channels cut into the pavers.

"There's running water here," Emily exclaimed as she crossed a wider channel.

"Yes. The spring waters the channels, and the channels water the trees."

"There's a spring here?"

"The spring of Rygel, one of my distant ancestors. It is said that he planted the first grove here. His descendants built this great palace." She gestured absentmindedly at the ruin behind them

"Who does it belong to now?"

"No one if not the dead," Vyara answered starkly as she hurried up the slope.

At the top of the incline they found several wide channels and a many-pillared pavilion backed by a rugged outcrop of natural black granite. Behind that outcrop rose a very high wall of quarried granite like an affront to the rose-gold of the dawn sky.

At the back of the pavilion was the spring of which Vyara had spoken. It gushed forth from a hole in the granite hill into three wide basins that fed the yard's channels. Emily would have liked to stop and dip her hands in its waters, but Vyara would not wait. The young Lady Cyronian was already clambering up the side of the granite hill. Neither she nor Emily had to climb far. About eight feet above the level of the spring a cleverly hidden path had been cut, and that path wound around the outcrop to its sheer-sided back. Here there was a concealed opening that led into a narrow tunnel.

"Hold this," Vyara told Emily when they were both inside. She handed the Midlander a small lamp. Then she threw back her veil and reached into her basket for tinder.

When the lamp was lit, they moved a bit deeper into the tunnel to where a steeply twisting stone stair plunged downward into the hill's heart. At bottom was another, wider tunnel that ran for several yards before ending in what looked like a stone wall with a rusting door set into it.

Emily looked at the door; Vyara probed the rough surface of the rock wall with delicate fingers, and when she found what she wanted, she reached into her bodice and pulled out a small key.

Emily looked on in wonderment as Vyara fitted the key into what looked like an unbroken wall of natural granite. Then her wonderment turned to astonishment as a large silvery mark blazed out of the rock-face.

"Stand back," Vyara said, and pushed. A whole strip of the rough rock shifted then rotated about a hidden pivot until it hung parallel to the tunnel floor. Vyara ducked beneath the bottom of the rotated slab. "Watch your head," she called to Emily.

272

"What was that?" Emily breathed when she had passed beneath the slab into the stone-lined tunnel beyond.

"A protection devised to fool trespassers. The metal door distracts intruders, and those determined enough to find a way beyond it step into a tunnel broken by deep pits."

Emily was shaking her head. "But the mark?" she insisted. "The leaf mark!" She struggled to master her own shock and amazement.

"Leaf mark?"

"The mark shining upon the door."

Vyara really looked at her companion. "Ah. You are unused to such things. Do not be frightened. The shield mark was put there as a message, to tell the initiated that the way is ready. The Shield is one of the ancient sigils of my family."

"Sigil," Emily whispered. "The Shield!" her mind shouted as she trailed after Vyara. The lady was now climbing a set of steep steps surmounted by a large set of bronze doors.

Upon these doors was a large and detailed relief of a spreading tree. And against the trunk of that tree rested yet another likeness of the Shield, which faded into a wash of daylight as Vyara pushed open the doors.

"What is this place?" Emily murmured when she had followed the lady out. For a moment, all her questions about the Cyronians' use of the Shield mark were forgotten. She and Vyara stood on a rise above an immense shaded depression packed with ornate buildings. At their back was the great black wall, and in the distance was a high hill whose crown was just emerging into early morning sunlight. Its peak shone green and gold.

"This is the City of the Dead," said Vyara, "the resting place of the noble scions of the Empyre."

"A cemetery," breathed Emily, looking around. "Why are we here?"

"To lay my mother's ghosts to rest. But we must go quietly, and you must speak of this to no one when we return. The members of my family belong to a noble order of guardians, but the living are not usually permitted to walk here except on funeral days."

"Why not?"

Vyara shrugged and lifted her skirts to begin the descent. "Most people think it is to protect the grave goods—many a prince has gone to his rest adorned with choicest treasure. But the truth is that the dead of this place rest uneasily. Great they were in life, and restless they are in death. They sense the passage of the living and, if the proper rites are lacking, they rise to meet them. That is why they have been given a city set apart."

They wandered into a cemetery like a huge maze, hurrying down lanes winding and straight between buildings like miniature mansions. All the buildings were gorgeous—decorated with friezes and statuary, mosaics and murals that seemed to tell elaborate stories. Emily saw statues of turbaned warriors, veiled women, kneeling children, and countless grotesques, probably meant to symbolize spirits of the underworld.

She was so absorbed in looking that she almost collided with Vyara. The young Lady Cyronian had finally stopped before a particularly large and magnificent tomb entirely faced in white marble. Emily, however, was craning her neck toward the high hill at the end of their road. It was much, much closer now, so close that she could see the trunk of the great tree growing upon it. "What a magnificent tree," she murmured as she halted beside her mistress.

Vyara looked up the hill as well. "Yes. It is very old. It watches over the dead as we Cyronians do. That is why it is another of our family sigils." Vyara pointed to the very large set of bronze doors on her family tomb. These were adorned with a much larger version of the same relief Emily had seen on the smaller doors at the end of the tunnel.

As Vyara mounted the steps leading up to those doors, Emily hung back, gazing up at the shield-shape. What could have prompted the Cyronians to put an image of the Shield Light upon their family mausoleum? And what connection did they imagine between the Shield and the cemetery tree?

She wanted to ask Vyara about these things. But the Lady Cyronian was deep in some ritual for which she had taken out a square of silk, a knife, and a small but beautiful golden bowl. She chanted over these items for a long time, her voice rising and falling as her hands wove elaborate patterns upon the air. Then she raised her little knife and set its edge against the creamy skin of her bared throat.

Emily gasped. "Don't!" she cried.

And Vyara's head turned sharply so that Emily saw it in profile against the bronze relief of the spreading tree. "The spirits require an offering," the lady intoned.

274

Emily lunged toward the steps, and the young Lady Cyronian turned the knife and stabbed its point into the end of one of her fingers. Emily halted, sagging in relief. She had been certain that Vyara was about to cut her own throat.

Now she laughed at herself as Vyara squeezed blood from her wounded finger into the golden bowl then mounted the remaining steps to the great doors. Murmuring low, the Lady Cyronian dipped her fingers into the blood and smeared it upon the shield-shape of the door relief.

A strange sound came from the tomb, a sound like a cornerstone shifting and cracking, and Emily cried out as a wave of energy engulfed her.

The Lady Cyronian turned around, saw Emily sinking to the cobbles, and hurried down the steps. "What is the matter? Are you sick? Is it the blood?" She spoke as if she were entirely unaware of the energy rocking Emily's world.

Emily was holding up a hand. She could see Vyara's lips moving, but she couldn't hear anything the lady said. There was a chorus of other voices in her head, and before her eyes, the white marble of the tomb was turning into a sea of stone-white faces all mouthing words at her from the semi-transparent depths of the stone. Somewhere high above it all a bird trilled. Then one of the faces in the tomb's stones hardened, acquired a body, and stepped out of the marble. "Greetings, sister Shield Bearer," it intoned in a voice like the ringing of a distant bell. "You come at long last."

"Tellers!" breathed Emily, "A real ghost!"

"A ghost?" cried Vyara, "Where?" Then her eyes jumped from Emily to a point above the Midlander's head, and her face twisted into an expression of horror. She would have screamed if a knot of shifting color had not swept out to silence her instead.

For the daughter of the Empyreor all was night even in the midst of fair morning. She had killed the man Yadak. Although she had not been in possession of her own body when she did so, she could remember every detail of the act clearly — the way Yadak had clung to her, the way the cold-consciousness had reveled in his devouring, the way it had delighted in commanding her mind, body and soul.

It fought to command her still, even though it had been three days since she had sucked Yadak dry of life. Nothing subdued it, not even the full light of the noonday sun.

I'm being eaten alive, Beth thought, as she wandered desperate among the Empyreal tombs, *like A'Carnis and Yadak, only from the inside out and more slowly. How fitting!*

"Let go," hissed the rough voice of Urttah. Beth turned and saw the witch-woman watching her from the shadows of a nearby tomb.

"Leave me!" Beth commanded.

"Come back to the tower."

"So you can drag me even deeper into the shadows, deeper into the dark! No!"

"You cannot avoid darkness by hiding out here. Night will come. Night always comes." The witch's usually raspy voice had softened to a snakelike caress.

"And day always follows," retorted Beth.

"With greater darkness waiting behind. For darkness is greater. As it was first, so it shall be last. But *you* need not fear it. For you, there is energy within the darkness and endless existence."

"Go away!" Beth cried and hurled an invisible lash of cold power at the witch that set her reeling. Urttah grunted and stumbled away. Beth broke into a lumbering run. Running made her heavy abdomen hurt, but she ran anyway. She ran until she had reached the great circle of Empyreal tombs facing the cemetery tree, then she fell against a wall of cold marble.

She rested there for a time, forehead pressed to her knees, and gradually her fear and despair subsided. Even the ever-hungry cold consciousness grew more quiescent.

Somewhere a bird trilled, and Beth turned her head to listen. The bird trilled again, closer, and she realized that there were words in the call. Her head came up. "Ogren!" she breathed.

A large blot of shifting color moved across one of the tombs.

"Ogren!" Beth cried softly. She would have jumped up to hug the nonman had she not been weighed down by the aching bulk of her body.

Ogren came to her instead, shifting his colors to match the sun-dappled shade, and cupping the side of her head in his nearly invisible taloned hand.

Beth raised her own hands to his great wrist. "Are you hiding here too?" she whispered.

Ogren warbled a gentle affirmative.

"But you shouldn't have come," Beth cried. "It is too dangerous. There is nothing you can do for me, and Urttah is always watching." Ogren's trill slipped into a basso thrum that shivered her bones.

Beth nodded. "Yes. I'm sure you are good at hiding from her. But you should fear her power nonetheless."

Ogren warbled more insistently.

"I cannot leave. Not now. My baby will soon be born, and my father needs me, as I need him. There is so much I still don't understand. But, for Miri's sake, I am glad you are near. You can watch over her. She is so focused on protecting me that she can't see her own danger. Promise me you will take her away from this place if things go badly." Ogren's warble sprouted soft notes of reproach.

Beth shook her head. "I will be fine. I should be alone. I deserve to be. I am that dangerous now, although Miri refuses to see it."

Shades of tree and stone and shade oscillated as the tone of Ogren's trill sharpened.

Beth laughed bitterly. "A friend? Who besides you and Miri would be so foolish as to befriend me?"

Ogren's colors spun like a kaleidoscope, and a disembodied dark purple arm suddenly appeared in the air. The arm pointed.

Emily rushed under the boughs of the great cemetery tree and skidded to a halt. The tree was truly immense, so large it dwarfed even the giants of the ancient Greenwood, but what stunned her was the energy emanating from it. Dark and light and so—so—alive! Like twilight fretted with gold and singing with energy. It vibrated the thoughts right out of her head and stirred the small hairs on her skin with ghostly fingers. Even the ground beneath her feet seemed to shimmer with a dusting of forgotten starlight.

Movement pulled her eye sideways, and another cemetery ghost, gray clad and gray veiled, materialized around the tree's trunk. "Emily?" it whispered.

Emily froze. Slowly, she lifted one hand to her chest and clutched the fabric there.

The ghost lifted its veil. "Emily," it sighed.

"Beth," Emily breathed.

Two girls, two women now, gazed at each other like old friends who, having been long separated, discover each other again standing on opposite sides of a deep, steep chasm.

"Beth?" Emily whispered again; then she cried the name more loudly and hurried forward to throw her arms around her friend. There was laughter and hugging, but few words at first. Words couldn't suffice.

Emily pulled away first. "Tellers, but I have been worried about you!"

Beth was laughing, sobbing really. "Emily! Emily! How I have dreamed of you! I dreamed that you said you were coming, but I never really dared to hope I would see you again."

Emily was scrutinizing her friend. "You're taller!" she exclaimed. "And thinner! And —" Her eyes moved down to Beth's swollen belly.

The princess' lovely face tightened.

Emily caught her arms, held her eyes. "How are you?"

Beth thought of any number of glib, reassuring responses, but they all failed before the reality of her friend. Emily's solid, pragmatic presence made the horrors of the past few months both more and less real. Beth saw herself as she had been in the Greenwood, as she was now, and felt the chasm between them grow wider.

Emily bridged it for her. "You are in trouble," she declared.

Beth shook her head. "Trouble doesn't begin to describe it." Her eyes swept across the places of shadow surrounding them.

Emily understood. "You are watched," she said softly.

"Always," sighed Beth.

"Well, Ogren is watching now. He will warn us if anyone else comes."

Beth smiled. "Yes. He is watching. And he found you."

"He did." Emily smiled back. "He nearly scared me witless in the process, but he did." She guided her friend to a nearby bench and sank down on it. "Now tell me what has happened."

Beth shook her head as she took her own seat. "You don't know what you are asking, Emily. You shouldn't even be here. However did you manage it?"

"That doesn't matter. I *am* here, and I am listening."

Beth threw her a grateful, yet despairing glance. "You won't like me when I'm done."

"Try me," said Emily, crossing her arms.

So, with a recklessness born of desperation, Beth did. She told Emily everything — how she parted from Blayne, how she escaped from Jazim, how she drained A'Carnis and Yadak — and when she was done she pronounced judgment on herself, flatly and irrevocably. "I am not just cursed," she said, her face to the ground "I am the curse. I am everything my father ever feared, a true monster."

Emily sat silent and so still that she might have been a piece of tomb statuary, so the princess reached out with the power to taste her friend's emotions and encountered an impenetrable slickness instead. Surprised, she lifted her eyes.

She could have wept at what she saw. The girl who sat beside her now was the same one that had befriended her ages ago in the

278

Greenwood. There was no horror in Emily's face, no shock of disbelief, only the same old abiding friendship.

"You have become a good listener," Beth commented.

Emily drew her knees up and set her chin on them. "Have I? Well then, I've learned one thing from my mistakes."

The words baffled Beth.

Emily tilted her head and smiled at her friend. "You aren't a monster, you know. Not really. Certainly not to me. You are just not entirely mortal."

Beth stared. "Not mortal?"

Emily looked up into the branches of the great tree. Her hazel eyes gleamed as if lit by scattered beams of sunlight. "You have wight ancestry."

Beth's brows came together. "Wight? You mean those darkling creatures who attacked your village?"

"Yes." Her friend studied her. "Didn't you know?"

Beth climbed to her feet, took a few tentative steps away from the bench. "They never tell me anything. They want me blind and stupid. Especially my father." She turned back to her friend. "Why do you think I am part wight?"

Emily fixed her with a steady look. "Because I have tasted a version of the same power you used on A'Carnis and Yadak. The wight that came for me didn't consume me, but it didn't want to. It had other plans. It tasted my emotions, however, and nearly killed me in the process."

Beth exhaled. "You were fed on?"

"Yes. And if Blayne and Alsandyr hadn't found a way to save me, who knows what I might have become."

"Blayne?" Beth's heart contracted, her throat went dry.

Emily looked sad. "He's half wight. But not a monster, Beth. He's different yes, and powerful and sometimes terrible, and like you, he's incredibly, absolutely beautiful. To see a wight as it really is is to long for it to consume you, to lose all fear of death."

Beth recoiled, remembering her own terrible longing during the deaths of A'Carnis and Yadak. "You sound as if you enjoyed it!" she cried.

"I did." Emily confessed, then she squared her shoulders. "But I loved my friends more. And I choose to believe that my love freed me for a reason, so that I might be a help to you, and Blayne. In my heart I know you and my cousin are meant to be . . . more."

Beth blinked. "You have a cousin like me?"

Emily's expression softened. Reaching out, she took Beth's hands in her own and said gently. "*Blayne* is my cousin."

Beth started, pulled back. "Blayne," she laughed. "That's not—"

"Possible?" Emily finished dryly. "Sometimes I don't really believe it myself, but it is true. Our grandfather—his and mine—confirmed it."

Beth gave her head a little shake. "You have a grandfather?"

Emily chuckled again and pointed to her forehead. "Blind and stupid sound familiar to you?" She sighed. "I didn't know. I didn't learn the truth about Blayne until after Millicynt died and Blayne took me to Cyr to meet our grandfather. I can't tell you how it has pained me to think of the way I treated him while she lived."

"Stop, stop! Millicynt is dead?" Beth exclaimed. Then her eyes widened in understanding, and she dropped to the bench. "Do you mean to say that Millicynt—"

Emily nodded, fighting to blink back tears. "Was my aunt and Blayne's mother—and his father was a twilight denizen, a wight."

Beth searched Emily's eyes. "How?"

"With power. More power than I, perhaps even you, can imagine. I still cannot fathom how Millicynt endured that rape and survived it. For it was rape, you know."

"Yes. I know."

"Yes. Well, somehow she did survive, and her half-breed son was born, Blayne."

"Is what is happening to me happening to Blayne?"

Emily shook her head. "I have never seen Blayne feed on a person. I don't think he can."

Beth's eyes fell. Then she tore the veil from her head and gathered the silken fabric of it into the balls of her fists. "You have seen him, often?"

"For a time, almost every day. He saved my life, several times, and he introduced me to our grandfather—but I told you that."

"I'm sorry. Here I am worrying about my own troubles, and so much has happened to you as well."

"It doesn't matter." Emily paused, then continued softly. "You were always in his thoughts, you know."

Beth looked away. "He spoke of me?"

"Sometimes. Usually he just lived and breathed you. I think you are the only thing in this world that really matters to him because you are the only thing that he can truly touch. He only stayed away from you because he thought it was what you wanted. I can't imagine what he would do if he knew you were carrying his child."

280

Beth laid a hand on her belly. "You know that this baby is his?"

"Beth!" Emily's voice was an admonishment. "You seem to forget that I was there when you met. I saw the way you reacted to one another. Trying to keep you apart would have been like asking the tide not to follow the moon. Now I understand why."

Beth deliberately unclenched her hands. Hiding her face from Emily, she said in a tightly controlled voice, "But you say that Blayne has never displayed powers like mine."

"I think Blayne's power is controlled, by the Council of Numyn, the leaders of my grandfather's order. It may even explain why he lacks regular emotions. Given the power that wights have over emotion, a power you also seem to possess, Blayne's utter lack of feeling seems unnatural. His perfect indifference has to be a consequence or condition of the control my grandfather exerts. Without that control, who knows what Blayne might do? He is a true half breed, whereas you . . . "

"What am I?"

Emily's gaze had turned more speculative. "If Alsandyr is right—and Alsandyr loves to be right—you have more mortal heritage than Blayne. How much more is hard to say. But the wight blood is definitely there. Your beauty, your ability to mate with Blayne, your own powers, all these things confirm it."

Beth's throat ached with suppressed emotion. "I should never have left him. If I had known myself better, I never would have."

Emily nodded. "Knowing what I know now, I wish you hadn't. But what's done is done." She looked into Beth's face and reached out in comfort. "You and Blayne will find your way back to one another. I am certain of it."

Beth recoiled at the thought. "Better we did not! I would rather die than see him become what I am becoming. What if I awaken in him the thing I have awakened in myself?"

All Emily could give her was empathy. "You're frightened. I know."

"Do you?" Beth rose and began pacing again. "Wights! Wights are Northlander legends. How could my father have become mixed up with them?" She paused, her wrist to her forehead. Slowly, she turned to look at Emily. "Or is he even my father?"

"He's always claimed to be, hasn't he?"

"Yes, but he speaks terribly of my mother."

"Who was your mother?"

"The Lady Janera?"

Emily frowned. "Janera of House Cyronian?"

Beth looked at her in surprise. "Yes. You have heard of her?"

Emily stood up. "For the last few months I've been living as a servant in her family's house. That's why I'm here. I came with Lady Vyara." She gestured at the tombs. "She is the niece of Janera Cyronian, the daughter of Janera's sister, Janys."

"What!" Beth came to her feet as well, and looked off into the tombs as if she could spot Vyara moving among them.

Emily began walking in a tight circle, wrist to her forehead. "But it doesn't make any sense, Benja told me that Janera's baby died with her."

Beth's following gaze locked on empty air. "What did you say?" she hissed.

Emily was still pacing. "The Cyronians' serving woman, Benja. She told me that Janera died in childbed as her son slipped from her womb. And Janys' tells a similar story."

Something in Beth's gut ripped. Crying out, she doubled over.

"Ogren!" Emily yelled, as she tried to hold on to a sinking princess. "Ogren, Vyara!"

The young lady Cyronian came running, trailing a gigantic swarm of cemetery colors. But so, from another quarter, did an older woman. Beth's eyes turned to that lady. "Miri," she sobbed.

"Miri!" gasped Emily, who had never yet had the privilege of laying eyes on the waiting woman she had heard so much about.

Inimiri Dahar focused on her princess, touching her abdomen with hands adorned with many rings and ignoring the tangled mass of shifting color that was the nonman Ogren coming to squat over her. "Easy, my dear one," Miri soothed.

Vyara, still pallid from the shock of meeting Ogren, knelt more slowly beside the princess. "I have some skill at healing," she said timidly to Miri. "May I?"

Ogren warbled, Vyara shied, and the older woman smiled. "Please," she urged.

The young Lady Cyronian, with gaze going distracted, laid her hands upon the princess.

"Is the baby coming?" Emily croaked.

Vyara hissed for silence, and furrowed her forehead in concentration. Slowly, Beth's groans subsided.

"How is the pain now?" asked Vyara, opening her eyes.

"Better," the princess whispered. Vyara flicked Miri a warning look that the waiting-woman answered with a slight nod of understanding.

Then Miri smiled down into her princess' face and spoke in a blithe tone. "Ogren will carry you back to the tower."

"No!" protested Beth violently. "Urttah mustn't see him. It is bad enough that she knows about you." Wincing, she pushed herself up into a sitting position and sucked in several quick breaths. "It is vital that she not know about any of this. Ogren, I want you to take Emily and Vyara out of the necropolis. Miri will help me to the tower."

Miri looked at Vyara as she spoke to Beth. "Can you walk, Highness?"

"Yes," Beth insisted, grunting as she rolled onto her knees. Vyara locked eyes with Miri and nodded.

"I want to come with you," Emily was saying to Beth. "I can help."

Miri's reproof was sharp. "No, Emilyn Sayers. The Princess is right. This is no place for you or the Lady Vyara. Let Ogren escort you home." She transferred her gaze to the Lady Cyronian. "I shall go to the Empyreor immediately. If you would, arrange to visit later."

Vyara nodded, "As soon as I can."

Emily, stunned that a woman she had never laid eyes on should so easily recognize her, tripped over her own effort at protest. "But—but—"

"Go now, both of you," Miri ordered, rising and fixing Emily with a level stare. To the nonman, she said, "Make sure that the witch does not see them. And I will help the princess to her rooms. Come, Highness." She bent to Beth and gently shouldered the princess to her feet.

Beth looked frightened, lost as a little girl, but she managed to smile at her friend as she hobbled away. "Goodbye, Emily," she said, setting Emily aquiver with foreboding.

As soon as Emily and Vyara arrived back at the Cyronian mansion, Emily went in search of Colin. She found him scrubbing soot off a fire-seared wall. "Nice of you to finally show up for work," he grumbled between vigorous strokes of his brush.

Emily closed the door and shouldered his grumpiness aside. "I've seen Beth," she panted. "And Ogren, and the lady Miri too—you remember me talking about Beth's guardian. I met them in the Empyreal cemetery of all places."

Colin had stopped scrubbing and let his knuckles rest flat against the wall. "The Empyreal Cemetery," he echoed.

"Yes. Vyara asked me to accompany her there this morning, and Ogren discovered us and took me to Beth. I think she will be delivered very soon. She collapsed just before I left her."

Colin said nothing.

"Did you hear me?" Emily demanded.

He turned his head, but his expression in profile was unreadable. "You know, there's only so much a man can take in at one time."

"Yes, well, I've talked to Vyara. She's convinced that the baby isn't coming for a few more days, but she's concerned enough about what she felt when she touched Beth to be afraid for her, and the baby too. I've persuaded her to take you with her when she is summoned to Beth's bedside."

Colin snorted. "You work fast."

"There's more. The Cyronians are linked to the Keepers. Some how, some way they are connected to my house."

Colin frowned. "How?"

"I don't know, but I'm sure of what I saw. The Keeper's symbol is a sigil of their house."

"Couldn't that be coincidence?"

"Nothing relating to wights or the Talisman is ever coincidence."

Colin dropped his right arm, wiped his sweaty forehead with his left forearm, and turned around. "Then why is the mark of the warders written all over Janeryc's hideout?"

"What? How do you know about the mark of the warders?"

Colin looked resigned to unpleasantness. "Faryn told me about it. He and I didn't make contact with Janeryc here, Emily. We found him in a very different part of town, among men who looked and acted almost as dangerous as Faryn. Janeryc's men all bore arms and vests marked with the warders' crescent. And that same mark was inlaid into the floor of their hideout. When Faryn stepped on to it, it lit up, and Janeryc recognized him as a member of House Warder."

Emily could not contain her astonishment. "The warders. How? Why? Why didn't you tell me?" she accused.

"Faryn said it would be best that way."

"Of course, he did, Tellers plague him! You, however—I expected more loyalty from you, Colin." Emily didn't bother to hide her disgust.

"Faryn's just trying to protect you. Anyway, I had my own reasons for keeping silent."

"Oh. And what might those be? Or did Faryn forbid you to tell me other things as well."

Colin put his back to the wall. "Be nice. I'm telling you now." Solemnity lent his words an unexpected authority. "Faryn wasn't the only one who managed to light up Janeryc's protective symbol. When I crossed it, it lit up for me as well. Don't ask me how, but apparently there is warder blood in my family. Faryn says he knew it all along, and Janeryc's symbol apparently proves it. It explains my ability to heal."

"Warder blood," breathed Emily.

"Hard to believe, isn't it? Just imagine how I feel. I used to think that only fools believed in the old stories. Every Midlander knows that warders and magic aren't real." He sighed, then amended, "Then again, in a strange way it makes sense."

Emily was staring at him like he had sprouted a second head.

He rewarded her with a lopsided grin. "It explains what Shade was playing at, and why he forced his damned staff on me."

"Oh, Colin."

"Yeah. Poor me. I expected leaving home to be hard. But that's nothing compared to being stripped of your identity."

Emily's face filled with sympathy. "Believe me, I know exactly what you mean."

She moved to stand beside him, pressed her own back against the wall. "So Janeryc is connected to the warders. Somehow, in hindsight, that doesn't surprise me. It explains why he seems so cold and isolated, so intent on his own purposes." Her fingers began tapping a rhythm on the tiles behind her. "So, why, why is the Shield Light depicted upon his family's burial place?"

"Don't heraldic devices usually appear on shields?"

"Yes, but the shield on the Cyronians' tomb is *the* Shield, the shape, the texture, and just like the Shield Light it is bare of any device." She saw Colin's doubtful expression and dropped her shoulders in irritation. "Oh, don't be so obstinate."

"If I am, you can blame yourself. I have asked you about the Talisman many times, and you have always refused to talk about it."

Emily raised her eyebrows. "Yes, well, if I needed any reminding, there's also this." She showed him the mark on her left palm.

Colin stared at the mark for a long time. "They match then?"

"Except for size, they match exactly."

"All right, point taken. Apparently, the Cyronians have a connection to both houses."

Emily thrust herself from the wall, took two long strides away from it, and turned back to him. "But such things aren't supposed to happen."

"I am not supposed to believe in warders, much less be related to them, but that has happened."

"You don't understand. Dominic, Lyr, Alsandyr, they all told me that crossing the bloodlines of the houses is forbidden. It's supposed to bring about the end of the world or something."

"Which fits your cloud of doom theory about this house perfectly."

Suddenly Emily was staring at him as if he had sprouted a third head. A small cry escaped her lips. "Tellers, that's it!" She flung her eyes ceilingward. "Oh, I'm such an idiot."

Colin frowned in bewilderment. "What? What is it?"

When Emily lowered her eyes, they had begun to glitter. She now spoke grimly. "What you said. It's absolutely right. It explains everything: the mood in this house, the strangeness of the family, Janeryc's manner. Worst of all, the tomb itself confirms it." She walked to the wall and dragged her index finger through the thick coating of soot. Squatting down, she began to draw an image on the floor, speaking as she did so. "I was so caught up in the sight of the Shield that I forgot to take into account the other parts of the relief." She swiped more soot, continued sketching. "The Shield has company. It leans against an intricate depiction of a tree, like this. According to Vyara, this tree represents the tree at the center of the cemetery, which the locals seem to have all kind of superstitions about. But above the tree there is this. I took it for the crescent moon. But now —" She stood and surveyed her work.

Colin leaned out from the wall. "The Warder's crescent."

Their eyes met. Neither one smiled.

Moments later, Vyara found them just so. At the suspiciously sharp turn of their heads, she paused and spoke in an unusually tight voice. "Am I intruding?"

Colin immediately blushed and bowed. Vyara stiffened. "I believe Dejan needs help in the great room, Emily," the lady said, head high.

With a huff, Emily swept her slipper across her crude drawing and marched from the room

Vyara watched her go.

But the Lady Cyronian did not follow her out. She remained at the door, her high-boned face smooth and her almond eyes unreadable. She stood there until all sound of Emily's departure had faded.

Colin, trying to control the slow bubble in his blood, watched her face and knew not what to say.

Vyara spoke for him. "Your friend tells me that you are willing to help me deliver the Princess Bethnara."

Colin ducked his head. He was trying not to think about the kisses she had given him the night before. "If you can arrange it, my lady."

"With the Empyreor's help I think I can. I also think that I will need your help. Something is happening inside her. Something I've never felt before."

"Then I will do all I can to assist you."

"Good," said Vyara and turned. Instead of leaving, she closed and bolted the door, locking the two of them inside the room. Then she spoke in a voice thick and dusky. "Now for the gods' sake, Colin Blackhammer, come here and kiss me."

Emily scrubbed and hauled and rubbed until the sun began to set, then she went up to her room to groom herself before she joined the other servants at supper. When she opened the door, she found Faryn lounging on her cot and tossing one of his several daggers.

"Back so soon?" she griped.

Faryn flipped his knife one way, then another. "I'm never very far away."

Emily closed the door and crossed her arms. In a cold voice she said, "You didn't tell me that Janeryc and his family have ties to House Warder."

His light eyes continued to follow the tumbling dagger. "No, I did not."

Emily pursed her lips. "But Janeryc isn't a warder. Not really. He's something else. Because he is also linked by blood to House Keeper."

Faryn's icy eyes slid her way. "What brought you to that conclusion?"

"Oh, let's just call it a gut feeling, one recently confirmed by a persuasive bit of physical evidence."

Faryn ran one thumb along the sharpened blade, then balanced its tip upon his finger.

"Doesn't Janeryc's mixed heritage concern you?"

Faryn only smiled.

"I thought the Houses never mingled their blood," Emily pressed.

"Never? The Steward's heir and Alysse of Cyr mingled power and more. And then he helped himself to you."

Emily felt his point sink in. Wanting to shrink from it, she refused to do so. "I was dying."

"No, you were being turned into a vessel suitable for filling. You were born to bear a child of mixed heritage—my Lord, the Twilight Lord, and the Steward's heir alike know it."

Emily shoved the personal issues aside and raised her chin. "So the rules are either changing, or they never really existed."

"They existed. For good reason. Long ago, two of the first in blood mingled both blood and power and bore a single child of mixed heritage. That one union cost the offending houses both power and the sacred artifacts of that power."

"The talismans."

"Yes."

"Illyria and Roland." The names were a sigh. "They had a child." Faryn's wild eye bit into her own.

Emily spoke flatly. "And the Cyronians are the result." She brought a hand to her forehead. "So they *are* cursed."

The warder rose from the cot and stalked toward her until he stood mere inches away. Emily felt the raw physical energy emanating from him as he said, "The Cyronians came too soon, and they have paid for it. But times change, and the rules change with them."

"And now the time is right for the houses to intermix?"

"Some believe so."

She tried to swallow the knot in her throat. "You think Alsandyr believed it?"

"Why else would he have defied the Steward and angled for Alysse's hand? She was a minor talent of meager blood, but a keeper all the same."

"Because he loved her," declared Emily. But her words lacked conviction.

"Keepers regard all things through the lens of the heart, but Stewards understand with the mind. What is love to one raised to the call of knowledge?"

"What is love to one who makes his body, heart, and mind into a weapon?"

Faryn did not answer.

Emily said, "What does House Warder believe the outcome of a second mingling will be?"

"Ask my Lord that. I only know what all my kind know, that the bones of the earth cry out that the time has come. But there have been other signs. You lay with the Steward's heir, and afterward you brought back the Shield Light." He touched her cheek with the tips of his fingers.

She jerked her head aside. "I did not come back with a child," she spat, breathing hard.

"Not from him. But then you were marked and sealed for House Warder. When you lie with an heir of my house, the outcome may be quite different."

Emily froze like the deer that suddenly scents the wolf, but there was very little else prey-like about her. Her eyes shone steady and bright while her hand crept toward one of the small blades hidden in her waist-band."

Faryn stared deeply into her eyes. "You don't think you can touch me with those?"

Emily stared straight back. "I think that if you move a hair's breadth closer, I'll try."

Faryn gave his hissing laugh and turned away.

Chapter 22: Night Mother

Just before sunset on the same day that Emily was briefly reunited with Beth, Janeryc Cyronian rode through the gates of his ancestral home. Dismounting in the yard, he swept past the waiting servants, including the two Midlanders he had ensconced among them, and climbed the stairs to his mad niece's nest.

When he came down, he sent for his great niece Vyara. The two remained sequestered in his library for some time. Emily did not see Vyara emerge from that conference, but she heard Dejan talking to Benja about it. According to Dejan their young lady was crying prodigiously. As soon as she left her uncle, she went to her room and locked herself in.

Later, when Colin was checking the lamps in the forecourt, he saw a group of bearers carrying a beautiful ebony litter pass through the main gate. The bearers were the stocky tunic-clad men usually favored for such tasks. But the men sitting fine horses behind the litter raised the hackles on his neck. They wore leather jerkins and bore heavy arms, and they milled in the shadows of a pillared portico until lean, elderly Janeryc swept down among them. He was dressed like a lord in a loose, flowing robe of black silk embroidered at sleeve and hem with bands of silver thread to match the silver in his tunic. His white hair was brushed back from his head, and his face looked proud and cruel.

Colin eyed the master of the house speculatively. But when Vyara emerged from the house, his heart turned over in his chest. She was clad in a shockingly sheer gown of rose silk and a veil that was little more than a wisp of mist sprinkled with gems that glinted like stars. She looked luscious and beautiful, for neither the veil nor the gown left much to the imagination and her white-gold hair hung loose to her ankles.

Colin watched Janeryc hand his niece down the steps. At the litter, she seemed to balk until Janeryc's hand closed firmly on her forearm. Then she climbed in, bearers drew the curtains closed, and Janeryc swept into his own saddle. The litter and its armed escort filed through the gateway.

Colin strode from the courtyard to find Emily scrubbing pots in the kitchen.

"Care to help?" she remarked flippantly over her shoulder. When he didn't retort, she turned to face him, read his expression, and dropped her scrub brush.

"You were right," Colin said. "We can't trust Janeryc."

Later that evening, when they were done with their chores, they discussed their options. "We can't stay here any longer," Emily declared.

"We can't abandon Vyara," retorted Colin. "Besides, we need her if I'm to help Beth."

Emily looked at him. "What's going on between you two?" she demanded.

Colin blushed to the roots of his hair, and Emily nodded. "So you've finally caught on to the lady's feelings. Tell me, has she begun to offer up any of her more winsome charms?"

"Shut up."

Emily dropped her eyes. "I'm sorry. I just want you to be careful. We don't even know what is going on with her. Nor is it our business to interfere. We have more pressing responsibilities."

"You didn't see her face, Emily, or Janeryc's."

"Still, he is her uncle, her family."

"He is hurting her."

"Vyara seems to have been very sheltered, Colin. I think many things could hurt her."

"You say that just because you don't like her. You want to belittle her."

"That's not true! I wish Vyara all the best. But for her I might never have seen Beth. I simply don't think we can do much to help her."

Colin turned away. "You keep saying that!" His voice was angry. "I keep saying what exactly?"

"We. We. But it's not necessarily we anymore, Emily. Up to now I've let you make all the decisions while I went along. But—I can't just go along anymore."

Emily stared at him in shock. "Colin! What are you saying?"

"That it's time for me to take my own life into my own hands. I want to help you, Emily. I do. But I won't do it at the expense of everything I care about. Not any more."

Emily swallowed that information with a big dose of silence. Finally she said, "And Vyara is one of the things you care about."

The realization of all that he was professing finally hit Colin. His face reddened, but he held firm. "Yes."

Emily closed in, then touched his cheek with a soft hand. "You hardly know each other, Colin. And you belong to very different worlds."

Colin moved his head away from her fingers. "So? I'm not like you Emily. I believe that people from two different worlds *can* make a life together. If what I've learned about my own heritage is true, I'm living proof of it."

Emily answered him with a sad smile. "Then I envy you." She threw her arms around his neck and said into his ear. "You have always been there for me, Colin. This time I promise to be there for you."

Colin felt her breath hot in his ear, and the scene around him blurred. Emily let go and took a step back. "What can I do?" she asked.

Alone in her tower room, Beth ached and dreamed. Somewhere in the distance, her little son was crying, prompting her to rise from her hot bed and stumble into the next room in hopes of comforting him. But the room was a dusty wreck of disintegrating furniture, and the baby's forlorn little cry came from an even greater distance. Beth broke into a run, rushing from room to room, each one more ruined than the last, until she arrived at the mouth of an enormous tunnel. The tunnel was dank and very wet, for water coursed down its sides and dripped from the ceiling to make a stream of the tunnel's floor. Her baby's cry echoed up out of the tunnel's depths, but when Beth dove into its darkness, she found an enormous gate barring her way. This gate was like nothing she had ever seen—it looked more like a tangle of vines than a series of iron bars. Some parts of it were as thin as a hair, others as wide as her waist and these tendrils crossed over and under each other like the threads of a tapestry. Every part of the gate was utterly black and yet within its blackness floated miniscule specks of multicolored light like countless stars. The whole great mass of it filled her with fear, but she grabbed hold of it anyway, determined to pull it down. Heat like a branding iron fused her flesh to the gate's blackness. She screamed and screamed, and out of the darkness came a childlike laugh followed by a coo. "My baby," the voice said, "My little one."

A cry of despair welled up in Beth. "Noooooo! Don't take him! Bring him back!"

The voice and the baby's cry receded, and Beth hung seared to the gate. "Blayne!" she cried out in desperation. "Blayne! Help me."

The tunnel melted into another reality. She stood upon a tremendous dune of sand between a sky spangled with stars and a desert spangled with fires. Around the nearest fires, she saw figures dancing.

"What is this?" she whispered, panning slowly from left to right. "Where am I?"

And then she saw Blayne. He also stood at the crest of the great dune, and star fire was in his hair, while from his hand jutted a sword that flamed every color of the rainbow. "Blayne," she whispered.

Though he remained standing looking out over the plain, he answered her, and his voice sounded in her ear like he stood right beside her. "Welcome, my mate."

Beth started. She had never heard him speak so warmly. "Blayne?" she asked in disbelief.

"Yes?"

"What's wrong with your voice?"

He laughed delightedly. "Nothing."

"But you sound so different."

"I am different. Wait for me, and you will see."

She tried to step backward in the sand but stumbled as it slid out from under her feet. "Blayne," she cried. "I'm afraid."

"Don't be afraid. I will be with you soon, and then all the world shall fear. We shall be like stars fallen to earth and our child will be the new sun."

The light-streaked head turned her way, exposing eyes that burned brighter than any star."

With a cry of horror, Beth scuttled backward off the peak of the dune and began sliding rapidly downward into darkness.

She awakened with a gasp to the coffers and dark stone walls of her tower room. Her abdomen was drum tight, her heart was racing, and her back ached abominably. She was so damp with sweat that the light silk of her gown clung to her swollen body. The warm room felt stifling. She stumbled up from her bed and saw Miri asleep on a nearby divan. Keeping quiet so as to not awaken her waiting woman, she made for the door. She had to get out of this hot, dead air. The tower stairwell was black as pitch, but she found her way down it.

The air outside wasn't much cooler, but at least it moved. She pressed her hands to her sore back and began walking, wandering without direction. The pain in her back spread to her abdomen. She felt as though she were being squeezed. She paused, resting her shoulder against a tomb and trying to breathe deeply—and saw a ghost.

It was tall and shaped like a man, but no man would have been so white beneath the light of the moon. She started to back away, but he smiled at her and beckoned her to follow. For no reason that she could understand, she did.

Just outside the shadow of the great tree he stopped. She stopped also.

He contemplated her for a long time. "You are indeed most wondrous fair, daughter of night."

"Why do you call me that—daughter of night?"

"Because it is who you are."

"Who are you?"

"A traveler. One who has journeyed a long way. Now my journey nears its end. Yours is just beginning, that is if you have the courage to do what must be done."

"What must I do?"

"Much the same as I did. In the words of the wise and beautiful woman who once instructed me, you must choose loneliness over love and set aside your own hopes to rule a nation."

"I do not understand?"

"I think you will, when the time comes."

A wondrous thought came to her. "Are you one of Emily's Tellers?"

The ghost man laughed. "Hardly. But I have benefitted from the wisdom and insight of those close to them. Now go to your father. He needs you."

In a ripple of moon-streaked shadow, the ghost was gone.

Beth went back to the tower and dressed, so quietly that Miri never stirred. Then she made her way through the underground corridors to her father's private apartments.

As she passed through the darkened corridor where Urttah had once ordered her and A'Carnis to douse their lights, she heard an odd mumbling. She paused to listen more closely, and the mumbling broke into sobs. The voice, Beth realized, was Urttah's. Not wanting to overhear more, Beth hurried on.

She came into her father's presence so quietly that he never looked up from the table over which he was bent.

"Father?" she whispered.

"Go away," said the Empyreor, his voice thick and throaty.

"What is wrong?"

"Nothing that concerns you. Go away."

"No, Father, I will not go away. I am your daughter, the only heir you will ever have, and if you wish to keep any part of your legacy alive, you will have to do it through me."

"My legacy. Hah! You hold that word out to me like bait, but you do not see the barb in it."

"What do you mean?"

"I lost my savor for power and preeminence decades ago. Only duty has kept me going this long, and now even that has died, as the Empyre itself soon will, for there is nothing I can do to save it." The words ended on a sob, and pushing himself to his feet, the Empryeor flung out his hand as if to sweep all the quiet splendor of the room from his sight. "Fine then! Let the would-be ravagers come. Let them all vie with one another until they rip themselves as well as this nation to pieces. Perhaps some of the little people shall worm free."

"But I am here, father?" said Beth. "Won't you let me help you? I care about the people, and you. It's why I came home, to serve the Empyre, if you will let me. It is not dead yet. Perhaps, together, we can save it."

Bethnarian hobbled around his desk. His cheeks were wet, his face strangely raw and vulnerable. He gazed at her out of haunted eyes. "So fair. So impossibly fair. The perfect poison for any man. It would have poisoned me too, but for Janera."

"So you did love her?" Beth breathed, face white, eyes beginning to glow blue.

Bethnarian's eyes hardened. "Until you took her from me!"

"A fact you can regret no more than I. You lost a wife. I lost a mother."

Lorraine DeWolf

Bethnarian's face seemed to cave in on itself while his eyes leapt to flame and his upper lip drew back from his teeth. *"Your* mother!" he snarled, *"Your* mother! No. No! I may have allowed my scheming nobles to believe it. But not you, Madame. Never you. You'll sully no part of the woman I loved, the queen I buried."

Beth was stunned. Pain shot through her abdomen. "Father!" she breathed, pressing her hands to her aching belly.

Bethnarian was ranting, raging. "You! You! They lured me with promises of power and the gleam of ten thousand pretty lies and for what? For you! For the very thing that would destroy the wife I loved, the Empyre I coveted. With one hand they gave, and with the other they took away."

Beth's back and abdomen hurt abominably, but the pain only fueled her own anger. "You are mad, old man?"

Bethnarian actually cackled. "Mad! The gods know I should be, considering all that those Sardic witches put me through. But no, dear daughter, my mind is sound. I see you for exactly what you are."

"And what is that, father? A darkling, a daemon, a wight? Which one of you made me this way? Not Janera, surely?"

"Do not say her name!" The words were a shriek. Footsteps came running. Two body servants and Caphal rushed into the room, took one look at the titans squared off within it and backed away.

"So the evil comes from you?" shouted Beth. "I should have known."

Bethnarian reeled, his reddened eyes blinking owlishly at her as he said in a low voice. "Yes, it comes from me. I chose power over the lives of my wife and my son."

"Son?" said Beth. Her human heart seemed to fail her as the cold fire inside her flared higher.

"The son I would have had — Janera's and mine — if I had not killed her as she tried to give birth to him."

"You killed her?"

"Oh, yes. But for me those Sardic witches I courted for a crown would never have had the power to strip her and my son of life and breath. But they did, and all so that a daemon child — you, dear daughter — might be born."

Beth moaned and sank to the floor, clutching her swollen, aching belly. Bethnarian hobbled nearer and his words poured down on her like an acid rain. "The Empyre was tearing itself apart. Someone had to do something. But neither of my brutish brothers had the intelligence or the honor to set their claims aside. They preferred to hack each other to pieces instead, using their armies and servants like strawmen.

Meanwhile the Sards were gathering on our doorstep. For centuries they had bred in their desert. Their strength had grown great. But only a few of us—Jazim's father, myself, Janeryc Cyronian, a few others—realized how serious a threat they were. Janeryc wanted to ask the aid of the warders in the northeastern mountains. But I had too much pride for that. I would not beg from those who had always despised and disdained us.

"I formulated a different plan, and to effect it, I turned to a man called Scryos, a Northlander with strange ties to the Sards. I thought I might be able to use him to negotiate a peace treaty, for my armies had just scored an important victory against the Sards. Scryos was ready to use me too. He agreed to arrange a meeting with the Sardic command on the condition that I allow him to establish a base of operations in the Empyre.

"Together we journeyed deep into the desert, and I presented myself to the Sardic high priestesses, offering wealth, influence, and territories in exchange for peace. They wanted none of those things, but they said they would sign a treaty with me if I agreed to participate in a special rite, a rite that would give them a child of both royal Sardic blood and the blood empyreal.

"I set my seal to the contract. I would give them their half-blood prince, and in return they would help me secure the Empyreal crown. I wasn't overly concerned about engendering a half-Sardic heir. No law of the Empyre would require me to recognize such a bastard.

"Of course, I did not tell Janera what I had done. It would only have upset her. Her opposition to the Sards was fierce, and soon afterward she was pregnant with our first child."

"Your son," said Beth hollowly.

"Yes. On the appointed day I descended into the ancient halls buried beneath this very palace and presented myself to an enclave of Sardic priestesses. There I submitted to many spells and tests. And there I was given the power to pass through the gate that holds an ancient power back. And there—"

"Please stop."

"I saw *her*. I cannot tell you what that moment did to me. In a way it was the worst moment of all the terrible ones to come. You see, when I agreed to father a prince for them, I had no idea what I was agreeing to. I was a politician, not a priest. I went into that place expecting to make fools of a group of superstitious barbarians and to sleep with one of them. I thought I would lie with one of their priestesses. I never imagined that I would mate with evil."

Beth was shaking. With heartbreak, with terror? She wasn't sure which. "No," she wept.

Bethnarian laughed. "Oh, yes. So beautiful, so terrible. It was blood and lust and ashes. It was life and death, ice and fire."

"She forced you?"

"Did you have to force A'Carnis or Yadak?"

"Oh, why didn't she kill you?"

"My pact with the Sards protected me. Their power gave me the strength to endure the monster's desire. So I delighted as I burned in my lust, spilled my seed, and all unknowingly sowed the seeds of Janera's death."

Bethnarian's head sank to his chest. "I was just another foolish pawn in their game. I did not realize that my seed was only one component of the spell. In order for the creature to actually bear a living child, she would have to receive another infusion of a kinder, more personal power."

"Janera's power"

Bethnarian closed his eyes. "She was so special, my wife. She could work miracles, and she brimmed with life. I suspect it was because of her that they agreed to our contract in the first place. They knew they could get the power they needed from her, through me."

"If they had not, I would have died."

"Or you would be even as Urttah is?"

Beth wanted to vomit. "Urttah! Gods no!"

"I was not the first Empyreor they tried their foul magic on. I was only the first to fully succeed."

"And for that may the gods curse you!" spat Beth, then she doubled over in pain as liquid gushed between her legs.

Chapter 23: Final Arrangements

The litter that had carried Vyara away from the great house returned just before dawn. Janeryc's men escorted it into the courtyard. But Janeryc was not with them, and the riders departed as soon as the bearers set the litter down.

Vyara emerged from the litter still wearing her veil, but beneath it she looked almost ghostly. All color had left her lips and cheeks, and her dark doe-eyes were enormous. She moved through the darkened house on limbs of lead.

Benja met her in the hallway before her apartments. The older woman helped her exhausted lady to undress and bathe. Then she wrapped her in warm robes and built up a fire for warmth. She would have done more, but Vyara dismissed her. Instead of going to bed, however, the young lady Cyronian went to stand by the window that looked out into the courtyard.

A few moments later, the door to her chamber opened, admitting another young woman. Vyara turned and looked Emily full in the face, noting how the Midlander girl's irises seemed to flicker with rainbow lights.

"Colin wishes to speak with you. May he come in?" Emily asked.

"Yes," said Vyara.

Emily nodded. "I'll be right outside the door if you feel your honor is being compromised."

Vyara's stony expression softened into a timorous smile. "Thank you."

Then Emily gave the Southern woman the first real smile she had ever offered her. It was a smile that warmed her eyes and Vyara's heart.

That heart beat faster as a taller person entered and closed the door.

Colin moved halfway into the room, then stopped. His voice when he spoke was rough. "Vyara. I do not know what is happening to you, and you don't have to tell me. But I do know that I cannot bear to see you suffering."

Vyara looked down at her hands. "I fear there is nothing you can do to stop it."

Colin stepped closer. "I believe *you* can stop it. If you want to."

Vyara turned dark, liquid eyes up to him. The liquid brimmed and ran down her cheeks in two perfectly matched tears. "How?"

"Emily and I cannot stay here much longer. We could be gone within the week."

Vyara put the back of her hand to her mouth and turned away with a little sob. "I understand."

Colin took three long strides and caught her free hand. "I don't think you do. I want you to come with us, Vyara. I'm not sure exactly where we are going, and I'll understand if you refuse. I could never offer you a life like this one, but I know I could ask for no blessing greater than to have you with me." He said this in his firmest, most persuasive voice.

Vyara's huge dark eyes battened on his face. Her voice shook. "You want me to leave—"

"Your home, your family. I know it is a lot to ask. Believe me. But I think we could make a home together, Vyara. Much different from the grand one that you have been raised in, but a home nonetheless."

"But my mother —"

Colin looked down at the soft hand he held. "I know. But we all have to leave our mothers sooner or later. And I do not believe that yours, even sick as she is, would want you to languish here."

Vyara ducked her head.

Colin released the hand he held with a sigh. "Do not be afraid, Lady," he said. "If I have asked more than I should, you have only to say so. I will never presume on your graciousness again."

"You!" said Vyara in an accusing voice. And then she was in his arms. Pressing her soft body tightly to his own, seeking his face with lips warm and intoxicating. She kissed him deeply, and pulled back. "I will go with you Colin of the Midlands, be it to the coldest heights or the bottom of the sea!" Then she kissed him again and again, calling up a hunger the like of which he had never felt.

When he finally left her rooms, he nearly stumbled on Emily sitting cross-legged on the floor with her head tilted back and resting against the wall. She smiled as he stood over her.

"You're still here," he said softly, looking up and down the hall.

"I told Benja that Vyara asked me to wait here. Besides someone had to play guard. I gather things went well."

He reddened, then smiled broadly. "She's agreed to come."

"Of course, she has! Who can resist you?"

He eyed her wryly. "You did."

"No, not entirely. I'm just not constitutionally made for marriage. And you are definitely a marrying kind of man."

She grew serious. "When do you want to make it official?"

He considered the situation soberly. "Vyara said that she is planning on visiting the princess today. I will wait to hear what she finds, and afterwards make my decision. Someone should tell Faryn."

"No!"

"Don't you trust him?"

"Yes and no. But most importantly, neither of us knows how deep this Janeryc business goes, and Faryn's not talking. He says he's acting on the orders of his Lord, and I'm inclined to believe him. But I'm in no position to judge." She looked deep into her own thoughts. "Everyone's playing a power game, and these players will do anything to win. To them, you and I are just two more pieces on the board.

Until I know exactly what the contestants are trying to win, I won't trust a single member of a single house. Did Vyara tell you what upset her so badly?"

"Janeryc has officially put her on the marriage market. The bidding opened last night because it was the first night of the Festival of the Ninth Moon. Apparently, there were riots in some of the poorer quarters."

"Tellers! They do it like an auction here?"

"Charming, isn't it?" Colin growled.

"Makes the elaborately negotiated marriages of the Northlander nobility seem almost sweet by comparison. Why now?"

"Vyara doesn't know. Janeryc has always protected her before. She thinks her uncle has finally gone the way of her mother. She said there was no reasoning with him when she tried protesting his plan."

"Fortunately, she's got you to rescue her."

Colin grinned. Real, undiluted joy spilled onto his face. "I love her, Emily. I don't know how it happened, but I completely and absolutely love her."

Emily smiled again. "Get to bed, young lover! You are going to need your rest."

As he slipped off down the hall, her smile faltered then faded. It was curious how love came to some while eluding others. "Must be nice," she sighed.

Colin floated back to his room on a cloud of elation thickened by disbelief—in short, a near perfect delirium. His head swam, his heart soared, his body seemed at once a delight and an encumbrance. He sailed through the door to his sleeping quarters to discover Faryn standing over his cot. The strain in the warder's every sinew shredded Colin's happiness like a hard wind.

"Wha—" he began.

Faryn looked away.

Colin turned his head and found another man standing in the room. This man's hair was snow white, and in his pale hands, he held Shade's black staff.

The sight snapped Colin back to the hard realities. "Put that down!" he ordered.

The white man lifted his white head and immobilized Colin with a red glare. "So this is the young healer."

"Yes, Lord," answered Faryn.

"Lord?" questioned Colin. He shot the warder a startled look, registered Faryn's warning one, and clicked his mouth shut. Faryn turned back to his master with a deferential expression. "He is raw, but quite gifted."

"He would be. The Cyros would see to that." The white man stepped closer to Colin. He seemed to be measuring the Midlander with his eyes. "And are you ready, young healer?"

Colin shifted his weight back toward the door. "Look, I don't know what—?"

Faryn interrupted, "Lord, it is not my place to—"

"To question?" The corners of the white man's mouth deepened in the merest hint of smile. "No, it is not. But, since you have already presumed—"

Faryn's head dipped lower. "Would it not be better to trust this task to one raised in our house? The boy has power, it is true, but almost no instruction."

The Lord Warder's red eyes remained on Colin, but the soft words he spoke were directed at the warder. "Would you question Roland as well as me? Your audacity is grown great indeed."

"You have always encouraged my questions, Lord. As for Roland, I cannot see the proof of him in this."

Red eyes latched on to ice gray ones. Pale hands raised Shade's staff and held it out to Colin. "If it is proof you need, you have only to ask the boy."

Colin blinked and stared. "Proof of what? I have no idea what you are talking about."

The Lord Warder's white head tilted. His ruby red eyes scoured Colin's mind. "Faryn tells me that this staff served you well on the road."

"I defended myself with it, if that is what you mean."

"Against a company of Sards no less."

"Only with *his* help." Colin nodded in Faryn's direction.

"And with the blessing of the staff's maker."

Colin swallowed. The white man's hint of a smile deepened into a real one. "What instruction I wonder did *he* give you?"

Colin took a step back toward the doorway. But even as he moved to pelt back through it, a pale hand seized him by the collar and yanked him back into the room.

It took Abreem Imharta a day and a half to finish cleaning up his library. His servants offered to help, but he refused to admit them.

He wanted to make certain that all evidence of his night visitors had been cleared away.

The servants shook their heads, but went on about their regular chores. Abreem locked himself in his library where he paced and pondered, and every now and then paused long enough to pile lumber or sweep the floor.

Finally, only faint stains in the mortar and the hole left by the ruined library table testified to the assassins' coming. The dead Sards were long gone, vanished along with the mysterious Northlander who had volunteered to dispose of their bodies. Abreem told himself that he should feel relieved if not grateful. Instead he felt edgy and oddly disappointed at the same time.

Almost, he wished that he could have had more time with the high-handed foreigner who had raided his library and saved his life.

So, when the dedicated scholar returned to his reordered library around noon on the second day and found the Northlander sleeping in one of his arm chairs, he almost shouted with — what? Satisfaction? Excitement? Fear?

He didn't shout. He collected his thoughts, then retreated softly, closing the door. Decency, after all, forbade throwing the fellow out.

Stumping to his larder, he gave his bewildered servants the rest of the day off and returned to the library carrying a tray of refreshments. The Northlander was still asleep. So Abreem settled into a chair with an open book, determined to wait him out while the sun slipped into the west.

At last the Northlander stirred and opened a dark eye. The eye rolled toward Abreem, and the dark head followed suit. After a long, still moment, the Northlander said, "I take it you haven't called for the Empyreal guard."

"A recent acquaintance of mine suggested there might be wiser courses of action."

"May the heavens smile upon him."

"It appears they already have."

"Let no one deny the graciousness of Abreem Imharta."

"You flatter as well as you threaten. Why does this not surprise me? Would you like some water, food?"

"Mmm. Since you are offering, both I imagine." The Northlander stretched his long limbs.

Abreem bent and lifted his tray from the floor.

The Northlander ate as if he had a very limited acquaintance with food.

302

"Did you come back because you were hungry?" Abreem asked him, "Or because you needed a few hours sleep?"

The Northlander quit chewing. Abreem raised a hand in apology. "You are welcome to both."

The Northlander's eyes gleamed. "I certainly didn't intend to fall asleep."

"The price one pays for too many nocturnal wanderings, I fear."

The man smirked around his mouthful of bread. "Even so."

"What *did* you intend?"

The Northlander wiped his mouth on his sleeve and leaned back. His expression had turned aloof, almost lofty. "Perhaps I just wanted to learn more about the harmless- looking scholar whom the Sards call the Chosen of the gods."

Abreem's brow contracted. "Your Sardic is better than you let on."

"Actually, it's not. I was guessing as much as translating. Thank you for confirming that I got it right. Mind telling me how you earned the title?"

Abreem put his fingertips together. "Many years ago, when I was a much younger and more foolish man, I liked stealing into the lands of the Sards. I liked to comb through the old, forgotten cities — two thousand years ago, the great desert did not reach so far and many groups of people dwelt in those lands. Inevitably, I was scouted out and taken."

The man grunted. "But not killed or gelded?"

"I had come into possession of some rare artifacts — and demonstrated a rare ability to read the markings on them. The priestess who discovered me was quite impressed by my skills. She had me taken before a group of high priestesses."

"And you said your story wasn't interesting."

"The ending disappoints. The elder high priestess was a filthy, superstitious crone. After confiscating my artifacts and grilling me on their translations, she turned me loose to live or die upon the desert."

"She could have eviscerated you and used your guts for fortune telling, like she does every other man admitted to her presence."

"She thought that I had been touched by her gods. She said that if I managed to make it back to the Empyre it would be proof that the gods had indeed marked me for their own."

"And you did make it back."

"By pure luck. A group of smugglers found me. They were a thoroughly despicable lot, but I had information they could use."

"What did you find that was so interesting to the High Priestess?"

"Tablets containing passages from the Book of Nyte."

"Night?"

"N-Y-T-E."

"Sounds familiar."

"It is the Sard's sacred text. Very rare and very secret, as it is supposed to be the testament of the greatest of their priestesses, an ancient and immortal queen named Nyte, who claimed to have found the keys to unlocking magic. There are few copies in existence, the Sards being a largely illiterate people, although it is said the Empyreor was gifted with one when he assumed the throne."

"Is the book the reason they are targeting you now?"

"I do not think so. They seem to want to know about my work at Ab Syminal."

"Ab Syminal?"

"A ruined city, well outside their borders. You might know it as Bin Edath. That was its ancient name. The Sards have many legends about the place. I spent a few weeks digging there."

"What did you find?"

"Nothing distinctive."

"The Sardic assassin referred to something called Heartbreaker."

At the sound of the name, Abreem stiffened. He stood and stepped angrily behind his chair. It felt like a rasp had been applied to the raw edges of his nerves "Yes, yes, I heard. I have thought and thought, but I have no idea what they mean. All I brought back from Ab Syminal were a few rubbings of the decorative carvings on the stones. Look for yourself if you don't believe me; my pack is in the chest over there."

Setting the tray aside, the dark man rose. "I believe I will," he said."

Abreem puffed, "Are you calling me a liar, Northlander?"

The Northlander was calmly lifting the lid of the chest. In soothing tones, he said, "No, Master Abreem. I know you are an honest man. But more than one curious thing happened the other night. Do you remember the crystal the Sardic assassin showed you?"

"Yes."

"When you looked into it, you spoke of Heartbreaker. In fact, you confessed to taking the thing."

Abreem swayed and grabbed the back of the chair for balance. "I—I don't remember that"

The Northlander didn't reply. He lifted Abreem's pack from the chest, moving so that the little scholar could watch him sift the items inside.

He laid out brushes and chisels and sheets of paper, and then he pulled out a bundle of cloth.

"That is just a dusting rag," Abreem sniffed, but the other man was already drawing back its folds to reveal a thing of metallic sheen.

"What is it?" whispered Abreem.

"The point of a lance I think. It appears to be broken. Have you absolutely no recollection of finding this?"

Abreem collapsed into a chair. "No." What he *was* remembering was a splinter of dark and a shining figure with a voice like fire.

The Northlander was muttering to himself. "These markings – all the houses represented." The long fingers of one hand moved to touch the metal, then jumped away. The broken blade flew, skidding across stone. The Northlander was standing now, his right arm stiff, his right palm open wide.

Abreem saw the black spot on that palm and blurted, "That mark!"

The Northlander's hand closed into a fist. All congeniality forgotten, he rasped, "You know this mark?"

"I – have seen – its like before." Abreem found he had to gasp to breathe, as if the atmosphere of the room had thickened to syrup.

In two strides, the Northlander was grabbing Abreem by the robe. "Where?"

"Please," Abreem wheezed. "I cannot breathe."

"Where?" demanded the Northlander

"On the palm of another man" – gulp – "a man called Scryos."

Colin squatted in damp dark and waited for the Lord Warder to return. Shade's staff was upon his knees, but defeat was in his heart. He'd learned the futility of trying to use it against a man whose ruby-eyed stare could send your blows like your curses crawling back down your throat.

He thought of Emily. He had begged the Lord to allow him to leave her a note, some word of explanation. He knew she would worry and that her worry might lead her to act rashly. Most of his thoughts, however, concerned Vyara, and not just because he wanted her so. Emily, he knew, would manage. She was used to grappling with mysterious powers, and she had Faryn to look after her. But who would look after Vyara? She was so fragile and vulnerable, so alone. She was counting on Colin to lead her to a happier life. If he did not return soon, she would think that he had deserted her.

"We can go now," said a quiet voice in his ear, and Colin started, falling back against the slimy tunnel wall. The Lord Warder made no sound when he moved, despite the water running through their narrow passageway. He also seemed to be able to see in the dark.

Colin felt a lean hand heft him to his feet. The hand moved to his shoulder and pushed him steadily forward. Colin heard the sound of his own footsteps splashing against the walls.

"Careful, there are steps here. They are slick."

Colin felt his way onto the first one, tripped on the edge of another and slammed to his knees.

"Are you hurt?"

"No. It's this damn stiff leg of mine." He jammed Shade's staff into the stone and pushed himself to his feet. "How much farther?"

"Not far."

"Tell me again why we are going this way. I thought you said the Empyreor was expecting us."

The cool dark warmed to a low laugh. "He is. His servants are not. I think we can risk a light now."

Colin blinked as their dank surroundings began gradually to emerge from endless dark. Two large holes of dark still lay before and behind them, but gleaming cobbles of stone appeared to either side, etched silver as if exposed to moonlight. Colin absently looked to the source of that light, then looked again. The Lord held neither lamp nor candle. The silver light streamed from his hand, at the heart of which lay a shining silver crescent.

"I've seen Emily's mark shine, but never as bright as that," Colin declared.

"Really?" returned the Lord with a shocked look.

Colin stopped and stared. A corner of the pale man's mouth twitched, and Colin snorted. "So warders do have a sense of humor."

"Of course."

"Faryn's doesn't seem particularly well developed."

"You don't know him well enough. Then again, you might not find his jokes amusing."

"I bet. I guess I shouldn't be surprised that you find me funny. Shade laughed at me all the time."

"Did he?"

"Yes, when he wasn't scaring me witless. Please don't take offense, but I think he intimidated even better than you."

Again, the Lord laughed, but the warmth seemed to have gone out of the sound. "I can imagine. There has never been another warder quite like him."

The hand in which Colin held the staff seemed to tingle. "Is that why you are willing to follow him?"

The Lord Warder showed his teeth. "Willing to follow? What I will, Colin, my brother, what any of us wills, is only as important as the power that we can bring to bear on it. I have a strong will and considerable power. Your Shade has more."

"Then in a way you are as much a pawn as I am?"

"More so, in fact."

Colin pondered those words as they trudged on—the Lord gliding as weightlessly and noiselessly as his light, Colin sloshing ever more tiredly—and eventually they emerged into a low arched chamber with three black openings in it. Here the Lord's light seemed to dim, and Colin saw a sheen like sweat on his pale brow. After a moment's hesitation, the Lord took the opening to the right, but Colin's staff tugged the other way. He took a step, and the staff tugged harder so that Colin's hand shook as he tried to hold on to it.

"Not that way, little brother," said the Lord Warder, rematerialized like a mist out of the other passage. "That way leads to the gate. But we have other work to do first."

Colin sent him a puzzled look. "It's the staff; it pulls so."

"Yes. It knows its roots, whence it shall lead us soon enough."

The staff's pull grew less intense as they moved away from the intersection, and soon they were walking through warm, dry corridors lit by sconced torches.

They stepped past a thick door that opened easily to the Lord's light touch into a round room covered with symbols. In the center of this room squatted a golden divan, and on the divan lay a woman.

Colin temporarily forgot his own problems as his instincts as healer took over. Moving without hesitation, or concern for the other people in the room, he took a knee at the woman's side and caught her limp wrist in his hand. "Beth? Princess? Can you hear me?"

Alabaster lids slid back from eyes a frighteningly deep and brilliant blue. "Colin Blackhammer," the princess breathed. Her bronze head, darkened by sweat, rolled his way. "You look—different."

"It's me though. How are you?"

"Tired."

"May I draw back the covers?"

The eyes closed in acquiescence.

As Colin gently lowered the rich covering lying atop her, a rather small older man stepped forward. His aquiline nose and bleak expression made Colin think of pitted steel. At his throat was a thick golden collar and his robes were white. "You are a friend of my daughter," he said with something like amazement in his voice.

Colin regarded him with surprise, only gradually realizing who he must be. "I suppose so, lord—I mean, highness. I met her in the Greenwood."

The man gave him a thin-lipped smile without humor. "Perhaps the Midlands breed them sterner than I thought."

The Lord Warder slid into Colin's peripheral vision. "Let the healer work," the white lord said.

The Empyreor's blue eyes gleamed, but he retreated toward the far wall. Colin finished pulling the covers back, sucking in his breath at what he saw. The fine silk of the princess' loose gown was sweat-plastered to her skin. Beneath it, her abdomen moved as if the child inside it were fighting to find its way out. But this was not what drew the rasp of shock from Colin's throat. It was the glowing light inside that envelope of flesh and fabric that took his breath away. The princess' womb seemed lit from within, as if what she struggled to give birth to were not a child at all but a being of pure light.

"Tellers be good!" Colin whispered as he slowly raised a hand to rest it upon the shining mother and child.

"How long has she been thus?" demanded the Lord Warder of those gathered round them.

A woman stepped forward, blonde, steady, and serious. "Since early this morning. After her water broke, the contractions began to intensify and the light came."

With a part of his mind Colin heard them, with the better part of it he was reaching out and touching living fire.

Suddenly he was bent double over his spasming insides. Someone took him by the shoulder, poured energy into him. Sick with horror, Colin looked up into the Lord Warder's white face and said, "I cannot do this. I don't even know where to begin."

He expected the Lord's face to register anger or disappointment, but the pale countenance remained calm. "More than your strength has been brought to bear on this situation, Colin of the Midlands, warder in waiting. Take up the Staff, the burden passed on to you, and do as its maker wills."

Colin looked at the staff lying beside him. Remembering Emily, he rose and held the staff over the dying woman's body. The round room disappeared. He now stood on a dirt track in a featureless wilderness roofed by stars and held his staff out over a dying fire like a many-petalled flame flower at whose core a knot of brighter fire struggled to burn. Across that flame flower waited a hatted man with fierce golden eyes.

"What do I do?" Colin cried as if trying to make his voice carry over a vast distance. Shade stood just beyond the fire, yet Colin felt certain that he was leagues and millennia away. Shade cocked his pale head and his lips moved.

"What?" Colin cried.

The lips moved again while the greater fire waxed and withered, and the smaller one flared violet, then green.

"I can't hear you!" Colin called.

Again, Shade's mouth seemed to move. Colin focused every ounce of his attention and energy on the movement, focused so intently that the muscles in his back ached as if weighted down by an immense, invisible load. He pulled and strained to hear, and grew aware of others standing behind him, focusing and pulling too. Across the flame came a whisper of sound.

"Reach," it said.

"Reach," the throng gathered behind him murmured.

So Colin reached, stretching his arm holding the staff over the flames till only his gripping toes saved him from falling face forward into what now looked to be a bottomless pit of fire.

He saw Shade's hands rise and take hold of the staff.

And Shade was finally with him, or he was with Shade. The golden-eyed man's strangely resonant voice was strong in his ear.

"You are improving," he said.

Colin wanted to curse him, but he knew that without the energy Shade was pouring into the Staff he would lose his grip on this reality altogether. "Just tell me how to save the Princess."

Shade looked down into the flames noncommittally. "Are we sure we want to save her?"

Colin was confused. "The Lord Warder says we do."

Shade leered, and the undertones in his voice leered with him. "Who am I to argue with the Lord Warder? We need the child at any rate. And Bethnarian's brat may be the only check we have on little brother."

"What are you talking about?"

As Shade's grin widened, his eyes disappeared beneath the brim of his hat. "Hold on then, young one. Let's give them all a sign to raise a blister in their minds."

The staff erupted in black fire like a dark veil that spilled into the fire below. That fire sunk down into the others and took root. Colin could feel the black flames licking his hand, sucking the energy from him so thoroughly that it seared the marrow of his bones. It took every erg of will he had left to continue holding on to the staff.

Across the fire, Shade bared his fangs. "You've seen a problem like this one before, boy. The life and will of one is bound up in the other. See how the fires feed each other and yet contest. Each life struggles to sustain itself by nursing off the other. But here the problem is magnified, for nature itself is set against the powerful unborn. How tricky then to separate them without destroying either life. Do you see how they are yoked?"

Colin looked down, moaned at the awful pull of the staff. "No."

"Find the fuel for their fire."

"Fuel?"

"Look hard. I can only do this through you."

Colin stared into the flames until his eyes felt as if they would crack from the heat, like balls of clay in a too-hot kiln. Meanwhile the staff gnawed away at his body. "Coals" he cried at last. "There are coals in the fire, coals like black diamonds."

"Yes, the dross of mortal lives refined. Is there more?"

"More?"

"Look deeper."

Colin ignored the pain and heat and looked and looked until his eyes like his vision dried up entirely, then he sensed it, the way the brighter smaller light hovered over a crack like a chasm in the world. The chasm was dark and deep and reminded him eerily of the cracks in the Lady Janys' broken mind. "The small light is drawing energy from somewhere else!" he exclaimed, and his voice came out like a husk of its real self.

"Ah. He is hungry. He draws too greedily on his other heritage and burns too hot for his flesh and his mother's as well. "

"What do I do?"

"Seal the breach, so he cools."

"I don't know how."

"Let the staff do the work."

Colin shook his head violently. "No! I'll die."

"Do it!"

"I don't want to die."

"No one does. Now yield to the staff and close the breach. Save the mother and you may save the Shield Bearer and Vyara as well."

"Vyara!" The word had hardly issued from his lips when he felt himself giving into the staff, becoming a bar to that other world, a line that none could cross. The black flames streaming from the staff grew blacker. They rooted in the ground, thickened over the crack in the world, and then sent up a black shoot that opened silver leaves.

From some great distance he heard Shade speaking, his voice rich in half-realized meaning. "That wasn't so bad, was it? You'll do well as long as you remember this: all life feeds on life. Life for life keeps true death at bay. When the time comes you must accept the life offered."

The images of night and fire faded as Shade's voice receded. "Take the staff to the tree!" the mysterious wanderer called.

Colin opened his eyes and realized he could see again. Above him blazed strange symbols, yet he felt utterly at peace. He figured he was dead. Then a silver limned head blocked the shining symbols from view.

"Is he still alive?" Colin heard a husky voice ask.

"Quite alive," answered the Lord Warder.

"And my daughter?" asked another harsher voice.

The white head turned away. "Perhaps we should let the healer answer."

Colin realized that the burning symbols were marks set into a domed ceiling. Peace receded and a chorus of aches rushed in. He lifted his head to see the princess lying upon the divan with the older blonde woman standing over her. The terrible light inside the princess was gone. Colin laid his head back on the floor. "How is her pulse?"

"Strong and steady," answered the woman.

"Is the baby still moving?"

Moments elapsed. "I do not feel it," the woman told him.

"Give me a moment, and I'll check."

The Lord Warder came to stand over him. Colin scowled at the hand he held out. "It is going to hurt," he said to the white man. "Try to be gentle."

The Lord's mouth quirked. "I shall try."

Fortunately the climb to his feet wasn't nearly as painful as he expected it to be. After a few moments getting his bearings, Colin felt steady enough to seat himself on the side of the divan and lay hands upon the laboring woman.

For long moments he did not speak, prompting the older woman standing near the princess' head to ask, "Are they well?"

Colin withdrew gingerly. "As best I can judge, they are going to be fine."

"The child too?" said the Empyreor.

"I believe so."

"Can they be moved?" asked the Lord Warder.

"I see no reason why not. The princess is tired but stable. She seems well able to deliver, and the baby is strong. Labor should progress normally."

"And if they have to be carried for many leagues?" pressed the white lord.

Colin frowned. "Carried?"

The Empyreor's interruption cut like his glance. "You cannot expect me to go along with your plans now, Sandyr. When I agreed to send my daughter south, I did not expect her to be in labor during the journey."

"And yet she cannot remain here," replied the white-haired man.

"So you say."

"So I say, and so you swore. He is twice the fool who thinks he can make then break a bond with my house. Night may yet be unleashed, Empyreor, that terrible and irresistible Night you know so well. If your daughter remains here when the prison of the ancient one fails, she and the child will be taken. What must become of them then would wring even your iron heart. Would you have that on your conscience as well? She must leave the city immediately."

All the bleak, hard steel in the Empyreor's nature cut through. His eyes even stabbed like drawn steel, but the Lord Warder only gazed back, implacable as winter. Caught between the two, Colin tried not to cringe. Then the waiting woman spoke.

"Great One," she said in her soothing voice, "I will take the princess south. My family can help. You know of my cousin Dahim I think. I can send for him."

"You expect me to trust my daughter to a mere merchant?" snapped the Empyreor. But the steel in his expression shattered as he turned gray and clutched at the collar of his golden robe.

"Yes, Bethnarian," said the Lord Warder in words that fell light and cold as snow on snow. "Your time is up, your work but partly done. Say farewell to your daughter, and let us go and finish what you started."

The Empyreor had begun to shake. Before their eyes, all the metal in him seemed to melt and drain away. His skin shriveled and sank inward. "The pain," he moaned.

The Lord Warder's eyes bled red. "I can help you bear the pain, but you must come with me now."

The Empyreor's mouth opened, his jaw wagged, but no words came forth.

The Lord Warder strode to the wooden door through which he and Colin had entered and held it open for the master of the Empyre.

Bethnarian lurched forward, stumbled, caught himself. He stared at the darkness beyond the door with mingled fear and longing. The Lord Warder's red eyes gleamed. "She is waiting," he said, "and so is your rest."

The Empyreor took another step and then another, while the Lord of the Warders stood and watched pitilessly, holding a door open on darkness.

As Bethnarian passed the place where his daughter lay, he looked down. His cold expression never changed, but his hand went out to touch a lock of damp hair. "So terribly fair," he rasped. "Perhaps she was right, and the Empyre is not dead yet. Jazim!"

The name drew a dark robed man from the wall. 'Yes, Great One?"

The Empyreor's expression said that every word he spoke was an agony, yet he managed to command. Pulling a ring from his finger and pressing it into his daughter's hand, he said, "Here is my last order to you. Escort my daughter and heir from the city. Defend her to the last and above all others, and may the Lord of daemons consume your soul if you fail them." Jazim inclined his head, and Bethnarian shuffled on through the door.

The Lord Warder did not immediately follow. He turned to the dark-robed man instead. "A word of warning, Prince of Serpents."

Jazim's dark countenance darkened some more. "I need no warnings from you, death dealer!"

"Then like Death, I'll do you the kindness anyway. Do not let mistrust rule. Your empyreor did and bitterness and loss are all it bought him. Now is the time for faith. But for darkness there can be no great light. Remember that, and you may yet outwit night's crueler masters.

The pale-haired man now looked to Colin, who still knelt on the symbol-etched floor. "Come, my brother."

"My Lord, the princess may yet need me."

"Her land and father need you more. Come. We go to the tree."

Chapter 24: Into the Lair

Emily spent the morning of the day Colin went to the tree doing laundry to Benja's exacting specifications. Her hands had dried papery. Her back ached. She considered her own fraying temper and decided, that it was high time to bring Colin in on some of the work. So she stomped up to his room and rapped solidly on the door. "Get up, lazy bones, and join the rest of the laborers," she called.

When she got no response, she rapped louder and called his name. "Decent or not," she called, "I'm coming in."

She opened the door to an empty and orderly room. She looked about. If Colin had ever gone to bed, there was no sign of it. Could the fool have gone back to Vyara's room? Surely, he would have known better. He must be working on one of the terraces. With one last look at the room's blank walls and empty corners, she turned to leave and ended up staring at the empty corner behind the door. After a moment it hit her: Shade's staff was gone.

She went over the entire room looking for it. When no amount of pallet turning or chest opening uncovered it, the worry kicked in.

She searched the whole house for Colin, interrogating a few of the other servants in the process. None of them had seen him, and most were impatient with her questions. The whole house had suddenly erupted into activity. Normally invisible servants were suddenly everywhere, calling to one another and rushing about with anxious looks on their faces. The unexpected activity made her all the more concerned about finding Colin. Thinking that she could approach Vyara without calling too much attention to herself, she made her way toward that lady's apartments. She met Benja instead, who scowled and grumbled and dumped a stack of linens in her arms. "Take these to the kitchen and begin ironing them," the old housekeeper said.

Surprised, Emily once again forgot to act like the servant she was supposed to be. "Why?"

Benja's eyes popped. "What concern is that of yours, sirrah? And why are you slouching about here when there is so much work to be done?"

Emily pressed her lips together, and Benja nodded in satisfaction and pushed her back down the hall. "When you are done with those, see Dejan about the plate for the Lord's table. We will use the blue porcelain and gold cutlery tonight."

From Dejan she learned a bit more. The old man was going about his work in a dither, at one point exclaiming to the ceilings, "Twenty years without a proper show of station, and he expects us to do justice by this house in one afternoon." He shook his white head.

Emily looked up from rubbing golden knives and forks and asked with as much nonchalance as she could muster, "What exactly are we preparing for?"

"Great and noble guests, girl! Lords of the Empyre."

"Lords of the Empyre?"

314

"Yes! So you had better be quick and attentive tonight. My lord will brook no careless service. He is like to whip any member of the household who displeases him. Now get back to work."

They rushed her from one task to another so that she had no time to further investigate Colin's absence. In the afternoon a small wagonload of foodstuffs arrived in the company of several hired cooks. She was ordered to unload the cartons and baskets and then sent to the kitchen to chop vegetables for a thin-faced man who repeatedly smacked her hand with a wooden spoon for cutting them too coarsely.

The whole time her concern about Colin was mounting, especially when she heard Benja complaining to Dejan that he had run off. The one bright spot in the entire the afternoon came when Benja ordered her to carry pitchers of bath water to Vyara's apartment. But her hopes of speaking with that lady were crushed at the door. Other servants took the pitchers and ordered her away before she got more than a brief glimpse of the room's insides.

It was while she was on her way back from this disappointment that she heard a ghostly whisper that pulled her into the tower stairwell. From the shadows under the stair a pale head was peering out.

"Lady Janys! What are you doing down here?"

The mad lady scuttled forward at the sound of Emily's voice. "You brought me flowers to draw," she mumbled. Her spiky head bobbed.

"Yes, lady. But you should be upstairs. Is there something you need?"

The head bobbed more furiously.

"What is it?" asked Emily gently and reached out a hand to usher the lady back upstairs.

"Quiet," whined Janys.

"Are we too loud for you? I didn't know the commotion would carry so far."

"I want him to leave me alone."

"He who? Is one of the other servants bothering you?"

Janys screwed her face up. "No, no. The servants do not know. They mustn't know. He'll hurt them. I ask him to be quiet. But he will not listen."

A terrible thought dawned on Emily. Her voice sharpened. "Janys, do you have Colin up there with you?"

The mad woman screwed up her eyes and spat. "Colin? Who is this Colin? I speak of the old one. He has grown most restless."

"Janeryc do you mean?" Emily had not seen the Lord Cyronian arrive.

Janys sunk frantic fingers into her hair and tugged hard at her locks. "Stupid, stupid girl!" Her face swung upward following the stair. She loosed a dry sob. "I want him to quit speaking to me. Light and death, light and death, it's always light and death."

From somewhere in the depths of the house Emily heard a voice calling her name. She ignored it. Janys was more important. The mad woman could not stay down here; the flurry of activity would only upset her more. "Why don't you show me what's bothering you," proposed Emily.

Janys' expression lightened. "You will come? Good! He will quiet down then; he does not like others to hear him."

Emily waved Janys up the stair. "Hurry then. I have work to do."

The tower rooms were as cluttered and dark as ever. Emily walked to the window, drew the heavy curtain aside to let in the orange glow of the setting sun. Janys' blinked rapidly in the sudden flush of light and scuttled back into shadow.

Emily looked carefully around the first room, even going so far as to poke behind the chests and piles of discarded garments. Then she followed Janys into her sleeping quarters. This space was even dimmer. Emily took her time meandering across it, looking for signs of any disturbance. Finding none, she moved toward the second curtained window. "All seems quiet, lady. But perhaps you shouldn't keep it so dark in here. It is easy to imagine things in the dark."

From the deeper recesses of the room, she heard Janys whimper. "Lady?" she called.

The mad woman was a blot of pale color standing directly before the narrow door leading to the topmost tower room, the room that Janys kept everyone but Janeryc from entering. The door was open.

Emily approached warily, though Janys' attention remained focused on whatever lay beyond that door. "Does the voice you speak of come from up there?" she asked in a soft voice.

The ill woman nodded vigorously and caught Emily's hand in a claw-like grip. Again, Emily felt that shock of energy passing between them. Janys stiffened and her vague, distracted expression sharpened into a look of cunning. "Sneaky," she said. "Tricksome. He is playing quiet now."

"Would you like me to follow you up?" asked Emily, speaking as much out of curiosity as concern. The mad woman had always been so protective of the upstairs room that Emily couldn't help but want to see it, although she suspected she'd discover nothing more than another horrible mess.

Janys' expression fluttered between suspicion and need. Need won. She nodded and tugged Emily inside.

The stair beyond the door was very narrow and twisting and littered with strange little puffs of colored dust. They swirled upon the stairs and floated across Emily's slippers as she climbed.

She emerged into a large, dark-beamed room like nothing she could have anticipated. The east- and west-facing walls each held a narrow window streaming light. But to either side of these windows and along a third solid wall of the great square room, stood looms of various sizes, large and small scaffolds of wood netted with thousands of interlocking rows of thread. Upon some of these looms hung half finished tapestries of such brilliant color and detail that Emily gaped to see them. She felt as if she had entered one of Alberyc's intricately illuminated texts. Images of splendor surrounded her—slender veiled women and robed men, prancing horses, desert sunsets, the great Empyreal palace, the densely packed city streets. Emily's eyes gorged themselves on world after world of vibrant color.

So this was where all Janys pent-up genius was spent.

"Oh, my lady," she breathed, "this is—"

"Mine," muttered Janys, "All mine." Her thin, worn face was set, and her eyes burned a hole through the far wall, where from great bars of wood hung still more tapestries.

Janys' fingers began to knead her forehead.

Emily reached out and gently snared one of the mad woman's hands. It fluttered like a trapped bird in her own. "Are you hearing the voice again?" Emily asked gently.

Janys shook her head.

"Well, perhaps we have scared your visitor away."

Janys looked doubtful. "He is only waiting for you to leave." Her eyes were fixed on the tapestry hanging near the center of the wall, a benign image of people in a terraced garden. "May I take a closer look?" Emily asked.

Janys kneaded her forehead more forcefully, but nodded.

Emily walked over to the tapestry with is rows of smiling faces sewn from tightly interwoven and layered threads. "This is lovely," she said.

"*He* doesn't like it."

Emily turned her head. "He who?"

"The one I've been telling you about. He knows I only put it up to spite him, because I was sick of him watching me."

The small hairs on the back of Emily's neck stirred. She turned slowly back to the tapestry in front of her. "He watches you from in here?"

Janys nodded.

Emily's eyes slid to her. "From inside this tapestry?"

Janys made her spitting sound of disgust. "No, stupid girl, from behind it. Push it aside and you will see."

Now the hairs on Emily's arms and back were rising. Part of her wanted to reach out and expose the space behind the tapestry, but another, equally substantial part was telling her to back away.

Janys' impatience decided matters for them both. Reaching up, she yanked the covering tapestry from its pole.

Emily yelped and stumbled backward. She was halfway across the room before she realized that the man she was looking at was only another image rendered in thread, just like every other figure in the weaver's lair.

Strangely enough the realization only made her skin crawl more furiously. The image was so perfect, life-sized and entirely lifelike — the eyes shadowed by the wide-brimmed hat, the generous, smiling mouth, the firm chin. He seemed to have materialized before her out of thin air just as he had so often materialized out of the fog of his road. "Shade!" whispered Emily and sat down hard on the floor.

Janys was whining to herself. "Shade! A shade! The shade. A ghost of the awful past, a portent of the even stranger future."

Emily shook her head. "This man is no ghost! I know him. I have seen him myself, spoken with him often. Colin too. We traveled with him on the road that brought us here."

Janys looked at her. "Then you traveled with Death," she said, her wild, strangely knowing eyes boring into Emily. "And you too speak with shadows."

Emily didn't want to hear those words, couldn't. She was pressing herself to her feet, anxious to leave, afraid she couldn't. Her stomach was churning, and the word "shadows" was making a terrible clangor in her head. Shade, who hid in the shadows. Shade, who avoided the light of the Sun. Shade, who had given Colin a staff inscribed with every permutation of the word "life." Shade, who had only appeared, after Emily had called out to the spirit of their strange road, Shade's road. Shade, the man who cast no shadow of his own.

"Oh Tellers, no!" said Emily. Her stomach cramped all the harder, and she vomited on the floor.

It was some time before she became aware that Janys was holding her like a nursemaid or a mother.

"Why do I always have to vomit when I cross a mental threshold?" Emily wondered tiredly.

"Because those are the hardest thresholds to cross," answered Janys. "As a woman with a broken mind, I should know." There was nothing of the childlike madwoman in her now. She sounded old and infinitely wise.

"Oh, Lady Janys," said Emily with a little sob. "I fear I've done a terrible thing."

"We all do terrible things."

"Not like me. I've crossed lines you can't imagine. I've touched wights and been touched by them. I've gotten myself joined to a Steward. I've walked the margins of the nether world, and I've brought things back across with me. But now I fear I may have crossed one line too many."

Janys' thin arms wrapped more tightly around her, and Emily raised beseeching eyes to Shade's image.

"How did this happen?" Emily asked. She spoke to the tapestry figure, but Janys answered. "I loved a young man once," the mad Lady Cyronian said, "though he couldn't love me. He had already given his heart to another, you see, a woman of his own country, but her father and his people absolutely forbade the connection. It made him so angry that he turned his back upon his homeland and his heritage to come here. My uncle took him in."

The distant reflection of a lost happiness lightened the lady's worn voice and drew Emily back from the brink of her own despair. "What happened to him?"

"He stayed with us for a time. Until Jana and her baby died." Janys said this calmly, as if her memories of her long-lost love were insulating her from the painful past.

"Did he know that you loved him?"

Janys nodded. "I think he did, but he was too kind to speak of it. When he left, I mourned for a time, and then Uncle introduced me to my husband."

"And you loved your husband?"

Janys patted her hand. "It was a prudent match," she said, "but one never forgets a first love. And mine was so beautiful, so quick and light, with hair the color of the whitest silk and eyes like rubies. I wanted to remember him exactly, so I began to weave this tapestry. But every time I tried to capture him, the color or the figure would turn." Janys' jerked her chin at the image of Shade. "He came out instead."

Emily could hardly believe what she was hearing. She wriggled out of Janys' hold and climbed to her feet, looking upon the offending tapestry with new eyes. "You were trying to render the Lord Warder — and Shade took control." She glared the woven image of the blue-robed man. "What exactly are you up to Shade? And what are you doing with Colin?"

Janys stood also. "He won't tell you," she warned. "He keeps his secrets well this one — until he wants to share them with you, and then he pounds them into you day and night."

Emily turned to the lady with real urgency. "Exactly what has he told you, Janys?"

The lady blinked, and the frightened but canny look of the mad woman began to surface in her eyes.

Emily sensed that she had only moments left in which to speak to the real Janys' Cyronian, so she grabbed one of the lady's thin hands and poured power through it. Again she felt energy arcing between them, but this time it was accompanied by laughter, low and rich and brimming with complex undertones. Janys' cried out as her true self convulsed and crumbled into the turbid waters of a rising madness. Emily cried out as well, grabbing her head in pain. "Damn you, Shade!"

A distant, deep report clapped the air, giving way to a thunder that shook the entire mansion.

As they journeyed deeper and deeper into the earth, Colin hung on to Shade's staff for dear life and prayed to see sunlight. What had begun as a disturbing mission to save a dying princess had turned into a waking nightmare.

He had followed the white Lord Warder back into the underground, accompanied by none other than the Empyreor himself. But the agonized ruler was not able to go far. Soon he collapsed convulsing to the floor, and the Lord Warder had to stop, kneel beside him, and touch his left palm to the quivering man's head. The white man stiffened then bowed his head. The Empyreor quit shaking.

"You are a healer," breathed Colin.

"No. The gifts of my house are many, and most are mine to call upon, but not that one."

The Empyreor coughed and opened his eyes. There was wonder in them. "The pain. It is gone."

320

Notwithstanding its hint of a smile, the Lord Warder's face looked grim. "Help him to his feet, Colin. We must go quickly."

He led them unerringly to the chamber with three openings. The tunnel they entered now was round and smooth and wet, and it sloped steeply down into darkness, so steeply that in places the floor had been cut into irregular steps to prevent slipping. Helping the failing ruler descend those steps was no easy task, especially when one was fighting the relentless tug of the staff, but the white lord did not offer any aid. The burden of the old was left to the young.

After a short time they emerged onto more level ground where darkness pressed heavily at the Lord's fey light. In the faint silver limnings, Colin could make out enormous and jagged wedges of stone like toppled walls leaning against one another.

"The antechamber," whispered the Empyreor.

"Lord?"

Bethnarian only leaned more heavily on Colin's arm.

Down a well-marked path they hobbled, among whispering immensities and corridors so narrow they had to slip sideways between the cutting stone. Then they entered another series of chambers where great stone spikes like teeth pushed out of ceiling and floor.

"The garden," nodded the Empyreor.

"Highness?" said Colin again.

Bethnarian's deep-set eyes glinted into his own. "Soon the serpent and then the gate."

Colin felt a chill deeper than the cavern's cold bite his bones. He could hear a strange whispering in the air. Slowly, insidiously, that whispering grew louder, swelling into a low roar that energized the air. From out of nowhere a cool breeze stroked their cheeks.

They came to a wide and shifting floor of silver-threaded movement.

"It's a river!" cried Colin, squinting.

"The Nersi," answered the Empyreor.

"The Serpent," translated the Lord Warder, the light in his hand glowing brighter, his face looking strangely pinched and ill. "This way to the crossing."

Soon the floor began to rise again, and the Empyreor's steps grew feebler, his breathing more strained. At a bend in the path he dropped to his knees.

"Lord Empyreor?" Colin cried.

The old man gasped. "I cannot."

"Are you in pain?"

The Empyreor shook his head. "My body refuses to listen."

Colin looked up to where the Lord Warder ghosted like some underworld spirit. The white man was already coming back to them, silver hair agleam.

"He does not have the strength to go on," Colin announced.

"He must."

"He can't!" The heat was rising in Colin's cheeks. He clenched his hand tightly about the pulling staff, for he remembered having a similarly infuriating argument with Shade. "Would you have me drag him?"

"If necessary."

Colin sucked in his breath, but a firm hand found his shoulder before the shout left his mouth.

"Patience, son. Why don't you try carrying him instead?"

"What! With this damn staff trying to pull me off my feet? You carry him!"

The Lord squatted down in front of him, forearms resting on his knees, gleaming hand dangling between and throwing odd shadows across his face. "I can not help you. I cannot touch him again. I took his pain on myself. If I touch him now, it will re-enter him, and it will kill him. He is too weak to bear it anymore."

Beside Colin, Bethnarian hissed and his bowed head lifted, revealing a dust- streaked and haggard face fractured by a cruel smile. "Fate's scourge stings even you, eh, Sandyr?"

The Lord Warder's white head turned. "Yes. But then the failing always was as much mine as yours."

Colin closed his eyes in disgust tinged with despair. "I'd like to curse you both. But I don't have words vile enough. Let the Tellers send you the justice you deserve." He opened his eyes and looked accusingly at the Lord Warder. "I don't suppose you can take the staff."

"Not here, I'm afraid. We are too close."

Colin's first attempt to lift the Empyreor nearly killed the dying man. Colin had hoped to sling Bethnarian over his back, but the pressure that the process put on Bethnarian's midsection, did serious things to his blood pressure. Colin revised his plan, and somehow got the tottering Empyreor into his arms while hanging onto the impatiently tugging staff. Carrying Bethnarian like a babe, he heaved his way painfully up the stony hill, sidestepping in places to accommodate his stiff leg. At the top he rested, setting the Empyreor down on a flat stone as he contemplated the swinging bridge before them.

He scowled at the Lord Warder. "This won't be easy. He's heavier than he looks."

"You will manage."

Those words and the rest of the journey dissolved in a fog of effort—the shining Lord Warder an ever-shifting point of destination in an interminable journey. When they finally reached their destination, it was long moments before Colin realized it.

"You can put him down now," said the Lord Warder. His voice was kindness over a ribbon of strained steel.

Colin laid the unconscious Empyreor on the rocky ground with a bass groan that echoed the quieter protest of his limbs. The staff, he realized, was no longer pulling. Looking up, he noticed faint stars of light glimmering all around him. There were Millions upon millions of them, so many that they filled the whole large cavern with a faint glow. Had they emerged topside? Was he looking at the stars? They couldn't be. Their colors weren't right. They scintillated too vividly through all the hues of the spectrum, and they seemed to be encased in snaking darkness.

"What in the—" he mumbled into his hand. Overhead and all around him, black tubes like great serpents as thick as a man's torso clung to the rock walls. Ahead of him more vines of varying widths formed a tightly interwoven glittering curtain.

"The Gate," said the Lord Warder.

"That's a gate?"

"Oh, yes."

"It's like no gate I've ever seen."

"I expect not. It is a living gate if you will. It was created, in a manner of speaking, by Roland."

Colin looked harder and realized that large areas of the gigantic vine were devoid of stars and ashen gray as if coated in chalk. "It looks sick."

"It is dying."

"Dying?" Colin looked down as the Empyreor began coughing and scratching at the stone.

The Lord Warder looked down as well. "And now I think you should begin preparing one of your energizing potions."

Colin shrugged and felt for his roll of herbs. "I'll need some water."

The Lord Warder moved away.

By the time Colin had finished crushing together a variety of herbs, the Lord had returned, with a shallow copper basin brimming with water. Colin emptied a little of the water onto a piece of cloth and laid that over the Empyreor's forehead. Then he carefully stirred the herbs into the rest of the water using a dusty finger.

Glancing at the white lord, he said, "If you would like, I can mix a dose for you. You look like you could use it."

His suggestion earned him a tight smile. "It would not help me. My problem is not exactly physical."

"You're wrong, you know," Colin argued. "Extreme pain does things to the body as well as the mind."

"Nothing that I have not been built to handle."

Colin slid closer to Bethnarian, but the Lord Warder laid a cool finger across his wrist. "Wait. There is one thing more." Reaching toward his belt he pulled out an incised leather glove, which he proceeded to draw over the long, lean fingers of his right hand. Then, with gloved hand, he searched beneath the collar of Bethnarian's robe and pulled out an oddly carved stone. A silver flash of his knife and the thong holding the stone about the Empyreor's neck parted. The Lord Warder held up his prize.

Colin looked at the veins of color in the stone then looked at the starry lights suspended all around them. Knitting his brow, he stretched a finger toward the glittering thing."

"Don't touch it!" the Lord Warder warned. "It is anathema to our kind."

Colin jerked his finger back. "The Empyreor will never be able to swallow that," he tried to joke.

A white eyebrow lifted and pale lips drew back from ivory teeth. "No? Well, young Colin, what do you know about wringing blood from stone?"

Rising, the white lord strode to the gate and, with a quick stroke of his knife, severed a loop of the gate's vine, one no thicker than his finger. It twined and snaked around the Lord Warder's gloved wrist as he knelt again beside the Empyreor.

The Midlander youth recoiled. "It's alive!"

"Of course, I told you as much already."

"You told me the gate was sort of alive."

"And this is a living part of it. Now, quickly, hold the basin underneath it. Try to catch every drop."

Careful to keep his hands over the bowl, the Lord Warder brought the stone and the wriggling vine together. Like a slug, the vine slithered off the Lord Warder's wrist and began wrapping itself around the gem's carved surface. Then it began sprouting tendrils like so many fine hairs. Like feelers the hairs explored the surface of the stone, penetrated into it. Snap! The stone cracked, and into the faint lines of those cracks dove more hairs. More cracks appeared, and the stone darkened as its veins of color withdrew into the vine.

A final report and a tiny plume of dust appeared. The dust wafted away. The vine unraveled, fell limp in the lord's gloved hand. The light in it began draining downward, pouring like liquid fire out of the cut end of the vine into the basin below.

In the lord's hand the vine shriveled and disintegrated.

Colin looked down into the basin. It held a cup of of melted rainbow salted with herbs. "What is it?" he whispered, half to himself.

"The source,"

"Of what?" Colin searched the Lord's face for further explanation, but the white man was looking at the Empyreor. "Lift him up, son."

Colin did as he was told, while the Lord Warder lifted the basin to Bethnarian's slack lips. "Drink, Bethnarian, Empryeor," the white lord said, pouring a small amount of liquid into Bethnarian's mouth. The Empyreor's head lolled. A few gleaming drops dribbled out of the side of his mouth. Then his eyes flew open, and he reached greedily for the basin. Lord Warder let him have it, saying, "Yes. Drink up. Drink it all. The sun will soon set, and our accounting must be made before then."

Bethnarian drank — like a man parched — and as he drank his sunken cheeks filled, his eyes lightened, his face took on the hawkish beauty of a much younger man. Colin's hands fell away. The copper bowl slipped from Bethnarian's fingers to ring against the stone. The Empyreor climbed to his feet, walked slowly toward the gate. "I feel her. Always I feel her, pulling at me."

The Lord's soft voice hardened to stone. "Do not lose yourself, Bethnarian! Husband your strength to hold to your resolve."

The Empyreor's response dripped contempt. "Do not fear me, Sandyr. What I have lost I cannot forget, even when I stand before her.

"Then let us be quick. Her strength will continue to grow as the night deepens, especially on this night." Turning to Colin, he said, "It is time for us to say farewell, Colin Blackhammer."

"I am not going with you?"

The lord's almost smile was a perfect mystery.

"Your time will come. Wait here. Once we have passed through the gate, the staff will show you the way."

"And if it doesn't?" The thought of being abandoned to this cavern of alien energy was only slightly less terrifying that the thought of following the Lord into the mystery beyond the gate. But Lord Warder had already turned away. Silver light blazed from his palm, and a strange litany of words began to pour from his lips. The light in his hand began to pulse, and the many lights suspended in the vines picked up its beat. Then the vines themselves began moving, so slowly at first that they tricked Colin into feeling like the whole cavern was moving. Soon, they were streaming over and under each other, moving so fast and in such set patterns that the gate no longer looked like a tangled mass of vines but more like an overlapping conglomeration of immense symbols. As the streaming light quickened, the symbols grew brighter, casting their net of light over the figure of the lord. His robes ignited in a smaller but equally complex series of symbols.

Then the central symbols of the gate rolled back on a narrow passage of purer darkness, and the Lord and the Empyreor passed into it.

Shortly afterward, the real nightmare began. It started as a strange, impalpable hum that lifted the fine hairs on Colin's arms and neck. Retreating to the cavern's far wall, Colin clutched Shade's staff tighter, but the carved rod remained dead in his hands while the hum crescendoed to a roar that caused his ears and bones to ache, his teeth to loosen in his head.

Then shadowy people began to appear. By ones and twos they came, by hundreds and thousands — handsome young men and pretty young women, grandfathers and grandmothers and children of all ages, the hale and weak, the proud and humble. They wore a variety of strange clothes and many had their skin painted. They spoke odd languages, and they called out as they ran or crept or hobbled in chains.

Many called to him. And this was the most terrible thing of all. They begged him for help even as their feet carried them forward in a relentless march. Although their cries wrung his heart, he dared not go to them. He took the coward's way out and wedged himself deeper into the rock while they went down into utter darkness. "I'm sorry. I'm sorry," he wept and turned his face away.

Then rays of sunrise burst upon the chamber, and striding out of them came Shade.

Colin's heart leapt up like a prayer. Forgotten was the fear and anger, the deep mistrust. He saw only that his savior had come. He gathered himself to run to the other man, then registered the terrifying expression on Shade's face.

This was not the Shade who had taunted and prodded and mocked him on the road. This man was not nearly that human. His bared teeth were fangs, and his movements were a killer's. With savage grace he strode to the center of the chamber and his eyes flamed. But at the heart of those twin flames was a vast and terrible darkness, a darkness reflecting the even more absolute black of the awful artifact topping his carven staff.

Colin shut his eyes and tried to think of home, of family, of Vyara — all the places where human hope and laughter and love existed.

He heard Shade cry out, or was it the Lord Warder's voice? The whole world rocked and rumbled in answer. Then it shattered.

If Colin had not already had his back to the cavern wall, he would have been hurled against it and smashed. As it was, the force of the blast bent his ribs and showered him with debris. More weight descended on him, stones that formed a half-completed cairn over his bruised body. His consciousness flickered, hovering just above extinction.

Even so, on some level he remained aware, of life, of death, of the radiant being that emerged from the darkness where the gate had been. The passage of that being was impossible to ignore, as was the mesmerizing song it hummed.

Chapter 25: The Ninth Moon

With the Empyreor gone, it should have fallen to the Lord Commander of the Empyreal armies to secure the city's peace until a new Empyreor could be crowned. Instead, the current Lord Commander was preparing to abandon the city altogether, in obedience to his Empyreor's final orders.

Confronting two of his best captains in the anteroom to the Emperor's apartments, he said, "Send word to the companies garrisoned at Sun Gate. I want them to move due west immediately."

The captains glanced at one another. The elder, Karzat, who often served as Jazim's aide, cleared his throat and bowed. "Is this the Empyreor's wish?"

The Prince of Serpents scowled. He did not like his officers questioning him at the best of times. For them to do so now, when he himself didn't know his own mind, was insupportable.

"You heard me, captain!"

"Yes, Lord Commander," the two mumbled together, bowing then turning to leave.

"Karzat! Wait."

The younger captain made a hasty exit while Karzat stiffened to attention. "My prince?"

"How many of our men are already inside the palace grounds?"

"Fifty at most, my prince."

Jazim wanted to curse. How many times had he begged Bethnarian to allow him to station a company of regular soldiers within the palace complex? But the Empyreor had stubbornly held to custom, which said that only the unshakably loyal and politically disinterested Empyreal Guard should patrol the Empyreal grounds.

Jazim ran his hand back and forth across the belt at his waist. "Gather them and meet me at the palace's south gate," he said to Karzat. He turned his back in dismissal, heard the door swing closed, and went back to stroking his belt.

He wanted to spit out the foul taste in his mouth—the taste of all the unspoken recriminations of the past.

Jazim had entered the Empyreal household as a young man. Being more than half in love with Bethnarian's pale-haired queen, he had chosen to serve Janera as a personal attendant and guard.

Then the mysterious Sandyr Ash had appeared, and disaster like death had followed. Jazim's first glimpse of the white-haired death dealer came on the night he tracked the pregnant Janera into the great necropolis. He had assumed that she was going into the great cemetery to make an offering at her family tomb; instead, he discovered her trysting with another man, a strange, pale man with hair whiter than bone. Other meetings would follow, all occurring in secret in various parts of the palace complex.

Although Jazim never saw the two do anything but talk, his suspicions about Janera grew, and he wrestled with himself about whether to expose her. Then came the terrible night when, summoned to the Queen's rooms, he came upon Janera screaming and dying in the white man's arms while Bethnarian stood back and looked on in shame and horror. The words the white man spoke to the Empyreor then rearranged Jazim's world.

Janera died, even as her stillborn son slipped from her womb, and it was Jazim who was ordered to wrap the infant body and conceal it in the Empyreal tomb. And it was Jazim who, a day later, went down into the chamber of falling waters to accept from the witch-woman Urttah a beautiful, healthy baby girl.

And now he had been ordered to put the safety of that girl child before the safety of the Empyre itself. It made him want to spit. Hearing a whisper of sound behind him, he whirled and saw Caphal, sere and silent as ever.

"You asked me to report on her condition," the major domo said.

"And?"

"Her labor grows more intense. She cries out in fear, and she curses—her mother."

Jazim looked toward the room where *she* lay.

Caphal cleared his throat. "Also, the Empyreal Guard has released Marbek. The prince has left the palace, taking his personal retinue with him."

Jazim's amber eyes narrowed. "And so it begins." He looked at Caphal. "Are the Empyreal bearers ready?

"Yes, Highness." The secretary bowed.

"Bring them!" Jazim barked.

When the great earthquake hit the city, Jazim and the Empyreal bodyguard were hurrying the princess' litter to the palace's southern gate. The jolt from the earth staggered him. The rumble that came afterward took everyone's feet out from under them. From the ground Jazim watched the great stones of the gate shift and begin to crumble in.

Men and horses screamed. A great plume of dust lifted off.

Jazim rolled to his feet and saw the silent Empyreal bodyguards stumbling to theirs. In the distance faint cries and the last of the sun's light were falling from the skies.

Into the stunned moment cut the princess' clear voice. "Jazim!"

Jazim turned and saw a tilted and mangled litter and the Lady Miri partially pinned under it.

Jazim ran and heaved at the corner of it so that Miri could clamber free. "Are you hurt?" he cried.

"Jazim!" cried the princess again. Throwing back the litter's curtains he locked eyes with beauty itself, sweat-sheened and desperate. "Help me to the gate!"

The Lord Commander scanned her. "Are you—"

"I can't walk far! Lift me up!"

He did as he was told, hauling her into his arms with a grunt. "I don't know if we can get through it."

"Then you must carry me over it."

"If I drop you—"

"Don't," she ordered, but she gasped sharply as he began to walk. "Hurry! She is coming."

Jazim was fairly sure he knew who *she* was. He quickened his steps, ignoring the low cries of the woman he carried, and calling over his shoulder for their escort to follow.

Before the ruin of the gate he paused, searching for the safest route through the rubble. The stones were piled high, but he thought he could pick out a fairly stable section stacked almost like steps.

"Hold tight."

"Go away, leave me alone," the princess hissed back. Then in a shockingly different tone of voice, she urged, "Quickly, Jazim. As you loved my father, take me out of here."

Gripping the soles of his boots almost as hard as he gripped her, Jazim launched himself first at one set of rocking stones then at another. Behind him one of the Empyreal guard let out a deep gurgling bellow. A rasping voice cried out, "Put my sister down, serpent lord."

"Don't stop!" cried the princess in his ear.

He set his foot to another rocky stone. "Duck!" screamed Bethnara, and Jazim pitched sideways, twisting as he did so as to break the princess' fall with his body. Something long and heavy whizzed past his face. He struck the tumbled stones hard and slid forward. The princess rolled from his arms. Though stone dug into his back and snatched the breath from his lungs, he scrabbled upward. Bethnarian's daughter was already on her feet.

"I've had about enough of you, witch!" the princess shouted. Jazim looked down the hill to see Urttah striding across the wrecked yard, dark robes flapping like crows' wings. "Foolish child, you cannot run," she cackled, "Don't you hear our mother calling? She is fully awake and eager to meet you."

With surprising speed the scarred woman ran and struck a swinging bodyguard down with a twist of her crooked knife, then she put her foot to their tumble of broken stone. "Come sister! Come and meet our mother."

"Why?" Beth cried. "So she can rip my child from my belly. I'll take my chances with the world outside."

Urttah shook her deep hood back from her naked and hideously scarred scalp. The crude folds of skin that passed for her lips split in an appalling mockery of a smile. "So you and I can both be free. Come. She will do right by your son, and by you. She will draw the pain from all of us."

Jazim drew his saber, shifting his stance on the broken rock so that the edge of his blade was out in front of him. "Go, highness! Hurry! I will delay her."

Urttah stretched out a claw-like hand, and Jazim prepared to swing.

"Don't you touch her!" came a shriek. Unnoticed the Lady Miri had clawed her way up behind the witch woman. Blood was running from her forehead, but she launched herself at the scarred woman with a tigress' fury. Silver flashed in her hand.

With a contemptuous slap of her own hand, Urttah countered the blow and sent the frantic waiting woman, rolling backward off the sliding stones.

"Miri!" screamed Beth.

Jazim lunged. The witch dodged his blade with ease and whipped her hand across his face. The blow rattled every tooth in his head and rocked the stones beneath his booted feet. He staggered but somehow stayed upright. "Seven hundred years!" Urttah rasped, as her knife scored a burning line across his forearm. "Seven hundred years of waiting to exchange service for freedom. I will not be thwarted now!"

Jazim raised his blade in a futile attempt to ward a second strike.

And a stone the size of a man's head sped over the broken rock and struck the scarred woman in the arm. Urttah howled. The knife spun up and away from her.

A massive knot of formless energy bounded across the rubble, faster and more agile than a wild bull, shifting enormous blocks as it went. It seized the witch, raised her into the air.

Ogren flashed his war colors, turning a purple so dark it looked almost black. The witch woman began to laugh, a horrible, croaking sound, and Ogren dashed her to the stones. Urttah gurgled. Ogren jabbed his talons into her chest and yanked out her beating heart.

Jazim tore over treacherous stone toward the now sobbing princess.

"Miri!" cried Bethnara, clutching at his arm.

"I will return for her," lied Jazim, "after I get you across the wall."

He heaved her up into his arms again, straining to keep his balance, and took one tottering step.

From out of the massive confines of the great palace came a voice like a love longed for, like hope realized, like the promise of life without end. "Come," it said, and Jazim found himself unable to take one step more.

The princess was pounding on his shoulder, screaming into his ear. "Don't listen to her!"

"I—" he strained toward—he knew not what.

"Come," the voice repeated.

"Jazeeeeeeem!" Bethnara screeched.

Jazim couldn't help himself. He turned back and saw walking across the garden a diverse crowd of persons—soldiers and palace menials, functionaries and great lords alike. All had the same intent expression on their faces, and all seemed to be looking at him and the woman he held. Fingernails raked his face, yanked it around.

The princess' eyes were burning with a pure, deep sapphire light. They flamed into his mind and cleared a corner it. "It's my mother.

She's sending them after us," the princess cried. "You must keep walking!"

"Yes," he nodded, taking fresh hold on the solid sound and feel of her. But he made the mistake of looking back again. Far across the great yard, a slender silvery shape was emerging from the eaves of the massive palace. It should have seemed frail and very small with distance, yet it dominated the grand scene like a single candle flame dominates a pitch-black night.

The princess spasmed in his hold. Suddenly, her mouth was on his, her lips sucking feeling and thought right out of him. A welter of strong emotion passed through him — passion, ambition, anger, loyalty, lust. On the crest of that emotion his spirit soared and his eyes closed.

The Prince of Serpents remembered who he was. Without opening his eyes, he turned, and trusting to luck or the gods, he dashed for the peak of the hill of rubble.

Half sliding, half running, he descended the other side.

The world outside the gate was chaos. Soldiers and servants and animals rushed aimlessly about.

Thinking only of putting as much distance as possible between himself and the thing beyond the wall, Jazim commandeered a horse from a young soldier, and shouted to those around him. "Get as far away from the palace as you can! Run! Plague has broken out. Pass the word and head for the foothills."

To the laboring woman he somehow still held, he said, "You shouldn't ride, but I can't think of any better way to get you out of here quickly?"

Her mouth moved against his shoulder. "There are no good choices left to us."

Jazim stiffened as a massive figure rose above him, dangling a child-like figure in its arms.

"Miri!" breathed the princess.

Jazim looked a plea into the nonman's splotchy lavender face. "I can take the Lady Miri with me on horseback. You must carry the princess. Keep up!"

Ogren trilled.

"Let's move!" Jazim barked.

As the tall Northlander strode through the unusually quiet streets, Abreem hurried after him, snatching at a trailing sleeve and saying, "Please, my friend, wait. Even if he is at home, you will never reach him. You would have to battle an entire company of his personal guard to force the issue, and that task, I fear, would exceed even your skills."

"He has a household guard?"

"Yes!" affirmed Abreem, finally snagging the sleeve. "And not any ordinary household guard. His are dangerous men, skilled mercenaries, many from your own land. I have heard that they disdain even the Sards."

The Northlander bared his teeth in a mirthless smile. "Sounds like a challenge." With a flick of his arm, he tossed Abreem off and moved ahead, loose robe billowing out behind him, exposing lean legs and an even leaner blade.

Abreem mumbled a curse under his breath and scampered after.

The house of the man named Scryos' lay tucked away in a quiet, elegant quarter of the city inhabited by people whose unorthodox roads to affluence made them value discretion. Abreem knew how seriously these citizens took their privacy, and he hoped to prevent the young Northlander from becoming their target, despite the fact that the Northlander looked and acted like a man bent on cudgeling death itself.

Abreem told himself that he should leave the man to his fate and go home. But then he considered what waited for him at home — more endless nights of fear and fire, the certainty of another visit from Sardic assassins — and, yanking his robes close about himself, he dogged the other man's heels. Even a high probability of death was better than the certainty of it.

When they reach the gates that marked the entrance to Scryos' neighborhood, the sun had just set. The cloudless sky was glowing that brilliant shade of cobalt that heralds the desert night when it belched thunder and the ground began to shake. Abreem grabbed at the Northlander's arm to steady himself. "What was that?" he asked, when the shaking was done.

The Northlander didn't appear to be listening. He grabbed Abreem's good shoulder and pushed him into a narrow alley between buildings.

"Stay here," he hissed and slipped back up the road.

Abreem waited. He had just gotten up enough courage to peer around the corner of the building when a hand jerked him back into a shallow doorway. Abreem swallowed a yelp while the Northlander whispered, "There are armed men ahead. An unusually mixed lot. Some look like Empyreal guard."

Abreem sagged against the wall. "Please don't surprise me like that," he whined.

"Shhh. They are coming this way."

Abreem held his breath, then whispered, "They are probably guards hired for the festival. It's customary for the elite of the land to join the mobs of the streets during the Festival of the Ninth Moon, but they rarely do so without protection."

"Quiet!"

Hooves on cobbles announced a trio of horsemen wearing short leather jackets and trousers studded with metal.

Abreem squinted, trying to get a clearer look. "Those look like the Scryos' men," he hissed.

The Northlander was grinning like a wolf. "Well, hello there, Captain," he growled under his breath.

Abreem stared. "You know them?"

"Yes, indeed. The Captain and I are old and intimate friends. But a short time ago we were exchanging pleasantries in the good old homeland. He must have ridden several horses to death getting here."

"I believe he is one of Scryos' more trusted retainers."

But the Northlander silenced him with a twist of shoulder.

Up ahead, the Captain, a shaven-headed man with a hard-planed face, had sidled his horse in front of the other two riders. His voice came to the concealed men faint but clear. "Davet, your men are responsible for securing the baggage train. Keep to the westernmost roads. The city will run riot tonight, and I do not need to tell you the consequences if any of the Lord's valuables are lost. Pellus, tell the other commanders to set up a camp at the dry wells north of the city. Keep a lookout for Empyreal scouts until the Sards have drawn the army out. We make for the border as soon as the Lord arrives."

"How long will that be?"

"What concern is that of ours, lieutenant? Be ready."

The captain waved the two other men off then swung his horse around as the sound of many more iron-shod hooves began ricocheting down the alley. More leather-clad horsemen passed at a brisk trot, followed by a contingent of red-robed footmen carrying tall pikes. Behind these footmen came a massive gold and black palanquin borne by bearers with arms as thick as young trees. Inside the unscreened palanquin sat a red-robed man.

"That can't be Scryos?" hissed the Northlander to Abreem.

The small scholar shook his head.

More horsemen followed, these wearing dark robes, and at that end of that train came a single horseman mounted on a fine gray whose hide rippled like moonshine. The rider was enveloped in a dark hooded robe that covered his head and shoulders and fanned out across his mount's flanks. On his booted feet shone sharp spurs and at his side hung a long metal-banded scabbard. He sat his mount with the easy composure of a man much used to the saddle.

Abreem reached out reflexively for the Northlander's arm. He dared not speak, he hardly dared breathe. There was an awareness seeping from the mounted man that even Abreem could feel.

The two hidden men remained still and silent for a long time after the single horseman had passed. Finally, Abreem exhaled, "That was Scryos."

"Yes," the Northlander agreed, his still, somber face fixed on the end of the alley,

"What now?"

The Northlander looked down at him. "Now, Master Abreem, you go home."

"If you are still planning on breaking into his house, I am going with you."

The shadowed eyes flicked back toward the rider's road. "I'm more interested in the man himself."

"But his information on bloodstone will be there. I know where his library is; I met him there once or twice. Now would be the perfect time for a raid. He will have fewer men there to defend it."

"A scholar and an adventurer as well," smiled the Northlander. "But it won't avail us. Didn't you hear what the captain said? Scryos is leaving the Empyre. He's already moved any objects of real value."

"So you are going to follow him?"

The Northerner's expression was bleak.

"Blood of the gods, Northlander! If you are so bent on throwing your life away, why didn't you just leap on him here and now? You saw the man! You felt his presence! Do you really believe you can defeat him?"

The shadows in the other man's face shifted to admit a slight smile. "Maybe I was thinking of you Abreem Imharta. And then again, maybe I was thinking of others besides you."

Abreem shook his head. "You will never take him alive, if you can take him at all—and I don't see how killing him outright will help you. You need him to tell you about the mark. But you would have better luck wringing words from a stone. I doubt the man knows the meaning of the word fear, but he is infinitely cautious and clever."

"Listen to me, Master Abreem. As of now, my concerns about Scryos go way beyond myself. If I understood the captain correctly, the Sards themselves will sweep into the city tonight. Go home. Collect your servants and a few belongings and leave. Pack only essentials and take the quickest roads out of the city heading north. Do not go east, and do not let anyone or anything detain you."

"The Sards?" Abreem choked. He could feel the stones of the wall scraping his hands.

The Northlander began to slip away.

Abreem caught his arm, held it in surprisingly strong grip. "What about the lance head, the Heartbreaker?"

The proud head swiveled back his way. "All the more reason to make haste. The Sards may be able to track you by it, but I recommend that you keep it with you at all times. Don't let go of it whatever happens. I am not sure what its purpose is, but it bears the marks of all the houses arcane, and it pulls at the life and spirit like bloodstone. If you manage to escape the city, make your way to the northeast border of the Midlands. Those borders are watched by the Warders. Your most immediate hope of discovering the lance's meaning may lie with them. Good luck, and may the powers protect you, Abreem Imharta. You have been a good friend."

"Good fortune, Northlander," answered Abreem in a voice so tiny it might have issued from the very bottom of the wells of hope.

As the last of the sunlight left the sky, Emily fought to hold on to a screaming Janys. Then Benja and another servant were bursting in upon them.

"What are you doing here?" the old servant cried.

"She asked me to come," panted Emily between Janys' shrill cries. "She said she was afraid."

"Get back!" ordered Benja.

But the old woman had even less success in restraining her mad mistress than Emily. Janys twisted free and ran for the opening to the stair."

"Janys wait!" ordered Emily, sending out a thought like a lasso.

The thought, picked up by the raging current in Janys' mind, snapped back at her like a whip. Emily gasped, bringing her hands to her head.

"Mother!" cried a distraught voice.

Janys' skidded to a halt. Vyara, clad in gleaming wine-colored silk, had emerged from the hole in the floor. Her pale hair gleamed, and her eyes were enormous and dark.

"Oh, Janera," moaned Janys and slipped to her knees.

"No mother," answered Vyara, going to the kneeling woman. "Janera is not here. I am Vyara, your daughter. What is upsetting you so?" Janys's head fell forward, and she began to sob.

Abruptly Vyara looked away from her stricken mother toward Emily. "What happened to her?" she asked in a voice devoid of accusation.

Emily opened her mouth, caught Benja's scowl, and spoke anyway, "She claimed a man was hiding up here. She wanted me to help her make him go away. And then the whole house shook."

"It was an earthquake." Vyara looked at Benja. "I will deal with my mother, Benja. You and Gerum go back downstairs. The guests will be arriving soon, and there is still much work to do. Close the stairway door please."

Emily watched the two servants leave with a sinking heart. The Tellers only knew how Vyara would excoriate her this time.

But Vyara's stare remained neutral. "Is what Benja says true? Has Colin left us?"

Emily's lips parted in surprise, and she took a moment to switch mental tracks. "Something has happened to him," she admitted.

"What?"

"I do not know. But it must have been serious and unexpected. He took his staff with him."

Vyara looked down at her mother's bent head. "Perhaps he has realized the impossibility of helping me."

Emily took a step forward and spoke sharply. "No, Vyara. Whatever has happened to him has nothing to do with you. Perhaps the Lady Miri sent word to him, and he felt it would be safest to leave without telling me, or you."

"Would he do that?"

Emily bit her lip in doubt. "It is very unlike him," she admitted.

Vyara averted her face and closed her eyes. "I knew I would never escape," she said.

Emily swept up to her and caught her hand. "Nonsense," she said in a voice brisk but kind. "If there is one thing I know about Colin Blackhammer, it's that he has a mind as sturdy as his father's anvil. He loves you, Vyara. Nothing will make him forget or forsake that. He will come back for you, somehow, some way. Give him a little time."

Vyara smiled. "I have no more time. Everything has conspired against us." Her eyes dropped to her mother's shaggy head. Janys began to whine.

"What do you mean?" demanded Emily.

"The men my uncle plans to entertain tonight include my future husband."

"What!"

"Yes. My Uncle intends to sign the contract of marriage tonight. Afterward, I will be a married woman, and my husband will be free to do with me as he wills."

Emily's eyes widened in horror. "Why didn't you tell Colin this?"

"I didn't know it until this afternoon."

As the implications of the situation began to sink in, Emily spun about, biting a nail. The still brilliant colors of Shade's tapestry caught her eye, and she looked to the woven figure in both trepidation and hope. "You must leave!" she said to Vyara. "Run away."

"I cannot. My uncle needs me to do this, and I owe him so much."

Emily remembered what she had learned about the Cyronians' origins and bit her lip. The two young women regarded each other helplessly as the muffled but unmistakable sounds of hooves beating against stone broke against the tower's windows. Emily hurried to the nearest one.

"The guests are arriving," she murmured.

"I must go," nodded Vyara, but her voice strained against the words and her feet did not move. Abruptly she walked to Emily, caught the Midlander's hand, and pressed something into it. "Put my mother to bed, and give her this to help her sleep."

Emily wanted to protest, to take Vyara by the shoulders and shake her, but the heavy cloud of despair that hung over the house seemed to have fallen upon her too. She let Vyara turn and leave without saying another word.

Janys' feverish eye snared her own. "Don't worry," the mad woman said, "Soon they will all burn."

She got Janys to bed, giving her a few drops of the cloudy liquid in the vial Vyara had handed her. Then she sat and watched the older woman toss herself into an uneasy sleep. Alone in a deepening dark, she thought of Colin and Vyara, of what must even now be going on below, and the whole time her practical self insisted that something even more dreadful was about to happen in this house. But she made no move to flee. A feeling had passed between her and Vyara in that tower room that was more than mutual concern and mutual respect. Vyara needed her, and in a strange way, she needed Vyara. For reasons she could not articulate, they were together in this, come what may.

She did not leave the tower room entirely alone, however. Before she departed it, she climbed back up to the now dark weaving room and ripped Shade's weighty tapestry off its bar.

"I've had about enough of your mischief, mister," she told him. "You are coming with me."

Back in the lower rooms of the apartment, she rolled him into a tight cylinder and threw several lengths of dirty cloth over him.

She was halfway down the poorly lit stair when she saw a strange, armed man standing at the bottom of it. He was a bald man with flat cheeks and an even flatter stare. That stare made her gut contract, but she put on a show of menial servility and scurried past.

More armed men ranged through the other rooms of the house. Some wore jackets and leggings of supple leather, others were clad in brilliantly dyed robes. A few of them wore badges bearing an all too familiar crescent mark, Janeryc's chosen insignia.

As she passed the hallway to the kitchen and larders, she heard Benja call her name in a harried tone. "One moment," she called back and rushed on past, anxious to dispose of the tapestry in her arms. Fortunately, the servants' quarters seemed to have escaped the visiting soldiers' attention. She ran to her room and hastily stowed the tapestry under her pillow. Then she dashed to the terrace above. "Faryn," she called in as loud a voice as she dared to use. "Faryn, if you can hear me, I need you. Please come."

She waited and waited, but Faryn never appeared. Briefly she considered reaching out with her mind. She had never actually contacted Faryn this way before, but she felt strangely confident that she could. Then she remembered Vyara's comment about her uncle's abilities and Faryn's cryptic warnings about other powers. Would Janeryc sense what she was doing? Looking down, she saw Benja stomping across the courtyard from the kitchens, so she abandoned all ideas of reaching out to the absent warder and hastened down the steps to meet her. As she slid off the last step, she nearly ran into the bald soldier, who was now standing at the bottom of the servants' stair.

"Excuse me," said Emily, sidling past him.

Bethnarian's daughter and her meager escort made for the southern edge of the Sun City. Jazim rode with Miri's bloody head and shoulders knocking against his chest, while somewhere behind him loped a confusing kaleidoscope of energy bearing a shrouded form in its nearly invisible arms.

As they bolted through one of the poorer quarters, Jazim heard the giant emit a sharp trill. He yanked his horse around.

Ogren was an appalling hulk of dark purple immensity standing on a crooked street against a backdrop of dirty, shabby edifices. In his arms Bethnara groaned and twisted. "We have to stop," the princess gritted.

"It isn't safe," insisted Jazim.

"Stop," she barked, grit deepening to groan.

Jazim slid off his dancing horse, walked to the nearest door in the nearest hovel and kicked it in. Inside, he found a thin, impoverished woman and her two scrawny children. "Get out!" he commanded.

The woman grabbed her children and ran.

Ogren squeezed through the door with the Princess in his arms.

Jazim looked about in disgust. "The blankets are probably full of lice," he said as Ogren fluted something untranslatable.

"Lay me down," gasped Beth.

The giant thrummed soothingly.

Jazim stood impatiently, stupidly. He had no children that he knew of and wanted none.

"Get Miri," Beth panted at him between short breaths.

The request made sense. Jazim went to fetch the lady, who still sat Jazim's horse dazedly. "Dreadful," she breathed as she ran her eyes over the houses along the street.

"Her time has come."

"Then help me down. I'm so dizzy I'm afraid I'll fall, but I must go to her."

"You are in no condition to go to anyone," he said, reaching up and hauling her off the horse. "You need to let me take a closer look at that cut on your head."

"Not now."

Steadying herself against the doorframe, Miri passed into the squalid little house.

Jazim secured the horse, scanned the street, then propped his back against the rough stucco. All was eerily quiet.

He looked north. Far off in the great plazas of the city, immense crowds would be gathering, people preparing to dance and game and feast away the Festival of the Ninth Moon. Perhaps most of the residents of this sadder quarter had already gone to join them, hopeful of forgetting desperation in drink and song.

The night wore on, and Jazim stood and watched a false dawn flare up in the eastern sky. The door to the house creaked open. The

Lady Inimiri stepped out. Even in the near dark, Jazim could see the strain in her face.

"Well?"

"It's over."

"Is she—"

"She's had a boy." The lady's soft mouth trembled. "He never cried. Ogren delivered him while I—." Her eyes slid toward Jazim's. "I was feeling faint."

Jazim exhaled slowly. "Is your head still hurting?"

"A little. She wrapped him up and would not let me see him."

"Let me see your wound." Carefully he pulled her to him, examined the margins of her clotted cut and tested the skull underneath. "You are lucky. Your skull is in tact."

"I'm lucky I'm not dead," Miri sighed. "Bethnara is worried about pursuit. She told me to warn you."

"The fire may help us there."

"Fire?"

"Look east."

Miri raised her head. "By the gods, half the city must be burning! How long before the flames reach us?"

"Hard to say. The wind seems to be in our favor. At any rate, I am less concerned about the fire than the Sards."

"Sards!"

"They are the ones doing the burning. Bethnarian had been expecting them."

Had it not been for the staff he carried, Colin Blackhammer would have died, undiscovered and unsung, in the belly of the earth. In a distant Midland village, a few people would have continued to ponder his disappearance, but soon even they would have set his memory aside to focus on their own troubles in the world.

There were times in the process of digging himself out of his giant cairn that Colin Blackhammer wished to die. Parts of him were bruised and bloody, and the heavy mound of stones atop him did not shift easily, but the staff, no less than its master, would not relent. It stuck fast to his hand and pulled.

He cursed it when he wasn't screaming with the agony of having to push with a stiff and badly abraded leg. He wept and called to the Tellers for mercy. But mercy had abandoned this dark place centuries before, and with the destruction of the gate, the last glimmers of hope had left it as well.

No matter. The staff knew exactly where it was going. It took hold of his flesh and his will and dragged him across dust-clogged and echoing spaces. It hauled him over boulders and across rivulets of running water. Somewhere ahead of him there was a silvery light. He limped, coughing, toward it, letting the energy of the staff share some of the work of his tortured limbs.

The light grew brighter, resolving eventually into a shape like a gigantic pillar. A thick braid of twisting vine-like shapes, it plunged through the ceiling of the high cavern he had entered and into the floor. About its thick central core, small vines like those of the gate twisted, forming an elaborate helix.

"It's like a staircase," he whispered, and limped eagerly forward, basking in its silvery glow.

At the point where he first reached it, its woven steps were too high to mount. So he began to limp around it. That was when he came upon the Empyreor.

In death, Bethnarian looked surprisingly peaceful. A gentle smile softened the hard edges of his face. His pale eyes, wide open to the ceiling, seemed to gaze dreamily into an unimagined distance, like those of a child watching the clouds drift.

"What happened to you?" Colin asked, and some trick of the light made the Empyreor's eyes seem to move in answer. Colin stepped back and felt a delicate crunch beneath his feet. Pale rubble littered the floor. He shifted his foot awkwardly and heard a louder crunch. The glowing pillar spread a soft light of definition over the white things beneath his feet, picked out their pattern.

Colin's stiff leg slipped out from under him, and when the cloud of pain cleared, he found himself looking straight into the eye sockets of a tiny skull.

Small skeletons. Several of them were laid out like offerings on the floor.

Whimpering, Colin crawled out of the strange graveyard, noting the odd deformities of the smallest skeletons.

Then he heard a whispered word.

The staff yanked him to his feet, heedless of the intense pain it caused. He cried out and tried to pry it out of his closed fist, but it dragged him forward anyway, so quickly that he nearly fell over the crumpled form it sought.

The Lord Warder looked physically uninjured and yet terribly drained, like a man who has come to the end of a long battle with a devastating illness. All his wiry strength and energy, that strange, predatory extra-aliveness he exerted, seemed to have been sucked out of him.

At another time, the sight would have made Colin weep, but he had no more energy for tears. "Oh, Tellers. My lord, can you hear me?"

After a long time the ruby eyes opened. The pale lips parted, but the sound that came out of them was so faint that Colin had to put his ear to the Lord's face to hear it. "Climb the tree."

Colin turned his head to look at the glowing pillar with a new understanding. Moments later, he began the slow and agonizing business of dragging himself and the dying Lord Warder up the gigantic twisted taproot that was also a stair.

Chapter 26: Revenge

For several hours, Emily scrubbed, hauled and cleaned while fears and hopes, certainties and speculations, impulses and stillborn plans went round and round in her head.

At one point, a servant handed her a pile of wet dishcloths and pushed her toward the laundry. Emily was halfway there when she realized she had to get outside or she was going to be sick all over again. Dropping the rags and holding her arms over her middle, she ran for a small courtyard just off an unused sitting room. At a small fountain, half hidden behind potted lemon trees, she splashed her face. The cool water eased her nausea, but sent her nervousness straight to her shaking legs. She sat down at the fountain's feet and waited for her stomach to settle. From elsewhere in the garden came the crunch of footsteps.

"How much longer?" declared a commanding Southern voice.

"But an hour or so more," answered a more cultured second.

"I tire of these games Scryos. You promised me the keys to mastery."

"And you shall have them, as soon as the remaining factors are accounted for."

The voices growing louder, Emily wedged herself more deeply into the fountain's shadow.

A low growl of discontent rolled across the dark. "While you speak of these mysterious factors, my time is wasted. Bethnarian is on his deathbed, if not dead already. My armies are in place, and more than half the nobles have sworn me their support. It is time I claimed my bride and the Sun Scepter."

"The Prince of Serpents might have something to say about both. You should wait if you want to have the advantage of him."

The Southern voice cursed. "Why do I listen to your vague promises?"

"Because," the cultured voice returned, "you know that I alone can protect you from the dangers of your more vaunted ambitions."

"Bah! I do not need you to scare an old man in line, and I'm sure there are many ways of securing stones of the blood."

"But not of controlling them," returned the other in perfectly reasonable tones. "Patience, highness. As soon as I have mine, I will see to it that you get yours,"

Boots scraped stone and a very tall silhouette came to loom over Emily's place of concealment. She saw a sharp profile against a dark sky, a powerful arm banded in gold. From out of that profile rolled the scathing Southern voice. "You have one hour, no more. You either finish your negotiations with Janeryc by then, or my men will take what I want. I am tired of waiting."

Again, boots scraped stone, one set following another. Emily tilted her face to the winking stars.

"You, by the fountain, come out," said the cultured voice.

Emily froze, and the stars winked more sheepishly.

"Come out," said the voice more persuasively. "Do not be afraid."

Emily knew better than to believe it, but an invisible tentacle of will suddenly latched on to hers. *Come out,* it said.

Emily rose on stiff legs and walked toward the source, a dark figure seated on a stone bench. "That's it," it said, not unkindly, while Emily strained to find a face within the shadow and her mind screamed for her to turn and run.

The seated man rose and, cupping her chin, tilted her face to the moonlight. "You have grown, Emilyn," he said.

Shock gave her the power to penetrate the darkness, decipher the features, the gleam of expression lurking deep in the shadowed eyes.

It also gave her the power to shatter his hold. Jerking her face from his hand, she spun and ran.

Covered in the night's shadows, Al Goodwin crouched atop a narrow garden wall and studied the movements of those in and around the house. Armed men were everywhere, and Scryos was among them.

He had followed the mysterious magician and his soldiers straight to this house, whose architectural style, and proximity to the palace screamed old nobility.

Safe atop his high wall, Al tuned his sharp ears and even sharper eyes to the talk of the three different groups of men guarding the outside of the great building. The red-robed ones talked liberally and loudly as they strove to outbrag each other while praising the majesty of their master, a prince named Marbek, indisputably the strongest of the potential lineal heirs to the Empyreal throne. The quieter gray-clad men spoke little if at all and only of matters essential to their duty. It was some time before Al figured out that they worked for the owner of the house, a man named Janeryc, Lord Cyronian. The last group of men, more raggedly and heterogeneously clad than the others, spoke not at all, but Al did not need to be told that these men worked for Scryos. He recognized several of them as he had recognized their captain.

Al shrank closer to the top of the wall as the large red-robed man who had ridden in the palanquin—obviously Marbek—emerged into the great courtyard at the side of a darker man who wore northern style pants and boots under a side-slit silk tunic of deep gray. About this man's waist was cinched the same long sword that Al had remarked from the alley near Scryos' home. Scyros.

Working his way along walls and rooftops, Al moved to a place where he could spy on the smaller courtyard in which the two men squared off. He listened to Marbek's threats, heard Scryos' unruffled replies, and absorbed the following key facts. Marbek was indeed intent upon taking the throne, by force if he had to. He had come to the Cyronian's house to secure Janeryc's political support, a wife, and a bloodstone, all three promised to him by Scryos, who also had vital information on the whereabouts of Marbek's only serious competition, Jazim, Prince of Serpents. Scryos, too, hoped to gain something, from Janeryc. What this was wasn't exactly clear, but Scryos clearly considered it important.

Seeing Marbek stride back into the house, Al was seized by a desire to leap down into the courtyard and set the bright, unequivocal edge of his saber to Scryos' neck, but then he heard Scryos call out. Thinking the magician was calling out to him, he froze while a woman answered the summons instead, a servant of the house by her attire. She emerged from the greenery of the courtyard moving in the rather boneless manner of a person under a spell. Clearly, her mind had been overthrown. Likely, she would never see her end coming.

Then the tall man reached out and raised the woman's face, and a name exploded into Al's mind, eradicating all his earlier thoughts and worries and narrowing his energies to a fine, killing point. Although he did not see it, the faint moonlit shadow he cast darkened and expanded into a shape far different from his own.

Emily hurtled through the house, ignoring the stares of nervous servants as well as the glares of armed men. Aware that the bald man was following her, she ducked into an unused room and then into one of the many carefully hidden back hallways designed to allow the servants easy and unobtrusive movement through the house. Dashing through several of these tight corridors, she wound her way to a door just behind the separate building that housed the servants' quarters. She was planning on taking refuge in Colin's room in order to give herself time to think.

On the stair she thought of Faryn. If ever she had needed the warder, she needed him now, so she took the rest of the steps two at a time and ran out on the terrace. He was not there, nor did he answer to her whispered calls. She looked behind her for signs of pursuit, saw none, then looked again at the roof. A hooded form was now dropping down from it. It landed lightly, but it wasn't Faryn. Emily turned to run. An arm caught her by the waist instead and pulled her into the house's shadows as a hand covered her mouth.

Terrorized and outraged, she kicked her heels and connected with flesh and bone.

"Ow," hissed a familiar voice and cursed. "Heaven's lights, Emily! Quit fighting me?"

Fear has a way of firing people's blood; relief can have quite the opposite effect. Emily crumpled. But for the arm about her waist she would have slid to the terrace stones. The arm, however, held her up, held her in close. A hand caught her lolling head and tilted it back against a firm shoulder.

Emily kept her eyes closed and concentrated on the feel of that hand, the bulwark of the body behind her. A connection she had thought lost forever flamed back to life. She didn't dare to move. If she did, she knew the magic would crumble to dust and drift away, leaving her lost and alone again.

"Are you still with me?" said the voice. She couldn't answer, but she whirled about and buried her face in rough cloth, choking on half a sob. Now she was the one holding on.

"Careful, I might begin to think you actually care about me," he teased.

She turned her head to free her mouth, pressing her cheek hard to the rising and falling chest. "Alsandyr Goodwin," she said in clear cold tones, "if you mock me now, I swear it will be the last thing you ever do."

He laughed softly, and she felt like she would have gladly died to bury herself in the sound of it. Its familiar warmth gave her the courage to pull back and look at him.

"Tellers!" she whispered. "What have they done to you?"

She instantly regretted the question. It seemed to draw a veil over his face heavier than the night's shadows, though his answering tone was brightly mocking. "That bad, eh?"

Her hand tightened on his robe, kept him from pulling away while her eyes moved hungrily over his face — the clean features, the tousled hair, the eyes like wells. It was the same beautiful, beloved visage, but there were angles and edges to it that she had never noticed before. There was something different in the eyes as well. She looked deep into them. Yes, the curtain of amusement that normally obscured what was going on behind them had been rent and frayed. Something raw and untamed looked back. It made her want to cry. "I was so afraid you had died," she whispered. "You were with me —" her free hand strayed to her heart, "and then — you weren't. What happened to you?"

He looked down at her. "So much. Too much for me to explain right now."

She could see the dark thing lurking at the bottom of his eyes growing restless, rising up. 'It doesn't matter," she said. "I don't know how or why you are here, but I'm glad you have come. You were right, I had no idea what I was getting myself into. Things are out of control — Janeryc, Beth, Vyara, even Colin's in trouble."

"Colin?"

"He came south with me. I am afraid —" The rest of the words stuck in her throat.

His hands caught her upper arms. "What is it? What's happening in this house?"

"There is a man," she said.

"Scryos. I know."

"Scryos?"

"The man who spoke to you in the garden."

"You saw that?" she shuddered, then shook her head. "He didn't tell me his name."

"That's what he calls himself. But whoever he is, he's a rogue practitioner of serious power, and he has tools at his disposal the like of which I have never seen. If he is in this house, Emily, you, as the bearer of the Shield, are in serious danger." He paused, reflecting, "He seemed to know you."

"I guess. I don't know how. But he's not the worst of it."

"There's more?"

She opened her mouth to try to explain, and realized she couldn't. How to describe what she had felt and seen, how to name her latest blunder? She could only think of one way. "There is something you need to see?" she finally said.

Checking to be sure that no guards had come, she pulled him into her own small room, drew the shutters, lit a lamp, and then dug behind her pallet to pull out the tapestry.

"Please just look at this, and then I will try to explain." Waving her arms sharply, she unfurled all the rich colors of Janys' remarkable work. Even in the dim light of the lantern the threads glowed jewel bright.

She heard his heels scrape the floor. "Roland!" he spat.

Emily's throat ached from rushing through her part of the story. Time was running out, and still she sat with her back to the wall and her knees drawn up to her chest while Al stood with his hands jammed into the loose sleeves of his robe looking down at the tapestry.

"Roland!" she said hollowly. She looked a plea at the Steward's heir. "Are you sure?"

"Positive. I've recently encountered him—not near so frequently as you and Colin, but just as forcefully. He's been dogging my steps since Cyr. Where did this come from?"

"The Lady Janys Cyronian wove it."

"Why would a Southern woman weave a tapestry of Roland?"

Emily stared at him in surprise. "Don't you know? The Cyronians are descendants of Roland's son by Illyria."

"How do you know this?"

"Several things point to it, but suffice it to say that Faryn, the warder who introduced us to Janeryc, confirmed it. He had the truth of it from his own Lord's lips."

"The Lord Warder," Al mused. "So the Cyronians held the mark during the lost years."

Emily's thoughts took a different track. "You and Lyr told me that such interbreeding was impossible."

He left off looking at the tapestry and cracked open the room's door.

"Are they coming?"

"No." The fact seemed to puzzle him. "Interbreeding has occurred," he said. "Obviously. But even then it is not easy and highly imprudent. Think of it this way. The members of the houses are like tools designed for a very specific purpose. We can do the work we do because the power shapes us to do it, and the powers of all the houses work to keep it that way. The histories of the houses suggest that it takes great power to break the prohibition on cross breeding, and when the lines are crossed traits become muddled, specific skills can be lost or, worse, twisted. At the same time there is a fearsome aggregation of power and potential in one person, which can throw the entire balance of power out of equilibrium. This may partially explain the Lady Janys' madness, as well as the deathly atmosphere that you say imbues this house. Fortunately, without further infusions of powerful blood, the Cyronians' own confused power has surely weakened over time."

"And you knew all this when you joined with Alysse—then me?" Although there was no accusation in her voice, she could not look at him.

"Emily," he murmured.

She waved at the air in front of her face as if clearing away cobwebs and used the wall to press herself to her feet. "No. Don't listen to me. The important thing is to figure out what Roland wants. Janys claims that he speaks to her, but her madness has prevented me from discovering anything about his aims. Meanwhile Colin has disappeared, along with the staff that Shade, I mean Roland, forced on him."

Al's solidity abruptly blotted out the lamp, the tapestry, all else. She tried to move around him, but he only caught her shoulders and turned her to face him again. "Stop it, stop trying to run away," he ordered in a voice low but crackling with authority. "Look at me," he ordered again. Emily found herself staring up into eyes that could swallow her whole. "I would never have done that to you, not ever. As for Alysse—" his voice thinned, "I will end up paying for that mistake with my life."

"What do you mean? Is Alysse—"

"Alysse is dead, may her poor, tormented soul find permanent rest. And I am cursed. You wanted to know what Roland wants. The answer, simply put, is revenge. You have seen for yourself something of the animosity existing between House Steward and House Warder; you once heard Blayne say that the source of that animosity was a woman. Guess which one."

"Illyria."

"Yes. Roland took what the Steward Ayr wanted, and Ayr withdrew his sight, invoking the oldest laws of the houses, the prohibition against interbreeding, to punish Roland for it. Undoubtedly, he meant his retaliation to strike only Roland, but he could not have been prepared for the power Roland possessed. Roland was more than just a warder, he was—"

"A half breed as well."

"Illyria was the weaker target. The punishment struck her first, drowning her land and killing her. But she must have used the Shield to save her son, and it was through her child that Ayr's retribution finally found its way to Roland. He came here to find his son only to meet his death instead—but not before he found a way to ensure that Ayr's act would rebound upon his own offspring, like a blade that turns in its wielder's hand. Roland laid his plans subtly and he laid them deep. He has waited centuries to strike at the house that destroyed him. And finally his time has come."

"Through you? Are you saying that Roland plans to take revenge on House Steward through you?"

He released her, turned away. "When it comes to House Steward I am the weaker vessel. Mistakes like Alysse prove it."

"The Tellers take your house and Roland! You have to get out of this city, now!"

"There's no point. It's already begun." He turned back to the door.

"Begun how?"

"It doesn't matter." But Emily saw his right hand tense and curl into a fist.

"Show me your mark!" she said sharply.

"Emily—"

She had his hand in her own. He did not fight her as she rolled the fingers back. She saw a spot of perfect black staining the palm where the Steward's golden mark had once gleamed.

"Roland did this to you?"

"A man called Scryos did this to me, with a stone that drinks power like the desert drinks water, but I have no doubt that Roland's hand was in it as well. That is why you have to leave this house immediately. We've wasted too much time already."

She remembered the untamed thing lurking in his eyes. "Promise to come with me."

He just looked at her.

"Why are you really here, Alsandyr?"

He met her question with silence as a soreness like the pain of unshed tears moved up from her chest into her throat. His stained hand clasped hers, but she tore her own hand away. She was so angry she wanted to strike him, so angry she wanted to scream. "How dare you do this to me!" she hissed. "How dare you come to this place intending to die!"

She wanted to drive him away, but he only caught her wrist as she raised her hand and gathered her in instead. Against her will, she found herself inhaling the scent of him and growing still against his chest. "Please try to understand," he whispered into her hair. "You know what happens to those who lose their power: you witnessed your aunt's decline. My power is gone, my time is done. I can no longer serve, or protect those most important to me. I do not know how much longer the energy vouchsafed me by Warder House will last, but I do know the name of the one who did this to me, who may even now be planning a far more terrible betrayal. By luck or the powers or the ghost of Roland, I have been given an opportunity to stop him, and I have to try. I may even be able to twist Roland's curse into something positive. Listen to me and try to understand."

She did listen, and she didn't pull away, but when she spoke, her voice, even and utterly empty, slammed a wall between them. "I understand. It's quite simple really. You have a calling and real obligations, a whole land to look after. Everything else is secondary. I know this. I can accept it. Just as I accepted your chidings, your station, your aid. What I can't accept is what you've done to me in the process. And now you tell me you intend to go to your death without so much as an apology for the fact that you will be burying a part of me with you. Do you feel nothing for me?"

He still did not speak, but his bearing changed. He now held himself so aloof, so still, that he might have become the wall she had set between them. Still, in the deepest, most foolishly irrational part of her she willed him to respond. Instants passed, and opportunity with them. He stiffened and turned his head toward a sound only he could hear, and she knew that his answer would never come.

"Men are coming," he said. He backstepped toward the window lying opposite the door. "Come. There is a way over the back wall."

"Not for you," interjected a voice so soft it might have been a distant call carried by the wind.

Faryn was a subtle vibration of air and darkness perched upon the window casement. How he had gotten there, Emily could not say, for the wall leading to the window was sheer and high and none of her senses had alerted her to his arrival. A hooded robe the color of scorched wood enveloped all but his knife hand and his face, but for all the uneasy shimmer overlaying his features, his eyes caught her lantern's feeble light like drops of ice.

Emily stepped between those eyes and the object of their cold stare. "No!" she breathed.

Faryn only stared past her. "You should have stayed away, seer."

"And you should have guarded her better," Al answered in a voice so brutally flat she hardly recognized it.

Faryn's mouth widened in a killer's sneer. "You would teach me about warding?" he asked almost gently. There was a short retort of splintering wood, and Faryn threw his knife. The blade whizzed past Emily's ear.

Her shriek died in her throat. She whirled in time to see the hilt of that knife protruding from a strange man's chest and to see Alsandyr throw his weight at the broken door, and then she was being yanked through the window.

What happened next crashed over her in a confusion of numbing sensations. First she was tumbling into air full of twanging and whirring streaks of movement. Bodies and stone cobbles broke her fall, and the bald headed man grabbed hold of her. "There!" he barked and pointed with his right hand as his left encircled her upper arm. "Shoot him!"

Arrows, even the pop of other, stranger projectile weapons, tore through the night. "Faryn!" she gasped and tried to look up to the window.

All around her erupted curses. Ahead in the darkness another yell sounded then fell off into a wet gurgle. But Emily had no time to understand more. As the vague figures of other men rushed toward the dying sound, the bald man yanked something narrow over her head and began dragging her back toward the main house.

He released her before the tall doors that opened into the great salon and, pushing them open, bowed her inside.

She did not acknowledge his bow, but walked past him with head high and shoulders back, aware that something slight but heavy was pressing into her chest and pressing her powers down with it. Her head and heart felt swollen to the point of bursting, but she would not allow her enemies to see it.

The salon was a cool, soaring space floored in vivid mosaics and filled with low furniture. Usually it was kept shuttered and shut up; tonight it shone in the soft radiance of many lamps and candles.

On the fringes of the large room hovered armed men. At its center stood two men more starkly realized. Emily's eyes went immediately to the spare figure of Janeryc whose hair and beard shone softly silver about his aged face. In truth, the bulk of her attention was on the man she did not look at, the darker figure standing near Janeryc.

It was the darker man who spoke first. "Do you have him?" he asked in an easy voice that invited trust and candor.

"Not yet, Lord," the bald man answered, tension crackling in his tone.

Janeryc's throat convulsed in a dusty laugh, and he threw up his left hand to the light. "Fools! If you didn't kill him outright, you will never take him now."

The bald man moved forward. "The warder was not alone."

"What?" demanded Janeryc. He turned sharply to the other man. "You said —"

"Peace, Lord Cyronian," said the dark man, raising a hand as if in benediction.

The bald man continued, "I am almost certain we hit the warder with some of the tainted arrows, but there was another. We subdued him."

"So not a warder," the dark man drawled meditatively.

"I do not know, Lord. He fought well. Many are dead."

Janeryc pounced upon this. "Men loyal to me among them, no doubt. You spend the lives of my warriors like coppers, and you wonder why I do not trust you."

"Trusting me brought you this," a lean brown hand gestured toward Emily.

"Don't give yourself too much credit," spat the old man. "She came to this house of her own accord without any meddling from you."

Now the dark man laughed, softly, gently. "Were it not for my actions, Janyerc. There would never have been a Shield bearer to so choose."

Janeryc's head swiveled back to Emily. "So young," he said, speaking in a sere voice. "So innocent of the disappointment and danger." His shadow-circled eyes seemed to caress the contours of her face.

The dark man answered him. "Do not let her youth distract you. She has waded deep in Twilight and tasted the power of the ancient ones themselves. By giving her to me, you turn aside the greatest weapon the Houses wield against you."

"Only to level it at you," returned Janeryc. A thin smile like the tart taste of pleasure's fruit pinched his sunken cheeks.

Emily felt more than saw the other man smile—she still refused to acknowledge him with her eyes. "A risk I willingly accept. Let her go, Janeryc. You have not violated your obligation to your blood. She is already linked to me. Hand her over and spare her the tribulations to come. Give the union your blessing and seize your inheritance."

"Sandyr will resist."

"I told you, Sandyr is finished. Even now he fails before the power he tries to lay to rest. The same power that has steadily eaten away at the foundations of this house and you."

"Sandyr tried to save Janera."

"If Sandyr had truly wanted to save her, he could have. The means was within his grasp."

"He chose to show you mercy."

"You have a strange concept of mercy."

"He spared your life when your own father would have taken it from you."

"Because he was weak and feared Roland's wrath. But his hesitancy has caught him out at last. Sandyr has only postponed the inevitable. What rises now waxes far stronger than it was then and will not be denied. Night will descend upon this city, and Roland will have his hour. I would not be Sandyr when the frustrated ghost of the Cyros comes forth at last. You have only to stand before the tree to assume the mantle of Warder House."

"As an old man sapped of vitality and strength."

"As the bearer of the second talisman and Roland's blessing. You are still capable of getting heirs of your own. Stand before the warders of the Crescent house with Roland's Talon in your grip and they will have no choice but to accept you, will it or no."

Emily could no longer see Janeryc's face to read its expression, but the slope of his aged shoulders bespoke doubt. She spoke to that uncertainty. "Do not do it, Lord. I say this to you as one who has borne the Shield Light. You cannot know the strange ends to which any of these vessels of power work. They are potent, yes, but not kind."

She half expected the dark man to step forward and strike her for her temerity, but he seemed content to let Janeryc weigh the merits of her words. The elderly lord Cyronian raised his head slowly.

"It should have been ours. Janera would be alive, and Janys—"

Scryos nodded. "You and your ancestors would have ruled two houses, the only bloodline to ever do so. Who knows what good you might have done if Ayr had not persuaded the other Houses to put forth their combined power to prevent it, interfering with the natural devolvement of that power and exiling the members of your house. So you have languished here instead, spending your vigor and your generations standing guard over what they refused to face while they reaped all the power and the reward. Who then are they to prevent you from taking your well-earned inheritance now? And who is anyone to judge you if you do?"

Janeryc raised his head; his silver hair gleamed. "I still need a steward's blood—unless you are volunteering your own neck." There was a menace in the old man's voice directed solely at the dark man, but the words struck Emily's heart like a killing blow.

If Scryos felt the threat, he did not show it. "The time is ripe, the way will present itself."

"Yet the time runs short for both of us. Perhaps the powers do not look as kindly on your schemes as you suppose."

A sharp rap sounded against the carved doors. The bald man slid to them. Emily heard a whispered exchange of information. She began to pray to every benevolent power she could imagine.

"Send them in, Captain Galden," said Scryos. "Let us see what they have caught."

Four men filed crisply in, followed by two more. Between them hung a bound and bleeding man. Emily watched leather-clad men heave their captive to the floor, and deep inside her something cracked. A part of her mind began to wail, even as a different part seemed to slip her skin to observe the moment from a pristine height.

The bald man said, "They had to use one of the tainted stones to subdue him."

Janeryc pressed stiffly forward. "This is not the warder."

"No, my lord," said Scryos. In three strides he had swept past Emily to stand looking down on the unconscious man. "This, Lord Cyronian, is the answer to your dreams. Did I not tell you that the way would be provided?"

Janeryc looked from the man standing to the one lying on the floor and back again. His washed-out eyes narrowed.

Scryos bent and touched a finger to the unconscious man's chest. "Wake," he ordered, and the senseless body convulsed, the dark head whipped back. A moan escaped the fallen man's lips

Scryos waited politely as the dark eyes opened and closed several times before gradually clearing. "Greetings, nephew," he said. "You come in most propitious time."

Power like black lightning dredged Al up from a thick ocean of darkness into a world of pain. Breathing was so hard. Thinking was even harder. It seemed that whenever he tried to reach beyond the empty bubble that encased him, a shadowy figure set a black bar in his way, a bar that for all its darkness writhed with lines of multicolored fire.

He clutched feebly at the light around him. Darkness dissolved into bleeding color; color took on shape and texture; shape and texture became a face, a face remarkably like his own.

"Scryos," he mumbled, his swollen jaw mangling the word.

"If you like. I am pleased to see you, Alsandyr. You cannot imagine how much so. Thanks to you, I have finally been able to properly monitor developments, and yet, you remained my one blind spot."

"Blind?"

"The price I had to pay for appropriating your power I'm afraid." The Scryos' smiled gently. "Captain, be so good as to take the Shield bearer's little knife."

Al tried to shift his position as sounds of a scuffle ensued followed by a woman's short yelp and curse.

The sound of Emily's voice snapped him fully awake. "You'll pay a higher price yet," he warned and mentally congratulated himself on the crispness of his words.

Something cold as winter iron broke through the other man's pleasantry. "And how will you ensure this? More to the point, what is there to lend your threat authority? Not a Steward's vision, for you are a visionary no longer."

Al screwed his aching mouth into a predatory smile. "Call it my killer instinct."

"Bravely spoken. Foolishly, but bravely. You have the family pride, if not the family prudence." A brutal hand caught him by the throat; an even more brutal consciousness raked into his own. But even as Scryos flexed the fingers of his will, the shadowy figure inhabiting Al's consciousness slashed back in a resounding crash of silver light. Scryos' brutal consciousness was pushed out, and the furred and fanged thing lying coiled at Al's core raised it hackles.

Al sneered. "I would be careful when speaking of my family if I were you, traitor?"

Scryos covered his surprise with calm. "Have my men cudgeled the wits out of you, Alsandyr. Don't you recognize me yet? I've already told you who I am. Think and you will realize that you know me, though you have never seen me before. Certainly, I know you. I have spent long years watching you as I waited for the right moment to reclaim what was stolen from me. You matured most satisfactorily. I don't mind saying I've taken more than a bit of avuncular pride in your achievements."

Al's head fell back. His eyes widened. "Dyre?"

Scryos smiled.

"You're dead! You were killed in a border skirmish thirty years ago."

"According to whom? My sanctimonious father? There is a good deal more to the subtlety of the Steward than you imagine, nephew."

"So you attack your own house? Why? To take revenge against the father who rested all his hopes in you?"

"Revenge! I am a steward, not a warder. I act only as the situation requires, to save the houses from themselves."

"You're insane."

"Am I? I took your sight, not your intellect. You have seen this city. Even without your power, you must feel the forces building in it. Did you know that the Empyreor's misbegotten daughter is about to give birth to a son, a child the likes of which this world has never seen? Yet your grandfather, my father, would let this monstrosity go unanswered. Meredyth Encanta and Sandyr Ash too. It cannot be borne. Men, not the Lords of Twilight, should rule both worlds."

"And your answer is to strip your own kin of power?"

"If it means that I can yoke the strength of all our kind, yes."

"Yoke them? The Keepers and the Warders are not oxen to yield to the direction of a Steward. It violates the most fundamental tenet of separation of the houses."

"Which is why I will give them little choice in the matter." Scryos rose. Wearing an almost fond expression, he said, "I have enjoyed speaking with you, Alsandyr. It is a pity we did not meet under different circumstances. But destiny would have it otherwise. Go to yours in the knowledge that you die in a good cause."

As rough hands dragged him from the floor, Al growled, "What makes you think I intend to die at all, Uncle?" He hurled the words at Scryos, but his eyes darted to the pale oval of Emily's face. Their gazes locked briefly before his captors dragged him away.

Chapter 27: Dyre Plans

Emily knew she should be thinking of her own peril as the bald man led her from the house. Fearing for herself would have been the practical thing to do. But her heart was bleeding, and the pendant against her chest was suffocating the rest of her.

Scryos' name was Dyre, and he was the son of the Steward, uncle to Alsandyr. She tried to remember what little she had learned of this vague, but much revered personage during her time in Cyr. Only fragments of facts came to her, none that might illuminate the man who had so coolly ensnared them all.

At least she understood her own violent reaction to him now. Seeing the two men together, so alike, so different, had forced her to recall a fact long buried. She had met this Scryos before.

The admission brought her disconnected selves crashing back together. Emotion, thought, sensation branched through her like lightning. Then thought entwined with thought, memory with memory like a tapestry being woven out of seemingly disparate threads.

The bald man swung her to a halt beside a box-like wagon.

"What is this?" Emily blurted, looking at the thick carven panels of its walls and the ornate wooden screens fitted to its windows.

"Your conveyance, lady," answered the bald man civilly enough. He reached up and pulled the door of the wagon open for her. Near the base of the conveyance a pair of metal arms moved, unfolding a sturdy step."

The bald man bowed.

Emily never moved. The bald man stared her down, and Emily stared back.

"Please, lady. I do not wish to hurt you."

"Tellers turn all your wishes to curses."

The hard planes of the bald man's face locked together.

"Spirited is she not, Captain," said an amused voice.

Emily stiffened. The bald man's expression eased. He bowed. "Even so, Lord."

"I will handle this. Thank you, Galden."

Emily kept her eyes on the wagon in front of her as the Captain moved away and the tall form of Scryos came up behind her.

"Your spirit pleases me, Emilyn. Your decision to exercise it now does not. I would treat you with the honor you deserve, unless you force me to do otherwise—a situation we would both regret."

Emily did not answer. Her chest rose and fell rapidly.

"Now, let us try this again." Scryos held up a hand. Emily looked at the symbol shining there amid a spot of black. The sight broke her resistance. Moving around the hand like she expected it to bite her, she stepped up into the dark interior of the wagon, holding onto the door frame while her eyes adjusted; and a jumble of color against the wagon's back wall resolved itself into silk-clad arms and long pale hair.

"Vyara!" she gasped, and lurched forward.

Behind her the door to the wagon slammed shut and a heavy bar was thrown across it.

"Vyara! Vyara! It's me, Emily."

Emily brushed the pale hair aside to uncover the unconscious woman's face. Gently she repositioned Vyara's head, stroking the smooth forehead and calling to the other woman repeatedly. Vyara's skin was cool, her features relaxed as any sleeper's, but neither Emily's voice nor her touch roused her.

In the courtyard outside, men called sharply to one another. Horses snorted, harness jangled, and hooves clattered against stone. The wagon creaked, swayed slightly, and lurched forward.

Emily put out her hands to the wagon's walls to keep her feet. She thought of taking the cushioned seat opposite, but opted to ease herself down beside Vyara instead. Although it took some adjustment to make room for the both of them, she took comfort in the other girl's physical closeness. With Vyara's head in her lap, she listened to the thump and grind of the cobbled roads rolling away behind them.

A long time later, Emily jumped as the door to the wagon opened. Blinking and rubbing her neck, she turned dazed eyes to the opening. A bald head presented itself, the face below it black and blank.

"Come out, lady," said the Captain.

Emily slid slowly out from under Vyara, whose head lolled onto the seat cushions. Not once during the journey had the Lady Cyronian stirred.

Emily stepped out onto open desert dominated by a dome of stars, and the Captain pulled her around the wagon and across dust pounded hard to a walled compound. At one edge of this compound she could see a smudge on the horizon that might have been the outliers of the Empyreal city.

She was led through wide, lantern-lit corridors to a pillared room with arched doorways that looked out on a walled and columned courtyard. At either end of the room stood ebony couches strewn with richly embroidered cushions. Across the center stretched a long, narrow table flanked by tall, carved chairs. As she moved to stand at the head of this table, a shadowy figure entered on silent feet, placed cups and a silver pot of tea on the table, and left as abruptly as it had come. Two more silent servants followed, bearing trays of food and wine. The last one came to stand behind the chair at the head of the table and with an open palm invited her to seat herself. Emily shook her head. The servant backstepped to the doorway and disappeared.

Emily studied the food, clearly meant for her, and touched again the strange dark gem cleaving to her chest. She settled for the food.

"Don't eat so fast, my dear. You will make yourself sick."

Emily paused in mid bite. Scryos was a dark pillar in her peripheral vision. With deliberate rudeness, she dropped her bite of cheese onto her plate.

Scryos did not appear to notice. He moved to the table and began loading a plate of his own. Emily watched him pull out a chair not far from her own and seat himself.

As he began to tuck away his food, she pressed her hands to the table and pushed her own chair away.

"Don't leave," he said.

Emily rose.

A sheen like ice coated his next words. "I said, don't leave. It wasn't a request."

He turned his head so that his black eyes might dig into hers. "Sit," he said. "Or I will ask the Captain to come in here and seat you."

Emily sat. "What exactly is it you want from me?"

"Right now? To enjoy the pleasure of your company, Emilyn. It has been a long time, hasn't it?"

"I don't know what you mean."

He laughed, "Come now! How could either of us forget that day on the village green? What a charming little thing you were! What an imagination you had! What revelations we shared!" His dark eyes sparked. He reached across the table, snared a carafe of wine and poured a generous amount of the red/black liquid into two tall goblets. Emily's drum-tight abdomen began to churn.

He held one of the goblets out to her. With a resentful toss of the head, she ignored it. He set it down within her hand's reach. "Join me in a toast."

"To what?"

"To family."

"After you consigned your own nephew to death? That hardly seems appropriate." Emily surprised herself with the sneering way in which she stated the fact.

"Seeming often has very little to do with reality. Personally, I like, even admire, my nephew. He has been such a thorn in my father's side. His cavalier behavior and unpredictability remind me more than a little bit of myself."

360

"Alsandyr would never seek to further his own goals by the death of another."

"Don't be so sure. He and I are more alike than you realize."

"A few moments ago I would have said that a certain family resemblance was all you had in common, but now I see that even that much was a mistake. The more I know you the less you look like him."

"And what, do you think, was Alsandyr's attitude toward the intermarriage of the houses?"

Emily's voice thinned. "Intermarriage?"

"Yes," Scryos sipped his wine, and his dark eyes grew distant. For an instant, Emily's mind imposed the vivid image of the Steward on the scene.

"What do you mean?"

"Come now. You know of his plans to marry, Alysse North, weak in Keeper's blood and power, but a Keeper nonetheless. You know how easily he transferred that interest to you."

"He would never —" she began, only to falter as her protest withered on her lips.

"Use you? But haven't you suspected that he has all along? And have you ever dared to ask yourself why?"

Emily's hands curled into fists against her thighs.

"You mustn't blame him for it, you know. It's a family failing, I'm afraid, this instinct to use the tools at hand, very steward-like. And you, Emilyn, are an extraordinarily useful tool."

"Alsandyr has my trust," she declared, lifting her chin.

"Don't lie to me, Emilyn. I know you too well."

"You know nothing of me."

Scryos chuckled and swirled the wine in his goblet. "Just because I haven't seen you since you were a little girl doesn't mean I haven't kept my eye on you, my dear." He watched her try to avert her gaze. "So you do remember. I knew your mother would try to bury those memories. I also knew that she would underestimate your strength."

The dark eyes snared hers, pried her dazed mind open. The summoned memories came—at once acutely vivid and tantalizingly vague. She was a very small child, screaming because there was dark presence watching her from a corner of her room. She was a little older, and standing dazed amid busy foot traffic as she held the gaze of the tall, dark man who watched her from the other side of the street. Most complete of all was the last memory. She must have been about nine. Her father had gone to sea, and she was playing on the sward outside the shop where her mother worked. So immersed was she in her game that she did not notice the shadow that fell over her. Like a gray veil it covered her and her makeshift toys. Then the shadow shrank and became a tall, dark man who squatted down to catch her eye, to slip through it and past her undeveloped mental defenses. She felt again how it was to begin gushing those strange and terrible words. Emily squeezed her eyes closed to banish the image.

"You invaded my mind."

"You mother was not training you as she ought."

"She died a month later." Emily's eyes shot open. "What did you do to her?" she demanded. How she longed for Illyria's knives!

"Nothing. Your mother brought about her own death, out of guilt and a perverse sense of retaliation. Perhaps something else," he added as his face acquired a speculative cast. "Capricious and unfathomable are the ways of the heart."

"Retaliation? So you did do something to her!"

"Nothing that she did not acquiesce in whole heartedly."

Emily flung herself to her feet. It seemed that a lifetime of anger and loss was building up in her. "What did you do?" she demanded in a clear voice grown ominously quiet.

Scyros leaned back in his chair. "I gave her you," he said.

I'm going to throw up again, Emily thought, and held her head tighter.

Nonsense, said an eminently practical voice in her head.

Get out of my mind, she screamed. Her stomach roiled more forcefully.

Calm down.

Get out!

"Bring the young lady a cool towel, Galden."

Emily spoke to the table. "You are a thrice-cursed liar."

"Then you are the thrice-cursed daughter of one."

Emily's head sank lower. She watched a small glassy sphere fall toward the table and burst with in an inaudible plop. A second tear followed the first one. "My father was a seaman from Seacrest," she whispered.

"Your mother was already pregnant when she married him."

Emily laid a hand across her eyes. For the first time in years, Madelyn's face appeared clearly in her mind's eye. *Oh, Mother,* she thought. *Why?*

"Because of what Meredyth did to Millicynt," answered Scryos.

Emily dropped the hand and looked at him. "Blayne. My mother had me to punish the Keeper for Blayne?"

"Punishment had nothing to do with it. Your mother and I acted out of a similar need to prepare our houses for the coming change."

"I don't understand."

"We both recognized that it was vital for the houses to do away with the prohibition on interbreeding. The key to building strength lies in the intermingling of our traits, not in the separation of them. Roland and Illyria realized this centuries earlier. Your mother and I saw it as well."

"You wanted to have a child of mixed heritage."

"Even as Alsandyr did?"

"Alsandyr said he would never—"

"What Alsandyr says and what he does appear to be remarkably different things, wouldn't you say? Whether you choose to believe that he knew it or not, he too worked to change the rules."

"What can you possibly hope to gain? I've been told that interbreeding is dangerous."

"And yet three times the houses have interbred far more dangerously. House Steward first, then the Warders, and lastly, in my lifetime, House Keeper. Now the third half-breed walks the world, and soon his son will arrive, the fulfillment of the power tested and honed through the first three. The time has come for the houses to unite in blood and power as well."

"How can you be certain of this?"

He smiled to see her emotions calm as her capacity for thought took wing. Lifting his glass, he sat back and settled in to tell his own story, knotting its threads carefully to form a net for his recalcitrant child. "For twenty-eight years I have dwelled in this land. When I first came here I saw it only as a prison. My father had gotten wind of my heretical ideas and knew my popularity among the people. His fear outstripped his love—not that feelings of any kind are our strong point. He called upon the other houses for aid in containing me. The Keepers sent to him a strange artifact, a stone of unusual properties. The warders sent him their most promising lieutenant, a man named Sandyr Ash.

"But I too watch and plan. After all, I am my father's son. I saw the blow coming and established a temporary haven for myself here with those most loyal and useful to me. Many others remained in the north, preparing for my return. I intended to return to my homeland as soon as I had the men and resources to overthrow my narrow-minded father.

Sandyr found me first. I tried to persuade him to join me. He used the stone on me instead and my power was diminished, my mark was blotted out, and a curse of banishment was laid upon my every step, my every road until such time as the Steward should decide to restore me.

"They thought they had defeated me. I thought they had too, until I came into contact with a Sardic witch named Nagga. The Sards, you see, are the remnant of the ancient Empyre, the one ruled by the first half-breed child of Twilight. She called herself Empyress. Her people called her Goddess. Her name, as it is recorded in the few fragments of ancient text that remain, was Nyte. For centuries the Sards have believed that she still lives, locked beneath the massive structure of the Empyreal palace and waiting for her time to rise. They believe this on the assurances they take from their most sacred text: the Book of Nyte."

"Why did her empyre end?" Emily interrupted, falling under the spell of the story in spite of herself.

Scryos stared into his glass. "Another story for another time. What you need to understand about her now is that she was of the Steward's line. Her twilight power, along with the gift she derived from my house, made her the most powerful visionary the world has ever seen.

"She wrote her testament at the height of her power, but it contained in it much that predicted her fall and her coming again. Of critical importance was what she had to say about the Houses in three short passages we might call verse. By trading certain secrets of my house to Nagga, I earned the right to read the book. What I found there added a new dimension to my own understanding."

Emily was listening with more than her ears and mind now, she was listening with the ache in her throat, with the pounding of her heart, with the pause between every breath.

Scryos took another sip of wine, and recited: *"Cold is the midwinter, but no colder than the heartless man for whom the earth alone can weep and gush gray tears. So, let the sea and land no harbor hold for men 'til the powers of the air weave from bitter sorrow and despair a crowned and crystal stair."*

Emily shuddered. How often had those same words haunted her dreams! "The translation in Alberyc's book, it was yours."

"Yes. My gift to you."

Emily narrowed her eyes. "I found it hidden in Alysse's apartment."

"Because I ordered it put there. As I have said, I've kept my eye on you."

"What does any of this have to do with your theory about interbreeding?"

"Nyte predicted it, just as she predicted the return of the Talismans. When the first and second Empyreal lines are made one, the power of the houses must also unite in one person."

Emily considered this. Sketchy as her understanding of what he told her was, the conclusion he drew had an elegant completeness to it.

"You hoped to do this through me."

"Yes, a steward who is also a Keeper, who could then be joined to a warder to engender the necessary heir." Emily swallowed and sat back. In her mind she was hearing not just Scryos' words, but Faryn's as well.

Then Scryos' tone changed. "Unfortunately, your mother's determination was not as strong as I had hoped. Even as she carried you, she did something, employed some unexpected dimension of her power."

"To do what?"

"To negate your ties to House Steward. You should have been born with an equal portion of my gift. Instead, your mother chose to cancel your Steward inheritance. I do not know how she did it, but I know she eventually paid the price with her life. She gave me a child. But a child of flesh and blood only. You are my daughter, but in terms of power and my hopes, you are incomplete."

Even as his words wrought a relief that loosened her limbs, her mind was crying a warning. She stared at this familiar stranger with resolute eyes and said, "So you cannot get what you want through me."

"Not entirely, no. Fortunately, I have found another way."

Chapter 28: At the Tree

The long night wore on, and Jazim, Prince of Serpentia, Lord Commander of the Empyreal armies, piddled while Sun City burned. Once he had doctored the Lady Inimiri's injuries, sharpened his weapons, stabled their horse in an unused room, and selected their exit strategy, there was nothing else he could do. The world outside might be turning to calamity, but he must wait on a young mother and her new child.

He looked at Miri, sleeping with her head and arms upon a rickety table. Then he let his eyes slide over the curtain screening one end of the little room. The nonman Ogren had hung that curtain, and now he squatted before it, a warning to all who might dare approach.

Behind the curtain reposed the princess and her child. Neither one had made any sound.

From time to time sound did float in from the world outside—carts creaking, feet running, anxious voices calling. Eventually, there came a din of hoof beats, a sound like a whole company of riders moving through.

Jazim rose and put his eye to a crack in the door frame.

"What is it?" asked Miri.

"A prince's personal army by the looks of it."

"Fleeing the city?"

"Maybe." Jazim put his hand to his saber. "They are stopping here," he said, and looked to the giant nonman. "Now might be a good time to disappear," he suggested. "One of us at least should remain free."

The nonman's unreadable expression never changed, but his skin underwent a rapid series of color shifts. A moment later Miri's chair rocked as his nearly invisible bulk edged past her and through the doorway into the room where Jazim had hidden the horse.

Miri sat up straight, pushing hair back from her forehead. "They cannot be looking for us?" she groaned.

"Anything is possible on this night," speculated Jazim darkly.

He took up a position near the curtain and drew his sword as fists began pounding on the barred door. There were shouts and grunts and a series of heavy thuds. The door flew inward. A tight group of red-cloaked warriors pressed themselves to the frame. Jazim smiled thinly and hefted his blade. The men floundered, one of them calling sharply to the company. A tall, auburn-haired figure pushed them aside.

"Prince Marbek," said Jazim.

Marbek smiled and stooped through the doorway. There was a feverish quality about him as he surveyed the scene. "How quickly you have come down in the world, Prince of Serpents," he sneered.

Jazim's smile grew even thinner. "Use caution, Highness. My ill fortune could be catching."

The auburn-haired prince glared down his patrician nose. "Sheath your sword, Jazim, or I will be forced to behead you for a traitor."

"A traitor to whom?"

"To your Empyreor."

"Then you are here on Bethnarian's orders?"

Marbek, never one to laugh, glared contemptuously at him. "Don't toy with me, Jazim. Bethnarian is dead or fled. Which one matters not at all to me. I am Empyreor now."

"I don't remember a coronation."

"A mere formality. My armies stand ready to enter the city, with the full support of most of the noble houses. When they do, those nobles who don't already support me will have an abrupt and absolute change of heart. Now, where is my betrothed?"

Jazim chuckled tiredly, maliciously. "Shouldn't you check with the Sards first before you claim the city?"

Marbek's big body didn't move, but something in the foundations of the hard planes of his handsome face seemed to shift. "A mere raid. One that the Empyreal armies can easily rout."

Jazim looked around. "What Empyreal armies? Do you mean to tell me you've stowed them in your pocket."

Marbek's handsome face seemed to contract around a single hateful point of malice.

"My prince," called a clear, compellingly feminine voice.

Marbek's head jerked, his feverish gaze glittered.

"No!" said Miri, backing herself against the curtain.

But the Princess Bethnara called again. "Let Prince Marbek come to me, Miri. You too, Lord Commander."

Jazim cocked his head as Miri threw him a look of bewilderment. Marbek's hot glare had melted into a sunshine smile.

Slowly, Jazim and Miri stepped aside so that the Prince of Cadash might sweep behind the curtain. Marbek's men fanned out across the room, and a stiff, wary stillness ensued that was marred only by the ring of harness from outside and the sound of low voices from behind the curtain.

When Marbek emerged, his triumphant face told them all they needed to know.

He ordered all but two of his men out of the house. Then, crossing his heavily muscled arms, he looked down on Jazim from his great height and said, "At my future queen's request, I will allow you to accompany us to my estate outside the city. Give up your sword."

Jazim stiffened.

"You promised to protect her," Miri whispered to him.

Growling on the inside, Jazim dropped his saber to the floor.

And Marbek set his booted foot upon it. "You, woman," he said to Miri, "ready my princess for travel. Her litter awaits her outside."

As Marbek swept from the room, Miri hurried to Beth. The princess was sitting on the edge of her cot holding a small, still bundle in her arms.

"What are you doing?" Miri hissed.

Bethnara raised her head. Even tired and clad in a poor woman's ragged robe, she still looked impossibly fair, but that goddess-like face belonged to a woman not a girl. "Do as Marbek says," she commanded.

Miri wrung her hands. "Highness, you know my love and my loyalty. But this man—I do not trust him. It is true that you are valuable to him—you are of the blood Empyreal and a woman. He stands to gain heirs as well as more legitimacy from you. But what of the child you hold? How will Marbek look upon it? Not as a friend I assure you. If you go with him, you put your son in great danger. Infanticide is nothing new to Empyreal heirs."

Beth smiled, but her eyes were wide and very, very blue, almost as if they glowed from within. "Trust me, Miri. What other choice do we have? Besides, Marbek does not frighten me, not nearly as much as my mother does. Marbek is a temporary solution to a much more serious problem."

Miri frowned. "He won't see it that way," she warned.

Beth stared until the waiting-woman's gaze faltered and fell.

Jazim poked his head around the curtain. "Your waiting woman is right to warn you, Highness. Marbek may be thickheaded, but he is not a complete fool. He will marry you and discard you just as quickly."

Beth laughed, a sound both rich and cold. "Let him try."

"Then you have agreed to take him as a husband?"

"Why should I not? My father promised me to him. So, I told Marbek I will gladly marry him when he sits upon the Empyreal throne."

A slow smile of appreciation spread across Jazim's face. "I wonder what your thrice-damned daemon mother will have to say about that."

Scryos escorted Emily down a stair into a round chamber with a domed ceiling supported by columns. The long curving wall of this room was lined with shelves containing books and odd implements. In the middle of it lay a long slab of perfectly flat rock, and atop the rock lay Vyara.

Scryos was speaking. "I told you I hated this land when I first came to be exiled here. But it has given me many gifts, dear daughter." He gestured toward the sleeping woman. "She, like bloodstone, is one of the finest of them."

Emily sucked in her breath.

"Ah," said Scryos, "Now you see it, the answer to my problem."

Emily turned to him in horror. "Don't do this," she pleaded.

"For all our sakes, I must. But do not worry. I know her frailty. In fact, with your help, I intend to remedy part of it."

A rush like a cold wind moved through Emily. With fearful gaze she watched Scryos move to stand next to a delicate plinth topped by a silk-swathed object. As Scryos removed the square of silk and let it fall to the floor, a jagged chunk of dark rock was exposed that glimmered with iridescent colors.

"Come," said Scryos with a gentle smile.

Emily stepped back. "No," she said feeling the power building in her in spite of the small bloodstone gem hanging about her neck.

"Captain, bring my daughter to me," said Scryos.

At the first touch of the larger piece of rock, Emily knew that she was going to die. Its hunger sucked at the very core of her being, draining her of not just power but the sap of life. So deathly was its kiss that Emily never heard Scryos' parting words to her.

Alone with the unconscious Vyara, she fought a futile battle to resist the stone. A pain that was more than mere physical agony ate away at the foundations of her mind and spirit. Her blood thickened, her power dissipated, her springs of self dried up and their banks began to crumble inward.

Her spirit fled, to a foggy hilltop in a landscape vaguely familiar to her. She still felt pain, but it had become a distant, manageable thing, like the old toothache one is resigned to living with. In the mists ahead of her, darker gray shapes prowled. One of them thickened, eventually coalescing into a girl child of about six years of age.

The little girl beamed and ran up to her, dark braids bouncing. As she reached Emily, she screwed up her little face in distaste. "That hurts," she complained in a serious little voice.

"Yes," agreed Emily.

The child tilted her head. "Do you like to hurt?" she asked with all a child's ingenuousness.

"No," answered Emily.

The little girl planted her hands on her hips and glared up at her indignantly. "Then why don't you eat them?"

"I'm sorry?" said Emily. Her vision was beginning to darken as the pain asserted itself ever more forcefully.

"Eat them," demanded the little girl, and she touched Emily's right hand.

Blinking away black spots, Emily raised her hand and looked down into her open palm. Resting atop it were four tiny black seeds.

"Go ahead," urged the little girl. "You will like them."

Emily tried to gather her muddled thoughts out of the welter of rising pain. "I'll die though. She told me that I would die."

The little girl's face grew solemn. She looked at Emily out of great, dark eyes. She has such earnest eyes, thought Emily. A little hand reached out and touched her own. "You are dying anyway. But don't worry. You belong with us, you know."

A young woman who might once have been named Emily raised a shaking hand to her drooling mouth. Her left hand had been squashed to the delicate-looking rock it appeared to hold. The fine bones in that hand were cracking. With what remained of her flagging strength, she tilted her head enough to catch the tiny black beads that her trembling right hand dropped. But for the strange chorus of voices in her head, she might never have found the strength to swallow them.

Like frozen tears they hit her tongue, but they slid down her throat like beads of cool glass. In her stomach they abruptly warmed and caught fire. The fire spread quickly, growing ever hotter, boiling her organs and bodily juices and scorching her marrow. A hot foam poured back up her throat, coated her tongue. She vomited light. Her tongue was forked flame.

"Life," she said with her flaming tongue, not sure whether she spoke to herself or to another.

Beneath her fractured fingers the stone shivered and cracked, the curious veins of color in it streaming upward into her palm. A short distance away the great slab of stone erupted in more transparent multicolored flames. The woman lying on it moaned and turned her head. The woman whose tongue was fire opened her mouth and called the flames to her. Like living things they answered. A flock of birds or a school of fish, they soared to her, and she opened her mouth to swallow them.

Sometime later men descended through dust and ruin to survey the body. "She is dead, my lord." A hovering voice said.

"Yes, and the transfer is incomplete."

"I am sorry, my lord. At least your lady was saved."

"How typical of Madelyn's child to choose death in order to thwart me. Or perhaps, the Shield played a part. If the artifact's link to her was strong enough, it may have overloaded the stone."

"What now?"

"We are done here. Locate what fragments you can, then prepare the men. I must see to my wife." Shattered stone crunched as footsteps retreated.

"My lord!" a voice called.

"Yes, captain?"

"My lord, your daught—the body. Would you have it buried?"

"What finer grave could you give her, Captain Madson, than the one she has made for herself? No, leave her to the desert. If jackals find her, they can take care of the rest."

It was cold lying in stone, lying in the dark. Cold, but peaceful. The dark embraced and suffocated all. Sound and sense subsided, and the settling dust and ash wove a shroud over crumbled stone.

The dark belonged to the dead, and here the dead were utterly content. No more effort, doubt, or defeat. No memory, no desire, no loss. The all-consuming heat had thwarted even the grave-robbing worms. There was only the dark and the dust. Here the fine granules of dissolved being would lie indifferent and unmolested until the desert winds came to scour them up and scatter them to the earth's ends.

Out of the starry desert night, a wind did come. It rushed over sandy flats and whirled into an eddy about the hole blasted into a conglomeration of fire-eaten walls that might once have been a house.

The settling dust rose up once again, lifted toward the glimmering firmament, whirled itself into a dust devil of impressive size.

In the heart of the whirlwind a pinpoint of radiance congealed. At first no bigger than a cloud-swept star, it flickered intermittently in the dusty foment. Then, as the whirlwind contracted, the light flashed and magnified until it flared everything to nothingness. Faint sparks of light dissolved into the night. Above the crumbling crater, a shining object hung, and from that object rippled irregular and overlapping waves of light like the sinuous lines of illumination cast in sunlit water. The ripples rained down into the deeper darkness of the hole and after a time, tiny twin lights appeared in answer.

Al swam in and out of a strange delirium. He felt the painful pull on his bound arms, felt his boots dragging across stone. He knew he was going to his death. Somehow he thought he had died already after being drained a second time by bloodstone. Now he was nothing more than a great, hulking beast—a wild bull or bear or lion—slung on a pole between triumphant hunters.

He heard the huntsmen's voices, felt his defeat keenly, but without any sense of humiliation. Death was simply an inevitable trade off, the price one paid for living in the first place.

He would die, and his death, one way or another, would nourish other lives.

As if his empathy for his captors bound him to them, he felt them tremble in a sudden alarm. He forced his head upward and looked at the cloudy world around him.

"My Lord," a man was calling. "The Guardians do not answer."

"That is impossible!" Janeryc Cyronian's voice was a whip crack. Al glimpsed him as a silver-haired ghost hugging the periphery.

"I have rung a dozen times."

Another man spoke diffidently. "Perhaps the earthquake—"

"It would take the end of the world itself to drag the cemetery wardens away," answered the Lord. He came directly into Al's line of sight and stood with his back to his captive, staring up at something. His blue-gray robes stirred in a faint breeze. The words that came from him next were meditative. "The end of the world, or the beginning of a new one." He raised a hand to his beard, then barked. "Force the gates open."

"My lord! What of the spirits locked within?"

"Quiet, you superstitious fool! There is only one spirit we need to concern ourselves with, and judging from events so far, he is on our side. Force the gates!"

"Yes, Lord."

Janeryc turned, met the eyes of his offering, and smiled. Al dropped his face.

They dragged him through a warren of close, cramped buildings and then up a long hill. Even though it was full dark, he felt the shadow that gradually engulfed them like a terrible weight. He was forced to his knees on cool stone.

Janeryc was giving his men orders. He heard the ring of metal on metal, the scrape of more metal being dragged across stone. Again he was lifted, hauled, and shoved to his knees. As the ground beneath them came into focus, he glimpsed faint flecks of light like the most remote of visible stars shining up at him. His awareness sharpened. He again lifted his throbbing head and saw the blackness of the vast trunk of an ancient tree.

Up through compacted layers of stone and natural faults in the rock Colin Blackhammer clambered, eventually finding the most efficient method of getting himself and the Lord Warder up the netted roots of the tree. First, he would drag himself the equivalent of two steps upward; then he would reach down and, grasping the Lord Warder's tunic, heave him up to the same level. Since only his weak left leg was damaged, he was able to prop himself with his right one. Finally, he would wait for the pain of his own wounds to subside before starting the process all over again.

Fortunately, instead of getting steadily wearier, he seemed to grow stronger the longer he remained on the stair. Even the pain in his scraped lower leg eased a bit. Equally fortunate was the fact that the staff had grown quiescent. He pulled and heaved and pulled and heaved and eventually came to a ceiling of solid stone. Here only the core of the great taproot continued upward through the stone.

"Now what!" murmured Colin. The sight of another stone impediment should have depressed him. Instead, he found himself eyeing it quizzically with a buoyancy of spirit that the day's events could not possibly justify.

The soft glow of the root cocooned him, and as he looked upward, he began to pick out faint patterns on the ceiling rock. The patterns stirred his memory. He looked down at the staff lying next to him and slowly picked it up. He held it gently for a moment and then lifted its tip to the hanging rock. The whole staff caught fire. Colin hastily let go, only to realize that the flames gave no heat. The staff hung from the rocky ceiling like a magnet drawn to a greater magnet. Above him the lines in the rock began to burn also. The earth rumbled gently. Stone parted, opening a door on fresh air and intermittent starlight.

"Bring him," ordered Janeryc.

Al was heaved upward, dragged several yards to the base of the great tree and thrown down again. A hand seized his hair and yanked his head upward. Janeryc's face was a narrow oval crowned by a faint silver halo.

"Are you ready to make amends, steward?"

Al bared his teeth and growled."

Janeryc's grip tightened. Al felt cold steel at his throat.

Then something whizzed past his face and Janeryc grunted and let go.

Men cried out. Fighting his bonds, Al shifted his position, looked out on the chaos that had overtaken them. Janeryc's men were stumbling about in the dark, running every which direction. A few pointed. Some shot arrows into the night. Al heard a couple of high yelps and blinked to see one of the bowmen jerked backward into shadow to the accompaniment of much growling and slavering. From behind another tomb a dark blur of energy leapt, landing on a second man, who expired with a gurgling scream. Moments later a third man dropped to his knees then fell forward on a knife hilt buried in his chest.

"The spirits!" cried one dying man. "We've angered them."

A seasoned veteran cursed him, then called out to the others. "Spirits don't need knives. Scryos had betrayed us." Whereupon a streaking arrow took him in the throat."

Many of the men broke at that point, running back into the tombs, and Al watched, supremely impressed, as one by one the remaining guards were felled, many with their own weapons. When the killing was done, only a single figure remained standing, and two dog-like shapes flanked it. Since all were remarkably hard to get a fix on, Al couldn't help but feel alarmed as the man shape began walking toward him.

Al looked up into the face of the warder Faryn. "You can't seriously be trying to save my life," he said.

Faryn looked impassively back. "Scryos has taken the Shield Bearer using bloodstone. I need your help."

From out of the tree shadows came a softer, dryer voice. "You are cleverer than I thought, warder. Tell me, did your master warn you about me?"

Faryn looked to the crumpled form of Janeryc Cyronian, whose chest had been pierced by an ancient bronze spear robbed from a tomb. "Warders never completely trust anyone, Janeryc, even their own kind. If you were truly one of us, you would know that."

"So you doubted me from the beginning."

"Let us say I kept an open mind. It was the Shield Bearer who decided me. She loathed you from the outset."

"Ah. Dangerous and deep are the ways of the heart."

"You would know better than I, Janeryc." Faryn looked back at Al. "Would you like to finish him, or shall I?"

Al shook his head. "Why bother. Just cut my bonds. He'll be dead by morning anyway."

"How very sensible and seer like."

Al was rising to his feet when the earth beneath them began to rumble again. Both men moved backward, Al with a stumble and Faryn in a single graceful bound.

"Another earthquake?" mumbled Al.

Two of the large stones about the tree pitched inward on darkness. The warder and the steward alike watched in amazement as a staff held by a dirty hand reached up out of the earth.

Colin heaved himself up onto the surface stones with a low groan and rolled onto his back gulping the rich, clear air. Above him the tangled limbs of the great tree formed a great net over the stars.

"Colin?" said a faintly familiar voice. Colin rolled his head sideways and saw a tall shadow rising near him. A moment later a second shadow joined it.

"Colin Blackhammer, where is my lord?"

Together the three men dragged the Lord Warder up out of the earth.

"He's dying," said Colin.

All three stared helplessly at the pale figure stretched out before them.

"What happened?" demanded Al as Faryn knelt down to lay hands on his lord.

Colin looked to the man he remembered as a journeyman smith. "He and the Empyreor, they fought some kind of battle."

"A battle? With the Empyreor?"

"Yes. I mean no. I mean they both fought with the thing that lived down there. With her!" Colin could not have said how he knew to call it a 'her'. He only knew that the fact lay as deeply ingrained within him as any other certainty.

"Nyte," said Faryn.

Al's head turned sharply. "Nyte! I've heard that name."

"You should have. She held this land and its people in bondage for a thousand years. She enslaved minds as well as bodies, and she has been growing stronger for centuries, even as the tree has grown weaker. We knew it could not hold her for much longer. My lord hoped to use the Empyreor to defeat her. They were bound through their daughter."

"Well, she's out now," said Colin flatly. "She blew the gate apart."

"My Lord's plan failed then. It explains what I sensed on the way over here."

Al's voice bespoke his incredulity. "The dark power in the palace is Nyte!"

"Yes, the half breed of the Steward's line. Naturally, her power to rule was unshakable. Only the warders stood between her and the North."

"A half-breed of Steward House. I never heard such a thing," Al said, forgetting for a moment that he once had.

"Nonetheless, it is true."

"And how is it that you knew of it and I did not?"

"You should ask that question of the members of your own house. The Steward knows it." Faryn looked to Colin. "You must heal Lord Sandyr."

Colin hung his head. "I don't think I can."

"You must."

"The boy is less than half alive himself," interrupted Al. "He will only kill himself trying."

"That is a sacrifice he may have to make. Our only chance of containing Nyte's power lies with my lord. Sandyr was a particularly powerful Lord Warder. If we lose him now, my house will be thrown into disarray, just when we can least afford it."

Colin only nodded forlornly at the warder. He had known this was coming. Ever since Shade had forced the staff on him, he had known that the price for carrying it would be his life. His only real regret was Vyara. Resignedly, he lifted the staff and touched the end of it to the lord's chest.

A hard hand came down on his shoulder. "Stop!" ordered Al. "You do not have enough energy to do this. You will only hurt yourself."

Colin gave the older man a bleak smile and squared his shoulders. "But I have to. It's the reason Shade gave me the staff of life."

The strong fingers of Al's hand convulsed, biting viciously into flesh. Colin winced and watched the shadows on the other's face grow ominously still.

"What did you say?" hissed Al.

"Shade gave me his staff because he knew this would happen, and he knew that with his staff I could heal the Lord Warder."

"Shade," said the other in a voice that sounded as if it emanated from a head as hollow as an empty skull.

Faryn spoke to Colin. "Do it now. Take power from me if you must."

"No," Al repeated.

"Enough, seer! We can waste no more time. My lord's life is almost used up."

"This is not Colin's task."

"Then whose? Neither you nor I can heal."

"It is Roland's."

"Roland again! Roland is a thousand years on the other side of death, thanks to the same power that threatens us now. How do you suggest we reach him?"

Al's face had moved completely into the tree's shadow. "By paying the price. Give me your knife."

"What price?"

"Just give me your knife."

Cautiously, Faryn handed one of his narrow blades over.

Al spoke to Colin, who crouched exhausted and injured at the Lord's side. "When the blood touches the stones, the power will come. Roland will have his hour."

Then, raising the knife, in one quick motion the Steward's heir slit his own throat.

A young woman who might once had been named Emily felt that knife slash deep in her own throat and awoke from a dream of death to the certainty of it. He was gone then. There really was nothing left to keep or regret.

The Shield rippled commiseration from her left arm while she turned away from the crater that had almost buried her to walk out into the desert night.

Colin watched the dark line on the steward's neck widen and spill a greater darkness. Impulses deep inside him told him to yell, to throw up his arms, to grab the other man. Instead, completely used up in body and spirit, he watched Al topple to the stones, thinking somewhat abstractedly, "Emily will never forgive me for this."

Faryn hissed and began cursing. He leapt for Al and rolled him onto his back as blood the color of ink spilled over his hands. Al coughed once and grew still. Faryn cursed more violently and began shimmering in and out of sight as if he were some sort of poorly summoned spirit.

From out of the black night, a high wind, cold as those that dip down from the stars, rushed in and scoured the hilltop. The great tree shivered and flailed, but the wind only wracked it more forcefully, and Colin brought his arms up over his head to protect himself from its lashing branches.

The tree shivered once more. Then, with a sound like lightning, it cracked. Immense branches thudded to earth, and Colin fell backward between two of them.

From out of the riven tree stepped a softly gleaming figure—Shade. His robes were the deep blue ones that he had worn on the road, although now they shone with a deep inner light, and beneath the brim of his wide blue hat, his lips were curled in that familiar mocking smile. The rim of the hat lifted a little to permit shining golden eyes to snare Colin's.

"Give me my staff, boy." His light voice sang out, crackling with darker undertones.

Bowing low, Colin held the staff out and felt somehow that he held his heart out with it. He watched Shade jam it deep into the very heart of the ancient tree, saw how with a great cracking groan, the tree opened wider. Something deep inside it clicked, and there was a ringing in Colin's ears like the reverberation of a giant iron bell. Shade lifted his staff and drew out a sickle of pure darkness, a thing so black it seemed a rent in the fabric of the world. In the same way, the sight of the thing rent the mind. Colin could not bear to look at it, but dropped his eyes and prayed. Even then, the terrible energy of the thing made itself felt.

The hem of Shade's glowing robes were before Colin's lowered eyes. A shining finger soft as a ray of light touched his brow. Colin followed it up into eyes like twin suns. "You have done well, healer," said the creature known as Shade. "Now, we shall heal my House." And he set his sickle of darkness on a dead man's chest.

Chapter 29: Desert

The Shield had drawn its bearer off the tracks leading down to true death and out into the trackless immensity of the desert night, but even it could not fill the void left by death's passage. Now, some distance away from the burned-out shell of Scryos' house, Emily lay curled into its concavity, being bathed in ripples of power that plucked at her burned-out mind and struck sparks off the cinders of her heart.

Eventually, the Shield tapped into her emptiness, and that emptiness became another's.

A man walked across a vast grassy plain. In a crudely woven net of rope at his back hung the strangely light mass of the Shield. The man looked west, but the Shield was focused like a great smoky lens on the bank of bruised cloud blanketing the east.

The sun was in the man's eyes, but when a tawny locust the length of his finger flew up from the grass in front of him, he caught it reflexively with his left hand. It felt at once tough and fragile as it wriggled against his palm. He willed it to stop moving, then peeled his fingers back. It lay stunned and stiff-legged across the lines of his hand. He studied the insect sadly, then popped it into his mouth and walked on.

The ground rose subtly. Even this slight incline, coupled with the drag of the grass, wore at his tired limbs. When he topped the long rise, he stopped, swung the Shield from his back, and sank down to rest. The tall blades of grass surrounded him, swaying like sea grasses, whispering hypnotically amongst themselves. Soon his lids began to droop. A bird called, the first he had heard in days. He opened his eyes and saw a human head so white it could only belong to one of the aged or diseased.

The head vanished into a trembling curtain of grass blades. Stunned, he sat motionless and then looked at the ground before him. On it lay a neat pile of dead locusts.

After eating the gift, he tried to track the stranger south. His own footprints were the only marks of passage he found. But later that morning, his westward route intersected a wide path of grasses flattened by the passing of sleds and many feet. He stood pondering it for a long time before adopting it as his own road.

When dusk came, he made a bed for himself in the grass and lay down on his back to watch the stars swim into existence.

He awoke in the night to feel his left hand tingling. The shield was a length of shadow at his side, but he could feel the hum of it pulling him back into consciousness. Very close by a soft, small voice rose in song. He looked down toward his feet and saw the singer.

His initial thought was that a ghost had found him. In the bright light of the gibbous moon the singer was a tangle of white-streaked darkness, except for her face, which lifted to the stars, seemed luminous, a young girl's face.

Very slowly, so as not to break the spell, he sat up.

Her head moved. Her face melted into shadow, but the moonlight made a delicate corona of her hair.

"You're just a child," he said.

She didn't answer, but neither did she run away. He slowly lay back down on his side and watched her until sleep reclaimed him.

She was still there in the morning. She could not have been more than eleven or twelve years of age. Her white hair hung in lank, snarled strands. Dirt encrusted the frayed edges of her clothing, but did not completely hide its sturdy fabric or the delicate embroidery adorning it. Her thin, expressionless face, beneath its streaks of grime, reminded him of chipped, abandoned porcelain. Her eyes were huge, dark circled, and their pupils and irises were ruby red.

He spoke to her, but she shied away from the sound of his voice, and when he attempted to approach her, she retreated, so smoothly and swiftly that he grew dizzy and afraid watching. Who was she? Had she too come out of the disaster in the east? If so, what had it done to her?

He decided to try putting her at ease another way. He ignored her. He collected himself, swung the Shield onto his back, stuck a juicy shaft of grass between his teeth to confuse his rumbling stomach, and set off down the beaten road, wondering if she would follow, afraid that she would not.

Reassurance was a long time in coming, but as the sun finally cleared the towering bank of cloud in the east, he caught a flash of white in his peripheral vision.

He cast a wary eye her direction and saw her loping effortlessly through shoulder high grasses. He shivered inside but never broke stride.

He studied her covertly for the remainder of that day and decided that she was more wild thing than human child, a difference her paleness only exaggerated. He could only assume that she, like himself, had been orphaned, forced to make her way alone in a world gone mad.

Together and yards apart they followed the road of beaten-down grasses westward. Although she never closed the distance between them, he took comfort in her presence. Wild though she was, she was the closest thing to a true person he had encountered since the disaster. He might still be adrift in a world turned to nightmare, but he had fought his way out of the black heart of it, and here on its sunnier margins, fate had rewarded him. He was no longer alone.

All too soon, the sun left them, and the bank of dark cloud roiled up out of the east and rolled over the moon and stars. The wind blew hard, scouring the whining grasses with sheets of choking dust. He set the Shield against the wind and leaned his shoulder into it, scanning its smoky ripples for the pinpricks of light that indicated that the enemy was upon them. Already he could feel the nauseating disorientation that came with the slip toward otherness.

He tried to persuade the girl to shelter with him, but she kept well beyond his reach, choosing instead to squat down in the tall grass and draw a strip of ripped skirt over her head.

He feared for her should the burning men come. Even the Shield might not keep them at bay if they sensed unprotected prey.

What found them instead was both better and worse.

They announced themselves with sharp barks that soared into high howls. From the sound of their haunting voices, he judged that they were still some distance away. But now the darkness was so complete it blinded, he swallowed dust and grasped the Shield more tightly.

"Come here, girl!" he coughed.

She did not answer. He half hoped that she had the instincts to run. Light and swift as she was, she might escape them if they attacked him first.

He gripped the Shield more tightly and wondered what help if any it would be against a pack of wild animals. His short blade hissed a warning at him as he drew it.

The sounds grew louder and then abruptly died.

The whisper of the moving grass underwent a subtle change. He tensed and blinked as he glimpsed specks of glowing light. They winked at him. One of the specks grew larger, acquired a mate and floated toward him. Glowing eyes rushed forward, and a great weight struck the Shield. Even as he flew backward, his attacker loosed a scream of pain. He scrambled up into a crouch, stabbing wildly with his knife at a second pair of approaching eyes. The eyes loomed over him, breathing frigid air. The eyes feinted. He followed them and struck with the Shield instead, throwing his weight and will behind his shoulder. He heard a satisfying crunch of bone and a second animal scream. But now there were several more pairs of burning eyes, and even as he spun about to gauge his stalkers' positions, he felt an exhalation of cold air on his neck. The growl at his back was more vibration than sound. Before he could move, the monster had sunk its jaws into his shoulder. This time it was his own scream of agony that cut the blackness. Cold that burned like fire sliced into his collarbone and shattered it. He stabbed upward at burning eyes.

White light cut the night. The icy jaws released him, even as the grass before him erupted in a whoosh of warm flame. The fire spread quickly, and a chorus of howls rose above its licking tongues. Trapped with him in a circle of fire was a snarling black shadow with banefully gleaming eyes.

He held off unconsciousness long enough to see the shadow monster rear up and away from a skinny whirling figure. In the light of the roaring flames the pale girl was painted the color of fire.

He opened his eyes again to cooler light. For a moment despair wrung his heart as the heavy smells of smoke and charred earth convinced him that he still wandered through brimstone chaos. He rolled onto his back and saw the moon overhead. A shadow oval eclipsed it, acquiring a silver corona.

When he sat up, the girl pressed him back. He winced, remembering his crushed shoulder, then touched it wonderingly. No blood, no broken skin, no pain.

"How?" he wondered aloud.

The girl crouched at his knees. He looked at her, "Did you kill it?"

Her silver-capped head turned. He sat up again, more slowly, and saw a mound of utter black lying not far from him.

Madness, he thought standing over the twisted bones and ligaments of the thing. Its shape defied naming. It was so black it might have been dipped in ink. It had a snout and ears like a fox, but its eyes were round and forward facing like an owl's. Its body appeared leonine, though stretched and attenuated in places where it shouldn't be and its heavy legs terminated in a dog's paws.

"It's changing everything," he said aloud.

He looked at the blob of shadow that was the girl's face. "We may never outrun it."

The shadow didn't answer.

Day returned, much to the man's relief. Together he and the girl watched the dead creature curdle beneath dawn's first silver glow. Like black snow, it melted and dissolved back into the earth.

The rising light seemed to lift him up and walking was easier where the fire had cleared the grass.

When mounds of smoothly eroded rock began to press up through the undulating plain, the man's pace quickened and he looked eagerly toward the towering, violet-tinted peaks on the western horizon. Energy filled him. His strides became sure and forceful, and his anticipation like his vitality grew until he felt his insides shuddering with it. The vitality became a wave that rolled him on.

Bounding up a steeper section of rock, he was abruptly jerked backward. He stumbled and skidded and came face to face with the girl. She held a corner of his ripped shirt, but her red eyes were fixed on the edge of tumbled rock above them.

"What's the matter?" he asked, clenching his jaws to stave off the compulsion that made him want to hurry on.

Her eyes briefly met his, slid up and over his shoulder.

He realized the source of all his energy.

Threads of darkness were snaking through the smoky translucence of the Shield. Here was the source of his compulsion.

The man turned and looked at the summit of rock. "Something's up there," he muttered to himself. "Something the Shield wants." He leapt to a higher rock and straight into the outstretched hands of the girl. In that dizzyingly effortless way of hers, she had anticipated him and now stood blocking his path.

He tried to sidestep her, but no matter which direction he turned she was always ahead of him.

Her interference cleared a space for him to think. He considered her, the Shield, the hills themselves. He laid a cautious hand on her narrow shoulder. "I think I have to see," he said.

The summit of the rock obscured a wide depression. The man looked down into it, feeling a terrible weight in his chest.

The dead, a hundred or more men, women and children, lay scattered in a large irregular circle about a half-finished cairn of rock. Beneath the shrouds of dust that half buried them, their flesh had shriveled. Here or there, it had peeled back to expose bleached bone.

Ignoring the Shield's tickling thrum, he went down and walked among them, noting the make of their clothing and gear, their position relative to the unfinished pile of stone.

They were Herdsmen, semi-nomadic rangers who drove cattle between the mountains they called home and the grassy plains. They must have been returning to their winter ranches in the foothills when the catastrophic storm rolled over them. They had set their tents and cook fires and then gathered to bury one of their own. Their animals had either died in pens beyond the ridge or fled before the blast.

"Is this what you want me to see?" he muttered to the Shield. "Haven't we already seen enough of death?"

Skirting corpses, he wound his way inward toward the cairn. It was a waist-high mound of carefully stacked stone. Absentmindedly, he peered into it. The far side had crumbled altogether. The center of it held only scattered stone, crumpled cloth, and a cluster of objects. One of those objects, a carved wooden doll and horse such as a child might play with caught his eye. He clambered over stone, reached in, groping for it. The doll had crudely painted features and a woolen dress, but it was the strands of long white hair wrapped around its clumsy hand that held his attention.

The hum of the Shield intensified. His eyes went to the girl standing on the depression's rocky rim, white hair obscuring her face, and his heavy heart went cold to see the perpetual vacancy of her expression crumble into a yawning ferocity.

"Were they burying you?" he breathed.

The Shield grew heavy as a six-foot plate of iron, pinning him to the stones. Inside the cairn a thing lurking beneath a thin skin of dust and cloth shifted into awareness, and sent forth a tentacle of blackness as perfect as the black beyond death's gates.

Curled into the womb of the shield, Emily shook like one fevered. Her hands and feet twitched, then stilled. The feelings of the man like his experiences passed away, but the hole they left was soon filled by another's.

In a city of tombs, a heart-sore young man, beaten and bruised but somehow drunk on life, leaned over a small campfire, and spoke to the light-eyed man sitting across from him.

"So we wait here all night."

"And all day, if need be."

"In a cemetery?"

"Yes."

"For what!"

"For the end." The light-eyed man kept his face and voice empty of expression, but the young man could sense the muscular tension beneath. The light-eyed man reached over the fire, handed the younger man a shallow bowl full of warm liquid.

"What's this?"

"Some of your own medicine."

"I don't need medicine."

The light eyes shifted deeper into shadow. "Plus a little something from my own stores."

"You aren't a healer," said the young man, peering suspiciously into the cup.

'No. But every warder knows how to use drugs for the easing of pain and the restoration of energy."

The young man glared at him disgustedly. "Are you blind, Faryn? Didn't you see what Shade did to me?"

The man named Faryn only stared into the fire.

The younger man looked over his shoulder to where the silhouette of a shattered tree sprawled. He avoided looking at the crumpled forms scattered beneath it as he turned his head back toward the flames.

"So we sit here among the dead and do nothing."

"What would you have us do?"

"I don't know. Join the living for a start? Help him?"

A grim smile curled the warder's lip. "Do you really think the Cyros needs our help?"

The young man swallowed, thrust aside a dark memory. "What about finding Emily? Vyara might know where they have taken her. If I could just speak with her – "

"Let it go, Colin," interrupted the other man patiently.

Colin leapt to his feet, smashing the bowl to the earth, sending drops of liquid like orange jewels flying into the fire. "I can't. I won't. You wouldn't either if you understood simple human feeling."

"Warders are not without feeling." Faryn locked fire-flecked eyes on his face.

Scalded by the heat in those eyes, Colin looked away. "I'm sorry. I guess I'm just fed up with taking orders from you people. I guess waiting isn't easy for you either."

"No. But I prefer waiting to dying. The Cyros had good reason for ordering us to remain here. The powers he is contending with now would snuff us like candles if we attempted to venture beyond this place. Here the ancient wards and the residue of the Cyros' passage protect us."

"But not the people in the palace?"
"No."
"What about those in the City?"
Faryn's fixed expression suddenly seemed bleaker than the empty sands.
Colin sank down before the fire and crossed his arms over the unbearable ache in his chest. "Vyara," he whispered.

Emily opened her eyes. Beneath her cheek the Shield felt as warm as sunshine, as invigorating as the promise of spring. But Emily felt nothing. Ripples of light playing under her hand grew into a sunburst blaze.

Millicynt Encanta ignored the void in her own heart and contemplated the pregnant woman standing before her. Madelyn's expression was as arrogant as ever, but her dark hair was lusterless, and her usually supple skin had a chalky cast to it, as if the least change in expression would cause her whole face to crack and crumble to dust.
"Don't you dare look at me like that, Millie? You of all people have no right to pity me."
"I do not pity you, sister."
"Your sickening courtesy says otherwise."
"I came here to offer you my help. I know what it is to be sick with child. Remember? I wouldn't want you to lose yours."
Ever quick to the curt reply, her sister snapped back, "Your child is not dead, sister. I would the Powers he were."
Millicynt looked down at her hands. Her voice remained mild, "Don't say that."
"Why? I'm sorry if it hurts you, but you clearly need reminding that the thing you gave birth to only looked like a mortal child. He's a wager, and an expensive one at that. Make no mistake, the debt of power our house incurred through him will be paid for thrice over, and guess who his daemon father will use to collect."
"Not if I can help it."
"You can't stop it"
"Perhaps I can."
"How."
"By loving him and believing in him as he is."
"You poor fool, Millie."
"Am I? Father and the council certainly thought so. That's why they chose me. If the Lord of Twilight had killed me, the loss to our house would have been minimal. I am not such a fool as to deny this. But do not think that

my foolishness has made me blind to my child's lack. Nothing hurts me more, not the violation by his father, not the knowledge that I will never have another child, not even the council's taking him from me. The one and only thing that broke my heart was knowing that he would never feel any of the things that made my foolish life worth living. Not happiness, not hope, not friendship, not simple compassion. None of it, not even the faintest trace of love."

Heavy grooves had formed in the corners of Madelyn's mouth. One rather swollen hand went out to her sister, and when she spoke her voice cracked. "I did not mean — Oh, Millie, must you always take so much on yourself."

Millicynt smiled to herself. "Is it taking too much on yourself to feel the guilt of having failed your own child?"

"It was the houses that failed him. We failed ourselves — and most especially you. But try to see the paltry mercy in what has been done. If your son does not feel friendship or compassion or love, neither will he feel heartache or hatred or grief or despair. None of those things that drive mortals to such dire and self-destructive ends."

"And none of the things that raise them up either."

Madelyn's mouth stretched into a travesty of a smile. "The powers only know what a half-breed would do with love if he could feel it."

Millicynt's hand caught hard at her sister's. "That's the crucial question, isn't it?"

"What?"

"That's the very same question the Teller asked me the night Blayne was born."

"The Teller? What are you talking about?"

"A Teller came to me the night Blayne was born.

"Impossible."

"You don't believe me?" Millicynt sighed. "Of course, you don't. She said you wouldn't."

Madelyn touched her cheek, said softly as if to a sick child. "The Tellers are a legend, Millie, a children's story."

"I have seen them, Madelyn. Spoken to them."

Muscles in Madelyn's face jumped, but she kept a tight rein on her voice. "No one has ever spoken to the Tellers, Millie. They don't exist. Every attempt of the houses to locate them or confirm their existence has failed. Even the far-sighted Steward himself knows nothing of them."

"I do. One came to me and said that Blayne would be made whole."

Madelyn closed her eyes. She pressed her lips together as if to forestall a sob. "It does no good to dream, Milly."

"It was no dream." Millicynt's voice was equally soft, almost serene. She regarded her sister without anger, without judgment. "The Teller told me that Blayne would know what it means to be human if — " She looked down at the *puffy hand she held and stroked it. Abruptly, she changed her approach. "How do you think I found you? Knew about the baby girl you carry? For the past two years, I've lived in this town waiting for the day when you would arrive. Because I knew you would come. Just as I knew you would be pregnant. Just as I know it is a child of mixed-ancestry you carry. I even know the name of the man who fathered her. Shall I give it to you?"*

Madelyn jerked her hand from Millicynt's grasp. She looked at her sister in horror.

Millicynt stood. "You broke the prohibition on interbreeding, Madelyn. You have only one choice left, to decide whether you or your daughter will pay the price for it."

Millicynt watched the hard crust of her sister's pride shatter, exposing the anguish beneath. "The Tellers told you this?" she said in a voice thick with desperation.

"Yes. Whether you want to believe it or not."

"Why?"

"They want your daughter."

Emily rolled away from the disturbing dream, and caught wind of a voice straining to make itself heard across the distance. The syllables were faint but familiar. "Emilyn!"

"Grandfather?" she murmured.

"Thank the Powers you are alive. We weren't sure what to think when the Shield vanished."

She sighed. "It found me. I'm sorry, Grandfather. I've made another terrible mistake."

"That you are able to hear me at all means that you have done something very right. Emilyn, remember what I told you. Find Blayne and hold on. Hold on to him."

"Blayne?"

"Allyn says he is on the eastern outskirts of the city, among the Sards. Go to him, Emilyn. You have what he needs. Share it with him before it is too late."

"How do I find him?"

"He is still bound to you. Call him as you have called him before, and he will find you."

"Shield Bearer?" It was a frostier voice that spoke now, but Emily recognized it instantly. "Lord Steward?" she answered.

"Be careful. Your cousin is much changed."

The awareness of these others ran out of Emily like a retreating tide.

She opened her eyes and saw the stars musing over her. The Shield had gone quiet; all was still and intensely clear. She looked at the stars and remembered their constancy, their imperturbable beauty.

She remembered looking up at the stars over Cyr and saying to Al, "You'd make a good big brother."

She remembered Scryos lifting his wine glass and saying, "To family."

She remembered Meredyth smiling his ironic smile and saying, "Welcome to the family, my dear," as Blayne looked impassively on.

She looked beyond the net of stars above her. Even more constant than those billion points of light was the connective darkness between them. Each star was distinct and different, and yet each was irrevocably bound to all the others by that darkness.

"Like family," she murmured.

She raised herself on her elbows and turned her head in what she assumed was the general direction of the City of the Sun. Then she closed the fingers of her left hand and called. "Blayne?"

Blood, fear, and fire—they swept across Sun City and pursued the company of Prince Marbek as it slashed its way south. Beth saw none of it. She sat motionless and vacant-eyed inside the Prince's curtained palanquin for her mind, like the city, was under siege, and she was using every bit of her strength, human and not, to hold the invader back.

In her mind, she was hurrying through the court of veils. She ran through the silken hangings as she had when a child, flinging them out before and behind her where they hovered like gigantic moth wings before settling. But no matter how hard she ran, or how far, she could not escape the court's colorful maze of curtains or the voice dogging her. The sound of it was as incessant and maddening as the constant tolling of a bell. "Come to me, daughter," it said.

Beth sobbed and ran on, thrusting aside streams of gold and turquoise, ultramarine and violet.

Before a hanging of deepest purple, she halted. Now the voice came from directly behind the curtain. "Forget these insignificant mortals, and come to me."

"No!" whispered Beth, her eyes on the vague form hovering behind the purple silk. "I know what you are."

"You only think you know. Come to me and learn."

Beth backed away. Somewhere a baby was crying. She turned around and ran toward the sound of it. Her son needed her.

Now the hangings she pushed aside were dry rotted and faded with age. Many disintegrated in her hands. She breathed so much dust she almost choked on it.

"You cannot reach him," said the voice.

"Try stopping me," growled Beth.

She ripped a black curtain from its hangers and found herself standing before a sunlit doorway. The light pouring through it was so bright that she had to throw up a hand before her starred eyes. Somewhere, lost in all that light, her child was crying. She stepped forward, and felt her foot drop into nothingness.

She reeled to one side of the doorway and held on. Faint areas of color and shape began to emerge from the general whiteness as her eyes adjusted to the light. She stood in one of the open windows of Moon tower looking down on a smoldering ruin.

"No," she breathed. Only the bones of the once great city remained, and devouring sands were prowling those. "Oh, no."

"Yesss," hissed the voice. "You didn't really think that running away would stop it."

"This can't be."

"But it will," the voice said, crawling out of the shadows of the room.

Beth spun. Her light-seared eyes strained to pierce the dark interior.

Something took shape in the general dimness. The room's shadows shifted and pulled back from a paler form.

The white woman moved so seamlessly, she seemed to float across the floor. Her garments, white gossamer beribboned with threads of silver and gold, foamed about her feet. Her head was down, shadowed by rippling hair, pearly white. She was small in stature, delicate in build, and as light of figure as a girl just coming into womanhood.

Beth stood dumbstruck, caught between the delicacy of the speaker and the sun-parched desolation at her back. "Why have you done this?" she accused, gesturing toward the charred world beyond the window.

The head lifted, though the eyes remained on the floor. Beth saw a full, sweet mouth curve in an innocent smile.

"Not I," the woman said in a maiden's voice. "All I wanted was to reclaim my domain."

"Was it the Sards?"

"You know better."

Beth clung white-knuckled to the stones. "My son?"

The smile wandered off the sweet lips. "My poor child. I told you that you wouldn't be able to reach him. There is too much that is merely human in your heritage. Give the boy to me. Before it is too late."

Beth looked at her in horror, shook her head violently. "Never! You are a monster."

"Only compared to some." With a delicate hand, she pointed toward the devastation beyond the doorway. "I would never do that."

For the first time, Beth's resolution wavered. The white woman sensed it and struck. Her head abruptly lifted and her lids rolled back, revealing a face that was a mirror image of her daughter's, only pearl pale and dominated by eyes that devoured. Those eyes penetrated and poisoned like fangs. They were colorless as mirrors and yet drawing on every color, and deep inside them a multihued inferno raged. Beth felt those eyes sink burning teeth into her mind. "Come to me," her mother said again, and under the shriveling heat of that gaze, Beth's volition melted and ran. The Princess felt the core of her self catch fire and knew the white woman's will had won.

Yet, in that moment, a distant reverberation shook the entire scene so that it rippled as if seen through running water. The world Nyte had conjured began to fade into a gray blankness as her fiery gaze turned inward. Beth seized upon the distraction. One slender foot reached back, found the doorway's edge. For a moment she still clung to the rock, then with a defiant thrust, she pushed herself out into a fall of relentless light.

After what seemed like an eternity of falling, her physical senses took over. The world settled. She looked out of her body and found herself in the palanquin, which now rested upon the ground. Her legs and arms felt stiff, but the fire and noise were over. The interior of her litter had turned hot and red with light. Its scarlet curtains rippled under the strokes of a steady wind. The wind and the relative quiet told her that Marbek's men must have won their way out of the city. She heard deep voices calling to one another, but she focused on the bundled form lying in her lap. Carefully, she drew back the blanket. Her son's eyes were open. She felt as much as saw them drawing on her, like they drew on everything they touched.

Though her own heritage was mixed, Beth was no stranger to the longing native to all mortal people, the inescapable longing to be understood, to be comprehended at the most fundamental level. Most people associate this desire with a dream of love and acceptance and so do not fear it. Few ever imagine what a terrible thing it would be to actually experience such complete comprehension in another. The princess knew. She learned it every time she looked into her own child's eyes. Something lurked in that small, helpless form that was capable of such comprehension, and even a mother's love had to quail before the naked power of it. Holding her son now, recollecting the vision the white woman had shown her, Beth shivered and wept, for herself, for her land, but most of all for the child she held.

It was Jazim who came and lifted her from the litter and carried her, still holding her son, into a lavishly decorated house nestled in rolling hills. He set them down in a large bedchamber.

Silent serving women with nut-brown skin and soft hands gathered about her, plucking at her robes, her hair. But when those hands reached for her son, Beth spoke sharply, and the hands retreated. An older serving woman approached. Bowing low she gestured toward a large, low bed topped by a cascade of net.

Beth settled her tiny son in a nest of pillows. The hands returned with sponges, warm water, and soothing oils, combs and cool silks. Clean and refreshed the Princess ordered everyone from the room, bolted the door and then stretched out beside her son and fell asleep.

She slept on and off for two days, rising only when awakened by the need of her son. She would feed him, clean and care for him, and then sleep again.

On the third day, she opened her eyes and found Miri waiting outside the netting with a tray of food and drink. Beth rose, feeling strangely buoyant with rest. "How did you unbolt the door?" she asked.

"I didn't. I had Ogren open it."

Beth looked about the room. "He's here?"

"He was a while ago. He seems to have vanished again. Marbek doesn't know about him, and Jazim wants to keep it that way."

Beth was still thinking of Ogren being in the room. "He didn't even wake me."

"Nothing did, and we both tried."

Prompted by sudden pangs of hunger, Beth accepted the food. She ate and drank slowly without speaking. Only when she set the tray aside did Miri speak again. "Your betrothed," she said in a carefully modulated voice, "would like his personal physician to wait on you, and — the child."

Beth stiffened, eyes darkening. "I feel fine."

Miri dropped her eyes. "The Prince is under a lot of stress at the moment, Highness. Rumors from the city suggest that things are very bad. It would not hurt to placate him. Besides, you have just had a child under most pressing circumstances. It might be wise to let a doctor assess you."

Beth noted the elegant emphasis Miri laid on the word "stress." There was a warning as well as a touch of reproach in it.

"Has he been treating you and Jazim well?" she asked.

Miri inclined her head, but fixed Beth with a steady look. "Most courteously. His guards bring me whatever I wish, and they are never more than a step away."

Beth raised her chin. "I see." She rose from the bed. "But Ogren managed to get by them."

"Apparently."

"Good," Beth murmured. She turned back to Miri. "Very well. The doctor may check me—but he will not touch my son."

Miri looked to the pile of pillows where the child lay concealed, then exited with the request.

The physician escorted into the room proved to be a sensible as well as efficient man, a wiser and more capable cousin of the palace flunkies who had hovered about her father. After a moment's silence taking in the elaborately screened bed and the flock of waiting women surrounding the thickly veiled patient, he turned his eyes and his hands to his work. He noted the princess' temperature and heart rate, before almost apologetically beginning a more thorough examination.

When he was done, he called Miri aside. "I believe I have misunderstood."

"Misunderstood what?"

"I was told that the princess had delivered a child two nights ago."

"Yes."

The doctor stared. "Impossible!" jumped from his lips and he rubbed his hooked nose with a finger. "Judging from her physical condition, I'd say she had never borne a child at all. He looked at the shrouded bed and flushed.

Miri dropped her eyes to hide her own surprise and raised them only when she was certain she could govern her expression. "Perhaps you have been in the field too long, doctor," she warned. "Tell the prince that all is as you expect. You wouldn't want him to lose confidence in you, especially at a time like this."

The physician's face whitened. He knew a threat when he heard one. Miri smiled and showed him out of the apartment, managing to hold off the shakes until she was alone with Beth in the bedchamber. The princess was standing at a window, holding her blanketed baby to one bare breast. The sight chilled rather than warmed Miri. She studied the white arms enfolding the motionless bundle, and her throat grew thick with an ache of suppressed emotion. She debated several utterances before saying, "The serving women have found you a wet nurse."

"Oh," said Beth, drawing the blanketed form more tightly to her. "Not yet. Let me nurse him for a little while longer."

Miri's throat tightened, her chest hurt. "It is a frightening thing to have a child," she said.

"Yes," murmured Beth.

"When your father summoned me to court and ordered me to take charge of you, I was more than apprehensive. You were a terrible obligation. Yet you were also sweet and beautiful, and lonely. You had never really had a mother, and I—I came to love you like you were my own. I needed you to be happy and to be healthy. So much so that it made me afraid in ways I could never have imagined. When the Family Carnis took you. I was frantic. I could not bear to think that you might be—"

The unspoken word hung on the air.

Beth's strangely luminous eyes brightened. "Why are you telling me this?"

Miri swallowed hard, and her hands clutched at one another. "We have been here for days," she rasped. "In all that time, I have never heard your son cry."

The Princess blinked at her. "What are you saying?"

"Children die. Newborns especially." There. The words were out.

Beth took a step back from the window, and Miri prepared to move in, to comfort and enfold. Then Beth lifted the baby from her breast, held him out as if preparing to drop him to the floor.

A tiny fist slipped from the blanket to pummel the air, and the creature in the blanket bellowed. Beth smiled. "He doesn't like it when you take his food away from him," she said. "Softly now," she told her son, and the baby instantly quieted.

Miri's mouth dropped open. She sank into the chair with an explosive sigh. "He's alive."

"Of course, he's alive," said Beth with mild exasperation.

Miri dropped her face into her hands, her fingers overlapping. "He was so silent. You acted so secretive." She lifted her head, said in a voice sharp with indignation. "Why won't you let anyone else touch him? Why not me?" Her eyes accused.

Beth's forehead crinkled in worry. "Do you really want to hold him?" she said in a small voice.

"Want to?" Miri gathered her dignity about her and rose. "Give him to me," she commanded.

Slowly, Beth handed the baby over. She watched as Miri looked at the baby and the baby looked back at her. She watched the waiting woman's rather silly expression of indulgence deepen into a frightening tension. Beth tensed and prepared to grab her child.

Then Miri rocked, blinked hard and turned her head slightly as if to avoid a blow. The baby cooed and touched Miri's face with a tiny hand. Behind Miri's face a door closed, leaving behind only softly determined delight.

"He is absolutely beautiful!" she crooned, looking at her princess and smiling. "Could the son of the most beautiful creature in the world be anything less?"

As evening came on, waiting women came and went, and Beth watched Miri bond with her son. What she saw forced her to turn away, relief having long since given way to a churning sorrow.

In a voice tight with concealed emotion, she asked, "Where is this wet nurse you mentioned?"

"In the servants' quarters, I imagine. Why?"

"He's hungry."

Miri looked up from her cooing. "He is?"

"Yes."

Miri frowned down at the baby. "How do you know? He isn't crying?"

"I just know."

Miri was staring fixedly at her. Beth watched the confusion in her face yield to understanding and then awe.

"Find the wet nurse," said Beth. "Bring her to me."

The wet nurse was a very simple-minded woman. Beth saw it with a mixture of pity and relief. Dismissing everyone else, she spoke with the heavy-breasted woman alone. Then sent her from the room with a fist full of gold.

As soon as she left, Ogren appeared, materializing as a strange hovering at one partially shuttered window. Beth gave him her instructions, then she sighed, "Blayne was right. I am nothing but a danger to them now.

Ogren chirruped softly, and Beth nodded. "It is a long way to the lands of your people from here. Leagues of desert lie between."

Huge brown eyes hanging on colors of stone and silk, regarded her expressionlessly.

"You can make it that far without aid?"

Another soft chirrup.

"Prepare then. Tonight I go to Marbek."

Marbek's guards had no intention of allowing the princess or her woman to leave their apartment-—their master's orders were clear. But one look from the eyes of the sapphire-eyed goddess who descended on them, and their orders and intentions evaporated, dew drops in a desert.

They escorted her to a room spanned by four great arches and strewn with thick carpets of elaborate design. Clumps of armed men were clustered in it, arguing and gesturing wildly about Sards and succession. When she entered the room, their rough, hard voices drained away.

The object of Beth's attention was seated at a broad table, his auburn hair burning in the candlelight. She saw the muscles in his thick arms ripple as he stood and set his fists on the table before him. *Marbek*, she thought, *is an undeniably intimidating man.*

His blue eyes glared through the smoke of her veil, but he spoke evenly. "You should not be here, highness."

Beth did not let his courtesy fool her. "Should a daughter of the Empyreor ignore the travails of her city and her people?"

"She should express her concern properly, as befits a woman and a consort."

"I could not wait any longer for news. I feared that you would ride off to meet the Sards before I had had a chance to speak with you."

Marbek's mouth smiled. His dark blue eyes did not. "If and when I depart, you will go with me." He spoke a curt word to the man at his elbow. The man gestured. The room emptied.

The prince reseated himself, gazing up at her with a proprietary air. He did not invite Beth to sit. "Where are your guards?" he demanded.

"Just outside."

"I ordered them to keep you safe, in your rooms."

"I convinced them of my need to speak with you."

"So they defied my orders."

"I persuaded them to."

He stood, came round the table. "Do you think to persuade me?"

The way his voice caressed the word *persuade* set Beth's alarm bells ringing. She raised her chin. "I would hardly know what to persuade you of, my prince. I only wish to learn what is happening in my city, so that I may decide how best to serve it."

"*My* city."

"Highness?"

"Sun City belongs to me."

The cruelty lurking behind his smooth words aroused the daemon powers dozing inside her. Suddenly, she could smell the heat rising in him, an intoxicating mixture of frustration, fury, denial, and desire. Things were not going as Marbek had planned, and he ached for an opportunity to take out his pent up frustration on something, especially her.

The daemon part of her sniggered. The moment he did so, it said, he would be hers.

Steeling herself for a blow, Beth smiled through her veil and said, "If the city is yours, highness, why are you not in it?"

The roiling emotions in Marbek surged to an explosive crescendo while Beth's eyes began to shine like cobalt stars. Marbek moved closer to those stars, lifted her veil and touched her face.

Beth made herself press her cheek to that hand. "I have heard that you sent scouts to the city?"

"From whom have you heard this?" His hand moved to her hair.

"My guards, and others," she lied.

"Then they shall each of them lose their tongues tonight."

Beth stiffened, her colder consciousness rising. "Should I not know the fate of my Empyreor's lands?"

"You should know what your Empyreor tells you."

Beth's eyes looked into his ruthless soul, and her power stroked it. "Then tell me," she said.

Marbek frowned resistance, but spoke anyway. "There is nothing to tell. The scouts have not returned."

"None of them?"

"None." His hand moved to her shoulder and slid along the silk covering it.

"And the other refugees, those running south? Have your men spoken with them? What do they say?"

"What we knew already, that the Sards are in the city."

"Nothing else. Nothing about the palace?" she asked, willing him to answer, yet feeling him pull back from her as a tangle of darker thought momentarily overwhelmed her siren call.

Marbek's mouth thinned. "The palace is quiet. Those fools who call themselves princes of the realm have abandoned it." He had pulled her close to him now so that Beth had to clench her teeth against the urge to feed on his hot energy.

"I have a request to make," she panted.

"What request?"

"You are going to war, a risky war with a terrible enemy. As your future wife and queen, I will remain by your side. But I fear for my child, for my waiting woman. Give them leave to go further south. Have a small group of your men escort them. You have me. They are of little use to you."

"Send your son away?" His desire-clouded blue eyes were welded to her own.

"Yes," whispered Beth. *Yes*, sang her cold consciousness, directing Beth to pull his head down to hers and set her lips against his in a long, deep kiss. "Set them free, my prince, and you shall have all of me," she whispered against his mouth, knowing that only the slenderest cord of resistance held her off now.

Marbek's hand moved to his chest, fumbled there a moment, then pressed something cold to her own breast.

Pain shot through Beth, and an impenetrable wall slammed down between her and Prince of Cadash.

Marbek thrust her from him, panting, laughing, and Beth stumbled backward into another table littered with maps and papers.

"What is the meaning of this?" she flared, her hands sliding over the tabletop.

Marbek's laugh died. His sensuous lips twisted in a sneer.

"Do you think me a fool, witch?" he said, wrapping his large hand around her upper arm like a shackle. "You are here to serve me. And serve me you will, on your knees." He held up to her face a tightly clenched fist from which dangled a silver-white chain. Then he grabbed her by the hair and, bending her head back, gave her a bruising kiss. Beth groaned and tried to squirm out of his hold calling on the inferno of power within her. The inferno was still there, but it could no longer reach Marbek.

Marbek held her head in his two hands and said, "You nearly killed me once. You shall not do it again, not with your beauty, not with your body, and not with your son. Those belong to me now. They are mine to use. The day they cease to be useful is the day they die. And should you defy me again, your son will die even sooner. Do we have an understanding?"

He shook her. "Do we?"

Beth wanted to scream her defiance, but she had her child and Miri to think of. Blinking back tears of fury, she nodded.

Marbek's smile was vicious. "Ah, compliant at last. What a pity it cannot last?" He stroked her cheek, bent to kiss her again.

A cry of protest slipped past Beth's lips.

Marbek's smile turned rueful. "You simply can't be trusted, can you, witch-child of Bethnarian? Not a creature like you. Oh, yes. I know about your evil soul. I even humbled myself to take a few lessons on the matter from a Northern magician. He told me many interesting things, including how I might possess you, without losing my life. So here my queen is my bridal gift to you." He raised his fist again and, holding Beth by the hair, slipped the silver chain over it.

Beth felt the silvery metal slide like ice water across her skin and settle with bone twisting force between her breasts. Her daemon self wailed and shriveled, while her mortal self struggled to bear up under the load.

Marbek watched her shoulders sag, her neck bend. He laid a hot hand on her shoulder. "Shall we consummate our union, highness?" he said.

Marbek left her eventually, and more silent servants appeared to attend upon her. She moved pliantly to their ministrations, and they left her seated stiffly before a great bronze mirror.

For a long time only the candle flames and shadows in the room moved. Then with a low moan the princess leaned in closer to the burnished metal. One hand wandered to her neck, touched ever so lightly the silver chain about it. Her fingers grazed it, then darted back, and a sharp hiss of agony escaped her lips.

She attacked the delicate silver chain with both hands, uttered a low scream, and yanked them away. Neither strand of the chain had moved.

Beth glared at the woman in the smoky depths of the bronze. She wanted to claw gouges into her perfect face. The woman in the mirror only glared back, her hands parting the silk at her breasts to expose the pendant hanging from the chain.

Inside an elaborately spun cage of silver wire sat a small, unpolished stone, black but threaded with opalescent veins.

Beth watched her reflection. *Time to pay,* it said.

Beth bowed her head. *Yes,* she thought. *I deserve it. I killed A'Carnis. I killed Yadak. Who am I to weep for myself?*

Her reflection nodded. One corner of its mouth quirked in a strange smile, as if to say, be glad you haven't done more terrible things.

Beth agreed, thinking one day soon Marbek would learn how terrible she could be.

When the guards came to take her back to the Prince, she was still sitting before the bronze mirror, her eyes intent on something deep inside it.

Chapter 30: To War

Marbek made her wait on his pleasure in a large courtyard lit by tall braziers and torches. The Prince sat on a raised platform in a chair draped in leopard skins. Before him stood an audience of noble followers, including many veiled women as well as armed men. All of them were working hard to project an air of courtly triumph, but fear stalked among them as well. They had heard the rumors coming out of the city, and more were coming every hour.

A personal guard of four men escorted Beth through the crowd to the Prince's makeshift throne. Jazim, Prince of serpents was already there. Even shackled and surrounded by burly guards, the Lord Commander of the Empyreal armies, retained his aura of deadly competence. His stance was relaxed, his expression unconcerned.

Marbek rose, looking as tall and masterful as an Empyreor could hope to be. Everyone in the gathered crowd bowed low, everyone, that is, except Beth and Jazim. Marbek glared, and one of Jazim's guards slammed his sheathed sword into the back of Jazim's knees. The Prince of Serpents' knees hit the stones hard.

Marbek surveyed his supplicants. His deep voice carried across the courtyard. "It has been a long time since the Empyre has had a master worthy of the Scepter of the Sun. My father would have been such an Empyreor, but for his conniving and traitorous brother. My father was a prince and a warrior, not a cowardly politician. He would never have made deals with the Sards. He would have chased them back into their desert and broken them over his knees like so many worm-eaten spears. Like my father, I am no coward to run from desert dogs. I am a desert lion. I eat dogs."

Delighted laughter from a nervous throng.

Marbek gave them a lion's smile. "In the coming days I expect to feast well. And you, my subjects, will feast also. We will give this land an Empyre like none it has seen since the days of Kendai the Great."

"As the Empyreor wills!" shouted many.

Marbek's ivory teeth flashed. He waited for the crowd to grow still. "There have been rumors of witchcraft and treachery. The ignorant say the Sards are using evil magic to take our city. Again, I tell you the Sards are flea-infested dogs. I ask you now, what kind of magic have you ever seen a cur wield?"

The crowd laughed, not quite heartily.

Marbek laughed harder. "Let the Sards put their faith in knuckle bones and ink stains. The proud people of the Empyre put their faith in their superior blood and might. We have ruled over the lands from Sun City to Inrak to Fumar to Dev'Umna for a thousand years. And I shall conquer many more. City after city, nation after nation has already fallen to me. I know how to win wars. The Sards may raid; they may break and burn, but when they face the well-disciplined armies of the Empyre, they will shatter, as they have before. They know nothing of true courage, nothing of discipline. They do not think like soldiers or even real men. How can they when they live their lives catering to the whims of soft women?"

The crowd jeered and rumbled their approval.

Marbek raised both hands, demanding silence. His handsome face had hardened

"I do not fear the Sards. And I am not a pretender like Bethnarian, who never once lifted a sword in battle. I am a true son of the royal line and a proven warrior. The blood Empyreal runs thick and hot in my veins. This is why Bethnarian feared me. And now Bethnarian is dead, destroyed by his own scheming. Tonight I ask you to bear witness to this, as you watch the last of his line humbled before me."

Marbek nodded at the guard standing closest to Beth, who turned the princess to face the crowd and pulled the veil from her face.

There was a collective gasp and then a surfeited sigh.

"Yes, my people. Look long. Look well. Bethnarian, who lacked the potency to sire sons, spent his seed in siring one daughter. I must say he did it well. He hoped to use her to buy me. But what he only pretended to give, I have taken. Come, daughter of Bethnarian. Kneel and kiss a true Empyreor's feet."

Beth's chest was on fire. Either the rage inside her or the anvil-heavy pendant was burning a hole through it. Marbek was making a public spectacle of her shame.

"Call me the daughter of Nyte," she turned and said to the prince.

Marbek rose, blood high in his face. Into this stand off came the sound of running feet. A sick-faced captain of the guard rushed up, prostrated himself before his prince, and babbled hurried words to the stones.

Marbek forgot the crowd. "What?"

"They are gone, highness—the waiting woman and the child. We are searching the rest of the house and grounds."

Marbek's face went slack, then anger began to twist it. His fists closed against his thick thighs.

Beth began to laugh, and as she did, her eyes caught fire, burning a deep but brilliant blue, despite the pendant pulling her earthward.

Marbek roared. He dragged her into the house and slammed her up against a pillar. "Where are they?" he thundered in her face.

"Highness, you will kill her!" his men were crying.

"Not before she learns the price of humiliating me."

The iron bands of Marbek's hands released her. Beth slid to the floor.

"He's broken her neck," a man cried

There was a short scuffle, a cry, and a thud, and a hard hand struck Beth's face. Her head whipped sideways, and the room around her jumped out of focus. Her chest hurt like it wanted to crack under the force of the pendant's pull.

Marbek's face, all brutal plains and ruthless edges, cut through the blur.

"Get up!" he screamed at her.

A circle of horrified guards and nobles surrounded them, but all Marbek's attention was on the woman at his feet. He spoke in a voice thick and garbled with ire. "I warned you not to defy me! But you will insist on being taught."

"Leave her alone, Marbek." The words came from Jazim.

Marbek swung away from Beth. "Do you want me to kill you now, Prince of Belly Crawlers!" he screamed.

"Don't be more of a fool, Marbek. If you kill her, you lose one of your most important bargaining chips with the Sards."

"*You* would school *me*!"

"I am hoping to clear your head, for all our sakes. If worse comes to worse, you can use her as a hostage. Bethnarian did. He knew the Sardic priestesses would value the life of the princess they helped create."

Beth, drowning in the pendant's cloud of pain, caught glimpses of Marbek's heavy hands beating the air, his face twisted by fury, his mouth foaming. "Kill him! Kill him, if he speaks again!" Marbek was shrieking.

The Prince of Serpents' voice cut through the shrieks, cool and sharp as his blade. "As you love your prince, don't listen to him. He is not well."

"*Kill him!*" Marbek roared again, spittle shooting from his mouth. The guards nearest Jazim reached convulsively for their swords, but couldn't seem to take their eyes off their raging master. Roaring incoherently, Marbek drew his own sword and swept the head off the guard standing nearest him. Blood sprayed. He turned on another.

All the on-lookers broke for the walls.

Jazim, in chains, moved closer. "You are a sick man, Marbek," said the Prince of Serpents. "And your political future is looking sicker."

The auburn-haired Prince roared and heaved his sword upward. Jazim caught the descending blade on the chain of his wrist shackles.

Snarling, Marbek yanked his saber free in a tooth-shaking screech of metal. He raised his sword again, but this time his arms and his blade were shaking violently. He tottered backward, slipped to one knee. His skin was flushed, his eyes glazed, and he panted loudly.

Jazim shuffled forward and leaned in to assess him. "I was wrong," he noted clinically. "You are a *very* sick man."

Marbek moaned.

Jazim sniffed in disgust. "That is what you get for trying to master daemons, and their kin."

Marbek seemed to be struggling to focus his eyes. He opened and closed his mouth. Finally a word escaped. "Scryos."

Jazim slowly stood up. "What about him?"

"Stone — protection."

Jazim's thin lips spread in a mirthless serpent smile. "You *are* a fool. That Northern magician is four times the machinator you are and eight times as dangerous. Short odds he meant his magic to kill you."

Marbek collapsed to the floor.

Jazim turned to the discombobulated guards. "Get your prince to bed," he said, then he looked to the gray-haired noble standing over Marbek. "Gather Marbek's generals, Lord Karek. Someone else will have to take charge now."

The gray-haired lord lifted his head. "You forget you are a prisoner here," he flared.

Jazim snorted. "And I was the master of Bethnarian's intelligence. The Sards will be coming, Karek. Marbek's not the only man out of time."

Chains rattling, Jazim made his way to Beth's side and squatted. She was staring wide-eyed at the place where Marbek lay. The cheek Marbek's fist should have crushed was as fair and smooth as ever, but her skin seemed stretched thinly over her bones and her right hand hovered just over her chest as if over a hot coal. Jazim's eyes caught the fall of silver at her neck, and lifting his shackled hands, he grabbed at it and yanked. The chain snapped. The princess melted into a groan.

Jazim studied the swinging pendant. When he looked back at Bethnara, she was watching him with flaming sapphire eyes. "Thank you," she whispered.

Jazim glanced at Marbek's men, who still stood arguing amongst themselves. "Where are Miri and the baby?" he whispered.

Beth's eyes dropped. "Gone."

"Where?"

"East, to the lands of Ogren's people."

"They could be running straight into the wide net cast by the Sards."

"The Sards are in Sun City."

"I do not think so. Not all of them, and not any more." He leaned in a bit closer, said in a low, firm voice. "Some of Marbek's scouts spotted robed riders along the perimeter of the estate and Marbek has been frantic for news from the rest of his army. They were expected, but they have not come."

"How do you know? You are a prisoner?"

Jazim's amber glare was cold and steady. "There are ways and ways of getting information. Your father kept eyes on Marbek at all times."

Beth blinked. "Spies? Here?"

"Everywhere. Look, if the Sards have left Sun City, it must be to pursue something they want even more."

Beth read his pointed expression. "Me?"

"Or your son. The Empyreor claimed that the Sards saw him as the fulfillment to a prophecy."

"Oh, gods! And I may have sent him right to them."

Behind them, the guards broke their conference. Jazim hissed, "Pretend to be ill."

Beth didn't have to call on her imagination to oblige. Moaning, she fell forward into Jazim's waiting hands. "Bring me water and wine, now!" the prince cried.

Two guards hovered over them. The youngest of them asked, "Is she badly hurt?"

"What do you think, imbecile! Get back! You are frightening her. If you make her worse—well, your master will be irritable enough if and when he wakes up."

The guards retreated, blinking and squeezing their saber hilts with indecision.

Jazim said to Beth through nearly motionless lips. "What we need is a distraction. Marbek's army would do nicely, what's left of it."

"And there's always me."

Jazim's lips thinned as another figure came to stand over him. It was the Lord Karek. "Rise, Prince Jazim. The generals and I would like to speak with you."

Emily assumed she would die walking in the desert, although it seemed a particularly pathetic ending for one who had walked in Twilight and carried the Shield back to the realms of men. Her mind said as much. Her heart didn't care. Where her heart had been a fossil remained.

She was dutiful about following her grandfather's instructions, however. Many times she sent out a summons to Blayne. It gave her an excuse to stop walking. After an hour or so of trudging through scrub, she would halt, drop the Shield, curl her fist, and call Blayne's name with her inner voice. She could feel the call fly from her straight and true as a perfectly balanced arrow.

Her calls received no response, not even the faintest flicker of awareness. She doubted Blayne even heard them. Meanwhile, the desert dismissed her with a thousand disinterested eyes.

As places went, she decided, it wouldn't be such a bad place to die. It offered no pretense. It was as relentlessly open as its light. It was also quiet. Its inhabitants—scorpions, sand-colored lizards, snakes—acted as averse to company as she felt. Emily had loved the wooded country she had been raised in, but the wide, beckoning horizons of the desert drew her as no forest glade ever had.

Even so, she expected it to devour her. She had no water and no food, only the Shield. She started off carrying it like any shield, across her arm. This wasn't hard since the Shield defied its own size and mass, but it was awkward. As the sun mounted higher, she took to balancing it on her head, one hand on each of the bronze armholes strapped to it. She must have looked like some bizarre, long-legged tortoise, winding her way across the sands, but the arrangement worked well. Not only was the Shield less cumbersome, but its smoky semi-transparency offered her protection from the direct light of the sun.

By noon, Emily had come to suspect that it was doing much more than shading her. The heat waves coming off the desert testified to fearsome temperatures, and yet Emily felt only mildly warm.

She did grow thirsty though. At evening, she stopped where a large flat rock protruded from the sands and made one final call to Blayne, then she set the Shield down for the night. The sky was a deep, vivid blue softening to lavender at the western horizon. The world seemed caught in a moment of timelessness.

404

At her feet something slithered, a lizard the blue of Roland's robes slipped out from under a stone. He climbed onto her rock and touched his snout to the little finger of her left hand.

"You wouldn't have anything to drink, would you?" she asked him. He cocked his head at her as if considering the question.

Movement in the sky drew her eyes away from him. A brown bird with a red crest landed on one of the puffy green cactuses nearby. She watched him jab the succulent ball with his beak. Soon his whole head was disappearing into the cactus. When it emerged again, his beak gleamed wetly.

Emily rose, her lizard companion scampering aside. The center of the cactus was dug out as if by the repeated foraging of birds. In the very bottom of it was a pool of juice.

Emily tested it with a finger, found it pulpy but very watery and palatable. "I'm probably poisoning myself," she said as she licked up more of it.

With some effort and a palm-sized flake of rock, she explored the interior of the cactus, smacking her lips as its juices flowed out. Getting the juice into her mouth was the hardest part. Her hands earned a lot of scratches before she discovered that she could hack the cactus up from the ground and drink from it like a huge prickly bowl.

Thirst quenched, she lay down on the rock, pulled the Shield over her like a shell and went to sleep.

Evidently, the cactus wasn't poisonous. She awoke physically refreshed from her sleep to spend another day walking and another night curled up beneath the desert sky.

On the third day, the terrain changed. She left the cactus and brush behind. Now the desert did begin to feel empty. As morning yielded to afternoon, Emily scanned more frequently what she believed to be the southern horizon. No signs of habitation ever appeared.

"I've gotten myself lost," she thought, "I'm probably heading into the deep desert now. Oh well. " Again, she wondered where all her instinct for self-preservation had gone. She might as well have been dead already for all the concern she could muster.

As dusk descended in all its exotic desert colors, she glimpsed a cloud in the distance. The cloud hung low and moved fast. She watched it grow larger.

Riders took shape among the dusty plumes, their long black and red robes flying out behind them. Emily planted the Shield in the sand and waited for them to stop. They passed only yards from her, still riding hard.

"I guess they didn't see us," she said to the Shield.

"They don't have the eyes to see you," a voice answered.

For a moment, Emily thought the Shield itself had spoken. She turned.

Blayne was enveloped in a desert-colored robe whose deep hood swallowed much of his gorgeous face. But Emily could see his eyes glittering like bright stars inside it. Those eyes reached inside Emily, searched for something to hold on to, found only echoing empty spaces where once a storm of human feeling had roiled.

Blayne smiled. Emily summoned up some bemusement—Blayne never smiled.

The smile widened. "You come ever closer to us, cousin," he said. He whistled high and long. Out across the desert, smudges that were horsemen turned.

She spent two days riding with Blayne, the Shield banging at her back. She was understandably dazed when they finally entered a large camp of Sards. It was full of odd, dome-shaped tents and hard-faced, tattooed men. Two young women came, offered her fresh clothing, water and food as well. Emily looked at the red tattoos on their checks and gripped the Shield more tightly.

A few hours sleep on a rough rug and she was in the saddle again, her own this time, the length of the Shield riding easily against her thigh despite its size. Judging from the movement of the sun, Blayne was taking them south. Blowing through two more camps, their inhabitants numbering in the thousands, they entered a land where tough dry grasses struggled to grow on parched hills. Ahead of them loomed brown peaks.

They were upon their destination before Emily ever saw it. The sea of domed tents was the color of the grasses and thatched with clumps of them so as to be almost invisible against the hills. No people milled about here. But Emily saw many eyes watching her between tent flaps.

Blayne dismounted before a tent lower and wider than most and disappeared into it. Men in desert robes came quickly to lead the horses away. After a moment Emily dismounted and followed her cousin. She nearly fell six feet to the tent's floor. It had been erected over a huge pit, whose bottom was reached by wooden ladders.

Blayne stood on the floor of the odd tent, a handful of thin-faced Sards kneeling before him. One of the Sards was speaking in Sardic.

Blayne listened and then spoke back.

In the dimness of the interior, his eyes were scintillatingly bright. He turned those eyes on Emily. "Rest here, cousin," he said and led the Sards from the tent.

Emily stood forlornly in the great tent for quite some time before finding a dirt wall to curl up against.

She awoke to the dim illumination of carefully shuttered lamps and found a prune-faced old crone watching her.

The old woman's eyes were dark. Her forehead and the sides of her face were elaborately tattooed. The way her eyes flicked here and there reminded Emily of Lyr, except that this woman was raw-boned enough to make two of him.

"Do you want something?" Emily asked her.

The woman loosed a string of hissing, clacking syllables and then cackled.

.   Emily reached for the Shield, but a rough, dry claw wrapped itself around her wrist. Emily took her wrist back. The old woman spoke as her dark eyes dug into Emily's. "You judged Ehkeshk."

Where Emily should have felt fear, she still felt nothing. "Who?"

The crone nodded. "You, bearer of the scale, found Ehkeshk wanting."

"If you mean the priestess who attacked me on the road, I did not judge her. I did not even know her."

"Your power judged. Power is the only judge."

"Let my cousin eat, Unashk," Blayne said, leaping swiftly and silently into the tent.

The Sardic woman rose. She hissed and clacked something at Blayne.

Blayne's star eyes flicked to Emily. "Soon," he answered.

The old woman's long legs carried her swiftly up a ladder and through the tent's flapping door.

Blayne smiled, a heart-stoppingly beautiful thing, if Emily had had any heart left to stop. "Come. The slaves have prepared food for you."

She ate mechanically because her body demanded nourishment After a while, she looked at Blayne. "Why aren't you eating?"

"I am not hungry."

"You could keep me company." She pushed a bowl of savory meat toward him. Blayne took it slowly. Then, seeing how she watched him, he lifted a slice between two fingers and folded it into his mouth. Emily noted the curious manner in which he chewed it, like a man who has never eaten meat before. At the same time, the star-fire in his eyes seemed to soften.

Emily looked down at the meat in her own bowl. "Thank you for answering my summons."

"You gave me no choice."

"I suppose that's true. I should explain why I called."

"It is not necessary. I had intended to track you down sooner or later. You made the task much easier."

"You've been looking for me?"

"Not actively. I have work to finish among the Sards first."

Emily wondered how far to push his apparent willingness to talk. She risked another question. "What work?"

"The expansion of my father's realm."

Something like the echo of a forgotten fear stirred the void inside Emily. "Your father?" she repeated hollowly.

"Yes."

"Your father's plans involve the Sards?"

"Yes. My father's reach into this world is limited. He finds the Sards useful instruments, especially for dealing with members of the Houses."

"People like me."

Blayne's eyes brightened dramatically. The smile on his devastatingly beautiful face held her bound. One perfect hand reached out and ran a finger along the side of her face. "Do I detect a faint hint of fear, cousin?"

Emily's fear, an infant aborning, died. She looked back at him with the same flat, incurious eyes that had looked into death.

Blayne's finger halted its tracings. "Ah. Gone again. It is just as well. The descent into Midnight will go that much easier for you."

"Is that your father's plan as well?"

"He hungers for you, Shield bearer, even though you are no longer able to give him a child. Alsandyr's interference provoked him mightily."

Emily jerked her head aside. "Do not say that name." Though she spoke with force, her voice remained flat. The void in her seemed to expand.

Blayne's eyes brightened again. "It holds great power over you."

"It's just a name now."

Blayne's expression grew almost sad, although the cold flash of his star-bright eyes ruined the effect. "Do not worry cousin, when my father claims you, you will forget even that."

"And when is this happy reunion to occur? Tonight, I presume."

"The priestesses would have it so. But I must make sure they hold up their end of the bargain before I turn you over to them."

"And they will give me to your father."

"They hope to please him with the gift of you."

"Really! Well, let us hope he gives them something really worthwhile in return?"

"They will consider it so."

Emily turned her head toward the place where the Shield was propped.

Blayne followed her gaze, saying in an even voice. "It will not help you, cousin. Not here. It is a thing of the darkling realms and cannot protect you from ten thousand Sards."

The next morning Emily rode south with a legion of Sards riding at her back, and pondered what her grandfather had told her. How was she to hold on to a cousin intent on handing her over to his soul-destroying father. She ought to hate him for it. Instead, she felt more bound to him than ever, as if the dark power driving Blayne were the answer to the cavernous darkness in herself.

Blayne seemed to feel the connection too. He issued short, terse commands to the Sards who sought him out. He spoke thoughtfully to her.

At one point Emily asked him if her conversation bothered him. He replied, "You are quiet in other ways. Your feelings do not clamor at me the way these Sards' do."

"You sense their emotions?"

He actually laughed, contemptuously. "I know them, like I know the shape of my own thoughts. It is a useful skill. At times, however, it can become distracting."

From Blayne, she learned that the Sards were riding to war. Emily assumed that this meant that the Sards were making for Sun City, but Blayne explained that he had already commanded another host of Sards in a successful sacking of the eastern half of that metropolis.

Emily tried to summon a feeling of sadness or dismay but to no avail. "If the city is yours, what else do you need to fight for?"

Blayne's eyes glittered into her own. "The city is not ours. Not completely."

"The citizens resist?"

"The citizens are grapes for the press. Those that we haven't crushed are being used by the ancient powers that now contend there. When those powers have spent themselves striving against each other, the Sards will take the rest."

"So you are biding your time attacking those who fled?"

"I am pursuing those who have my son."

Emily looked off into the distance. "Beth had her baby," she sighed. "Is she well?'

"I know nothing of the mother except that she fled the city, taking my son with her. Now she and the child are prisoners in the camp of a pretender called Marbek."

Emily stared at him, felt the reins of her mount slipping from nerveless hands. "You mean Beth," she prompted firmly.

"That is her name," he returned.

Emily slowed her mount. Although a steady stream of dark-robed horsemen swept around her, shutting out her sight of Blayne, he was sharp as an awl in her thoughts. "Changed indeed," she muttered to herself.

The battle came to Marbek's men exactly as Jazim had said it would. Because Marbek was still incoherently ill, his commanders deployed their troops according to their own plans. They did not listen to Jazim. They did not trust him, and none of them could really bring themselves to believe that the nightmare he described was about to descend on them from out of the peaceful hills.

The commanders sent several companies north toward the city to confront what they thought must be a traditional raiding party of Sards. They also sent out dozens of riders with messages for the city's refugees and the Empyreal armies normally quartered at Sun Gate.

By noon, gravely injured men were being carried into the house from the field. Marbek's men had engaged several companies of Sards, and caught glimpses of the massive army Jazim had predicted. Beth came out of her rooms to do what she could to help the injured and the physicians who operated on them. Some of the bleeding, dying men spoke of the viciousness of the saber-wielding Sards.

As day melted into night, the skirmishing continued and the numbers of injured increased dramatically while the dead piled up. Hollow-eyed commanders rushed to and fro when they weren't arguing and pulling their hair over piles of maps. Weighed down, Beth lurked about the periphery, listening to their lamentations and arguments, watching them struggle to bear their own burdens.

At dawn the next day, the generals' talk turned to escape, not that such talk lasted long. A few of the people who did try to flee, returned hours later, dead and mutilated and tied to their horses. The generals hung their heads in defeat. No one spoke of escape any more, or surrender. The Sards did not offer anyone terms of surrender, and they gave no quarter.

Lord Karek, one of those generals, finally approached her. Together they went to Jazim.

"No!" he barked, glaring at Karek and ignoring the hand Beth held out to him. "As the princess' protector, I forbid it. And if you try to go to anyone else with this, Karek, you'll be dead before you hit the door." He swung to Beth. "It is suicide."

Karek raised his head. "You are a prisoner not a protector, Lord Commander."

"Am I?" threatened Jazim, widening his hawkish stare.

Karek seemed to second-guess himself, and Beth stepped forward. "You said they want me."

"I said they *might* want you, or your son. They are Sards. They might just be bent on eradicating us all. Have patience. I have sent word to my men—that's right, Karek, I still have men, and unlike yours, mine know what to do. The armies of Sun Gate will come."

"And which of us will live to see it?" answered Beth. "The Sards might overrun us at any time. You yourself wonder why they haven't done so already. Perhaps it is because they are afraid of harming my son. If they want him that badly, I can talk to them, at least delay them, and give the rest of you a little time."

"And if they torture you? They say their magic is foul," Jazim warned.

"No more foul than my own," said Beth wearily. She turned away, planning to go with Karek anyway.

Jazim caught her arm. "Running to the Sards won't help your son or your people."

"No? What greater help could I be to them than to find a way to prevent your slaughter?"

"And if you die?"

"I've lost nothing. There will be nothing left for me to lose."

All in all, Emily decided, war was at least as tedious as it was bloody. For her it amounted to a lot of waiting. From her seat at Blayne's side, she saw fifty or so enemy riders toppled from their mounts and pounded to pieces beneath flailing hooves, then her cousin sent her away.

Catching her horse by its bridle, he calmed the animal to stony stillness while his star-fire eyes stabbed into hers. "Time for us to part, cousin," he said in a voice throbbing with energy and the anticipation of the kill. Then he spurred his own horse into the rush, his dust-colored robe lifting and flapping like wings.

Emily was left with a group of heavily robed and tattooed women who led her to a crude pavilion made of coarse fabric strung between four wooden poles. Briefly she thought about using the Shield to escape from them, but that would have meant abandoning Blayne, and that she could not do, either because of herself or some power emanating from him.

She sat under the pavilion as the sun dragged the day into the west. At dusk she looked up from contemplating the smoky ripples in the Shield to see a long supply line snaking its way out of the darkening east. The Sards had come prepared to stay.

Beth got her way. In the afternoon, she was escorted from the house of Marbek by a group of captains and Prince Jazim. On her finger lay Bethnarian's signet ring; between her breasts hung the pendant that Jazim had ripped off her. It still pulled painfully at the power inside her, but she took that as a positive sign. If it could turn her power, it might turn the Sards' as well.

Her escort took her on a circuitous route toward a higher range of hills that would allow her to look out over the main battlefield. She seemed to look down on a battle of the ants. Movement was everywhere amid a tiny litter of bodies, human and animal. She could make sense of almost none of it.

Beth heard the captains grumbling behind her, then the captain nearest her raised a curved brass horn and blew it three times. The bright metallic sound floated out over the battlefield. A second captain unfurled a hastily patched together banner carrying the personal emblem of the Empyreor Bethnarian. But the wholesale slaughter continued.

Then, from behind the hills opposite soared the breathy moan of rams' horns. The line of the battling Sards surged mightily and turned back toward their own battle lines.

Marbek's men hastily retreated to higher ground.

One astounded young captain blurted, "If I didn't know better, I would think that the barbarians are actually agreeing to talk."

"I am not yet ready to believe it," remarked Jazim.

Beth spoke over her shoulder. "Send word to the men on the line. If the Sards wish to send us a messenger, we will entertain him."

412

It took time for orders to be relayed and communications established. The sun was halfway behind the hills when the Sardic messenger finally arrived.

Beth expected a youth or a slave. She looked with surprise on a tall tattooed old woman wrapped in voluminous robes. The crone halted her mount a short distance from Beth's and spoke in a voice heavy with rough and hissing accents. "Who raises the emblem of Bethnarian?"

"I do," answered Beth.

The old woman's mouth spread in a travesty of a smile. "And who are you?"

"Bethnara. Daughter of Bethnarian, Empyreor of the South, Scion of the Sun." She held out her ringed hand.

The old woman's tattoos crinkled. "Welcome, Daughter of Nyte. I am Unashk, priestess of Ishenesh."

Jazim pushed his horse forward. "And we are the princess' servants."

The old woman stiffened and glared at Beth. "Does this slave seek to offend me?"

Beth raised her hand. "No, Unashk. He only wishes to answer your question."

The woman cursed in Sardic and thrust her gray head forward. "The Daughter of Nyte would not let a mere man speak for her. Show me your face?"

Beth sat straighter. "It is not the custom of—"

Unashk cackled. "More insults! The priestesses of Ishenesh do not treat with cowards who hide behind flimsy screens of cloth! When I saw a woman come to the field, I thought that the Empyre had grown some wisdom. But I see now that it remains as barbaric as ever!" With a sharp gesture, she spun her horse back toward the Sardic line.

"Wait!" ordered Beth. She lifted the veil from her face, felt the breeze loft it back from her head.

Unashk's horse stilled. Unashk's seamed face confronted Beth's. No muscle or wrinkle moved. Sibilant Sardic poured through nearly motionless lips.

"I do not understand," said Beth.

The seams of the face deepened and fanned out. The mouth widened. "I said you are exactly as promised."

"Then you recognize me. Will you negotiate?"

"I do not have that authority."

Beth clenched her reins in frustration. "Will you take my request to the one who can?"

Unashk continued to stare at Beth, the breeze seeming to sigh for her. "I will," answered the crone at last.

Beth and her escort waited while the Sards erected a structure that was nothing more than four cloth walls in the middle of the battlefield. Around these walls, they set burning torches. To either side of it, they posted two large companies of Sards. As they watched Unashk ride back to them, Jazim could barely contain his concern. "They could be planning to slit your throat."

Beth didn't bother looking at him. "In that event, act as you see fit. I will send you word if I can."

"Take at least a few of us with you," urged a captain named Faruk.

"No. It is too risky. They are invested in me. I will go alone."

Beth followed Unashk into the walls of cloth, which were given a soft red glow by the torches burning outside the space. Carpets had been laid. A stool sat in the middle of the room, and a short distance from it stood a tall robed and hooded figure.

Unashk moved to the center of the room and bowed low. She spoke swiftly in Sardic.

A softer, deeper voice answered her.

Unashk departed, still doubled over in a deep bow.

Beth regarded the figure in surprise. "You are a man," she said.

"You wish to discuss terms?" he answered.

"That depends."

"On?"

"On what you are willing to offer."

The shrouded man spoke clinically. "Your army is outnumbered and exhausted. It has been retreating for three days. Unless you plan to pull reinforcements out of a pocket, it will not last another."

Beth knew she was out of her depth, but persevered anyway. "You agreed to meet with me. That tells me there is something you and your people want."

"Nothing that we cannot take."

Beth looked down. Must men always be bent on taking? She spoke to the carpet. "Are you sure? Marbek is a ruthless man. He and his captains will do their utmost to inflict heavy losses on you before the end. Do Sards' lives mean so little to their leaders?"

"Sards lives mean nothing to me. Where is my son?"

Beth froze, and with a shake of his head, the robed man cast his hood aside. His incredibly bright eyes speared her mind. "My son," he repeated.

Beth reeled, falling toward him at first and then away, her hands shoved to her mouth as if to stifle a scream. "Blayne!" she choked into them.

The name flashed to nothingness before those eyes, which stabbed mercilessly at the core of her. "You have power," he remarked disinterestedly, "But not enough to resist me. You will deliver to me my son," he said and assaulted her with his own frigid multihued fire.

"No, no, no," she wailed as his star-bright eyes dissected her being and found it wanting.

His hands were hard on her forearms, his eyes growing brighter, irradiating her soul so as to burn away any and all obstacles to the knowledge that he sought.

Beth heard herself sobbing his name like a prayer, a prayer which his white-fire eyes incinerated. Her own fire roared up in contest, the heavy earth power of the stone between her breasts awakened so that Beth's prayers turned to screams.

Emily was jarred awake. Somewhere there was screaming and desperation, and it involved Blayne. She could feel the hum of his troubled consciousness in her teeth. He was more than troubled; he was almost frightened.

Emily raised herself to listen. The screaming continued, high and agonized. With no thought for the Sardic women surrounding her, Emily scooped up the Shield and ran toward the sound.

Although the scream was in her mind rather than in her ears, she knew exactly where to go, as if the knowledge of the place had come through Blayne's awareness into her own.

There were footsteps behind her. Hands clutched at her wrist, her clothes. Emily gritted her teeth and jammed the Shield into them. There came a sound like twigs breaking and sharp cries. She ran through them, over and around hills and onto a field still littered with bodies. The screams were fading now.

Sentries stood between her and the torch-lit square of cloth. Then a Sardic voice rang out. "Come, Shield Bearer. Hurry!" It was the ancient priestess Unashk. Her tousled silhouette motioned Emily on and parted the cloth for her so that she might pass into the structure's interior.

Emily instantly absorbed the scene — a large, almost empty space, Blayne standing at the center of it, and on the ground at his feet — "

"Beth!" Emily hissed as somewhere below the void inside her something stirred. She rushed to the prone woman and knelt at her side, laying the awkward length of the Shield alongside her. Beth's skin was waxy, her perfect features pinched. Even her hair seemed to have lost its luster. This, Emily thought, is how Beth would look if she were only human.

Emily glared an accusation at Blayne. "Tellers take you, Blayne! What did you do to her?"

Blayne looked coldly back, his eyes flashing like burning pinwheels. Emily rose to better confront him. "Tell me!"

"I compelled her to tell me the truth."

"And this is the result?"

"She has power. She tried to resist. The thing about her neck awoke."

"What—" Emily didn't bother to finish the question. She dropped to her knees and parted the silk at Beth's neck.

"Another one!" she cried and began to curse. She tried to slip her fingers beneath the exposed chain to rip it off Beth's throat. Not so much as a fingernail could she slide underneath it. She opened Beth's collar wider and scratched at it. The chain clung tight to Beth's skin as if welded there.

Emily uncovered the pendant and inhaled in one long hiss.

"Bloodstone!" she heard Unashk say as she broke into a litany of Sardic.

Emily nodded but only to herself. Deep in her gut she began to tremble, and the void inside her at last began to fill with a deep, puissant anger as she recalled the servant of Scryos slipping a similar chain over her neck.

Unashk said to her. "This is potent magic. Both stone and charm. He who made this is strong in mind as well as in magic. The stone seeks her power, and the chain twists that desire to new purposes."

"Then I'll twist it to mine!" grated Emily. She adjusted her position on the carpet slightly, so that she could touch the Shield with her right hand. With her left she reached out toward the silver-caged stone.

She had only the faintest glimmer of a plan. She was being driven mostly by the anger within her. The vague notion had come to her that the stone would be drawn to her power in the same way as its sister stones in Scryos' house. If so, she might be able to draw it onto her and off Beth before it killed her.

416

At first the pendant was cool against her palm. But then she willed the mark on her hand to flare to life. Bright light flashed beneath her hand, fanning out like a corona, lighting the inside of the flesh covering it.

Emily felt the stone begin to pull. Drawing on the Shield, she poured more power into it and the pull intensified, sucking at her flesh as she rained power down on it through its delicate silver net. Beside her the Shield began to ripple light.

Now Emily could feel the nature of the spell, the way the stone hungered after power and the way the chain limited that power. She released more power into it and let her awareness follow it down into the matrix of the stone itself. She could feel the opal-threaded rock begin to resonate with the power it drew. Was there a limit to how much any one stone could hold? She intensified the stream of power, felt the vibration of the stone deepen. The stream became a torrent. A hairline crack formed, expanded.

The stone cracked. The silver flared white and crumbled to ash.

Intent as she was on her inner vision of the stone, Emily did not know that both she and the Shield had begun to shine with the enormous volume of power she was drawing. When the stone cracked, all the power drawn into it flashed out of it in one enormous burst of light. People on the plain saw the cloth walls of the shelter disappear behind white radiance. People in the hills beyond, saw the horizon lit up by a white corona like a thousand simultaneous strokes of lightning.

Gigantic as the flashover was, the power in it went only so far before the Shield drew it back. As it had the wight's power, the Shield sucked at the escaping energy and drew it back into itself. The bubble of power shrank. Whiteness cohered again and then failed altogether.

In the sudden darkness, Emily's stunned mind and body slowly adjusted. Hovering only an inch or so above Beth's dust-peppered chest was a tiny softly glowing ball of liquid crystal.

"What is this?" murmured Emily.

Blayne loosed a breathless curse.

The priestess Unashk fell on her face and began muttering frantically in Sardic.

Emily spared her only the most cursory of glances. Her attention belonged to the tiny ball. Gently she extended the index finger of her left hand out toward it, intending to prod it ever so slightly. But just before she touched it a yet stranger thing happened. Emily felt the heavy ring she wore constrict. Looking down, she saw its sinuous surface move and saw how it split into three concentric bands of differing widths. The thicker top band lifted up revealing a triangular head with tiny eyes like a beads of iron. In the middle of these eyes were the merest slits of pupils, infinitely dark.

The ring had become a tiny, perfect serpent. Emily looked at the little thing in amazement and the snake moved toward the ball hovering before it. Its tiny tongue flicked out, black as the slits of its eyes. Once, twice—on the third flick it struck, swallowing the liquid crystal whole. Then it curled itself tight about Emily's finger and lowered its head.

The first thing Emily did when she shook off the surprise of the whole strange affair was to grab hold of the ring with three fingers of her right hand and test her ability to remove it. The sinuous band of black iron remained glued to her digit, as tight as if it truly were an iron serpent constricted about it.

Then Beth stirred, diverting attention. Emily leaned over her friend, who turned her head and mumbled. Emily called her name, Blayne said something in Sardic, Unashk crawled backward to flee through the fabric wall.

Emily called to Beth many more times, but though the princess stirred, she did not wake. This worried Emily, who scanned her friend's form and wished for Colin's healing sight. At least, the princess' old ethereal beauty had returned. Her features were smooth and relaxed; her skin luminously clear.

Emily sat back on her heels. She looked up at Blayne, whose eyes still shone like stars.

"I think she will be all right."

"Very well. I will resume my interrogation when she wakes."

Emily stared at him. "What?"

"I must learn what she knows about my son."

Emily lurched to her feet. "*Your* son," she said, leaning hard on the first word.

"Yes."

Emily stepped closer to him, spoke with careful, clipped precision. "No. *Your* son. *Yours* as in both of you, yours and hers."

"The woman no longer matters."

"I wouldn't tell her that. For one thing she's not just a woman." She looked deeply into Blayne's starry eyes and for the first time, she was able to see beyond them to the power-blinded being inside. "I'm beginning to look forward to seeing that dreadful father of yours again. I have quite a few things I want to say to him." She pointed a stiff finger at Beth. "She's your son's mother. She's your love. But most of all she's your kind. You share a nature as well as a child." She paused and took in a deep breath. "She loves you, Blayne. Do not turn away from that. You will be lost forever if you do. You will be lost to yourself."

No sooner had those words left her lips than Emily knew what she had to do. She could hear her grandfather's words rolling like a wave through her mind. *Hold on. You have what he needs.*

There was only one thing of any value that scruffy Emilyn Sayer possessed that her gorgeous, unnatural cousin might need. She had given a piece of it to him once before when she pulled him through to the twilight world, and it had nearly killed him. Since then they had both journeyed far and come back changed. The Tellers willing, those changes would be enough.

Emily took one final, irrevocable step. She wrapped her arms around her cousin and set her ear to his chest as if to listen to the strange stirrings of his heart. Then she began to remember, for herself as much as for him. She had to resurrect a dead feeling. Starting with Blayne, she recalled it. She remembered him as she had known him when he was alien and feared. She remembered Beth, and then Beth with him. Then she remembered them as she had seen them together in that first cataclysmic moment of soul recognition, and later on that night when their natures had met and merged. When she had remembered all she could of that, she remembered him on the journey to Cyr and afterward when he had turned to her for understanding. *She sent me away because I could not love.* Love, Emily thought. That was the key. It opened up a door to a whole world of feelings.

The void in Emily filled again with a feeling as deep and broad and full of restless yearning as the sea. The dull roar of it filled her ears, drowned out thought and memory, closed her throat, and cleft her heart in twain. But when it had passed it had taken with it all the dusty despair of death, leaving her clear, heavy hearted, and free.

It seemed that she stood on a narrow strand, on the margins of an endless sea. The sea lapped at her feet, glinting in the sun. Its clear waters robbed the sand from beneath her feet, but gave back to her glimpses of all those whom she had loved. She saw them raw and unvarnished, as life had cast them. And it came to her that love was less about the loved one than the one who loved. Love for these people had filled her days like the sea filled the deep places of the earth, giving an otherwise vacant life color and energy, beauty and deep mystery.

This was the gift that Emily gave to Blayne. One small, simple, true thing. A shell through which to hear the relentless call of that strangest of seas. Across the bond that Millicynt Encanta had forged, it flew and came to lodge in a heart untried.

The pressure of Blayne's convulsing fingers brought Emily back to the present. She stepped back. For a long moment, she contemplated what she had done, and her hand, as Millicynt's had once done long ago, cupped Blayne's cheek.

"Love, cousin," she said, then turned, picked up the Shield and walked away.

Beth awoke to strange sounds and even stranger surroundings. Images flickered in her mind like the flame in the strangely wrought lantern sitting near her. Her mind cast back through the days and stumbled over one moment. *Blayne.*

She turned her head to take in more of her surroundings, found the man to match the name sitting near her.

Reflexively, she shrank back into the cot that held her. Then she saw the look in his shining eyes, more green now than white.

"Blayne?" she whispered.

And he smiled. It was a slow, uneasy smile, but it seemed to well up from the deep, unexplored places within him, and it carried with it a mortal joy and mortal sorrow. Like sunlight it lit up his already radiant face. "My love," he said.

Beth cried out as he reached for her. She fell to weeping on his neck.

When Emily left Blayne, she was heading nowhere. She had nowhere to go. Then something hard struck her in the back and then the head, and nowhere found her instead.

When its blackness at last began to recede, she heard voices. Hands were running over her, grappling with her arms and legs. Her head was lifted. Liquid rushed into her mouth, choking her. She gulped it and gasped for air.

Liquid seemed to fill the world. She sank back into it.

She awakened more slowly the second time, seeing fuzzy stars that sharpened to points with agonizing slowness. She tried to move her arms, gradually realized that they were bound together in front of her.

A shadowy blob swam into view. A vaguely familiar voice, thick with Sardic sibilance, issued from it. "Are you awake?"

"Unashk?" She garbled the priestess's name. Her tongue seemed twice its regular size and half as fast.

"Yesss."

420

"Where—"

"Your cousin is with his woman. That was a nasty thing you did to him, but the Lord of Darkness and Light will make it right. Your Shield lies where you dropped it, as it shall until the end of days, for none after you will be able to lift it. We will move on, but it shall remain, until the dust and grass claim it for the new earth."

Different voices, approaching fast. More blobs swam into view. With a nauseating lurch Emily was lifted to her feet.

Although it made her stomach churn, the change to an upright position did much to clear her head. The blobs became the intent faces of Sardic priestesses.

Emily could see Unashk speaking heatedly to another group of Sardic priestesses and gesturing broadly.

Emily was dragged up a hill and over it. The clutch of priestesses preceding her, spread out, giving her a view of a broad depression filled with people holding torches. Flame-etched faces swung her way, and a murmur began that crescendoed into a throbbing chant. She was dragged forward into a cleared space marked by six seated women—three on the left and three on the right.

A summons began. As it pounded to its conclusion, Emily could feel the air around her thickening with a power that emanated from every woman present. Alone their power was feeble in comparison to hers. Together it became almost irritating.

She could do nothing about it, however. Her head ached; her power would not come. Had it not been for the priestesses supporting her, her knees would have buckled. From the edges of the circle six children were led forth. They looked to range in age from four to six and they wore little kirtles and nothing else. All of them stared into the air with eyes glazed.

Now slaves were coming forward, bent men with heavy slabs of irregular rock. Emily took one look at the veins of multicolored fire glowing in those rocks and began to struggle in earnest. She threw her weight about, only to feel the priestesses' grip on her tighten. She reached for power, found it stifled and twisted by the drugs she had been given.

In a rictus of helpless fury, she watched the men press the little children into kneeling postures before the stones while the priestesses raised sharp knives.

"No," mumbled Emily, as one by one the priestesses swept their knives across the children's necks and the little heads fell at awkward and extreme angles. Blackness gushed forth onto stone until the emptied bodies were cast aside like so much refuse.

The veins of color in the stones began to pulse then to flow, and power thick as congealed blood filled the air. Emily felt it condensing about her. She blinked with painful slowness as the landscape before her began to bend and wave like a world seen through ripples of water. The hills before her undulated, and the stars too. Emily followed their wavy streaks to the focal point of the power, a place low down in the air where darkness stretched like a bottomless well.

Far down this infinitely dark tunnel Emily saw a flaming figure. The figure was moving steadily closer, or perhaps she was falling toward it. She could not tell, for the rippling was now all around

The daemon lover called, and Emily quite forgot to resist.

Then a wind howled out of the western hills, snuffing the torches and flattening people like grasses. It dashed Emily to the ground. It felled priestesses like trees. It slammed into the expanding ripples of power and shoved them back. The tunnel into Midnight imploded. The wind departed as swiftly as it came.

Emily clambered onto hands and knees and scrubbed the dust from her eyes. Other people were crouched upon the ground or crawling along it. A few cried out and pointed to the crest of the tallest hill.

Emily looked to where they pointed—

Dark against the starry sky stood a shape all too familiar to her, a figure hatted and cloaked and holding a long, thin staff. Only now that staff was crowned with a terrible living blackness that swept like a scythe through the mind.

It had been a thousand years since human eyes beheld the thing atop that staff, but Emily knew instantaneously what it was. "The Warders' talisman," she breathed.

Adrift in her own frayed thoughts, she watched the hatted figure point the dark crescent earthward.

From out of the dust and sand of the little valley burst tiny blades of inky darkness. Like grass they grew but blindingly fast. They shot skyward and multiplied. They unrolled runners like spiked tentacles and raised tall black awns which dusted the earth with tiny black seeds that, in turn, sprouted more blades. Faster than the people could move, the black tentacles grew and entangled them, grasping legs and arms, twining over toes and fingers, drawing them tight against the earth and rooting in their flesh to suck the nourishment from their blood and organs. And when at last the feeding was done, the black grass retreated and not one human being besides Emily was left standing or sitting or lying in the sandy dell.

With the cries of the dying Sards still ringing in her ears, Emily watched the black crescent lift skyward and its bearer begin to descend the hill.

She had trusted Roland once, and he had delivered her heart and soul to death. She would not trust him again. His ways were as dark and twisted as the talisman he wielded, his gifts as devious as his mind.

"No," she breathed swinging her head slowly from side to side. But Roland only came on. "No," she spat at him. He raised the crescent higher. "No!" she cried, a third and final time. She doubled over clutching at her gut as there came a rending deep inside her. At long last the terrible soul-eating anger that she had kept buried deep down inside her ever since the night of Alsandyr's death finally burst forth. No longer was she an indifferent, hollow shell of a person. No longer was she devoid of feeling.

She straightened and shook her fist at Roland's shadowy form. "You have taken too much," she said. "You will take no more." Then she spun around and ran across the sand, feeling the dark tentacles of the Crescent reaching out to snare her.

She remembered well enough where the tunnel to the wights' realm had formed. She who had the poorest of senses of direction in the sunlit world had an unerring inner compass for twilight.

In a blink she stood again upon the crystal bridge spanning obsidian mountains beneath a diamond sky. On the road below her stood a beckoning flaming figure, but his allure no longer held sway. She burned too hot for his cold fire. She sought a place where she could bury for once and all her soul-consuming anger.

Chapter 31: Night's Flight

In the days before Emily shook her fist at the Crescent Lord and vanished into Twilight, the ancient power of the second talisman stalked the City of the Sun.

It began during the Festival of the Ninth Moon, while the Empyreal princess and Jazim and Miri sprinted for the city's border and the vast majority of its other citizens swarmed to its heart, drawn by the promise of decadent revels, of mayhem and madness, of fire and blood and, yes, even death. Not even the earthquake felt at dusk blunted their appetite for merrymaking.

By full dark, residents and rustics alike cavorted in the broad torch-lined streets, drinking deep, dallying, and dancing. Even the lesser nobility paraded across the broad squares, overawing the commoners with their panoplied retinues as they made their way from lavish feast to lavish feast. Many a bottle as well as a skull was broken. In the haunted old quarter, mad-eyed fanatics with glowing faces spun and leaped and held snakes up to the spire that was the Tower of the Moon. In more commercial districts, the members of the merchant class drank to their profits, celebrating with a bit more sobriety. For the moneymakers it had been a very good year.

Inside the Empyreal palace even greater changes were taking place. At first, the great rooms squatted in their own incongruous dark, entertaining only shadows and echoes. Even the servants' quarters were silent.

As the night deepened, however, all this changed. One looking down on the palace with a steward's sharp eyes would have seen the transformation begin in the halls and corridors nearest the great throne room and ripple slowly but steadily outward.

Unlit lamps and torches flared to life with a fire like nothing in the mortal world. Their flames gave off no heat, yet burned with a fierce multihued radiance that dyed the gilded halls myriad colors. Long after they sprang to light their radiance continued to build, and soon, the very stones and furnishings of the palace seemed to take up their glow.

Eventually, the people emerged. Vacant-eyed and stolid as sleepwalkers, they set to work. Doors and shutters were flung open. Floors were swept and polished. Flowers were picked and woven into elaborate wreaths or shredded so that their petals could be scattered across the floor. Precious stones and pearls were unpacked; the wealth of generations of Empyreors. Far below the rooms and corridors of power, the vast kitchens roiled and thrummed like a great hive.

Music poured out to match the light, sweet and compelling. Harps and horns, cymbals and drums interwove their distinct magics.

The rainbow glow from the palace overflowed onto the streets. Those who saw it were immediately drawn to it. Nobles and pariahs alike collected at the great palace gates to be admitted by blank-faced guards who hardly seemed to see them pass. Had the guests been more clear-eyed themselves they might have recoiled from the cloudiness of the gazes beneath those conical helms.

The majority of mesmerized commoners were left to crowd the streets outside the palace and gaze longingly at what they could see of the great edifice rising above the walls. Soon they numbered in the thousands, forming a living wall beyond the palace gates, until more guards emerged and pressed them into a living corridor for princes.

By midnight, bodies clogged the palace gardens and receiving rooms. Movement of any kind became difficult, but that did not stop the people from acting. Empty-eyed nobles and grandees bowed and scraped, drank or danced. Empty-eyed guards stood stiffly at attention. Empty-eyed servants cleaned and served and cleaned and served even as their hands grew red and sore from use. None slowed their activities no matter how their bodies ached and sweated.

The eastern half of the city was now burning, but no one in or near the palace cared. They sensed nothing.

In all that vast Empyreal complex only one person escaped the strange spell. His name was Caphal, and night found him sitting alone in the Empyreor's study and working hard by firelight to dispose of Bethnarian's personal papers. Some of those papers Bethnarian had ordered destroyed. Others he had ordered stored. Still others he had ordered preserved for his daughter.

Caphal tried to work fast—he hoped to leave the city before the following morning, well before the civil unrest that always accompanied an Empyreal succession—but sorting Bethnarian's private correspondence proved tedious work.

By the time he had finished, he was sore-eyed, thirsty, and suffering from a slight headache. He rang for servants, and went on to other work. Another stack of papers later, he realized that the servants had never come. He rose and rang again. He waited, and waited, tapping his nails on lacquered wood and thinking that it didn't take long after the passing of an Empyreor for the servants to slack off. Finally, he made his way to the apartment's main doors. Heaving one open, he looked up and down the hall in irritation then amazement. Not a single guard!

He was about to investigate when he heard the unmistakable sound of marching feet. Four guards came into view, and he summoned them with a peremptory snap of his fingers. They marched on by.

Stunned, Caphal moved after them, calling.

As one, the guards stopped, turned. The next thing Caphal knew, he was crashing into a wall. The guards had gone.

As he lay there, his skull ringing like a bell, it came to him that he was hearing music. Shaken and sore, he used the wall to get to his feet, then followed the sound to more public areas of the palace. What he saw sent him scurrying back into the Empyreor's apartments, where he bolted and blocked the doors.

It was her! Her! The white daemon! The Empyress of Night! She had gotten free! He thought of his Empyreor and sagged against a wall, clutching at a lump concealed beneath his robes. If the Empyreor and the death dealer had failed, the Empyre was doomed.

He drew out from under his robe a gold chain from which hung an elaborately wrought Sardic pendant with a fleck of black stone. The chain had come with the title Secretary, and Caphal had accepted it as a sort of seal of the office. He thanked the gods he had it now.

He looked about the rich apartment and remembered the secret passages leading down to the old palace. Should he dare those?

Before he could decide, he heard the creak of wood and the whine of hinges. Caphal froze. Only two people ever used the secret door leading to the chamber of runes, Bethnarian and the witch who served the white woman.

Quietly, he began to slide along the carved wall. It must be the witch. If she caught him here now, alone—she would haul him before the daemon Empyress herself.

He considered the barred door, the other rooms. The great sitting room led to the private garden. He could hide there.

From an adjacent room came the scrape of shod feet. Bending low Caphal took off for the library. He would take the secret passage leading to the necropolis and Moon Tower instead.

His sandaled feet slapped loudly as he rushed into the darkened library.

Behind him, shadows thicker and darker than ink began oozing out of another doorway and snaking their way across the floor.

Caphal slipped and slammed his shoulder painfully against one of the library's wide pillars. Grunting, he ran on, hands outstretched into darkness. He hit the curving wall of books, followed it around to the wooden door. Behind him steady footsteps were ringing on marble floor. He pawed at the wood, found the lock, and blessedly, the key in it. A quick twist and the wards snicked back. He pressed the gold plated handle.

The key turned back. The wards rolled to locked position. Caphal jerked frantically at the golden handle, choking on fear like a stone in his throat. Beneath his hands, the handle softened, elongated, sprouted metal tentacles that threaded themselves across his fingers.

Caphal cried out. The footsteps came on.

With a soft thunk they stopped.

Caphal heard a loud tap like the sound of a metal-shod pike hitting the floor, and the darkness in the room rolled back before a soft silver glow. The tentacles about Caphal's hands unraveled, turned back into a door handle. Caphal pulled his trembling fingers away and took hold of the pendant at his chest. Slowly, he turned around.

In the middle of the library stood a man holding a staff. His face was half hidden beneath a broad-brimmed hat. His tall form was draped in a long blue robe. Surmounting his staff was a thing that seemed to tear a crescent-shaped hole in space at the same time that it writhed with energy, exuding shadows like long licking tongues that curled about the man's face and form. The man held his left hand out, palm up. Silver light emanated from it.

Caphal gulped and tried to look away.

"Who are you?" the man said in a voice shimmering with layers and undertones.

Caphal found he had to answer. "Caphal Nuhamna."

"Why are you in Bethnarian's rooms?"

"I—I—I." Caphal swallowed hard to steady his voice. "I am the Empyreor's secretary."

"Then you are familiar with the Empyreor's library?"

Caphal opened his mouth, searching for words. The question seemed an odd one coming from a man such as this. "Yes."

"You are not enslaved like the others." The head beneath the hat tilted. The living shadows caressed the lower half of the face.

Caphal flinched. 'N—no, gr—great one."

A boot shifted. The staff scraped across the floor. "Ah, Sardic magic and a piece of stone." The undertones darkened and deepened. "I should snap the power of that little trinket right now."

Caphal ducked his head. "Please . . ." he pleaded. "She will eat my soul."

The man laughed, a ringing sound that caromed off the polished marble and stirred up strange echoes. "She always was a glutton."

Caphal's eyes jumped up in surprise. "You know her!"

"More than I would like, and less than I should. But now I have you."

Caphal's right hand began to shake so hard it played a counterpoint to his racing heart. "Me?"

The man moved closer, his hat brim lifting. With long fingers made of shadow and a predator's stare, he pinned Caphal to the door. "Show me where your master keeps the *Book of Nyte*."

Dawn came. An army of Sards moved through the charred easternmost quarters of the city, and camped amid the houses and streets they had spared, waiting.

At the very edge of the Sards' military lines, priestesses prowled. Each one carried a bloodstone next to her heart and kept her eyes trained on the southwestern skyline.

Beyond this point, the city slept. The easternmost streets swam in the detritus of the night's revels — forgotten cook fires, discarded clothing, bottles, and cups as well as uneaten food — but no people. One had to move deeper into the city to find these, a few at first and then in hordes as one approached the palace complex. Like animals they had lain down where the night had abandoned them. Some were curled up in doorways or huddled against brick walls, but most lay in the streets, heedless of whether they wore tatters or pearl-encrusted silks. Though the sun poured down on them, they neither snored nor stirred. They might have been dead so still did they lie. By noon their bodies, like the garbage, were baking. The air reeked of smoke and sweat and rotting food, the decay of an Empyre.

Caphal worked hard through the remainder of the night and for most of the next day. Now, as dusk descended, he plunked down a fresh stack of books and sagged back against the wall. His terrible new master was still perusing *The Book of Nyte.*

Caphal was one of only four persons who knew that Bethnarian even possessed the text — the others being Bethnarian himself and two priestesses of the Sards. As custodian of the Empyreor's most private papers, he had been allowed to know where the Empyreor kept it. He had never opened it, never wanted to. As far as he was concerned the book's only purpose was to serve as a token of the treaty made between Bethnarian and the Sards some twenty years earlier.

A spurred boot rose and came down hard on Bethnarian's gilded writing table. Caphal winced, but held his tongue. Daylight had done nothing to diminish the strangeness of the creature sitting at the Empyreor's desk. Nor had the darkness of the thing atop his staff waned. Even propped against the study walls, it snarled and lunged like a barely leashed animal.

Caphal took its threat quite personally. Once when raging thirst had driven him momentarily mad, he tried to slip away while the staff's bearer was distracted and his magic staff out of reach. But as soon as Caphal touched the library door, the wood sprouted black tentacles that sewed him bodily to it.

He had hung there for a long time. Then the staff's bearer had called out, "Bring me the next volume of Finhar's histories," and the shadows dumped Caphal in a boneless heap on the floor. When Caphal returned to the study with the requested tome, the man, without even looking up from his reading, said, "Binder doesn't like it when you try to run away."

"Binder," bobbed Caphal, bowing deeply and trembling.

The man gestured with his head. "My staff."

Caphal bowed again.

Predatory eyes snared him. "Did you really think you could get away?"

Caphal wanted desperately to look somewhere else, wanted even more desperately to be able to equivocate. The eyes gave him no quarter. "I am very thirsty, great one."

"Thirsty?" The man rewarded him with a terrible smile. Caphal tensed, thinking he was about to be eaten. A water skin hit him in the chest instead.

"Drink that. Then go back to work."

"Yes, great one."

From then on Caphal waited on his strange new master as patiently and loyally as any old dog. And now as twilight shadows began to slink through the room and rub themselves against the more ferocious darkness of the thing atop the staff, he reminded himself that his situation could be worse. He was at least free to think as he chose, unlike the mindless fools downstairs.

Wood scraped against the floor. In a ripple of blue robe, the man rose. He pressed long fingers to the pages before him, then bent down to scrutinize them more closely.

"A — a light, great one?" suggested Caphal.

The man raised his left hand and snapped his fingers. The lamps closest to the table and the whole great fireplace shot up flames that burned a healthy red-gold. The man's downcast eyes drank in that golden color and spilled it back onto the page he perused.

"Children," he said in his layered voice.

"Great one?"

"Children," he repeated looking at Caphal. "Not one child, but two."

Caphal opened and shut his mouth confusedly.

"The final pages of this book appear to be missing," said the man in a deceptively mild tone.

Caphal gaped. "Why I . . . That is impossible. It is kept locked away, I swear to you. Only Bethnarian ever touched it and he — "

"Calm yourself," said the man sharply. Caphal squeaked. The man's mouth widened slowly into another feral smile. "Really, Caphal," he said almost lazily, "A man of your age and station shouldn't squeak like a frightened little girl."

A fresh thought penetrated Caphal's alarm. *Is this creature actually laughing at me?*

The man cocked his head. "You said Bethnarian acquired this book when he made the treaty with the Sards."

"Yes, yes. Unless the Empyreor himself tore pages from it, it is exactly as it has always been."

Tap, tap, tap went one of the long fingers against the pages of the book. "So either the Sardic priestesses deliberately gave him an unfinished copy, or the final pages have been lost." The man shrugged off a thought. "No matter. I have done enough here. Prepare these books and manuscripts for travel."

Caphal jumped. "You are leaving?"

"I have work to do."

"But the white woman . . . "

"What about her?"

"What am I to do once you are gone?"

"You are to pack books, as you have been instructed."

"And you?"

The man donned his hat and reached for his staff. Tendrils of the living darkness in it snaked out to caress him. "I am going hunting."

Again the palace blazes with beckoning otherworldly light. Again the people outside yearn toward it with their whole being, while those inside wallow in service to an alien glory, lost to themselves and the lives they have led before. All is as Nyte ordains.

In an upper hall, a door cracks open on darkness.

The disruption, when it begins, is so slight as to go unnoticed, a fly buzzing at the feast, a hairline crack in a foundation stone, a thimbleful of inky darkness dropping into an ocean of rainbow light. A slave sweeping empty halls glimpses a flicker of blue-edged shadow and forgets to swipe her broom. A guard hears the beat of steady footsteps across gleaming floor and tilts his head to listen. A noble sees a finger of black smoke snuff a glittering fairy light and remembers the rest residing in true dark. The buzz, the crack, the darkness spreads. Flesh casts off the false promise of a daemon's dream and remembers itself.

In the great throne room the rivers and walls of gold still run with color. Everything except the clayey flesh of the throng has taken on an iridescent sheen. The people dance and sing and cavort for the pleasure of the one sitting on the Seat of the Sun. She is clad in a skirt of cloth of silver. Her torso is bare but for the mounded ropes of precious stones falling over her breasts. The gems scintillate madly as if lit to their depths by a living light. Not one rivals the diamonds of her eyes. Thousands of mortals have died in their fire. Their bodies carpet the steps before her throne.

The hatted man enters the room unseen. Brilliant as Nyte's eyes are, long and relentless as their vision has been, they cannot easily penetrate to the heart of this darkness. The ripple of disruption he brings with him, however, is not so easily missed.

Heads turn, eyelids flutter, bodies droop. The crowd gives way. The man steps through.

Nyte rises, a pearl beyond price borne up on a tidal wave of worship. The silver of her skirt ripples like water. Her eyes stab at the shadows beneath the hat. Their rays ricochet onto the crowd.

She speaks to the man, but no one in the assembly hears her voice except him. It is her thought rather than her mouth that moves.

"Well met, brother. A thousand years of mutual captivity, and we are both finally free. Come and celebrate. I have prepared a splendid repast." The cup of her pale hand encompasses the crowd.

"You mistake me," answers the man and shifts the long rod of wood he holds. The folds of his robe flare where they cover the dark thing attached to it.

Nyte is not deceived. She knows all too well what lurks just out of sight. She can feel the shimmering power of it pulling this world closer to the next. She smiles, decimating the mortals who look on.

"What! Would you continue the old argument even now? Have you not yet shaken off the disease of your mortal mother? Or has a thousand years feeding the tree weakened your mind? I won the fight. I was always stronger. I am the eldest and purest. And as I am first, I shall be last. You did not defeat me at the height of your power. You have no hope of defeating me now. You chose to cleave to the mortals. You sacrificed a part of your power mating with a mongrel stepchild, a usurper. You spent much of the rest containing me. While I manipulated weak minds and fed and waited, you poured out your energies on holding me. Now you are diminished, but a shadow of yourself."

The head dips until the hat hides the entire face. The hand tightens on the staff, the knuckles gleaming whitely.

Nyte sees it and her smile softens. An expression suspiciously imitative of sympathy comes over her face. She flows down the steps of the dais, her skirt flashing like fish scales and approaches the waiting man.

431

Her mental voice becomes a mother's cooing, a gentle nursery song. "It hurts you, doesn't it, brother? You shroud your pain in shadows, but I can feel it. Weakened as you are, you cannot fight the terrible pull of it, the heaviness of untransmuted matter, the dull, sticky web of mortal flesh. You have grown thick and corrupt with it. You are closer to them now than you have ever been."

She reaches out white arms.

"Let me help you. Feast with me. Drink deep and slowly your power will be restored. The talisman can be chained, and you can finally escape this mortal coil. I will sit you at my right hand. We can even engender children of our own. Together we will harness enough power to force even our terrible father to share dominion with us."

The hat wags side to side as the man shakes his head. He keeps his face hidden.

Nyte laughs. "Hah! You refuse to believe it. Perhaps you do not know about the child. Oh, yes, my brother. The youngest of us has engendered a child, a son, and by my own get. A hybrid of two lines, he is fruit ripe and ready to be plucked. We can claim him and the inheritance that can be his when all the lost pieces are rejoined. The knowledge and power of the True Immortal can be ours if you give yourself to me, brother. What is your answer?"

The man slowly lifts his head. Nyte's bright gaze breaks on the lashing darkness of the other's stare.

The man spins his staff. A hungry black crescent sails into the air and snaps at the power within the room.

He smiles. "As I said, you mistake me."

Nyte bares her teeth in a snarl. "Touch my power if you dare! I will see you imprisoned again. And this time, you will not last a thousand years."

The hatted man laughs. The resonant sound seems to draw the air out of the room. It dims the multihued lights and sucks the milky blindness out of the eyes of the men and women present. "Bind your power! I wouldn't dream of it. I'd rather set it free and see it returned to its true realm."

"And how will you accomplish that?" sneers the white woman.

"By binding the very part of you I know best."

Nyte's starlight eyes flash, but she retreats one step. The man takes one step forward. Now he speaks aloud, and the rich undertones in his voice spin a complex and irresistible web of enchantment across the room. "Much as you strive to forget it, you too are shot through with mortality. It is warp to your power's weft. Your mortal mother made it so. And as you well know, what is mortal is mine to bind."

432

Nyte flees.

Into the Well she flies and deeper, past the caves where she has so long been held captive and into the cataract of the river far below. No matter where she runs the shadow of her mortal self follows. Night passes and another day follows. Still Nyte flies on, and mortality made infinitely dark and infinitely strong pursues her as she first runs then crawls through secret passages leading up into the great necropolis.

At the top of moon tower it catches her at last. The white woman, glowing like a miniature moon, shines there for a moment for all to see, and then darkness like a mass of thorny canes pierces her to the heart. It clutches the half of her that was mortal fiber and binds it fast in the form of a great vine.

Rainbows cannot normally be seen at night. They are a trick of sunlight and cloud mist. But in the last hours of the last night of the Festival of the Ninth Moon a vast corona of rainbow filled the night sky and rained down into the earth seeking fragments of stone buried far below. People throughout the City saw the rainbow through clearing eyes and knew in their hearts that a different kind of star was about to rise.

BOOK THREE: After Dark

Chapter 32:   Parting

How do you hold on to the perfect moment? Beth wondered this as she held on to Blayne, hoped for it even as she knew it was a feat impossible to accomplish. All moments pass, and the answer to the riddle of their perfection lies in their passing.

Still, it was hard to contemplate letting go, especially when one could still feel all that would be lost. The dawn's light increased, brightening the interior of the tent, but Beth only pressed her cheek more tightly to Blayne's chest.

He stirred and sighed in his sleep. Beth sighed as well.

This, she thought, is how it feels to finally come home.

All her life she had wondered about that mysterious place that other people spoke of so casually, so thoughtlessly. Perpetually in exile, Beth had been preordained a stranger to every world she entered. She had been born a stranger to her father and her land, had been shut away a stranger in the Greenwood, had loved a stranger as a stranger to herself, and eventually returned to the Empyre as a stranger to its ways. Last night she had lain with Blayne, not in the heat of an overwhelming and unfamiliar desire, but in the full understanding of the heritage they both shared. Last night, she had hungered as she had burned, dangerously bright, and that hunger, like the burning that went along with it, had been matched and embraced. In Blayne's arms, she had finally come home to her entire self. Home—the place where the self exists if not unfettered, free.

She ran a hand across his ribs, felt the silky skin move beneath her fingertips. Blayne moved, long lashes sweeping back from smoldering green eyes?"

"That tickled," he said.

Beth smiled. "Really? I didn't know you could be tickled."

He set warm lips to her chest, to her throat, to her mouth. More than their lips touched. Beth felt the power inside both of them kindle and interweave like flames. She dove into it, felt it flickering in her flesh, filling her with transforming light. She could live in that light and never feel hunger or thirst or suffer again. She could dance with the fire, and thrill to its power and beauty.

Voices outside the tent.

Beth turned her head away from the filling fire. "What is that?"

"Ignore them," he said in a voice like the crackle of flames. He claimed her lips again.

Voices growing louder, coming nearer. Calls from just outside the tent door.

Beth felt Blayne press himself upward. She opened her eyes and saw colder stars kindling deep in the green.

He rose with ineffable grace and slipped into a loose robe. But as he started to leave the tent, she could not keep herself from crying out softly, "Don't leave me."

He turned, smiled. "It will only take a moment."

But she was on her feet, melding to him like flame melds to flame. "A moment is too long. Let them come in."

He called out to the Sards, telling them to wait. When Beth was dressed and seated on the edge of the camp bed, he bade them enter.

Four men—heavily tattooed, venerable in age, frightened in appearance. They spoke quickly in sliding, sibilant Sardic.

Blayne spoke back sharply. His head turned. He fixed his eyes on one tent wall as if to look through it toward yesterday's field of battle.

The Sards groveled, their words coming faster, higher.

On a wave of Blayne's robe, they dispersed.

Beth, her throat tight with presaged ending, swallowed. The moment was almost gone. "What is it?"

Blayne's eyes were on the billowing tent flap. "The priestesses have disappeared."

Beth blinked, rose, and went to him. "I don't understand."

"Neither do I."

"Have they run away?"

"The Sards seem to think not. They believe they were taken, swallowed by the earth."

"That's impossible! They must have left. Perhaps they mistrust you now and fear for their own power."

"Whatever happened, it was unexpected. It has frightened them. They spew terror like vomit."

Beth nodded. She set her lips to the flesh above the open collar of his robe. "I can sense it too."

"There is something else."

"Yes."

"They are reporting sightings of a large army of Empyreal soldiers moving this way."

Beth stepped back. "From the city?"

"More likely from the West. If the armies at Sun Gate had tried to move through the city, they would have encountered the Sards encamped there, or something far worse."

"My mother."

"They would have had to go around the city to reach us so soon."

Beth gasped, "I must get to Jazim or the fighting will start all over again!"

Blayne caught her by the shoulders. "You can not go back there."

"I must!"

"So that a fool like Marbek can rape you again? No." He said it without malice or anger, which made the negation in his words far more terrifying.

Beth's shoulders tightened. The memory of Marbek's violation still hurt, though Blayne had washed away her sense of shame. She raised a hand to his mouth. "I will deal with Marbek."

He slid his lips past her fingers. "There will be others, men enamored of you who will try to grasp what their mortality cannot comprehend. How will you protect them and yourself?"

"Blayne please!" She was trying to pull away now.

He caught her tightly to him, stilled her struggling with a wave of his own clear, bright fire. "I do not say these things to hurt or compel you."

She bowed her head to his chest, weeping silently. "You never do." In voice tight with strain, she said, "I shall never be ready. Not for this. There are things that I want to do and things that I choose to do. In heart and body and mind I will always want and choose you. But above and beyond my desire are things that I must do. This is one of those things."

He stepped back. "You will not let me come with you." He stated it like a fact.

She choked out a "No," and saw the old cold disinterest settle over his face. "You are turning me away again."

"You must understand. To them, you are simply the enemy. Even if I could keep them from learning your role in this war, I could never make them accept you. I already terrify them. And I am Bethnarian's child and a woman. I cannot imagine how they would react if confronted with the likes of you. I am willing to do many things to try to help this land, to help its people. It is the price I choose to pay for being my mother's daughter. But I will not risk you. I'd sooner risk my own soul. Without a soul, I am nothing. Without you, I am alone."

She raised her head, kissed him fiercely, feeling the brilliant energy and color of their union. She wanted to wrap herself in it like armor.

His hand brushed at her hair. "I will order the Sards back to their desert."

Amazed, Beth tried to focus on him through tear-streaked eyes. "Will they listen?"

"They are under my command. They swore it to my father. And now that they are without their priestesses, they will welcome my orders. Even if the priestesses resurface, the bulk of them will obey me. I will give them no other choice."

"You are that powerful?"

The star-fire in his eyes quickened. "I am my father's son, forged, tempered, and honed in his cruel fires. I carry his power within me. And I choose to use that power for us now." He wrapped her face in his hands and followed the trail of her tears with his brilliant eyes. "To think that I could ever have forgotten you."

Beth swallowed. "He might try to punish you."

"He loosed me on this land. He could not tie me to him too tightly or I would have been unable to bear the sun's light. Now that I am unleashed, even he cannot call me to heel so easily. You must not fear for me."

"How can I not when every threat to you feels like a direct assault on myself?" Then she was melting into him again, marrying herself to him as if she had no intention of ever departing. *I cannot do this,* she thought. *I gave up my son. Must I give up this too?*

436

He gave her the answer they both already knew. "It is time for you to go."

Beth sighed. "You once told me that you would not let me go."

"I did. And I never will again, no matter how far apart we are."

She turned her face into his shoulder. "Will you stay among the Sards?"

"No."

She was weeping silently again. "I thought — I hoped — if you stayed close, we might be able to meet. From time to time."

"I do not belong with the Sards."

"Then you will go back to the North?"

"No. There is nothing for me there now."

"Emily said you have a grandfather there, and other friends."

"My friend is dead. My relationship with my grandfather is problematic. As for my cousin, I fear she has slipped beyond my reach. I felt her leave last night, and under her own vastly increased power. Once again, she seems to have saved me from my darker self."

"What do you mean?"

He met Beth's eyes squarely. "Last night, before I remembered you, I intended to give her to my father."

Beth's lips parted in horror. Blayne gave her a sad smile. "I told you his power is cruel."

"Cruel enough to make you betray your own blood."

"Cruel enough to make me betray my own love."

She rose up and kissed him thoroughly. "Your love forgives you," she said when she was done. Then drawing back she gave him a forlorn little smile. "So I am sending you out into the world homeless."

"There is one place I might go."

"Where?"

"East. To find our son."

Beth's hands clutched reflexively. *"Our* son."

"Yes. He is still in great danger. My father wants him for reasons that he has not made clear to me. He is important, my love. Very important. Someone must protect him."

Beth's eyes had begun to shine. "Yes!" she whispered. "Yes! Find him, Blayne. Find him for me and keep him safe."

Blayne helped her mount in a circle of Sards. Four of them would go with her as escort. As she watched his tawny head lift, she saw that his eyes were green again. "Tell our son about me," she said.

"I will." He caught her ankle in a hard hand. "Do not go back to the City. Leave it to its ghosts."

Beth sighed. "But how many of my people will have the strength or will to build a life elsewhere."

"After what has happened there, many. Now go!" He slapped her horse's flank and sent her mount trotting off toward the hills before she could utter another word. The last she saw of him, he was raising a hand in farewell.

She had her tears under control by the time she reached the hilltop where her generals waited. All but one of them looked at her as if dazzled by the light of the rising sun.

Jazim faced her with relief. "I was beginning to think the Sards had slit your throat," he said sourly as he steered his mount near hers. "You took your time in coming back to us."

"Do I look like I've had my throat slit?" she asked almost flippantly.

His amber eyes narrowed. "No. You look surprisingly well for a woman who spent the night in an enemy camp."

"What say the Sards, highness," asked a younger commander looking rather worn for wear.

"They will be returning to their desert in two days time"

They gaped to a man. Even sardonic Jazim couldn't keep his mouth from falling open. "How by the daemon's dark mother did you accomplish that?"

"I used my considerable powers of persuasion, Lord Commander."

He snorted. "You believe them?"

"I believe in their reasons."

"Which are?"

"Their priestesses have abandoned them. They are almost leaderless and in disarray. More importantly, the armies of Sun Gate are only a few hours away."

There were cries of elation. One young general whooped loudly. "Now we can give those desert devils some of their own back."

"No!" said Beth sharply. The fiery power in her shot up, consuming doubt like dross, fueling her will, and filling her eyes with blue star-fire. The men before her froze in mid movement, utterly captivated. Even their horses stilled. She spoke slowly and clearly. "There has been enough killing. More will not undo the damage done. Our people need peace and time to recover. There is work more difficult than bleeding and hacking to be done. And I expect each of you to put your backs and well as your minds to it."

One by one they bowed their acquiescence.

Beth nodded. "Now, let us meet the armies of Sun Gate and give them the good news."

"Handled like an Empyress," remarked Jazim as they turned their mounts for home.

Shed of mortal memory and name, a girl, sometime called Emily, stood high upon an enormous cliff face under darkling skies. The stars, clear and cold, stared at her, fixed and unblinking as if holding their breath or holding back time. Below the cliffs lay a vast plain, and far away on that plain stood a shining city. A gleaming road straight as moon beams ran to that city, for those willing to risk the dangerous descent from the cliffs.

She would risk it. She knew well the path, its sparkling twists and turns. She knew the spot where it divided, one branch diving into a cleft in the rock, the other diving down to the darkling plain.

She took the path to the plain. It was a slow and treacherous descent, and many times the winds rising up off the plain tried to turn her back. They whispered strange stories in her ears, tales children would hang their dreams upon; full of treasures, enchantments, fair princesses and resolute princes; full of beauties light and dark.

She only clung more grimly to the steep way. I am no child, she told them. Blow your stories elsewhere.

One last winding turn and she put her foot to soft horizontal ground. The cliffs became a black wall rising behind her.

She reached the plain only to discover that it was a vast glassy sea and the road across it was only a beam of light cast by the shining city.

She crossed the gently sloping black sands of the narrow shoreline on which she stood and bent to touch the little waves lapping. The water bit her fingers with cold, numbing them instantly. She drew them back and looked at them curiously, for in this place pain, like all things, seemed less important than the place itself.

The sands behind her whispered.

She turned her head, and a robed woman came to stand next to her on the shore. The woman, too, looked across the sea out of a face as familiar as the place in which she stood, as serene as the placid sea.

"Have you come from the City?" she asked the woman, scattering drops like diamonds from her fingers.

The woman smiled. "No," she said in a voice of many voices.

"Are you going there?"

"No."

"I would like to go there."

"No one goes there?"

"Why?"

"It is still being built."

"By whom?"

"By you, by me, by many, many others."

"But I have never been there."

The woman's smile grew secretive. "Some cities start as stone; others as ideas or dreams; but it always takes many to build them, many ideas, many people, many ages, many loves, many lives."

"It is still beautiful."

"It has known its dark ages. We work enthusiastically to build. But we can lose sight of our goals, or the work can go awry. Sometimes we abandon it altogether. Sometimes, even when we build well, others come behind us and wreck what we have created."

She turned from the woman and looked out over the water. "I hope someone goes there. Even a dream city shouldn't be empty."

The woman's eyes gleamed like the sea. "If you work faithfully, the day may soon come when someone will."

"Who?"

The woman swept an open palm back toward the cliffs. "Her for instance." The voice of many voices frayed into a rising wind.

She turned from the shore to follow the woman's gesture and found herself standing among hills that climbed toward towering red rocks. Tatters of mist floated across the rolling land. Over her head the sun was muted to a silver disk by rising fog.

"I've been here before," said Emily, for her name had returned to her. Then she saw the little girl. The child, about five or six, was tossing a ball that looked to be made of glass. With all her meager strength she would hurl it into the air and then run, skipping and hopping, to catch it while her long dark braids skipped and hopped behind her.

The girl noticed Emily when her ball slipped through her reaching hands and rolled to Emily's feet.

Smiling, Emily bent to pick it up. It was cool and smooth and light as the thinnest crystal, but none of the child's rough play appeared to have damaged it. Emily held it out to its owner.

The little girl beamed. "Hello!" she said.

"Hello," said Emily.

"You aren't hurting anymore."

"No."

"I told you the seeds would help."

"I guess they did. Thank you. Are you out here all alone today?"

The little girl scrunched up her face. "Well . . ."

One corner of Emily's mouth twitched. She fought to curtail a knowing smile. "Do your parents know where you are?" she asked in a sterner voice.

The little girl's dark eyes shifted side to side. She seemed to consider her answer carefully. At last her face brightened and she said triumphantly, "Byrn knows where I am!"

Emily wasn't fooled. She knew an evasion when she heard one. She set a hand on her hip, thinking, *How precocious!* "And is Byrn your mother or your father?"

The little girl laughed delightedly. "Neither, silly!" Then she realized what she had done and drooped into a pretty sulk.

Emily chuckled silently. "This is lonely and wild country for a little girl. You should go back to your parents. They could be very worried about you."

"My father worries too much. Do this, go here, study that!" said the little girl with a sniff and a flippant toss of her head.

"That's because he loves you."

The child scuffed a guilty foot through the grass. "I know," she whined. "It's just that sometimes I want to be alone, just for a while. To do the things I want to do. You know!"

Emily sobered. "Yes," she answered. "Still, it can be dangerous."

The little girl's cheeks dimpled. She directed at Emily a smile of alarming charm. *What a minx,* thought Emily, as a warm little hand slipped into her own. "You are here," the child said.

Emily had to admit the ploy was hard to resist, but she gave the hand a little squeeze. "Go home!" she said, punctuating the command with a firm look.

The girl laughed again. "Oh, very well. Father will probably start looking for me soon anyway, and he always finds what he looks for." She leaned closer to whisper. "Sometimes I think he can see straight through the mountains! Are you going to go home too?"

"Maybe. Maybe I'll just stay here for a while. It's a peaceful place."

The child gave her a cunning look. "But it could be dangerous," she emphasized.

Emily had to laugh. "Oh, fie. I'm a big girl and you are not! Now get going."

The little girl gathered up her ball and went dancing back up the hill. Just before she disappeared over it, she turned and gave Emily a wave.

Heart warmed, Emily sat down in the grass. Whatever she had told the child, she had no intention of going back. Not yet. Let Roland seek for her through all the worlds, sunlit and twilit. She'd elude him until he got tired and gave up the hunt. But then she wondered. Did Roland get tired? In a thousand years, he'd not once given up the hunt for revenge.

Emily hugged her knees as a shiver of foreboding ran up her spine. Then she put Roland's relentlessness from her mind and lay back in the grass, tucking her arms under her head.

She was awakened by a strange stirring in the air. The pockets of mist had thickened to a true fog, and the dimness told her that beyond the screen of cloud the sun was lowering itself to its rest. Emily's skin prickled; the small hairs on her neck rose. Something or someone was coming. It was time to move on.

She stood up cautiously, tasting the air, and listening for the howl of dogs. With a part of her mind she reached for a different twilight, but just before she slipped into that other place and plain, she sent out a summons. In a blink the Shield was there, waiting on her like any good foot soldier. Immediately its ripples of light became infected by threads of darkness like worms swimming just beneath its rippled skin. Emily knew what the darkness meant: Roland wasn't far behind. She forged a path into beyond and stepped onto it.

Chapter 33: Back to Life

Emily spent weeks slipping in an out of Twilight. After the initial journey, she never went deep or far. She shifted just enough to keep a jump ahead of Roland. She always had a general idea of where he was from the peculiar resonance of the talisman he carried. A barely perceptible shiver inside meant that he was quite far away. A deep hum meant that he was getting too close.

Then there were the worms of darkness in the Shield. Never again was it as clear and full of light as it had been. Its ripples were always shot through with threads of dark, spider-silk thin or broad as her arm, depending on the other talisman's location. The Shield seemed permanently tuned to its brother talisman's call.

Emily never again took the Shield into Twilight with her. She didn't know if she should. Not that it mattered one way or another. She had only to issue a mental summons for it to appear. As time went on, it even took to anticipating her. She would slip into a dusky world of silver-barked trees and emerge in a new part of the Midlands to find it waiting for her.

She took to living like a rootless, half-wild vagabond. She haunted the roads running through the southern Midlands. Travelers were frequent here. Never the woodsman, she depended on them for much of her sustenance. She became quite adept at lifting fruit and vegetables off farmers' carts. She would lurk in the trees and hedges until a likely-looking candidate came along. Then she would scamper after it, leap up on the back, and snatch what she wanted. Most of the time the driver never even saw her. Once or twice she was spotted and pursued. The drivers chased the female thief into the trees only to lose her completely after a few steps.

Snagging meat was a bit more difficult. For that, Emily often resorted to stealing from cottage larders. She never took much, just enough to fill her belly, and occasionally she got lucky and happened upon a loaf of freshly baked bread or a hot pie.

She avoided the Greenwood religiously.

The worst part of the whole business, she soon discovered, was the hygiene. After a prolonged period of living in the woods, she looked and smelled and felt as filthy as a pig in a wallow. Eventually her condition so disgusted her that she stole some extra articles of clothing. The closest she came to getting caught was when she entered a house to steal some soap. The farmer who found her actually got a hold of her before she shattered his stolid mind by half-dragging him into Twilight.

A soapy bath did wonders for the spirit she learned, even if taken in a bitterly cold stream. Still, she never stayed clean or satisfied for long—until Roland finally decided to give up the pursuit. Perhaps he did tire of the chase. More likely, he decided on another method of snaring the Shield Bearer. Whatever his motivations, when the weather began to shift, bringing in much cooler nights, he began moving away from her. He disappeared into the eastern mountains, and she lost her sense of him completely, though the Shield retained its fine threads of darkness. The utter lack of him made her extremely anxious at first. As more time passed without incident, she relaxed and took more careful stock of her situation.

One day when she happened upon an abandoned shepherd's hut in the rocky eastern hills, she decided to make it her home. It needed some patching, and it did little to keep out the evening chill, but at least it prevented most of the rain from finding her head. Now she slipped into Twilight only to steal food or gather information. She soon learned which places along the road afforded her the best opportunities for overhearing gossip. In this way, she discovered that a new conflict had come to the Northlands and that the governor of the Midlands had joined forces with the enemy. The men she overheard speaking of the conflict called it a rebellion and claimed that it was being incited by a man of remarkable strength and charisma with close ties to the Steward. To hear the Midlanders tell it, fully half the lords and districts of the Northland had gone over to him. Whatever their governor's views, the citizens of the Midlands obviously found the rebellion a deeply unsettling event, all the more so because it was unprecedented. Not once in the nearly two-thousand year rule of the stewards had that noble House been divided against itself.

Even after hearing this, Emily made every effort to avoid thinking about Scryos. She had two good reasons to keep him out of her mind. First, it only made her sick with rage to contemplate his connection to her and to know how easily he had escaped accountability. Second, she never thought of Scryos without being reminded of Alsandyr. That two men could resemble each other so strikingly and operate so differently turned her stomach. For the first time she reflected on her initial distrust of Alsandyr and wondered if it was rooted in those early, half-erased memories of the man who claimed to be her father. But she dared not think on this question for long. There was a gaping hole inside her where love and life had once resided which threatened to consume the little meaning that remained.

Occasionally, as the days passed and she settled into a routine of scrounging food and fixing up her makeshift house, she thought of Colin and her aunt, or she wondered about Beth and Blayne. But all of these thoughts brought her pain. She had failed them all in one way or another. And deep down inside she knew she was failing them again. She had only to look at the Shield to be reminded that there was a world of people waiting to be served by one strong enough to wield it as it should be wielded.

Perhaps that was why she tended to dream of the shining city. In her dreams, she heard a layered voice saying, "Work faithfully, and the day may come soon."

Dream or no dream, Emily would have remained hidden in the woods indefinitely if one day she hadn't looked up from picking through a sack of apples to find Faryn standing a few yards away.

He and his pony had come upon her so stealthily that she had not heard a whisper of their passing.

Her first instinct was to reach for Twilight. But a pained expression wrinkled Faryn's face. He raised a hand. "Please," he said. "It has taken me weeks to find you."

Emily relaxed ever so slightly. "Did Roland send you?"

Faryn drew a boot through the grass. "No."

"Where is he?"

"Your guess is as good as mine."

"You have not seen him?"

"Not since the night he appeared before the tree and took his staff from Colin's hand."

Emily frowned, thinking. "Very well. I'm stumped. Why are you here?"

"I came to bring you this. May I?" He took a few cautious steps closer and held out a folded piece of paper to her.

Emily rose just as cautiously and reached for it.

Looking at the address written across it, she had to laugh. "You mean to tell me that the seventh warder has been reduced to a letter carrier!"

Faryn's light, unreadable eyes glared into her own. Then a corner of his mouth twitched.

They both laughed this time, and before long Emily was passing him an apple and encouraging him to tell her all about his journey round the southeastern Midlands looking for her. She was surprised to find herself hungry for human company and human talk.

"What made you think that I was in this area?"

"The Lord Warder told me where I might find you."

"He can feel me way over here?"

"You are a ward of our house, remember? That gives him a certain connection to you. Then there are all those rumors among the people hereabouts."

"Rumors?"

"Yes. About a mysterious apparition of the forest, who haunts the roadways stealing men's souls—and apples. Lots of apples."

Emily threw her core at him. He tilted his head, smooth as ever, to let it fly past. Then he gestured at the letter lying on the ground near her. "Are you going to open it?"

Emily glanced down at the wrinkled paper. "I'm afraid to," she admitted. "I hate to think of what he has to say to me. He did me a huge favor. And I returned it by handing him to Roland and misplacing the woman he loves. Vyara's lost to him now."

Faryn's light eyes flashed. "You cannot blame yourself. Not even the Steward himself was prepared for what Scryos did."

Emily gave him a measuring look. "Are things as bad as I hear tell?"

"Worse," said Faryn bluntly. "Both Numyn and the capital city are under pressure from Scryos' supporters. House Warder may have to intervene."

"You will go to war!"

"It is likely, yes. And we will need all the aid we can muster. We cannot allow Dyre to get his hands on the third talisman."

"The third talisman! Has it also appeared in the lands of men?"

"It never left. The third talisman has been in the custody of the seers for as long the Stewards have existed, though very few people have ever seen it. It is what gives the Steward his extraordinary sight, far above and beyond the considerable skills of the other members of his house."

Emily looked at the letter she held, and then back at Faryn. "So what's the real reason why you are here?"

"To bring you back to a place of relative safety."

"No!"

"Relax, Shield Bearer. I have no intentions of forcing you. I couldn't if I tried. You've grown beyond me I'm afraid. I only want you to know that we, I, fear for your safety and the safety of all the houses. As the bearer of the Shield you figure heavily in many futures."

"And what of the second talisman? Why aren't you trying to round that up? Or does Roland command too much respect and fear?"

"Those are questions you should ask the Lord Warder when you see him. Why don't you open your letter?"

Emily was on the verge of ordering him to leave. Not because she wanted him to. Now that he had found her, she realized how much she had missed him and his odd ways, how worried she had been about what might have befallen him. She jammed her thumb under the flap of the letter instead.

Her eyes flew over the words written there.

Emily, I am with the warders. I need to see you. I'm worried about you. Please come.
Colin.

It was the one summons she simply couldn't resist. An hour later she was ready to ride, and Faryn was pulling her up on his pony's back.

They spent three days riding through rolling hills. It was good to have a warder for company. Faryn managed to make camping in the woods feel comfortable and look easy. There was always a warm fire and hot food.

446

On the fourth day, Faryn turned the pony's head toward the mountains.

"What are you doing?" asked Emily, seized by a sudden suspicion.

"Taking the trail to Hidden Pass."

"Why aren't we going to your camp near Cyr?" Her tone was shrill, her body tense.

"That place is no longer secure. I'm taking you to the Settlement instead."

"What's that?"

"My home."

"You have a home?"

Faryn actually sighed. "Are you trying to be insulting?"

"I just asked a simple question."

"You have asked four questions. I have answered three of them. How about giving me and your mouth a rest?"

Emily shut her mouth, but kept her guard up. She had felt Roland cross over the eastern mountains too.

The pass was narrow and high and cold. It offered some shelter from the wind, but little else.

Eventually they rounded the easternmost peaks and hit a steep downward sloping trail. Coming out from behind a massive slab of sheer rock, Emily was afforded her first ever look at the dawn side of the mountains and the great eastern plain. Faryn, hearing her gasp and feeling her hands tighten against his sides, obligingly reined in his pony.

"Impressive, isn't it?" he prompted after a while.

"Yes. I feel like I can see forever," she breathed. Then she shook herself. "Is the Settlement far from here?"

"A few more days."

Emily spent most of those days riding with her head turned to look out over the plain. She could not explain her fascination. She only knew that the vast distances of it drew her the way the openness of the desert had, only with ten times more allure. Even when they made camp within the tree line, she usually found her way to the place that gave her the longest and best view.

They entered the Settlement without her even realizing it. They came down out of the trees onto a long sloping mountainside that terminated in minor peaks like the horns of a gigantic buried bull. The great eastern plain shone like the promise of gold between them. The arms of the forest to either side were emerald green. The long meadow between rolled in wind-stirred waves of chartreuse spangled blue and yellow. A strange, shifty, hard-to-define atmosphere hung over the entire landscape. Almost she felt as if she had wandered into the formlessness of a dream.

"It's beautiful," she said.

"Yes." They cantered into the trees. Emily heard water running in the distance. Soon they crossed a fast-running, foaming stream spanned by a low bridge of mossy stone. Then they skirted a string of ponds like green glass beads, one spilling into the other. They halted before a ferny wall of stone. A woman in a sand-colored tunic and pants waited for them. Her hair was completely white, but her tanned skin was only lightly lined, and her lean body appeared hale and strong

Faryn helped Emily slide to the ground, then dismounted lightly. He nodded his head. "First Healer."

"Faryn. You bring me the Shield Bearer."

"Yes. Emily, this is Zamyra, the head of our healers."

Emily bobbed her own head in acknowledgment.

Zamyra slid forward in the seamless, perfectly balanced way of warders. "I see your aunt in you."

"You knew Millicynt?"

"I taught her for some years."

"I remember now. Master Lyr told me that she had studied among you."

"Yes. And now we welcome another generation."

"I do not have Millicynt's gift of healing, I'm afraid."

Zamyra raised one white brow. "Do you not?"

Emily gave her a wry smile. "No."

Zamyra glanced at Faryn. "The Lord Warder wishes to speak with you," she said to him, then gestured for Emily to accompany her. As they moved down the track, she picked up the conversation as lightly as she moved. "Healing is a complex process that encompasses many disciplines and many dimensions. There are those who mend bodies and those who mend spirits. Both gifts are important. A person's health resides as much in spirit as in body."

Emily shrugged. "I can't take credit for either. I tend to cause disruption wherever I go."

"That too can be integral to healing."

Emily stared at her in surprise.

Zamyra smiled. "Sometimes we must break bones and cut flesh to bring about healing of the body. Why should we not break spirits as well, if the breaking produces a healthier, stronger spirit? The spirit can stand quite a bit of disruption. It is ten times more resilient than the body."

Emily looked down at the path sliding away beneath their feet. "That's an interesting way to think of it."

They passed into a cavern that proved to be a long tunnel leading to a honeycomb of other caverns. Eventually they emerged into a secluded canyon surrounded by sheer mountain walls. Large tents lined the canyon walls. Most had their front walls rolled up to reveal empty interiors. Near one stood a group of warders. One of them was speaking. He was tall and crowned with hair the color of rust.

"Your friend," Zamyra said, "is remarkably gifted in both the physical and spiritual aspects of healing."

Emily stopped walking. Colin turned his head as if to respond to one of the warders near him and saw her. He took several long deliberate strides away from the others, then stopped and stood still, waiting for her.

Emily began walking again and met him in the middle.

He gave her a half smile. "Where have you been this time?" he asked calmly.

Emily wrinkled her nose. "Hiding in the woods, I'm afraid."

"The world appears to be ending, and you hide in the woods. What a terribly brave and noble thing to do." He said it so good-naturedly that she couldn't take offense.

She snorted a laugh instead. "Isn't it though? I can't imagine what the Shield was thinking when it picked me for its bearer. The wisdom of these magic talismans is clearly overrated."

It was Colin's turn to laugh. He shook auburn hair back from his face. "How about we make ourselves scarce for a while? It's a really easy thing to do hereabouts. These warders love their privacy."

She turned to fall in beside him. "If they can spare you, I'd like nothing better."

Near the lower end of the long meadow, they found a large rock. Together they sat, knees hunched up to their chests, looking out through the twin peaks framing the gateway to the East. They spoke desultorily of things they had experienced over the years, together and apart. Their talk turned briefly to the night Sun City fell. Both sensed that they were taking care to avoid the most wrenching subjects. There were things they could not tell and things they would not tell. *We're like two old soldiers,* thought Emily, *considerate of one another's aches and pains, knowing all too well where the irreparable damage lies.*

It was Colin who first dared to touch one of those broken places, but then he had always been the more direct of the two of them.

"Is it true what they say about Vyara?"

Emily bowed her head. "She had no choice in the matter, Colin. Janeryc sold her into a marriage she didn't want. She longed to be with you." Almost immediately she regretted the last statement. Judging from Colin's rigid features, the way the muscles along his jaw moved, he hardly needed the reminder. It certainly wouldn't ease his pain.

He checked his emotions quickly however. "At least she's alive. She got out of the city before the end. We can thank the Steward's despicable son for that!"

Emily's throat and chest began to burn. She tasted acid and bitter gall. "If I ever see him again, I'll thank him for both of us – with one of Illyria's daggers through his heart. He took them from me, you know."

She didn't see the solemn expression of concern Colin directed at the side of her face. "He took a lot from both of us," he said gently.

Emily rose from the rock. "That doesn't matter now."

Colin caught her hand, pulled her back down to the rock. "I've heard the warders say that he almost killed you trying to strip you of your power."

Emily's mouth quirked in a nasty little smile. "Yes. Well, that's one part of his plan that went awry. I hope he lives to regret it with every ounce of his being."

"I'm sure he already does. Now you have even more power."

"I guess. In the end, I shattered his damned stone easily enough. Pity he waited so long to try to take the power from me. A few months earlier and he might have prevented me from aiding Roland."

Colin studied his knees. "Shade," he said.

Emily's smaller hand came to rest on one of his kneecaps. "I understand if you hate me for my part in releasing him," she said. The hand squeezed. "Believe me. I hate myself for it."

Colin's head snapped up. He searched her bitter expression. "Don't," he ordered. "Don't do that to yourself, or to me. Things happened that night, Emily, that had to happen, that had been building for a thousand years. You and I were only a part of it."

"He kept you from being there for Vyara."

Colin looked torn between his pain and hers. He opened his mouth to speak, then closed it again, shaking his head slowly. "Emily, there are things I wish I could tell you, but—"

Feeling her throat beginning to close painfully, Emily forestalled him. She pressed a hand to his mouth, then stood. "Forgive me, Colin. You are right. There are things that talk can't solve. That part of the story is over. We have to move on. You seem to have found a way.

450

It's time I learned to do the same." She gave him a brave smile and wandered away.

Thereafter, Emily saw relatively little of Colin. He spent most of his time with the healers learning new tricks of the trade. He carried himself with a new gravity and confidence too, a maturation that suited him. He had the respect of the warders as well. He even seemed to make friends among them, if one could ever really count a warder a friend. Sometimes Emily wished for his easy and open manner.

Left largely to her own devices, she spent much of her time prowling the Settlement and looking out at the plain. Almost she expected to see it send her a sign. But all she ever saw were cloud shadows drifting across it.

She was never called before the Lord Warder. He was preparing for war.

The people she encountered most frequently were Faryn and Callyn. That Faryn should make an effort to keep her company did not surprise her. Hadn't the Lord Warder himself appointed him her watcher and guardian? Hadn't he at one time intended the young warder to be something more?

The mystery of Callyn defied ready explanation. The tawny-haired woman clearly disliked Emily as much as ever. She took no pleasure in Emily's company. More often than not they ended up in petty verbal squabbles uncomplimentary to both. Still, Callyn insisted on seeking Emily out, though Emily never made any effort to return the dubious compliment. She wouldn't have known how to find the female warder in the mazy, shifty confines of the Settlement if she had wanted to. Nonetheless, hardly a day went by when Callyn didn't appear. At least she treated Emily with less overt aggression. Now her manner was almost meditatively ungracious, as if she were bent on watching Emily to see what she could learn.

Once Emily adjusted to the uneasy atmosphere enough to realize that she was being almost continually watched, she thought she had the answer. The realization that someone of power was monitoring her with the mind's touch came to her one day when she was alone and sitting on the big rock in the meadow. Watching the play of light over the plain had put her in a peaceful, hazy frame of mind. She seemed almost to float free from her body, light as thistledown borne up by the mountains' breezes.

Then she felt the watcher—a cool, predatory gaze lingering on her back.

Zip, her consciousness contracted. She returned entirely to her body and felt the hairs rise on her neck. So, she thought, even when I'm alone, I'm not really alone. The Lord Warder is preoccupied, but not as indifferent to my presence as he appears to be.

This, she concluded, was the obvious explanation for why Faryn and especially Callyn came around so often. They had been set on her like the Lord Warder's hounds. But they would not actively interfere unless she tried to stray from the fold.

She tested the theory the next day by walking down the meadow all the way to the great horns of the gate. This close, they looked like the smaller mountains they were. She loitered in their great shadows but a moment, feeling the watcher's gaze deepen to an almost tangible pressure, and then she stepped into the gate itself.

Out from the shadows of the rock slipped a man she had never seen before. His hair was coal black, his eyes bright blue. He was all warder in dress and bearing.

"Shield Bearer," he said with a bow.

"Yes," she answered in a startled little voice.

"You should turn back now. The gate is no place for a guest in these uneasy times."

Emily lifted her chin. The blue eyes held hers without compromise. Resentfully she turned back, feeling as she did so the flickering awareness of the watcher skipping over her like a laugh. She made other attempts. Some of these were forestalled by the shifty nature of the Settlement itself, which seemed to want to turn her steps like a rider with a headstrong horse. Once or twice she must have made it to another border, for one or more warders stepped out of nowhere to block her path and send her back the way she had come. Every time the watcher's satisfaction raised an unscratchable itch in her skin.

The more she tried, the more intensely she felt the watcher's presence. It made her tingle as if she had a rash. She eventually took to lurking close to places where warders could routinely be seen, including the houses of healing, just to get some relief. At least in these places the watcher eased up the scrutiny.

In this way she discovered the warder children. Like other children they played, performed chores, and went to school. Unlike other children they were parented by the entire community and deadly by the age of five. This was brought home to her the day she saw a six-year-old boy coming down out of the mountains carrying the huge gray carcass of a wolf. Callyn was with her that day. The female warder saw the little one toiling toward them and went to meet him. The little boy dropped the head of the animal at Callyn's feet. Callyn squatted down and stroked the furry mound. "Ah, how sad," she said.

"Yes," said the little boy. "I tried to warn him to stay away from the sheep, but he wouldn't listen"

"Then you had to kill him," agreed Callyn. "He would teach his pack to hunt our sheep, and more wolves, his brothers and sisters, would die."

She stood and let the little one continue on his way, lugging the wolf homeward.

"That little boy killed that wolf all by himself," breathed Emily.

All Callyn's sympathy evaporated. Her mouth thinned with disgust. "Of course," she snapped. "He's a child of warders not a silly woman from the Midlands."

Emily came to enjoy spending time among the children, and they accepted her readily enough. She made them laugh with her ignorance of their ways and her clumsiness. They delighted in inducing her to join their games just to see how silly she looked trying to compete with them. Emily didn't mind. Their laughter lightened the heavy places inside her, and Colin occasionally joined in as well.

Finally, the day came when she uncovered the heart of Callyn's mystery. It happened quite inadvertently.

Faryn was entertaining Emily by introducing her to a very simple game entitled "Snatch the Stone." He said it taught warder children how to think patiently and creatively while honing their skills and reflexes. The rules of the game were very simple. A stone was placed on the ground between two or more people. The person who snatched the stone first won. Contestants were allowed to use almost any means available to them to claim the stone or to prevent another person from grasping it as long as they relied only on their upper body and wits. Blows, arm twisting, and head butts as well as lies and distractions were perfectly legal.

After the first few illustrative bouts, Faryn basically quit trying for the stone. It was obvious to both of them that he could snatch it at any time he chose without even thinking about it. So the game disintegrated into an exercise in which Emily tested every method she could devise of drawing Faryn's attention away from the stone long enough to get a finger on it.

She'd already been through every version of "Lookout behind you!" and "What's that?" she could think of. Now she sat chin in hand, lower lip protruding as she blew an annoying strand of hair off her forehead.

Faryn was lying on his side propped up on one arm. He looked half asleep. Suddenly, Emily had a rather wicked idea.

She sat up a little straighter and leaned in as if to get a closer look at his face. "Come here," she said.

"Why?" asked Faryn, acting for all the world as if his mind were a million leagues away.

"There's still dust on your face."

"Because you kicked it at me. Which is illegal, as I told you."

"Well, let me make up for that breach of the rules by removing the rest, before it gets in your eye. Here."

He pressed himself up to comply.

Emily ran her thumb across his cheek as if to remove the dust and then she leaned in and kissed him, snatching the stone.

As she pulled back, she clenched her fist tightly to reassure herself the stone was actually there. Then she crowed her triumph.

Faryn's eyes had opened a little wider. A smile played about his mouth.

"Why are you smiling?" Emily demanded. She laughed and shook her clenched fist in his face. "I have the stone!" she announced.

"Are you sure?"

"Of course I'm . . ." she stopped, scowled, and opened her fist. There was a stone there all right. It just wasn't the right one."

"You wretch! You switched them on me! I thought you said that was illegal."

"It is. But I didn't want you to feel you had kissed me for nothing. You have been working so hard."

Emily dropped the stone. "I hope your pony bites you!" she said.

"He won't. But you should be careful about kissing warders."

"Why? Do they normally lop people's head off for it."

"No. But they might kiss you back."

And he did.

Caught completely off guard, Emily could hardly digest what was happening. But that didn't stop the kiss from sinking in and turning her bones to water.

She opened her eyes to find Faryn's light, unreadable gaze on her. She blinked, remembered to breathe.

"We are masters of the body, Emily. It is our domain, as the heart is yours. Remember that the next time you kiss one of us."

And then he was gone, leaving Emily to begin sorting through the jumble of her thoughts.

"Why don't you just mate with him and get it over with?" came a bitter voice from behind her.

Emily jumped and half spun around to find Callyn's tawny cat eyes on her. Her mental shields shot up crackling. "I have no intention . . ."

"Don't be a fool, Emily!" spat Callyn. She came to where Emily sat and actually flopped down on the ground next to her. Emily struggled with a different sort of surprise. To her knowledge, Callyn had never before called her by name.

"Why are you so nasty to me, Callyn?" she demanded.

"Because you can be so blind and stupid. You are going to sleep with one of the men of Warder House, you know. Why else do you think you were brought here? We are about to go to war, with a sizable portion of Steward House no less. We need all the power we can get. And we can get quite a lot from you once you are properly joined to this house. A joining was always the plan. Even you know that much."

"Joining," murmured Emily. She licked her lips, and her shoulders began to shake with a barely suppressed laugh. "Wrong again, Callyn. I'm not a fool. I'm a complete imbecile."

When she calmed down, she loosed a long cynical breath. "Who?" she asked, pinning the warder with glittering eyes.

Even Callyn had to squirm beneath the power in that gaze. "How should I know?" she said moodily. "For my part, I hope it's Faryn. You'd enjoy it immensely I assure you, and he needs to get you out of his system once and for all. Maybe then he—" Callyn stopped in mid sentence and moved as if to rise and leave.

Emily's eyes had narrowed. "Maybe he what?"

"Nothing."

But Emily's lips were spreading in a slow smile. "I thought warders didn't need to be exclusive."

"What do you mean?"

"I thought they didn't get jealous. You know, share the wealth and all that."

Callyn bristled. "This isn't about sex, you stupid woman. Faryn can help himself to you or anyone else as he likes. It means less than nothing to me."

"I guess you are right. This isn't about sex. It's about love. The heart, you know, plays by different rules than the body. You might not care who Faryn sleeps with, but you care very much who he loves."

"Nonsense."

"You are in love with Faryn."

At that point, Callyn did the most surprising thing of all. Shoulders slumping, she gave up the fight. "So now we know that we are both fools," she said.

Emily actually found herself feeling sympathy for the woman. "Why don't you tell him?"

"He would never understand."

"You won't know until you try."

The warder rose. She looked almost tired. "Would you, Shield Bearer, tell a man you loved him if you weren't certain that he loved you?"

Emily started to lie, then told herself not to bother. Her history spoke for itself. "Never."

Callyn gave her a genuine smile. "Then maybe we have something in common after all."

The warder turned to walk away. "Callyn?"

"Yes, Emily."

"Just so you know. There are times now when I wish with all my heart that I had said 'I love you.'"

Emily returned to the tent in which she slept in a pensive, even depressed, mood. She found Zamyra waiting for her. "Colin tells me that you have begun complaining of restless nights."

"Yes, well, I'm still getting used to things and all."

"Our lands can be disorienting to outsiders."

"Well, that's me obviously. The outsider."

"Try drinking this before you sleep. It should help." In a flutter of tent flap and without another word of explanation, Zamyra ducked out of the tent and departed. Emily was left holding what looked like a vial of clear water. She gave the Shield a long conspiratorial look. "Now what do you suppose was that about?"

The Shield answered her with the same old invincibly cryptic rippling.

She had no intention of drinking Zamyra's concoction. She'd been alerted to House Warder's plan. If they wanted to join her to a member of their house, they had better come and present their request formally, like good little warrior magicians.

She ate well, played with the children, and went to bed with the Shield leaning against her left side. The sky had been overcast much of the day, and toward evening it had taken on an ominous greenish light. To top it off, the shiver that she associated with the second talisman had returned, although the Shield's appearance did not change.

456

Between the niggling in her gut and the itch caused by the watcher's scrutiny, she came dangerously close to kicking something.

She must have slept for a while. When she awoke, moonlight was sketching riddling shadows on the roof of the tent. She pushed herself up on her elbows and felt the air quivering like a live thing. She did not need to see the Shield to know that bands of darkness like long fingers were snaking across it. Her eyes found the door to her tent. The shadows on it shifted in an unfelt wind, pulling back to reveal the silhouette of a head wearing a broad-brimmed hat.

The old anger came surging back.

"Come on then, Roland," she sang out softly. "Let's see what you've got!"

The shadowy head moved closer to the gap. Emily tensed. Then it sank down and disappeared.

Emily was on her feet and sticking her head out of the tent door. She could make out nothing but the trunks of trees in the fitful moonlit darkness ahead of her. A cloud crossed the moon. The darkness mellowed and uncovered a deeper man-shaped darkness disappearing into the trees.

Fed up with hiding and waiting and warders, spoiling for a fight, Emily took off after it. It skimmed on ahead of her ducking in and out of shadows, sliding in and around the dark trunks of trees.

She picked up her pace, but she couldn't close the gap. "My, how times have changed," she panted under her breath as she trotted faster. "First the hunter, now the hunted. Why are you running, Roland? Don't you *want* to talk to me?"

So intent was she on the pursuit that she failed to notice the intoxicating thickening of magic in the air. She had followed the shadow down slope in the direction of the great gates, only to watch it dart sideways and deeper into the trees. She veered after it and came upon a pair of irregular stone steps laid into a slope of rising ground.

There was no sign of anyone ahead. The moon peeked out from behind a cloud, laying a dusting of silver over the stones. Emily put her right foot to the first step then paused and turned to look behind her. Nothing but trees. Slowly she climbed the steps, brushing her way past the sticky arms of thick-needled conifers. Her passage filled the air with a clean, resinous scent.

At the top she found herself strides away from a clearing dripping with moonlight. Overhead the full moon had freed itself of its attendant clouds. Now it swam in a clear pool of stars. It beamed down into the oval-shaped clearing like the white pupil of a great dark eye.

Emily stood uneasily at the clearing's margin. Instinct told her to be cautious, but no matter how she strained her eyes, she picked out only the knotty, tangled darkness of trunks and branches and leaves. Roland was not here. In fact she had lost altogether the quivering associated with him. He had proved as elusive as his reputation. But the air of the clearing hung still and pellucid. It smelled frosty green, full of peace and promise.

The first step was the hardest. After that the moonlight seemed to seep into her bones and waft her toward the mound at the center of the clearing. It was a great flat rock. With her fingers she explored the textured surface of it, and the great crack that had split it in half. She ran the fingertips of either hand down the edges of it as if working a spell that might marry the severed halves. That was when she heard the voices.

Her head shot up. Her glittering eyes darted and swooped into the darkness beneath the trees. The clearing looked empty, yet the voices went on speaking, and they came from all sides, men's and women's voices. They whispered to each other, overlapping like waves. The soft roar they engendered might have been the crashing of the sea or the sound trees make rustling in high wind, except there was no sea or wind and these whispers were full of words.

"The Shield Bearer."

"So young."

"A woman."

"Full of anger."

"Full of loss."

"Full of heart."

"Last of the line."

"Marked by the Tellers as well."

"A fitting vessel."

"Strong enough to bear the binding."

"Strong enough to bear."

"Yessss."

Emily pressed her hands to her ears. "Stop!" she cried, but her voice fell small and faint on her own ears. The world roared to the rushing sound of a thousand voices.

The voices ceased.

Moonlight streamed into the tree shadows. It teased out new shapes from the tangled weave of leaf and branch and bark—a fold of cloth, a rounded arm, a lean hand, a hollow cheek . . . and eyes, many, many pairs of gleaming, knowing eyes. The eyes sank into her like teeth and held her bound.

Emily tried to break free. She slid one foot away from the rock, then followed it with the other.

A sudden lunging darkness brought her head round so that she looked beyond the end of the great rock and into a much wider gap in the great ring of trees. Something was congealing in that darkness and twisting itself into a familiar shape. Emily saw the broad brim of a hat cut through the shadows. Beneath the brim, eyes glowed hot and gold.

The moon was swallowed up by bubbling dark clouds. Heaven's lights went out. The air erupted in a silent roar. An invisible, intangible wind howled straight through the core of her. Emily leapt away from the rock.

Straight into the waiting hands of another.

She tried to yank herself out of those hands, but she was eaten up with alien magic and shaking so hard she could hardly stand. The hands held her up. The hands reeled her in. Just their touch sent shivers of desire running up her back.

She wanted to scream out her fury, but all the power of Warder House was pressing down on her, crushing her voice, suffocating her willpower.

Roland, you daemon bastard, she thought. *Not here. Not now. Not like this. How dare you treat me like fruit for your warders to pluck and eat as they choose!*

The problem was she wasn't just arguing with Roland now. She was arguing with all the ancient might of his house, and the considerable physical presence of the man chosen to represent it. His arms held her and his lips were at her neck, her ear, her mouth. They made her want more, so much more.

Hadn't Faryn warned her? All too late. As she opened her mouth to her lover's lingering kiss, her resolve dissolved and her body caught fire. She heard Faryn's words ring mockingly in her mind's ear. "We are masters of the body, Emily. Remember that when next you kiss one of us."

She remembered. After this night she would never be able to forget it.

Emily opened woolly eyes. She blinked once, twice, three times. The world was soft green and gray. Relief. She was in her tent. She sat up slowly, trying to shake off the dream and saw Roland standing right in front of her. He wore a maddening half smile, and his golden eyes were cold as a cat's. "There," he said, "that wasn't so bad. I believe you quite enjoyed yourself."

She opened her mouth to scream—

And woke up for real. No reassuring tent. No rush of relief. No happy dismissal of a night's fantasy. But no Roland either.

She lay on thick green grass clutching blue fabric to her thudding heart. The sky overhead was a lighter blue. Sunlight kissed the tops of the trees. The air was cool, but she did not feel cold.

She sat up and discovered that she was stark naked beneath the dark blue robe covering her. She sat near the edge of the same clearing she had visited in the night.

She called on her outrage. She called on her shields adamant. She sent a sharp command to the Shield Light. She tried to whip herself into a frenzy of anger.

She recollected the night's events and flushed with desire instead.

Even the Shield didn't take her seriously. For the first time ever, it ignored her call.

Didn't it know that she had been taken against her will?

Trouble was, she didn't feel taken. Quite the opposite. She felt well and whole and ready for anything. Just remembering the night's sensations filled her with shivers of delight. He was good, that warder. Damn good. If she ever discovered who he was she'd scratch his eyes out but good, provided she didn't agree to bed him again first.

So now there was only the pretense of shame to deal with. The awkward act of getting up, walking out of this thrice-cursed clearing, and pretending to everyone who knew damn well otherwise that nothing whatsoever had happened.

Good grief, Emily! What would the people of Greenwood village say if they could see you now?

She moved to wrap the robe around herself and uncovered her rumpled garments. She dressed quickly, and then she climbed to her feet. As she moved to step over the discarded robe, her imagination was caught by the color of it. It glowed a deep but unbelievably brilliant blue against the green grass. It reminded her of Lyr's blue, of Beth's eyes, of the desert sky at the very edge of night. Most of all it reminded her of the strange blue flowers that grew on the very edge of Twilight. Its irrepressible color seeped into her and opened her inner eye. She looked inside and discovered that all the bleakness of heartache was gone, along with the terrible scorching anger it had fueled. Zamyra had been right. Body and spirit were bound up together. Heal one and you help to heal the other.

Feeling more buoyant than she had in months, she turned to bid the clearing farewell—

And saw that she was not alone after all.

What does a person do when the world suddenly decides to invert itself? When up becomes down, black becomes white, and wrong takes on all the virtues of right? What is the answer to the lie that becomes truth, the truth that becomes lie?

Nothing. One can only wait for the world to right itself again. Only, if Emily could have had any wish granted to her, any wish at all, it would have been for the world to stay just as topsy-turvy as it had become in that moment. For this reason she did not move, she did not blink, she did not breathe. She willed even her heart to stop beating. She could not risk shifting the world back to the way it had been.

He looked at her out of night-dark eyes and tapped one booted heel against the stone. His soft dark curls were tousled. His shirt was gleaming white. A stream of water gushed past his hand, trickling to the stones below. The moss at his feet was emerald green and glistening.

She must have fainted. Either that or the earth righted itself in one awful, wrenching moment.

"Emily? Emily?"

"What?" she answered irritably. Couldn't he see that she was busy trying to figure out which direction was currently up? Tedious business that. Almost as tedious as his constant prodding—go here, read this, try that.

She lay propped against something lumpy and warm. She opened her eyes and saw him looking down at her. She could see a white line like a scar at his throat.

"I love you," she said. The words came straight out of her soul, bypassing her will, her shields, her prickly personality, everything.

"Really?"

"I've said it once. I'll not say it again. You can forget it if you like."

The lumpiness shifted. He was kissing her, a soul-jarring, mind-stirring, body-burning kiss.

Damn, he really is that good, she thought.

"Do you know how long I've waited to hear you say that?" he whispered into her ear. Then the lingering currents of his kiss dredged up another thought.

She pushed at his chest as his mouth moved to her neck. "You!"

"Hmm?"

"Last night, that was you!"

A startled black eye skewered her. "Of course it was me. What did you expect?"

She wriggled free, found her feet. She wanted to find a way out, but the trees were all around, hemming her in. "What did I expect?" she repeated. Her eyes beseeched the trees for an answer. Her shoulders slumped.

Strong hands gripped her elbows. His voice darkened. "Perhaps I should ask whom did you expect?

The whole clearing darkened too. It wasn't as if the illumination dropped. No cloud dampened the sunlight. Rather the whole clearing shifted to give her a glimpse of its darker underpinnings. The sky, the trees, the grass—all were edged with blazing dark.

She shut her eyes. "You are impossible," she said.

He leaned in closer, laughing softly. "Is that all? You aren't exactly easy, you know."

She turned around, steeling herself against the leap of heart that came with really seeing him. "Don't deliberately misunderstand me." She paused, trying to contain a sudden terrible surge of bone-crushing emotion. "You are supposed to be dead." She struck her chest with a fist. "Do you realize that I felt you die?" Her voice dropped into a forlorn little wail. " I felt you die!"

"Yes," he answered, all solemnity for a change.

"Then . . . how?"

He averted his gaze, but not before she saw the outlines of a horrible dark thing rearing up in them. "Let us say, I gave Roland what he wanted. And he gave me something in return."

"Your life," she breathed.

"In a manner of speaking."

"In a manner . . . What is that supposed to mean? Are you really here or not? Oh Tellers, is this one of Roland's tricks? If I turn my back for a moment, will I turn around again to find you dissolved into mist?"

He crushed her questions against his chest. She smelled wood smoke and leather and something utterly intoxicating. "I'm here," he said into her hair. "I'm really here."

He held her for a long time. But eventually she felt his body tense. She tensed too. "What is it?" she whispered.

His hands swept through her hair, turning her face up to his. His eyes were like deep wells. "I have to go."

"What? No!"

He smiled his old mocking smile. "Don't be such a doubter, Emily. I'll see you soon. There's someone waiting for you at the bottom of the steps."

He stepped away, sliding through her grasping hands, and disappeared into the shadow-filled gap in the trees.

With all that had happened, she had to work hard on the stone steps to convince herself that she wasn't descending from a cloud of dream. More than once she fought the urge to look back.

At the bottom of the descent she came face-to-face with the imposing black-haired warder who had turned her away from the gate.

He bowed his head to her.

Completely taken aback Emily mumbled an awkward, "Good morning," and straightened her shoulders.

"Lady," he said. "Shall I escort you back to your tent?"

"I can find my way," she returned.

"It would be better if I escorted you."

"Why? Am I a prisoner?"

The idea seemed to shock him, although anyone not intimately familiar with the ways of warders would have missed the slight tensing of facial muscles that signaled it. "The area near the clearing can be misleading and difficult to navigate. Without guidance, you would get lost."

She had to clench her teeth to keep from retorting, "I found my way last night, didn't I?" Remembering Roland's shade and everything that came afterward, she thought the better of saying anything.

Her tent was exactly as she had left it. Zamyra's vial lay on the ground next to her cast-off blanket. The Shield rippled serenely at her.

She glared at it. "I hope you are happy with yourself," she said.

She tried to throw herself into the activities that normally filled her day. But she felt restless and jumpy as a cat in heat. Where was he? What was he doing? Why had he left so suddenly? Did the master of Warder House call him away? Emily knew that every gift of power must be repaid. She had learned that lesson well, but she could not imagine how Al would ever repay Roland's gift of life. What is the price of life but life? That made her think of the Lord Warder, and then a new worry began to gnaw at her brain.

By afternoon, she had given up trying to bat away the thoughts circling and circling like buzzards in her mind. She retreated to the meadow rock.

When Colin found her, she was kicking it. He shook his head and crossed his arms. "Has that rock done something to you?"

Emily jumped like a startled deer. "Tellers! Colin, you scared me!"

He gave her an odd look. "Watching you beating up on that rock, I'm thinking that I'm the one who should feel scared. You could decide to beat up on me after all, and I'm a lot softer."

"I'm sorry. I'm just irritable."

"In that case, thank the Tellers you aren't angry."

She had to smile at that. He came and stood next to her. "You know it might help if you got some real rest. How did you sleep last night?"

She stared at him out of wide eyes. "Fine!" she snapped.

"Really?"

She tried to feign nonchalance. "Absolutely."

"Even without this?" He held up Zamyra's vial and wagged it side to side like a warning finger.

"Hey! You aren't supposed to go digging in my tent." She snatched at the vial.

Colin only held it up out of reach. "I wasn't digging. I was looking for you, and I stepped on this." He went all serious and earnest. "Look, Emily, tonight you need to drink it. When I told Zamyra about your trouble sleeping, she seemed quite concerned. She said this place can have an odd effect on people, especially people with power. She seemed to think that you are having a sort of reaction that could result in more serious symptoms. She gave you this potion to keep it from worsening."

Emily stopped kicking the rock. She felt cold inside. "What sorts of serious symptoms?"

"Oh, I don't know."

"Hallucinations?"

"I guess it's possible. Are you trying to tell me that you are seeing things?"

She uttered a weak little laugh. "Of course not." She felt sick.

The stomach-churning feeling didn't go away, though Colin hung around for a long time, as if he sensed how deeply troubled she was.

Along about dusk, they said farewell. She made her slow, meandering way back to her tent, and there he was, sitting up against a tree in all his dark-haired handsome glory. His long legs were stretched out and crossed in front of him. He had stuck a stem of grass between his teeth.

When her heart finished turning over, she walked up to him and placed her hands on her hips "You," she said earnestly, "are driving me insane." She looked about, saw no one but themselves, and threw her hands up. "Where are the witnesses when you need them?"

"Still the doubter, I see. Come, sit."

"Only if you tell me where you went and what you've been doing all day."

"My job."

"What job does a seer have in the land of warders?"

"Talking to warders, and seers for that matter."

She sat down. "There are other seers around here?"

"A pair of the Steward's representatives made their way here just today."

"To speak to the Lord Warder?"

His eyes had gone even blacker. They seemed to drink in the light. "Yes."

She wanted to ask about the war, but her own particular fears pushed it aside. "Did you speak to the Lord Warder?"

"Why?"

"I guess I'm just curious about what he's thinking. After last night and all."

He slid an arm around her shoulder, pulled her in, spoke softly into her ear. "Well, I will tell you what I think."

"What?"

"I think that I'm tired of thinking about what the Lord Warder thinks. I'd much rather think about you."

But Emily wasn't about to let the first statement go. "So you're worried too!"

"Emily," he growled in her ear. "Shut up."

He stayed the night, left in the morning, leaving Emily to wonder how she could feel so wonderful and so terrible at the same time.

It simply didn't make sense. He shouldn't be here. He definitely shouldn't be with her. Even if Roland had given him back his life, he was the Steward's heir. Well, former heir. House Steward and House Warder detested each other, an enmity that went straight back to Roland. Why would the Lord Warder allow Alsandyr to represent House Warder in a joining with the Keeper's heir?

Unless he didn't know.

Was that even possible?

That question set her to biting her nails. With Roland and the second talisman in the mix, anything was possible. He'd used Alsandyr once. He could be using him again. But to what purpose? Could he be bent on deepening the rift between Steward House and Warder House?

Fortunately, Callyn appeared later that morning, catlike and contentious as ever. "Come on, Midlander," she ordered.

"Come where?" said Emily suspiciously.

"To the stables. Your blade-work may be hopeless, but we can at least try to improve your horsemanship. It would be an absolute disgrace if you still couldn't ride after being joined to Warder House."

After being joined? She started feeling sick all over again.

But Callyn proved an excellent cure. Malicious and efficient, she criticized every move that Emily made, setting Emily's blood on a low boil. Emily ended up shouting at her and stomping her feet like a child. It felt wonderful. Even the rearing and kicking of her vicious wild-eyed pony — infuriated by all the unwarder-like ruckus — only fed her satisfaction.

When he whipped his head forward to take a big bite out of her arm, Emily left off yelling at Callyn and rounded on the horse with glittering eyes. "Be still, you wretch, or I'll ride you straight into the frozen wastes of the netherworld and leave you there!" The pony sat back on his haunches and whickered meekly.

Emily turned back to Callyn and saw the warder wearing a half smile. "Not bad, Midlander," she said. "If you remember to do that to your enemies, you may not need a blade."

By the time she had stumbled through the baths and back to her tent, it was nearly midnight. All she could think of was flinging her saddle-sore body into bed. She ducked through the flap and tripped over a boot.

"Ouch!"

"Where have you been?" said a voice.

"Humph. Back again, I see. Actually, I can't see. Where are you?"

"Over here."

"Hey, that's my cot!"

"As cots go, it's not bad."

"Well you can just get out of it. I've been breaking horses and weathering Callyn's insults all day, and I'm dog tired."

"Me too. So get over here and settle down and let me go back to sleep."

She rolled over early the next morning to see him shoving his foot into the boot she had tripped over.

"Going back to your job?" she asked sweetly.

"I'm afraid so. We can't all lounge around in bed like you."

"My, how funny you are in the mornings."

466

He stood, stretching. "Go back to sleep."

Watching him closely through narrowed eyes, she said, "I would love to get some more sleep, but I can't help thinking. What do you suppose Roland is up to these days? Or, more interestingly, what do you think the Lord Warder plans to do about it?"

He was standing before the tent's door, but he turned his head to speak over his shoulder. "Do you enjoy making worry for yourself?" he asked, then slipped outside.

She was leaning through the flap before he'd taken three strides. "Maybe worrying is *my* job," she called to his back as he disappeared into the trees.

She was about to take his advice and tuck her stiff and sore body back into bed, when a flutter of garment caught her eye. Faryn was only visible for a moment, but it was long enough for her to see the grim expression on his face as he looked at her.

She couldn't find Callyn. The children were in school. She went to the place of healing hoping to throw off the sick feeling of premonition that followed her like her shadow.

The canyon and caves were almost empty. A young male healer materialized at her side.

"Is there something I can help you with, lady?"

"Oh, no. I mean yes. Is Colin Blackhammer here?"

"No, lady. He has gone with Inryn's company?"

"Where?"

"A place called The Crow's Nest."

"Will he be back soon?"

"No. It is many leagues from here, and it will take my brothers and sisters some time to clear it and the surrounding countryside."

"Clear it of what?"

"Those loyal to the rogue seer who calls himself Scryos."

The cold finger of fear tapped Emily on the chest. She nodded her thanks and left. You should have asked Alsandyr about the war, she told herself. You've been stupid and self-absorbed. The Lord Warder has concerns far greater than you.

The day crept along. Eventually afternoon yielded the land to dusk, and dusk succumbed to night.

Only, night brought no relief. She spent hours tossing and turning, wondering what Colin and the warders were encountering out there in the world, debating what, if anything, she could or should have done. Worst of all, Alsandyr never came.

But the next anxiety-ridden afternoon brought the summons she had long been expecting.

Callyn met Emily at the meadow rock. "The Lord Warder wants you," she said.

Emily swallowed a lump of fear-salted guilt. "When?"

"Now."

The journey was a long, cold, and arduous one that gave Emily ample time to run through her lines. The ones that she especially rehearsed went something like this. "I'm sorry, my lord. I'd like to help you, I really would. But, you see, either this place is making me crazy, or Alsandyr has interfered again. But you really shouldn't blame either one of us. Blame Roland. He's the one behind it all."

She listened to the tinny sound of those words banging around in her mind and hung her head in despair.

They neared the top of the mountain without Emily really noticing. She took the last step on the path's steep and winding stair and walked out onto a great flat, frosty terrace. The view momentarily robbed her of her worries. From the edge of the terrace, the world fell away into a stunning miniaturized landscape of fir forest, sloping meadow, and the twin peaks of the gate. But it was the plain beyond that claimed her attention. Beyond the mountains' shadows a portion of it gleamed sunset gold. Never had she beheld so much of it or seen it so clearly. One day, her heart whispered to it. One day, it whispered back.

Callyn touched her arm. "This way."

They walked between wide pillars holding up a cloth pavilion. Emily heard water running, but before she could trace the source of it, they entered a wide, open room roofed by the rugged natural rock of the mountain. Ivory candles burned in tall brass stands. A man stood before a blazing fire that helped to hold back the mountain's chill.

He turned.

Emily's lips parted, "Grandfather!" She flew into his arms and hugged him fiercely. How she had missed the terrible old man.

"Hello, Emilyn!"

"What are you doing here? How did you get here?"

"It wasn't easy I assure you, but the Lord Warder anticipated my coming. His warders met me on the road."

"You had to fight your way here?"

His lined face hardened. "Yes."

"So it's that bad."

He seemed to measure her character against the weight of what he knew. "Yes," he answered.

She drew herself up. "Is there something that I can do?"

He caught her shoulders in firm hands. "Haven't you done enough already?"

Emily looked away. "I know, one blunder after another."

"Hmm. You have your aunt's knack for self-deprecation. Why don't we set all the so-called blunders aside for a moment and talk about right now?"

"All right."

"Very good then. You will have dinner with me. I've quite missed our dinners, you know."

He slipped an arm through hers and led her through a series of chambers to a room where the rock walls of the mountain had been carved into elaborate reliefs. A table and chairs sat before a hole in one wall that might once have been a natural cavern door, but beyond that door was a large pool of clear mountain water that seemed to run straight into the sky.

"Take a seat, granddaughter. I'm afraid we will have to serve ourselves. Warders don't go in much for footmen and the like."

The aromas certainly tantalized. "It is so beautiful here."

"Yes. Warder House is perhaps the most beautiful of the Lairs."

"Lairs?"

"A common term for places like this house, the Keep of Numyn, a few such others.

"Seems an unusual choice of word."

"I'll tell you the story behind it some other time."

Emily watched her grandfather serve her plate and remembered why she had come. "Is the Lord Warder going to join us?" she asked. She felt a good deal less alarmed now that her grandfather was with her, but by no means comfortable.

"He is otherwise engaged, I'm afraid. But he knew how much I wanted to see you."

Emily let out a long breath and relaxed.

The food was good. She'd grown used to the peculiar spices favored by warders, but her grandfather's presence added new relish to the meal.

He spoke in a roundabout way of things going on in the outside world and of the acquaintances they had in common. Emily was interested to hear that Cyr still held its own against the rebels. Syrene and her consort helped Lord North govern with a firm but capable hand, and Corwyn Abrille was loyal to the Steward to his last drop of blood. Apparently, he and Dyre had something of a history, although he was a decade younger. The Steward's situation and his city's were much more precarious. Lyr was there, but Meredyth did not dwell on it. She did ask him to give her all the news he had of Greenwood Village. She didn't expect it to be much, but he surprised her. It seemed that he'd kept a careful watch on that village ever since her return there.

"So it wasn't just Faryn monitoring my movements," she said raising her brows.

"No. We had agents from all three houses following you."

"Did Faryn know that?"

"Certainly. Not that it mattered in the end. Not even Allyn expected you to find Roland's road. I for one never really believed it existed."

"Roland," she whispered. "What do you know about him, Grandfather?"

"Compared to you, Emilyn, relatively little. To me, he is merely a collection of legends. You, on the other hand, have actually spoken to the man. You walked his road."

"And still he shrouds himself in a mystery. I might as well be lost in the fog of that road for all I can see. But all my instincts tell me that I need to know more."

"Then you will have to speak to the only person who does know more."

"Who is that?"

"The Lord Warder of course."

Emily leaned over the table searching her grandfather's face. "You think that the Lord Warder understands Roland?"

Her grandfather's eyes gleamed over the rim of his goblet. "As well as anyone but Roland himself."

Emily pondered that for a long time, staring out over the water. The stars were reflected in it, and it made a soothing sound. Suddenly, other sharper sounds rang out over its gleaming surface, voices calling.

Emily lifted her chin from her hands and shot her grandfather a questioning look.

"Ah, yes," responded Meredyth. "That would be the Lord Warder returned."

Emily rose slowly, steadying herself against the table. Then she followed her grandfather from the room.

In the great room fronting the terrace, the fire still burned brightly. But stands of torches now lit the terrace itself. Warders milled there, graceful, predatory. None of them took any notice of the Keeper or his granddaughter. Most were looking in the direction of the stair.

Emily didn't have to wonder why. Already she could feel the resonance of the second talisman like a cataract's roar. Moments later she saw it rise above the heads of the assembled warders in all its writhing, twisting midnight glory. Emily saw the Darkness and knew it, and the Darkness knew her.

She felt her grandfather slip a firm hand beneath her elbow as if to prop her up. The wall of warders parted revealing the Crescent's bearer. Wreathed in his talisman's fingers of shadow, he stood tall, his deep blue robe flaring out around him as he turned. The hatted head swung back and forth, issuing orders to those near him. Then he spun and strode forward into his domain trailing living darkness like tendrils of smoke.

Emily was already backing up. *I'm not ready for this*, she thought. *Even after all I've seen and done, I'm not ready.* She tried to reach for Twilight, but something in the mountain's rocky walls seemed to block her.

"Wait, Emilyn," said Meredyth firmly.

The Lord Warder was bearing down on them, his head bent to the floor beneath his feet so that his broad-brimmed hat hid his face.

Emily loosed a little sob. The head lifted. Firelight slid beneath the brim and washed across the face underneath to be swallowed by startled blacker-than-black eyes.

"Tellers!" breathed Emily, just before she slid into a gentler dark.

Voices. Familiar, beloved. She must be back in Cyr. Any minute now she would wake up to find herself in her grandfather's apartments.

"I'm glad you agreed to wait for me. I was able to cushion her."

"It doesn't seem to have helped much. You could have warned me that you planned to tell her tonight."

"In the end, I doubt it would have made things any easier. Best to get it over with in one swift blow."

"Then why isn't she waking up?"

"Patience. You have given her the shock of her life."

"The shock of her life was supposed to have occurred three days ago. She handled that well enough."

"Is it so hard to understand why? She is my heir. Through the remarkable strength of your joining, she felt your death, and her mind digested it, but her heart—Who can convince the heart to accept what it will not abide? Only time. And not enough time had passed for her heart's hope to die.

"On the other hand, to find that you are Roland's heir goes against everything she knows about Roland and you. It's like her heart has betrayed her to her worst enemy, and yours. Ah, she is waking up."

A gentle rising movement, like her body was being lifted on an ocean swell. Her grandfather's voice receding. "Talk to her. But go gently."

Light crept under her eyelids. Emily breathed deep and opened her eyes. She saw firelight washing across tight folds of silk — a canopy — and turned wooden posts. So she *was* back in Cyr.

A slight sinking feeling as someone sat on the edge of her bed.

"I wish you would quit fainting on me," he said.

She resettled her head on the pillow. "You quit being impossible."

He laughed, wrapped a warm hand around her wrist. "You're shaking. Are you cold?"

"It's that damn talisman of yours. I can feel it vibrating from a thousand leagues away. It makes my teeth ache."

She felt the pressure on her wrist increase. Suddenly, her bones quit rattling.

"Better?"

"Much. So you can control it?"

"Control it? Not really. It's more like coming to terms with an old adversary."

"Like Roland."

"Hmm."

She rolled her head a little and looked straight into the heart of darkness. It was breathtaking. "So how does a seer, a child of Stewards, become the Lord of Warder House? I know Roland is crafty and powerful, but that feat seems extraordinary even for him."

He dropped his eyes to her wrist. "I have a theory."

"I'm swooning to hear it. Literally."

One corner of his mouth quirked. "I'd like to confirm it first."

"Oh."

"But as soon as I do, I will tell you. I promise."

She balled her hand into a fist. "And do you have a theory about what Roland wants from us?"

"Perhaps we should talk about something else tonight. You need to rest."

"Why don't you just tell me?"

"Emily, I've been wrestling with Roland and what he wants for months now. I could use a little rest too."

Her eyes slid down to the white line across his throat. "Sometimes I want to strangle Roland," she said, but then she smiled mischievously. "Well, if rest is what you need, you have a very comfortable bed for it." She opened her eyes wider and popped up onto her elbows. "Hey, you have a bed!"

In a bounce and a bound he had launched himself over her to stretch out at her side.

"That's a neat trick," she commented.

He grinned. "I'm full of neat tricks."

She propped herself on one elbow and frowned down at him. "So, if you have a real bed why have you insisted on crowding my little cot?"

"You want the convenient truth or the shocking one?"

"Is the shocking one any way as bad as the revelation that you are the Lord Warder?"

He ruminated, frowning attractively. "Depends."

"Good grief! Then the convenient truth by all means."

"Well then, here it is. I wanted to make sure that you were recovering from the initial surprise. Resurrections can really jar the mind. I figured the more I could be with you, the quicker you would regain your equilibrium." He paused, his eyes running up and down the folds of the canopy. "It helped me too. I don't know who I was when I first awoke at the tree. And I wasn't myself for a long time afterward—It's probably just as well you ran from me when I found you in the desert."

"You saved my life. But all I could see was Roland."

"In a way, I was more Roland than myself. Fortunately, you finally agreed to come here. Watching you, being near you, these things helped heal the wounds in my mind as well."

"I could feel you watching, you know. I figured it was the Lord Warder but—" She paused and nestled down in the pillow. It gave her heart a sweet ache just to look at him. "Okay, that truth wasn't so bad. What's the shocking reason?"

"You are sure you are ready?"

"Hit me."

He rolled onto his side and touched her face. "I couldn't stay away. I've waited a long time to be able to share your bed."

"My," she laughed, "that is shocking,"

He stood in his shirtsleeves looking down from the heights. So clear was the air, so sharp the details of the view that he could almost believe he yet retained the power of sight.

"Heady, isn't it?" said the man lurking in the shadows.

Al shifted. "It's the thinner atmosphere."

"I was talking about the view from the heart, not this terrace. Love can go to a man's head quicker than his loins, but a man in your position needs to keep his head clear."

"Don't patronize me."

"But I am your patron. I have a thousand years of spilt power, blood, and seed to prove it. You ought to call me Grandfather. You can leave off all the greats."

Roland strode out of the shadows, stopped with the toes of his boots hanging over the terrace's edge. From beneath the wide brim of his hat he scrutinized the Settlement below, a hawk eyeing his domain. The locks of his pale yellow hair fluttered like feathers; the edges of his blue robe billowed up like wings. "Inryn has returned, with the stone."

"Those extracted from the city should be here within days."

The hawk's eyes alighted on the Lord Warder and smiled. "The game begins."

"Dyre will be expecting a fight."

"So we give him one. The best way to snare a steward is to give him what he expects. House Steward's arrogance has always been its downfall. The action will be good for you. You have always enjoyed a good fight. Even the astringencies of Steward House could not exorcise that daemon from your blood."

"It will mean leaving the Settlement."

"You are letting that woman cloud your thinking again."

"She's vulnerable. Now especially."

"She is no less dangerous than you. As you well know. She may seem helpless as a kitten lying in that bed, but she is full grown, and she has a nasty set of claws. You will see them again soon enough. Wait until she learns what you have done."

Roland watched Al press his fingers to his eyes, and he flashed his feral smile. "Afraid, Lord Warder? You have captivated her mind and possessed her body, but you can feel her hand on your heart. When those claws bite, you will bleed no matter how fast you move."

"I can handle her claws. It's her talent for escape I'm worried about." His dark eyes rested gloomily on the plain.

'Leave her to Illyria."

Al's head shot around. The golden eyes flickered, the mouth grew sober. "Oh yes, the Shield Bearer has her guiding spirits too."

Al heard footsteps approaching.

Meredyth came striding onto the terrace, his hands clasped behind his back. "Good morning. How did she sleep?"

"Well."

474

"And you?"

"Better."

"Perhaps I should leave you alone with your thoughts."

"No. Stay."

But Meredyth still sensed preoccupation. He came and stood at the younger man's side only a foot or so short of the place where Roland had stood. He whistled. "It's a long way down from here."

"Too long."

"It is difficult being the orchestrator of an ending. The burden you bear is great, I know. But try to remember that you aren't bearing it alone."

The harshness of Al's laugh surprised the Keeper. "Believe me, I know."

Chapter 34: Promise

An early blast of winter was closing the mountain passes when the dark-haired woman rode through. Warders met her at the high pass and led her and her guard through the shifting waves of obscuring magic to the foot of the central mountain.

A black-haired, blue-eyed warder held her horse as she dismounted. He gestured toward the paths leading upward.

"Not yet," she said, lifting her head above the sable of her collar to scan the iron gray sky. "Will you take me to the clearing?"

The ethereally close quiet that comes with heavy snow had claimed the woods around the meadow. The conifers gleamed deep green beneath their burden of white. Their drooping limbs seemed to reach for the woman as she mounted the stone steps.

She stepped out of the trees and tasted the whiteness in the air. Here branches were bare or leafed or needled depending upon each tree's variety, yet each seemed wrapped tight in its own isolation.

"I shall wait for you below," said the warder.

She acknowledged his words with an absent-minded nod, then stood a moment gazing at nothing. The soft, reflected light stripped the years from her face, lending a heart-rending purity to her already fine features and an emphatic darkness to her eyes and hair.

Eventually, she walked to the great flat rock. Her gloved hand brushed wet snow aside.

Cold might have sealed the moisture of the air in ice, but the stream still bubbled out of the rock and poured itself out on the brilliant green moss at the rock's foot.

The woman gazed into the fast running clarity of the water for a long time. Then she hung her head and gave in to soft racking sobs.

When Alyra Goodwin entered the Lord Warder's house, no trace of that woman remained. The lovely face expressed only aloof serenity. The eyes were cool as jet. She waited a long time for her audience, standing before a blazing fire, sipping warm wine. Beyond the wide doors opening onto the terrace, the night flaunted a crystalline glory that put the glittering patches of ice to shame.

The master of the house announced himself with a firm tread and a chill wind of irritation. He tossed his snow-dusted coat onto a chair and followed it up with a broad-brimmed hat.

"My Lord," said Alyra inclining her head in an exquisite display of courtesy.

"Mother."

He moved to the nearest table and poured himself a goblet of wine. "I thought we agreed that you wouldn't come," he said evenly, looking down into the glass.

"I wanted to see you. I thought we should speak face-to-face."

"Dyre has spies everywhere, and he sees far these days. You could have been taken."

"If Dyre were interested in taking me, he would have made the attempt before now. And he would regret it."

"He could use you to blackmail members of Steward House or sway the loyalties of the people."

"The people and their loyalties do not concern him. He knows that his road to power lies through us. He must consolidate support among members of Steward House, or eliminate those members who try to oppose him. Where House Steward goes, the people will follow, sooner or later."

He sank into a chair, draping his arm over the chair's arm. He swirled the wine in his glass. "Isn't it ironic? House Steward prides itself, in part, on being a successful answer to the kingships that led to the Great War. The Stewards were supposed to be the servants of the people, to guide through knowledge and understanding and insight, but never to rule. And two thousand years later what do we have? Stewards living and ruling like kings."

"We are not kings."

"No? You have the elevation, the wealth, the military might, the political authority, everything but the title."

476

"We are also the people's first line of defense against the onslaught of Twilight. If some class distinction has come with that service, so be it. It was inevitable."

"Was it? At the moment, it seems to be a big part of the problem. More members of Steward House are thinking about their political power and intrafamily alliances than the growing threat of Twilight."

Alyra moved to sit across from her son. "So this is why you refuse to declare your existence to them. You doubt their worth and therefore the worth of your birthright."

"Birthright? What birthright?"

"You are the designated heir of House Steward. Dyre was stripped of that honor. If you step forward, you might help end this conflict."

"I will end it all right. But not by courting House Steward." He held up his left hand. A silver crescent gleamed there. " Look at it, Mother, and then remember yourself. No house is more jealous of its power or more adamant about the prohibition against interbreeding than the House of the Stewards. Ayr set the standard a millennium ago. Even if I still possessed the powers of a Steward, how many members of that House would continue to accept me as Allyn's heir if they saw the mark I now bear? As I recall, most questioned my fitness for the Stewardship when I chose Alysse. Nor has Grandfather hesitated to express his own doubts about me."

"You and Father have had your differences, but you must know that he would support you over a rogue like Dyre, Alsandyr."

"Dyre's blood is not tainted." His black eyes bored into her. "Grandfather knew all along, didn't he?" His voice smote the air like the dull, dry thud of an ax.

Alyra closed her eyes. "Apparently."

"Why did you do it? Were you, like Dyre, interested in erasing boundaries?"

"I had my reasons."

"Does my father know?"

"That is not—"

"Does my father know?"

"He knows that you are not the child of his body."

He stood up, set his glass on the table, and walked around his chair, running a hand through his hair. "And my brothers?"

"Of course not. Wilhem forbade it. He wanted no distinctions made between his natural sons and the son he was adopting. He loves you, Alsandyr, and he takes great pride in you. It devastated him when he heard the rumors that you were dead."

"So you married him just to hide your guilt. It explains a lot."

"Wilhem is a good man."

"A good man who had the misfortune to fall in love with you. Do you have any idea how angry it made me feel to see how indifferent you were to him? To all of us?" His long fingers dug into the back of the chair.

Alyra was on her feet. "How many times must I tell you! I have never been indifferent to you! How could I be?" Her voice cracked. "You were the one small piece of Sandyr that I was allowed to keep?"

He looked stunned. "Sandyr Ash? The Lord Warder?" He stepped back, then stood still, arrested by a thought. Abruptly, he tilted his head back and loosed a low laugh. "My name. It was there all the time."

Alyra reined in her surprise, forced herself to stay calm. "No one told you."

"No." His wide eyes seemed to drink in the light. "I didn't think there was much point in asking. It being a warder and all. They generally ignore issues of parentage." He reached for his goblet, downed the wine in one gulp.

"What is it?" she whispered.

"Nothing."

She approached him cautiously and laid a hand on his arm. "My son?"

He was staring into the shadows.

"Alsandyr."

He looked at her finally, but his eyes didn't see her. He spoke to a memory. "He knew. He chose death at the tree because he knew."

He refused to let her into that memory or his mind, but he could not entirely shut her out either. She sat near him, a calm, faintly maternal presence. Her fingers rested lightly on his arm. After a long time, she began to speak, compelled by some specter of grief in herself. "He loved you. I know it must sound strange to hear it, but it is true. He was a warder, and you never really knew him, but he knew you, far better than you can imagine. The circumstances of your birth and station required us both to keep a close watch on you. We knew from the beginning that we were taking a huge risk—we both believed it was necessary, but that didn't make it any easier."

"So it was planned," he said, in a dull voice.

"Of course. How else? You know Lyr's theories, Alberyc's claims. I admit that I, like my brother, was influenced by both. The warders have long held similar beliefs. They have not broadcast it, but their history has shaped their attitudes."

"He sought you out."

"Heavens no! Our initial meeting was entirely accidental. My horse broke its leg while I was exploring a place I should never have visited. He gave me aid, grudgingly, condescendingly. He quite despised me I think. I considered him unworldly and savage." She smiled. "Even his own people thought him wild, if you can imagine that. But he had such power, and a strange affinity for Twilight. The first time I saw him I thought I had been discovered by the Lord of Twilight himself."

She sighed, touched his hand.

"We knew it would be hard for you. We spoke often about it through the years. I know you think I wasn't a very good mother, but believe me, without Sandyr's wisdom and advice, I would have been a far worse one. In a way I loved you too much. The violence and impetuosity of your other nature frightened me. But for him, I would have worked too hard to curb it. But the things that disturbed me only made him smile. 'Alyra,' he would say, 'You are raising a wolf not a lady's lapdog. Put the books aside and let him cut his teeth.'"

Her mouth twitched. "He was the one who saw to it that you and Blayne were introduced so young. It was right after you had that terrible fight with Lord Andrik's sons — all four of them. I can laugh about it now, but when I saw what they had done to you—" Her hand tightened on his arm. "It's the closest I've ever come to wanting to do physical injury to someone. They were almost grown; you were just a little boy. Then your brothers told me how you retaliated. I began to wonder if I would have to send you to Father. A few days later I received a message from Sandyr. 'Quit fretting, Alyra,' it said, "I am sending the boy a sparring partner." The next evening Meredyth appeared at our door, Blayne in tow."

Al allowed himself a grim smile. "And I hated him too."

"Only for a while. He was so strange and imperturbable, I think he actually helped to calm you down. Finally, there was someone to make you feel less restless, less set apart."

"Andrik's sons certainly got their own back, and then some."

Alyra rose and went to stand before the dying fire. She smiled down into it. "I never said his coming didn't introduce a whole new set of problems. But you were happier."

She turned back to her son.

"You will claim the Stewardship, you know. I have seen it. Your father, Sandyr, counted on it. The Keeper too. The powers of our houses must be united."

"It can hardly be prevented now."

Her lips parted. "Then you will declare yourself."

He rose. "I will not."

Alyra's dark eyes flashed. "Foolish—"

"Don't worry, Mother. I will claim the Steward's power. I certainly have no intention of allowing Dyre to savor it. But I will do it in my own way and in my own time."

His mother lifted her proud head. "Do you realize the extent of my brother's plans? He intends to get a healthy child of mixed power on his young bride. And not just to control Steward House, but to challenge the Lords of Twilight themselves. With the aid of a talisman or a seat of power, he can do it. Father has confirmed that the girl is a descendant of Roland and Illyria. If Dyre gives her a child under the right circumstances, it will have the blood of all three houses in its veins, and it will be primed to inherit more. The members of Steward House do not want to believe it. They refuse to acknowledge the closeness of our connection to the Twilight brethren. But the Steward knows, the Keeper knows, and Sandyr knew it as well."

A grim hint of smile played about the Lord Warder's lips. "It's all about children, isn't it? From Nyte on down."

His mother knelt at his knee. "Night?"

His eyes flicked to her. "Let Dyre give the girl a child. Let him give her a hundred children. It won't do him any good."

"Why do you say that?"

"Didn't you know mother? Didn't Sandyr tell you? I am a descendant of Roland and Illyria, as was Sandyr himself."

Her beautiful face stilled.

Her son smiled at her. "So you see, technically I am a child of the three houses."

Her words came out as a whisper. "Then you—"

Standing up, he brushed her aside. "I'm afraid not. It's a bit more complicated than that. First of all, there will not be one heir to Twilight, but two. Two children from two very different branches of the same tree. Second, the conditions of inheritance require the child of our branch to be the chosen heir of *all* the houses. That includes the Fourth House."

"The Fourth House? There is no Fourth House!" she scoffed. "It exists only as a story and a few snippets of folklore."

"So speaks the stewards' cool voice of reason. But others are not so sure. Did you know that Midlanders put little stock in the other three Houses, but believe wholeheartedly in the Tellers?"

"What does it matter what Midlanders believe? Most of them look no further than their shops and fields."

"It's easy to dismiss their faith, isn't it? Then again, old instincts die hard. What do your instincts tell you, Mother? Have you ever tried dredging up that thrill of wonderment watered down by a millennium of careful inbreeding?"

She rose. Her beauty and her power were palpable. "My instincts tell me to look for answers that make sense. Assuming that the Tellers do exist, in some realm or manner heretofore unencountered, they do not pass on their power through the blood."

"That doesn't mean they can not have an heir."

Alyra measured him with her eyes. "You think you can find this heir."

Her son was smiling as he turned away. "Maybe I already have. Good night, Mother."

It was snowing heavily the next morning. Restless with thought and the sense that something important was unfolding in this place somewhere just out of sight, Alyra spent her morning indoors exploring the portion of the house open to her. It proved to be very large. The maze of its caverns ran through the mountain in all directions. Many rooms were furnished or stuffed like pantries. Many more were empty. She routinely happened upon warders ghosting through them. Only a few acknowledged her. None spoke with her.

She knew that she was monitored though. While the aura of the place blunted the sharpness of her sight, it could not entirely veil the movements and shadows of her guardians.

Eventually, she found a library. It was large and lined with shelves and cubicles full of books and scrolls. To her amazement, its only occupant was a small, neat Southerner who was too busy comparing the three or four works he had open in front of him to notice that she was watching.

Alyra departed.

Hours later she came upon another outsider, a young woman standing and staring moodily out of a natural window in the cavern walls at the fall of snow on a pool of frozen water. She wore warder attire but lacked their physicality and grace, and she looked as pent up as Alyra felt. Something in the depth of emotion running beneath her still features held Alyra's attention. An impulse came over the Steward's daughter to leave the darkness of the narrow tunnel in which she stood and go to the younger woman. But then a female warder appeared.

She stalked over to the table near which the girl stood and set a cup upon it.

"Take it away," said the dark-haired girl without so much as a glance in the warder's direction.

"Drink it," said the warder. She made Alyra think of a mountain lion, all tawny coloring and lean, effortless power.

Now the young woman did turn her head. The challenge in her eyes was clear. "Forget it."

Alyra felt a pang of sympathy for her. The contest was one-sided in the worst way. The girl could only end up losing.

"Drink it," said the warder again and pointed to the cup.

"No."

"You must drink it."

"It makes me ill."

"Zamyra's medicines don't make people ill."

"I feel ill."

"Which is why you need to drink it."

"I wasn't feeling ill when Zamyra insisted I start drinking her potions."

The warder woman narrowed her eyes. "I don't have time for this, Midlander." Ah, thought Alyra, that is the accent. Curious. "Drink it or I—"

"You'll what?" The Midlander woman stood straighter, crossed her arms, and leaned on a challenging smile.

That's a mistake, thought Alyra.

The warder smiled in turn. "You realize that with a slight twist of your an arm I could have this brew down your throat. You wouldn't even have to think about swallowing."

The Midlander sweetened her smile. "Do it and Faryn and I will have a little talk about exclusivity."

The warder glared. "You wouldn't."

The smile showed its edge. "Not as long as you lay off arm-twisting."

To Alyra's amazement, the warder abruptly discarded her threatening air. "I will have to tell Zamyra."

"Go ahead, but just so you know, making this her problem won't accomplish anything."

"What exactly is the problem?" said a new voice.

Both women glanced toward the speaker before again locking eyes. The Midlander glowered. The warder smiled clear to the bottom of her amber eyes. Alyra slipped further into the shadows.

Alsandyr strode into the room. "There is a problem, isn't there?"

"No," snapped the Midlander.

"Yes," purred the warder woman.

Alsandyr adopted his most congenial air. "Well, at the very least we have contradictory interpretations of the situation. I'd call that a problem."

The warder kept on smiling. "Yes, Cyros," she said respectfully.

But the Midlander turned on the Lord Warder and snapped, "Stop being clever! This doesn't involve you."

Alyra's eyebrows went up. She watched her son. He accepted the reproof mildly.

The warder woman, however, hissed a little laugh. "Oh, he's very involved," she purred.

Snap! all the Lord Warder's congeniality vanished. His black gaze engulfed the female warder and bound her like a mountain lion in a huntsman's trap.

But the Midlander was digesting the female warder's words. She frowned, "What is that supposed to mean?"

The Lord Warder's eyes released the tawny woman. "Thank you, Callyn, I will handle it from here."

Freed, the female warder slid quickly away, allowing herself the smallest of smiles as she swept from the room.

The Midlander stood, lips parted, watching her go. She seemed to suck in her breath as she placed one hand on her hip and looked up at the Lord Warder. "Exactly what do you expect to handle?" she said in a dangerous voice.

Alsandyr raised a hand in apology. "My mistake. *Handle* was entirely the wrong word."

The young woman fed him a smile of poisonous sweetness. "So, we are finally learning to admit that we make mistakes. I'd call that progress." She rather ruined her sarcasm's effect, however, by pressing her lips tightly together as if to suppress an urge to throw up.

He looked down at her. His face was sober; his eyes glittered. He doesn't know whether to laugh or to shake her, thought Alyra. She watched him lean back against a rock wall. "You really should drink that, you know."

"The next person who says that to me gets the whole cupful in the face. That includes you."

"You would feel better."

"It's making me feel sick."

"Why do you say that?"

"Have your wits turned to water? Or are you just too preoccupied with schemes and strategies to notice anything else? I've been queasy for weeks now. I can hardly stomach food. And I can't seem to think straight either. Even the power of the Shield doesn't help anymore.

I'd swear that someone has stuffed my head with wet wool. This place fogs the mind in the worst way."

Alyra found herself having to hold on to the rock wall to keep steady. *Oh, my son, my son*, she thought.

"I have noticed. I'm simply wondering why you blame Zamyra."

"I'm not blaming Zamyra. I'm sure she's doing what she feels is best, but just thinking about the stuff turns me green."

Careful, Alsandyr, his mother silently warned. *Remember your training. Ease her into the truth.*

"But after you drink it, you do feel better."

"Why do you say that? How would you even know? You're never here."

Alyra closed her eyes.

"Come. Let's take a walk." He caught one of her wrists, but she only jerked it free.

His mother sighed. *It's too late now, my darling.*

"Have you been monitoring me again? You have, haven't you?"

Alyra saw him catch the Shield Bearer's face in his hands. "These are dangerous times."

"Dangerous for anyone who leaves the Settlement. But I'm locked up in here. You won't even let me leave the house these days. What are you so afraid of?" She abruptly stopped speaking to put her hands to her head. "Damnation! My head is spinning." She lowered her hands and noticed that they were shaking.

The eyes she raised to the Lord Warder's face were brilliant with color, almost as if the irises had caught fire. "You!" she breathed.

She tried to leap away, but he only caught her upper arms. "Emily, listen," he said in his calmest, most soothing tones.

"Get your hands off me!" she spat.

He only pulled her closer.

"How dare you use the power of that thing against me?"

"I'm not using it against you."

"You're not clouding my mind?"

"I'm trying to make things easier."

"You are trying control me, and you don't even care that it's making me ill."

"Will you please just listen?"

"No! Thanks to you I've been utterly miserable for weeks, and all you do is try to cover your tracks with one of Zamyra's potions."

"I'm not the reason you feel ill! Zamyra is not the reason you feel ill!" The whip crack of his voice matched the lash of black fire in his eyes.

The girl in his arms froze. His grip gentled. He brought his face close to hers. Alyra watched his lips move against her cheek.

Alyra didn't see the girl move. She was too busy weathering the flash of power. When she could see again, the Midlander stood free and her son's hands were empty. The Shield Bearer looked at the Lord Warder with eyes deeply sad and profoundly wise. Watching her, Alyra was struck by the thought that Illyria must have looked just that way when she first beheld Roland. "You promised," she said in a flat little voice.

The Lord Warder could only bow his head. The girl vanished.

Emily sat beneath the cold, beneath the stars.

The great plain was a pall of gray on the horizon. Still it beckoned to her. Now more than ever.

You love him, one part of her said. He used you, said another.

Must having his child be such a bad thing? she asked herself

She sighed and said to the air, "You should have known better."

"He loves you," said a warm voice.

Emily turned her head and saw a woman standing only a few feet away from her. The torchlight caressed a face strikingly beautiful in its hauteur.

The woman moved closer. "May I?" she asked, gesturing to the furs on which Emily sat. Emily nodded once. The woman sank gracefully to the stones, seemingly indifferent to the fine fabric of her gown. She looked out at the plain for a moment then turned her face to Emily.

"He does love you. Of course, it in no way excuses what he has done."

"No it doesn't," agreed Emily.

"He always was difficult," admitted the woman. "But I forget my manners; I should introduce myself properly."

"I know who you are," answered Emily. "I've seen you in his mind."

"Hmm. That can't have been complimentary to me."

Emily turned her eyes back toward the plain. "Actually, he adores you. He resents it though."

Alyra permitted herself a small smile. "I have given him reasons. Perhaps the people we love the best always do. I loved his father desperately and resented him terribly at the same time."

"Did you want to have his child?"

"Very much."

"I never saw myself with a child," Emily said. She looked out at the plain. "But then I never saw myself with him either. It just happened."

"Then you must trust in that, and each other, no matter how difficult it may be."

Emily breathed deep. "But it's not just about him and me. It never has been. There are things we both have to do. I'm not sure a child fits into those things."

"It will have to fit into them now."

She took her medicine and climbed wearily into bed. She hoped for a deep, dreamless sleep. Busy with preparations for an assault, the Lord Warder kept odd hours. Lately he slept whenever and wherever it was convenient.

She awoke to a fireplace full of coals. Alsandyr was a warm darkness sitting on the edge of the bed.

"Is it time for you to leave?"

"Not just yet, but soon."

She tucked her hand under her head. "Try not to get yourself killed this time."

He shifted, lifted a hand as if to touch her, but held off. "That's gracious of you."

"Not really. I'd like to kill you myself."

He sighed. "Would it help if I said that I think you are well on your way?"

"You look healthy enough to me."

He leaned in, ran a hand up her arm. "Why are the things we want the most always the hardest to hold on to?"

'I wish I knew," she said.

Days later, the warders seat of power played host to an unusual convocation. In addition to five of the top seven ranked warders, the clearing was occupied by a small neat Southern scholar, a gray-haired man with a lined but resolute face, and a black-haired woman of striking beauty.

They did not speak amongst themselves. The warders lazed in the tree shadows, self-centered as cats. The old man and the woman stood near the great rock rapt in their own thoughts. The scholar stood apart fidgeting. Although the snow had deepened, the trees loomed taller as if they too waited expectantly.

The Lord Warder eventually made his appearance. The deep, yet vivid blue of his robe and hat challenged the winter colors of the clearing. The dark thing atop his staff pulsed and hummed and sent out faint probing fingers, slipping dark threads into the onlooker's minds. Even the snow's white seemed to take on an added dimension of shadow. The scholar cowered away from its energy and raised a hand to his eyes.

The Cyros walked to stand before the gap in the trees. He seemed to commune with its shadows for a moment and then said. "Cayne and Insyra?"

A black-haired blue-eyed warder and a lean woman with hair of graying chestnut shifted their eyes to their master.

"Lead your companies north as we agreed. Employ the tactics that seem best to you, fight when you need to, and use screens. He will still see you coming.

"Andryl and Wyndan, the southern districts are yours." Two other warders exchanged looks as their master continued, "Defend them as if they were vital to our long-term interests. Syrene of Cyr will give you what support she can."

The Cyros turned; his face was in shadow despite the snow's reflective light. "I will see all of you in the capital."

Four pairs of eyes gleamed. Four predators melted back into the trees.

"Master Abreem," said the Cyros.

The scholar bowed low.

The Cyros smiled, "You know how grateful we are for your aid."

"My lord is too kind."

"Work fast. We haven't much time. When you are ready, Zamyra will know how to reach me. And be well, my friend."

Abreem Imharta actually grinned then bowed again. "May your road continue to run true, Northlander." he said and walked as rapidly as the snow would permit toward the other end of the clearing. The great trees seemed to swallow his small form.

The master of the house looked at the two standing near the rock. "Cayne and Insyra should divert attention away from Numyn," he said to the Keeper.

Meredyth nodded. "As soon as I leave the Settlement, I will contact the council about beginning preparations to make the move east. There will be resistance."

"You will manage. You always do."

The lines at the corners of Meredyth's mouth deepened as he gave in to a rather bitter smile. "Yes." He clasped his hands behind his back. "Now, about my granddaughter."

"She stays here, Meredyth." The words though spoken softly reverberated with dark and dangerous undertones.

The Keeper nodded good-naturedly. "Certainly. She is safest here. Provided you can keep her here. She will need to be watched most carefully, Cyros. If you will allow me to send her a representative of the council—"

Alyra spoke. "That won't be necessary, Lord Keeper."

Both men looked at her in surprise.

"I will stay. Watching is what I do best after all, and your concerns, Meredyth, are justified—the Shield Bearer needs very close watching."

The Cyros drew himself up. "Your power is needed to counteract Dyre's sight."

"There is nothing I can accomplish that my father cannot do far better. He is the Steward. We members may preen over our individual gifts, but they are paltry compared to his. A fact that Dyre appears to have forgotten, to our advantage."

"Which is all the more reason for you to return home, Mother. I was counting on you to mediate between me and your father."

His mother raised her eyebrows in mock surprise. "Does the Lord of Warders need a mediator? Really, Alsandyr, you take your personal issues with your grandfather too far. Clearly, I should have stopped intervening years ago. Allyn is waiting to hear from you. Set the past aside and reach out to him. It's high time you two quit baiting one another and worked together like masters. I will stay here."

"Well," said Meredyth lightly, "now that that's settled. I think I shall be on my way." He nodded to the younger man. "Since you refuse to let Emilyn contact Blayne, I will concentrate on doing so. I will send you word as soon as I have located him." With a gracious bow to the Lady, the Keeper departed.

Alyra held her ground and waited.

"Why are you really doing this, Mother?" the Lord Warder asked once the Keeper had vanished.

"I told you: the Shield Bearer needs watching. I can offer her experience and support."

"Alysse could have benefitted from your experience and support. You refused to even acknowledge that relationship."

Alyra regarded her son with knowing eyes. "Alysse was not the Bearer of the Shield or my grandchild."

As her son's eyes bored into hers, Alyra raised her head. She could feel the dark power in him stretch out its hand, but she would not bow before it. "I wonder, my son, if you really know what you have done."

"Why I have only finished what you and Sandyr Ash started, Mother," he replied softly.

"I know the power it takes to break the prohibition. I know the power you poured into the Bearer to open her womb. I bore you. This pregnancy will not be easy for her. It confuses her power as it augments it. It makes terrible demands on her mind and body. To make matters worse, she is conflicted in her own nature. Already, she is in a struggle between what she is and what she must become. She is in real danger."

He closed his eyes. "What am I to do about it now?"

His mother's look was stern. "You do what you have always done so well. You fight—for your land, for yourself, for the Steward, and for her. Leave the rest to me."

When he opened his eyes, the expression in them made him look young and almost vulnerable. She smiled and touched his forearm. "I will contact you if anything happens."

A sudden breeze rattled the trees of the clearing and disappeared into the gap in the trees with a sigh.

It seemed to stir the roiling energy in the Crescent, which sent out long dark tendrils that wound lovingly about the Lord Warder's form.

"Faryn," he said.

"Yes, Cyros?"

"The hounds are yours. Sooner or later she will try to make for the plain. You must not lose her this time."

The light eyes of the warder flashed. "On my life I will not."

The Lord Warder nodded and with a shift of his hand on his staff donned the shadows that marked him the Cyros. He turned and disappeared into the trees.

EPILOGUE

In a moonpale boat on a midnight river, a girl who is more than a girl shudders as her mouth froths words that shake the very stuff of the darkling world around her. Substance and dimension shiver, collapse, twist, unfurl, so that the girl's companion must work frantically to steer a navigable course from a boat that is not always a boat on a river that is only sometimes a river. Now with pole or sail or rein or rudder, he pulls and heaves and slips them around sudden dissipations of darkling forest and explosions of moonstone desert, past whirlpools of obsidian ocean and eruptions of crystal mountains.

Spaces, landscapes, worlds are born and die aborning, but the girl senses none of it. Her consciousness belongs to her telling, and her telling has sunk her in the body of a man standing in a tall tower overlooking a radiant city.

The city unfolds like a complex multi-petaled flower, all radiating lines and mounting saffron rooftops. The eye of this flower is the point where the serene but deep-running river that enters the city from the north divides into two symmetrical channels so that the city is trisected by the river's waters. What sits upon massive bridges above this dividing point is Farview Tower.

The old man who stands in the highest room of the tower stares dreamy-eyed into space and interrogates history. He thinks about the magical artifact resting serenely on the plinth at the center of the room, considers the rainbow lights it casts upon the wall and the structure of the tower that houses it. He smiles humorlessly. He of all people knows that history cannot be trusted, for he is the Lord Steward and he has looked far and deep—beyond the child's sketch that is mortal history into the unimaginable complexities beyond.

As usual, the merest reference to the obligations of his office brings on the pressurized blindness that precedes the brutal touch of the Orb. The dark-eyed Steward rocks on his feet and tries to summon the meditative state that sometimes helps to mitigate the talisman's violating touch. One cannot see as the Orb sees and remain unviolated. So every Lord Steward has learned to fall back upon a keenness of intellect and a stark objectivity that spares nothing and no one, most especially not himself. Other people might regard the Lords of Steward House as cold and unfeeling, as relentless and remorseless in their aims and judgments, but that is only because ordinary people cannot know what it means to be the Steward, to be both a frail, petty, sentimental mortal man and an all-seeing eye. Every vision vouchsafed by the Orb brings with it an instantaneous and brutal reckoning, for what the Orb sees, it sees into and through and in multiple dimensions. And the Orb sees its Stewards—sees them as absolutely and unequivocally as it sees everything else—until they cannot act for good without seeing the wrong impregnating it, cannot mete out justice without spotting the injustice that is its conjoined twin, cannot triumph without tasting abject failure, or gain knowledge without plumbing their ignorance. So profound is their clarity in sight that it should have destroyed their acceptance of self.

But power takes care of itself. Familiarity breeds habit. Great handicaps teach resourcefulness. And the flexible mind seeks out the safest and most useful path.

The Orb adapted to each Steward, tempering its power to the channels of mortal consciousness, and the Stewards, tempered by its energies, adapted as well.

Clarity of sight, the eureka of insight, the power to reason and perceive possibilities as well as increase probabilities, these were the Stewards' gifts, the powers that allowed them to anticipate history before it became history and choose from among infinite courses of action.

Allyn Teleos, Lord Steward of the North, calls upon the Orb's illuminating fire and, being struck blind by it, sees beyond sight.

He sees fire burning in a hollow between hills. Sees two women lying beneath rough blankets — one fair-haired and slender, the other coarse-faced and heavy-breasted. Across the fire a massive creature the shade of the night's shadows crouches. Its color would hide it completely from ordinary eyes, but not from the Orb. The fair-haired woman stares into the fire, her arm curled protectively about a bundle of blankets. The Orb hovers over the thing inside the blankets, but chooses not to see into it.

Wind whips the fire, spins it into a shifting cylinder. A man steps into the light. He moves with a preternatural grace to match the preternatural symmetry of his face and form. But the Orb sees through that form to the light decanted within.

The woman raises herself. The Orb sees the tiny muscles of her face move in directions suggesting doubt and fear as well as hope and wonder. The nearly invisible giant explodes upward and strikes. The man evades its blow, prepares to react to another, wasting no movement, giving no ground.

He opens his hand and shows the ring he holds in his palm. "She sent me," he says to the looming ferocity.

The giant subsides.

The woman clutches the bundle to her chest.

The man turns and faces her, and the woman melts. "It breaks my heart just to look at you," she breathes, helpless to stop herself.

The man regards her out of burning eyes, now green, now star-white. "Give me my son."

Biting her lip, the woman rises and brings her bundle forward. The man takes the small form, looks down on it. The light inside him changes.

The Orb looks elsewhere. With a lurch, the Steward sees the man called Scryos, who is also Dyre, the Steward's own son. He is older than when the Orb last looked at him, but no less handsome, maturity has lent him a beguiling aura of wisdom with which to cover the corruption curled underneath. He stands beside a bed where a girl with hair pale as ivory pretends to sleep. The gleam in Dyre's eyes says he knows the girl is not sleeping, that she has in fact been crying, again.

Dyre lifts his head, his eyes look through empty air as if hunting for Allyn's. *Are you watching, father?*

Another woman enters the room, distracts Dyre. She is petite and pretty despite the gray threaded through her ash-blonde hair. Her filmy garment floats enticingly about her body. The Orb sees fading beauty and the ravages of a gluttonous heart.

"Come back to bed, my love," she says to the man standing at the bedside.

The Orb looks south and east. Allyn feels the energies in it build to a searing crescendo, but the mazy wards of Warder House hold firm. Never have those wards been stronger, shiftier, more obscuring. Although they cannot entirely stop the Orb from seeing, they can shift and jumble its images. Images of warders overlap one another; trees and towering rock jump in and out of focus. The Orb scrutinizes the Settlement. Something hides behind its rippling curtain of protections, something that the Orb wants to see. House Warder has grown powerful indeed.

With an agonizing mental wrench, Allyn feels the Orb shift its focus and penetrate into Twilight. It sees the flexible substance of that realm as a net of woven fibers through which energy light and dark dances. And within that substance it glimpses the Lords of Midnight like distant candles flickering across a burning darkness.

It turns its gaze to the nearer layers of that strange and ever unfolding land. At last, in a nest of intertwining tentacles of darkness, it finds what it has been looking for: a figure in a hat and robe that glow a deep, resilient blue.

What are you doing? wonders Allyn, curious despite his physical agony. The Orb is curious too. It slips a narrow ray of its power between writhing arms of shadow to get a closer look.

The shadows feel it and rub up against it like cats. The figure turns and lifts its head, reveals a smiling mouth.

The writhing arms of shadow increase their twisting. Some close about the figure, even as others come together into a clawed, fanged agent of darkness with glowing golden eyes. The huge shadow cat leaps upon the Orb's ray of power. Orb-light clashes with taloned fingers of darkness, but the wrestling powers do not so much make war on each other as greet each other roughly and then negotiate a dance of compromise. The Orb pulls its power in. The shadows, satisfied, retreat.

Allyn opens his own eyes to find himself curled into a fetal position upon the tower's floor. He can tell from the roughness in his throat that he has been screaming. When the pain finally subsides enough for him to move, he rolls onto his back and begins laughing.

Here ends *Abiding Darkness,*
Volume Two of *The Tellers' Tale.*
The story concludes in
Volume Three, *Making Magic.*

Glossary of Terms and Characters
(Characters listed by first name)

Abreem Imharta — scholar and translator residing in Sun City.

Ab Syminal — an ancient ruined city on the edge of the Sardic desert, also known as Bin Edath.

A'Carnis — First Prince of the powerful Empyreal family Carnis.

Alberyc of Numyn — 27th Keeper of Numyn, an artist and scholar who was later stripped of office for his controversial theories concerning the intermingling of the Houses.

Allyn Teleos — current Lord Steward, head of Steward House, bearer of the Orb talisman of that house.

Alsandyr Goodwin — son and only child of Alyra Teleos Goodwin and current heir to the Lordship of Steward House as a result of his mother's abdication of that position.

Alyra (Teleos) Goodwin — daughter of the current Lord Steward, Allyn Teleos; she abdicated the heirship of House Steward after the birth of her son Alsandyr Goodwin.

Alysse North — only child of Lord Cyrill North, one-time heir to the lordship of Cyr, betrothed of Alsandyr Goodwin, and minor member of House Keeper on her mother's side.

Artie — a mysterious, very uncommunicative ex-comrade of Garvin Blackhammer who assists Emily and Colin in escaping the watchful eyes of Faryn of House Warder.

Ayr — a famous Lord Steward of ancient times, believed by some to be the Lord Steward who betrayed Roland and Illyria.

Benja — elderly female servant of the family Cyronian.

Bertran — deceased half-brother of Bethnarian I.

Beltand — deceased half-brother of Bethnarian I.

Bethnara (Beth) — daughter and only living child of the current Empyreor, Bethnarian I.

Bethnarian I — Empyreor of the South, father to Princess Bethnara.

Betrice Kolmarden of Ancyr — Lady in Waiting to and long-time friend of Syrene Malamot.

Blackthorn Manor — the ancient and long-abandoned manor deep in Greenwood Forest where for many years Beth was held in exile.

Blayne of Numyn — half-breed of House Keeper and son of Millicynt Encanta by the Lord of Twilight.

Callyn Holly — female warder of House Warder.

Cal Whitfield — young citizen of Greenwood Village, friend and peer of Colin Blackhammer.

Caphal Numhana — Head Secretary to Bethnarian I.

Catastrophe, Great — a common term for the mysterious event that changed the nature of the world in ancient times. Also known as the Great War and the Cataclysm.

Cayne Ash — Second Warder of House Warder, close confidante and aide to Sandyr Ash.

Claire Raines — friend of Regina Waxman and daughter of Henley and Reanne Raines.

Colin Blackhammer — youth of Greenwood Village, close friend of Emilyn Sayer, apprentice healer under Millicynt Encanta, and son of Garvin Blackhammer.

Corg — trusted lieutenant to Galden Madson.

Corwyn Abrille — high-ranking member of House Steward, close relation and trusted lieutenant of the current Lord Steward, husband to Syrene Malamot.

Countess Beck — a noblewoman of Ancyr and Lady in Waiting to Syrene Malmot.

Crow's Nest — a large estate near the eastern border of the Northland that was abandoned sometime after the death of Dyre Teleos.

Cyr — the seat of the family North, a powerful and influential southern district of the Northland that includes both the city Cyr and many leagues of town and farmland extending around that city.

Cyrill North — Lord of Cyr, father of Alysse North.

Daemon — a term employed by southerners and Sards to describe the fire-wielding immortals that dominate their legends and religions.

Darkling — a descriptive term for the masters and other creatures of Twilight, used because that realm is without sunlight and withdraws from the touch of it.

Dax Blackhammer — the third child of Garvin and Kaitlyn Blackhammer.

Dejan — a male head-servant of family Cyronian.

Dominic — the librarian of Lord Cyrill North of Cyr.

Dorlan of the Forest — the legendary folkhero of the Midlands who is alleged to have a hidden hideout deep within Greenwood Forest and who is famous for his elusiveness and ingenuity.

Dyre Teleos — first child and only son of the current Lord Steward, Allyn Teleos; he was heir to the lordship of Steward House until he was killed in a border skirmish as a young man.

Elnora Norven — Lady in Waiting to both Alysse of Cyr and Syrene Malmot; she subscribed to the beliefs of the Color Guard and became a worshipper of the Twilight Lords.

Emilyn Sayer — daughter of Madelyn Encanta, retriever and bearer of the great talisman of House Keeper that is known as the Shield Light.

Ehkeshk — the Sardic priestess killed by Emily Sayer on the road to Sun City.

Faryn Linden—Seventh Warder of House Warder, a rank he is quite young to have achieved, who was appointed personal warder to Emilyn Sayer.

Ferne Blackhammer—sixth child of Garvin and and Kaitlyn Blackhammer.

Fyre—the pet fire cat of Princess Bethnara, presented to the princess by the nonman Ogren while she was living in the Greenwood.

Galden Madson—longtime captain of Scryos' household guard.

Garvin Blackhammer—smith of Greenwood Village in the Midlands and sometime citizen of the Northland whose children are Colin, Sara, Dax, Nell, Mack, Ferne and Chip.

Great Confederacy—a great alliance of northern and southern nations that existed more than two thousand years before the time of Emily Sayer and her friends.

Great War—the legendary conflict that resulted in a dramatic alternation to the world; also known as the Great Catastrophe.

Half-breeds—the term used for people of mixed Twilight and human ancestry. Although mortals may tell many fantastic stories about mortals interbreeding with immortals, the lore of the Houses indicates that the birth of hybrid children is actually extraordinarily rare because it involves both a tremendous influx of Twilight power and the mating of the Lord of Twilight himself with a mortal woman of considerable magical ability.

Heartbreaker—the mysterious, oddly marked artifact that Abreem Imharta discovered in Ab Syminal. It may be a piece of a broken lance.

Henley Raines—man of Greenwood Village, husband to Reanne, father to Claire.

House Keeper—House Keeper is the house of remembrance and preservation. Its goal is to preserve and develop the memory and knowledge of the realm. Its members tend to be scholars, craftsmen, teachers, artisans, builders. Its powers are those of the heart—intuition, inspiration, empathy. The great talisman of the house is the Shield

Light. Its mark is a shield shape commonly believed to be a "leaf" until the return of the keepers' talisman. Its motto is "I stand fast." Its seat is the ancient fortress of Numyn that lies on the border of the great eastern plain.

House Steward—House Steward is sometimes called the ruling house of the Northland. It should more aptly be described as the advising house. Although its activities are often political in nature, House Steward only rarely intervenes in the work of the governing bodies of the Northland, which include both noble and common representatives from all the major districts. The primary function of the house is to anticipate threats from the denizens of Twilight and ensure that the people of the land work together to respond to those threats. Therefore, an important secondary function of the house is political guidance and mediation. The members of the house often serve as advisors or arbitrators in negotiations between districts and representatives. And because they are seen as nonpartisan protectors of all the Northland, their advice is both sought after and generally followed. The Lord Steward has historically been the marshal of the Northland's regular armies and the custodian of many of its armaments, including the advanced weaponry of firearms and mortars, which are only rarely seen and used. The great talisman of the house is the Orb. Its mark is a circle divided by two arcs. Its powers are those associated with the mind—reason, judgment, insight, extrapolation. Its motto is "I look to serve." Its seat is the capital city of the Northland, Farview.

House Teller—House Teller is the least understood of all the houses. Very few members of the other houses even believe that it exists. There is little historical information on the Tellers and no physical evidence of them. It is known (or believed) that, unlike the other houses, they did not pass on their powers through blood descent. In lore they have been called the House of the Spirit, the Lost House, and the Forbidden House. But Alberyc, 27th Keeper of Numyn, who devoted many years of study to this house, called them the House of Revelation and Transformation. Their mark, their motto, and their seat, if they ever existed, have been lost.

House Warder—House Warder is the house of combat and protection. Its members are only rarely encountered since stewards keep the peace between ordinary mortals. The warders' energies are almost exclusively directed against the creatures of Twilight, and the bulk of their protective work is done upon the borders of Twilight's various realms. The powers of the house are those of the body — physical strength, grace, and vigor; sensory awareness; sensitivity to the things of the material world. Its great talisman is the Crescent or Talon. Its mark is a crescent shape. Its motto is "I protect." Its seat is the Settlement, of which none but the warders know the exact location. It may lie somewhere near the easternmost tip of the great eastern mountains.

Houses Arcane — a term for the magical orders of Keeper, Steward, Teller and Warder that protect the lands of men from the encroachment of Twilight.

Illyria — lover of Roland of House Warder, leader of House Keeper in ancient times, lady ruler of the drowned lands that were the home of the keepers before their migration to the ancient fortress at Numyn.

Inimiri (Miri) Dahar — waiting woman and appointed guardian-in-exile to Princess Bethnara.

Janera Cyronian — wife and first queen of Bethnarian I.

Janeryc Cyronian — current Lord of the Empyreal family Cyronian.

Janys Cyronian — sister to Janera Cyronian, mother of Vyara Cyronian.

Jazim Veris — Prince of Serpentia, current Lord Commander of the Empyreal armies and Master of Intelligence.

Justyn Baryns — the master smith-magician who trained Al Goodwin.

Kaitlyn Blackhammer — wife of Garvin Blackhammer, mother of Colin Blackhammer. Her children are Colin, Sara, Dax, Nell, Mack, Ferne, and Chip.

Kevyn of Esande — a gifted sculptor and member of House Keeper who was born in the land ruled by Illyria.

L'eret Carnis — First Lady of Carnis and mother of Prince A'Carnis; her mother was a Sardic priestess.

Lettie Harrington — a young female resident of Greenwood Village and wife to Cal Whitfield.

Lyr Feyone—a master magician and teacher who is both a powerful elder member of House Keeper and a widely respected teacher. His students have included many of the heirs of House Keeper and House Steward.

Mack Blackhammer—the fifth child of Garvin and Kaitlyn Blackhammer.

Madelyn Encanta—mother of Emilyn Sayer, eldest child of Meredyth Encanta, candidate for succession to the Keepership before she deserted her house.

Marbek of Kos—only son of Empyreal Prince Bertran, a nephew of Bethnarian I.

Marks—Every one of the Houses Arcane is associated with a specific mark. This mark always appears on the palm of only one member of the house at a time, and it may not appear on any member for generations. Both the warders and the keepers have endured long periods of time without any bearer of their mark. Only the stewards have maintained their mark in unbroken succession from Lord to heir throughout the generations. This may be because the marks are closely associated not only with lordship of a house but with the great talismans they commemorate. Unlike the keepers and the warders, the stewards have never lost track of their great talisman. The mark of the stewards is a circle broken by two opposing arcs; the mark of the warders is a crescent; the mark of the keepers is a leaf or shield shape; the mark of the tellers is known only to Emilyn Sayers.

Melodie—a young maid in the house of Lord North of Cyr, friend to Emilyn Sayer.

Meredyth Encanta—current Keeper of Numyn, grandfather to Blayne of Numyn and Emilyn Sayer. father to Millicynt and Madelyn

Micah Fairway—the young nobleman of Cyr who guides Emily to the inn of the prophet and his tower.

Midnight—an otherrealm alleged to exist either beyond or deep inside Twilight and sometimes identified as the Dark Heart of Twilight. Midnight is traditionally regarded as the home of the Twilight Lords.

Millicynt Encanta — the second and youngest child of Meredyth Encanta; she was the mother of Blayne of Numyn, the aunt of Emilyn Sayer, and a gifted healer.

Motley Men — Emily's term for the disaffected extremists collectively known as the Color Guard. Members of the Guard distinguish themselves by wearing parti-colored clothing or motley and by challenging authority wherever they go. They belong to no particular nation, but act in opposition to current political powers. They worship immortals that they regard as the true masters of the world and work in the cause of these immortals in return for the gift of immortality.

Nell Blackhammer — the fourth child of Garvin and Kaitlyn Blackhammer.

Niall Waxman — head of the village council of Greenwood Village, a wealthy man by local standards.

Nonmen — a mysterious race of nonhuman, sentient beings that, according to some legends, first made their appearance in this world after the Great Catastrophe.

Nyte — legendary Empyress of the First Empyre, an age never referenced or acknowledged by official historians of the Empyre.

Ogren — nonman protector of the Princess Bethnara.

Reanne Raines — matron of Greenwood Village, wife of Henley, mother of Claire.

Regina Waxman — acknowledged beauty of Greenwood Village and daughter of Niall Waxman.

Reggie — a mysterious, very talkative ex-comrade of Garvin Blackhammer who assists Emily and Colin in escaping the watchful eyes of Faryn of House Warder.

Roland — lover of Illyria of House Keeper and the most famous warder of Warder House, known as the Cyros because he was the only warder to ever bear the deadly talisman of House Warder.

Rycard — a master scholar of House Keeper whose particular skills lie in identifying the origins of ancient ruins and artifacts.

Rygel — the name of the founder of the Empyreal family Cyronian who lived at the dawn of the Second Empyre.

Sara Blackhammer — the second child of Garvin and Kaitlyn Blackhammer.

Scryos — mysterious resident of Sun City and a foreign merchant who is believed to possess magical powers.

Sandyr Ash — current Lord Warder, head of Warder House.

Sards — a nation of many loosely affiliated tribes of desert dwellers whose ancestors once occupied the northernmost lands of the Empyre, including Sun City.

Shade — the name of the mysterious vagabond that Emily and Colin encounter on their strange road south to the Emprye. He may be a warder, a half-breed, or something else entirely.

Shadow Brethren — another term for the people of Twilight.

Sun City — also called the City of the Sun. It is the capital city of the Empyre and the seat of the Empyreors, a vast metropolis situated on the plain west of the great desert of the Sards.

Syra Malamot — Lady of Ancyr, mother of Syrene Malamot Abrille, half sister of Lord Cyrill North through their father Cyrian North, and member of House Steward through her mother's family.

Syrene Malamot Abrille — Current heir to her uncle Lord Cyrill North of Cyr, first cousin to Alysse North of Cyr, wife of Corwyn Abrille, and a longtime friend of Alsandyr Goodwin.

Thom Humbolt — a young man of Greenwood Village who is the younger brother of Will and another friend of Colin Blackhammer.

Twilight — a mysterious, fluid, and many-layered otherrealm that can be entered and endured only by those with magical ability.

Twilight Denizens—one term for the creatures existing in or arising from the various dimensions of Twilight; more specifically the humanoid masters of those creatures and realms, who are the enemies of mortals and especially the members of the Houses.

Unashk— a Sardic priestess encountered by Emily and Beth during the Sardic invasion of the Empyre.

Urttah—the ancient witch responsible for guarding the labyrinthine underworld beneath Sun Palace.

Wilhem Goodwin—Lord of the small northern seaport of White Harbor, husband of Alyra Teleos Goodwin, father to sons Jorge, Dale, Jules and Alsandyr.

Will Humbolt—young man of Greenwood Village who was a friend to Colin Blackhammer until he joined one of the Midlander militias.

Vyara Cyronian—daughter of Janys Cyronian and great niece of Lord Janeryc Cyronian, who is head of the ancient Empyreal family Cyronian.

Wights—Midlander term for the mysterious magical beings that drink the souls of ordinary people and flee the light of the sun.

Yarbek—a count of the Empyre.

Zabet (the Conjurer)—a professional thief and smuggler residing in Sun City.

Zamyra Willow—First Healer of House Warder

.